Other Lovers

Erin Pizzey is well known for her work in the Seventies with battered wives and their children. She has had a successful career in magazine journalism and is now a full-time novelist. Her previous novels include *First Lady*, *The Consul General's Daughter* and *The Snow Leopard of Shanghai*.

ERIN PIZZEY

Other Lovers

Fontana
An Imprint of HarperCollinsPublishers

Fontana
An Imprint of HarperCollins*Publishers*
77–85 Fulham Palace Road,
Hammersmith, London W6 8JB

Special overseas edition 1991

Published by Fontana 1991
9 8 7 6 5 4 3 2 1

First published in Great Britain by
HarperCollins*Publishers* 1991

Copyright © Erin Pizzey 1991

The Author asserts the moral right to be
identified as the author of this work

Printed in Great Britain by
HarperCollinsManufacturing Glasgow

DEDICATION

Every woman writer needs a wife. I have Annie Walton, who made the writing of this novel a pleasure. My cherished Miss Annie, I dedicate this novel to you.

I also wish to dedicate the book to Nan Socolow, who gave me unflagging support and cups of Chinese tea. To Don, Richard, Randy, and Troy, the Brac's most eligible bachelors. To Leon Jackson, for keeping the island physically fit. To Dr Louise Davids, for being a friend and for the help during revisions. To Gary Callan at Visage, for taming my hair in wild surroundings. To all of Cayman Brac and its children.

To Jill Savager at the Lloyds Bank for her unfailing help. To Kate Perry and Jill Coleridge at Girton College, who answered my many research questions. To my white knights – David Morris, John Elford, Alan Cohen, and John Faure – for being my white knights. To my handsome agent Christopher Little, for making everything possible.

To Kate Parkin, my dear editor, and her talented team at Collins and Fontana, and to Simon King, my publisher and fellow lover of fine food. To Eddie Bell, for having the faith to publish me in America. To Mark Le Fanu at the Society of Authors, who does sterling work on authors' behalf. To Laurie Wiseman, for being such a gifted filmmaker. To Eddie Sanderson, one of the world's very best photographers. To Mary Emma Baxter, PR par excellence.

To Singapore Airlines for their courteous help in research.

To Susan Miller at the Public Library on Grand Cayman who helped with research almost daily. To Walter Wiggins, who owns Tiara Beach, the prettiest hotel in the Caribbean. To Emilio, Sue, Barry, Bruce, Seamus, Roy, Philip, Ron, Olive, and Starrie, who look after me and share my tea break at the hotel. To Miss Nellie at Foster's Food Fair on Grand Cayman, who hunts for otherwise unobtainable gourmet delights.

To my two favourite restaurants in the world – The Savoy's River Restaurant and Gaylord's on Mortimer Street. Please save me a seat.

To my beloved husband Jeff Shapiro.

Finally, to all Souls everywhere.

God bless you all.

'The restraints they acknowledged were of their own imposing only. They read the Bible and they read the *Morte d'Arthur* in the same spirit and with the same reverence, and they have founded on both a code of superior morals suited, as they considered it, to women of their own superior kind. It allowed them almost every latitude of feeling, including passion between the sexes, for they held it that without passion life would be colourless and the higher emotions could not be enjoyed . . . It was a maxim of their set that "Every woman shall have her man; but no man shall have his woman."'

WILFRID SCAWEN BLUNT,
in his *Secret Memoirs*, 2 June 1891,
describing the Souls

And now good morrow to our waking souls,
Which watch not one another out of fear;
For love, all love of other sights controls,
And makes one little room, an everywhere.
Let sea-discoverers to new worlds have gone,
Let maps to others, worlds on worlds have shown,
Let us possess one world, each hath one, and is one.

JOHN DONNE,
from 'The Good Morrow'

PROLOGUE

'Nah.' Molly leaned across the table in the River Restaurant at the Savoy Hotel in London. 'I think she has an F.F. of about three and a half.' Molly's voice was throaty and full of gravel. She ran her hands through her wild black hair. Her generous mouth smiled.

'Don't be beastly, Molly,' laughed Glenda. 'At least give the poor woman a five. She must have been beautiful. Once.'

Four pairs of eyes watched a tall, elegantly dressed woman move across the restaurant floor. The woman wore a man's tuxedo jacket over a thin black skirt. A white blouse and a bow tie sat neatly at her neck. She carried a briefcase under her arm. She walked quietly up to a group of men who sat at the table behind Molly. There were two empty chairs. Three of the men struggled to their feet and then sat down again, continuing to talk. The woman quietly sipped her iced water.

A moment later there was a commotion at the door and a young woman walked in, surrounded by waiters.

'Wow.' Molly grinned at Glenda. Her body corkscrewed around. 'Now this one I'd give at least an eight.'

Fatima narrowed her dark eyes in careful appraisal. 'No, seven. She won't age well. No bones.'

Georgina inspected the girl as she made her way to the remaining empty seat at the men's table. 'They all remind me of hounds about to hunt,' Georgina said. 'I'd give her a nine. She really is quite beautiful.'

Glenda looked warily at Georgina. Then she saw that, whatever had happened, Georgina evidently did not hold Glenda to blame. Glenda relaxed. She had already arranged

3

with Georgina that they would have coffee after the others left.

Molly motioned the wine waiter to fill her glass. 'Here's to us, and may we all remain within the F.F. Zone until the day we die.'

Glenda protested. 'I don't think of myself like that,' she said. 'I don't care if I'm in the F.F. Zone or not. I don't want to be like that girl. Men slavering all over her. Look at them.' The girl leaned forward. Her golden breasts like cantaloupe melons dangled in front of her.

'What's wrong with a bit of slavering?' Molly asked. 'Sounds like the answer to me. I mean, look at the men. They're all entranced.'

'Men.' Fatima sipped from her glass of Perrier. 'Hopeless.'

'Not all men,' Glenda reminded her.

'No, not all men. But most.'

The four women sat at the table comfortably aware of the years they shared between them. Molly lit her after-dinner cigarette and they all chose small chocolates from a silver tray. Glenda looked out of the big picture window. Even recent events could not spoil this place. It had a life of its own. The Savoy sailed like a mighty ship over all waters, smooth or stormy. The years of worry and stress were over. 'Hard to believe we've all known each other since the Sixties, isn't it?' said Glenda. 'Tell me, Molly. What do you remember most?'

'Those were my hippy dippy days,' she said. 'I guess I remember the Sixties as mostly jammy and bonking.'

Georgina laughed.

'It wasn't all jammy and bonking,' Fatima said.

'No,' Glenda agreed. 'Not all of it.'

'And now,' said Georgina, 'here we sit. Married. Well, most of us anyway.' She cast a reproving glance at Molly. 'Do you think you'll *ever* marry again?'

Molly took a deep breath from her cigarette. 'Well, maybe sooner than you think.'

4

'Really?' Georgina was incredulous. 'You mean it?'

'Hey, I only said maybe.'

'Why only maybe?' asked Fatima.

'*Because* . . . Because sometimes I get scared by the idea. Maybe I'm a bit long in the tooth to share my life with someone else. And what happens if I want some time on my own? Then there are other times when I think that the guy I'm with is the best guy in the world and I'd be crazy not to marry him right away. And I do love him, so why wait? I don't know. He wants to get married. What do you all think?'

Glenda laughed. 'I think you should do what you want. But you're the one who worries most about the Fuckability Factor, even though you have nothing to worry about. I mean, I'd give you at least a Fuckability Factor of eight, and I think you'll be in the Fuckability Factor Zone for life. But you're always preaching that women become invisible once they reach fifty.'

'And isn't it true?' said Molly. 'Take the older woman over there. Men no longer even see her. She should have stayed home. Why'd she even bother to come when she was only going to end up sitting across the table from Miss Extra Fuckable? And won't that be me, not many years down the road?' She stamped out her cigarette. 'Oh hell,' she said. 'Ageing sucks.'

Georgina raised her glass. 'To Molly,' she said. 'The last of us four Souls to marry.'

Glenda picked up her glass. 'To all of us Girton girls,' she said. 'To the Souls.'

'Older and wiser Souls.' Fatima raised her glass. She gazed at Glenda.

She knows, Glenda thought. Damn, Fatima could always see through her.

Molly was the first to leave and then Fatima.

Georgina sat at the table, the debris of an excellent meal

5

quickly disappearing as unseen hands took the plates and the glasses away.

Glenda warmed a brandy between her palms. She swirled it around the *ballon*-shaped glass and she sniffed it. The smell was thick and strong. It reminded her of the earth before winter when the grapes were dry on the vine. It was the smell of the bountiful earth of Dorset. Her husband had forgiven everyone now, but she still felt a dreadful sense of failure. She had betrayed a friend.

'Have you decided what you will do, Georgina?' Glenda's voice was tense.

'No.' Georgina shook her head, her hair fair swinging against her face. 'Not yet, Glenda. But I will have made up my mind by the time you two return from your trip to Hong Kong.' Georgina was obviously not yet ready to talk. They finished their coffee and Georgina left the restaurant.

Glenda sat for a few minutes by herself. The room was nearly empty, apart from a few couples sitting in the flickering candlelight. The woman in the black tuxedo was by herself, making notes on a yellow legal pad. She looked up as Glenda walked past. There was a sadness in the elegant face, a sadness that hurt Glenda. Molly is right, she thought and she went through the doors. Women are anonymous after a certain age. Invisible, faceless.

In her room upstairs at the Savoy she lay in her midnight bath. On the fat rim of the tub was her bath oil. Femme by Rochas. Hard to find now, but still the only purchased smell she enjoyed. The oily drops covered the water and her body in a light, fragrant film. Little globules formed a lifeguard around her buoyant breasts. She closed her hazel eyes and lay back in the water, her rich chestnut hair fanning out around her delicate narrow face. I do love this place, she thought. The bath was deep enough for her to float.

Now it's safe for me to remember. In the heat of this water, I feel as if I'm in my mother's womb, safe from the horrifying world, safe from the garbage and the smell of poverty. She opened her eyes and looked at the ceiling. Above her was a small hairline crack. Brown at the edges, it beckoned her. Glenda floated up through the crack in time until she reached her first memory. She heard her own baby wails, echoing off the walls of the two rooms that she shared with her mother in Hounslow, London. Horrible, grim, grotty Hounslow.

BOOK ONE

Chapter 1

She fell from the drawer she slept in and the impact hurt. Glenda lay on her back and howled loudly. A fearful Minnie came running in and clutched Glenda to her full bosom. 'You're all right, you're all right.' She carried Glenda to the window that looked out on a school playground. The grey asphalt lay disconsolate in the February rain. Glenda stopped screaming and watched from the window, hoping to see some children playing, but school was out and the usually busy school house was empty. 'I'll have to get you a proper bed soon,' Minnie promised. 'Can't have you sleeping in a drawer forever. Jack!' she yelled. 'Put the kettle on! There's a love!' The answer to all problems in life, Minnie knew, was a good cup of tea.

Glenda's cries quietened in her mother's arms. The trauma of the fall over, she sat astride Minnie's hip as Minnie strolled from the one room into the only other, the room Minnie used as her bedroom with her many lovers. For now it was Jack. He sat by the small fireplace, poking the coals under the teapot on a trivet. Minnie was proud of her trivet, lovingly polished with Brasso. And she was proud of her coal scuttle and the brass fender. She put Glenda on the floor and watched her daughter waddle towards the brightly burning fire. 'Careful, duck,' she said. 'Don't go near the fire.'

Glenda paused. It wasn't the fire that deterred her; it was the smell of sweat from Jack. He sat in his grey, grimy undershirt and his equally unclean underpants, a stubble across his chin. Glenda knew he would not be around for long. None of them ever was. She also knew that whatever happened in her little life, she was safe in Minnie's arms. Her mother and herself against the world. Even the McCluskies downstairs were not part of their world. In these two rooms on the long road that led to the sweet shop, Minnie reigned supreme. Although she got pregnant at fifteen and had Glenda when she was sixteen, Minnie was a naturally wonderful mother. 'Haf to be,' she explained to Mrs McCluskie who liked her and took an interest in Glenda. 'Me mum passed away and I was the youngest. I did all the running about and fetching and carrying.'

'And Glenda's father?' Mrs McCluskie asked sympathetically.

'Oh, 'im.' Minnie raised her eyes to the ceiling and shook her head. 'Best looking boy in the school, 'e was.' She smiled at the memory. 'I fancied 'im no end. 'E thought he 'ad *me*, but really . . .' She glanced impishly at Mrs McCluskie who, she knew, counted the menfriends that climbed the stairs to her secret lair. She laughed a deep throaty chuckle. 'Really I 'ad *him*. But then I got pregnant and Glenda looks just like 'im. I 'ad to leave school, didn't I, and the welfare put me in this place.'

Glenda knew that her mother talked to Mrs McCluskie when Mrs McCluskie's husband, Police Constable McCluskie, was out of the house. Mrs McCluskie was big and fat and smelled of bubble and squeak. If Minnie wanted to pop up the road, Mrs McCluskie looked after Glenda, or rather one of the eldest of the ten McCluskie children kept Glenda occupied in the packed four rooms that made up the downstairs flat.

Between the two flats there was a steep stairway and a narrow corridor and a lean-to bathroom with a tepid, grey, cracked bath, a fearsome hot water heater and a lavatory with a chain. At the end of the chain was a white porcelain hand-pull. Glenda was getting to know the hand-pull because she sat beneath it, looking at the yellow potty which she used to use and which Minnie never got around to throwing away. The potty had a peeling teddy bear emblazoned on it. Glenda resented the cheap likeness of a teddy bear. She wanted a whole, live, furry teddy bear like the ones on the potties she saw in Boots the Chemist, her most favourite shop after the sweet shop. Minnie was adamant. 'We 'aven't that kind of money,' she said firmly as they trailed through yet another jumble sale.

Saturday mornings were spent up the High Road. Minnie was a demon jumble saler. Glenda did her best to keep pace with her mother, though from Glenda's vantage point she saw little else of the jumble sales but the knees of fellow shoppers. By the age of four, she had seen all the knees she could bear for the rest of her life. They all looked alike. The women seemed to have fat, cracked knees throbbing with varicose veins. Most of them wore lisle stockings with garters gripping their swollen legs.

The smell of the jumble sales bothered Glenda. Wet wool, mountains of stuffy, dusty fabrics, and rows and rows of books, torn and yellowing with age. Minnie made a point of buying any book that gave instructions on child care.

Last Saturday, Glenda's fourth birthday, Minnie made the great find of a high chair for a present. 'See?' she said, breathless with excitement. A forest of legs surrounded Glenda. She could tell her mother was thrilled.

Minnie did not wear lisle stockings, ever. Minnie wore fashionable nylons with long black or scarlet garter belts. Usually in the commotion of the jumble sale, she would develop a run and Glenda watched the snag become a veritable torrent as it reached down her mother's shapely legs. She liked her mother's body. It was cuddly and soft and she always smelled nice. 'There,' Minnie said with pride when she had paid for the new high chair. 'Off we go, ducks! I got you an Ashley Cooper chair! Who says God don't answer prayer?'

Quite why Minnie should have made so many references to this chair bemused Glenda. When they got home and the object of veneration was carefully pushed into place at the little drop-leaf table that Minnie dusted with care, Glenda soon found out. The Ashley Cooper chair had been designed by some fiend who wished to torture small children's backs. Glenda fidgeted and fussed. She thought she was too big for the chair anyway and deserved a grown-up chair, but she knew better than to object outright. Minnie was determined that her daughter was going to escape to the finer things. From the age of four, Glenda realized she was not going to be like other children.

Other children were the McCluskie children downstairs. 'No future for them,' Minnie sniffed when she went over her long-term plans with her daughter. As for the children in the playground, Minnie was not hopeful. 'I've got me own flat at least,' Minnie said fiercely when she sat by the fire and Nick or Jack or Ron was down at the pub. Glenda lay on her mother's lap and listened, her double-lashed eyelids falling over her big, slanted hazel eyes, her tummy full of porridge after her supper. She loved the way her mother cooked the rolled oats and then sprinkled dark brown sugar and smooth cream over the wonderful grey crenellations. 'Hmm,' Glenda agreed.

Minnie looked down at her daughter. 'And you're not to waste y'self on any old man, like I done,' she scolded, gently kissing the tips of the copious young hair that cushioned Glenda's head. Mother and daughter gazed at each other in absolute trust. 'I think it's time for Jack to move on, don't you?'

Glenda nodded through the hazy sleepy feeling. Behind her mother's head she could see the drying rack. On it hung yet another pair of Jack's dingy underpants. She felt a calm descend. For a while they would live alone and not too quietly. When PC McCluskie came home from being a policeman, drunk, Glenda could hear loud thuds and smacks and the children screamed and Mrs McCluskie would come upstairs. PC McCluskie might be big and brutal, but he was frightened of Minnie who stood on her doorstep and dared him to come near his wife. 'Fuck off, you rotten bastard!' Minnie would shout. 'Fuck off out of this 'ouse and leave your wife and kids alone!'

Only once PC McCluskie had made a murderous launch at Minnie, but she had her heavy cast iron frying pan in her hand and she brought it down full force on his head which he had unwittingly lowered to charge. Glenda crowed loudly from her place on the sitting room floor as she watched McCluskie topple to the ground. She was still laughing when PC McCluskie crawled back down the stairs, clutching his head.

And then Minnie made a cup of tea for Mrs McCluskie whose face was wet with tears. 'It's only when he drinks,' she said softly. 'Most times he's the best husband there ever was.'

Minnie made a face but didn't argue. ''Ave a cup of tea, pet. And next time call me first and I'll kill him for you.' Glenda never doubted her mother's ability to keep her safe.

None of Minnie's men dared even to raise their voice to her. Minnie ran away from her own violent home and, in the lonely years it took to set her life up and take care of her daughter, she vowed no harm would ever come to Glenda. Glenda felt protected in an uneasy world which, unbeknownst to her, was still recovering from the Second World War. Glenda saw the uncertainty and the real poverty in the cracked streets of Hounslow, but stomach-twisting want managed to brush by the woman and her child.

Glenda grew up knowing her clothes were secondhand, but not her shoes. They were always new even if the dinner on the table consisted of an awful lot of potatoes. 'Nothing wrong with potatoes and gravy,' Minnie would say after a shoe-buying expedition. 'Nothing wrong at all.' But Glenda knew she would always have shiny shoes to walk down the long grey stretch of road to the sweet shop presided over by skinny Mrs Jones.

Mrs Jones was as thin as a stringbean and nearly as green.

Her face was long and unrelentingly sorrowful until she saw Glenda grinning at her with her farthing in her little pudgy hand. Then Mrs Jones would come to life and give Glenda a black silken string of licorice with a bright, gloriously vulgar tip of red chewy sugar. It took ages to strip off between the front teeth and left a warm brown slime all over the mouth as she sucked the candy until it was all gone. 'Licorice is good for the stomach, I always says,' Minnie observed and Mrs Jones agreed. 'Otherwise I wouldn't let Glenda eat sweets. I read in this book that if you start them off on sharp things like pickles, they never get a sweet tooth and gorge on sweets and then get spots.' Minnie detested spots.

'I got a spot!' Minnie announced a few weeks after the chair purchase.

Glenda's mood fell. If Minnie had spots, they didn't go out. Minnie had no intention of facing her public with a spotty face.

But by now, to Glenda's relief, Jack had gone. Minnie and Glenda were on their own again. Delicious evenings spent over supper followed by Minnie reading to her by the fire. Minnie's favourite books were love stories borrowed from Boots library at a penny a time. Minnie read with great concentration, her finger underlining the words and her eyebrows working hard. '. . . and he dragged her through the underbush . . .' Glenda remembered this story particularly because it had a horse in it. 'The great steed reared . . .' Glenda listened nightly to the stories of derring-do and romance. When Minnie had finished the night's chapter, she read a children's story for Glenda.

By her fifth year, she had heard all the Winnie the Pooh books. Glenda lived with Winnie the Pooh. She had an old battered bear that Minnie had salvaged months ago from a jumble sale at the Salvation Army. He was Glenda's best friend and confidant. He lived with his one eye on her new bed in the corner of her bedroom. Glenda loved her bedroom. Minnie, with love in her heart, had transformed the bleak square room into a tiny palace. Fluffy curtains swung in the London breeze. White billowing nets adorned the plate glass and the matching bedspread was swagged with bunches of flowers. Beside the bed was a rocking chair that Minnie sat in, singing songs, whilst waiting for Glenda to go to sleep. 'Go to sleep, little baby, go to sleep. By your bedside angels will keep . . .' She paused to check the closed eyes. '. . . watch over your tired head.' And Glenda drifted off into another safe night to the sound of her mother's gentle melodious voice.

Chapter 2

Glenda learned to read by the age of five. Mondays Minnie took her to the library. Glenda loved the big book-filled room. Minnie usually stopped at the newspaper rack and pulled out three newspapers. Trembling with excitement, Minnie would sit Glenda down and, with her mouth close to Glenda's ear, she would read of the Royal Family's engagements for the day, moving on to who had been born, given birth, or died. The list was usually long on a Monday. It seemed to Glenda that a lot of very wealthy people made a habit of dying over a weekend. But if she was bored, Glenda would never hurt her mother's feelings by saying so. Rather she would gaze at her mother's neat ankles with her Monday morning new pair of stockings. Minnie was not at all immodest; instead she quite naturally took her body and her daughter's body for granted. Glenda often felt she was interchangeable with her mother. Her left leg, for instance, could just as easily sprout out of her mother's thigh as her own.

Minnie opened the *Telegraph* and looked for the latest books for herself and for Glenda. To write down the list of books they must take from the library, she used a tiny pad and an old, very precious, fountain pen. Minnie treated the pen carefully, for it had a real gold nib. 'Must be worth a fortune,' she told Glenda. 'A bloody fortune.'

Today in the library, after giving the pen a lick to get it started, Minnie wrote down some names and then took the *Telegraph* back and surreptitiously drew out *The Mirror*. This time Minnie sort of slid into the back row of tables followed by Glenda. Glenda realized that Minnie was ashamed of being seen with this newspaper, but she didn't see why. *The Mirror* had nice clear headlines and Glenda was almost able to guess and make the sounds of the letters so that she could read about murder and that lovely easy word: SEX. The two of them sat until it was time to go to lunch. Lunch on a Monday never varied. Minnie took Glenda by the hand and lugged a bag full of books in the other. They walked the long ribbon road, walked down past the pub and then on to Joe's Cafe. Minnie promised Glenda tea and buns at Joe's Cafe. Joe was a strange, white, thin man. He sat in his cafe pouring out cups of lugubrious tea from a tea urn, but the buns he served . . . Glenda could swear they were made by magic. Nowhere else had she ever tasted such delights.

Joe's Cafe was quite full today. Three large lorries were standing in the forecourt. The smell of men who had travelled excited Minnie. She liked long distance lorry-drivers – they made good lovers. They usually arrived carrying with them presents from Stockton or Ashton under Lyne. René, her Frenchman, used to come over from France bringing with him stockings and perfume.

Minnie looked about her to see if he was anywhere around. Joe was sitting in a corner looking miserable. 'Seen René, luv?' Minnie put her hand on his. Joe's hand was always white and scaly. Must be the hours he spends mending and making shoes, she thought. ' 'Ere, Joe. I've got some of those high heeled shoes you like to mend.'

Joe's eyes lit up. 'You mean the black spikey jobs?'

'The very ones.' Minnie pulled out a wickedly-pointed shoe with a five inch heel.

Joe took the shoe into his hands and for a moment his face burned. 'Just like my mother used to wear,' he said reverently. 'What a smell. Reminds me of brown lino down the hall and the smacking of the shoes walking on it. My mother wore silk petticoats. The sound of the petticoats and the silk stockings . . .' He grinned, his thin lips revealing a row of ferret-like teeth. 'Better than a shot of champagne,' he said. 'A man could go mad for a sound like that.'

Minnie cleared her throat, not sure where this conversation was heading. Joe was an odd sort.

'Minnie,' Joe said, seeing her discomfort and turning his eyes to an elderly man who walked in, 'here's someone I want you to meet. This is me old friend Phil Clough,' he introduced. ' 'Ow are you, mate?'

Phil smiled and the long bitter lines broke rank and re-assembled themselves into a rather gentle face. 'I'm okay, as okay as a man can be at eighty-one, but I've got my health.'

Joe reached for the thick white cups. 'How do you have your tea, Phil?'

'Hot and wet with sugar,' Phil said. 'What's the word of the day, Joe?'

'Why, yesterday Minnie here and me was just discussing . . . Say, what was we discussing, Minnie?'

'The new Town Hall, Joe. Good to meet you, Mr Clough. Joe was saying what a stupid idea it is for old man Councillor Oppenheim to force his Town Hall down our throats, and I told Joe 'ow right he was. What do you think of it all?'

The elderly man looked startled but he laughed. 'Not much. We have a perfectly good Town Hall already. We don't need a new one. But our aldermen feel the old seats are too tight for their arses and they want a mausoleum in their remembrance.'

Minnie snorted. 'Waste of taxpayers' 'ard-earned money,' she said.

The old man smiled. He held his hand out for Minnie to shake and said, 'Call me Phil. Nice to see you young ones taking an interest in politics.'

'Minnie Stan'ope,' she said, 'and this is my daughter Glenda.'

Glenda gave a small hello while Phil Clough shook her little hand.

Phil looked admiringly at Minnie. Even at eighty-one, he still felt a jolt of pure joy when he beheld a pretty girl. 'Live around here?' he said.

Minnie nodded. 'A bit of a way, really,' she said, 'but we walk, Glenda and me. Please do sit with us and drink your tea.' Minnie was all formal. She felt Phil had been a somebody, and her curiosity was piqued by his clean, long hands with well-trimmed nails. He wore a greatcoat which, though shabby in places, had probably seen service in both wars. Its shoulders spoke of hours of attention and his shoes were shiny and clean. Minnie approved of clean men and men who looked as if they had done something with their lives. In fact, Minnie liked men of distinction but usually ended up with those who took advantage of her good nature. Somehow the men of distinction were to be admired and kept at a distance, while the rotters were invited home and mothered.

'Can't beat these houses round here,' said Phil, sitting down at a table with Minnie and Glenda. 'I live in one. Warm as toast in winter. Council offered to put me into a council flat. "What?" I said. "Take my road and my friends and stick us up in the air? No, thank you, sir," I said. "Sod off," if you'll forgive my French.'

Minnie laughed and gladly forgave him. 'That Mr Oppenheim, our alderman,' she said. ''E comes smarming up to visit us when he wants votes. Makes loads of flashy promises, and then we don't hear nothing from him again, except he's voted to put up the rates.'

'It's the way they treat people nowadays, isn't it? I mean,

I'm an old soldier,' Phil said, visibly straightening his back in his chair. 'Fought for King and country twice and both times I came back to Blighty with nothing. Now, if I'd been an American, I would have been all right. America looks after its boys.' Deep lines embittered his mouth.

Minnie knew how he felt. She had met many men like Phil Clough. Thank God, she thought, I'll never have a son, never have to face his going off to fight. She looked at Glenda and a surge of love flowed through her. Glenda would one day leave these streets forever. Her Glenda would not pass away her years on jumble sales and the Sally Army. Glenda would shop at Harrods, get her silks from Liberty, and telephone Fortnum and Mason's for whatever she desired. For now, when Minnie felt she needed a glorious day instead of just an ordinary day, she took Glenda up to the West End to mooch about the great shops and finally to sit in Harrods' banking hall: 'Please give me the forms necessary to open an account with you.' Minnie smiled as she sat with Phil Clough. How she enjoyed the play-acting! And she loved the way that Glenda, now old enough to join in, said, 'Shall we put a million in, Mother?' It was the word *mother* that cracked them both up.

Glenda stopped paying attention to the adults talking and concentrated instead on the bun which Joe put down in front of her. Her mouth moistened as she tasted the sugar reamed around a light brown puff of air, and she savoured the melting moment when she scrunched down into the bun. While Minnie and Phil talked, Glenda remembered that after her bath and the six o'clock news, she would sit at her mother's feet while Minnie brushed her hair a hundred times in front of the fire and they would listen to *The Goon Show*. The bun itself was happiness made real, and she had even more happiness to look forward to tonight.

Chapter 3

Important things happened in Glenda's life that year, the year when she was five, the year that was the last of her childhood. September loomed ahead and the narrow wire doors of the school behind the house yawned uncomfortably in her face when she pressed her forehead to the window, pushing with all her might.

Some of the myriad McCluskie children from downstairs came romping into the house every afternoon from the hellhole. Glenda watched from the top of the stairs as they poured through the door, jamming their way into their big untidy front room, yelling for sandwiches made from loathsome fish paste or sickly pink, rubbery Spam. Glenda shuddered and knew that before the summer was out and the harsh plane trees dotted along the Hounslow roads turned to gold and withered, she too would be standing behind the great wire fence – a prisoner without redress.

The thought made her very miserable, but Minnie had first promised her a summer holiday without an uncle. Nobody at all but Minnie and Glenda, a holiday paid for by the church at the end of the road. They were not going to a camp site or a Butlin's or anything common like that, Minnie explained. 'We're to 'ave a chalet all of our own. We 'ave a bedroom for you and one for me, and then we 'ave a sitting room and a kitchen on the beach, right on the beach. Can you imagine?' Going to bed in the hot July nights with the window open and the air puffing listlessly through the net curtain, Glenda imagined the billowing curtain to be blue sparkling waves and the white foam enveloped her and carried her away into tidepools of rocks where long pink-fringed prawns tickled her bare feet.

August the fifteenth arrived full of promise. The bus to the south coast smelled of the inside of crisp packets and

22

Player's Weights cigarettes. Minnie bought two packets of ten to see that she didn't run out. Travelling made Minnie excited but nervous.

Glenda lay back and shut her eyes. Every so often she would open them for a second to see trees and houses flashing by. First they passed the airport and the pregnant planes lumbered up into the air, their great bellies vulnerable. Then the airport fell away and the trees became greener and soon there were hills and valleys and miles and miles of grass with cows and sheep dotted about. In between dozing, rocked by the shuddering bus, Minnie and Glenda played noughts and crosses or hangman's noose. Minnie was reading another Georgette Heyer romance. 'What you reading, mum?' she asked.

Minnie shielded the book with her shoulder. 'You're far too young.'

Glenda let her head fall back against her chair. Her head bounced slightly, in rhythm with the bus.

By the time the bus stopped in the village and Minnie and Glenda got off, awkwardly carrying their suitcase and various bags between them, the evening was dark and the first stars were high in the sky. Far down the beach Glenda could see the receding tide. In her nose lodged the smell of burnt seaweed. Their feet sank into soft white sand drifts. 'I'll take me sandals off,' Minnie said, putting down the suitcase and huffing a little.

Glenda stood by her mother and gazed across the beach. She felt almost afraid. The two of them had never been exposed to so much space, such emptiness, such lack of noise. The harsh suck of the waves a long way away and the goodnight cry of a bird were the only sounds. Further up the beach, lights could be seen, twinkling and inviting.

The chalet, a white clapboard house, sat by itself along the shore, hollow and ambiguous. 'Do you think there's a witch in there?' Glenda asked nervously.

'Really, love!' Minnie laughed. 'Don't be so silly.'

Glenda felt her mother brace her back and straighten her shoulders. Well if there *is* a witch in there, Glenda thought, mum's ready to give her a piece of her mind. Minnie only straightened up like that for a rude shopkeeper or for Mr Oppenheim. Minnie hoisted the suitcase and Glenda clutched the shopping bag full of Mrs Jones' contribution to the holiday. ('Never know,' Mrs Jones had remarked glumly as she parachuted Eno's Fruit Salts, kaolin and morphine, Vick chest rubs, Fishermen's Friends, and other necessities of life into the bag. 'You just never know what germs those folks at the seaside may carry. Heathens, most of them. Bloody 'eathens.')

They trudged the last few yards to the door, which was shut tightly against them. 'Key's under the mat,' Minnie said to Glenda.

'The cat sat on the mat,' Glenda said, with a smile, rhyming with her mother. 'The key is under the mat.' Glenda was keeping her mind very busy with information. But underneath, fear lurked, getting bigger by the minute. The little house looked very like every house of horror she had ever heard described. Hansel and Gretel's wicked crone of a kidnapper might have lived there. Little Red Riding Hood's bad wolf grandmother would fit in quite naturally.

'Go and get the key,' Minnie directed. 'I'll 'eave the suitcase up to the door.'

'I'm scared, mummy,' Glenda was ashamed to hear herself whine.

'Glenda.' Minnie's voice was sharp. 'You've too much imagination. That's your problem. Nothing's about to scare us, is it?'

'I guess not.' Glenda put one foot in front of the other, each step taking at least a century. At the last minute, when her eyes accustomed themselves to the gloom, she saw the edge of a rough sisal mat. She dashed the last few feet and scrabbled wildly under the square which repaid her by twisting and gyrating as her hands grabbed for the key. She let out a yell of pure terror as she pushed the mat and saw a large grey wolf spider leap from the mat onto her arm. The day had been too long for Glenda and the spider was the end. She screamed.

Minnie brushed the spider to the ground and stamped on it. Glenda clung to her mother and sobbed. Minnie sat on the step with the suitcase at her feet and cuddled her daughter. 'There, there, little'n. Don't cry. We're here now. Let's get the door opened and I'll make a nice pot of tea and some sandwiches. Come on '

Her mother's warm lips touched her forehead and Glenda was consoled. True, the house had not yielded up any wolves or kidnappers, but there had indeed been a life-threatening situation when the monster spider crawled up her arm. But Minnie knew just how to handle it without fear and without fuss. Glenda felt very safe.

And safer still later, with a stomach full of sweet hot tea. She lay beside her mother in a large bed hemmed in by thick cotton sheets and a light blanket. 'Good night, mum,' she whispered. She could hear her mother's faint snore. She rolled over in snug tiredness.

Chapter 4

Glenda awoke, feeling as if she were sailing on a sea surrounded by a light yellow wind. The colour that struck her so forcibly was streaming through the window behind the big bed. She yawned and inhaled the smell of the sheets: honey mixed with hot sun. The sheets shone white and further down the bed the bedspread, thick candlewick, fluffy and yellow, became married to the colour from the window. She looked across at Minnie. Minnie lay curled with one hand under her chin, her mouth slightly open, and long whips of hair lay in strands across her face. Glenda felt very protective. Poor mum, she thought. And then she wondered why poor mum . . .

She stretched and sat up. From where she sat she could see across the sand outside the cottage. The sea was far closer this morning than last night, and the sky was clear and blue, not a cloud to be found anywhere. Glenda slipped onto the floor and felt the bare varnished boards under her feet. She looked down at her toes. Her feet struck her as ugly white and the toenails faintly blue. Now, where's the toilet? she asked herself. Last night in the horror and the exhaustion she had made no map of the other rooms. With a sense of adventure she walked down the small corridor until she found the bathroom next to the kitchen.

Sitting on the lavatory, she watched her knees swinging her feet off the floor. The lavatory was old and had a heavy mahogany seat. Her feet many inches off the floor, Glenda felt like a queen giving an audience to her subjects, which happened to be a row of blue towels draped over a wooden towel rail next to the bath. The bath looked clean and had been repainted a great many times, unlike the bath they shared back home. Whoever repainted the bath in this cottage had done so with care and enthusiasm. Over the years the different layers had become a multi-hued desert.

Gingerly Glenda leaned forward off her throne and twisted the big pronged horns of the cold tap. Water gushed into the bath and raced to the end of the tub. Water, hissing and spitting, tumbled out with such force that Glenda sat back and watched with fascination. The water in their flat at home trickled and burped its way into the basin and the bathtub. Hounslow water smelled bad most of the time, but here Glenda was overjoyed to see the water well up abundantly.

She heard Minnie calling. 'I'm coming, mum! Don't worry, I'm coming.'

'Put the kettle on, will you, pet?' Minnie shouted. 'It's gas, like home.'

Glenda made a face. If the gas was like home, then she

would risk her life here as she did there. Their gas cooker had come from the Sally Army. Ten shillings – a bargain. But it was a big, spiteful, growling affair with burners like a many-nostrilled dragon.

Each morning at home Glenda would light the sulphurous match and hold it to the hissing holes. The stove sucked in the flame and then WHUMP – it would spit out blue-edged jets of fire.

'Glenda!' her mother's voice came down the corridor. 'Don't daydream. 'Urry up.'

Glenda sighed. Even on holiday, Minnie would set the pace. Left to herself Glenda preferred to take the morning slowly, but tea had to be made.

She wandered next door into the kitchen. There was a little four-legged pine table with a blue and white tablecloth. The cooker was a younger model than theirs at home. Younger and cleaner. She lit the match and turned the dangling brass handle. The cooker responded with a polite burst of flame and Glenda let out a happy laugh. This was going to be a safe house. She and her mother would have a wonderful week in Cambersand.

She left the kitchen and trotted back to the bedroom. She had done her part in putting on the kettle; Minnie would do the difficult bit, the actual pouring of the boiling water. Maybe if she was very lucky, her mother might bring a tray into bed and they could sit side by side eating Robinson's marmalade on toast in between sips of hot sweet tea. Minnie grinned. 'Everything all right?' she asked.

Glenda nodded her head enthusiastically. 'Can we live here for ever, mum?'

'Not for ever, luv,' said Minnie. 'You 'ave to get an education, and I 'ave to get a job.'

Glenda looked startled. 'A job?' She slid into bed.

Minnie sat up, her arms wrapped around her knees. 'Yeah, Glenda. Now you'll be in school, I'll have time on me 'ands. And so I'll go looking for a part-time job and we'll have some extra money. We could do with a bit extra,' she smiled.

Glenda felt a momentary pang. Her mother out working. The flat empty during the day, empty of both of them. 'What sort of working?' a troubled Glenda asked.

'Oh, maybe some big 'ouse in Chiswick. I like to keep other people's things tidy. If we get a bit more money, I can see about a new carpet for the front hall. And a few new things. You know, Glenda,' she said, as the rising scream of the kettle shrilled from the kitchen, 'it'll be nice to 'ave some things new about the place.'

Minnie left the room.

Glenda lay back against the pillows. The smell of toast wafted across the room and she imagined new carpet in the hall. *Really* new, she thought. Not scuffed or bare in patches, not curled in the corners. Just *new*. Smooth, and with a pile that you could brush with your fingertips. It would be nice, she decided. Very nice.

Glenda smiled at her mother's face as Minnie approached the bed with a tray. 'Toast,' Minnie said.

'Robinson's marmalade!' Glenda chimed.

Minnie put the tray down on her sidetable. Mother and daughter gazed at each other in silence. The silence was a moment of suspended happiness. But behind the happiness was a fragment of time, five years of time encapsulated like the honey in a honeycomb. It was separated from the other cells of the comb, impenetrable, but there, locked away.

Glenda reached for her cup of tea and Minnie bit into her plump piece of toast, neither of them realizing that the honey years were now contained in the past by a wax veil. They were facing a new beginning.

Chapter 5

On Sunday, Glenda heard the church bell tolling in the village of Cambersand. The sound made her pause from digging a hole in the sand outside the cottage. Far away the pealing bells sounded young and fresh, not heavy and dolorous like Hounslow bells. The sun was shining on her back. She was wearing her new striped blue and white bathing suit. Her feet were bare and she felt the bite of sudden sunburn. To relieve the heat she lay down in her hole and was glad of the moist granules of sand that stuck to her body. Lying with the sun now in her eyes and the blue sky above her, she felt at peace, very much part of this time away from the rest of the world. Minnie, she could hear, was sweeping. The shhh shhh shhh of the broom became the only sound. Glenda wondered how she would ever go back to the world the two of them had left behind . . . Glenda dozed off until she heard Minnie calling.

Lunch time and Glenda was hungry. 'Pork pie. Glenda, look at that!' Minnie held up a large slice of pie, pink and running with aspic. 'It's 'omemade. And look what I picked outside – tomatoes off the vine.'

Minnie thrust a fat tomato under Glenda's nose. 'Smell it, Glen. Just smell it.'

Glenda sniffed. The skin of the tomato was warm and soft and she plunged her teeth into the swollen fruit and gurgled as the seeds slopped into her mouth and the thin juice ran down her chin.

'Ain't it amazing?' Minnie marvelled, looking at the food on the table. 'All this stuff, all fresh, and only a few hours from 'ome!'

Food was one of Minnie's favourite topics. Glenda just wanted to eat and eat until she burst.

Finally, both of them replete, they pushed their chairs

away from the kitchen table. 'Umm.' Minnie wiped her mouth. 'What you doing this afternoon, Glenda?'

'I'll take my new shrimp net and bucket and see if I can find some shrimps. What do you think?'

'Okay, love. I'll have a sleep. You know, it's queer, I can't keep awake down here. Don't go too far, mind. We don't know anybody around here.'

'I won't,' Glenda promised.

The idea of being able to wander off by herself at all was so exciting. This is my first real life adventure, she thought as she collected her bucket from her hole and went to unwrap her shrimping net. She walked across the tightly packed sand and saw nothing but more sand until finally she came to the edge of the sea.

The water curled around her feet in invitation. The beach was hot but the water cool. Her net trawling the sea-floor, she extracted small brown shrimps and put them into her bucket. Soon she had half a bucket of wriggling, writhing bodies.

As she walked she became aware of a man and a boy digging in the sand. The man had a long-handled spade. The edge of the spade was corroded and rusty and the handle was bleached by years of work in the sun. The man's hands were thick and Glenda noticed the forearms were made as if all flesh had been stripped away, only the ridges and furrows of muscle remaining. The man looked at her and he gave a thin lopsided smile. Glenda smiled back and offered her bucket. 'Are these shrimps, mister?' she asked.

The man bent his head and gazed into the sandy water. 'They be shrimp,' he said. 'Nice Boston shrimp, we call them. Just boil 'em in water, peel 'em, and put them in butter. Very, very tasty.'

The boy was scrutinizing her. 'You from London?' He lifted his chin for a reply.

'Yes.' Glenda's heart beat fast. In her deepest secret heart she had so much wanted to make a friend on this magic holiday. She had never had a friend, except for Minnie, Mrs Jones, and Mr Clough. Now here, standing in front of her, was a perfect, fair-haired, upturned-nosed boy.

He wore an old pair of stained shorts and a grey shirt. He was tanned by the sun. Glenda liked him. 'What have you got there?' she asked.

'Lugworms to bait the night hooks.' Glenda looked into their bucket. In hideous squirming piles, the lugworms protested against their captivity.

Glenda shuddered. 'Oh, how horrible!'

The boy laughed.

'I better get home now.' Glenda was suddenly afraid. 'My mum will be waiting.'

'My name's Sam,' the boy said, sticking out a small hand decorated with bitten fingernails. 'I'll be by later on to see if you want some mackerel. Does your mum like fish?'

'Loves it,' said Glenda.

'Done then,' Sam said. 'See you this evening.'

Glenda ran all the way back to the cottage. 'Mum,' she said as she rounded the corner, 'look at my shrimps!'

Minnie was in the kitchen. 'You're tramping in all that sand, Glenda!' Minnie was yet again pushing the broom around the place.

'Don't worry about sand, mum. Look at the shrimps. And,' Glenda paused, 'I met a boy who says he's coming to bring round some fish.'

'That's nice, dear.' Minnie brushed hard. She wondered if this holiday had been such a good idea. No uncles meant no dancing, and no dancing meant no beer. Still, the pubs opened late on a Sunday. Maybe she could take a walk down to the village with Glenda and see what was what.

'I don't know,' she muttered under her breath so as not to deflate her exuberant daughter. 'The city's the city, I suppose. But the country . . .' She shook her head. 'There's an awful lot of country.'

Chapter 6

'Come on, mum. Let's go.'

'Why?'

Minnie was enjoying herself. The little garden tucked behind the Village Arms was pretty. Minnie sat with Glenda on a wooden bench gazing happily at a young dark-haired man who was leaning on the fence talking to a man in the car park. Nice bottom, Minnie thought, and then she looked away. In front of her she had a shandy. The beer was cool and the pot-bellied half-pint glass sweated in the afternoon sun. Glenda had finished her soda pop and wanted very much to go home. Pub gardens were never of much excitement to Glenda.

'You promised, mum.'

Minnie smiled innocently. 'Promised what?' she said, cursing the fact that her daughter knew her almost better than she knew herself. Clever cow, she thought. She saw me look. The dark-haired man straightened up and stretched. Minnie felt a sudden explosion, a racing tide of lust that threatened to drown out the garden and overflow. She clenched her shaking hands as she caught his deeply amused blue eyes sizing her up.

The man ambled over to the table. He was tall and broad-shouldered and said, 'You must be visitors.' He had a soft accent and Glenda noticed he wore thick fishing boots. At least she imagined that was what fishing boots looked like. Wellingtons, but bigger and blacker with swelled toes. Minnie noticed the clean bridge of the man's nose and the curl of his lips as he smiled. Nice teeth, Minnie thought. She was particular about teeth. Jack got the boot because his teeth came out at night and Minnie could only take so many months of waking up to Jack's teeth. So for some time now Minnie had been a woman on her own. And that is no condition for a woman to be in, she complained to Mrs Jones. Shit, she thought. I promised Glenda. But he isn't half handsome.

Minnie turned her face up towards the man and Glenda groaned. 'It's time to go, mum. Please, let's go back,' she pleaded.

'Glenda, don't be rude.' Minnie put on her best mother's voice. 'Say hello nicely to the gentleman.' Minnie put out a limp hand and the man took it into his. 'My name is Thomas,' he said, 'and you . . .'

'Thomas.' Minnie melted. Her eyes grew wide and her mouth tremulous. 'Minnie. Minnie Stanhope. And this is my daughter Glenda.' She flashed a warning look at Glenda.

Glenda screwed up her face. 'I want to go home,' Glenda announced. She looked up at the still, strange man. 'A boy is bringing fresh fish from the sea and we have never eaten fish straight from the sea.'

The man smiled. And Glenda thought, At least he has a nice smile. And if mum *has* to have an uncle about the place, he might not be too bad. At least Thomas looked healthy.

'Call me Tom,' the man said to Glenda. 'Do you know how to gut fish then?' He raised an eyebrow at Minnie.

'Well, no, actually I don't. But I expect we can learn.' Minnie felt embarrassed and inadequate. The women in his life must all know how to do basic things like gut a fish, she reckoned. Minnie looked anxious. 'How do you do it?'

Tom laughed. 'I don't think it's a woman's job anyway,' he said. 'Round here, the men catch the fish and leave the gutting to the women. But I don't think it's right. Gutting is a dirty business. Look, if you're not doing anything, I'll come round later and show you. Where are you staying?'

Minnie pointed across the road towards the beach. 'In the little white cottage.'

'Ah! My aunt's cottage! Good,' Tom said. 'See you there in a couple of hours.' He raised his hand and for a moment Minnie thought that it might blot out the sky.

33

Inside Minnie was still quivering. Maybe the holiday might be all right after all. 'Quick, Glenda,' she said. 'We'd better get going. I've loads to do.'

Well, Glenda mused, if mum spends the afternoon dressing up and doing her hair, it will make a change from sweeping the floor.

Glenda sat alone while Minnie went into the pub to powder her nose before the walk back to the chalet. Maybe she could dig an even deeper hole with her friend or maybe they could go for an adventure somewhere in the dunes and the hillocks of the beach. Glenda sat dreaming in the sun, looking at her hand which was already tanned.

'Come on,' Minnie called and Glenda jumped from the bench and ran down the path.

'Oh, mum,' she said grabbing Minnie's hand. 'This is such a good holiday.'

Minnie laughed to see her daughter so happy. 'I wonder what we should have with the fish.'

'How about chips?'

'Of course. Yeah,' Minnie said thoughtfully. 'Chips. And peas. I got some peas. Fresh peas. We'll have to pod 'em. My goodness,' Minnie said, suddenly lost in time, 'it's been ever so long since I podded peas. My dad used to grow them in the back garden. Long trailing rows of peas on poles, all black from the soot of the railway engines. But when you podded 'em, the soot came off all over your hands. And then out popped the pea, bright and green, so pretty you couldn't believe anything so pretty could grow in a back garden like that.' Minnie's throat was tight.

Glenda looked at her mother. Only rarely did Minnie ever say anything about her childhood. 'Was that my granddad that grew the peas?'

Minnie was walking quickly towards the cottage. 'He died. I told you, he died before I really knew 'im.' Minnie's nose gave a quick twitch. 'Most of us kids lost fathers and uncles. Really, they just went off to the war and the next thing you knew they didn't come back. Just mum crying and crying. She never did stop crying after he died. Us kids just went to school with black armbands and then everybody was nice to you for a few days and didn't rag you until someone else came to school with an armband and then they were nice to them and you got ragged again. We didn't talk much in those days. Not like now where everybody talks about everything. In those days we kept ourselves to ourselves. But I missed him, Glenda. Still do in a way, I suppose.'

'Don't be sad,' Glenda pleaded. 'Not today.' Glenda didn't understand. For her the future stretched away into this endless adventurous week and maybe beyond. 'Race you, mum!' she shouted and she started for the house.

Chapter 7

The rest of the afternoon Minnie hummed in her bedroom while Glenda napped.

Minnie cursed the fact she had vowed not to fill her luggage with her frills. She impatiently pulled out a slim black dress with bright red polka dots. Seersucker, she remarked. At least it won't crush and the material is light and spongy. She slipped the dress over her naked body and did a twirl. She smiled at herself in the fly-blown mirror tacked onto the wardrobe. Minnie's eyes lit up. She liked Tom. She liked his even white teeth. She liked the brown back of his neck where the sun had kissed the rough ends of his hairline.

She shivered. How many lovers? she thought as she wandered down the corridor. Many, she grimaced and slid into the tub of hot water. So many of them over the years. Still, Glenda knew she was the one and only person in Minnie's life. And Glenda didn't seem to mind the men that passed through. They never stayed for long. Would Tom stay for a little while?

Minnie stared at her feet. She made a note to herself that

she must do something about the nail varnish. Her feet were well-shaped, but the bright red nail varnish looked out of place against the quiet, soft colours of the sands. Maybe pale pink, Minnie considered. Could she live here with Tom in a little cottage like this away from the stink and roar of London? Minnie wasn't sure, but she enjoyed the thought so much that she overstayed her time in the bath.

She pulled out wisps of cotton wool. The thick red nail varnish caught the tufts of cotton wool which curled them-selves into sinister blood-stained vines. Minnie could feel a rising panic and then she saw Glenda's sleepy face still crumpled and surprised at the door.

'Come in, love,' she said. 'Give your mum a hand. Get the dustbin from over there and I'll drop this mess into it.'

Glenda walked over to the table. She glanced at her mother who had four painted toes stuck up in the air and the little toe of her left foot still bare.

'I know, I know,' Minnie scolded herself irritably. 'I ought to put one layer on at a time. But in London I never have the time.'

Glenda handed her back the basket. 'There. Ta, love. I don't know, Glenda. Whatever will I do without you?'

They both grinned at each other.

'Look out there,' Minnie said suddenly. 'Is that your friend coming up the path?'

Glenda looked pleased. 'He's got his bucket of fish with him. He said he would.'

'Right, then. You go and let him in, and I'll finish me nails and be out in a minute. Give him a drink. He must be thirsty. There's a bottle of Ribena in the pantry.'

Glenda heard the knock on the door and she ran down the passage to let Sam in. As the door swung open, she saw him standing on the doorstep with the bucket between his hands. Glenda looked down into a mass of shining fish. Their backs gleamed silver and blue in the sun. Dying, their eyes lost their clear vision and the mouths twitched. Blood ran from the gills.

'Oh!' said Glenda.

'I got the best I could for you,' Sam said. 'I've been out with Grandpa and the nets all day. We had a good run.' He lifted the largest mackerel by the tail. It hung limp from his hand. 'What do you think?'

Glenda paused and checked on the turmoil rolling in her head and her stomach. 'They look very nice,' she said solemnly. 'You want a drink?'

'Yes.'

Glenda led the way to the kitchen. 'Mum'll be here in a minute. She'll give you money for the fish.'

'They're a present from me and Grandpa. Grandpa sends the rest of the catch up to the restaurant and the fish and chip shops and he sells what's left to the tourists. Grandpa owns the fish station at the end of the pier. Have you seen it?'

Glenda shook her head.

'I'll take you tomorrow. Come on. I'll show you how to clean fish.' Sam reached behind his blue shirt and pulled out a long thick knife with a fierce blade.

To Glenda, the honed edge looked as sharp as her mother's razor blades that nicked Glenda's tender skin when she played at shaving under her arms when her mother wasn't looking. The other side of the blade had big teeth. 'Is that *your* knife?' Glenda asked, her voice rising.

'Yeah.' Sam looked at it nonchalantly. 'Dad gave it to me when I was seven. That's two months ago. He reckoned I was old enough to have a real fishing knife.'

Glenda felt a hand close around her throat. Her face went red with longing. 'Oh, if only,' she said, 'I could have a knife like that.' Underneath the wish for a knife was the thought of having a father who would give her a knife. She had no father and no knife.

'Here.' Sam held it out. 'Take it. Feel the weight.'

37

Glenda's hand was not quite big enough to grasp the hilt, but she watched her fingers curl around the knife and then she tightened her grip until her knuckles went white.

'Want to cut up the belly?' Sam offered, selecting his first victim. He threw the fish into the kitchen sink. 'We need some newspaper for the guts.' Sam's tone was practical.

Minnie came through into the kitchen and caught sight of the bucket of fish. 'Oh!' she said, peering in. 'They look lovely.' She saw Glenda clutching the knife. 'You helping clean the fish then, Glenda?'

Glenda looked uncertain. Her idea of a knife like this was to be used to chase Germans or to play cowboys and Indians, not to plunge the lovely gleaming blade into the belly of a fish.

Sam, a little bored by all the hesitancy, took back the knife. 'I'll do the first one. Look, start at the hole at the bottom of the belly and then run the knife up.' The belly split open neatly and a mass of slimy, smelly worm-like things spilled into the sink.

'I think I'll go and brush the porch,' Minnie said, leaving quickly with the broom.

'Now,' Sam demonstrated, 'lay it flat like this, and cut out the back bone. And there you are.'

'What about the skin?' Glenda asked, trying not to breathe.

'You cook that,' Sam said. 'It's delicious. All crispy.' Sam laughed. 'If you don't want to do it, I'll clean 'em for you.'

Glenda's relief was evident. 'You do it this time,' she said. 'I'll do it next time.'

'Okay, but next time it might be a big crab with claws that will chase you all around the boat.'

Glenda laughed, pleased that her friend was talking about a next time. And tomorrow she was going to see a fishing station. Life was busy, but a different busy to Hounslow. A moment-to-moment busy, not a jagged busy. She heard footsteps. Must be Tom, she thought. Mum's friend. She watched as Sam bent over the sink, gutting the fish, saying nothing, his fair hair falling down his face and his tongue protruding out of his mouth, concentrating. Mum has a friend, she thought, and so have I.

Later that evening the four sat in the kitchen with a plate of fried fish in front of them. 'You can eat the skin, Glenda,' Tom said.

'She doesn't like the skin,' Minnie interrupted.

'Oh, yes, I do.' Glenda smiled at Sam. 'I love the skin.'

Minnie arched her eyebrows. Dear me, she thought. They learn young these days, don't they. She caught Tom's eye. 'As of now, Glenda eats skin.'

Tom laughed. 'We'll change your London ways yet, my lady,' he said, winking at Glenda.

Glenda crunched down a piece of skin. She couldn't wait.

Chapter 8

In the daytime, Sam showed Glenda everything. He took her to his grandfather's fishing station. He took her for a picnic lunch on the beach. He even took her out in a row boat, out to where a buoy marked the location of a crab pot, and he hoisted the crab pot into the boat. A hard, rattling crab fell into the boat and scratched about under the seats. Glenda kept her feet up off the floor the whole row back. Tom helped Minnie cook the crab for dinner.

Two nights later Glenda lay in bed listening to Tom and her mother talking. As usual, Tom came round after he had laid his night lines and sat with Minnie in two deckchairs decorously sitting side by side outside the front door. Glenda could hear their voices floating on the wind. Tom's voice was deep and melodious. It had none of the London whine. Minnie, relaxed by her days on the beach, trilled and cooed, her light high voice soaring. The two voices comforted Glenda and she wondered if Tom was going to be around for a while. If he was, Glenda realized she would be pleased. He had been good company the other night, and had done a good job of helping Minnie cook the delicious crab that she and Sam had caught. Glenda was growing to like this man.

Glenda was drifting off. Once upon a time, she told herself (which was a favourite way of going to sleep), there was a little girl called Glenda . . .

In front of her was a crab, a gigantic crab, even bigger than the Biggest Crab Ever Caught at the Natural History Museum. But this was no spider crab. This crab's legs were thick and his claws alone were as big as Glenda's body. He guarded the doors, the doors to the school. She *had* to get past him, *had* to go into the school, but the crab would not let her simply walk by. He waved his eye-stalks at her and reached out to snap his claws . . .

She leapt out of her bed and ran down the corridor. Minnie would comfort her. She would understand.

Minnie lay with her nightdress up over her bare bottom. Sheets and the counterpane swirled around her. And behind her, with his huge arm across her shoulders, lay Tom. Both of them were deeply asleep.

Glenda turned and walked back to her own bed. Tears were streaming down her face. Something had happened that night that would forever set her apart. Nothing that would show or that any adult could discern. Just a little bit of her soul had slipped away from this world to be held for ransom in the next.

Glenda sat on her bed and waited. She waited for her mother to leave her private world with Tom, the new man in her life who would need cups of tea and goodbye kisses at the front door. After that ritual Minnie would restore life to Glenda. Maybe, Glenda thought, that's what men are: kisses at the front door and cups of tea. And real life begins when they leave.

But there was another life, a life that existed over the rim of the huge sea that lay outside the cottage. Glenda waited and the sun began to climb. Only two more days, she thought, and all this will be over. She decided to think about Sam. She tucked her feet under her and thought about his bright hair and how it stuck up at the back of his head.

These thoughts, however, did not take away the pain or the emptiness. Minnie asleep alone looked like a young girl. Minnie in bed with a man looked like a Minnie Glenda did not know. It hurt, it still hurt, and no amount of dreaming would take that hurt away. Glenda realized that she wanted a mother and a father like Sam had, and a grandpa thrown in for good measure. She could do without a grandmother if she had to. What she wanted was a proper family.

Glenda swung her foot and began to tell herself a story about a girl called Glenda who married a fisherman and had six children. She got to the fifth child when she heard Minnie talking. Good. Breakfast soon, she thought. The day had begun.

Chapter 9

On their last dusk, Sam showed Glenda how to make a fire. Beside the fire they had a plate of naked pink sausages and a pile of chips. Inside the cottage Minnie entertained Tom. Their voices punctuated the crack and the snap of the dry burning branches.

Glenda sat cross-legged, watching Sam, who held the frying pan over the fire waiting for the fat to seethe and bubble. She held a stick, and had whittled a fine point with Sam's knife. At the end of her stick a sausage curled and charred, dropping hot fat into the fire.

Sam piled the chips into the fying pan. They sat in stillness listening to the noises of the night and suddenly, after a week of talking together, found very little to say.

Tomorrow lay before Glenda like a desolate road, the kind

of road that led out of Hounslow to the great nowhere. She imagined herself walking down the road with no Sam by her side. All week long, his cheerful face beaming from the moment he came to collect her in the morning until the moment he pressed her hand goodnight, he had been her ever present companion, her friend. And now they had to go their separate ways, he to his family and his fishing, she to the little flat above the monstrous McCluskies.

'Will you be sorry to go?' Sam asked.

'Very sorry,' she said.

'You can come and visit with Tom. Mum says he's coming to see us.'

Sam grinned. 'Can we see the lions in Trafalgar Square?'

'Yeah, and we can go to the Natural History Museum.'

'Battersea Fun Fair?' Sam's eyes were alight.

'Sure. There's lots to do in London.' They were silent for a moment.

'Look. Your sausage is ready. Can you do one for me?'

The shadows lengthened as the children ate their supper. The first taste of grit in Glenda's mouth was quickly followed by the blackened taste of the burnt flesh. 'Lovely,' she said dreamily, lying back with the end of the sausage between her fingers. 'Best sausage I've ever had, Sam.'

Sam attacked the pile of chips. The fire whistled and occasionally tossed a meteor of flares into the sky. One side of Glenda felt the heat of the fire and the other the cool of the evening. Sam lay beside her. His fair hair in the firelight gleamed silver and his eyelashes were long. Glenda watched him and he her.

'You ever kissed a boy?'

'No.' Glenda said. 'I'm only five.'

Sam smiled. 'Of course,' he said. 'But you're so grown up for your age, you know.'

Glenda was pleased. 'Everybody says that. Mrs Jones — that's the lady in the corner sweet shop, you know, the one I told you about, that gives us dinner?'

By now they knew each other's lives intimately. 'The one with the back-boiler that burps,' Sam added.

Glenda burst into a fit of giggles. 'That's the one. Well, Mrs Jones says I'm precocious.'

'That's a long word.'

'Yes,' Glenda beamed. 'I looked it up in my dictionary. It means I developed too soon. Mrs Jones just snorted all funny when I told her that, and said I was too clever by half.'

'Then, Miss Precocious, do you mind if I kiss you?' Sam's voice trembled and there was an awkward pause.

'Of course not, silly.' Glenda closed her eyes. She was glad she was lying on the ground because she had no idea of what was coming next. Did kissing lead to writhing and rolling around like her mother and her boyfriends? Or did it mean a mouth-to-mouth struggle like Glenda had seen in the romance magazines that Minnie read and then hid under her mattress only to be retrieved by Glenda when Minnie was out shopping?

Sam's face loomed over hers. His back blocked the fire and she felt a cool wind take the heat from her cheeks. Sam lowered his face and briefly held her lips with his own. 'I'll miss you, Glenda,' he said.

Glenda opened her eyes, relieved and saddened. 'I'll miss you, too, Sam. Very much. You're the first friend I ever had.'

'But you'll make friends at school. You'll see.'

Glenda heard Minnie opening the door of the cottage. 'I've got to go, Sam. It's time for bed.'

He jumped up and kicked sand over the fire. 'I'll help you take the things back to the kitchen, and I'll be at the coach tomorrow to see you off.'

'We leave at six in the morning.'

'I don't care, I'll be there,' Sam said.

They put the pan and the dishes in the kitchen sink. 'I'll do those with Tom,' Minnie offered. 'Glenda, you get to bed. We're up early tomorrow.'

Glenda knew that Minnie wanted her out of the way. But this time she didn't feel resentful. This time she had a friend of her own and she had been kissed for the first time in her life. Glenda went to bed feeling a little overwhelmed.

The coach pulled away. Minnie, sitting next to Glenda, had tears in her eyes. 'He was ever so nice, Glen,' she said. 'He really was. He says he wants me to marry 'im and live down 'ere.'

'Why don't you, mum?' Glenda found herself immediately excited. Oh, the thought of being with Sam for good and of never having to leave the seaside! And Glenda, in all honesty, did like Tom very much. He'd be a good stepdad.

Outside the window, Sam's figure seemed smaller and smaller. Then both he and Tom vanished as the bus trundled around a corner.

'I couldn't,' Minnie sighed. 'I just can't. Besides, you have school to go to and the Hounslow primary is supposed to be a good one. Anyway, he's coming to visit.'

'And Sam says he'll come with Tom. That'll be fun.'

'Yeah.' Minnie's eyes held a distant look. 'That'll be fun.'

But Glenda knew that look. It foretold several weeks of going over to Mrs Jones's for phone calls, followed by ecstatic plans to be made for the great visit, then the phone calls dying away, and then nothing. Not because of Tom, not because of Sam. But because Minnie tired easily of relationships and the fun of it all was in the talking. Talking, that's what Minnie did. Which was why the holiday was such a miracle: It actually *happened*. Most years they spent talking about the summer holiday and they talked about it so much that Glenda ended up believing that she had actually been on holiday. But this time it was all true. Glenda sat back in her seat and looked at Sam's knife. Before the bus left he had slipped it into her hand. 'Here,' he said, 'it's for you.'

'But it's your favourite,' she protested.

'You take it. I want to know that you have it, so whenever

44

I think of you, I know you have something of mine.'

Glenda smiled and clutched the knife. Will I ever be so happy again? she thought as the bus returned Glenda and her mother to the real world.

Re-entry into the real world took time. The flat seemed so little and cramped. Hounslow rose before Glenda's eyes: tall buildings, grey faces, and hunched shoulders. Mrs Jones had kindly cooked dinner for Minnie and Glenda on the evening of their return, and Glenda sat and listened while Minnie recounted for Mrs Jones's sake all that had happened at the seaside. In the process of the re-telling, Cambersand was somehow transformed from a reality to a memory.

At night, instead of lying in bed with the sound of the sea outside the window, Glenda heard only the noises of the loud McCluskie clan in the flat below. She said goodnight to the absent Sam and included him in her prayers.

Chapter 10

Minnie searched the local paper, *The Hounslow News*, for job adverts. 'Look,' she said one morning while Glenda sat picking at her cornflakes. ''Ere's one for a cleaning job. It's just up the road in Ealing. Remember those big posh houses past the post office?'

Glenda nodded. She did know those houses very well. They passed them on the way to the park. Before the big houses they also passed the Hounslow Hostel for the Homeless. There, children hung out of the grimy windows and the doors were leaning off the hinges.

'I don't want you to clean floors, mum.' Glenda's eyes filled with tears. Even now she hated to watch Minnie scrubbing the floors of their own flat. It didn't seem to matter how hard they both tried to battle with the soot and the dirt, the little flat never sparkled the way the white clapboard house had sparkled in Cambersand.

'But I don't mind cleaning. Honest I don't. Anyway, it's all for you and your education.' The word *education* fell heavily from Minnie's lips.

Glenda knew that her mother's whole life was devoted to the idea that she break out of this cluttered flat, and that Glenda was going to be *Somebody* – a somebody who walked down the street, people staring at her, hands over their mouths, and eyes shining. 'Did you see Glenda Stanhope go by?' they would whisper. 'I remember her when she was just a little girl and her mother used to clean houses to buy her school uniform . . .' The somebody called Glenda wore minks and sables, even in the summer. And high-heeled shoes . . .

'Come on, Glen,' Minnie commanded. 'We're going to see Phil Clough at Joe's Cafe. Phil's got the latest on the old bastard Alderman Oppenheim. He ain't building no palace for himself on taxpayers' money, not in Hounslow, anyway.' Minnie was snorting with indignation as she carried the breakfast plates to the sink. 'Who does 'e think 'e is?'

Glenda walked back to her bedroom to dress. She picked up *Winnie the Pooh* and read the reassuring passage where Pooh finds Eeyore's tail. I wish I had a Pooh-bear, a real live bear who could look after me, she thought as she pulled on a plaid skirt and a jumper. She picked up her teddy bear, put him on her pillow and made her bed.

Minnie was waiting impatiently. 'We're walking today,' Minnie said and Glenda made a face but said nothing. It was the end of the week and they had to walk everywhere, but anything was better than ending up in the Hounslow Hostel for the Homeless. Glenda kept the hostel in the back of her mind as the most awful thing that could happen to anybody, her personal nightmare.

Minnie forged ahead on the pavement and Glenda hurried along behind. An eternity later, when Glenda had shut her mind down completely and was just concentrating on taking the necessary steps to propel herself beside her mother, they arrived at Joe's Cafe and Glenda fell into one of the chairs.

'Tired?' Phil asked sympathetically.

Glenda released a loud exhalation to show how tired she was.

'Never mind.' Phil ruffled Glenda's hair. 'I've ordered two big buns for you and a glass of root beer.'

Glenda smiled. She liked Phil. He was a kindly, gentle presence in her life.

Minnie threw herself into a chair and let out a sigh. 'Well, what's the word on the new Town Hall, Phil?' Minnie's cheeks were red and shining, as they always were when Minnie was worked up about a particular pet grievance. Alderman Oppenheim had been her most consistent grievance for some time now.

'There's a council meeting on Saturday,' Phil said, 'and they've put the building of the new Town Hall last on the agenda.'

Minnie squared her shoulders. 'Trust Oppenheim to schedule it last. He hopes everybody will've gone home by then, clever bastard.'

Glenda wished that Minnie did not have to fight over whether there was a Town Hall or not. Personally she did not care. The two adults talked earnestly over their cups of tea until Phil cleared his throat and looked nervously at Minnie.

'Minnie,' he said, 'before you go, there's something I'd like to discuss with you.' He flushed and moved uneasily in his chair. 'You see, I've got my war pension and a little bit of money put aside. I'm an old man, no family and all that, and I know Glenda starts school next week. What I would like to do is give you some money to help towards her school uniform and for you to get her a satchel and things like that.' He lifted his hand as Minnie opened her mouth to protest. 'You can make an old man very happy by just accepting the

47

money, please.' Phil's voice was urgent.

Glenda looked at him. She understood that Phil really did want to give Minnie the money. And it was for Glenda to have the thing she most wanted in the world: a proper satchel. Glenda had been looking at them for weeks now, hanging bright and shiny in the shops. All of Hounslow seemed to be carrying satchels. So far Glenda had feared that hers would have to be secondhand, a cast-off from a Saturday jumble sale or from one of the charity shops. 'Thank you very much,' she said firmly, before Minnie could ruin a perfectly good offer.

Glenda got up and threw her arms around Phil. 'Now I can have a real shiny new satchel all my own!'

Phil put a fistful of notes into Minnie's hand. 'It's only fifty quid,' he said, 'but it might help a bit.'

'Fifty pounds!' Minnie's eyes filled with tears. 'Oh, it'll help and all . . . I've been praying for a break. I really didn't want my Glenda going to school in secondhand, like I had to. This means I can get her a new pair of shoes and a blazer.'

'And a satchel,' Glenda said desperately.

Minnie smiled, relieved. The usual worried line around her mouth had softened. 'Thanks, Phil,' Minnie said. 'You're a duck. Really, you are.'

Phil patted her hand.

'And now,' Minnie said with determination, 'we have an appointment with Miss Blanchard. Come on, Glenda. We'd best be off.' She grinned. 'And with our lolly, we can take a bus all the way there.'

Glenda climbed on the bus and sat in her seat looking out at the rest of the poor unfortunates who had to walk everywhere. One day, she thought, as she glided into her dream world, one day I'll have a big shiny Rolls Royce. One with the roof down so she could wave at the people when she went past, as the Queen did.

Chapter 11

Minnie and Glenda walked up the gravelled road towards the big Edwardian house and Glenda could hear a voice ringing out of the wide square windows. 'Pah, Pay, Pee, Poh, Poo . . .' The voice swooshed into the thick dusty air. Glenda thought it all sounded rather rude and looked up at her mother. Minnie had braced her shoulders. The voice was at it again and the top note sounded perilously close to the sound of a train going through a tunnel.

Minnie marched to the big white front door and grasped the knocker which was in the shape of a fist. Thud, thud, the sound reverberated through the house and the voice went silent. Minnie stood clasping Glenda's hand in her own.

The door swung open and an immensely tall, immensely black man stood staring down at them. Glenda was frightened. There were a few black people in Hounslow, but very few. The man grinned. He had bright white teeth and big brown eyes and he was totally bald. 'I've come about the cleaning job advertised in the paper,' Minnie said. Minnie's voice had lost its usual belligerence.

The large black man turned on his heel. 'Follow me,' he said.

The man pushed open another big white door and said, 'Renée, it's about the cleaning job.'

Renée Blanchard was six feet tall and very thin. She wore a rag bag get-up of scarves and a pair of old gloves with the fingers cut off so her long, pointed, chipped red nails stuck out like the talons of a raven. In fact, Glenda observed, looking at Renée, that was just what she seemed like – a great big bird.

'Can you clean, darling?' Renée enquired of Minnie. 'I do so need someone to look after me, as the song goes. Or something like that. Actresses,' she said as she swooped down

49

to the end of the room, trailing pieces of clothing and the smell of a costly scent, 'actresses mustn't do everyday things like sweeping and cooking. One quite loses the fantasy in life.' She passed by the man and put her arms around his neck. 'Don't you think, Abe my baby?'

Abe smiled widely. 'Quite,' he said. 'Quite right. And a man should never do women's work.'

Minnie stared at them. So did Glenda. Then Glenda slowly looked about the room. The room looked like its mistress: exotic, elaborate, unusual, yet beautiful. Huge puffy chairs were covered in silk shawls. A grand piano withstood the weight of music stacked in piles. A very old phonograph and a large wireless stood in the middle of the room.

'How many rooms have you got?' Minnie asked.

Renée frowned. 'About eight, I think,' she said. 'There's only Abe and me here now. It used to be full of my friends – other actresses, poets, painters – but most of them are dead now. Died of booze and drugs, things like that.'

Minnie looked horrified.

'Oh no, darling! Don't look upset.' Renée flew up the room to Minnie's side. 'We bohemians have to die an improper death. None of this departing in bed with your hands crossed. Life,' she screamed at the top of her voice, 'is a challenge! You live like a flame and you go out with a bang. Don't you, Abe?'

'Sure, honey,' he said. 'Sure thing.'

'You already know how you're going out?' Minnie asked nervously.

'Of course. I shall fling myself off Big Ben when I get too old to enjoy my vices,' announced Renée.

Glenda didn't know what vices really meant, but it sounded interesting and definitely worth looking up.

Minnie thought it was time to get back to the matter in hand. 'With eight rooms, you'll be needing me most days. I can come after I drop Glenda in school and stay until it's time to collect her.'

'How marvellous!' Renée looked pleased. She shook Minnie's hand. 'Then the position is now officially taken.' She put her hand under Glenda's chin. 'You poor little thing,' she said in tones of drowning sweetness. 'You poor, poor little thing, locked up in school for the next hundred years.'

Glenda looked confused and Minnie stiffened.

'Glenda is not "locked up in school",' she said strongly. 'And certainly not for the next 'undred years. But she 'as to get an education, same as anybody else.'

Renée threw back her head and she laughed. The laugh was housed somewhere deep in her throat and it came out like a thunderclap. 'Of course she'll get her education like anybody else,' she said, 'but I'll teach her the things that really matter.'

Glenda looked into the huge black eyes. Down, down she watched herself falling headlong into the canyon. She smiled at Renée. She wanted to be this strange woman's friend. Renée and Sam and Glenda, three good friends. Renée could keep secrets. In those big dark eyes, huge secrets lay hidden. She grinned and Renée grinned back.

'Off you go,' she said, patting Glenda on the back. 'Baby, see them out for me. I am tired.'

Glenda last saw Renée lying on a deep old sofa, her head back and her long black hair hanging. 'Good heavens!' Minnie said as they exited the house. 'What a pair!'

Glenda trotted after Minnie. 'Mum,' she said, 'do you think it comes off?'

'What comes off?' Minnie was in a hurry to get to the Co-op.

'The black, I mean.'

'No,' Minnie said. 'I don't think so. But you never know. Chops tonight, Glenda,' Minnie said, the bundle of notes rolled tightly and safe in her handbag.

'Oh good!' Glenda felt happiness rising through her body. How perfect! Chops tonight. And soon hopefully a new satchel, too.

Chapter 12

All Saturday Minnie and Glenda walked the streets of Hounslow. Minnie was like a bloodhound. 'A bargain is a bargain,' she said tucking and pulling at the seams of garments in shops up and down the High Road. 'Look at this!' she demanded, her tone loud and hectoring in one shop. 'Do you call this a blazer? Look!' She pulled mightily at a small piece of thread which hung from the cuff. 'It's ripped. 'Ow much off?' she demanded of the salesman.

'Come on, mum,' she whined. 'Can't we leave yet?' But it was a lost cause.

Glenda had been hoping for a neat pair of brown shoes with lovely pointy toes and perhaps a tassel; Minnie insisted on Clark's sandals. 'I've always wished I had a pair of proper sandals,' Minnie said reverently as they left the hallowed portals of the shoe shop, and went down the road to W. H. Smith's.

First Glenda got to pick out the eraser. There was an assortment of erasers to choose from; long thin erasers, one end green and the other white . . . Not quite right. Alone at the end of the row sat the one eraser that completely captivated Glenda. It was thick, a light brown, nearly yellow in colour, and squashy. Above all it smelled right and when she erased a line of pencil it left lots of bits of itself attached to the paper. Glenda held it in her hand and smelled it. A deep rubber smell. She imagined waiting for the rubber to pour out of a rubber plant in the Far East. Her rubber.

Now it was time to study pencils, a much harder task for there was much more choice. Finally she settled for six perfectly matched green pencils with erasers at the end on their elegant gold-lettered backs. Minnie favoured a pencil box made of tin. 'Look, love,' she said. 'If you don't like that, there's always the little bags with zips.'

Glenda would have none of it. 'No,' she said. 'I know what I want,' and she found it. Glenda's pencil box was unblemished white wood. The lid slid on its grooves to shut the box up, shut tight enough to keep any secrets Glenda may have. The top section took two pencils and had a square hole for the rubber. With a sophisticated swivel the box swung open to expose a deep tray which would take the other pencils. Glenda gave a long sigh of pure happiness. 'Mr Clough'll like this pencil box when I show him,' she said.

'Hurry up,' Minnie said. 'We've still got to get your tunic.'

Glenda found a navy blue satchel. It had an inside zip pocket and an even bigger outside zip pocket. The main zip was shiny and the strap which hung off her shoulder was black. 'This one, mum,' she said. 'I'll take this one.'

Minnie smiled. 'Great,' she said. 'Let's run and do the last odds and sods.'

Keeping up with her mother, Glenda was in a state of exaltation. She had her eraser, her pencils, her miraculous pencil box, and – best of all – her beautiful satchel. She couldn't wait to get home and sit on her bed and play with it all. Glenda was really and truly happy, but amidst the happiness was a pang of loss, for she had dreamed of this moment for a year now and the dream was gone, leaving the ache of reality. And reality was school.

Chapter 13

On Monday morning Minnie was up early. Glenda awoke gazing at the chair beside her bed where a pile of brand new clothes lay complacently. September now had a tinge of winter; foremost on the pile of clothes was a navy blue jersey with shiny navy blue buttons. Glenda lay in bed contemplating all this newness with great satisfaction. When she had gazed her fill at the clothes, she turned her eyes to the little dressing table where her satchel sat, fat with promise.

'Glenda!' Minnie called, her voice high with excitement. 'We got a letter.'

Glenda sat up. A letter? Who would send us a letter? Maybe Tom.

Minnie ran into the room. ''Ere you are,' she said and she handed Glenda a small square picture.

Glenda looked down at the photograph. A warm feeling of remembered happiness crept over her. 'Sam!' she said.

Minnie's face was bent over two sheets of white lined paper. The writing was neat and orderly. 'Tom wants to visit,' she said, 'and he'll bring Sam up for a day trip.' Minnie sighed. 'Why do people always want to hang on?' she asked Glenda.

Glenda did not like the question. 'I want to see Sam again,' she said.

'Well, maybe. But it'll 'ave to be in the Christmas holidays. You have your school to go to now. Hurry up and get dressed, Glenda. I'll make breakfast. You'll have to eat more than just cereal. You need a proper cooked breakfast.'

Glenda pulled on her tunic over her white cotton shirt and she struggled with her tie. Why, she wondered, didn't her mother want to see Tom? People had a way of blowing into Minnie's life and then they were gone. Glenda very much wanted to see Sam. She stood dreamily at the window looking out at the empty school ground, realizing that in an hour and a half or so, she, Glenda Stanhope, would be in the playground looking back at her half past seven o'clock self in her bedroom window. Glenda felt for a moment that she was inside out. Today was a giant step in her life. One of many she would take, this was the first. Life was beginning to fill up, like the parrot house at the zoo, with exotic birds. Mrs Jones was less than exotic, but a safe crow, whereas Renée and Abe were definitely exotic.

'Oh, *do* come on, Glenda!' Minnie called.

'I'm coming!' and Glenda ran into the small sitting room and sat down to a pile of toast and fried bacon.

''Ere, let me do your tie.' Minnie's hands flashed around Glenda's neck. 'After I drop you at school, I'm off to give Renée a hand, and then I'll collect you after three-thirty.'

'Mum, what if I don't like it?'

'Don't like it? Of course you'll like it. Best years of your life, school years. You'll make lots of friends and then you can invite them home for tea.'

'I'll miss you, mum,' Glenda said tremulously.

Minnie smiled. 'I'll miss you too, ducks. But I'll be round to collect you, so you'll be all right.'

Glenda felt more and more nervous.

'Don't leave me, mum.' Glenda began to cry.

But Minnie hurriedly steered Glenda through the school gate and across the playground. 'Take a hold of yourself, Glenda. You'll be all right. I promise.'

Once in the brightly lit classroom, Minnie walked up to the young school teacher. 'This is our Glenda,' Minnie introduced. 'It's her first day at school. Ever.'

Glenda threw back her head and began to cry in earnest. 'Don't go, mum. Don't leave me.'

The young teacher put her arms around Glenda.

'Here's the money for your school dinner,' Minnie said, bending to shove the money into Glenda's pocket. Then Minnie turned quickly and fled from the room. She could hear Glenda's shrieks from the playground. She bit her lip to stop the tears from pouring down her cheeks. She's got to go to school, she promised herself. I owe that to her. I can't let her do what I did. Not the dole and cleaning floors for the rest of her life. Minnie hurried to the bus stop and threw herself into a seat. Oh dear, she thought, I never knew it would be so painful. Please God, she prayed to a God whom she usually neglected, please God let Glenda have a good day. Once the prayer left her lips she felt at peace.

Glenda did not hear the prayer nor did it have an effect on her. She sobbed hopelessly at the back of the class.

Mrs Turner, her teacher, observed Glenda and shook her head. Single parent mother, no socializing, no peer group. Why, she thought, do these women do it? She approached Glenda while the rest of the class put their heads on their hands for a break. 'Here, dear,' she said, pushing a book into Glenda's hands. 'Do you know your letters?'

Glenda said, 'I can read.'

'Really?' Mrs Turner was surprised. 'Who taught you?'

'My mum taught me. She taught me arithmetic as well, but she's not as good at arithmetic as she is at reading.' Glenda forgot her unhappiness. She looked at the book. 'I can read this easy,' she said.

Mrs Turner smiled. 'All right then, why don't you go and choose a reading book to take home with you? I think you'll do very well at school, Glenda.'

'You do?'

Mrs Turner laughed gently. 'Really.' This was one pupil she would enjoy teaching.

Later Mrs Turner said, 'You can help me sort out pencils. My, what a lovely pencil box, Glenda!'

Glenda, from that moment, fell in love with Mrs Turner. Mrs Turner was tall with yellow-gold hair and blue eyes. By the end of the day Glenda was euphoric. When Minnie picked her up from school she chattered all the way home about her teacher. Minnie sniffed as they entered the flat. Mrs Turner this and Mrs Turner that, she thought, feeling quite put out at the pall of misery and guilt that had hung over her day. Obviously Glenda had not missed her at all.

That night she went into Glenda's bedroom to tuck her up with a kiss. Glenda hugged her hard. 'I like school, mum.'

'I told you you would, silly,' she said. 'I'll just be downstairs for a hot bath, Glenda. You go to sleep.'

Lying in the grubby bathroom in the faintly hot water,

Minnie felt sorry for herself. The day, apart from worrying about Glenda, had been enlivening. She had shared her coffee break with Renée who was rehearsing for a play. Abe made the coffee. It was hot and strong, dispensed from the coffee machine, the latest model from America. But the floors of the house were endless and Minnie's back was not used to bending.

She heaved herself into a sitting position and then inspected her breasts. No stretchmarks, she thought. She held a leg up into the air. Her thighs were still taut and supple. Still, if Renée, with her wild hair streaked with grey, could hold on to Abe, maybe there was hope for her yet. She didn't really know what to make of Abe. She wondered if he ate a lot of watermelon. That's what black people did, she thought. She climbed out of the bath and pulled her dressing gown around her shoulders. She wandered up the stairs and into the flat. How cramped and small it seemed after Renée's house. But tomorrow, as they say, is another day, she reminded herself and laid her slightly stiff back on her mattress for the night.

Chapter 14

As the week passed, Glenda found herself venturing out of the safety of the classroom into the playground. Slowly the various bells and rules fell into place and she was able to relax. By Friday she had learned that her teacher Mrs Turner was married to the Very Reverend Turner and that Mrs Turner liked little girls like Glenda who loved to learn.

School lunches were another matter. Glenda was glad she did not have to join the queue for free dinners. Those children, usually ragged and faintly grimy, formed a separate queue and were given green tickets which they handed over to the dinner lady, Mrs Prewett. She was short and fat with a hairy face and cruel red hands, and appeared as greasy as the food she cooked. Glenda hated the way Mrs Prewett splattered her great serving spoonful of food onto Glenda's plate. She hated the way Mrs Prewett talked and the way Mrs Prewett lit one cigarette from another and then ran her hands down her old rusty black skirt tied down with a fly-blown apron. Glenda could not wait to escape back into the calm classroom where Mrs Turner sat at her desk, the sunlight falling on her long blonde hair and she smiled a clean tranquil smile that quite drowned the sound of the music coming from her radio.

'What's that music?' Glenda asked after one particularly disgusting wrangle with Mrs Prewett.

'That's Mozart, darling. Mozart was one of the most wonderful composers the world has ever known. Do you like it?'

Glenda put her head on one side and listened. The notes fell out of the square radio serene and measured. 'It sounds like a lovely drink,' she said.

Mrs Turner smiled. Friday, she thought, is always a long day, but a child like Glenda makes it all worthwhile. 'It does indeed,' she said. 'I have a book for you to take home, Glenda.'

Glenda could feel her heart beating faster. There was always something thrilling about a new book. An adventure between two covers, places to get lost, fathoms to be explored.

Mrs Turner handed her the book.

'*The Secret Garden*,' Glenda read the title out loud.

'It was my favourite when I was your age.'

Glenda was thrilled. The book was not very thick but it had a picture of a beautiful garden, dense with rose bushes, and a boy wrapped in a blanket, just his nose and eyes showing over the blanket. What was he doing there, Glenda wondered, those eyes gleaming? What was the secret? And then the bell rang for the afternoon lessons. Glenda slipped the book into her satchel and took out her maths text book.

Clarence, a thin white-faced little boy who sat next to her whispered, 'Can I copy?' for Glenda was already seen to be someone to copy from.

'Okay,' Glenda said nonchalantly. 'You can if you want.'

Clarence copied furiously, his tongue sticking out of his mouth. He was one of the kids from the free dinner line. He had the same blonde hair and blue eyes as Sam, but he wasn't shiny in the sunshine like Sam; his hair was dingy and his face green. His teeth were decayed and his breath sour. 'Let's be friends,' Glenda whispered, glad at least to have someone to talk to.

Clarence looked up and then smiled nervously. 'All right,' he said. 'Let's.'

Glenda sat back in her seat and watched Mrs Turner move around the room. I've been at school for a week, a whole week, and I have a new book and a new friend. She felt her cheeks rising in a smile, and she waited for Minnie to come and collect her.

Chapter 15

'When Mary Lennox was sent to Misselthwaite Manor to live with her uncle, everybody said she was the most disagreeable-looking child ever seen.'

Glenda wriggled with pleasure. She was hunched up in her bed with the book on her knees. She read quickly and with great concentration, because Minnie announced on the way home from school that she was working Saturday mornings. Saturday felt precious, now that Glenda had spent a whole week rising early in the morning and returning home at four in the afternoon. Time had lost its elasticity; no longer did one day meander into the next. Time had definite slots and bells and lines of shuffling children. Glenda looked up, leaving the world of The Secret Garden and returning to her world, a world with no secrets, just events. Today the main event would be Renée's household.

'Hurry, Glenda!' She could hear Minnie's high heels tap-tap-tapping as Minnie flurried around the flat, getting breakfast, boiling water, flipping a duster over the surfaces of the furniture, busy rushing. Glenda stretched and yawned. She dressed herself and went next door to join Minnie.

'Let's go, pet, or we'll be late.' Minnie wore a tight black pencil skirt and a blue and white striped blouse. Her fingernails were painted a bright shocking pink.

'Do you like working for Renée?' Glenda asked.

Minnie tossed her head. 'Miss Blanchard is a very fine actress,' she said, waving her hand in the air. 'She's got lots of friends as well. Finish your tea, Glen. We'll run for it.'

Glenda was pleased to see a sparkle in Minnie's eyes and a set to her shoulders. Minnie, Glenda realized, usually only looked this well-groomed when she had her eyes set on a man. Glenda hoped that working for Renée would keep her busy enough to take her mind off other 'uncles', the kind that moved in and mooched about the flat. Glenda hoped that the only uncle she would ever have to live with would be Tom, and maybe even Sam could move in with them too.

While she sat beside her mother on the bus she thought about Sam and then, for a change, she thought about Clarence. I have a lot to think about now. Glenda gazed out of the window and allowed her eyes to blur the scenery until the outside of the bus passed by like a back-drop in the films.

The bus jolted to a stop and Minnie pulled Glenda along the road, past the tall privet hedges which smelled of cat. They rounded the corner and then turned into the driveway of the big house. Crunch crunch crunch, then up the shallow stone stairs to the front door.

'I saw you coming,' Abe said, holding the door open. The smell of coffee wafted behind him. He wore a bright red, silk dressing gown. 'Come on in,' he said. 'Renée's in bed. She says to go on up. I'll be along in a minute.'

Minnie, walking ahead of Glenda, led the way up the wide oak staircase. Glenda ran her hand along the thick mahogany handrail. Everything around her in this huge house had been carved and detailed. Even the ceilings were decorated with

60

plaster oak leaves and corniced with cornucopia dripping fruits and flowers. The carpet under her feet was deep and soft. Glenda pretended that she and her mother lived in this house.

Glenda was unprepared for the sight of Renée lying in her bed. She blinked and then, startled, reached for Minnie's hand. Beds in Glenda's world were functional things. Minnie's double bed had a Salvation Army multi-patchworked blanket and two pillows, one for each person in the bed. But Renée's bed, Glenda noticed, had at least six big square pillows, and the huge puffy cloud that lay across Renée definitely was not a blanket. It was quite like an eiderdown, the sort you saw in posh shops in Chiswick and were impossibly expensive.

'Good morning, Minnie. Ah! You have little Glenda with you. Come here, child, and give me a kiss.' Renée extended one long white arm.

Glenda approached the bed hesitantly.

Renée's hair fell over her shoulders, and Glenda could see a mound of hair under the outstretched arm. Renée was wearing a black silk negligée, her enormous breasts swaying loose in the cups. She scooped Glenda up with her long arm and pressed her close to her face. 'What a huggable little darling you are!' Renée cried, kissing Glenda like a pneumatic drill. Renée's breath was cigarette-laden, but Glenda forgot to be afraid and found she was rather enjoying the petting and the hugging.

Behind her she heard Abe enter the room. 'Put the poor kid down, Renée,' he said. 'Here's breakfast.'

Glenda came to sit beside Renée. She felt as if she was sitting on the roof of the earth. The bed was tall and high off the floor. Minnie seemed miles away at the other end of the room.

'Here, child, have some toast.'

Glenda picked up a piece of toast. Several pieces were jammed into a silver toast rack. This toast was not thin like

61

the bread from the Co-op; this toast was thick and fat and square. Glenda bit into it when Renée had applied a large amount of butter and jam. She realized that nothing the poor have faintly resembles what the rich enjoy. Renée, she thought, lying back on the big square pillow, must be awfully rich.

Minnie and Renée were talking about the night before.

'Absolutely riveting, darling!' Renée was saying. 'Couldn't believe it. The old fart was pissed!'

Glenda closed her eyes. She held on to every word coming from Renée's mouth. People, she thought, didn't talk like that in Hounslow, not even in the cinema. But this was real life. Renée said words that sounded murky. 'You wouldn't believe it, Minnie. That old bag Julia, the one who plays opposite me, well she's balling the producer. Can you imagine?'

Abe slipped into the other side of the bed, and Glenda still lay curled in the crook of Renée's arm.

Minnie stood beside the bed, her eyes alight. 'Really?' she said. 'Really?'

'You'd better believe it.' Renée's voice was like the scrunch of a shoe on thick gravel.

Glenda decided she'd believe anything Renée said for ever. At this moment she couldn't decide who she loved most, Renée or Mrs Turner: Mrs Turner with her wide apart blue eyes and luxurious silken, long blonde hair, or Renée with her grey-streaked tresses streaming down her back and over her shoulders. Renée whose arms were long and thin but whose bosom was massive and smelled of perfume and a light tinge of musky sweat.

Glenda looked across at Abe. He had an enormous black hand wrapped around a pretty little porcelain cup of coffee. Well, she thought, the colour certainly does not come off. The sheets and pillow cases remained a glistening white. Abe, she noticed, was not wearing anything under his dressing gown. The thought crossed her mind like a jolt of electricity. Glenda had seen uncles in grey Y-fronts and not thought much about it. The men were thin grey wraiths in her life, but Abe lying there, all sleek muscles, casually sitting or lying beside Renée, seemed to have secrets that were unknown to Glenda. She wriggled herself into a fold in the pillow and sighed. How lovely to be rich, she thought. One day, one fine sunny day, she would take her mother by the hand, throw open the door of a lovely house and say, 'It's all yours, mum . . .'

'I'll get started in the kitchen,' Minnie said and Renée stretched.

Glenda felt Renée's spine arch. She watched Abe as he slid his hand behind Renée's back, and felt the heat from Renée's body. She also felt Renée's spine curve to fit Abe's hand, and was afraid. 'I'm coming with you,' she cried. She jumped off the bed and ran across the room to join her mother. Something was about to happen in that room and Glenda knew she did not belong to that happening. Way ahead of her she saw a small door marked PRIVATE. Whatever the something was, it belonged for now behind that door. 'I'll help you, mum.'

'Thanks, love.' Minnie clip-clopped down the stairs. The sound of Minnie's platform shoes was muffled in the thick carpet, not like the sound of the same shoes this morning in the flat, tip-tapping on linoleum.

Glenda followed her mother into the kitchen. Not long now and Glenda could sit on her bed and drown herself in *The Secret Garden*. There were lots of secrets in this house, Glenda thought, but for now she was content to find her secrets in books. Books didn't hurt you; they just let loose a flood of words and you could always put the cover down firmly and compress the words back into the book and walk away. Glenda was reminded of the story Minnie read to her about Pandora's box. In that room upstairs it felt as if a corner of the box had been opened and a piece of Glenda had slid into the box. Nothing would be the same again because in the flash feeling of heat and energy that passed between Abe and Renée, Glenda sensed a dangerous current. A high tension wire like the wires along the road on telegraph poles. Better to think about the secret in the garden, not the one upstairs. Glenda vigorously polished the silver after-dinner tray and mentally added the tray to her list of belongings to be owned in the future. 'Isn't it nice, mum?' Glenda said.

'Yeah,' Minnie said thoughtfully, 'but all that polishing.'

Glenda said nothing. One day she would have someone to polish *her* silver, someone to open her door and to usher her into her own big square hall. Some day.

Chapter 16

Time began to stretch out now. Glenda found that her days were spent in the peace and safety of her school under the calm gaze of Mrs Turner, and Saturday mornings were spent in the wildly thrilling company of Renée and Abe. Sunday dinnertime she sat with Minnie who retold the stories of the week to Mrs Jones who *well-I-never*ed. Several times a month they went over to Joe's Cafe to talk to Phil Clough. 'I'm worried about Phil,' Minnie said once.

But Glenda only smiled. 'You sound like *Mrs Dale's Diary*,' she said. Mrs Dale's worries and concerns over her Jim were an important part of their wireless ritual. Because Minnie had no family of her own, they both took the Dales to their hearts and they worried, too, over the doings in the English countryside.

Letters of invitation had been dispatched to Tom and to Sam and a date had been set for a day in London just before Christmas. Now, with Christmas approaching, Minnie had her Co-op savings book and the extra bit of money that Renée paid Minnie for her cleaning job meant that life was not such a tight squeeze. Minnie could take out her purse without a heart-stopping anxious look on her face. Glenda was glad for that. At times, when the money had been so low it was absent, Minnie and Glenda had memories of crouching on the floor when the rent man came knocking. He was a large kindly man, but even he had to collect the rent.

'It's not that I don't know that you do your best,' he would say, shaking his head. 'There's plenty that'll thieve the rent . . .'

But now on a Friday, Minnie could open the door and invite the rent man in for a cup of tea. He even stayed for dinner once or twice, for Minnie, always a good cook, could now afford some decent ingredients. Yes, Glenda thought, Renée made a lot of difference to their lives.

This Saturday was the first Saturday in December. Mrs Turner was arranging the school nativity play and Glenda was the third angel on the left. Nights were spent with Minnie working over Glenda's nativity costume. The grim grey streets began to assume a festive air. Bits of tinsel hung in tobacconists' windows. Woolworths had piles of presents on their counters, and Christmas crackers exploded into all the shops. Sprigs of holly adorned boxes of chocolates. Horses pulling carriages appeared on biscuit tins. Every week Minnie bought something towards the great day.

Glenda was hoping for a bicycle, a fat, shining, pink two-wheeler to ride in the park. She had seen the one she wanted in a shop up the road and Minnie nodded saying, 'We'll see, we'll have to see, love.'

Downstairs in the McCluskie flat the family seethed and boiled. PC McCluskie arrived home most nights in a less than festive mood. Minnie found Mrs McCluskie in tears more and more often. The muffled yells came through the ceiling and sometimes sitting by the coal fire, Glenda looked at her mother and frowned. 'Is he hitting her, mum?' Glenda asked, as a series of thumps and shudders rattled the window frames. Sometimes the children could be heard screaming and running from one room to another. Angry curses caused both

Minnie and Glenda to pause. Sometimes Minnie took the broom handle and banged it hard on the floor, but lately she interfered less and less because, although Mrs McCluskie cried and sobbed and tried to cover her black eyes with thick pan stick make-up from Woolworths, she never left her husband. But then, Minnie said after yet another conversation about leaving, where could she go? The Hounslow Hostel for the Homeless was just round the corner. But all that would happen was that they would take away the kids. Put them in a home. And you don't want that, not a home . . .

The tension in the house tightened, and after a happy day at school Glenda dreaded the return. PC McCluskie was on a late shift, so all was safe until eleven o'clock at night when the pubs emptied out and McCluskie came home. 'Can't we tell someone, mum?' Glenda pleaded.

'No point, love,' Minnie said. 'There's only the Social, and they don't do nothing.'

Glenda sighed. Between the covers of her books there lived an orderly world. She finished *The Secret Garden* in an orgy of tears. In *The Secret Garden* a boy was reunited with his father. How bitterly Glenda wished she had a father of her own! Downstairs was a huge cruel man who beat his wife and abused his children. Never, even if he lived for a thousand years, would PC McCluskie love or respect anyone. He was a nasty, shallow bully. Books, Glenda decided, were better than real life.

Mrs Turner was worried about Glenda. She saw the shadows under her eyes. 'Is there anything the matter, Glenda?' she asked.

Glenda shook her head. 'No, Mrs Turner,' she replied. 'Could I have some more books, please?'

Mrs Turner smiled her golden smile and Glenda knew that her teacher would not make head nor tail of the life lived in Glenda's house. The life of Minnie and Glenda and the life of the Reverend Turner and his beautiful wife were so far apart they would never cross.

Mrs Turner had been brought up in the country. When she read poetry to the children it was all about the sea and the Dorset coast she loved so well. She had five sisters and brothers and a father that she idolized. At the age of eighteen she made her father the happiest man on earth by finishing her schooling and going to a place called Cambridge. When Glenda heard the word Cambridge on Mrs Turner's lips, she saw her face change and a warm soft glow take over. Memories about Cambridge must be like memories of Joe's buns, Glenda thought. You know what those memories taste like, but each time you go back it's like the first time. 'Can anyone go to Cambridge?' Glenda asked in the second week of December when the turkeys hung upside down off the struts of the awnings of the butchers' shops.

Mrs Turner smiled. It was the end of a long Friday. Rehearsals were over and Minnie was waiting in the shadow of the classroom to take Glenda home. 'No,' Mrs Turner answered. 'Not anyone. But exceptionally clever people who work hard have a chance.' And a clever little girl like you, Mrs Turner thought, might some day have a very good chance.

On the way home, Minnie walked up the cold pavement with Glenda beside her. Glenda practised breathing steam in and out of her nose. Under her arm she had a pile of books.

As they pushed open the door of the house, Glenda glanced into the McCluskie doorway. The children were ominously quiet. Mrs McCluskie, she could see through the kitchen door, was cooking tea. Down by the fireplace Glenda saw the big old poker. There was no fire in the fire place, just the big black poker.

'Come on, mum,' she said hustling Minnie past the door. 'Let's have some tea. I'm hungry.' Glenda didn't want Minnie down there tonight. Without really knowing why, Glenda found her skin crawling, as if an earwig had run across her back. 'Come on, mum.'

They walked upstairs past the bathroom and then onto their own safe landing. Minnie opened her Christmas cupboard and admired her stack of tins. 'Mrs Jones invited us for Christmas dinner. And Phil Clough. And then,' she grinned, 'we've been invited to a party on Boxing Day at Renée's house. Oh, Glenda! Life is exciting, innit!'

Glenda looked at her mother and marvelled at how much better Minnie seemed. Her mother had put on a bit of weight, and with a few extra new clothes and the lively company at Renée's house she was very different. In a week's time Tom would be here for the weekend with Sam and then it would be Christmas. A bike-filled Christmas, Glenda fervently hoped. A windswept rush down the hill with two wheels under her weight. 'Mum,' Glenda said, 'Mrs Turner went to a place called Cambridge.'

'Oh yes?'

'And I want to go when I grow up.'

'How you talk!' Minnie laughed. 'Well, that's a long way off, love.'

Glenda pushed her mince around the plate with her fork.

They got ready for bed. The lights were out and Glenda had a marker in her new book, *What Katy Did*. Glenda was the first to hear the commotion in the downstairs flat. 'Mum!' she called and she heard Minnie get out of bed and come across the room in her bare feet.

'Move over, love, and I'll get in with you. It's just one of their usual fights.' The thumps and banging escalated. Glenda could hear the children running about and screaming. Soon, other neighbours were adding their complaints. Shouts came through windows. 'Can't you bloody well shut up?' 'Sling a hook in it!' was the angry reply.

Minnie propped herself up on one elbow and switched on Glenda's night-light. She shook her head. 'I don't like the sound of this,' she said. 'Sounds like a right knuckle-up.'

Glenda froze. There was a peculiar piercing quality about the children's screams. One particular voice rose above all the others – Mrs McCluskie's. Her voice shrieked to an unbearable pitch. The sound rose higher and higher until it was sharp and cutting into the night. Glenda heard windows thrown open and was aware that people were hanging out in the cold December air. A stillness seized the house for a moment, and then came a loud thudding, a pounding sound. Minnie was on her feet. 'I must stop this,' she said.

Glenda got out of bed and clung to her mother's arm. 'Don't, mum. I'm frightened. He'll hurt you.'

Minnie pushed Glenda behind her. 'I can't let him kill her,' she muttered to herself. 'I'd never forgive myself.' Minnie went back to her own room and put on her dressing gown. 'You stay here,' she commanded.

Glenda followed her mother to the door and stood at the top of the stairs, looking down into the stairwell. Minnie flipped up the light switch and the dim electric light seemed only to add to the gloom. She gazed into the darkness. A loud thud was heard, followed by more thuds, each one more rapid than the last. 'Don't! Don't!' She could hear PC McCluskie's voice take on a pleading tone.

Coming towards her, Minnie heard a shuffling sound. Someone was making their way towards the light on their hands and knees. A shuffling sound and then the choking. Minnie stood motionless with Glenda behind her. McCluskie put his big hands on the first step and seemed determined to slither his way up towards Minnie.

McCluskie's head ran in rivulets of blood, pouring out of the side of the head and down his face. His huge nose poked out of the blood and his mouth was a black cavern. 'Help me,' he called. 'Help me. She's done me in.' His hands stained the walls. He put his head down on the second step, his body twitching in a series of short convulsions. Behind him Minnie could see Mrs McCluskie standing paralysed, still clutching the fire iron. Nobody moved.

Over Minnie's shoulder Glenda saw PC McCluskie, now completely immobile. 'Go back into the flat, Glenda, and close the door. I'll be with you in a minute.' Minnie slipped down the stairs, stepped over McCluskie's prostrate body, and went up to Mrs McCluskie who was staring speechlessly in the corridor. She could hear the children beginning to move around. A general babble of noise, and then she heard a police car in the distance. The high panicky whine. Please, God, she prayed, someone has called them.

Someone had. A big bang on the front door and the room was filled with large men in uniforms.

Minnie took Mrs McCluskie by the shoulder. 'Can I take her upstairs for a cup of tea, Officer?' Minnie asked.

The constable took a look at the huge body on the floor and at the bent and shaking figure of Mrs McCluskie. The police photographer was snapping shots of the body from every angle. A reporter from the local newspaper was already squeezing his way in the door, trying to get information from anyone who would talk to him. The police constable shook his head. 'A bad business,' he said.

He took the poker out of Mrs McCluskie's hand. 'Well, she won't be going nowhere,' he said. 'Tell you what. We'll get this mess cleaned up and then I'll come up and talk to her. This been going on long?'

Minnie knew what he meant. 'For years,' she answered.

'I dunno.' The constable was tired. Why, he thought, do they always go at it before Christmas? Most of his last week's duties had been domestic events. He hated domestic events. There was no shape and no plan to them. Walking into the houses where enraged husbands cornered their wives was more dangerous than chasing armed murderers. 'Come on, lads, give us a hand. You,' he pointed to the older McCluskie daughter, 'take the kids into the kitchen and give them a cup of tea. I've phoned for the social worker. Get the kids' clothes packed.'

'We'll not be split up?' the girl asked.

'I can't promise anything. Move, love.' He heard the doctor's car pull up, and looked at Minnie. 'A bad business,' he said. 'A very bad business.'

'But she had to do it,' Minnie heard herself saying. 'She had to. Or 'e would 'ave killed her.'

'He's one of our own, dearie,' the constable said. 'We don't like nothing 'appening to one of our own PCs.'

Minnie put her arm around Mrs McCluskie's shoulders. 'You come upstairs with me, love. Glenda and I will give you a lovely cup of tea. Don't worry. I'll speak up for you. You 'ad to do it. He would have killed you if you hadn't.'

Mrs McCluskie's body was wracked with sobs. 'I know I know, the bastard.'

Upstairs, sitting at Minnie's dining table, Mrs McCluskie was still sobbing. 'I hated him, you see.' She raised her haggard face from her arms and looked at Minnie. 'I really hated the fucking bastard.' And then she let out an animal wail. 'But I loved him. Do you understand, Minnie? Do you?' She held on to Minnie's arm with such force that Glenda was startled.

'But he hit you,' Glenda put in, feeling she must help her mother out.

Minnie shook her head. 'No, Glenda,' she said. 'You're much too young. Yes,' she said gently putting Mrs McCluskie's grasping hand back on the table. 'I do understand. Loving and hating's very close together. I've made me own mistakes in my time. Yeah, I understand.'

For Glenda, it was too many hours to stay awake before Mrs McCluskie and the children were taken away.

Thank goodness, Minnie thought as the tears of the children hung in the cold morning light, Glenda was fast asleep. The three older ones were going to a children's home in Ealing and the four youngest to somewhere in Hammersmith.

71

Minnie tried to get the addresses from the social worker. 'So as I can visit,' she said.

The social worker had a face like a rat trap. 'No visiting,' she said, and indifferently she swept the howling children off to her car.

Minnie grimaced. She was one of the lucky ones. She had Mrs Hopwood, a good social worker. But the new breed, she thought, just in it for the money. Mrs McCluskie went off with the police and the last sight of Mrs McCluskie was a thin hand waving through the window. 'I'll be up to see you!' Minnie shouted. 'Tomorrow after work!' Mrs McCluskie heard her and Minnie turned back into the now empty house which looked as it had always looked, except for the suspicious splashes of blood which had been hurriedly and inexpertly wiped. Must give it a good scrub-down tomorrow, Minnie thought as she climbed the stairs.

She checked on Glenda. There were tears clinging to the child's face and Minnie felt dreadful. Why, she thought as she got into bed, do I have to expose her to this sort of thing? Still, I can at least buy her the bike she wants. She fell asleep and was tormented by the last look on McCluskie's face. His hollow mouth hung open.

Chapter 17

Minnie woke up with a strangling feeling around her neck. She sat up and heard the silence. She was amazed she had slept at all. Last night's events suddenly appeared before her mind. The flash of the camera belonging to the local newspaper reporter seemed to catch the whole sordid story, the body in the hall and the weeping of the wife and the children . . . Minnie lay back defeated. She felt alone. A failure. Minnie, who had jauntily left her childhood behind her and promised her own child a future free of the stench of crime and poverty, had inadvertently led Glenda into a situation where a man had been murdered, the wife taken off to jail, and the children collected like little brown parcels. In one night everything Minnie had fought for was taken away. She had failed Glenda.

Now, no doubt, the local paper would blast the story across the front page and Minnie's failure would be public knowledge. She felt a deep sense of shame.

Of course, everybody knew that men beat their wives, but no one ever discussed the matter. And if a woman's face was bruised, it was a cupboard door or a fall downstairs that was to blame. Minnie sighed and decided she must get up. Not only must she get up, but also she must plan to get out of this house. The fearful events of last night would not just go away. The shadow of the death and the blood would be there always. She must go and telephone her social worker, kindly Mrs Hopwood, and ask to be transferred.

Minnie put the kettle on and called Glenda. Glenda came into the kitchen in her pyjamas. 'Did last night really happen, mum?' Glenda asked, her eyes fearful and her mouth trembling.

''Fraid so, love.' She pulled Glenda to her. 'We'll both go over to Renée's and you can help me. I've a lot of dusting to do.' Minnie talked on while her mind whirred and sprang. I hope we get a transfer, she thought, but not too far, so Glenda can stay at the primary. 'Come on, Glenda. I'll make you your favourite pancakes and then we'll stop by Mrs Jones's on the way. I have to phone Tom and tell him the visit is off.'

Glenda understood. 'Sam wouldn't like it here, not with that mess in the hall and a dead body. It was all right while we played in Cambersand, killing Germans, but not like last night.'

'Please, love, let's try and forget about last night. Let's think of something else.'

'What like?' Glenda was willing to be distracted.

'Well, let's talk about Christmas coming up.' They both

tried, but reality lay downstairs in the appalling silence that seeped from under the front door.

Finally, the breakfast things back in place, Minnie took up her vast handbag and, becoated, they went down the stairs holding hands tightly. Glenda tiptoed past the McCluskie front door, trying not to breathe. Somehow without the McCluskie clan in the rooms the place smelled even more sour. Only the Clorox used to remove the bloodstains cut the smell. Minnie wrinkled her nose. 'Phew!' she said and her body crawled with fear and loathing. One day, she thought as they banged the door shut and left the house, soon we'll leave and never go back.

As they walked down the road Minnie saw the curtains twitching. She imagined the muffled comments and the remarks. People she vaguely knew brushed past. No smiles, no nods of recognition. They were embarrassed to know someone who had been so nearly involved in a murder. Minnie was embarrassed also, deeply embarrassed. She dragged Glenda at a fast pace behind her and took courage as she flew through the door of the shop, her presence announced by a sharp ping of the bell. Several people stood around the shop with eager looks on their faces.

'Take what you want and get out,' Mrs Jones said loudly. 'Don't be standing gawking there all day.'

There was a shuffling rush to the counter and money changed hands, and then Minnie breathed a sigh of relief as the last customer left the shop. Mrs Jones took off her glasses, rubbed her eyes and put out the CLOSED sign.

Mrs Jones's eyes were bulging with excitement. She had a copy of the Hounslow newspaper in her hands. 'You poor souls,' she said, addressing Minnie and Glenda. 'What a night you must've had!'

Minnie nodded wearily.

'Come on, then,' Mrs Jones said. 'Let's have a good cup of tea.'

Glenda followed the two women into the kitchen. The back-boiler hurrumphed reassuringly and Glenda sipped from her cup. Mrs Jones, she reflected, always kept the pot hot. You have to wait at our house for the tea to boil and for the pot to sit, and then for it to be poured into the teacup. But here it came up immediately and comfortingly. Tea solved everything, Glenda thought. Minnie was repeating the details in a low monotone, glancing occasionally at Glenda. Mum is really upset, Glenda thought. Glenda was upset, but still, behind the blood and the thumping and the noise, she also felt curious. What were they going to do to poor Mrs McCluskie? And anyway, with her old man being such a beast, why isn't everybody pleased he's dead? 'I'm glad he's dead.' Glenda's voice crashed into the conversation.

'*Please*, Glenda!' Minnie looked shocked. 'What an 'orrible thing to say!'

'Are you sorry, mum? He was so awful.'

Mrs Jones's nose twitched and Glenda could see her eyes were laughing.

Minnie said slowly. 'Well, if I 'ad to be honest, I'm not sure just what I feel, but I do feel sorry for poor Mrs McCluskie. And if Mrs Jones don't mind, I'll borrow the phone and see if 'Ounslow Police Station know where she's gone.'

'Probably to Holloway, I should think,' Mrs Jones put in.

'Imagine that,' Minnie said. 'Imagine somebody we know in 'Olloway.'

Mrs Jones shook her head. 'I don't know,' she said. 'I don't know what things are coming to these days. Wives killing their 'usbands . . . In my day your old man gave you a thump or two on 'is way 'ome from the pub, and you knew he loved you.'

Minnie raised her head sharply. 'Getting thumped has nothing to do with love. If any man hit me, he'd better lie awake in the dark. I'd bide my time and then I'd kill him.'

Glenda was amazed at her mother's vehemence. 'Yeah,'

Glenda joined in loyally. 'And I'd help her, too. Nobody hits my mum.'

Mrs Jones smiled. 'You modern generation. You just don't understand.'

Minnie said, 'I understand only too well. That's why women die all the time. Nobody wants to do anything about it.'

'Well,' said Mrs Jones somewhat haughtily. 'For better or worse. That's the way we went into marriage.' She coughed, her old chest rattling. 'Until death us do part.'

'I'd better telephone the police,' Minnie said again. 'I'm a material witness.' She made a face. 'I don't mind helping poor Mrs McCluskie, but I don't fancy the idea of standing in the dock.'

'I'll be in late today,' Minnie told Renée over the telephone. Then she telephoned the police station. She came back rubbing her hands. 'Well! Mrs McCluskie *is* in Holloway after all. I can visit her, if I get a slip, and a police sergeant will come by at some point for another statement. Thanks for the tea and the telephone. Mrs Jones, I'd best be going. I've told the school Glenda's off for today. Come on, love. Let's catch the bus.'

Glenda sat on the bus and marvelled at her new life. Once it had been her mother and herself against the world. Now Minnie and Glenda had friends. And Glenda was looking forward very much to spending a whole day at Renée's. Maybe it was worth old man McCluskie getting killed. Minnie was crouched over the local newspaper. Sure enough, there on the front page Glenda could see their front door hanging open and some shadowy, looming figures bent over what she knew to be PC McCluskie's dead body. She gazed around the bus and wondered if anybody else knew that the picture was of their house and that she, Glenda Stanhope, was in the newspaper front page, too: the small child in the background of the photograph, sitting scared at the top of the stairs.

76

Chapter 18

Minnie telephoned Mrs Hopwood from Renée's house. 'I'm sorry, Minnie.' Mrs Hopwood sounded tired. 'I'll do what I can, but I don't think we have any immediate accommodation. There's always the Hounslow Hostel for the Homeless, of course.'

Glenda, who was leaning against her mother, saw Minnie's face go grey. 'No, Mrs Hopwood. I'd rather stay in the flat than go to the Hostel.'

Glenda grabbed Minnie's hand. 'We can't go there,' she whispered fiercely. A few of the children at the primary came from the Hounslow Hostel for the Homeless and nobody talked to them at all. Glenda felt frightened and shaken.

And suddenly the events crystallized in Glenda's mind. Before and during the awful moments the whole thing had been blurred. But now a terribly clear reality emerged – PC McCluskie was dead, very dead. His wife was in jail and his children dispersed. The awful inhuman form dragging itself up the stairs with the misshapen head and pouring blood once had been a human being. Glenda felt her legs twitching with revulsion.

Minnie put the phone down and Renée came into the room. 'I've been talking to Abe,' she said. Her long fingers were pulling at her hair. She looked at the two forlorn figures: Minnie perched on the chair beside the telephone, Glenda sitting on her mother's lap. 'We decided that it would be much better if both of you took the flat downstairs. It's been empty for ages and I need someone to live down there. If I go off on tour Abe and I need someone to babysit the house. Besides you can't go back and live in the house after that frightful murder. It's all decided. Abe's bringing round the car. Minnie, you go and get packed, and I'll stay here with Glenda.'

77

'Live here? With you?' Minnie's eyes filled with tears. 'You really mean that, Renée?'

'Absolutely,' Renée said firmly. 'We're still in Glenda's school district, so she won't have to change schools. And this way she gets a garden to play in. What do you think of that, Glenda? While your mother and Abe are packing, we'll go downstairs and have a look at your new home.'

'I don't know how to thank you,' Minnie said.

'You don't have to thank me. Just having you here every day makes my life possible. Before you came it was a nightmare, trying to keep a career going and a house. Abe's a good cook, but a housewife he is not.' Renée's tip-tilted eyes were warm and shining. 'Anyway I could do with a good woman about the place. I don't have many women friends. Most women are such bitches. Don't you think?' Renée glided up to Minnie and, leaning down, she gave her a big hug.

Glenda was surprised to see Minnie's small form crumple into Renée's arms.

Renée continued to hold Minnie, but she looked at Glenda over Minnie's shoulders. She said, 'Don't worry, Glenda. It's much better for your mother to have a good cry than to keep it all in.'

Glenda stood terrified. This was Minnie, her strong indomitable mother, in the arms of someone else. Glenda began to cry.

'Hey.' Abe walked into the room. 'Quit the crying, will you?' He picked Glenda up and carried her to the window. 'Look outside. See?' he said. 'Know what that is out there? That's your fairy coach, princess, all ready to get your stuff and move you into your palace. Dry those tears and let your Abey Baby take care of you.' He kissed Glenda on the cheek.

Glenda felt safe in his big warm arms. She gazed shyly at his earnest brown face and his soft dark eyes. She would be very happy here.

Abe put her down and she ran to her mother. 'Look, mum!' she said. 'Have you ever seen such a car? It's big and green and it has huge silver things wrapped around it. Come, do look.'

She pulled Minnie to the window. Minnie's tears were drying on her face and she rubbed the end of her nose in a handkerchief.

Outside Minnie saw a large green Lagonda parked at the kerb. 'It certainly is a lovely car,' she said.

Abe took Minnie's hand. 'Come with me, doll. Let's get going.'

'I've got to go and see Mrs McCluskie tonight. I promised her before they took her away.' Minnie's voice faltered.

'Don't worry about that.' Renée waved a nonchalant hand. 'Abe'll take you. He knows a lot about prisons. Don't you, baby?'

Minnie looked up, alarmed, and Abe laughed. 'Yeah,' he said. 'One of life's little trips, you know? We'll be back for lunch, darlin'.'

Glenda looked at darlin' who stood in the sunlight with the rays pouring over her shoulders. Somewhere in Glenda's heart a small ball of ice was melting. Maybe, she thought as she saw her mother leave the house with Abe, maybe mum feels it too and that's why she's crying.

Minnie looked small and exposed sitting in the open Lagonda beside Abe. He gunned the car and they roared off down the street.

Renée put her hand on Glenda's shoulder. 'Now you come along with me and we'll go and inspect your new bedroom.'

Chapter 19

Later that night Glenda lay in bed reviewing the day's events. Today, Glenda thought, has to be the biggest day in my life. How come I just had the most terrible day in my life and today I am in this room, lying in a comfortable big bed, with mum lying next door in a beautiful bedroom of her own?

She listed the rooms in her new flat: a sitting room, a real dining room, a big kitchen, her mother's room, and her own bedroom done out in pink striped paper with deep rose curtains. Beside her bed she had a glass night table with an electric clock that showed the time. And even now in the dark Glenda could see the green comforting face radiating the time.

From the kitchen, French windows led to a long green overgrown garden. And just as in *The Secret Garden*, there were clumps of roses here and there and a large bed of blue delphiniums. Glenda lay in the dark with a feeling of enchantment all around her. Perhaps Renée and Abe were sorcerers. If they were, Glenda decided, she didn't mind being bewitched.

The Stanhopes were not on welfare any more. Mum had a real job and they had a proper place to stay, not a sour, mean little flat but a fairy tale palace. The sofas in the sitting room were covered in slippery brocade and the carpets were unstained. Everything was new and shiny and smelled of polish. Before mother and daughter hugged each other good night, Minnie bent over Glenda. 'Good night, my love,' she said. 'We'll be happy here.'

Glenda smiled. She stretched out her arms to her mother. 'Mum, will Mrs McCluskie be all right?'

'I hope so, love. Abe took me to see the assistant governor. She was very kind and says that since Mrs McCluskie hasn't ever been in trouble before, we might find a judge who'll let her off on probation. That means he'll let her go 'ome and then she can 'ave the kids back. Holloway is no place for the Mrs McCluskies of this world, poor soul. She's no criminal. She was crying so when she saw me. I said, "But you always called him a pig." ' Minnie sighed. 'I don't know what to make of it all. Mrs McCluskie said yes, he was a pig. But then she gave a really sad sort of cry and said, "But he was *my* pig." I'm glad you wasn't there to see it. It was ever so sad,' Minnie said.

Glenda, too, was glad she hadn't been there.

Now alone in the darkness, Glenda thought about the school nativity play at the end of the week. And then it was Christmas. Hopefully the brand new bicycle would materialize by the same magic that was touching everything in her life.

Chapter 20

Glenda was very nervous. She found herself regarded as a sort of heroine at school. Little groups of children came up to ask her about the murder. The pack of McCluskie kids that usually infested the playground were noticeably absent. Clarence treated Glenda with great respect, Mrs Turner with sympathy. 'I'm so sorry, dear,' she said, resting a long slim hand on Glenda's shoulder. 'What a dreadful thing to happen.'

Minnie told Mrs Turner about her change of address but without any details. 'We don't want people knowing our business,' she said. Glenda knew her mother's attitude to *our business*. 'Nobody's business but our own' was a well-worn refrain. It was rather a relief for Glenda to live with Renée and Abe who seemed to find everybody's business their business. There was an openness about the two of them that made Glenda feel relaxed. With Minnie, Glenda was always on guard, her mother's faithful protector. If Glenda didn't worry about Minnie and take care of her, there was no one else who would.

But now in the last few days, Mrs Turner noticed a small change in Glenda. Her face was more at ease and she smiled more often. Sometimes Mrs Turner worried about Glenda. She seemed like a little miniature adult. She had no ability to play with other children and she did not make friends. Mostly Glenda stayed in the classroom, her head bent over books, books that were really far too advanced for her. But then Mrs Turner recognized that she was an exceptional child.

Mrs Turner made a point of commenting to Glenda what a nice nativity costume she had. She could see that Minnie had taken hours of expert sewing to make the child a really delightful costume. The blue cloth hung to the ground and Glenda's wings were straight and true, unlike several other angels whose wings and halos hung crooked. 'Don't be frightened, Glenda,' Mrs Turner said during rehearsals when Glenda showed signs of stage-fright. 'Just take a deep breath and count to ten.'

Glenda was counting. One, two, three, four, five, she counted, trying not to pant loudly with fear. Then Glenda saw Renée and Abe sitting with Minnie in the fourth row. All around them sat mothers next to fathers, flanked by aunts and uncles, all of them white-skinned, their cheeks flushed with the heat of the room and the importance of the event. Brothers and sisters who weren't in the play sat also in crumpled suits with socks hanging around ankles, while the girls perched on their chairs in stiff shop-bought dresses. Bits of pink and white lace peeked out of the skirts. Tight bodices encased nascent breasts beating with pride as the girls watched the magic of the nativity.

On stage Mary bent over her Baby Jesus, and Joseph (the tallest boy in the school) put a patient hand on Mary's shoulder. *Silent Night* drifted through the air, the small, thin, sweet voices of the choir welcoming the birth of the Christ-child. Glenda lost her fear.

But suddenly an overwhelming feeling of sadness came down upon her. For a moment she was confused, for her sadness did not form words in her mind. Instead she suffered a shapeless feeling. What did she have to feel so sad about? In the house she had just left there were two Christmas trees. One stood in her own sitting room, lovingly decorated by Minnie and herself, and upstairs was a six-footer filled with baubles of light and a-tingle with gold and silver ornaments.

But Glenda still felt sad. Had she words to give precision to her thoughts, she would have recognized the overpowering longing to have her Dad sitting next to her Mum like everybody else. Instead she was vaguely embarrassed, not just by Minnie who normally would be sitting there alone and friendless, but also Renée and Abe, her new-found friends and employers. Glenda could see people surreptitiously leaning forward to glance at the ill-assorted threesome. Glenda hung her head and hoped that the tears that rolled down her cheek were invisible to the audience.

They were to all except Renée, whose perceptive eyes saw the bend in the child's neck and the sudden droop. Poor little thing, she thought. Renée looked compassionately upon the simple scene, now being re-enacted on the auditorium stages of countless other primary schools in England. Like other people you are not, Glenda, and the sooner you learn that the better. She squeezed Minnie's hand and Minnie gratefully squeezed the hand back. 'She looks lovely,' Renée whispered.

'Yes, don't she though?' Minnie glowed. Tomorrow was Christmas Day, and she and Glenda would spend the meal with Phil Clough and Mrs Jones. I have so much to tell them, Minnie thought as she sat back in her hard little seat. So much.

Chapter 21

When Glenda awoke in the morning, she thought she was still in her old room in Hounslow. Slowly the room righted itself from an early morning spinning and she remembered that she was safe. And that it was Christmas Day.

She jumped out of bed and ran into the sitting room. There, propped up against the Christmas tree was her longed-for pink bicycle. On closer examination, she found it even more luxurious than the one she had seen in the

83

Hounslow Co-op. This bicycle was more of a Rolls Royce than a Mini. Her new bicycle must have come from a real bicycle shop, not the sort of bike that stood in a row of others waiting for a Co-op shopper to come along and wheel it home. No, Glenda was proud to see that this bicycle came complete with a light in front and a bell and a basket. A big, square, useful, taking-your-lunch-to-school basket.

'Mum! Mum!' Glenda called a sleepy Minnie out of her bedroom. She stood grinning with the bike between her legs. Minnie laughed, happy to see Glenda so entranced. 'Abe and I found that bike,' she said. 'It was ever so far away. A great big shop!'

Glenda sat on the saddle. The stabilizers held firm. Then she noticed two other presents and her stocking. Minnie sat under the Christmas tree with her daughter. Renée had picked out a twin set for Minnie, and Abe had given her a string of pearls. Minnie was silent for a moment. 'Everything's so sudden, love,' Minnie said. 'I can't quite take it all in.'

Glenda could. She ripped open her parcels and laughed. 'Look!' she said as a black and white taffeta dress fell onto the floor. 'Look, mum! It's got petticoats! Lots of petticoats.' The dress made a lovely expensive rustling sound. Abe's present was a pair of black patent leather shoes.

'Real leather,' Minnie said appreciatively.

Glenda stuck them on her bare feet and looked at them in wonder. 'Can I wear these to Mrs Jones's?' she asked. 'And my new dress?'

'Sure thing,' Minnie said, imitating Abe. 'Sure, honey.' And she put her arms around her daughter and hugged her. 'Let's get up. I must go and wash up last night's dinner for Renée, and then we can go.'

After the washing-up marathon, Minnie and Glenda were ready to leave the house. As they walked out the front door, Glenda could smell the gravy from Renée's kitchen. Abe, she knew, was cooking Christmas lunch for Renée and a few friends. A disloyal thought crossed Glenda's mind: She wished she could have stayed to have her Christmas lunch with Renée and *her* friends. Renée's friends were much more interesting than Mrs Jones and Phil Clough. Renée's friends used bad language. They had all sorts of different accents and many of them got drunk. When they were drunk they would tell Glenda all sorts of things that Glenda thought only happened to people who lived in places like Tottenham or Hackney. These people lived in places like Chelsea and Westminster. Glenda thought only the Queen lived in Westminster and Hyde Park and St James's Park where she fed the pelicans. No, these people got drunk and did things to each other that even *The News of the World* forgot to mention . . . But Glenda and Minnie were off to see Mrs Jones and Phil Clough and that was that.

At Mrs Jones's house, Phil Clough was there already. He looked even thinner and older than he had the last time she saw him. 'How are you both?' he said, worried by the stories he had heard from Mrs Jones.

'All right,' Minnie said cheerfully. 'You know, mustn't grumble.'

'How is poor Mrs McCluskie?' Phil asked.

Minnie made a face. 'Spending Christmas in Holloway, I'm afraid, but the hearing will be in the New Year. I'm a witness, and her solicitor says if I tell a good enough story she should get off with probation. I'll do me best, Phil. Lord knows the poor woman had to put up with so much. I'd have killed him years ago, the rotten bastard.'

Glenda noticed that when her mother used bad words they sounded ordinary. But Renée could use bad language and make it sound sophisticated. Life was difficult, she decided, hugging Phil.

Mrs Jones retried the McCluskie case throughout the meal, Phil nodding and tutting as the grim details fell from her lips. Minnie sat in on the discussion adding extra bits and pieces. When that conversation wore down, Phil gave a report on the Council meeting about the plans for the new Town Hall. 'Doesn't matter what we say,' Phil said world-wearily. 'Always the same. If they want to build it, they'll build it. Oppenheim'll have his way in the end. Nobody cares what we want.'

Glenda wished she was back in the big house with Renée and Abe.

Chapter 22

Glenda rode her bike. Winging down the road, pedalling speedily, she felt the freedom of the wind blowing in her face, and her feet had a life of their own. Minnie was nervous about letting her go, but Abe was insistent.

'You can't pen her in, honey,' Abe said, as yet again Glenda tried to leave the house. Snow was falling around Abe's massive shoulders and Minnie stamped her foot.

'You don't understand, Abe,' Minnie said.

'Sure I do, I do,' Abe's soft low rumbly voice reassured. 'But you have to give a child liberty.'

If Minnie had seen Glenda's antics once she got round the corner, her mother, Glenda knew, would have had a heart attack.

Very soon Glenda could ride her bike with her hands tucked behind her back. Whizzing in and out of the traffic she especially loved the little fat Morris Minors, with their rounded behinds, and the Austin Sevens – very spinsterly those cars. Little matchboxes on wheels. Then there were the Daimlers with the bowler hats – city cars. Occasionally a long gleaming Rolls Royce cruised past on its way to disgorge its rich occupants at the airport. First class, of course, Glenda reminded herself as she veered towards the tinted windows to see just who the really rich were.

Renée had a friend called Chinchilla who was really rich.

She had a Rolls Royce Corniche, cream coloured. Glenda would very much like to have licked the car all over. Glenda licked the thick Cornish cream from her muffins, and the car gave off the same sweet smell. 'The sweet smell of success,' Renée remarked when Glenda came in one day after she had been rubbing her hands over the bonnet of the car.

Chinchilla grinned and ruffled Glenda's hair. Grown-ups, Glenda decided, couldn't keep their hands off her hair. 'So pretty, darling,' Chinchilla said in her slightly breathy voice. 'So absolutely adorable.' Chinchilla was also an actress, a hugely successful actress. Her face and bosom protruded from posters everywhere. Glenda was amazed by Chinchilla's bosom. It stuck out like the boxes that sat empty in the Hounslow cinema. They were firm and very white. Chinchilla had mauve, silvery hair, big blue eyes, and she was small and neat except for this edifice.

During the holidays Minnie had meetings with Mrs Hopwood – on Mrs McCluskie's behalf, for Minnie no longer needed a social worker. Renée had become involved in the cause of freeing Mrs McCluskie, and New Year's Day had been chosen for a benefit to raise money for Mrs McCluskie's legal defence fund. 'We need the best barrister we can get, and we need to raise three thousand guineas for his fee,' Renée announced at dinner one night.

This particular night was a council of war. Chinchilla had volunteered herself as secretary and Renée took the chair. Minnie was chief caterer and Abe just nodded a lot and said 'Sure thing.'

Chinchilla cried easily, and the thought of Mrs McCluskie incarcerated in Holloway prison and deprived of her children made Chinchilla weep. From Boxing Day onwards Minnie cooked. Her repertoire of dishes was now greatly expanded, thanks to Renée's shelves of cookery books. When she wasn't cleaning or cooking, she visited Mrs McCluskie who cried and cried.

Minnie was confused. 'I don't understand it at all,' she

confessed to Chinchilla. 'How on earth can she miss that dreadful bastard?'

'He might have seemed a dreadful bastard to you,' Chinchilla said, 'but he was her husband for seventeen years.' Chinchilla's round, innocent eyes widened. Minnie felt a shiver crawl up her back. Somewhere in Chinchilla's life, she must have known a PC McCluskie. She must have heard the thumping and the rumbling of a fight. The sharp knock on the wall. The wail and the blood. Minnie liked Chinchilla.

Glenda still had nightmares. So did Minnie.

'If men like that were all bad, it would be easy to forget them,' Chinchilla continued. 'But it's not that simple.' She shook her head. 'Sometimes you think you will never survive them, but then when you do survive, and you leave, you find you will never love again like that, if *love* is the right word,' she said in a small voice.

She walked to the window and looked out. Her hand clenched the curtain. Snow whirled down outside the house and Glenda, eavesdropping on the conversation, could see her face reflected in the windowpane. 'So long ago,' Chinchilla whispered. 'So long ago.' She turned and smiled. 'Oh dear,' she said, 'how silly of me. Just practising a part in a play, darlings. Don't mind little old me.'

Minnie laughed. 'For a moment I thought you were serious, Chinchilla.'

'Me?' Chinchilla put her hand under her chin and threw Glenda a kiss, a big raspberry of a kiss. 'You should know me better than that, darlings. When is Chinchilla ever serious, except where money and sex are concerned?' She smiled. 'Now I must get ready for tomorrow, darlings. What does one wear for a prison benefit?'

Minnie giggled. 'I don't know,' she said. 'Stripes and arrows?'

'She's a rum one,' Minnie said as they heard the Rolls pull out of the drive. 'Still she's got a guest list as long as your arm. And I've cooked so much food, between the lot of us we should raise the money.'

By the time the guests were due to arrive Glenda was in a nervous state. Her job was to open the door and take the coats. Renée bought her a black velvet dress with a big lace collar. She wore her patent leather shoes and a pair of white socks that came up to her knees. Minnie plaited her hair into a French roll. Glenda was very pleased with the result.

The first guest pushed the door open so hard he very nearly slammed Glenda up against the wall. 'Can I take your coat please?' Glenda gasped.

'Oh. Yes, dear.' The very tall gentleman was obviously used to a great many servants. He peeled off his topcoat, dumped it on top of Glenda and then removed his gloves and an enormous round black hat.

Glenda staggered off to the temporary cloakroom which was in the library.

'Well?' the tall gentleman bellowed. 'Renée, Chinchilla, what in hell is this all about? Why am I here? I get a perfectly incomprehensible telephone call from Aubrey who says I am ordered to appear at this house. I hope you're not raising money for one of your wretched causes again, what?'

Glenda had only seen this sort of person in films at the cinema. Now she was seeing one in real life. Renée flashed past and winked at Glenda. 'Don't worry, darling. He really is a dear. And we'll get some money out of him. Just you wait and see.'

The door opened again. In staggered a very old wrinkled lady followed by a much younger man in a green velvet suit. 'That's Lady Chartres and her lover,' Chinchilla whispered. Glenda's eyebrows rose even higher. She knew about lovers. Minnie had the uncles, and Renée had Abe, but this old woman didn't look as if she would survive the night. Her mink was heavy and smelled as if a forest of flowers had died that day. Glenda sank her face into the mink coat and imagined the coat was her own – and with that smell . . . It was a million miles away from the smell of the shop assistants in Woolworths or the smells on the bus when too many women had splashed themselves with too much California Poppy. Those smells made Glenda feel sick.

She found a special place for the mink coat. She draped it over a chair and promised the coat that she would pay it a visit before it left on the ungrateful back of that very old woman. Still, Glenda thought, imagine having a coat like that!

Glenda walked back into the hall, pretending that she was at least as old as Chinchilla and just as pretty. No good thrusting out her chest; there was nothing there to thrust. But she could pretend, couldn't she? Quickly the house filled up with guests. The food, piled high in the dining room, kept most of them busy. Minnie had excelled herself. Though she had been learning how to cook all sorts of foods since coming to live with Renée and Abe, her steak and kidney pie and her beef with dumplings were still favourite dishes. The night was bitterly cold and the smell of the dumplings and the wine gravy intoxicating.

Renée swooped about the room giving a little pat here and a small kiss there. Glenda watched her and she saw the men's eyes as they flitted about. People didn't look at each other, at least not for long. Their eyes were restless: pursuing Renée and Chinchilla, looking towards the door as each new knock allowed another character to enter into this night's theatre. Glenda felt as if she was watching a film at the cinema. Here were all these people, the men in black suits with bow ties, and the women in long gaudy evening dresses. Many of the women wore diamonds twinkling under the lights. Their hands were laden with gems. Glenda knew from her geology book that emeralds were green and rubies red, and her favourite gems were sapphires. But then nothing, she decided, nothing could beat a good diamond. Chinchilla had the biggest of them all. The other women in the room couldn't take their eyes off her finger. Wherever Chinchilla moved this burst of light moved with her.

'You like my ring?' Chinchilla said, seeing Glenda's eyes. Glenda nodded. Chinchilla laughed. 'See that little man with the fat tummy over there?' she said, pointing across the room. 'He gave it to me as a little present.'

'He must like you very much.'

Chinchilla laughed again. 'Oh yes, darling. He likes me very much.'

'Do you like him?'

Chinchilla shrugged. 'It depends on what mood I'm in. He has a very nice aeroplane, and at the moment I am rather taken with aeroplanes.'

'Oh, I see.' Glenda was puzzled.

Full of food, the people filed obediently into the drawing room where rows of gilt chairs lined the floor. In front of the chairs Abe had arranged a head table of sorts. Renée and Chinchilla had a chair each and a very tense and frightened Minnie had the other. Minnie had been practising her speech all week in front of Glenda. 'You sound really good, mum,' Glenda said after the morning's rehearsal. 'And if you get frightened, just hold your breath and count to ten.'

'But I hate speaking to people like this,' Minnie said. 'Why did I get myself into this? Why didn't I mind me own business?' Then Minnie remembered Mrs McCluskie's stricken face in the gloom of the prison lighting. 'Well, I'll do me best. That's all I can say,' she said.

Now she stood wringing her hands in front of this rather large audience. 'Ladies and gentlemen,' Minnie began. Glenda thought she would burst.

'Ladies and gentlemen . . .' Minnie's shoulders dropped and she put down the pieces of paper she was clutching in her soggy hands. 'Look,' she said, 'I'm not an actress and I'm no good at talking in front of people. But Mrs McCluskie was my friend and our neighbour. She knew Glenda from the day she was born and I knew 'er and that man.' Minnie was getting angry. 'Why didn't she leave him? Very simple. She didn't have no place to go. There was the Hostel for the Homeless round the corner, but he'd have found her there. He was a policeman, so even if she did find somewhere to go, he'd find her easy, wherever she was.' Minnie, gaining confidence, looked into the faces listening to her. Nobody fidgeted and nobody spoke. Minnie thought: Maybe even some of these women know what I'm talking about.

'Anyway,' she said, 'the night it happened, my little Glenda and I saw it all.'

There was a horrified intake of breath and eyes shot over to Glenda who sat next to Renée. Minnie nodded.

'I couldn't protect Glenda. The house was small, and PC McCluskie tried to climb our stairs after she beat 'is head in with a poker, but there was no other way. He was a big man and he was very drunk. She 'ad to kill 'im or be killed. Do you know 'ow many women get knocked about in Hounslow?' Minnie's face was bitter. 'I don't know how many,' she confessed. 'Well, not the actual number, I mean. But it's far too many. Saturday night the men come home and they beat their wives and their children. It gets so as the children think it's all right to beat your wife. They don't even notice the bruises. Don't even see 'em after a while. But I do,' she said. 'My dad was poor, but 'e never hit my mum. Maybe that's why I notice the bruises. I never saw my mum bruised, but believe me, women get beaten all the time. Mrs McCluskie's lucky now. At least she is alive, even though she's in jail. If her husband 'ad still been around, she might not 'ave been alive.' Minnie hung her head and she felt her eyes stinging with angry tears. 'It's not fair,' she said passionately. 'It's just not fair that Mrs McCluskie should be in jail, 'er children in children's homes, and 'im buried. He made her life hell for all those years.' Minnie stopped talking. She felt drained.

Renée stood up. 'I am supposed to say something at this

point,' she said, walking up the aisle towards Minnie, 'but I think Minnie has made the events of that night clear to you all. We need to raise money for a top-notch barrister and we need to get Mrs McCluskie out of jail and reunited with her children. Mrs Hopwood, her social worker, is here and has very kindly arranged a transfer, so Mrs McCluskie need not go back to the same house. Chinchilla will accept cheques or cash for the legal defence fund, darlings. So now dig in your pockets and give to a very worthy cause.' Renée smiled. 'Of course,' she said, 'there are a few of you who know very well, perhaps personally, about the matter of wife-beating. Do please give generously.'

Her eyes floated around the audience. Every so often the eyes stopped and stared impassively at a man who blushed furiously. 'Yes, darlings,' Renée said, smiling dangerously. 'There are not many secrets among us, are there?'

Renée knew what she was doing. The rustle of notes intensified and Chinchilla stood by the front door waylaying the guests.

'Well, if one must get mugged at a party,' drawled the tall, exquisite man, wearing the big floppy hat, 'I suppose one might as well get mugged by a pretty lady.'

Glenda carried his huge greatcoat and hat across the floor. Chinchilla smirked. Exquisite took out a thick gold pen and his cheque book. Glenda watched. The cheque book was fat. Coutts Bank, it said.

'Just add another nought, darling,' Chinchilla breathed.

Exquisite gazed down at Chinchilla, his eyes firmly resting on the bust. 'I'd intended to, anyway,' he said coldly. He swept out and banged the door, handing Chinchilla the cheque.

Chinchilla grinned. 'Most notorious wife-beater in Kensington,' she said. 'And look across the room, Glenda. See that famous face with the blue eyes?'

Glenda looked. She could see a man standing by the wall. He was by himself and she noticed his hands were shaking.

'He looks like he's sick.' Glenda observed.

'No.' Chinchilla shook her head. 'DTs. Too much whisky. He regularly beats his wife. She's a famous actress. And he throws her out of the house naked.'

'Why doesn't she run away?' Glenda asked incredulously.

'She's famous. He'll always find her. She says it's better to stay and know where he is than to hide and wait for him to find her.' She sighed. 'Makes you wonder why people ever marry. But we all live in hope, dearest. At least I do.'

Abe came across the floor. 'How are we doing, doll?' he asked.

Chinchilla said, 'Very well indeed. Looks like we're raising enough to cover the legal fees and more.'

Abe picked Glenda up in his big warm arms. 'Come along, little darlin'. Let's go find you some milk and cookies. All these grown-ups get to be too much, don't they?'

Glenda nodded, her cheek resting on his comfortable shoulders. 'Why are grown-ups so awful to each other?' she asked.

Abe grunted. 'Depends on how they were brought up, honey,' he said. 'When I was your age we lived in a shack. Would you believe it?' He nodded, 'A real shack, like the ones you read about in *Tom Sawyer*. But nobody did any hitting in my family. No matter how rough things got. You ever read Mark Twain?'

Glenda shook her head.

'You should some day. I'll get you a copy.' And while he carried her to the kitchen, he told her all about his own family background on Merritt Island, Florida.

In the kitchen, Glenda picked up her glass of milk. 'Do people hit each other in Florida?' she asked.

'Sure they do. Happens all over the world.'

Minnie came running into the kitchen. 'Abe!' she cried. 'There must be thousands here.'

Her hands were full of cheques and large five-pound notes. She plonked them down on the table. 'You count them, Abe.'

Chinchilla floated in, followed by Renée. Both women were talking at once. 'Did you see Moira, darling?'

'What an old bag,' Chinchilla interrupted. 'But then Colin was there. He usually doesn't turn up for a fund-raiser. Guilty conscience, I shouldn't wonder.'

Renée put her arms around Abe. 'Well, that's the barrister's fees covered. Now it's up to the jury.'

Abe smiled at the women and then he said, 'I think Glenda needs to go to bed. She's a tired little girl, Minnie.'

Glenda followed her mother down the stairs and sighed when Minnie tucked her up. 'Thank goodness you don't hit me, mum,' she said.

'The things you say! Of course I don't, love,' she said. 'I'd never hit you. You're far too precious.'

Glenda snuggled down into her blankets. Tomorrow I'll ride my bike, was her last waking thought.

Chapter 23

'Who's that?'

Glenda was sitting on the front steps, watching Abe lovingly clean his Lagonda.

Abe squinted into the bleak sunlight. 'That's the attorney fellow,' he said. 'Caspar Alexander. Supposed to be shit-hot in court.'

'Is he going to get Mrs McCluskie off then?'

Glenda very much hoped he would. Recently, as she lay in bed, she found her nightmares about the murder less troubling, but the thought of the children locked away in a children's home while she had moved into a life of glamour and luxury made her feel guilty.

'Hope so,' said Abe.

This morning Glenda had spent time in her secret garden. 'Abe, do you think I could have a rabbit?'

Abe paused for a moment. 'I don't see why not,' he said,

thinking, poor little thing, no friends and so lonely. 'Tell you what. Let's go in and see what the grand old man proposes to do about Mrs McCluskie. And then I'll take you for a run down to the pet shop. Let's surprise your mother. Not a word now, okay?'

Glenda giggled. 'Mum'd say no, but she can't if we do it first.'

'You got it,' Abe agreed. He stood up and stretched.

To Glenda he looked huge, outlined against the sky, but not as huge as the man who had just entered the house. 'What's his name again?' Glenda asked.

'Caspar Alexander,' Abe answered. 'The man has a fierce reputation and lots of wives.'

'Really?' Glenda was interested. More *News of the World* stuff. Now Minnie no longer bought *The News of the World*. She struggled through *The Guardian* and *The Times*. Renée left the newspapers in the kitchen. Talk no longer centred around Mr Oppenheim and the Town Hall (opposition had proved a lost cause anyway) or the doings of Mrs Jones's customers. Now life was far more interesting, full of pink bikes, murders, events in far-off places. Names like Anthony Eden and wireless programmes like The Goons. Glenda loved The Goons, especially Spike Milligan. She sat in the kitchen with Renée and laughed, both of them swaying backwards and forwards while Minnie disapproved. She punctuated the programmes with a constant, 'I don't see what's so funny.'

Now Glenda could see Minnie's face. She knew Minnie was worried about Mrs McCluskie. Minnie and Abe were her only visitors. But help was at hand.

'Who's the solicitor on the case?' Caspar Alexander's voice boomed around the house.

'Um. George Pinney,' Chinchilla replied.

'That's right. Pinney. One of the Dorset Pinneys, I take it.' Caspar stood in front of the fireplace, warming his huge bottom. 'Good,' he growled, glaring at Chinchilla, who looked visibly put out. She was not used to being ignored by anything male, even if it did resemble a rhinoceros deprived of a week's food. 'Ah!' Caspar's face brightened as Renée came into the room carrying a bucket of champagne. 'A bit of the old bubbly, what! Who's *that* fellow?' Caspar glared at Abe. 'Your houseboy?'

'No,' Renée smiled sweetly. 'My lover. Abe darling, do you want to dish out the champagne? Let's sit down everybody. Glenda, come and sit by me and we will hear what Caspar Alexander, QC has to say.'

Caspar took his glass of champagne very gingerly from Abe's large black hand. He studied the foot of the glass carefully and then took out a large white monogrammed handkerchief and wiped the stem. 'Can't be too careful,' he remarked. 'Ummm.' He sucked in a mouthful of champagne. 'Not bad, my dear. Not bad.'

'It's an unusual bottle,' Abe said. 'I found it myself. Bought a whole case in Arcachon. On my way to get some fresh oysters.'

'Didn't know your kind ate oysters.' Caspar tried to smile.

'Why, yessuh,' said Abe. 'And lots and lots of watermelon.'

Renée could feel the tension in the room. 'Come on, Abe,' she said. 'Let's not talk about wine. Let's stick to business, shall we?'

'Well,' Caspar began. 'We'll see that there are plenty of women on the jury. I don't think the jury will find her guilty. I've had a look at the brief. It was self-defence, but it will all depend on the judge. If we get old Robertson, we don't stand a chance. Knew him years ago. Went to some minor public school. Not quite one of us, oh no, not one of us at all. Can't hold his drink. And he's been known to give the wife a wallop or two. Don't want him siding with the deceased, do we?'

Caspar rocked on the balls of his feet. Renée and Chinchilla sat wide-eyed and waiting.

'Don't worry,' Caspar said. 'Don't worry at all. I'll see to everything.' He finished his glass of champagne and strode out of the door issuing orders. 'Tell young Pinney to get in touch with me. And you, get in touch with my clerk over the fee. For the trial, I mean.' He began to leave the room. Renée followed to show him out. 'This visit's gratis,' Caspar said over his shoulder, 'unusual though it is. Your West End producer friend is an old chum. Said you needed some help. Doing this for him. Otherwise, wouldn't be here at all, you understand.'

'Oh dear!' Renée said when she returned to the drawing room. 'That was quite an experience.'

Glenda sat on the sofa, her legs swinging in the air. 'Can we go now, Abe?'

'Sure thing.' Abe stood up. 'What a son of a bitch!' he said.

Renée cocked her head. 'Nevertheless we need him. He'll get her off.'

'How?' Chinchilla said. 'With his elephantine charm?'

'No,' said Renée, 'he won't need that. It's all in the Old Boy system. Same as me asking my producer if he knew any good barristers. And now that we have Caspar Alexander on our side, he'll get the judge to do him a favour and let him win this one. And later on he'll owe the judge one. It's English justice. It's what made us famous all round the world. You squeeze my arm and I'll squeeze yours. It's a lesson my father taught me and I never forgot it. She glanced down at Glenda. 'Now you see how it's done, don't forget it.'

Glenda looked up at Renée. Her head was full of rabbits. 'Yes, Renée,' she agreed. 'I won't forget.' Somewhere in the back of her brain Glenda registered Renée's words. And years later, many years later, they would come back to haunt her.

Chapter 24

ALDERMAN OPPENHEIM WINS AGAIN! The headlines screamed their local news. Oppenheim's fat unctuous face smiled blandly at everybody who passed the newsstands. Minnie was philosophical. 'You was right, Phil,' she said down the phone. 'Doesn't matter what folks like us say. The Town Hall's going up, anyway.'

Glenda watched her mother's face and wondered why Minnie wasted her time getting so upset. Glenda couldn't care less if they had a new Town Hall or not. But somehow the question of Oppenheim and the new Town Hall had now passed its lifetime as the issue which everyone discussed in pubs and cafes and corner shops. The McCluskie case was due in court soon, and this was by far the newer and fresher popular cause. Let the Establishment have their Town Hall, was most people's opinion, but let's have mercy for poor Mrs McCluskie.

Glenda got to watch much of it firsthand, as Renée's house became the headquarters for many meetings and strategy sessions. 'And do you know,' Minnie informed a very tired Mrs Hopwood over a cup of coffee in the immaculate kitchen, 'as soon as Mrs McCluskie gets out of prison – *if* she gets out – she wants me to take her to her husband's grave. Fancy that now, after all the bleeding bastard did to 'er! I can't imagine wanting to see someone who'd beat the living daylights out of you.'

Mrs Hopwood made a face. 'I don't know,' she said. 'I've been dealing with these cases for years, dear. I sometimes don't know what people want at all. Some leave and start a new life for themselves, but many don't. They just don't. You get them a new place, a safe place, and then just when you think everything is going right, they go back to the person who made them miserable in the first place.' She sighed. 'Human nature is a puzzling thing.'

Minnie lit another cigarette. 'Well, all I know is that if some bastard hit me he'd better sleep with one eye open for the rest of his life.' She snorted.

Glenda smiled. In two days Sam was visiting with Tom, and she was looking forward to showing Sam her bike.

'I must go, dear,' Mrs Hopwood said. 'I've so many cases, so many cases.' Mrs Hopwood left in a trail of scarves and a huge overflowing satchel. Behind, the air lay heavy with lost hope and dying aspirations.

'Poor Mrs Hopwood,' Minnie said. 'She's a good woman, Glenda, but she don't know much about life. All her knowing is from books and you can't learn about life from books, can you?'

Glenda shook her head. Living with Renée during the last few weeks had taught Glenda that. Until she had met Renée and Abe, life had been written in small letters. Now that they had moved into the house, real life in huge capital letters had begun. Now Glenda felt she was sitting in front of the great Wurlitzer that rose from the well in the cinema until mighty and glorious bursts of music streamed out of the organ. But now Glenda was in the seat conducting. She grinned at her mother and said, 'Mum, you got any lettuce for Lady?' Today was cage-cleaning day for the rabbit which Abe had got her – a large white rabbit with pink eyes and long downy ears. She called her Lady because that was what Glenda was going to be when she grew up: a lady.

At the coach station, when Tom clutched Minnie's waist, Glenda saw her mother's dress climb up her thighs. Glenda could see that Minnie was wearing a new, very frilly, black underslip. Glenda noticed that other people were looking.

'Oh, Tom!' Minnie straightened her clothes. 'Please, you're messing up my skirt!'

Glenda stared at Sam who was standing behind Tom. Sam blinked in the sunlight. Glenda showed him that she had brought with her the knife which he gave her.

Tom said, 'We're here. Two of us from the country in the big city. The lad and I have been excited, haven't we, Sam?'

Sam nodded and Tom went off to collect their suitcases from under the coach.

'I've got a rabbit,' Glenda offered.

'Have you?' Glenda remembered with a start that Sam talked with a soft country sound.

'Yeah. Her name's Lady. I'll show you as soon as we get home and,' she said, walking along beside Sam, 'I have a bicycle.'

'We heard about the murder,' said Sam. 'Seen it in the papers. You saw it happen, did you?'

'Oh yeah. Wasn't much to it really. PC McCluskie tried to kill Mrs McCluskie, so she hit him on the head with the poker. Splat.'

'Was there much blood?'

Glenda looked at Sam and realized that this was all *News of the World* stuff to him. He didn't know Mrs McCluskie or the kids that were now languishing in a children's home. 'Lots,' Glenda said, trying to sound nonchalant, trying to forget her nightmares and the picture of PC McCluskie's head coming round the stairs. 'Lots and lots. Mum had to spend a whole day bleaching out the stains. I had to jump the last two stairs so as I didn't stand on his blood.'

'Imagine!' said Sam. They climbed onto the local double-decker bus. Sam gazed out of the window at the unfamiliar wonders of the city around him.

Glenda kept an eye on her mother. Minnie's head was bent and she was smoking a cigarette. Minnie looked happy, Glenda decided. Her face filled out and she was gazing up at Tom. Maybe Tom would be the man in Minnie's life. Glenda rather hoped so.

The bus stopped and they all got off. 'Nice house,' Tom said as they walked up the drive.

'Yes,' Minnie giggled. 'Life's taken a turn for the better.

No more welfare and no more council flat. Here,' she said, opening the door to the flat.

Glenda followed Sam into the sitting room. There was a moment's silence. 'Where should I put my suitcase?' Tom asked, his cheeks going pink.

Minnie smiled. 'In my bedroom,' she answered cheerfully.

Glenda watched Tom's shoulders relax. She looked at Sam. Sam stared impassively back.

'Sam,' Minnie said, 'can sleep on the couch.'

Sam smiled. 'I'll sleep anywhere just to be in London.'

After lunch Minnie decided that they should visit Trafalgar Square. Sam and Glenda spent the afternoon feeding pigeons and climbing on the statues of the lions. Minnie and Tom sat on a bench and talked while the children played.

Later that night when Minnie's door was firmly shut, Glenda crept into the sitting room. 'Are you still awake, Sam?'

'Yes.' Sam sat up. The moonlight streamed into the room.

Glenda cleared her throat. 'Do you think Tom wants to marry mum?'

'I don't know,' Sam said. 'But I want to marry you.'

Glenda curled up beside him. 'I don't know, Sam,' she said. 'I don't know if I ever want to get married.' She remembered Mrs McCluskie's face. 'We'll wait and see. All right?'

They lay in silence looking out of the window.

'Good night, Sam,' Glenda said. She kissed his cheek and slipped off into her own bedroom. She lay back and was pleased. Sam wanted to marry her.

Sunday, and Abe had promised to take Sam and Glenda to the zoo today. Sam had enjoyed playing with Lady the rabbit, and at the zoo Glenda would show him Mr Creswell's bear, fourth pit on the left. He was huge and furry with big white teeth and he had a friendly look on his face. If Glenda leaned over the pit and called 'Here, Mr Creswell's bear,' the bear would rise with his paws in the air and wave to Glenda.

Abe had also promised to give them lunch at the zoo. Not fish paste sandwiches, but a real lunch. Glenda was excited.

After breakfast in the flat, Glenda led the way up the stairs where Abe was waiting for them. 'This is Sam,' Glenda said very seriously.

'How are you, boy?' Abe replied, holding out his big black hand.

Glenda had told Sam that Abe was black. Sam had never met a black person before, but he resisted the impulse to pull his hand away in fear. Then he smiled. Abe's eyes shone and his bald head nodded briefly as he shook Sam's hand. He led them out to the car.

'Today,' said Abe, 'will be a humdinger of a day.'

'What's a humdinger?' Sam asked with a laugh.

Abe laughed, too. 'It's like this.' He walked across the drive and opened the door of the Lagonda. 'Hubba hubba ding ding,' he said, motioning Glenda into the car with a regal bow. 'Baby, you've got everything.' He bowed low and Sam scrambled into the car, sitting upright and nervously beside Glenda. 'And now, my dears, I'll climb into the front of my car and drive you to the zoo. Everybody will stare at my car and at you. And of course,' he said, 'they will all assume that you are two very rich little people with a big buck nigger as your chauffeur.'

Glenda winced. 'Mum says it's not nice to say nigger.'

'Your mum's right,' Abe snorted. 'But it's better to say it than to think it. If I get called a nigger, at least I know where I am.'

Sam wanted to change the subject. He felt uncomfortable.

Glenda said, 'Abe, sing something American.'

'Okay.' Abe gunned the throttle of the Lagonda. *'Binga banga bonga, I don't want to leave the Conga, oh no no no no no. Ain't got no ice cream, candied yams and jelly babies . . .'*

'That's not how it goes!' Glenda cried out, and they all laughed.

At the zoo in Regent's Park, the bear looked as if he had been waiting for a long time for this moment. 'We can't feed him buns because he'd get too fat,' Glenda explained. 'Hello, Mr Creswell's bear!' she called. 'See?' Glenda pointed to the plaque on the wall. 'He was born in Persia, and Mr Creswell brought him to London and donated him to the zoo. And he's my special bear.' She leaned out over the pit. 'Here, Mr Creswell's bear!' she shouted. 'I'm here!'

On cue, the bear stood up on his massive hind legs and waved his paws happily in the sunlight.

At the zoo's restaurant, Glenda ordered the steak and kidney pie. 'I've never had lunch at the zoo before,' she said. 'Not at the restaurant, I mean. I used to come here with mum and we'd sit on a bench and eat our fish paste sandwiches and watch all the rich people go into the restaurant and sit down at a proper table and sit in proper chairs. I told mum that one day I'd be in there too. And today's the day.' Glenda chattered on to Sam. Abe gazed down at her mane of chestnut hair with affection.

He said, 'Your fish paste days are over.'

Glenda turned to look out the restaurant's clean, airy windows. 'I wonder how many of the people outside are looking in at us and thinking how nice it must be to be us.'

'Hundreds,' said Sam.

Chapter 25

Abe delivered them back to the house singing loud songs. '*Chicaboom chicarack, chicaboom chicarack!*' he bellowed. Soon Glenda and Sam joined in.

The three of them got out of the car, thoroughly pleased with themselves and their day at the zoo. Renée opened the big front door and came down the steps to meet them. She put out her hand to Sam and said, 'Sam, I've heard so much about you from Glenda. Have you enjoyed your day?'

Sam nodded, quite overcome with shyness. Glenda watched him. She remembered when she first met Renée and how awesome Renée's tall figure and her long hair seemed all those months ago. Now Renée was Renée and Abe was Abe. Renée put her arm around Glenda. 'Happy, darling?'

Glenda glowed. 'We saw the rhinoceros and the seals. And best of all we saw Mr Creswell's bear. He knows me, you see, and when I call him, he sits up and waves at me. Didn't he, Sam?' Sam nodded mutely again. 'And,' Glenda went on, 'we had lunch in the restaurant. Imagine! Steak and kidney pie.'

Renée smiled at Abe. 'Thanks for taking them.'

'Thanks for taking them? Ha! I needed an escort myself. I love the zoo. I really do.'

'Off you go then, children,' Renée said and she turned to climb the stairs.

'I'm not a child,' Glenda found herself suddenly uncontrollably furious.

Renée raised an eyebrow. 'Glenda,' she said, 'you are six.'

Glenda felt herself blushing. Sam beside her was tense. 'But that doesn't make me a child.'

Renée shrugged. 'All right,' she said gently. 'You're not a child, and perhaps that is a problem for you. We all need our childhoods. Off you go, darling,' she said. 'Your mother will be waiting for you.'

Glenda marched off, her back stiff with outrage. Why, she thought, must grown-ups say such hurtful things? Children only existed in books. Little girls and boys dressed in sweet clean clothes. Children who lived in beautiful houses. Children like Anne of Green Gables or Katy in *What Katy did*. Even Jo in *The Fives* books. Jo dressed like a boy and had a parrot. She had real adventures in caves frequented by pirates.

Glenda opened the door to the flat. Her mother's bedroom

door was still closed. Nobody's mothers in the books she read had men in their bedrooms. In fact bedrooms were never mentioned in children's books. Neither were the visits to the welfare office or the sour smell of poor people all living together in council houses. Poor children didn't have childhoods, Glenda decided. Therefore she did not want to be called a child. Anyway, she sort of knew the door wouldn't be open and said, 'Sam, do you want a cup of tea?' Unexpected tears were threatening to roll down her cheeks. 'Or let's go and see Lady,' she said, desperately trying to gain control.

Sam wanted his cup of tea, but he would rather be out in the fresh air. In the two days he had been there, he had enjoyed himself very much indeed, but he didn't like being inside quite so much. As much as he enjoyed Trafalgar Square and the zoo, he wished himself home again. Home, where nothing much happened but everything did. Home to grandpa who probably was collecting great big fat orange crabs from the crab pots. 'Let's skip tea,' he said, 'and go outside.'

Lady was pleased to see them both. She snuffled and nuzzled. Time ticked away. Glenda looked at Sam. 'Do you think you'll come again?'

'I don't know.' Sam sat on the cold ground. 'I'd like to, but I guess it depends on Tom.' They could hear Tom and Minnie moving about in the flat now.

'Well. Let's go in and see if mum has anything for tea. Hope she made a cake.'

Minnie, dressed in a wrap-around skirt and a halter-neck top, had indeed made a cake. 'Carraway,' she said, taking down the cake tin from the top of the fridge. 'Abe says he'll drop you both off at the coach station,' Minnie said to Tom as she apportioned the cake onto the four plates. Minnie collected the kettle and poured the boiling water over the tea leaves.

Glenda watched her and remembered that Renée always poured boiling water into the empty teapot and then swirled it around. 'Always warm the pot first,' she reminded Glenda in their frequent afternoon tea sessions together.

Minnie poured the tea into dainty cups and then Minnie lifted her cup to her mouth, her little finger carefully stuck out at a right angle.

Renée, Glenda observed, never did that. Glenda kept her little finger tightly furled.

Tom picked up his cup, which was swallowed up in his big hands, his thick fingers nervously shaking. 'I always like a mug, myself,' he said.

Minnie laughed. 'We're going up in the world, Tom.'

Tom looked at Minnie and in that look he said his goodbyes.

When the time came to say goodbye, Glenda wished she could put her arms around Sam and hug his thin body tightly. But her mother was there saying a stately hand-shaking goodbye to Tom and then to Sam. Abe sat in the car waiting. Sam climbed in stiffly beside Tom and waved at Glenda. 'See you in the summer,' he called hopefully. Glenda did not answer.

'I think I'll go to bed early, mum,' Glenda said that evening, back in the flat.

'Are you all right, Glenda?' Minnie looked anxious.

Glenda felt a lassitude descending upon her. 'I'm fine. I'm just tired. We walked so much today.'

'Why don't you sit in the kitchen while I iron your school clothes for tomorrow, and tell me all about it,' Minnie suggested.

'No thanks.' Glenda shook her head. Somehow she wanted to keep the day at the zoo to herself. Maybe as a memorial for Sam. She didn't want to let her mother into that part of her life. If she re-examined the day and recounted the events, letting Minnie in with her oohhs and ahhs and well-I-nevers, the day would lose some of its pristine beauty. She said, 'I just want to go to bed.'

'Deary me,' Minnie said. 'You must be tired. Run along then and I'll look in on you a little later.' Minnie got out the ironing board and turned on the wireless. '*Chicaboom chicarack, chicaboom chicarack,*' she hummed along with the singer, imagining she was singing on BBC radio. That Glenda, she thought, she really is growing up. Minnie felt slightly sore, but very contented. He can't half make love, she mused, but he'll have to go. He don't belong in a place like this. That was why Minnie spent the day in bed making love to Tom. Tom, she realized, was miserably unhappy in London. The crowds made him nervous. He felt out of place, and the best they could do was to stay in bed.

'I'll miss you,' Tom said as he slid into her naked warm body for the last time. He held her against his chest as he began a long slow ascent to a final thrusting. Minnie wrapped her arms around his tanned, strong back and desperately wished she could keep the body in a cupboard somewhere and dispense with the head.

'I'll miss you too,' she said, feeling her body tingling its way back into a life of its own. 'Ohhh,' she breathed as she slid down the slide into a comfortable blackness. 'Ohh. That was nice, wasn't it?'

'Lovely,' said Tom, utterly spent, thinking, I do wish she made it sound less like a purchase in a grocer's.

Bending over the iron now, Minnie smiled. Tom was safely on the coach. Minnie was satiated, but this was the moment Minnie always liked best. She was on her own again with the wireless going and her ironing board. On one side of her lay a pile of newly-washed clothes. Rhythmically she moved a wrinkled, depressed blouse onto the ironing board and within a few minutes she had restored the blouse to its well-pressed glory. Neat and smelling of starch, the blouse blossomed into a thing of great beauty. The blouse was reverently put on top of the pile. Minnie was making sense of her universe.

* * *

In her bedroom Glenda lay staring at the ceiling. She could hear the thumping and the bumping of the hot iron from the kitchen. She could imagine the familiar smell of clothes being ironed with a slightly too hot iron. Why had she exiled herself from this warm human scene? She didn't really know, but she had, and now she lay alone and miserable. Missing Sam, but not missing Sam. Angry with Minnie, but not angry with Minnie. Upset because Renée had called her a child and made her feel small in front of Sam, but wishing she had been able to rush up to Renée and hug her and be a child. She turned her face to her night table. There lay a book with a picture of a little girl in a poke bonnet with a frill of flowers around her neck. Glenda took the book and hurled it against the wall. She turned her back on the room, wound her blankets around her body, and buried her face in her pillow.

Minnie poked her head around the door a little later. She must have been tired, she thought, as she returned to her own bedroom. The bed and the sheets were still warm from their lovemaking. Minnie took off her clothes and fell into bed. 'Mmm,' she groaned, her nose pressed in the sheets.

Chapter 26

Abe and Renée drove up in the front seat of the Lagonda; Minnie and Chinchilla sat in the back. Minnie was nervous. 'I've never been to a murder trial,' she said.

Chinchilla leaned towards her to be heard over the noise of the engine. 'Neither have I. Only in films. Once I played a part where I was convicted of murder, but of course I was innocent.' She sat back in her seat and looked out of the window.

Chinchilla wore a black shirt with a matching black blouse, which showed off her breasts, and a cream sable coat. Beside her Minnie felt like a small grey pigeon perched next to a glorious bird of paradise.

Abe parked the car, and the little band of McCluskie supporters walked up the road to the Old Bailey and passed through the dreaded portals, up huge marble steps, into a wide hall. Renée addressed a uniformed porter. 'Over there,' he said, pointing down a long corridor.

'Come along.' Renée smiled at Minnie. 'It's down here.' Minnie heard her own high heels tapping on the stone floor.

All along the corridor people stood talking. Outside Court No 1 they met the barrister, Caspar Alexander. 'I've reviewed your affidavit,' Caspar said, standing tall above Minnie. 'Very good, very good. Now, are you prepared to be cross-examined?'

'I'll stick to the truth, if that's what you mean.'

Caspar shook Renée's hand and glanced down at Chinchilla's shining bosom. He ignored Abe who stared with evident amusement at Caspar's white wig. Caspar said, 'The judge is Souter. Went to school together. Rather set in his views, but not too bad. We may have a chance. Up to you, my dear,' he said to Minnie. 'We have to prove to twelve citizens that your friend had no intention of killing the fella. She was just defending herself. D'you see?'

Minnie saw only too well.

'How many women on the jury?' Renée asked. 'Takes a woman to understand a woman.'

'We managed to get four,' said Caspar. 'Should be able to pull some sympathy out of them.' He held out his arm, indicating the old oak door to the court room. 'Shall we?'

Inside the court Minnie found herself entranced by the setting. Once long ago, before she had Glenda, the local repertory company in Hounslow had put on a Gilbert and Sullivan play called *Trial by Jury*. Minnie and her girlfriend had gone to see it because Minnie was interested in the man who played the judge. Now, all these years later, Minnie was standing in almost the same setting as she had seen on stage, but not because she fancied the judge; she was here to save her neighbour's life, if she could.

Minnie saw Mrs Hopwood sitting on a bench among the spectators. And then Mrs McCluskie herself was led in. Minnie gave a small wave. Mrs McCluskie looked back for a split second. Minnie was struck by the sadness on her face. She had put on weight in prison, but her face was sallow. Sorrow bowed her shoulders, and she watched Mrs McCluskie's hands writhe and plead for forgiveness. Minnie knew that not much of what was about to happen in the court would ever give relief to those grieving hands. Nothing Minnie could say about the night of the murder would bring solace to her. All her life she would carry the burden of guilt knowing that she had destroyed another human life. The fact that she had taken her husband's life to save her own was merely a legal nicety.

When the usher instructed all present to rise for the judge, Minnie could feel herself shaking. Chinchilla took her cold hand and squeezed it. 'Courage, darling. Pretend it's a film set.'

'I can't,' Minnie gasped. 'I'm not that good at pretending.'

Minnie was called to the witness box. She was on her own. She thought the trip to the witness box would take forever, and tried not to look at Mrs McCluskie. She kept her eyes on the box until she reached it. From her position there, Minnie felt as if she was standing in a small, defenceless boat, adrift in treacherous seas.

Minnie heard someone's voice swearing to tell the truth, the whole truth, and nothing but the truth. The voice sounded very far away and surprised Minnie. It was her voice. It had a distinct wobble.

'Are you all right?' She saw the judge lean towards her.

She nodded her head. 'Yes, my lord,' she said, wondering if she had said the right thing. Do you call him my lord, she wondered, or was that only for Jesus. She was so distracted that she misheard the first question. 'Oh, I'm sorry,' she said and then she settled down.

Gradually, as the trite questions of names and addresses were answered, she let her eyes turn toward the jury. Reassured, she saw only kindly curious faces. Caspar Alexander treated her carefully. Finally, after exhaustive questions of how she lived with Mrs McCluskie as a neighbour and a protracted questioning about the night of the murder, he walked away from the dock and left Minnie feeling lonely, unprotected, and vulnerable. Now it was the turn of the prosecution.

The counsel for the prosecution looked mean, Minnie thought. He was small with slicked-back, black hair showing underneath his wig, and he had a small toothbrush moustache. When he smiled, his lips barely moved and only his rabbit front teeth showed for a moment. 'Miss Stanhope.' Standing behind the long table in Counsel's Row, he leaned forward on the balls of his feet. 'We have heard at great length the virtues of living with Mrs McCluskie as your neighbour. She seems to be, by your remarkable account, a woman with an impeccable past. It is your opinion that Police Constable McCluskie comes home after a hard day's work caring for other people and then – you want us to believe – beats his wife. You go on to tell us not only that he beats his wife, but also that he attempts to take her life. And she had to defend herself by beating him to death with a poker.'

He seemed to Minnie to be more of an actor than a lawyer. He shrugged his shoulders and raised his eyebrows, a seemingly small gesture which nevertheless created the strong effect of making Minnie appear a liar. And then, his expression changing abruptly, he blurted out in a percussive voice that reverberated off the walls of the court, 'Why?'

For an instant, Minnie felt it was she who had been battered. 'Why did she do it?' he gasped. 'Why?'

Minnie was frightened. The man's face was white and his

hands were shaking. 'I don't know,' Minnie said. 'I really don't know.'

'No, you don't know very much, do you, Miss Stanhope?' the counsel for the prosecution snapped sarcastically.

Caspar was on his feet. 'M'lud,' he said, 'the counsel for the prosecution is intimidating the witness.'

The judge gave a silent but eloquent tilt of his head which reminded the counsel for the prosecution that we are, after all, gentlemen.

Minnie felt awash in her boat and only Caspar's huge figure could protect her, but he was on a far shore. She glanced across the room at Mrs Hopwood. Mrs Hopwood appeared dazed as if she had always sat in this court listening to case after case until she had habitually switched off from all proceedings. Then Minnie dared to look at Mrs McCluskie in the dock. Mrs McCluskie looked drained, her face grey and tired. She returned Minnie's stare with such pleading in her eyes that Minnie slowly felt an ember of anger beginning to burn in the pit of her stomach. This was the same ember that burned when she struggled to bring up Glenda on a few pounds a week and she heard that Mr Oppenheim intended to build himself a brand new Town Hall. It was the same anger that made Minnie yell at shopkeepers who refused to serve her or treated her as the welfare recipient that she had been. There were the bigger flames when she realized that she must go out and clean other women's floors to have sufficient money to send Glenda to school and pay for school dinners so her daughter might be spared the humiliation that Minnie suffered in her childhood. Mrs McCluskie was a good decent woman, married to a savage sadist. And Minnie decided then and there she was not going to let this little wanker of a prosecuting barrister get the better of her. Only watch your language, she heard Renée's voice in her head. She looked at Renée and she saw Renée's huge tip-tilted eyes aglow with battle. Chinchilla waved her lavender covered fingers. Abe gave her what she took to be a go-ahead nod.

113

'Mrs McCluskie always had a good cooked dinner on the table when 'er 'usband came in of a night,' Minnie spoke up. 'The kids were always washed and tidy.'

'How do you know that?' The weasel's teeth were pointed.

'Because they shared the bathroom on the landing and I could hear them.'

The weasel breathed in sharply. 'You have told the court that Police Constable McCluskie often attacked his wife. How often? Once a year?' The man's head was thrown back and his eyes were slits in his face.

'No,' Minnie said, determined not to be bullied. She let the silence hang until the counsel for the prosecution opened his eyes.

Tough little bitch, he thought. 'Well then, once a month?'

'No,' Minnie said again, folding her hands. I can wait this out, she thought.

'Once a week?' the man's voice was hustling and cajoling. 'Come along now, Miss Stanhope, we have heard your evidence once before. How many times and how often?'

'Two or three times a week. Sometimes more.'

'I see, and how did you know this?'

Minnie looked at her hands. The thumbs lay protectively around the fingers. 'I could hear it,' she said, faltering. 'My Glenda and me.'

'Glenda? Your Glenda? Who is your Glenda?' The weasel pounced.

Minnie looked up at Caspar and she saw a cloud form on his huge face. 'Glenda? She's my little girl.'

'I was not aware that you had a little girl.' The counsel for the prosecution's voice softened. Maybe he likes children, Minnie thought, desperate not to upset the man any further. 'Is your Glenda in the court at present?'

'She's at school.'

'And how old is your Glenda?'

'Irrelevant, M'lud,' Caspar jumped in.

114

The judge shook his head, saying, 'The child was a witness to the events. Go on, Miss Stanhope. Answer the question.'

'Six, now,' said Minnie.

The counsel for the prosecution reared back. 'And tell us, is there a *Mister* Stanhope?' he asked. The court was quiet, waiting.

'No.' Minnie felt her head wilt on her neck.

'I see,' the word hissed through the man's teeth. 'No Mr Stanhope. Divorced, Miss Stanhope?'

'No.' Minnie felt a storm-cloud of colour descending on her face.

'A widow then?'

'No.'

'So your child is . . . illegitimate?'

'Yes,' Minnie whispered.

'Objection!' Caspar was furious. 'Relevance?'

The counsel for the prosecution flapped an arm at Caspar beside him. 'I am only trying to determine the credibility of the witness for the defence, m'lord. This witness is an unmarried mother giving evidence on behalf of a woman who committed an act of murder. I need to establish whether or not there was collusion between the two women.'

Minnie tried not to cry. She could see several faces in the jury box harden. Ever since Glenda was born Minnie was ashamed that Glenda had no father. And now here, in an open court, her shabby secret lay bare. 'Glenda is my daughter and she is six years old. We lived upstairs from Mrs McCluskie from the day I brought Glenda home from the 'ospital. For all the years I've known Mrs McCluskie and her family I've always known her to be a good wife and a good mother. But 'er husband, he used to come in any time day or night, and if he felt like it he would beat her and often the kids.'

'You say this, but what evidence do you have?' The unpleasant man stood quietly. 'I mean, I don't want to hear about noises downstairs or thumps in the night. We have heard all that. What *real* evidence do you have, or, for that matter, does anybody else have? Why did Mrs McCluskie never go to the social services?' That question really rated with the jury, Minnie could see. All twelve faces looked relieved. There had been an answer all along. They felt comforted. Faced with the possibility of their having to make a decision that might let a murderer go, they knew now that all Mrs McCluskie ever had to do was to go down the road to the social services, paid for by their taxes, of course, and there should have been no problem.

'You can't just go to the social like that,' Minnie explained. 'If you went to the social, they sent a social worker to see your husband, and then you got beaten twice as bad.' Minnie desperately wanted to make the jury understand. 'If a woman is beaten by 'er 'usband, she's much too embarrassed to go out even. Many is the time I've seen Mrs McCluskie beaten black and blue. Her face a mess, her eyes out to here.' Minnie cupped her hands over her eyes. 'The kids run errands for 'er. I sometimes did the shopping until the bruises faded.' She felt she was getting back the sympathy she had lost from the jurors. 'Believe you me, Mrs McCluskie tried and tried and tried. She was scared of Mr McCluskie, dead scared. There was nothing she could do. If you do run away, they put you in the Hostel for the Homeless, and that's only just round the corner. Where's the safety in that? He would've found her. He is, I mean he *was*,' she corrected herself, 'a policeman. They take care of their own.'

'How right to say *was*!' the counsel for the prosecution put in.

But Minnie knew she had won. The counsel for the prosecution had lost the fight. The jury believed Minnie and now he might as well sum up and go home. 'You see . . .' Minnie said.

'I see all too clearly,' he interrupted. 'I believe you have said enough. We've heard sufficient fabrications from your lips to last us . . .'

'Let the witness speak,' the judge instructed. 'What she says is of interest to the court.'

'Thank you, m'lord,' said Minnie, giving the judge her prettiest smile. 'You see,' she continued with increasing confidence, 'Mrs McCluskie never did stand much of a chance, really. 'E used to come in the front door and bellow at 'er. "What did you do all day long, you lazy 'ore!" he'd shout, and then she'd have to tell him her whole day, where she went, who she saw, if she spoke to any men. But whatever she said, something would make him angry, and then he'd begin to 'it 'er. I don't blame her that night. I thought she was a goner.' Minnie's voice grew faint as she remembered the figure crawling up the corridor. 'She didn't stand a chance,' Minnie said quietly. 'Poor woman, poor woman.' And Minnie felt the tears rushing from her eyes and down her face. She held her hands over her eyes and rocked in silent grief.

'You may step down now,' the judge said. 'Take your time. If it is of any help to you, I would like to tell you that you have assisted greatly in our consideration of this case. The court is grateful to you.'

Minnie nodded and stumbled from the dock. She slid into her seat beside Renée who put a reassuring arm around her shoulder. 'You were marvellous,' Renée said.

'What a performance!' Chinchilla whispered. 'I couldn't have done better myself. Oscar material, you are, Minnie. Really. At *least* an Oscar!'

Minnie found herself comforted. Really, she thought, Chinchilla. Trust her not to notice how upset Minnie had been. Life for Chinchilla was a broad silver screen with events projected on to it that never touched Chinchilla. How I wish, Minnie thought, I could be like that.

In the corridor outside the court, Caspar Alexander came lumbering up to Minnie during a recess. 'Well done,' he said grasping her hand. 'Very well done, my dear. The jury won't be out long. I think you've saved the day. Renée, I'll telephone you as soon as I have the nod that the jury are ready to give a verdict.'

Renée thanked him and led a shaken Minnie out of the Old Bailey.

Chapter 27

Glenda whined and pleaded until Minnie, distracted and tense, agreed that they would pick Glenda up from school after lunch and take her to the court with them. 'But I'm sure they won't let you in,' Minnie said.

'I don't care. I just want to be there when they let Mrs McCluskie off. They will let her off, won't they, mum?'

'I hope so. I very much do hope so.' Minnie had a bottle of port in the kitchen. 'I need it,' she said, taking a sip. Before her was a comforting pile of ironing. Abe's silk shirts were a real trick, and Minnie loved to see the creases disappear as she stroked the material with her magic iron. Once this is over, she thought, I'll go dancing. I'll call up someone and go dancing. Who can I call up? All the young girls from years ago were married and living quiet lives in Hounslow. Now, Minnie realized, she had no friends except old Mrs Jones and Phil Clough. Well, I'll ring Phil and we'll go over to Joe's Cafe and eat buns. Just me, Phil, and Glenda.

She pressed the clothes and waited for Glenda to fall asleep. I need a man, Minnie decided, a nice young, good fun fellow to go dancing with. She put away her own clothes and took Glenda's clothes into her bedroom. I'll put them away tomorrow, she thought, looking at the clean vests. She is growing, she thought. remembering the tiny white baby vests she had when Glenda was just born. She really is growing.

Minnie undressed and fell into bed. I'm too tired to wash or clean my teeth. She fell asleep with the sugary taste of port on her tongue.

*   *   *

The jury reached a verdict by lunchtime the next day. Abe ushered his small tribe into the corridors of the Old Bailey. Glenda held Abe's hand.

In the court room, through a haze of fear, Minnie heard the Foreman of the Jury say the words 'Not guilty, m'lord,' and then a wave of emotion poured around the court. Renée was hugging Minnie, and Chinchilla was bouncing up and down. 'Hurray! Hurray!' Chinchilla yelled in her inappropriately high voice.

When silence was restored, the judge allowed the verdict of not guilty of murder in the first degree, and he agreed 'to set Mrs McCluskie free to rejoin her children and hopefully to be able to make a new life for herself and her family.'

Minnie sighed. The judge had believed her. All the humiliation heaped upon her by the counsel for the prosecution was worthwhile. Minnie felt herself floating. Little Minnie Stanhope, mother of an illegitimate child, had left her mark in the world. Minnie smiled broadly. Renée pushed Minnie down the stairs towards Mrs Hopwood. 'Do you need a lift home?' Renée offered.

'Yes, we do,' said Mrs Hopwood, taking Mrs McCluskie by the hand.

'Can I ask you a favour?' Mrs McCluskie's face was bathed in tears, but there was a purpose to the corner of her mouth.

'Of course,' Renée said. 'Anything. I am so glad it's all over.'

'So am I,' she whispered. 'But on the way to the social services, could we stop at the graveyard? I'll only be a moment, I promise.'

'Sure,' Renée said. 'We've got all the time in the world.'

'Well, well, well!' Caspar's voice engulfed the group.

'Thank you very much,' Renée said, shaking his hand. 'You did an excellent job.'

'I did, you think?' The man gazed at Minnie.

Minnie felt a question bursting on her lips. 'Why did the prosecution behave as if he hated me?'

'Oh, old George Pecker!' Caspar laughed. 'Old George is

known for giving the missus the odd wallop, you see.'

Renée lifted one immaculately plucked eyebrow. 'It happens,' she said, 'in the best of families.'

Caspar flapped his hands. 'Bye, darlings,' he said and he walked off down the hall. 'Don't forget to call my clerk,' he said over his shoulder. 'School fees for the little Alexanders, y'know.'

'School fees?' said Abe who had joined them. 'School fees my ass. Alimony and mistresses is more like it.'

'What's alimony and mistresses?' Glenda asked.

'You're too young to know,' Abe said and they marched down the corridor.

Minnie walked beside Mrs McCluskie with Glenda beside her. 'Are you all right?' she asked.

'As right as I'll ever be,' Mrs McCluskie answered. 'But at least I have the kids back. And that's a miracle.'

They climbed into the big Lagonda and pulled away. Most of the drive was silent. Everyone sensed the woman's sorrow. The car pulled up at a pair of wrought iron gates and then slid through into the centre of the graveyard. Minnie got out of the car with Mrs McCluskie. Glenda quietly followed her mother and the sad figure. Soon they came to a recent grave with no headstone. Minnie stood back a few feet, holding Glenda's hand. Mrs McCluskie moved forward and Glenda watched her cross herself. They could hear Mrs McCluskie mumbling to herself. After a while they could make out the words. Mrs McCluskie was giving her husband a full account of the time she had been separated from him.

Slowly, as the litany ended, Mrs McCluskie fell to her knees and then she laid her face on the brown earth and sobbed. Glenda watched and she promised herself that if she ever married she would never never abandon her husband. If this was the price Mrs McCluskie had to pay, it wasn't worth it. Watching the woman, Glenda wondered if Mrs McCluskie would ever smile again. Maybe if you take the vows of marriage, Glenda thought, you could never break them. Until death us do part was one of them.

Minnie moved forward and helped Mrs McCluskie to her feet. Brown earth still stained her face. Minnie brushed away the earth gently. Mrs McCluskie stood like an obedient child. 'We'll go back now,' Minnie said and she took Mrs McCluskie's hand in hers. She led the way to the car.

Chapter 28

Minnie felt as if she had been zapped by electricity. It took weeks for her to return to her usual calm way of life. 'You know, Phil,' she said as she sat in Joe's Cafe with Glenda beside her, 'I never want to go to court again.'

Phil coughed. He coughed a lot these days. Not the usual Hounslow phlegmy soot-ridden cough, but a dry one like the sound of tissue paper tearing.

'You sure you're all right?' Minnie said.

Phil had become thin, far too thin, and the sun almost shone through his wintery hand. As he bent his head to drink his tea Glenda could see long strands of neck muscle straining to hold his head above the steaming cup. The cafe was warm, packed with bodies, and the windowpanes dripped with water. The coffee machine gurgled and moaned and the tea urn boiled and bubbled. Glenda could see the three witches of the heath writhing in the steam from the coffeemaker. (Renée had started rehearsals as Lady Macbeth in a West End production. She practised her part nightly in front of Glenda who sat mesmerized.) 'Double, double toil and trouble; fire burn and cauldron bubble!' Glenda murmured to herself in ecstasy, as Renée had taught her to recite.

'Shakespeare.' Phil laughed in recognition. His laughter turned into a long, crusty cough. 'But you can't be doing Shakespeare at school already?' he said when his coughing had subsided.

'Not at school,' Glenda said. 'Renée gets to be Lady Macbeth. Do you know *Macbeth*?'

'Course I do.'

'Renée says Macbeth and Lady Macbeth killed the king,' Glenda explained.

'Macbeth was a weak man, Glenda. A very weak man. It was the missus who was the strong one.'

Minnie was bored. She usually left the room when they started, but if it occupied Glenda and kept the child from asking endless questions, Minnie didn't mind. She looked around the cafe. Over in the left-hand corner she saw a young man with a mischievous twinkle in his eyes. He had Irish blue eyes the colour of cornflowers and a sweet curled red mouth. Minnie liked his teeth. The teeth were delightful and they were smiling at Minnie. Minnie rolled an eye in his direction. He wore his hair quiffed at the front and long at the back. He had on a navy blue suit with a thick velvet collar. The man stood up. Oops, Minnie thought. He's coming over. A familiar feeling of excitement shot through her.

The man lazily sauntered up to the bar and threw down some change. He paused for a moment and seemed undecided. Should he leave or should he stay? He flipped a coin in his hand and peered at the answer. 'Tails,' he said loudly. 'I'm staying.' He walked casually up to Minnie's table. 'Hi.' He bent over a very long way. 'My name is Tony. Everyone calls me Big Tone. May I have the honour?'

Phil stopped talking to Glenda and looked startled. 'I don't believe,' Phil said, 'we've met.'

'We haven't, pops.' Big Tone put a large hand on Phil's shoulders. 'But everybody knows me here. Don't you?' he asked the room. The cafe had fallen silent when Big Tone rose to his feet. There was a ripple of yesses and a flurry of nods. Big Tone surveyed the room for a moment. Then he bent his head again and took Minnie's hand.

Minnie looked at her hand in his and very much wished she had repaired the chip on her fingernail. Her little finger lay naked, exposing its wound and the fact that Minnie had been too lazy to repair it. 'My name,' Minnie said, a little haughty out of guilt, 'is Minnie Stanhope, and this is my daughter Glenda. And this is our friend Phil Clough.'

'Mind if I sit?' Big Tone lowered himself into a chair.

Glenda's heart sank. Mum was at it again, she thought. But at least he looked as if he had a laugh in him. Goodbye, Tom, she thought. And goodbye, Sam.

When they left the cafe Glenda was cheered by the fact that Big Tone owned a black Ford Consul. The seats were covered with furry fake zebra skin and from the back window two large square furry dice swung to and fro. Glenda got into the back of the car and enjoyed the feel of the fake fur against her legs. She knew Renée would hate the car. Utterly ghastly, she could hear Renée's voice. Too, too terrible, Chinchilla would back Renée up. 'Wow!' Minnie said, perched in the front seat with both her legs knee-locked together, exposing as much thigh as she could. 'What a fab car!'

'Fab?' Big Tone hooked one eyebrow up over his eye.

Minnie said, 'Fab.'

Big Tone switched on the radio. Tommy Steele's voice boomed out into the road. Passers-by looked at the car and its occupants.

Minnie felt she could try a little wave, like the Queen. She was so preoccupied with Big Tone she forgot to register the fact that she was really worried about Phil Clough.

Chapter 29

Phil Clough died in February just a few days before Glenda's birthday. The new year stretched its fingers into February and the light was thin and the wind piercingly cold. Glenda stood by Phil's grave, holding her mother's hand. Renée and Abe were also there, but Chinchilla was somewhere in America, a place called Los Angeles to see about a film. She had told Glenda all about the hot weather and the beautiful red hibiscus flowers and the palm trees. Now standing on the freezing ground and looking at the deep hole dug for Phil's coffin, Glenda cried. She cried because she knew Phil, because she didn't want his body to go down into the cold ground. But she also knew that it had to go down there in order for Phil to go to heaven. Glenda had a hazy idea of heaven. The Reverend Turner preached that heaven was somewhere good people went when they died. Phil was definitely in heaven because Phil was a good man. Glenda was dreadfully afraid that she was not a candidate for heaven, and she fervently promised God that she would clean Lady's cage three times a week as she knew she ought. 'And please look after Phil,' she prayed.

Renée looked down at Glenda. Poor little thing, she thought. First the murder and now a friend gone. Such a burden in a young life. Still, we'll give her a good birthday. I wish Glenda made friends with other children. Renée had discussed this with Abe. Abe said, 'She's not a child's child, Renée. She's deep, that little kid. Very deep and very smart.'

Renée shifted her weight to ease her quickly freezing feet. The local grammar school is excellent, Renée thought. And there's no reason for Glenda not to make it there, seeing the strong way she had started school already. She went through a list of presents for Glenda. 'Thank you, Lord,' Renée prayed, 'for giving me Glenda.'

Renée was forty-eight now. Her forty-eighth year had not been easy. With menopause stalking her heels, she had to rethink herself. While the monthly blood had flowed, Renée had taken her childlessness with equanimity. Now she looked at babies hungrily, imagining them hers and Abe's.

Abe did not mind the absence of children in his life. All he lived for was Renée, but Renée minded. She longed for the clasp of a pair of small fat arms and the round-eyed goggling of an interested baby. She felt as if she were a tidal basin without a tide, so used was she to the ebb and flow of her desires. For now there was no desire, there was no heightened crescendo to a month and the diminuendo until, shortly before her monthly period, desire sparked again. Her body had held her in its biological tempo ever since she was twelve. Now all these years later, she was returning to a time when her head could again dictate her heart.

The Reverend Turner was coming to a close; Renée castigated herself for daydreaming.

The little group of people, which included Mrs Jones, trooped off to Renée's house for tea. Minnie had laid out a large table full of cakes and biscuits. 'These,' she pointed out to Mrs Jones, 'are almond drops. Ever so expensive to make.'

Glenda sat by her teacup and thought, Why does everything happen with cups of tea? She was cross because Minnie was going out with Big Tone tonight. Glenda didn't think it was right to go dancing, when Phil Clough was in the cold ground. But on the other hand she could spend the night in Renée's part of the house and have a bath in Renée's big French bathtub. Glenda loved the nights with Renée. After a proper dinner with lighted candles on the table, Abe washed up if Minnie was 'off', and Renée and Glenda sat by the big fire in the drawing room while Renée read her stories. Currently they were reading *One Pair of Hands* by Monica Dickens, all about a girl living in a flat in London, or trying to live in a flat in London, because the girl was very poor. Glenda knew one day she would live in a flat in London. But Glenda knew she would not be poor.

Chapter 30

'Guess who I've had?' Minnie was preparing supper in her kitchen and Glenda was bent over her homework. Chinchilla was paying a downstairs visit. Chinchilla, when she was downstairs in the flat with Minnie and Glenda, was quite different from the upstairs Chinchilla. Now she had arrived to see Minnie and she regularly brought presents for Glenda. 'My home away from home,' Chinchilla called it. She kicked off her high heels as soon as she came through the door and sat over her cup of coffee with her cigarette no longer at a jaunty angle, as she and Minnie got down to the nitty gritty of life and love in the fast lane. If Minnie thought life in the fast lane was Big Tone, well, she learned a lot from Chinchilla, whose life in the fast lane included a lot of men whose faces beamed down at Glenda from billboards in Hammersmith Broadway and also graced the pages of magazines from America.

'What was he like?' Minnie asked, glancing at Glenda who seemed buried in her homework.

Chinchilla inserted her thumb between her first and second fingers.

'Oh no!' Minnie giggled. 'And he's such a big man!'

Chinchilla laughed a raucous belly laugh. Her high-pitched little-girl voice completely gone. 'Nah,' she said, her posh English accent falling away. 'Minuscule. You could play hide and seek for a week before you found it. And then it wasn't much use.'

Glenda felt her ears burn. 'The dog sat by the fat cat,' she wrote laboriously, copying from a textbook.

'Cutest balls, though,' Chinchilla's eyes were wide. 'And you should see the mansion, Minnie! I could marry the man just for that. I don't know.' Chinchilla sighed. 'Men. I wish I could find a man I truly loved. What've you been doing while I've been away?'

Minnie turned from the stove and looked at Chinchilla. 'I met Big Tone.'

Chinchilla was interested. 'Really? And who is Big Tone?'

'He's ever so nice,' Minnie explained. 'He's been in trouble with the police, but he's promised me that if we go together he'll keep his nose clean.'

Glenda moaned. She'd heard that before. Why her mum did not become a social worker, she never knew. At least that way she'd get paid for it. Big Tone tried hard with Glenda, but Glenda just did not like him. She didn't like the way he bossed Minnie about nor did she like the fake fur pouffe that he produced soon after he met Minnie. Now the fake fur horror sat luridly alone in their sitting room. Glenda hadn't the heart to tell Minnie she hated the thing, but even now as she sat at the end of the kitchen table she could see it smouldering in the sitting room. Every time she went past Glenda kicked the pouffe, but it was seemingly indestructible, rather like Big Tone himself, whose hectic voice and large frame haunted the small flat. Tone fancied himself a rock and roller. As soon as Big Tone arrived in the flat he put on the record player and belted out rock songs, charging up and down the flat pretending to play a guitar, his leg up in the air.

Tonight Chinchilla was not happy and Minnie tried to cheer her up. 'I'm cooking corned beef and cabbage, Chinchilla. Want some?'

'I'm on a diet.' Chinchilla's small nose smelled the corned beef. 'Oooh, it does smell good. You know, Minnie, I would like to be married again.'

'Again? Again, Chinchilla? But you've been married three times already.'

'I know.' Chinchilla cupped her chin in her hands. 'But it was easy to get married when I was younger. Men loved me, Minnie. Loads of men. Everywhere I went. Now I'm getting over the hill. I'm thirty-six, you know, give or take, and you can see the lines and the wrinkles coming. Every morning when I get up I look in the mirror and say goodbye to some part of my face or my neck. And then there's that bit under your arms. See?' She held out an arm and pulled gently at a small flap of flesh. 'It's not tight any longer. Men notice that. Most men need to be with young women. As long as the women beside them are young and pretty, they forget their own fat tummies and balding heads. Men live through women, you know.'

Minnie didn't know. She had never sat down and thought about men as a subject for philosophical speculation. 'I suppose so,' she said.

'Well, they do. And I should know. Mind you, there are enough of us women who live through men. Not Renée, though. Renée's all right, but she's one of the few women who are. She's always been a strong woman with or without a man. She has Abe and they live in a tight little world of their own. But for me, I've always needed a man. In a way, it's a curse. Without a man I don't feel whole. I feel half dead inside, if that makes sense.'

Minnie looked at Chinchilla. 'I know what you mean, but for the last six years I've had Glenda, and ever since I had her I felt complete. You ever had a kid?'

'No.' Chinchilla paused. 'I never wanted one. I suppose I'm such a child myself. Once I got away from Yorkshire and my awful family, I promised myself I wouldn't bring a child into this dreadful world.'

Minnie lifted the corned beef onto a serving dish. 'Put away your homework for now, Glen,' she instructed. 'I'll lay up for tea.'

Glenda carried her homework into her bedroom. And as she neatly piled the books beside her bed, she wondered why someone like Chinchilla who was so beautiful should be so alone. After all, Minnie had Big Tone. During dinner she decided to ask.

'If you want to get married, Chinchilla, maybe Big Tone has a friend who would like to marry you.'

There was a moment of silence and Glenda realized that Minnie was embarrassed.

'It's not as easy as that,' Minnie said. 'One day you'll understand why. When you've grown up.'

Glenda sat back while the two women talked. She did not understand. But perhaps it was something to do with Renée's furniture in the flat and the awful fake fur pouffe. Certainly Big Tone was awfully quiet on the few occasions he had come across Renée or Abe when they were entering or leaving the house. And, come to think of it, Minnie never asked Big Tone to go upstairs. Maybe it was something to do with that. Glenda ate her corned beef and cabbage and wondered if she would have time to finish her English homework. Her teacher was very pleased with her work.

Before bed Chinchilla gave Glenda a soft feathery kiss. 'Don't be sad, Chinchilla.' Glenda hugged her sweet-smelling body. 'I know you'll find somebody to marry you. You will really.'

Chinchilla hugged her back. 'I hope so, Glenda.' The little-girl voice was back and Chinchilla's lavender eyes looked desolate.

Chapter 31

Glenda was at school when the phone call came. Minnie had finished cleaning upstairs and was in her own kitchen preparing macaroni cheese for Glenda's tea. The voice was old and peppery. 'You are Miss Minnie Stanhope, I take it?'

Minnie stood quiet for a moment, the black telephone receiver in her hand. 'Yes, that's right.'

'I have to tell you that Mr Philip Clough left the sum of five thousand pounds to you, Miss Stanhope. We shall be writing to you in the next few days. How do you want the sum presented? A wire transfer to your bank?'

'No,' Minnie said nervously. She did not have a bank account. 'Not a wire transfer.'

'Well then,' the voice said slightly more impatiently, 'by cheque?'

'Yes, yes, a cheque would be fine. Make it out in my name.'

'Very well then. Good day.'

Minnie put the telephone down quickly. 'Good heavens,' she said breathlessly. 'Good heavens!' She walked back to the kitchen and turned down the stove. She sat down and reached for a cigarette. Five thousand pounds. Enough to buy a little house in Hounslow for me and Glenda. For a moment Minnie had a dream. A little house in one of the long roads leading to the airport. A freshly painted picket fence and a back garden where Minnie imagined she would grow tomatoes in the summer and big thick-headed cabbages in the winter.

She looked around her and out of the window. No, she thought, I can't take Glenda away from all this. This new world that Renée had introduced them to entranced Glenda. From being a shy, remote little girl, Glenda had blossomed. She loved having Renée and Abe upstairs and indeed she was to be found more upstairs than down. At times Minnie awoke in the middle of the night and sat smoking, with her knees drawn up under her chin. She thought of their lives together when it was just Minnie and Glenda against the world, but even then she recognized that their lives now were fuller. And if she was to have her dream come true for Glenda, then she must let her go. Let Glenda explore and meet other people.

Perhaps, Minnie thought, sitting in the kitchen, I will put the money in the bank and keep it there as a nest egg. Minnie had often read novels about people having nest eggs.

When she collected Glenda, Minnie told her the exciting news. Glenda hopped and skipped through much of the retelling but she was bursting with her own news. 'Ruth Schwartz has asked me to tea tomorrow. Can I go?'

Minnie looked at the beloved bright-eyed face. 'Of course you can go. Why shouldn't you go?'

Later that night she approached Renée with her new-found luck. 'Marvellous!' Renée said. 'Why don't you rush off on a world tour, Minnie?'

Minnie stood aghast. 'I can't do that.'

'Why ever not? You might find yourself an exotic rich

lover. Just think! You can go anywhere in the world!' Renée had been drinking.

Abe sat in the corner of the drawing room. He was busy sketching, his back against the window behind him. The curtains were drawn against a cold spring night. He watched Minnie's face. 'Don't listen to Renée,' he said comfortingly. 'Renée's the one who needs a trip. She's been getting edgy lately. Haven't you, baby?'

Renée turned her blazing eyes towards Abe. 'You know me so well. We do need to travel. England is such a small island and one gets stale after a while.' She turned to Minnie. 'Put the money in a savings account, darling, and sit and watch it grow. That's what I do, don't I, darling?'

Abe nodded. 'When the cheque comes in, Minnie, I'll take you down to our bank. Lloyds. They'll look after you.'

Minnie smiled a grateful smile. As she left the room, she saw Renée lope over to Abe and bend down to kiss him. Between them Minnie saw ropes of gold and around them a light shone. That's what real love must be like, Minnie thought. I must get rid of Big Tone. Minnie was getting bored with him. He was more likely to look in a mirror than he was to look into her face. Besides, Glenda really did not like him.

Minnie went back downstairs and shut the door. She passed through the sitting room and walked into the kitchen. Glenda sat in her usual position at the kitchen table. 'Mrs Turner taught me how to say something in French, mum. *Comment ça va? Ça va bien, merci*. And when I'm older I can take French in school. The French teacher looks like a witch, but I like French anyway.'

'That's good, love,' said Minnie. 'Maybe when we get our money, maybe you and me can go to Paris some day.'

Glenda was immediately excited. 'We can go with Abe and Renée. They both speak French.'

Minnie felt the wound, but she gave no sign. 'All right. We'll all go together.' Of course, she thought as she tucked

Glenda into bed, of course the child wants to go with Abe and Renée. Maybe I'll get Chinchilla to go too. Minnie wanted some company of her own.

Chapter 32

The trip to Paris never did happen. Days passed, then months, and then years. As she grew, Glenda showed a maturity and an intelligence that made other people usually believe her to be two or three years older than she actually was. Throughout the middle years of her childhood, Glenda found herself sucked more and more into her life at school. Her friendship with Ruth introduced her to another way of life. Mrs Schwartz, Ruth's mother, was large and smelled of cooking. The Schwartzes' home straddled the borders between respectable Ealing and suspect Hounslow. Dr Schwartz was known locally as a dangerous socialist. He tended to the poor and refused to take private patients. Ruth was a plump, smiling girl who loved to compete. 'Look at you!' she said, leaning over Glenda's workbook. 'You're so tidy!'

Glenda envied Ruth. When they were both nine, they promised each other eternal friendship. 'I don't want ever to get married,' Ruth said. She was sitting beside the rabbit cage in the bright garden behind the house. Lady hopped about, nibbling a bit of grass here and there. Glenda watched Lady's long hind legs as they stretched, ready for the next leap. 'We're a bit like Lady, you know,' Glenda said. She was lying on the ground with a piece of long sweet grass in her mouth. Her teeth were searching for the right spot where the plump grass would release its thick juice into her persistent mouth. 'We have to take a big leap soon, past the eleven-plus, and then go on to the grammar.'

'But what do you want to do with your life after that?' Ruth asked.

'I dream about going to Cambridge,' Glenda replied, thinking of the fondness with which her teacher spoke of the place. Indeed, at this age, Glenda's thoughts of Cambridge could be described only as dreams. But she worked hard at school, always with the goal somewhere in mind that her work might make her dreams come to life.

Long luxurious talks about their future were the hallmark of this nine year old season. After school Ruth either came home with Glenda and they both did their homework at the kitchen table, or they went back to Ruth's house where they immediately entered into the fat fussy life of Ruth's mother. Homework could not be attempted without plates full of cakes and buns and tea. Not Lipton's tea from a teapot, but Russian tea from a samovar. Glenda enjoyed the tea sessions and sometimes she thought of old Mrs Jones in her shop and felt a twinge of guilt. She and Minnie no longer saw old Mrs Jones. In fact Glenda didn't know if old Mrs Jones was still alive. Other people now lived in the house that backed onto the schoolyard. Other children hung out of the window that had once been her room. Long days well passed.

Now Glenda grew as did her breasts and the beginning of down under her arms and between her legs. Sometimes as she lay in the sun she felt stirrings and a pounding. An intense longing for she knew not what.

Glenda knew all about periods. Those dangerous days when Minnie became short-tempered and disappeared into the bathroom to struggle with her sanitary towels. Glenda often inspected the snowy white pads kept under the sink. She knew that once she bled, she could also have babies. It all seemed very mysterious and very dangerous. This bleeding happened to her mother and she, Glenda, was the result. Whoever had put his penis into her mother's vagina had not waited around long enough to celebrate the arrival of the inevitable consequence. No, Glenda did not look forward to her periods, nor, in some ways, to the process of growing up.

Ruth, she decided, was ignorant of this most secret side of

life. Mamie Schwartz and her husband Danny Schwartz covered Ruth in such a protective coating of love that it was hard to imagine Ruth as anything but a permanently industrious, plump, willing, little doll. Still, Ruth too was growing breasts and they were bigger than Glenda's. Glenda looked down at her small, flat, brown nipples. She sighed to the mirror in the bathroom. Her slim, hipless body stood before her. Her chestnut hair fell to her shoulders. Her brown hazel eyes, ringed with long lashes, stared back. Who am I? she thought.

Glenda felt that she was changing. As much as she loved Lady, her rabbit, she did not spend as much time as she had in previous years squatting on the ground outside in her secret garden. The garden was no longer her especial refuge. The trees were no longer her clandestine friends, nor the bushes and the flowers her co-conspirators. The house and its occupants were still the major influence on her life. She loved to roller skate with Abe. She loved the ebb and flow of Renée's visitors upstairs, and Chinchilla's warm friendship with her mother, but now she watched television avidly. The Suez crisis was over. Anthony Eden, with his disappointed chin, no longer dominated the screen. The Korean War finished, the world seemed to be at peace.

When she was out shopping with Ruth on a Saturday morning, they no longer went to the matinées at the local cinema. Ruth was reading *Frenchman's Creek*, by Daphne du Maurier. Glenda was reading *Wuthering Heights*.

At school both girls worked hard. Mrs Turner, big-bellied with her second child, supervised her two girls. 'Only another two years,' she said to her class, 'and then you will take the eleven-plus.' A terrifying thought. Your whole life – the rest of your life – depended on pages of paper covered in squiggles. Either you passed and went on to the grammar school, or you failed and it was the secondary modern school.

The lines were very clear in Glenda's primary. The well-dressed, well-spoken children with their clean well-pressed clothes would naturally take the eleven-plus and move on to the grammar. Occasionally there was a hitch in the social arrangement and a child like Cyril O'Mally would get through.

Cyril O'Mally was one of a family of seventeen. He was huge, with holes in his pants, and scuffed shoes. He stood in line for his free dinners and finished off all the bottles of free milk left half-empty by the children of the better-off. Cyril was an awful embarrassment to everybody. Glenda hoped that God would grant her slightly guilty prayer and not let Cyril through to the grammar. He reminded Glenda of G. K. Chesterton's poem 'The Donkey'. He brayed even more furiously than usual when he saw Glenda.

Ruth teased Glenda. 'Here comes your boyfriend,' she whispered as Cyril cantered about the playground after Glenda.

'He's not,' Glenda hissed back.

'Yes he is.'

The school year trickled away down a long drain of recurring events. Glenda filled her notebooks with hieroglyphics, English language, English literature, Shakespeare, Pyramus and Thisby, Puck, Peaseblossom, arithmetic, geography . . . All the time she knew, as the months passed by, that she was changing.

After her tenth birthday her periods began. Somehow with the monthly flow, Glenda felt a door was now closed between herself and her mother. Not a door closed in anger or even indifference. More that a separate path was beginning to emerge. Glenda watched Minnie, sometimes tired and a little strained, run the house well and efficiently. She often helped Minnie in the evenings with the ironing. I'll never, she thought as she ironed another of Abe's silk shirts, iron anyone else's clothes when I grow up. She felt a tight knot of resentment build in her throat. The anger was not towards Renée or Abe, but more towards the fact that Minnie was condemned to serve others. Even the five thousand pounds which sat reproducing itself in the bank was not enough to give them a lifestyle where they owned a roof over their heads and could afford to pay the bills and put food on the table.

Sometimes when Danny Schwartz held forth at his own dining table groaning with food, laden with kasha and brisket, Glenda found herself arguing with him internally. Ruth, her face pink with so much food, chewed with her mouth open and the food could be seen in mid-mastication. Cyril should be here, Glenda thought, as she watched the overweight family stuffing themselves. Cyril could do with some real nourishment. Despite a generally barrel-shaped chest, Cyril had the cleft in the breast bone that showed on all the boys who queued for their free dinners. 'Welfare,' Danny declared, waving his spoon. 'That's what we have to be proud of. England has the best welfare system in the world.'

'Eat, Danny. Eat.' Mamie pushed another bowl of food into the centre of the table.

Glenda looked across the table at Ruth. What does she know of welfare? Glenda thought. What does Mrs Schwartz know of standing in a queue, waiting for money you didn't earn? Tins. That's welfare. It was a long time ago that Minnie and Glenda ate beans. Now they never ate beans. Even the smell of beans made Glenda feel slightly sick. They no longer had margarine in a round tub squatting in their fridge. Glenda's thoughts returned to the ironing. Damn, she thought. The iron is too hot.

She sprinkled some water over the shirt. Minnie looked at her ten year old daughter and she smiled. 'You've grown up so fast, you know, Glenda. Seems like only yesterday we came to this house.'

Glenda ran the iron up and down the shirt. 'I've got to go upstairs and do some maths with Abe, mum. I've got ever such a lot of homework to do.' Glenda wanted to escape from the ironing. She felt as if she were in a pack of cards. She and Minnie lived in the bottom of the deck. She was the two of clubs, and Minnie the three. Above them the other fifty cards stacked up in claustrophobic layers. Minnie took over the ironing and Glenda grabbed her notebook and fled out of the door.

Once she was outside in the fresh air, she gasped to breathe. Before her the house stood silent. Renée, she knew, was at the theatre. Renée was the Queen of Hearts, Glenda decided, Abe the King of Spades. They were on the top of the stack of cards. She, Glenda decided as she climbed the front stairs, would also end up on the top of the deck. She grinned to herself. She would be the Queen of Diamonds. But who does the Queen of Diamonds marry? The Joker, she thought, as she pushed open the front door. Of course, the Joker. But then she remembered Abe saying, 'In poker, the Joker is wild.' Of course, Glenda thought. The Queen of Diamonds looks for the Joker.

She had a sudden vision of her Joker: a tall fair man with thin hands and two eyes blazing like diamonds under a bright light. She sang to herself. '*Chicaboom, chicarack, she's singing, her shoes paddiwack at the front and the back, and her yellow curls go swinging.*'

She found Abe in the drawing room. 'You're in a good mood,' Abe said, sitting her down at a table.

'I've decided to marry the Joker,' she said. Inside she was bursting with excitement. 'I didn't used to want to get married, but today I decided I would. The Queen of Diamonds belongs with the Joker.' Abe leaned back, his long intelligent hand playing with a pencil. Glenda watched his fingers. These were the fingers that did those yearning things to Renée, the same fingers that sometimes made Renée's eyes shine brightly. Glenda felt a huge impatience befall her. 'Why does it take so long to get on with life, Abe?' she asked.

Abe stretched. 'Don't be in too much of a hurry, honeypot,' he advised, amused at her vehemence. He recognized that Glenda was crossing the thin line between childhood and adolescence. She's crossing early he thought as he watched her bent over her sums. Abe felt concern for Glenda. He had spent many years alone in what often seemed to be a hurricane, tossed and turned by circumstances, until he met Renée and there, in her warm passionate arms, he had known safety, and in that safety the knowledge of rapture. Rapture had never been part of his experience in life. All his adventures with women had left him lonely and spent. Now he realized that most of the women he left abandoned all over the world were false. The promises they made to him were nothing but a need for a security they lacked themselves. Only Renée offered real security. She, like a majestic ocean liner, was afloat in the sea of life for herself. With him or without him, this great ship sailed on. If he abandoned her, the lights would not blaze less brightly. But then Abe knew that he would never abandon her. Never. In Renée he found the one thing he had always dreamed of. His greatest fear and his greatest triumph: a woman he could love forever.

He heard the crunching of a taxi's tyres in the drive. 'Renée's back,' he said joyfully.

Glenda looked up. She watched Abe greet Renée at the door. Abe's mouth pressed hard on Renée's cheek. She was wearing a thick black trench coat. The smell of autumn clung to her. Glenda felt the chill wind penetrate the house. Both adults stood in the hall, their bodies intimate. Glenda felt a sharp stab between her legs. She pushed her hand down against her belly. A feeling of terrified longing engulfed her. This is what it's like, she thought. 'Had a good day, darling?'

Renée was in the room. Her coat was open. Her breasts were encased in a low halter neck sweater. 'I've had a bastard of a day. Get me a martini, Abe, will you? The damn director is a bitch. He doesn't know what he's doing, so he shouts and yells at everybody. I'm too old for all this.' She stretched out on the sofa.

Abe came back carrying a martini glass. 'Here,' Renée said. 'Have a sip, Glenda.'

Glenda obediently walked over to the sofa. She put her

lips on the chilled glass and she sipped. The gin slid down her throat. She felt an icy tide slide up her nose. 'Take the olive,' Renée said.

Abe stood beside Renée. He massaged the back of her neck. 'That's wonderful, darling,' Renée purred.

Glenda sat in her chair watching them, the sweet taste of gin still in her mouth. 'Glenda says she wants to be the Queen of Diamonds,' Abe said. 'She says she'll marry the Joker.' His voice was light and amused.

Renée kicked off her shoes and wiggled her escaped toes. 'They say diamonds are a girl's best friend. But what's wrong with the King of Diamonds?'

'He's too old and boring,' Glenda laughed. 'The Joker is wild.'

Renée made a face. 'If you play with a wild thing, you'd better be careful.'

Glenda looked at Renée lying there on the sofa, and she saw in Renée's eyes a warning. 'I mean it, Glenda. If the Joker is wild, anything can happen.'

'I know,' Glenda said slowly, 'but I like the kind of poker Abe taught me. When the Joker is wild, you're right. Anything can happen.' She laughed. 'Otherwise, it's all too boring. Anyway, I'd better get back. Mum's cooking my favourite. Roast chicken and Paxo stuffing.'

Abe smiled and relaxed. 'She's still a child,' he told himself as Glenda left the house. He heard the door slam. He bent over and Renée pulled him on top of her. 'Here,' she said. 'Now.'

Later that night Glenda put a hand between her thighs and finished what had begun in the drawing room upstairs. Within a few seconds, release arrived. Now Glenda knew, as she dropped off the continent into a deep, deep sleep, she would never be the same again. She had eaten and tasted the knowledge that divided the world of the adult and the child. The taste, she decided, was definitely of gin.

Chapter 33

Glenda knew she would pass the eleven-plus. The world, before she discovered sex, had often been confused. Grown-ups made decisions about her life. She seemed to float about two feet above the ground. Sometimes only Lady seemed to understand her, Lady with the pink eyes. Those eyes rolled in Lady's head and her long soft furry ears felt like corn silk between Glenda's hands. Sometimes in the winter her hands were pale from lack of sunlight. During the exam time her hands were brown and Glenda made a promise to God that she would not touch herself 'there' until the eleven-plus was over. Glenda very much wanted to be first in her class, mostly to please Mrs Turner, but really she knew that she wanted to know that she was the best. The cleverest person in the classroom.

For months she worked at her books. Sometimes she wished she could eat them and thereby retain the knowledge in her weary brain. Ruth often worked beside her in Minnie's kitchen. Minnie left the girls alone. If they studied at Mamie Schwartz's house, Mamie fussed and puttered about the room, peering over their shoulders, correcting spelling or the shape of a sentence. 'No, no, no,' Mamie's voice nagged. 'Don't you remember, Ruth? A gerund.'

Ruth muttered under her breath, 'Let's go to your place.' And they went, Ruth grateful for Minnie's anonymous presence, Glenda guilty because she knew her mother couldn't interfere. Abe was her tutor for maths, and Renée her guide to literature.

Glenda was stricken by guilt. Her body at times behaved normally. But then there were days when she felt on fire. The earth moved and buildings swayed, pulled by the incessant tides of her feelings, feelings that were confused between what she imagined must be lust – as described in her Bible –

and her urgent need for relief. She struggled to keep her body pure and her thoughts clean, but many times she failed miserably. Most of the day she kept herself busy, but at night, when she lay in the warm hollow of her bed, she felt her spine tingle, and the slow melting of honey between her legs, and her fingers itched, she softly made the luxurious foray into the soft hollow between her thighs. She slept peacefully after her body had finished its ecstatic shuddering. She woke up into a silent and guilty world.

She wished she could talk to someone, but there was no one. Certainly not Ruth. Glenda could not imagine Ruth or her mother and father ever talking about anything. Dr Schwartz, with his small pink hands and his neat shiny face, looked so fastidious that Glenda could not even imagine him sticking his penis into Mrs Schwartz, assuming he had a penis at all. Glenda imagined Dr Schwartz must have a penis very like the little finger of his left hand, which was usually crooked at a right angle. No, Ruth must have been a virgin birth. Another *News of the World* story, like the woman who had one white baby and one black baby, or the woman who was spirited away by a yeti. When Glenda was not struggling with herself, she was studying hard.

When the long wait was over and the results were through, Glenda was pleased that she had passed but was enraged to find that the awful lout Cyril O'Mally not only had passed but was also top of the class.

'Don't take it too 'ard, love,' Minnie said. 'You done well, really you have. I'm so proud of you.'

Renée screwed her nose up in the way that she had when she was feeling sympathetic. 'Look, Glenda,' she said. 'You've done your best. You've done really well.'

Abe agreed, but in her heart of hearts Glenda felt she had betrayed herself. At least she was second in the class, with Ruth a close third.

Renée invited the Schwartz family over for dinner to

celebrate the exam results. The dinner went well. Minnie sat beside Chinchilla who was feeling in a mischievous mood. Dr Schwartz talked to Abe about the National Health Service. Abe listened amiably but disagreed. 'People respect what they pay for,' Abe said at the end of the lecture.

Minnie nodded. Glenda looked at Chinchilla. Chinchilla wore a very large new diamond ring. Her face was younger and softer. 'Diamonds,' Chinchilla interrupted, catching Glenda's eye. 'Now there's something I can respect.' Renée saw the look on Chinchilla's face. Glenda watched both women. In their faces was a superior knowledge of the way women knew how to rule the world of men. The knowledge Glenda had so recently acquired was part of the jigsaw puzzle. Even Mrs Schwartz, as she sat in the light of the dinner candles, knew some of the mystery. Not much, though. Her little fat hands occasionally patted her husband's thigh if she felt he was talking too much. She pushed and prodded Dr Schwartz rather as she might push and prod an unyielding piece of dough on her well-floured chopping board. Minnie, her mother, knew also, but her knowledge was practical. Only women like Renée and Chinchilla knew about power from the inside. They knew all the technical information that one could read about in books, and they practised their knowledge. They held their men. 'Who is he, Chinchilla?' Renée raised her eyebrows.

Chinchilla waved her left hand under the flames. The stone exploded and refracted under the lights. Glenda, sipping her splash of champagne, smiled as the bubbles popped in her nose. 'A very well known actor, darling,' she said. 'I have invented a charity called Pets. He is my chairman, so to speak. You see, it works this way.' Chinchilla leaned forward, her alabaster brow lined in an effort to make herself understood. Dr Schwartz found himself gazing into the valley between Chinchilla's breasts. Good heavens, he thought, restraining a wish to bury his head up to his neck in her

142

welcoming bosom. He patted Mamie's plump thigh. Good heavens. And I'm a doctor.

'You see,' Chinchilla went on, 'he tells his wife he's collecting money for my charitable work with animals, and she just *loves* animals. That way we get lots of time together and I get to throw parties in her house.'

'Oh boy,' Abe whistled through his teeth.

'I think we'd better be going.' Mrs Schwartz looked at her watch. Half past ten, the watch reassured her. Outside this big house with its lush furniture and exotic food there was a real world of normal people who waited in queues in Dr Schwartz's surgery. Some of them, admittedly, were not at all clean, but they posed no threat to her way of life. She could pity them. Mrs Schwartz found it hard to feel pity for Chinchilla. The woman was mistress to a married man. She even boasted about it.

The Schwartzes said goodbye and Minnie saw that Glenda was tired. 'Time for us to go to bed,' Minnie said. 'Leave the washing-up. I'll do it in the morning.'

Renée put her arm around Minnie's shoulder. 'Don't worry,' she said. 'I'll do it with Chinchilla. It'll do her diamond good to do some honest to God housework.'

Chinchilla laughed. 'Yes,' she said. 'Renée and I will get a chance to catch up on the latest gossip.'

Minnie left the home. On the way downstairs she suddenly felt excluded. Why was she going to bed at half past ten, when she would much rather be upstairs having a good gossip with Renée and Chinchilla?

Minnie kissed Glenda good night and lay in her bed, disconsolate. She had no man to give her diamonds. Glenda was on her way to grammar school and independence. She, Minnie, had no one. The salt tears moistened her pillow.

Chapter 34

The grammar school was a big barren place. True, the primary school had looked that way at first to Glenda, but after years of attendance it appeared finally cheerful and almost cosy with Mrs Turner's devoted loving care. Even the witch of a French teacher became bearable with hindsight. The unfamiliar grammar looked daunting.

Glenda and Ruth were deposited at the door by Mrs Schwartz. She had clucked her way nervously through the traffic, and the car was full of strings of words of warning. 'Now, Ruth, you talk to no one you don't know.'

'But I don't know *anybody*, mother. So who can I talk to?' Ruth rolled her eyes. Glenda smiled nervously. Ruth's eyes looked like poached eggs when she argued with her mother.

'If you don't watch out, you'll end up with one foot in *tsimmis* and the other in *tsooris*. Boys are only after one thing. Remember that.'

Behind her both girls were mouthing the well-worn phrase. *No chupi, no shtupi.* 'Chance would be a fine thing,' Ruth grumbled.

Glenda felt surprised. Maybe Ruth is growing up, she thought. Maybe she feels some of the things I do.

Minnie had hugged her tightly this morning. 'Goodbye, love,' she said, ''ave a wonderful time.' There was an ache in the hug and a chasm between them as Glenda left the flat in answer to the impatient bleat of the little Austin Seven.

Now, walking down the long dark hall, the autumn sun poking its fingers through the windows, vainly trying to play with the students who ignored the sun and the furious wind tapping on the windowpanes, Glenda looked out of the windows. They both marched down the silent corridors towards the locker rooms and then their classrooms. Most of the first day was spent sorting out piles of books. Glenda was happy to have so many unknown books at her disposal. By the end of the year the hieroglyphics in the maths books would be resolved. The codes in chemistry would make perfect sense, and her Latin and French sufficiently learned to make Mrs Turner beam with pride. The only sour note was Cyril, who sat next to her. 'You don't mind?' he said with breathless determination. 'I don't know anybody else, do I?'

Glenda was cross. She didn't want to know, let alone be seen with Cyril. But Cyril stuck to her side. Ruth laughed. 'At least you're safe,' she said. 'No hope of *chupi* or *shtupi* with him around.'

Glenda frowned. 'I'm not interested in boys, Ruth.' She looked at the motley collection of males in early adolescence that slouched in their seats, the be-pimpled, nail-bitten denizens of another land. Unfamiliar girls sat around the classroom. For the most their faces were bright, their hair pulled back and clean. But the boys were hopeless, their long, lank legs sprawled out into the aisles between the desks, their wrinkled socks exposing thin protruding ankles . . . Glenda wondered how anybody could ever be interested in boys. She buried her head in her books.

Her form teacher, a Mr Maynard, was a shy man with a nervous lisp and a passion for Thomas Hardy. Glenda was pleased. She too had a passion for Thomas Hardy. This was the first day of her life in her senior school. Although the grammar was bleak and forbidding, Glenda watched the sixth form boys and girls sauntering around the playground.

During assembly the Headmaster read out a list of names, names of people who had passed their A-levels and were now at universities. 'Sommerfield and Peters, Oxford. Angela Williams and James Beck, Cambridge.' Edinburgh, St Andrews, Aberdeen, and then on down the list. Glenda realized that the list was indeed impressive, and that seven years from this very day her name would be read out. 'Glenda

Stanhope, Cambridge.' She could hear the words now. Several of the teachers didn't look as if they would survive the six years. Two of them sat moribund and constipated on the platform.

'Latin teachers,' Cyril grinned, his rotten teeth hanging like fronds of leaves from his jaw. 'Always look dead. Just like Latin.'

'Do shut up, Cyril.' Glenda grabbed Ruth. 'Let's go to the toilet, Ruth. At least we'll get away from Cyril.'

'Lavatory, not toilet,' Ruth reminded Glenda.

'Lavatory, then. I don't care what it's called. I just have to get away from Cyril.'

The bus stop was at the front gates of the school. Ruth and Glenda waited nervously for the Ealing bus. Both of them felt small and insignificant beside the tall teenagers who loomed over them, shouting, pinching, and flirting. Glenda drew Ruth aside. 'What a stupid way to be!' she said. 'We'll never become like that.'

'*Goyim*,' Ruth said. 'Loud and noisy. We're never like that at Hebrew school.'

Glenda had often collected Ruth after her Hebrew lessons. She rather liked the peace and the quiet in the temple, the boys bent over their books. 'It's Sammy Goldstein you're after,' Glenda teased, feeling a sharp jab as she remembered a different Sam, now years away, already at big school. Still, her satchel was full of thick books and new notebooks. Her pencil box was also full of pens. Now they wrote their names with real ink and carefully blotted it dry with blotting paper. She liked blotting paper, even if it did mean that Cyril used his to shoot pellets at her.

The bus arrived and sucked in the children from the front of the school, like a giant Hoover. The children threw themselves into the bus and rearranged themselves into the seats. 'All aboard!' the bus conductor smiled. He was lighter than Abe, but he was black. Glenda sat back in her seat. She watched as the bus deposited children and passengers at various points on its route. Now the faces on the streets were not all pale white. A few turbans with dark Indian faces peered out. Jamaicans, Pakistani matrons with their dark-eyed children trailing behind them. 'Karma,' Abe said once. 'England's colonies coming home to roost.'

Ruth got off the bus first. Her place was taken by a young pregnant woman. The woman was poor. Glenda could smell the lack of hot water in her life. The smell of the poor was a sour smell, Glenda was reminded. It made her uncomfortable. Never again, she said to herself as she sat next to the woman. The woman's belly was hugely swollen. There was an attempt at a ring on the woman's wedding finger, but it didn't look like a real wedding ring. The woman's dress was too thin for the autumn weather. Little bobbles of material told Glenda that the dress was probably from the jumble. She didn't want to look any further at the woman. Another baby without a father, she thought. Another bastard like me.

The word *bastard* flashed involuntarily into her brain but Glenda knew the word. It had often been used against her in the playground. Cyril may well come from a slum family, his father a well-known alcoholic bully, his mother a permanently pregnant manic depressive, but Cyril had both a mother and a father, so he was respectable. Not so Glenda. Sometimes she caught a sad look in Mamie's sweating eyes and she knew what she was thinking. Why must my Ruthie, such a nice respectable girl from a nice respectable family, make friends with Glenda, Glenda who is not Jewish and worse, who hasn't got a father? Glenda knew that look. The only people other than Minnie who never looked at her like that, but only with love, were Renée, Abe, and Chinchilla.

As the bus neared her bus stop, Glenda was glad, very glad, to be home. She left the bus, struggled past the pregnant woman, and walked the few yards to the house. The house was tall, strong, and welcoming.

Chapter 35

Work obsessed Glenda. Cyril effortlessly topped her marks. He grinned at the end of every week when their papers were returned. Glenda set her lips and went home more determined than ever. 'I want to be top,' she told her mother.

'That's my girl,' said Minnie, fondly fussing around Glenda's diminutive form.

Some nights Glenda felt she was forever chained to her pile of books, her fingers cramped from writing. 'All Gaul is divided into three parts,' hammered her brain at night. Whether Gaul was divided into three parts or not, Latin declensions became a fierce battleground between Cyril and herself. Ruth trailed along behind. Cyril had a photographic memory.

'*Amabo, amabis, amabit,* errr,' a nervous student stuttered in class. The Latin master wearily ran his fingers through his hair. 'Finish it off, O'Mally. Just finish it off.'

Cyril jumped to his feet, his long arms flailing at the sky, as he raised his demented face to the high ceiling and bellowed the answers.

'What do you want to do when you leave here?' Glenda asked Cyril after a particularly hair-raising virtuoso performance in the classroom.

'I want to go into the Foreign Office and travel to all the different places. I want to see China and Japan and Egypt. You ever read Somerset Maugham's stories?'

Glenda shook her head. 'Nah. I'm reading Jane Austen, and a book called *Middlemarch*.'

'Dried up old spinsterish stuff,' Cyril sniffed contemptuously. 'You should be reading Graham Greene.'

Slowly Glenda was beginning to like Cyril. He had no pretensions, no wish other than to escape his own background. 'I've got to get out, Glenda. I really 'ave. I can't live in Hounslow me whole life. I don't want to be a gas inspector or a post office worker. And even if I do well at university, I don't want to go into the Civil Service and be a clerk behind a desk. I want to travel and see things.'

By now Glenda was in her teens, and she heard the yearning in Cyril's voice. Ruth had finally netted Samuel Goldstein and Glenda, with no interest in the boys around her, allowed Cyril to accompany her to the school dances. There was an unstated agreement between them that whatever the rest of the school might think, they were friends. If people sniggered at the unlikely sight of a small chestnut-haired girl accompanied by a huge shambling oaf of a boy, they could giggle. Glenda put her nose in the air and commanded her friend to shine his shoes, straighten his tie, and brush his hair. Sometimes Cyril and Glenda made up a foursome with Ruth and Sammy and went rowing on the pond at Gunnersbury Park. Minnie liked Cyril and felt comfortable that her daughter had a formidable friend who would protect Glenda from the often violent eruptions in the playground.

Their fifteenth year was marked by the beginning trauma of O levels. Glenda had chosen to take eight subjects for her O levels along with Ruth. Cyril took ten. After O levels there were two more years to go, when the three of them would be sixth formers faced with the hurdle of A levels. Glenda felt like a race horse. She imagined her fetlocks bandaged for the races.

Outside the safe shell of her life, the world spun by. The decade of the Sixties was approaching its middle years, and America, having lost a favoured president, seemed suddenly propelled into the troubled whirlwinds of upheaval. English television sets showed American protesters shaking their fists at the old orders, now recognized as oppressive. Fire hoses were aimed by white Americans against black Americans. American university campuses, once the imagined home of the imagined character 'Joe College', now seemed poised to explode. Riots were in the offing. Assassination had become the way to quieten brave dissenting voices. But all of it passed Glenda by and England waited to see what the outcome would be in America before endeavouring to change itself.

The pressure of exams continued. Internally, occasionally, Glenda realized she was lonely. Upstairs, Abe and Renée continued to live happily together, but now Abe talked often of America. He wanted to be part of what was happening there, he said. He wanted to see it first-hand. Renée, her huge eyes silent, listened quietly. She still worked hard in the theatre and was now a well-established character actress. Minnie worked tirelessly around the house. 'We'll both be old maids,' Minnie joked with Glenda.

Glenda made a face. 'I don't care if I am an old maid. I'd rather do that than end up like Ruth with Sammy Goldstein.'

'But he's such a nice boy, Glenda. She'll be happy enough with him.'

'You said it yourself: Happy *enough*.' Glenda gazed out of the window. 'I'm sure she will.' She looked at the empty rabbit cage. Lady had died during the winter. There had been no warning. One morning Glenda went out and lifted off the sacking that protected the cage from the cold night air. She found Lady stretched out. She lifted her beloved rabbit into her arms and felt the stiffness and the coldness seep into her own bones. For a moment all Glenda could do was to stand still. The shock of Lady's death hit her first. No longer would she be greeted by the pink eyes or by the snuffle of her rabbit's nose, the long velvet ears under her chin and the thick smooth coat – a playground for her fingers. The ache left a rabbit-shaped hole in Glenda's life, a hole that could never be filled, not even by another rabbit. No other could take the place of the ebullient, loving, intelligent Lady. No, Glenda realized as she gazed out of the window. 'I'd rather,' she said slowly, 'be alone for the rest of my life than end up living like Dr and Mrs Schwartz. You know, mum, sometimes when I'm around there, I think I want to scream. They don't live, those two. They exist. And that's not living.' Glenda's voice was shaking.

Minnie tucked her legs up into her armchair. 'Well, it is for most people, Glenda.'

'Maybe. But I'm not most people. I don't want to be like most people. I want to be me.'

Minnie shifted uncomfortably. Glenda recently seemed to be so fierce, she thought. It's all those books. 'What you reading, then?' Minnie asked, hoping to calm Glenda down.

'Camus,' Glenda said.

'Who's Camoo?'

'He's a French writer who doesn't believe in anything. Nothing. Not God, not eternity, just the here and now. Cyril thinks he's great. Can I have a black skirt for my birthday?'

Minnie laughed softly, relieved that she had her Glenda back.

'I'll ask Renée if she'll give me a black jersey. Existentialists wear black, mum, and they smoke Gitanes cigarettes from France.'

'I hope you won't smoke, Glenda,' Minnie said, reaching for a cigarette. 'It's an awful 'abit.'

Glenda stared at her mother. 'Of course not,' she said. She ignored the Pinocchio-nosed puppet that laughed silently at her lies. After all, she reasoned, I've only tried a few times with Cyril in the park. Cyril was already hooked and his fingers were beginning to yellow.

Throughout the summer of their sixteenth year, most evenings she and Cyril walked in the parks, talking animatedly about their studies. Cyril stretched Glenda. He bullied her, he pushed her out of her reclusive position.

Cyril was comfortable when he visited the downstairs flat, but when faced with Renée and Abe, he froze. His feet became weapons of war and his voice alternately quivered in a high falsetto or a deep bass. He sweated and grunted. Renée was amused by this intense young man who seemed to be like a desperate character in a Dostoyevsky short story.

One time Renée gave Glenda tickets to the theatre for both of them. 'I'll see you backstage,' she said.

Glenda loved the theatre for the work it encapsulated. She loved the moment she walked through the doors into the womb-like foyer, down the aisles, and then the moment her bottom hit the plush seats. All around her people rustled in the darkness while on stage the story unfolded. Funny, intense, mediocre, or occasionally so back-breakingly beautiful that Glenda never thought she would breathe again.

Cyril, sitting for once in an intense silence, was drunk on the words. He watched Renée as she brought the house to its knees with laughter, or she held their hearts with a tilt of her head, the magic words pouring like molten gold from her mouth. Abandoned and betrayed, she stood by herself in the glow of a spotlight. The audience was in tears, and Cyril was finally, irrevocably in love.

Later, when the curtain swished down for the last time, Glenda took his hand and led him backstage. 'You were wonderful, Renée.' Glenda threw herself into Renée's arms and hugged her.

Abe grinned at Cyril. 'Did you enjoy the play?' he said. He could see that Cyril was infatuated by Renée. He thought, Join the queue, buddy. Cyril nodded his great head and he blushed. Renée put an arm around his awkward shoulder. 'I'm glad you liked it, Cyril,' she said.

Chapter 36

The results came in and Cyril swept the board. For once the Headmaster did not frown at him. He beamed. 'These are the best marks we've ever had.'

Cyril, standing stiffly to attention, tried to suppress his trembling body.

Such a pity, the Headmaster thought, that such a good brain should be given to an O'Mally. They were a slum family, but surprisingly all the children of the two sullen parents seemed to inherit a wild streak of genius – an inheritance which mystified the Headmaster. The working classes should know their place, the Headmaster maintained, and that was that. But some of his students seemed hell-bent on transcending the futures which he had envisioned for them.

Then after Cyril came Glenda Stanhope. Her mother wasn't up to much, but her mentor, Renée Blanchard, was famous. An excellent actress. Pity about the black paramour.

'Ruth Schwartz, six O levels,' he intoned. She should have done better than that. Jews are really quite clever. Cunning really. Dr Schwartz a bit of a red. The Headmaster long-windedly read on. He was due to retire in two years. Thank goodness, he thought. I'll see this lot through A levels and then I'll be gone, down to my little Devon cottage where I can get away from the dirty streets of London and from children who drop their Hs.

Glenda looked across at Ruth. The results had been sent by post to their homes a few weeks before school started, but Ruth had been away and Glenda had not seen her until to-day. Glenda caught her eye as Ruth's results were read out. To Glenda's surprise, Ruth didn't flinch. She was changing, Glenda realized. Changing from a young girl, Glenda's best friend, to a rather matronly sixteen year old woman. Even though they were sitting next to each other, on Ruth's other side sat her other friends of the last year. Dawn, Debbie, and Wendy. Glenda had privately dubbed them the three witches. After school she decided she must really have it out with Ruth. Either they were best friends or they were not.

'You failed two O levels, and you didn't tell me. Ruth, what kind of friendship is that?'

Ruth, sitting in the ABC Cafe in Ealing High Road gazed at her espresso coffee and played with the sugar cubes neatly wrapped in her saucer. 'I'm not taking sugar because I'm on a diet,' Ruth replied. 'Sammy thinks I don't need to diet, but Wendy says I do.'

'What has dieting got to do with O levels? I thought we agreed that we would both work hard and try to go to Cambridge together.'

'Did we?' Ruth squinted at Glenda. 'That was a long time ago. That was before I met Sammy. What's the point of me going to university for years and years, when I could be married? I want to have my own house and two children.'

Glenda felt she had been hit on the head very hard. 'Ruth, we always told each other we *might* get married, but not until afterwards.'

Ruth smiled. 'I want what my mother has, Glenda.'

Glenda felt a hot surge of rage rising in the back of her throat. 'And what does your mother have?' Between them, the coffee cups put up their steam. Glenda wished there was sufficient steam to shroud their faces. The conversation was becoming dangerous and terminal. The words unsaid between them were lying in an open grave of friendship. Mamie had a white wedding, a husband, a baby. Mamie had Danny. She did it the right way. She didn't open her plump white thighs until her wedding night, and then only occasionally thereafter to keep Danny living in an eternal netherworld of lust. Yes, Mamie didn't need a degree from any university to know how to catch and keep her man. As much as she had rebelled in her early years, as much as she studied Kant and Rilke

154

and Nietzsche with her best friends, as many times as they swore rebellion and emblazoned Simone de Beauvoir as their mentor, Ruth finally watched her mother and knew that she had no intention of risking herself and her future by leaving Sammy, who was a stock clerk in his father's warehouse.

There he invoiced bales of elastics. Elastic for belts, elastic for braces, and even thinner elastic for knickers. From such productivity hung Samuel's future, the heir to an elastic factory. Ruth calculated (even without her failed O level in Maths) that if she married Sammy in the next year she could start her married life in a house a few streets away from her mother-in-law. Then as they shared the High Holidays with both families, they could move district by district until Ruth could make it to Richmond where all rich Jews finally migrated to live on Richmond Hill and gaze down at the *goyim* who didn't have the money to live on the Hill. Next year on Richmond Hill, and the year after that in Jerusalem . . . It was her mother's little joke, but now it was a joke they both shared.

No, Ruth decided. Glenda was all right, and a friend, but a dangerous friend.

But then Glenda never knew the rules of the game, even if Ruth tried to explain them. 'I love Sammy,' Ruth tried again. 'I want babies, not degrees.'

Glenda sulked. 'You can have all that later.'

'Can I? Don't you think some little *shiksa* might come along and pinch my Sammy? Then what? No, Glenda.' She shook her dark head and slurped her coffee loudly. 'I'm not taking that chance.'

Glenda sat silent. Well goodbye, Ruth, she thought. 'I'd better go, Ruth,' she said. 'I've got a lot of books to sort out for A levels.'

Ruth smiled. 'Okay, Glenda. I'll invite you to my engagement party.'

'You don't waste time, do you?'

Ruth looked up. Glenda could see a real sadness in her

eyes. 'There is no choice, Glenda. I don't think the world is a very good place for women if they're not married. Do you?'

Glenda felt stuck. She remembered her mother's face, years in Hounslow. Now, although her life had improved, her mother was lonely – a loneliness shared with Chinchilla. Women of a certain age without men. Glenda knew exactly what Ruth was trying so desperately to convey. As she stood up she smiled at her old friend. 'I can't wait for the invitation,' she said.

'Thanks.' Ruth put her cup down.

'Really, I must run,' Glenda said. She patted Ruth on the shoulder and as her hand came down to touch the well-padded body, Glenda knew their days together were over. Like the pop song she listened to often in her head, the words *over, over, over* swelled.

Chapter 37

Ruth left a hole in Glenda's life, a much larger hole than she had expected. When the phone rang at home it was usually Chinchilla for Minnie. Sometimes it was Cyril who had a job in a fish and chip shop. He fried the fish and the cod's roe in deep fat from 7 to 11 pm when the pubs shut and the last late night revellers went home.

In his newly-found reverence for Renée, Cyril tried very hard to renounce his old slovenly habits. Now he spent his hard-earned money on new shoes, new trousers, and a magnificent black donkey jacket. The only problem, Glenda learned with regret, was that he smelled perpetually of fried fish. She didn't have the heart to tell him, though. The new improved Cyril minded his table manners and tried very hard not to eat with his mouth open.

Renée realized that Ruth no longer came to the house. Abe was sympathetic. 'One by one,' he said, 'they drop out, honey. When the going gets tough, the wimps run for cover.'

'Huh,' Glenda mumbled, her brain aching with tightly packed information. 'It's not the same for men.'

'Oh no?' Abe gave his wide-eyed minstrel look. 'Whadja mean it's not the same for men? Whadja think is going to happen to little ol' Samuel Goldstein there? He's going to invoice elastic. Then he's going to pack the stuff. Then, if he's lucky, he can follow his father around while they sell the merchandise. All so that he can buy a mortgage for Ruth's little, or not so little, ass. Then come the babies. He has to sell more elastic. Finally he can become Elastic King of Ealing! What a life.'

Glenda sat by the fire in Abe's drawing room. 'Money seems to be the answer to all this,' she said quietly. 'Look at Cyril. He works all hours for a few measly pounds so that he can buy some decent clothes and eventually get an old motor car. He has no friends apart from me. There are other boys in the sixth form all taking A levels to go to university, but they're all boys from posh homes. They don't like Cyril. They imitate the way he talks and the way he walks. I get furious. He says he doesn't care, but I know he does. He gets them back by beating them hands down with his marks, and they hate him for it.' She sighed. 'I'm not much better off. There are girls who talk to me in the playground or at lunch, but you know, Abe, I'm the only girl that really wants a career. The others, when we really get down to talking, just want to get a man. Even if they pretend they don't want to get married, they honestly do. I wish all this was over. I wish I could shut my eyes and when they opened, I'd be at Cambridge.'

Abe sat in his chair and watched Glenda's mobile face. How she had grown from the tiny cowering little thing that first shivered on their doorstep! What an influence she had been on Renée. From almost the beginning, Renée had changed. Her long-checked maternal nature blossomed once she took Minnie and Glenda in. Minnie, with her neat, organized ways, cleaned up the chaotic side of Renée's nature.

The house, in those early years, slowly changed too as Minnie washed, cleaned, and cooked. Soon Renée appreciated the organized peace as she came through the front door. A frantic night at the theatre no longer meant a night of heavy drinking and drunken regrets the next day. The house welcomed Renée and reassured her. Meals were on time, properly planned, and Glenda was there to kiss and hug her. When Renée sang, her great voice cascading out of the window, the notes were no longer full of pain and sorrow. Glenda fulfilled Renée's need to love a child. 'You know, honeybunch,' Abe said, smiling, 'there is nothing quite like a glass of champagne and a little bit of jitterbug to lift the spirits. You roll back the carpet and I'll get the champagne.'

Two sips of champagne and a five minute jitterbug demonstration with Abe left Glenda laughing. 'I'd better go, Abe,' she said. 'I've got an absolute stack of algebra to do.'

'Bye, honeybunch,' Abe said. His eyes closed, his fingers snapping.

Glenda stood watching this man who had so much to do with her life. Abe hadn't chickened out and gone to the suburbs of life. He was still the same huge bald Abe she had known for ten years. Always there, always comforting, but not dull like Danny Schwartz. 'Is the Joker still wild, Abe?'

Abe paused and looked at Glenda. 'Sure, honey. The Joker is always wild if you want to play it that way.'

Glenda took a deep breath and she smiled. 'I do, Abe. I do.' She walked on the steps and she felt as if a huge weight had been lifted off her shoulders. All those rows of little houses with identical windows, identical cat-pissed hedges, her idea of hell, receded. Abe restored her balance. She did not have to live in one of those little houses. Fine for the Ruths and the Wendys and all those who came after them. She, Glenda Stanhope, was on her way to Cambridge – she hoped. She hummed . . . 'And we will not be moved. I'm on my way to Cambridge and I will not be moved . . .'

Chapter 38

'I got the car!' Cyril's voice over the telephone was triumphant.

'Great,' said Glenda. 'Take me for a drive.'

'Be round in a minute.'

Minnie, addressing her eternal pile of ironing, smiled. She approved of Cyril. Grotesque as he was, she had come to like the shy, serious boy with his erratic, brilliant mind. Now that Ruth no longer came to labour at the kitchen table with Glenda, Cyril often arrived before leaving for the fish and chip shop. Only a few afternoons ago Glenda and Cyril had a furious battle over whether Ophelia was a more powerful literary figure than Hamlet. 'Who do you remember, then?' Cyril bellowed. 'Fucking 'amlet, poncing about in his leotard, or Ophelia, lying drowned in the river? 'Scuse the French, Mrs Stanhope. Didn't mean to offend.'

Minnie was so intrigued by his description that she spent the rest of the evening reading the play. 'Do you good, love, to go out for a spin. You look tired.'

Glenda stretched and grinned. 'I am,' she said. 'But, you know, there's such a great beauty to these chemistry equations. Once you understand how they work, they flow just like a piece of Mozart.'

Minnie nodded. Gibberish, she thought, looking at the squiggles on the paper. Such gibberish. What use will all this be to Glenda? She kept her disloyal thoughts to herself. As she ran the iron back and forth, back and forth, Minnie daydreamed her favourite daydream. Glenda in cap and gown stood on a platform, her hand outstretched to receive her degree . . . She was interrupted by the arrival of Cyril.

'Come and look at 'er, Mrs Stan'ope. She's beautiful.' Cyril's face was alight and his eyes were bulging with excitement. 'See? I got my driving licence, passed the test first go.'

The car was an ancient cowl-nosed Morris.

Glenda approved. 'She really is pretty, Cyril. What will you call her?'

'Ida, after me mum.' Cyril walked around the car. 'Ready, then, Glenda?' He held open her door. She climbed in. 'Where to?' he asked. ''Ow about Ealing Common?' He revved the engine. There was a spluttering whine and a strangled cough. 'Come on, old girl. Don't give me that.' Then Ida took off.

They flew down the road, Cyril crashing the gears and letting out great war whoops of excitement. 'See 'er go, Glenda!'

'Do slow down, Cyril. The police will catch us.'

'Nah!' Cyril yelled. 'I've the luck of the Irish.'

Glenda looked at the huge bulky figure squashed into the small Morris and sighed. Maybe the local police knew the O'Mally family well enough to leave them alone.

Finally the little car turned up Acton Lane and Cyril slowed down. 'Innit beautiful, Glen? Just beautiful. Look at the colours turning on the trees to get ready for winter.'

Glenda felt a deep moment of sympathy for this boy. Not really a boy any more. His voice now remained deep. His face, though covered with pustules, needed a shave. But at moments like this she recognized a tender sensitive side of Cyril that he never showed to anyone else. In school, he was Cyril the bully in the playground. In class he was Cyril the brilliant. With her he was Cyril the gentle giant. She put her hand on his thigh.

Cyril stopped the car by a huge rhododendron bush. The flowers were a bursting colour of red. Cyril lay back in his seat, his huge hawk-like nose pointing directly at the ceiling. His hair was thick with Brilliantine. He said nothing for a moment, but Glenda felt his thigh muscles tighten. 'Can I kiss you, Glenda?' he asked. 'Just once. Can I?'

Glenda was taken aback by the ferocity of the question. She saw a misery in Cyril's eyes. 'Of course, Cyril,' she said, not wanting to hurt her friend. 'Of course you can.'

Cyril turned towards her and then brought his full lips down on her unsuspecting mouth. Glenda was transfixed with horror. Cyril's tongue rooted around inside her mouth and she felt him struggle with his clothes. She was pinned down by his weight. She could not move. 'Hold it for me,' she heard Cyril's hoarse voice. 'Please, Glenda. Just hold it for me.' Cyril moved her hand from his thigh onto what she realized must be his penis. Her small hand obediently held this huge indecent object until Cyril finished thrusting and collapsed again back into his seat.

Glenda sat absolutely still. The shrunken penis lay on his lap. She looked up at Cyril. Tears were dripping down his face.

'No one,' he said, 'has ever done that for me, Glenda.' He talked in great shuddering gasps. 'No girl has ever let me even kiss her. You don't know how lonely I've been.'

Glenda moved her fingers. 'It's all right, Cyril,' she said. 'It's all right.' She looked about the car for a bit of rag to clean her fingers. 'Really, it's all right.' She saw a red and white duster in the open glove compartment. She pulled it to her.

Cyril stretched himself and zipped up his fly. 'This must be the best day of my life,' he said.

Glenda tried to smile. She hoped very much that she was not going to be sick. The setting sun threw shadows across the grass of the Common. Glenda felt a huge sadness rise in her throat. If that's what sex is like, Glenda knew she could leave it alone. I'll be celibate for the rest of my life, she promised herself as they drove back to the house. Strangely, however, she did not find her feelings for Cyril changed. She still liked him and felt sorry for him, he seemed so trapped in his lonely life. She had Renée and Abe and Chinchilla . . . Who did he have?

Cyril talked quietly. 'When I get to Cambridge,' he said, 'I'll study Oriental philosophy and literature. I want to go to

China. I want to find myself a little Chinese girl who'll love me and take care of me. You know, Glenda, girls like Ruth are a trap for a man. She doesn't love poor old Sammy. She just wants to be married. When he comes home at night after the first few months of marriage she'll be hanging over the stove in her curlers, nagging.' Cyril imitated Ruth's voice. 'For what you want steak? You don't earn enough money to eat steak! You think you're a big man like your father? I cook good kugel, macaroni and cheese! The baby likes macaroni cheese! Eat, eat!'

Glenda found herself laughing. 'You're right, Cyril. That is how she sounds even now. Have you been invited to her engagement party just before Christmas?'

Cyril shook his head. 'She doesn't want to know the likes of me.'

'Then you can take me,' Glenda said firmly, deciding that there would be no more drives to Ealing Common but that she wanted their friendship to continue nonetheless. The car drew up at the house.

Cyril leaned across Glenda and pushed open her door. 'Glenda,' he said softly as she stood on the pavement. 'Thanks. Yeah?'

Glenda nodded. 'Sure thing,' she said, imitating Abe. 'Good night.'

Glenda spent ages in the bathroom washing her hands. She then borrowed her mother's face cream and smothered her hand. That night she dreamed that a sonorous voice from the sky demanded that if her right hand offended her, she must cut it off. She woke up with a start. The moon grinned at her, a cruel slice of pie in a dark world. Never again, she promised herself. Never again.

Chapter 39

Ruth's engagement party was a deeply embarrassing occasion for Glenda. Cyril took the entire evening in his stride. Glenda could see Cyril, his huge head bent over some little fat aunt, his loose lips smiling benignly, and Glenda realized that Cyril would do very well in the Foreign Office, if only he would do something about his dreadful accent. Living with Renée, Glenda automatically learned to remodel her voice. Now she rarely dropped an *h*, except when she forgot herself. She listened to the sound of the grammatical structures that made sentences and phrases fall so easily from Renée's wide mouth. 'English is a beautiful language, Glenda. Don't murder it.' Glenda learned. She wanted to be accepted when she got to Cambridge. If she got to Cambridge.

The small cramped sitting room was full of Ruth's newly found friends. Glenda put her engagement present on the dining table. She had thought long and hard about a present for Ruth but she could not bring herself to buy kitchen equipment or mixing bowls or any other form of the usual nuptial paraphernalia. Standing in a shop in Ealing High Street she had gazed at a long row of bowls and teapots, coffee grinders, glass fruit bowls . . . Behind every object she could see Ruth's fat complacent face. Sell out, Glenda thought. Then she saw a salad bowl. It was big with a beautifully rounded big-bellied belligerence. She lifted the salad bowl. It was made in Sierra Leone, Africa. Whoever carved that bowl did so with such love and creativity. She marvelled at the wood – thick red mahogany. The bowl had a life of its own and even Ruth would not be able to destroy it. She could suburbanize everything in her new house. She could tame her husband, polish her silver into submission, but this African bowl would live malevolently and permanently in exile from the country it loved. Inside the bowl at night, herds of wild animals would roam its plains and bright parrots would fly from palm tree to palm tree. Bougainvillea and hibiscus would blossom. And some time in the deep suburban nights when Ruth was asleep, her head on a fat pillow, her unsatisfied husband beside her, his hand covering his rising and falling erection, dreaming of his frowsy blonde secretary, the salad bowl would let out a strange lingering smell. The stench of the jungle floor, guano mixed with dead leaves.

And now she handed the bowl over to Ruth. Ruth looked doubtfully at Glenda. 'What a surprise!' she said.

Glenda made a face. 'I know it's rather big for just the two of you, but I couldn't resist it.'

Ruth picked up two serving spoons. She gave a little tinkling laugh as she saw the two nude African women carved into the handles. 'Well, we'll have to put these away for the time being, won't we?'

Glenda watched Ruth's fat little back leave the dining room and run down the familiar hall to the kitchen. She walked on impossibly spiky heels. The shoes pitched her body forward. Everywhere there seemed to be hordes of relations. Uncle This and Aunty That, all of them chattering. Mrs Schwartz was sweating with pleasure. Her Ruth was doing right.

Sammy wandered about. 'You look hot, Glenda,' he said. 'Let's go outside for a moment.' They left the sitting room and stood in the pre-Christmas garden. Around them other houses had early Christmas trees winking and blinking. The Schwartzes had no tree. Glenda knew all about the Jewish Chanukah holiday. For years she helped Ruth light her candles for the eight nights and envied her her eight presents. But still she loved her own Christmas celebrations. As they stood in the garden she felt sorry for Sammy Goldstein. He was a good decent boy and he didn't look happy. 'Are you sure this is what you want to do, Sammy?' The question hung coldly on the wintry air.

Samuel looked at Glenda. He had always been fond of her direct, friendly manner. She never giggled or simpered like the other girls. 'Not really,' he began. 'But then my family expects me to marry Ruth. My mother likes her. She'll be a good daughter-in-law, and celebrate our traditions. My parents want grandchildren. Especially my father, so . . .' He made an expressive gesture with his hands.

'But what do *you* want, Sammy? It's your life, your marriage.'

A forbidden thought came to Sammy's mind as he looked at Glenda. He decided he might as well trust Glenda with it. 'I'd like to run away with a big busty blonde with tits like Diana Dors, and just have fun.' Sammy's small frame shook with laughter. Then he sighed. 'But I won't, of course. I'll marry Ruth and sometimes we'll be happy. I'll mow the lawn and go to temple. Ruth will join Hadassah. We'll live and we'll die, always "next year in Jerusalem". Only Ruth would never cope in Israel. She could never live there. Maybe if they get a Marks and Spencer's.' He laughed. 'Come on, Glenda. We'd better get back.'

'Funny people, Jews,' Cyril said as they drove back.

'Funny people, Irish,' Glenda replied. Nothing worse than the English, they both agreed and they laughed.

'Good night, Glenda,' Cyril said as he deposited her upon the pavement. 'Friends?' he said, looking up at her.

'Friends for life,' she said. In a funny way, Glenda thought as she walked up the drive, even if that event on Ealing Common was a horrible memory, she felt closer to Cyril. She saw him at his most vulnerable, without his usual card-sharp brilliance to act as armour. She was glad she still had him as a friend, because after tonight she knew Ruth was part of her past.

Chapter 40

Glenda passed all her A levels and Ruth had her first child. Both events coincided, but Glenda, who had seen Ruth heavily pregnant, decided not to attend the circumcision ceremony.

'Certainly not,' Cyril said, crossing his legs firmly. 'What an 'orrible idea. Savages.' He, too, had passed with distinction.

Glenda realized that they would not be in assembly when their names were read out. She thought of the many years it had taken to get to this point. A piece of paper in her hand to say that she had passed her exams and then the thick envelope full of pieces of paper to tell her that her dream was to come true. She had been accepted at Cambridge to read English Literature. Cyril was also accepted.

Both of them felt dazed and a little punch-drunk. 'Nobody in my family has even been to university,' Cyril said.

'Nor mine, I don't think. I don't know much about my family, except they were all poor.'

'Do you think Renée and Abe would give me a lift when they drive you up to Cambridge?'

'Aren't you taking your car?'

'Alas, poor Ida! No, I've sold the old girl. Most of me fees are on scholarship, and all, but there's still so much to pay for, so many expenses. And anyway parking in Cambridge is a beast, I'm told. So good old Ida was offered up as a sacrifice to the great god of Furthering Meself.'

'I'm sure Renée and Abe would be glad to take you then. Actually, Renée has offered to take us both shopping for clothes next week as a present for us passing the exam. I said yes on your behalf.'

'Jolly good show.' Cyril grinned.

'Oh don't.' Glenda punched him affectionately. 'Come on. Let's go down to the river and get a drink.'

'Promise me one thing,' said Glenda as they settled in the corner seat of the busy pub. 'You won't change, will you? I couldn't bear to think of us becoming like them over there. Those men with no chins and the girls with silk scarves over their hair.'

'Never.'

'Promise?'

And Cyril promised her he would never change.

BOOK TWO

Chapter 41

Abe arranged for Glenda's new bicycle to travel by train to Cambridge. Both Cyril and Glenda were extremely nervous. Cyril arrived at the house in time for breakfast. He had two shabby suitcases. 'Mostly full of books,' he said. He was wearing the new grey wool suit that Renée had bought for him. Glenda chose to wear her pleated black wool skirt and a turtleneck jumper, which Minnie had made a point of paying for herself, out of the money which Phil Clough had left her. Some of the money was also going towards Glenda's fees, though the bulk of them were covered by Renée and Abe.

It was generally agreed that Minnie should save most of Phil's money and let it turn over in the bank until some day it would have grown enough to set Minnie up in an independent life and to help out Glenda in any way necessary. But Minnie took particular pride in matching Renée's offer to buy some clothes for Glenda. 'So you can wear it and remember while you're away,' she had said to Glenda.

Indeed, for her drive to Cambridge, it was the skirt and turtleneck which Glenda chose to put on. These days Glenda also wore black eyeliner and a very pale pink lipstick. For this particular great day she tied her hair back in a pony tail and slipped on a pair of black pointed shoes with a small heel and a plain strap.

She could hear Minnie frying her favourite breakfast. She stood in the bathroom breathing steam onto the small mirror of the medicine cabinet. She traced her initials with her forefinger. From today on I no longer live here, she thought. Next time I'm here, I will be a visitor in my mother's flat.

She turned her head to look at her left profile. Not awful, she decided. She looked at herself full-face. Her chestnut hair was thick and glossy. Her intelligent eyes sparkled with excitement. Looking at the face in the mirror, Glenda could see her own emotions so clearly that she felt sure everyone else would be able to see through her as well. Before her was an eighteen year old girl who, Glenda had to admit, might well be described as pretty. Her skin was clear, her eyes showed thoughtfulness, and her lips quite naturally turned upward in a smile, even when at rest, betraying an instinctively optimistic disposition. But Glenda also saw a girl who had spent the early year or two of her life sleeping in a bottom drawer in a council house in the least attractive part of Hounslow. She saw a girl for whom speaking well was not an inevitable inheritance. She hoped these aspects of her were not as immediately visible as she felt them to be. She also saw a girl – no, a young woman – whose years of work had earned her a place at Cambridge. She knew there would be some girls there, but not many, who had come from similar situations. She hoped she would not look too much out of place.

Part of Glenda was genuinely terrified by the idea of stepping out alone. No Renée to guide her or Abe to advise her or Minnie to fuss over her. In a matter of a few hours, she really would be on her own in a land of strangers.

Of course she already knew what Girton, her chosen college, looked like. Why had she chosen Girton? A chance remark from many years ago. Mrs Turner was describing the differences between the Cambridge colleges to the French teacher at the primary school. 'Girton women are a formidable lot,' Mrs Turner said, smiling. 'I was at Newnham. We were a lot more fun.'

Glenda remembered thinking that the words 'formidable women' sounded excellent.

Today she looked at herself in the mirror again. She didn't look very formidable yet. Actually, she decided, she looked rather small and anxious. She went back to her bedroom for a last check around. Goodbye, window, she thought. Outside were the rotting remains of Lady's cage and a little way away was the small wooden cross under which Lady lay buried. Goodbye, Teddy. She gave the bear a hug. 'You sit there and take care of my room until I get back.'

'Breakfast!' Minnie shouted.

As if on cue, Cyril presented himself at the door. 'Smelled bacon,' he said. Cyril and his two suitcases and several parcels came in like an avalanche. Still, Glenda realized, organizing Cyril into a chair, it'll be easier for mum and for me to have company this morning than to be alone. Glenda knew her mother was suffering. Minnie had spent the night before reminiscing over their lives together. By the time Glenda was ready to go to sleep she could tell her mother dreaded the loneliness. 'It won't be long, mum. Then we'll be back for Christmas. It'll go like a flash, you'll see. I'll phone every Sunday, cheap rate.'

But when Minnie came into Glenda's room to kiss her good night, they clung to each other. 'I *will* be all right, mum,' Glenda said.

'I know you will.' Minnie sat on the edge of the bed. 'Glenda, promise me one thing. You will be sensible about men, won't you?'

'I won't even bother about men. I'm going to Cambridge to study, not to chase men.'

Glenda remembered the conversation as she sat at the breakfast table. I don't want to end up like Mrs Turner. All that brain only to end up marrying the Very Reverend Turner and teaching in a primary school.

Cyril shoved forkloads of food into his mouth. His arms were milling about his head and he was explaining the details of his scholarship to Minnie. 'There's not that many of us on scholarship. At least not from grammar schools. But Trinity is the best, as far as I'm concerned. It has a magnificent library. Books from all over the world.'

173

Minnie smiled at both of them. She had not slept much. During the night she had found herself wondering if she had done the right thing for Glenda. Maybe if she hadn't been too ambitious, Glenda could have married a local boy, and by now Minnie might have been a grandmother pushing her grandchild in a pram up Ealing Broadway like Mrs Schwartz. At about five in the morning, Minnie decided that maybe she would be comforted by a role as a grandmother with Glenda living nearby. But by half-past five, Minnie realistically knew that Glenda had never shown any interest in any of the local boys and still less interest in children. Well, maybe I'll go and visit Chinchilla in the New Year, after Renée has gone and come back from New York . . . Such were the thoughts that had turned themselves in circles in Minnie's brain throughout the night.

Breakfast was over, the teapot drained dry, the side plates full of crumbs. It was time to leave and to get on with the great adventure. The time between yesterday and today seemed fluid to Glenda. Yesterday was the day before any-thing had to happen. Bits of yesterday intruded into today, the day it would *all* happen. Now it was the day. There was no talk of tomorrow. She found herself rushing about checking on yesterday's packing. Invisible threads of memory and affection bound her fingers and her legs to parts of the flat. A last look out of the French windows at the garden mourning its falling leaves, roses with their brown, blown, dead heads nodding a dismal goodbye, a few already hipped and hawed, blushing from the touch of chilled wind from the north. Birds crying in the tree tops. Time to go, time to go, time to go. Yes, Glenda thought. Time to go indeed. You birds go to Africa and I go to Cambridge. Both great adventures.

Minnie stood beside her and mother and daughter gazed into the garden. 'I'll miss you, love,' Minnie said.

'I'll miss you, too.' Glenda put her arm around her mother's waist. They turned and walked together to the door.

Cyril had done an efficient job of loading the car outside.

Abe and Renée were waiting in the car. 'All aboard!' Abe shouted. 'All aboard.' Glenda took a last look at the flat and then she followed her mother into the back of the car.

Glenda had never been away from her mother, except for the odd night she had spent at Ruth's house. Now she sat next to the window with her mother squashed like a teacake between herself and Cyril. On the way back from Cambridge there would be no one in the back of the car, just Minnie. No longer a teacake, but a woman on her own. Glenda tried not to imagine how she would feel when the car pulled away from her college.

It was Saturday and the roads were busy. Glenda concentrated on reading the number plates of cars going by. It was better not to think. Please, God.

Chapter 42

Glenda and Cyril had been to Cambridge before, for their interviews and entrance exams. But the sights of the town and the colleges, still so new to them, struck them again as beautiful and unfamiliar. It was a fairly late, quiet Saturday afternoon when the car arrived in Cambridge. No one said very much on the drive there. Lunch was a hurried pit-stop when they stopped for petrol.

Glenda still marvelled at the flatness of Cambridgeshire. Seen from afar, the town itself reminded her of the fairy castles that rose so majestically out of the American pop-up books. Slowly, as they drove towards the city, she could see spires over which hung a teatime golden haze. Tourists wandered about clutching guide books. To her surprise she saw everyday women and children shopping, pausing to chat. It seemed somehow odd that the streets here would include people who did not go to the university. She had always imagined the streets of Cambridge to be lined exclusively with students wearing gowns and mortarboards. Maybe a proctor or two, with their bulldog attendants, porters in bowler hats. Long-headed dons in steel-rimmed glasses, quoting Greek at each other. But no. It was not like that at all. There were students about the place, but they were not wearing gowns, no proctors or bulldogs. There was a Woolworths and a Co-op, just like Ealing.

Glenda felt rather disappointed. She had hoped to escape Woolworths and British Home Stores and British housewives with their hair in curlers, carrying bulging string bags and messy infants. Still, King's College looked magnificent as they drove past. 'We're here, Cyril.'

Glenda leaned across her mother and prodded Cyril who was snoring loudly.

Cyril woke up on an inward whistle. 'Where?' He opened his eyes.

'At Trinity. Look over there.' Glenda pointed to a great gatehouse.

'Just drop me here,' Cyril said.

'Don't you want us to come in with you?' Renée leaned back over the seat.

'No, if you don't mind.' Cyril blushed.

'Of course not.' Renée smiled gently at him. 'This is your new life and you want to make it for yourself.'

'Something like that.' Cyril got out of the car and collected his suitcases and his parcels. 'Thanks ever so much,' he said, standing on the pavement looking huge and forlorn.

Abe leaned out of the car. 'Here,' he said, handing Cyril some paper money. 'Take yourself out to dinner on us.'

Cyril grinned. 'I'll phone you, Glenda, when I'm set up in the next few days.'

'Do that. Good luck, Cyril.' She watched as he walked purposefully into the gatehouse. Behind him the long green lawn of Trinity lay like an emerald carpet. She leaned back against the car seat and then she put her head on her mother's shoulder. Her heart was beating fast. This really was happening. Cyril had at this moment already begun his life at Cambridge.

Renée was looking at the map. 'Girton is two miles out of the city centre that way,' she pointed.

The car crawled slowly up the crowded streets. Once out of the city they entered a loose sprawl of suburbs. A big turn right and a small gatehouse barred the way to the college. Afraid and nervous, Glenda was immediately comforted by the impressive towering portico. 'So Victorian,' Renée muttered. The stone architecture was warm and the building friendly. Glenda felt a little less nervous. Here there were no tourists. The grounds were beautifully kept. The grass long and soft. Trees let down their overloaded branches and there, sitting reading in the autumn sunlight, was a girl, her back up against a tree, her head nodding as if nearly asleep. Her hair was very blonde and fell over her shoulders.

The girl rose to her feet and approached the car. 'My name is Georgina Lampsetter. I came early, so I've pretty much been assigned to helping people settle in.' She held out her hand to Abe.

Glenda looked at the girl and felt an instant sense of her own inferiority. There was something so cool, so calm, about her person. She reminded Glenda of the Queen. It was as if this girl, who must have been Glenda's own age, was now welcoming them to her own home. Abe took the proffered hand and said, 'Where can I park?'

Georgina looked at Glenda. 'Are you new, too?' Glenda nodded. 'Oh good.' Georgina hoisted herself up on the running board. 'Go back to the road and then you'll see a turning a bit further down. I'll hang on and hope the police don't see us.'

Abe drove carefully. The car found the opening and, once past the end of the building, they stopped in a car park. 'First years are all in rooms on the second floor. I'll take you up. After that we can have a late tea in Old Hall.'

'How do you know all this in one day?' Minnie asked.

'I've visited here many times. My parents used to bring me often.'

'Then you always knew you'd come here?'

'There never was a question, even if I had wanted to make a different choice. The Lampsetter women have been at Girton since it was founded in 1872.'

The room was small, comfortable, and square. It looked out over the pond and the greenhouses. Now Abe, Minnie, and Renée stood about disconsolately. This was not their world. This was a young woman's world. Cars were arriving, disgorging luggage, happy shouting between girls.

Tea was served. Mothers, fathers, aunts, and uncles, walked up and down corridors. Minnie wished it was all over. She felt alien in this world. She tried to smile at the harried waitresses. She poured the tea for everyone and then the time came to say goodbye. Georgina turned away for the moment it took for Glenda to kiss Abe and Renée. When Glenda put her arms around her mother she could feel Minnie shaking with pain. 'Don't, mum,' she said. 'I'll write to you all the time.'

Minnie hugged her. 'No, you won't, love,' she said. 'You won't have the time.'

The car pulled out, its three occupants waving. The last Glenda saw of Minnie was her straight little back sitting erect and alone in the wide back seat. 'Smashing car,' Georgina remarked.

Glenda nodded.

'Don't mope, Glenda.' Georgina took her by the hand. 'Come and meet some people. You'll like them.'

Glenda cleared her throat. This is Cambridge, she thought. And I'm here. Better make the best of it. Part of Glenda, the unseen part, was clinging to the door handle by the passenger seat. 'Don't leave me, mum! Don't leave me!'

'*Noblesse oblige*,' Renée's voice admonished. '*Noblesse oblige.*'

Chapter 43

Glenda very much wished she had brought her teddy bear. Georgina left her alone in her room to unpack. First Glenda gazed out of the window onto the kitchen garden and the fields and trees. She opened the window and leaned out. A smell of late summer evening reached her face. Black loamy soil. Something in the smell of the soil caused Glenda to feel an excitement stirring in her body. Electricity ran up and down her spine. The sweep of the arms of the trees. The rows of corn below her, some already picked and harvested. Ducks in the duck pond. All spoke of fervent activity.

For so long, Glenda had suspended any personal or sexual feelings, and she was aware now, leaning out of the window, that she had perhaps missed out on the mysterious pastime pursued by most people. Ruth had already taken the plunge. Whether Ruth enjoyed sex with her husband or not, she had given birth, that primordial sacrificial rite which seemed to separate the girl-child from the fully fledged woman. Glenda was conscious of the difference between her own inexperience and the experience known to Minnie, Chinchilla and Renée, and especially Ruth.

Ruth, from the first day Glenda had seen her pushing her pram, had a look of superiority in her eyes. Those eyes said, 'I can create a living human being. How can that compare with a few mouldy books? In order for me to work this miracle, I have procured myself the prerequisite, a man, who will love me and take care of me for the rest of my life.'

Glenda sat with her chin cupped in her hand. But now, after all these years of hard work and dedication, Glenda was going to confer upon herself a gift, and that gift was that she would work and play for the three years she was up at Cambridge. She shut out the afternoon smells, the evening call of the birds, and pulled the curtains across the three windows. Kneeling down, she put a match to the gas fire and the white mantles obligingly popped blue and then red. The heat slowly reached out to embrace her. She got up from her knees and sat back on a small Victorian nursing chair. The fireplace had a carved wooden surround. The single bed was covered with a blue and white check counterpane, and by the bed was a night table with a lamp. Under the window she had a small table with three drawers and a spindly chair. There, she thought, I will do my work.

All alone in the room she felt a tinge of melancholy. No more sadness for a habit. If I were back with mum, we would put the kettle on and have another cup of tea. How odd to be in a room in a place that did not include Minnie! The silence from the outside was overwhelming. The walls of the college were thick. She thought, somewhere out there, hundreds of girls were milling about or maybe like her they sat alone in their rooms just dreaming.

She got up and opened her suitcase. She took her brush and her comb and put them on her night table. A small torch and a pile of favourite books, including her King James Bible. I'll try to read it every day, she promised herself. Then she grinned. I'll never read it every day, she thought. But I'll try.

She was hanging up her clothes in the square Edwardian cupboard when Georgina knocked. She saw Georgina standing in the doorway. Behind her she saw another girl. Focused in the mirror of the cupboard, Georgina was smiling. 'This is Molly,' she said. 'She's also new here. You both looked like you could use some company. I thought we might dine together. Glenda from London, meet Molly from . . .'

'From New Jersey,' Molly added.

Glenda turned around. Georgina had changed her clothes and was now wearing a full skirt and a white blouse. Her waist was pinched by a black elastic belt. Around her neck a milky string of seed pearls shone pink against her white skin. Molly, in sharp contrast, wore a plaid skirt, a silky black turtleneck, and brown penny loafers.

Glenda was very aware of her own lack of interest in clothes. She still vividly remembered the jumble sale years. But now, with her mother earning, and Renée and Abe generous to a fault, the relative paucity of her wardrobe reflected only her disinterest. Maybe she would learn. Maybe Georgina would teach her.

'I promised I'd keep an eye out for a student from abroad. We just have to collect Fatima, and then we can go to Hall for dinner,' said Georgina.

Glenda followed Molly and Georgina down what seemed to be endless corridors and flights of stairs. They stopped before not too long to collect Fatima, who was thin and dark-haired. She was not just thin, Glenda frowned, she looked skeletal. Her hair was a dark mass of silk tied up in a chignon, most of it escaping down her back in wisps. Her eyes were slanted, not like Renée's, but more Middle Eastern. But now they were wide. And her mouth was twisting. Glenda realized that Fatima was very afraid. 'Where are you from?' she asked gently.

'From Turaq,' Fatima said. 'But there are troubles at home, so my parents sent me to safety. Now I am here for three years.'

Glenda walked beside Fatima. At least, she thought, there is someone else who feels as out of place as I do.

The Hall filled up. Glenda watched the senior girls and the professors take their seats. It's not all that different to the grammar, she thought. But then she smiled. It was very, very different. Each and every girl had struggled to get here. She looked at all the faces as they sat at table – animated faces. She gazed at the ceiling of the great hall and she felt a strange kind of exaltation. For a moment she hung above her body in a golden bubble. That bubble commuted back into history and connected her with the first much smaller group of determined women who fought their way into Cambridge. Coming back into the present, her bubble stretched out into the future. A great mass of running energy . . . 'Earth to Glenda, earth to Glenda. Come in, Glenda. Glenda!' she heard Molly's nasal twang. 'Wake up and join the real world. You're dreaming.'

Glenda laughed. 'Am I?' she said. For the rest of the meal Glenda pushed her food about her plate.

Fatima ate her food as if she was tasting everything for the first time. When she saw that she was being watched by the other girls, she blushed a little and said, 'This is different from what we eat in Turaq,' she said quietly. 'We have rice and shashlik. But this is good,' she said, evidently making the best of everything. 'Very good.' Fatima was very close to tears.

'You'll get used to it,' Glenda comforted her. Her heart went out to the poor girl.

Molly was explaining her life history to Georgina. 'I've got four brothers, all going to business school, but I wanted to get an English education. Harvard, Yale men . . . yuck. So juvenile.'

Glenda had to laugh. 'I see your interests in Cambridge aren't entirely academic. What brought you here? The education or the men?'

'Both,' Molly said with relish. 'And where better than Cambridge?'

'How about you, Georgina?'

Georgina smiled. 'Oh, I'm engaged to be married.' She held up her left hand. There on her engagement finger the three other girls saw a square-cut baguette diamond.

'Ooh, how beautiful!' Fatima leaned over and took Georgina's hand in her own. 'Who is he?'

'Jonathan,' she said. 'Jonathan Montague. He's in his second year at Harvard Law School. So I decided to go along with family tradition and attend university while I wait.' She shrugged. 'And, as I told you, there really was no choice where to go. Lampsetter women have always been at Girton.'

Glenda sat in her chair and was surprised to find herself

feeling outraged. When she considered the effort it had taken her to get here, she was startled that anyone could speak so casually about attending what Glenda believed to be the finest university in the world. 'Why don't you just get married?' she said rather sharply, feeling that Georgina was occupying a space that another grammar school girl could well have lost.

'Because Ma wants me to get my degree. You know. All this modern stuff about girls being independent. Ma was one of the first. She was an independent feminist before there were feminists. Poor Pa. He doesn't complain, though. He just says "Yes, dear. Anything you say, dear," and locks himself in his study with his *Times* and a bottle of Glenlivet.'

'I have a boyfriend,' Fatima interjected shyly. 'His name is Majid. He runs his family's restaurant in Paris since they had to leave Turaq. I wish I was there now.' Her eyes filled with tears.

Molly grinned. She filled her mouth with chocolate cake. 'Well, that leaves you and me, Glenda. We'll have to go fishing.'

Glenda shook her head. 'Well, good luck to you, but I'm not much of a fisherman. I'm here to work.' She felt very embarrassed. How could she sound so self-righteous? But as she looked around, she imagined all these girls, all attached to boyfriends or fiancés. Only Molly and herself . . . Well, at least she had Cyril. That was small comfort indeed.

As the four girls spent the evening together, an unarticulated awareness grew up between them. Though each had come from a different background, they had nevertheless quickly become friends. Within a few hours, each girl felt she had known the other three for innumerable years. Maybe it was the simple fact that they were all new that drew them together. But no, it must have been something deeper, a natural sympathy of spirits. For the girls were to meet many other newcomers, but these were treated as cordial strangers. Only in each other's company did Glenda, Georgina, Molly, and Fatima feel immediately at home. It would have been hard for any of them to give rational reasons why they should be friends; perhaps friendship between kindred souls needs no rationale.

Chapter 44

Glenda was up early on her first Sunday morning. Bells had been ringing since dawn. Far away she heard the six o'clock Angelus bell pealing out from some Catholic church. Girton College lay quietly, still asleep.

Glenda sat up and looked around. That, she thought, was my first night away from mum. She promised herself that on her next visit home she would definitely collect her teddy bear. After all, Molly seemed to have imported half the contents of a stuffed toy shop. 'Surrogates for sex,' Molly called them. Glenda was shocked. Her teddy bear was a reminder of the days of innocence spent sitting with Minnie beside the little coal fire, watching the flames leap and dance in the back of the grate while Minnie read stories of Pooh and Eeyore and Owl. Teddy bears for Molly, evidently, held a different connotation.

Glenda decided it was no use letting herself hang about only to make herself homesick. I'll go and collect my bike from the train station, she thought. If I get up and leave now, I can catch a bus into Cambridge and then maybe I can have an adventure.

The thought cheered her up. After all, this is what I'm supposed to be doing. Cambridge *is* an adventure.

She transferred her two five pound notes into her handbag. She selected a pair of black slacks, a big comfortable warm jersey, and a dangling pair of black plastic earrings. She smiled at herself in the mirror. This was the same face she had pondered in yesterday's mirror at home; already it looked more independent. I may not have an hourglass figure like Molly, she thought, but at least I'm slim. She tied her long hair up in a pony tail and then, feeling very daring, she took her new black eyeliner and carefully drew two doe-like black lines over her eyelids. She gazed at her face in awe. Her eyes looked enormous. She sucked in her cheeks and made a kissing pout of her lips. Then she laughed. 'How ridiculous!' she said out loud. She grabbed her dark glasses and left the room.

The halls were quiet. A few servants were moving about in the Great Hall. She let herself out of the side door in the magnificent entrance and walked down the path towards the road. The dew lay heavily on the thick green grass. It was not yet cold enough for the dew to be turned to frost, but the smell of winter was just perceptible in the air. Glenda felt as if she were walking to a shivering, trembling future.

She stood by the bus stop, a map of Cambridge in her hands. The railway station was somewhere below Lensfield Road. She saw the outline of Trinity College on the map and wondered how Cyril was getting on. She looked up and saw the bus arriving. Not red and cheerful like a London bus, but green and business-like. Single decker. She swung herself in and sat down behind the bus driver. 'New girl?' He smiled at her over his shoulder and leaned forward to shut the door. Glenda nodded. She liked the gentle sound of his accent. 'Yes, I am,' she said. 'I need to collect my bike from the train station. Is that far away?'

'Other side of Cambridge, but I'll take you there.' The bus driver settled back to listen to the radio. 'I can't get no satisfaction . . .' The complaining voice irritated Glenda. She wanted to sit either in silence or listen to Mozart. Something like that. Something appropriate to the surroundings. She wanted her Cambridge to be the Cambridge that nurtured Byron, who kept a tame bear in his Trinity suite of rooms. She sat on the bus watching the green fields flash by.

Loveliest of trees, the cherry now/ Is hung with bloom along the bough . . .

She recited Housman to herself, trying to create for the day a proper learned atmosphere.

The bus picked its way through the city. Glenda watched avidly as the famous colleges made their appearances — Magdalene, Sidney Sussex, Emmanuel. She ticked off the colleges on her map.

Cambridge was just beginning to swing into Sunday action. Bells rang more loudly, one college calling to another, 'I have more celebrants than you have!' For now the bells were a cacophony. Hopefully, Glenda thought, one day I will be able to know the bells well enough to tell which college they belong to. She imagined Trinity bells, with the college's long and distinguished list of successful graduates, would ring out imperiously, the bells telling everyone that they had sent men all over the world. Trinity men, with their fine educated minds could and would be found in African jungles, in the Sahara sands, quietly translating from Greek or Latin. Never bored and never lonely, a Trinity man had his roots in Cambridge. Wherever he is, he is also always there. Glenda hoped very much that she would feel that strongly about Girton.

An hour into her adventure, she felt the pull, the steady embrace of Cambridge slowly sucking her into a different world, a world that belonged to only the tiny minority who raced and struggled to get to a place called Cambridge. Glenda hugged herself, content with the knowledge that she had run that race and here she was.

At the train station, her bicycle leaned like a friend in the storage room on the platform. Another train to London choo-chooed its way back, but Glenda was not sorry to see it go. She pushed the bike out through the station and nodded to the station master. He smiled back. They get younger and younger, he thought as he punched her platform ticket. 'You ride carefully,' the old man said.

'Thanks.'

'Maniacs on the roads these days. Not like when I was a

lad. It was all horses, you know. Mind you, my first job was shovelling manure. Don't 'ave to do that nowadays. But then, the manure was good for the roses . . .' The quivery gentle voice disappeared as Glenda swung her leg over the bike and took off out of the station.

She headed towards the middle of town. This morning she was just going to roam about. Here she was, one little red corpuscle in a huge body called Cambridge. Excitement surged through her veins. Adrenaline caused her legs to fly and the bike to go faster and faster until, after half an hour of pedalling, she slowed down. She passed Trinity College. There was no point in looking for Cyril. Besides, this was her day alone. She pedalled on until she reached the gatehouse of St John's College. Intrigued by its great beauty, she left her bicycle outside and walked through the first court and then through the plummy red, second courtyard. She wanted to find the chapel and see King Henry VIII's head in the outer arch of the main door.

As she approached the chapel she heard loud organ music pouring from the building. The music was baleful, the notes piled one on top of the other, higher and higher, fuller and fuller.

From afar Glenda imagined she could hear her own footsteps approaching the chapel. *Chicaboom, chicarack, chicaboom, chicarack, chicaboom, chickarack, she's singing.* The song from her childhood played in her head in rhythmic counterpoint to the music that grew from the stones of the chapel.

She did not want to get devoured by the organ music. The last time she heard loud organ music was when she stood by Police Constable McCluskie's coffin in the church. Then the organ music was soothing, offering hope for eternal salvation, even for him. Now the music was threatening. It was strange music. The notes were not discordant, neither were they in harmony. Instead, they were simply not at peace with each other. The notes sang out at once, like dissimilar elements, and refused to mix. The sounds invaded Glenda's head. *Her shoes paddiwack at the front and the back*. Even Glenda's song no longer sounded innocent and cheerful. The notes were glacial and jagged. *And her yellow hair was swinging*. Glenda was swept by the music into the building. Before her rose up the stern splendour of a Victorian Gothic chapel. But what stunned her was the sight of a small thin figure labouring over an organ keyboard. The figure writhed, the head rolling as if in pain.

Glenda, as if against her will, walked down the aisle towards the only other human being in the chapel, the organist himself.

Now her song was absorbed by the music. It was almost as if the man in front of her could read her mind. She stood transfixed staring at the thin stalk of a neck and the ash-blonde hair. In the middle of a wretched chord the head turned and two large, desperate, blue sky-washed eyes glared at her. 'Do you know what this is?' His voice was high and cracked. Glenda shook her head. He stopped playing the piece, and held down two notes of the queerest interval, the interval on which the piece was built.

He stared at Glenda while two fingers held the notes. He held on to them while they blared like antiphonal trumpets, echoing harshly off the walls. He held the notes and fixed his eyes on Glenda until the sharp, cutting sound forced its way through Glenda's ears and into her skull, making her head vibrate with the noise. His eyes, too, pierced her entirely. Suddenly he released the notes.

'*Diabolus in musica!*' he said to her with a weird smile when the reverberated after-sounds had quietened. 'The devil in music.' And he laughed. 'Quite something. Don't you think?'

'I beg your pardon,' Glenda said, feeling suddenly denuded. 'I didn't mean to interrupt your practice. I'll go.' She turned and started walking away.

'You don't have to go,' he said.

Glenda looked back over her shoulder and saw in his eyes a look of utter need. She paused, said, 'I'm sorry,' and left.

Outside the building, Glenda found herself running. The music started up again and chased her across the courts of St John's College.

Outside the college she climbed on her bike. Puffing, she paused for breath. I'll go home, she promised herself. As she rode back up the road, she realized that there was no home to go to – only a room in a college called Girton. But for now it meant safety. As she pedalled, her heart went back to normal. The fear receded and she wondered why the music had affected her so much. Was it the man who seemed in torment, or was it the music of the devil? Or maybe it was the shock, the shock of seeing what she had only dreamed about. Why did the man look so like the Joker – the man in the pack of playing cards? She saw Abe's face as she pedalled back to the college. Don't worry, she reassured him. If that's the Joker, he's too wild for me.

Later that night, her second night at Cambridge, she sat in Molly's room nursing a cup of coffee. 'And,' she said, talking to a rapt audience consisting of Molly, Georgina, and Fatima, 'he was playing the strangest music. Then he turned to me and said the music had something to do with the devil. It certainly sounded like it did.' She was silent for a moment. 'But it was the look on his face I can't forget.'

'I'm impressed,' said Molly. 'You've found a man already, and I wasted a whole day unpacking.'

Georgina said, *Diabolus in musica.*

'Yes, that's it. That's what he called it.'

'An interval of two notes, forbidden to be played in the Middle Ages,' Georgina explained. 'An augmented fourth.'

Georgina would know, Glenda thought. Georgina sat on a cushion on the floor. Her hair hung in silken skeins down to her shoulders. Her blue eyes gazed benignly at the world in general, her long slim legs drawn up under her. She wore a peasant wool skirt that reached her ankles and a long tie-dyed shirt. At her throat was a small, elegant gold cross. Georgina laughed. 'You wanted adventure and you got one. Not bad for your first day.' Georgina's engagement ring flashed in the fading light from the window.

Molly sighed. 'I'm beginning to think I consigned myself to the boondocks. You know, I did think about going to the London School of Economics instead. At least I'd have been in the middle of London. Get a piece of the action.' Molly wore a pair of skin-tight Levis and an even tighter red sweater. Glenda wondered how Molly managed to sit down without splitting herself in half, the jeans were so tight. Her dark hair cascaded in curls down her shoulders and her big bright eyes sparkled. 'Tomorrow,' she said firmly, 'I'm going down to troll Cambridge.'

Georgina said, 'But we all have appointments all day.'

'Not this girl,' Molly grinned. 'Anyway, I have to go buy a car.'

The room was silent. 'A car?' Fatima spoke up from a corner of the room. She had been sitting quietly, wrapped in a filmy gossamer sari. The gold-embroidered material lent a fragile air to her delicate face.

Molly got up and walked over to her window. 'Yeah,' she said. 'I plan to get myself the perfect JAP-mobile. Besides, we can't bring men up here, can we?'

'No,' Georgina agreed. 'We can't.'

'Well then. Makes sense.'

Molly's room, Glenda decided, seemed to be in a general state of rebellion against everything. On the walls were posters of Mao, Che Guevara, and Fidel Castro. There was also a poster that declared, 'A Woman Without a Man is Like a Fish Without a Bicycle.' Even more confusing were posters demanding liberation from men and other posters showing fierce women brandishing guns. Buttons for peace. Glenda felt as if the room was in a turbulent maelstrom of undecided war. On Molly's night table sat a big silver-banded photograph of what she assumed must be Molly's mother and father beaming contentedly. They held hands, sitting on a multi-coloured sofa. A warm rug hung over Molly's mother's knees. Her father, small and squat and balding, held a photograph of a much younger Molly with braces on her teeth. 'Shot of brandy, anyone?' Molly asked.

'Sure thing,' Glenda said, in her best American à la Abe voice.

'Wanna come and buy a car tomorrow? Come on, Glenda. I could use the company. And those two are already bartered brides. Let's leave them in their misery. I've got Scraggs – can she really be called Scraggs? I guess so, you English with your quaint little names – at twelve noon. I'll do that and then we can quit after lunch.'

'Okay,' Glenda said, sipping the brandy-laced coffee. 'I'm seeing her just before you.'

'Have you heard from Majid?' Georgina asked Fatima.

'Not yet. But I'm sure he'll write to me soon. I've promised to write to him every day.'

'Every day?' Molly was amazed. 'You write to him every day?'

'Why not?' said Fatima.

'What, are you scared some other woman might Shanghai him?'

Fatima laughed. 'No. That is not possible. In our country we still arrange marriages, and ours has been arranged. It will take place.'

Molly was interested. She squatted down by Fatima's pillow. 'You mean you *have* to marry the guy?'

'Of course,' Fatima said simply. 'Our families are close. We have known each other since childhood. Majid will make a good husband for me.'

'And can you, you know . . .'

Fatima frowned. 'Can I what?'

'Oh, you know what I'm talking about. Have sex?'

191

'Molly!' Georgina protested. 'Really, it's none of our business.'

'Lighten up, Georgina. You're telling me you're not the least bit curious?' said Molly.

Fatima shook her head. 'I was raised a Muslim, and women are expected to be virgins when they marry.'

'How about men?'

'Men . . . It's different for them. It's not so important. Men don't have children.'

Molly rolled her eyes. 'I see you have a long way to go, Fatima.'

Glenda was surprised to see a hint of cool steel in Fatima's smile. 'Perhaps,' she said kindly, 'you are the one who has far to go, Molly.'

Molly for a moment looked nonplussed. Fatima held her gaze. Molly nodded her head and said, 'Far out.'

The shadow from the table lamp fell on Fatima's graceful body and on her beautiful, long tapered hands. To Glenda, Fatima looked as if she had been carved out of alabaster years ago. Glenda looked at Georgina. She sat back on the cushion on the floor. Molly and I are newcomers in all this, Glenda thought. Fatima and Georgina have families stretching behind them for centuries. They have certainties. I have no certainty, only myself. Georgina will marry Jonathan Montague. She will live in a big house with blonde-haired, blue-eyed children. She will have horses. I will either make my way to a fortune or end up like my mother, and she knew that there was no way she was going to end up like her mother.

'Okay, Molly. I'll go with you tomorrow. Good night, everybody,' she said, getting to her feet. 'I'm tired.'

Molly gave Glenda a quick unexpected hug. 'Sleep well,' she said, and Glenda felt her eyes fill with tears. Molly looked up at her. 'We'll hang in there together,' she said.

Glenda smiled. She waved her hand at the other two and went back to her room. 'One is one and all alone,' she thought as she got ready for bed. 'And evermore shall be so,' an owl hooted mournfully back. As she pulled the curtains shut, she saw the wind lift the huge branch of the tree outside the windows and she remembered the man's hands crashing down on the keyboard. *'Diabolus in musica,'* she said out loud, trying the sounds of the words in her mouth. She strained her ears to listen to see if she could catch the last remaining notes of the organ. Vaguely she imagined the music stalking over the vast, black, wintry fens. How many drowned faces, ears blocked by the mud of the fens, heard that demented music and rose from their damp funereal beds to dance in the dead of night, watched only by the moon? That full, green-tinged, monstrous moon ushered in by the owls, devisers of the haunted night . . .

I must stop now, Glenda told herself seriously. Or I'll never go to sleep. I've got to face Miss Crompton in the morning. I wonder why she's called Scraggs.

Chapter 45

Glenda soon found out why Miss Ivy Crompton was nick-named Scraggs: she *looked* just like a Scraggs. She was tall and very thin. The bones of her ankles and her wrists stood out. Glenda, her back to the door of Miss Crompton's study, wished she had at least rehearsed a few pleasant sentences. The silence tumbled around Glenda's ears. Miss Crompton sat down after an eternity and turned her attention to a folder on her desk. 'Come here, Miss . . . ,' she said finally. 'Miss . . .' She pointed to a chair.

'Stanhope. Glenda Stanhope.'

'Miss Stanhope. Grammar school gel, are you?'

Glenda blushed and wriggled. What a curse blushing is, she thought. 'Yes, Miss Crompton.' There was another silence.

'Hm. Rare species round here, y'know.' She turned her eyes fully to Glenda. 'But it speaks well of you. Shows you've worked even harder than most to get here.' She had quite a nice smile, actually, Glenda noticed. 'I know you'll work hard. That's important, Glenda.' Her face turned severe. 'I'm not here to waste my time on young women who want to chase the boys. Girton was built for exceptional women to achieve their ambitions. Women who want to be leaders in their fields.'

'The first time I ever heard of Cambridge was years ago. Mrs Turner at my primary school once said that Girton produced formidable women, Miss Crompton. When I heard her say that, I decided that formidable had a special sound to it.'

Miss Crompton's face softened. She leaned back in her chair. Under the shy exterior of the young woman before her, Miss Crompton could see a very determined will. 'You live with your mother in Renée Blanchard's house?'

'My mother,' Glenda said, aware that her voice was defensive, 'is Renée's housekeeper.'

'What a wonderful actress she is, your Renée Blanchard,' Miss Crompton smiled again. 'I saw her first in Ibsen's *A Doll's House*. She was very young then. And after that she played Hedvig in *The Wild Duck*.'

Glenda clasped her hands. 'Oh, I love *The Wild Duck*. I suppose I was particularly caught by the awful image of Hedvig's duck in the attic. They believed that the wild duck had forgotten the sky and the water and the reeds because it had been so long in the attic. They all imagined that the duck locked away in the attic with a bath full of water would forget.' Glenda twisted her hands. 'People or ducks who are trapped never forget. If they are living in attics or are trapped by poverty, you still don't forget. Especially if you've seen the possibility of a life outside that trap. The duck knew the moonlight and the stars and the bottom of the muddy river with the reeds.' Glenda knew she was talking too much, but she couldn't help herself. 'I always felt when I read *The Wild Duck* that I understood the duck best of all.'

Miss Crompton chuckled softly. 'I think we'll get on

together very well indeed. I'm teaching a course on women in early nineteenth century England. I'm looking at women who not only wrote books or were part of a literary or political circle, but also women in various fields who made positive contributions to the positions that we now take for granted in our society. Would you be interested? It's a once a week lecture in the evening.'

Glenda realized she was being dismissed. 'I'd love that,' she said.

'Fine then.' Miss Crompton returned to her work.

'Wow!' Molly shot into Glenda's room and threw herself on her bed. 'What a tartar! No wonder she's called Scraggs. Her neck looks like the bleached end of an old chicken bone. Boy, did she give me a hard time. She doesn't like Americans, and she's probably anti-Semitic.'

'Maybe,' Glenda observed as Molly rolled over and fished out a cigarette from her back jeans pocket, 'maybe Miss Crompton just doesn't expect students attending their first tutorial to turn up dressed in jeans covered in anti-war buttons.'

'Could be,' Molly replied, her eyes half-closed against a plume of smoke. She was lying sprawled on the bed. 'You Brits can be really uptight.' She inhaled a deep drag. 'But I'm an American and I have my constitutional rights to dress as I please.'

Glenda let out a little laugh and Molly laughed, too.

'Hey, listen, Glenda. You got any aspirin?'

Glenda shook her head.

'My period approaches, thank goodness. And if I don't get a couple of aspirin, I think my head will pop.' Molly took another deep breath of her cigarette. 'Tell you what, I'll track down the aspirin in my room, and then we'll head into town. We're off to see a man about a car. Sound like fun?' She waved a hand and departed.

Glenda did not have time to answer. If she had had to

answer, she would have said yes, it did sound like fun. Somehow, though Glenda could not explain why, Molly made everything sound like fun. For all that Molly appeared slightly abrasive, she had enormous energy that made Glenda smile. Glenda smiled now, thinking that she was indeed looking forward to walking around the town with Molly.

Glenda opened her window. Minnie smoked but not like Molly, who seemed intent on inhaling as much smoke as her lungs would hold and then shooting out grey jets through both her nostrils.

Finally Molly decided on a smart little red MG. Two in the front, and luggage space in the back, or a crumpled human. Glenda was impressed by the obsequious bank manager. Molly coolly wrote out a cheque. The bank manager spoke into the telephone to find out whether or not the cheque would clear. When he received his reply he seemed suddenly to genuflect to Molly.

During her interview with the bank manager in his inner sanctum, Molly sat in front of him, her short be-jeaned legs swinging above the floor, the imperious toes of her pointed high-heeled boots occasionally kicking his desk. 'It appears your father deposited a large sum,' the manager began, eyeing Glenda, she felt, with disfavour. Glenda knew her presence as the poor relation was going to ensure that no amounts could be mentioned. The bank manager leaned over and scribbled some figures on a bank complimentary slip.

'Twenty thousand?' Molly said, her voice dripping with satisfaction. 'Is that dollars or pounds?'

'Pounds,' said the bank manager.

'Thank you, Daddy.' Molly stood up. Glenda followed her out of the bank.

Twenty thousand pounds, Glenda thought, as Molly flagged down yet another taxi. The ride from the college had cost an arm and a leg. Glenda thought of the remainder of Phil Clough's hard earned five thousand lying in the bank struggling to produce interest for Minnie. Life had obviously been different for Molly.

Now she sat beside Molly in the red car while Molly zoomed and squeaked around corners. 'I've got to check in on Cyril,' Glenda screamed against the wind. 'He's at Trinity.'

'Okay,' Molly shouted. 'We'll stop at the next pub I see and ask for directions.'

Chapter 46

Glenda was exhausted. For Molly, driving on the English side of the road was a trial. When pedestrians pointed at her and shouted probably well-meaning advice, Molly, in a fair panic, instructed them to fuck themselves. She wrenched the car around, causing the tyres to squeal. Glenda decided that she would make sure that she learned to drive, even if it meant that Molly would have to teach her.

Finally they manoeuvred their way to Trinity College and parked. Up the road at St John's lay Glenda's adventure of yesterday. She shivered as she remembered the music and the saddened face. Fortunately Cyril was a face from her past and a well-remembered one.

Both girls walked through the main gates into the courtyard. For a moment Glenda felt lost. Trinity seemed impossibly inhuman. She stood on the path looking across the bright green grass. Even Molly was quiet for a moment, letting out only a whispered, 'Wow.'

In forty-eight hours Glenda had absorbed some of the older history of Cambridge. Girton spoke of only a hundred years, but Trinity existed for some four hundred. Now all those years appeared to drain Glenda of speech or movement. She stood breathing in. All she seemed to have done since she arrived at Cambridge was to breathe in history and breathe out wonderment. How could she really be here? Not just to walk around the city like the tourists, but because she really belonged here. For the next three years, and hopefully forever, Glenda Stanhope was part of this piece of history called Cambridge.

The college stood around her, its darkened doors full of mystery and its turrets and windows blinking in the sun. Molly struck a match and threw the spent match on the ground. 'Molly!' Glenda felt a surge of fury.

'Litterbug, huh?'

'No, not even that. Can't you see how perfect the lawn is? Look at it, and then look at your match.'

Molly bent down and picked up the match. 'Peasant little me. Come on, let's find your friend.' Molly set off at a lively walk, her rounded buttocks warring with her tight jeans. Glenda envied her curly hair which swung over her shoulders.

Eventually they found Cyril's set of rooms. Banging on the thick oak door, Glenda heard a foot-shuffling and a nose-trumpeting that could only mean the appearance of Cyril. His head stuck out of the door and his eyes peered around him suspiciously. 'It's me, Cyril. Glenda.'

A wide smile stretched across Cyril's face. 'I was thinking of ringing you,' he said. 'Come in.'

Glenda led Molly into a small, square sitting room. Cyril stood with his head slightly bent. 'What on earth have you done to your forehead, Cyril?'

He blushed. 'I keep hitting my head on all these damned low door frames. The place was built for midgets,' he grumbled. ''Enry!' he shouted suddenly. 'Come and meet the girls.'

Molly looked across the room expectantly. Her eyes lit up and she brushed her lips with her tongue. Until Henry came into the room. Henry was short and plump. His black hair curled around his tonsured head and his wire spectacles gleamed. 'Ah!' he said. 'Friends of Cyril's. From the great metropolis, I suspect?'

Glenda giggled, Henry looked so much like the Rabbit in

Alice in Wonderland. All he needed was a watch and a few whiskers. 'I'm Glenda Stanhope. Cyril and I grew up together. And this is Molly Rosenthal. She's from New Jersey.'

'Ah. New Jersey.'

'Oh, you know New Jersey, do you?' Molly said hopefully.

'Well, never been there, but know of it anyway,' Henry replied. 'Across the river from New York, isn't that right? Poor unfortunates reside there for lack of any other welfare housing.'

'Ha!' Molly burst. Glenda tried not to laugh. Cyril, fussing about in his own rooms, made the offer of tea.

'I've joined the Labour Party,' Cyril told Glenda. ''Enry and I agree about politics. Will you be joining?'

Glenda shook her head. 'I don't know anything about politics, Cyril, and I haven't even found my way round my college yet. We seem to have miles and miles of corridors. The only time I've been into Cambridge was yesterday to pick up my bike and then I pedalled up this way looking for you until I reached St John's and then I heard this strange music. You won't believe this, Cyril, but there was the strangest young man playing in the chapel. It's really quite spooked me.'

'Maybe it was a ghost,' Cyril suggested. 'All these places have ghosts.'

Glenda laughed. 'You know you could be right. I never thought of that. Girton has a ghost. Georgina was telling me. The ghost of a young girl who died before she finished her exams. I must say I don't blame her. Cyril,' Glenda handed her nearly empty cup of tea to him, 'are you pleased you're here? I mean, do you think it was worth all the work and all the effort?'

Cyril smiled. His huge lips elasticated around his mouth, and his bad teeth, that spoke of years of neglect and decay, gave his face a derelict appearance. He raised a protective wish in Glenda to hold him in her arms and to tell him that his teeth were not his fault, nor were the crumbs of chocolate Digestive biscuits that ran down the front of his old jersey.

She always did feel protective of Cyril. A brief memory of Ealing Common flashed through her mind, making her feel even more sorry for Cyril in his awkwardness. 'I think it was worth every bone in my body,' Cyril said. 'I mind the stupid arses who snigger at me because I don't talk like they do, and I come from a grammar, not a public school, but then I've as much right to be here as they do. And in the end they'll see. I'll top the lot of them.'

Henry put down his teacup. 'He will, you know, he will. Our Cyril is ferocious when it comes to knowledge.'

Glenda looked again at Henry. There was a twinkle in his eye, a twinkle hinting that he took the world with a very large grain of salt, if not black pepper. He had a small black toothbrush moustache that hovered over his little red lips. His chin was round and pricked with black hair shafts. The type of man who must shave twice a day. A nice man, Glenda decided, a kind man. The sort of man, she realized with a start, that she ought to like very much. Henry raised an eyebrow. 'A penny for them, Glenda,' he said.

'We must be getting back,' Glenda replied, blushing. Drat the man, she thought. He can read my mind.

'When do we get invited to tea?' Cyril asked.

'Soon,' said Glenda.

Outside, the girls climbed into the car, after Cyril and Henry had elaborately admired the vehicle. They drove off and Molly demanded, 'You're not seriously going to ask those two to tea, are you? We won't have a reputation left to lose.'

'Of course I will,' Glenda said, holding onto her side of the car. 'Left, Molly, left, and stay on the left hand side of the road, or there won't be any Cambridge, let alone tea parties. Look, Cyril's my best friend. And Henry looks all right.'

Molly put her foot on the accelerator. 'Then you really

are in love with the grotesques. Ever read any Sherwood Anderson?'

'Who's he?' Glenda yelled over the wind.

'Who *was* he. Was, you idiot,' Molly shouted back. 'A writer. He got ripped off by Ernest Hemingway. Anyway you should read him. Writes all about grotesques. Should be right up your street.'

'I'll give him a try,' Glenda promised. 'If we get back to college alive.'

Chapter 47

The days and weeks flew by. Soon Glenda felt completely at home. It was almost as if she had been born at Girton. The four girls spent most of their free time together. Molly became her best friend, but it was Georgina who taught her the many things she did not know. Playing tennis with Georgina, she realized that she would never look at home on the court. Even if Georgina carefully showed her ways of holding the racquet, she would always feel a bit of an orphan.

Georgina and Fatima both walked like princesses. But then Glenda recognized they had never known anything other than a richness and a fullness of life that had only recently been given to Glenda. As she watched both the girls bend over their books, she was grateful to Minnie for the early years when she had tried very hard to read to Glenda, reading not just any old books, but the classics of literature. Even if middle class manners and customs were occasionally elusive for Glenda, her literary background was not bereft.

When she did have time Glenda bicycled into Cambridge to spend some hours with Cyril and Henry. Henry was a grocer's son, so she felt a kinship with him as a fellow outsider. So intelligent was he that he had been able to pass all his examinations with ease.

Cyril, having joined the local Labour Party, gave Glenda

splendid socialist lectures. These lectures rather irritated her and she reminded him that she wanted all the things that life could give her for herself. 'I don't mind if other people share what I have, but I do want to live in a nice house with a big front door dripping in brass. And I'm quite happy for someone else to do the cleaning. No, Cyril, I'm not a socialist.'

'Surely,' Cyril said in disbelief, 'surely you must have *some* political leanings, some outrage at injustice, some . . .'

'If anything, I'm probably a rampant capitalist, so there. And when I have my own house you can visit and sit in the kitchen and eat a morsel of sour socialist bread.'

Cyril grinned. 'Oh no I won't. I shall be outside on your front lawn stubbing out my fags and holding a placard saying *Down with Capitalism.*' Glenda was not impressed.

'Don't mind him,' Henry stepped in. 'He's just found socialism like a new religion. He'll calm down.'

Glenda grew impatient. 'You don't know Cyril like I do,' she said. 'He's like a dog with a bone.'

Cyril stood still for a moment. Then, without warning, he stuck his hand deep into his trouser pocket, pulled out a fistful of something, shoved it into his mouth, and walked out of the room, his face a curious colour of red and his cheeks puffed and lumpy. 'What on earth are you doing?' Glenda asked.

The noises that Cyril made over his shoulder were indecipherable.

'Learning to speak through a mouth full of pebbles,' Henry translated the grunts for Glenda. 'He read all about Winston Churchill doing the same thing so that he could become a great orator. And now Cyril stands on the banks of the Cam bellowing at the swans with stones in his mouth.'

'Good Lord,' Glenda said faintly. 'Don't tell anyone we know him, will you?'

Henry walked Glenda out of the college. 'Cyril's had a very hard time,' he remarked.

'So have we all,' Glenda replied.

Henry inclined his sleek head. 'You watch, Cyril will make something of himself.'

Glenda looked at Henry. 'And you?'

'I'll go into Parliament. There are other ways of making a country more equal. A little less histrionic than Cyril's way perhaps, but over time more lasting.' Henry smiled. 'Look, Glenda, let me take you out for dinner one night and I'll tell you all about my plans for the future. You are one girl who doesn't seem to think that the whole purpose for being here is to catch a man and get married.'

Glenda laughed, embarrassed for a moment. 'Of course, Henry. I'd love to.'

She imagined Molly's face when she told her that she had a date with Henry. Still, she thought, Henry is a nice man and good fun, even if he is not exactly my big moment. And who knows? I might see that man at the organ again. Then she very carefully stepped on the thought. No, she reminded herself, not the Joker. Henry was kind and safe and he had a future . . . That was precisely the problem: she did not find Henry exciting. Try Russian roulette, she nagged herself as she struggled with her bicycle up the hill.

Leaving her bike outside, she walked into Girton College and she heard the sounds of feet trampling into Hall for dinner. I must find Molly, she thought, and then she too ran.

Chapter 48

Fatima felt alone and very isolated. She had based her ideas of life at Cambridge on the books she read during her teens. Sitting under the mulberry trees in her mother's garden, Fatima had imagined young English girls of her age running around the tennis courts at Girton wearing rather long vague lawn and lace trimmed dresses. She knew that English girls, like girls of her own class and race, now shopped in the very latest Paris boutiques. Indeed she had a wardrobe full of clothes from Paris and from Rome, but she still wore the purdah veil when at home in Turaq, as did all the women in her family. She preferred it that way. She had not attended school like her brother Ali, but stayed in the women's compound under her mother's eagle eye with her other three sisters. She had been educated by the governesses and tutors imported from England, which was why her English, though slightly accented, was impeccable.

At home she did not mind purdah. Her family was very large and the women lived together in the compound with four houses, one for each wife. Fatima's mother was wife number one, so Fatima and her sisters and brother were the number one children. By the time she left for Girton, she had eighteen brothers and sisters in the other houses, and about twenty uncles and aunts. When the women walked outside the compound, they wore the veil.

Fatima enjoyed the anonymity of the veil on the streets. Men were not able to ogle her lustfully as they did the more modern women. Once back inside the compound she could throw off the veil and relax with her family, sitting about on the big puffy cushions, eating from little trays of jam, and sipping tea through lumps of sugar.

Only Fat Aunt was a modern woman in Fatima's family and she brought disgrace to them all. Fatima believed Fat Aunt became a modern woman because she knew no one would marry her. To be fat in Turaq was not shame, but Fat Aunt was both fat and hairy. She sang about the compound like a restless bird and she was always chattering about the men she picked up in the bazaars. She had no shame.

Fatima's marriage had been arranged when she was four, so she had always known that she would be safely married to Majid. She sometimes saw him at big events and then she would hide her eager eyes under her veil. Fortunately he was rich and handsome with a kind face. When, later in his life, Majid's political activities became conspicuous and potentially dangerous, he and his family moved to Paris, though they had to leave behind them their wealth. They opened a restaurant, still a meeting place for like-minded political thinkers. The situation in Turaq was becoming more uncertain with every passing month, as rival factions struggled for leadership. Indeed, now it appeared doubtful that Fatima's family would be able to stay much longer. Fatima was safe from any peril at Cambridge – much of the reason her parents had sent her so gladly, even if it was unusual in the Nicnojad family for a woman to get a degree, never mind to live abroad on her own.

Very early on Fatima had made it known that she wanted to go to Cambridge and get a degree. In the long drowsy after-lunch hour, when the head felt like a thick wooden spoon leaning on the baking walls of the compound and all the other women slept under their white mosquito nets, Fatima lay on her bed buried in her books. She read Willa Cather and longed for the American West. Then she read Walt Whitman and longed for the American Eastern seaboard. What must New England look like, with its cool blue days and its sea curling and swirling so blue and so cold? Her sea was far away, and when you got there it was as hot as the sun that beat down upon it. Mud sludge and faces slid by. The stink filled her nostrils as she remembered the sea. Long slivered boats rotting, sails patched brown and red before the sun set. The call of the *muezzin* for prayer, the minarets tall before the setting sun. The men all around her pulling out their prayer mats. The women running for their houses or to the compound, in her case, to get together behind their doors to say their prayers. Men and women did not pray together because women, being lustful objects, distracted men from higher contemplation.

All this Fatima missed as she sat in her small square room in Cambridge so far away from her loving mother, so far away from home. The only palpable remnants of her country were a box of Turkish delight to set her teeth on edge and a small homesick pot of Turkish coffee.

Fatima raised the tiny coffee cup to her mouth and sat quietly, feeling the heaviness of homesickness and the acute pain of missing the hibiscus and the bougainvillea. England was flat and dull compared to the great mountains and the wild foliage of Turaq. True, the historic buildings of Cambridge filled her with delight, but many of the women gathered at Girton filled her with horror. They seemed crude and immodest. Some of them walked around in trousers like men. Some wore no underwear and their great breasts swung as they walked, like a camel's.

Understanding Molly was a particular challenge to Fatima. Glenda she thought she liked. Glenda was quite and modest. And Georgina was her friend. But Molly surprised her with her frank talk and her sexual references.

Yesterday Molly had explained to Glenda and to Fatima that the women's movement meant that women in the future would be able to have cheque book sex, just as men do. 'Cheque book sex?' Glenda asked.

'It's like if you're attracted to a guy, you go up to him, and if he sees that you want him, he says, ''Make me an offer to get my attention.'' So you write out a cheque for a hundred dollars and he's yours for the night, or however long you want to screw him. Personally I prefer to fuck them and then ask them to leave. I mean who wants a naked, hairy guy wandering around in the morning?'

Georgina was smiling. 'Really, Molly,' she said, 'you're just making this up.'

'Nope,' Molly replied. 'It's just that, being English, you're a natural prude. We Americans have been swinging our way through the Sixties while you've been hiding your refined selves in convents.'

Georgina was undaunted. 'You're not implying that there's harm in being a virgin when you get married, are you?'

Glenda backed her up. 'Yeah, what's wrong with that?'

Fatima joined in at this point, feeling intensely irritated.

'If women don't respect themselves, what makes you think men will respect them?'

'Oy vey!' Molly ran her hands through her long wild hair. 'I'm surrounded by a bunch of virgins. Just my luck!'

'But don't you worry,' Glenda laughed. 'We'll civilize you yet. And,' Glenda added, looking at the table beside Molly's bed, 'you can start by losing the habit of putting out your cigarette in your cold cream jar. Molly, you really live like a pig.'

'Glenda!' Georgina said, with mock sharpness. 'That's unkind. To pigs, I mean. We keep pigs at home, and their domestic habits are far cleaner than Molly's.'

Molly grinned. 'Mock on, my virginal sisters, mock on. I'm above your barbs. Experience has a way of elevating a person, you know. Though you probably wouldn't know. Besides, I was raised to live like a well-kept piggy. I'm used to maids picking up after me. And Dad has an English butler who says things like "Quite right, sir." "Are you leaving the house, Miss Molly?" Very Bertie Wooster. I thought England would be very Bertie Woosterish, but it's not.'

'No, it's not at all,' said Fatima with feeling. 'It's all a bit grey and sad.'

'Grey and sad? Not all of it, I promise you.' Georgina smiled at Fatima. 'I asked my mother if I could take you home for the Christmas hols. You'll love the grounds and all the animals. Should be some good hunt balls. We can go hunting, if you like. Do you ride?'

Fatima smiled back. A little knot in her stomach untied. She liked Georgina. She liked her room and her silver-backed hairbrushes. Georgina spoke of good manners and comfortable furniture. 'I do ride,' Fatima said, remembering the exhilarating gallops with her brother along the ridges of the mountains and the smell of her little Arabian in her nostrils . . . But Christmas with Georgina would be good. She might even be less homesick.

Today she sat with the coffee hot in her mouth and her

heart full of pain and longing. Days like yesterday in Molly's dirty room made her long for her own *budgi* who took care of her from the day she was born. Were all American women untidy? She thought not, but Molly was funny at times. Her ruthless energy and her good humour made Fatima laugh, in spite of herself.

Now she was tired and the day was coming to an end. The sun was setting, time for her to take out the Koran and say her prayers. She sighed and looked out of the windows. How very English the trees are, she thought. And the little round pond could have Peter Pan sailing in his giant nest, or perhaps the three little pigs trotting by on their way to meet the dreadful Big Bad Wolf, for in the right light England was indeed the land of fairy tales and nursery rhymes. She smiled and began to recite.

'*Ashadu an la ilaha ill-Allahu . . .*' As she prayed, her tired thin shoulders swayed and the words comforted her. Her room felt as if the shadows of her mother and her sisters were with her.

Chapter 49

Georgina felt very much at home at Girton. Scraggs had taught her mother. Often she had visited as a child all the reunions when her mother and her contemporaries came back to 'That Infidel Place', as the college was known. Georgina's mother was a formidable matron who ran the local magistrates' bench with a rod of iron. Georgina was in awe of her mother, but she enjoyed her mother's rather advanced views on the rights of women now so eagerly debated among the girls at Girton. Georgina found her eyes tended to glaze when her earnest feminist fellow students held forth.

Though she might hesitate to confess it too loudly, Georgina rather liked Molly. At least Molly liked men, which was more than some of the more radical feminists would admit about themselves. Molly's attitude towards men had very little to do with feminist causes and more to do with a personal quest to pursue and capture any man she chose. Molly seemingly had a rapacious desire for sex. Georgina rather admired Molly.

Jonathan, her own fiancé, came into her life when she was in her last year at school. For Georgina it was very much as she imagined love at first sight to be. She saw Jonathan coming across the garden, walking slowly with her brother Harry. It was the bored restless season of awaiting the results for her application to Cambridge. The roses hung heavily on their stems. The manor house, elegant and white, stood above the Dorset farmland. Georgina had been sitting in a deck chair, her arms over her head, gazing at the blue sky and wishing that the exam results might come in. From far away she heard Harry's deep voice rumbling. She squinted into the sun and then she saw another taller head beside Harry's. The man was Harry's age and Georgina had been expecting him, but she had been expecting an American with a crew cut and wire spectacles, or perhaps one of the long-haired beatniks that graced the front of her American folk albums. This man, as he walked steadily into her life, was tall and graceful. He had light brown hair combed back off a wide forehead. His eyes were also brown and his wide mouth was smiling. 'You must be Georgina,' he said. His voice was soft with the sound of the wind blowing through the word *Georgina*. Why she could hear a wind blowing, she had no idea, but she felt herself blushing, and then shamefully wondered how his moustache would feel if he kissed her.

So far Georgina had restrained her lovemaking to lying in the bath, imagining the great event of kissing a few of the callow boys at hunt balls. Now she stared at Jonathan in an embarrassed silence. 'Cat got your tongue?' Harry grinned. 'I told you I was bringing him for the summer. Now that he's here, you're struck dumb? Most unusual,' he remarked, turning to Jonathan. 'Usually you can't stop her talking. You

209

take Jonathan off to the stables and show him the horses. I'll get Brooks to carry our luggage, unless he is in one of his communist moods and is on strike.'

Georgina grinned. 'He had a binge yesterday. He's got such an awful hangover, he's being nice to everybody. Besides, mother let him off last time he came up before the bench.' She shook her head. 'It's hard to get people to work now. We have a factory not far away and they all rush off in droves. Though quite why they want to sit in rows listening to awful music, when they could be out in the fresh air, I don't really understand at all.'

Jonathan listened quietly. Georgina felt Jonathan would always listen quietly to anything she had to say. 'Are you involved in politics?' he asked after she had finished speaking.

'I know it's fashionable to be political,' she said, 'but I'm afraid I have no interest. I suppose I should try and keep up with what's going on, but apart from mother, who's up to her neck in local politics – and that gets heated enough – I mostly tend to live among the horses. If I'm accepted to go to Cambridge, I want to read literature. I am interested in women's literature, but . . . Well, I don't expect you'd understand. Harry tells me you're from New York, and I know that all New Yorkers talk politics all the time.'

Jonathan laughed. He had a delightful laugh. It was spontaneous and caused him to throw back his head. 'You see,' he said when he had finished, 'I've had such a battering of political in-fighting among my friends that it will be a real relief just to spend a summer in this beautiful valley without worrying whether I should be supporting the Black Panthers, or Abbie Hoffman, or some lady who wishes to burn her bra.'

They arrived at the paddock. Flame, Georgina's horse, looked up and saw her mistress. Flame was a chestnut. Her mane was untrimmed and her tail was full. She trotted up to Georgina and her large, brown-fringed eyes looked into Georgina's face. Her breath disturbed the air. She whinnied, looking sideways at Jonathan. 'This is a visitor from America,' Georgina explained.

Jonathan looked impressed. 'She understands just what you say.'

Georgina patted Flame's neck. 'I had her from when she was born. I waited two years before I trained her to a saddle, and from then on we've been inseparable.'

By the evening Georgina knew she was in love. By the end of the week Jonathan confirmed that he felt the same.

Although the parting from Jonathan and the excitement of arriving at Girton had caused a turmoil in Georgina's soul, she knew Jonathan had to finish his legal studies at Harvard, and she would spend the time getting her degree. Then would come the marriage. Georgina was guilty of long secret daydreamings, planning the moment when Georgina Lampsetter would become Mrs Jonathan Montague. For this reason she was determined to learn all she could about America from Molly – to know Jonathan and his world even better.

Glenda seemed an odd little character to Georgina. She respected the girl's fierce need to get ahead. She also realized from Glenda's slightly imperfect accent that she had come from a poor background, rescued no doubt by the odd couple whom she had met in their magnificent Lagonda. Renée she recognized as a very famous actress. The mother, the quiet mouse that sat in the back with Glenda, had a kindly face. Cyril she had come to know from several rather embarrassing visits when he popped up to see Glenda. Usually he was accompanied by Henry, who had at least the semblance of manners. But Cyril made Georgina cringe. And as much as she deplored her father's attitude towards 'the working classes', as he called them, Cyril made Georgina feel her father might have a point. Glenda, she thought, would take time to get to know.

Fatima however made Georgina feel at home. There were several Middle Eastern girls during her time at boarding school. They had always formed a fairly isolated little group, but Georgina's father had been in the army and he generally made the girls welcome when Georgina brought them home. The girls were always grateful to stay with someone like her parents who could listen to their talk of homesickness.

Georgina could listen to Fatima and sympathize with her. Besides, both of them were betrothed. That beautiful safe word that would protect them in a rapidly changing world. 'Jonathan telephoned . . .' Georgina could begin. And then Fatima would say, a slight reddening to her cheeks, 'Majid wrote.' Both girls talked into the night about their hopes and dreams. Georgina felt sorry for Molly and Glenda. There were no certainties in their lives, only the knowledge that they *must* get their degrees because they did not yet have the security of marriage. But in the turmoil of the revolution that was to change family life forever, Georgina could walk over the safe bridge into Jonathan's arms, and she would never have to put a foot into the big, yellow swirling chasm which marked the beginning of the bursting banks, first in America and now all over the world. The new religion, as preached by Molly, stated that men and women were to be equal, both in the boardroom and in the bedroom. Georgina saw that Molly had a point on paper, but then Georgina had no wish to attack the boardroom. And as far as the bedroom was concerned, she knew she would leave it all to Jonathan on that wonderful day when she walked up the aisle dressed in white. If such a day ever came for Molly, she would have to wear a startling pair of red knickers, if she wore knickers at all.

Georgina finished her night reminiscences and sipped her cocoa. It had been a good full day and she was happy. Girton closed her in her loving arms. Georgina went to bed, thinking of Flame.

Chapter 50

'Shit.' Most mornings Molly lay in bed and swore to herself. Fishing about on her side table, she found a packet of dreadful English cigarettes. They tasted terrible, but she had run out of her American Marlboros. With her head hanging over the end of the bed, she groped for her lighter and then groaned. Last night she had been out with Hugh. He was one of those upper class English gentlemen that spoke with a turkey gobble. But he had nice buns and the cutest pair of balls she had yet seen at Cambridge.

If Molly wished to discuss his blessings and her fortunate find, her best bet would probably be talking to Glenda. Molly had only to mention sex and Fatima just froze. Georgina always looked as if she'd surprised the servants in the car park. Molly marvelled that the English could be so backward. Amazing that they managed to repopulate the country for so many centuries if sex was so taboo.

Molly's skull pounded and her stomach twisted with a rising tide of nausea. She fought back with a drag on her cigarette. There were some dregs of last night's coffee in a cup by her bed and, damn, she had put out last night's cigarette in her cold cream jar and she had promised herself that Glenda was right: the habit was gross. She breathed deeply and watched the room readjust itself.

Mid-term and Molly was in trouble with Scraggs. Miss Ivy Crompton did not like her, but then Molly admitted, lying in her small bed in her small room with a hangover, she wasn't all that sure about too many people here herself.

And to make things worse, there was no shower. Molly couldn't believe that the English could be so unclean, preferring to sit in dirty bathwater. And they seemed to find virtue in freezing themselves to death for lack of central heating. Girton was a cold place for Molly. She ached for her father's house, the big mansion in Upper Montclair, New Jersey. She missed her lush bedroom, she missed the maids. She missed her friends who all slept with their boyfriends and had endless lunches in the mall to discuss the details. She couldn't have the same discussions here. Glenda was pretty good fun, but still she was more interested in talking about the paper she was currently writing: an essay on the three basic features of the European novel. And that Cyril guy just wanted to talk politics. Sociological realism was hardly a lunchtime discussion, as far as Molly was concerned. Oh why had she decided to go to Cambridge? Why hadn't she gone to Smith or Vassar, like her friends?

Perhaps it was to get even with the boys. Several years ahead of her, her brothers were in the Ivy League, and Molly was tired of seeing their framed faces climbing up the walls of the mansion in their caps and gowns, each clutching a musical instrument. Molly wanted to have her picture at the top of the stairs in *her* cap and gown. 'Cambridge. Can you believe it? A nice Jewish girl from Upper Montclair at Cambridge!' her father said to all his colleagues. Molly simpered her way into yet another gold bracelet and yet another disgusting frilly dress. Dad had never understood that she was now eighteen, not eight. Every month after a trip to another part of the state, he came back with a dress for his baby.

Molly smiled as the room began to slow down. 'My heart belongs to daddy,' she hummed to herself as she levered her body out of bed. It did indeed, but her body belonged to anyone she fancied. A few rooms had basins and running hot water; Molly's did not. She put on her bright red taffeta dressing gown and walked down the hall. Around her other girls walked in their beige and fluffy muted dressing gowns. Molly grinned. Old maids, all of them. While she washed she thought about Glenda's invitation to her home for Christmas. Chanukah was not a particularly high holiday, but maybe Christmas in London in her little red car could be fun. Glenda had sworn on her honour that Renée and Abe had several bathrooms, all with showers. Molly realized that she would do anything for a shower.

This evening promised to be a frosty night out. They would be going to listen to the St John's choir. All four of them. Georgina and Fatima scrunched up in the back of the car, and Glenda with her in the front. Hopefully there would be some religious rugger buggers to admire. Molly felt she needed something to look forward to, and she had never before been inside a Christian church. God might strike her dead upon entering, she feared, which, on second thought, might add a touch of the perverse to the proceedings.

On the way back from the bathroom she saw Glenda. 'Okay for tonight?' she shouted.

Glenda nodded back.

Molly liked Glenda. There was something tough about Glenda. She did not shy away from conversations, even if they were about sex or abortion or all the issues that rocked her friends in the mall. The same conversations that her mother had in their big sitting room with her girlfriends. Molly was made privy to all the discussions and was amused to find out how many of her mother's friends were unhappy with their prestigious marriages. Her mother, of course, said nothing by way of open complaint about her own marriage, but just passed the plates of soft, buttery cookies and saw that the wine glasses were refilled. No, Molly thought, my little bustling mother is far too clever to be indiscreet.

Still, even if she was landed for the next three years with this relatively inexperienced bunch of women, once the three years were over, Molly would show her family that she was made of sterner stuff than her mother. For now she was studying for a business degree, although the English called it PPE, which sounded a lot less capitalist. Molly intended to make money, lots of it, and to troll the world. Life, she felt, had to be one big party, otherwise what was the point of the planet?

She reentered her room and wrinkled her nose. Maybe if she picked up a pizza in town she could persuade the fastidious Glenda to help her clean her room. Maybe. Scraggs was cross enough with her. She might as well get really cross. Molly intended to cut the morning's classes and take a spin into town. Glenda would fill her in later. Good old Glenda, she thought, as she poured herself into her jeans. She grimaced. Hugh had a blue for rowing, a fact that he forgot when he was screwing her. She felt herself walk bowlegged down the corridor. How many of you bitches, she thought as she passed rooms full of girls carrying books, would know about that?

Chapter 51

Glenda was looking forward to the Christmas carols. The Michaelmas term was now coming to an end and she felt the old familiar excitement of Christmas. Even in the days when she and her mother had no money, Minnie always made Christmas an exciting time. Now, with her mother's cheerful tones relaying messages from Abe and Renée down the telephone, she heard the snow in her mother's voice and she remembered the cans of frost that she traditionally sprayed over the big windows of the house. Molly would be with her so they could explore London. How odd! Glenda thought. I've lived all my life in London and I really don't know the whole city. There were lots of things she didn't know about life. She knew about contraception, because she had seen Ruth's rather revolting little pink tin. Inside it was a round object that had nothing to do with desire, but more to do with a pharmaceutical company. How on earth, Glenda had wondered as she gazed at the thing, how on earth could anyone want to make love after pushing that revolting object up inside you? Ruth seemed cheerful enough about it all. She had been practising in the lavatory, but then Ruth was a very cheerful person. Glenda always thought she would just swoon away in her husband's arms and let him take care of the details, although she knew from Cyril that men didn't like using French letters – 'Like waltzing in Wellington boots,' he said.

Cyril by now had a small girlfriend called Beth. She wore rimless National Health spectacles. Cyril was so proud of himself he was fit to bust. '*And* she's an International Marxist!' he announced.

Why, Glenda asked herself, am I thinking about French letters, Dutch caps, and International Marxists when I'm getting dressed to go and listen to Christmas carols? She pulled on a long red skirt. Maybe it's because my life has become very complicated. Before Cambridge and before Girton, life was all about working hard and passing exams. Now at Girton, Glenda felt she was at home. True, she did not fit in socially with many of the girls there, but Girton had a no-nonsense, down to earth attitude, and Glenda was already one of the most successful students in the college. Scraggs, she knew, appreciated her diligent study and her efforts at seeing that her papers were in on time. Unlike Molly, whom Scraggs seemed to loathe. But then Molly deliberately wandered into tutorials with her hair unkempt, her eyes red from smoking joints, and her walk provocative . . .

It was time to run for the car. Most of the other girls had pushbikes or mopeds, but Molly kept her car in the garage down the road. The dons knew she had a car, but decided to leave her alone. Glenda was glad for the car. The night was cold and frosty. Glenda saw Fatima's anxious face. 'I've never been to a Christian church before,' Fatima said nervously.

'Don't worry, sweetie.' Molly drove fast. 'They won't bite you. Anyway, imagine a Jew like me entering a church. About as good as a Christian dick at a nude circumcision ceremony. Uncomfortable, I would think.'

Georgina leaned forward. 'Somehow, Molly, I knew I could count on you to set just the right mood for the evening. But once we're inside the chapel, let's keep it clean, shall we?'

Glenda sat in the front seat and was glad for the warm air circulating around her feet. Dark trees waved their arms at her as the car drove by. The trees looked like hanged men in supplication for a pardon. It was late and the rooks had gone to bed. The fields and the fens were quiet. Soon the lights of the outskirts of the town shone into the car. Four girls, Glenda thought. All facing life ahead of us. The huge bulk of St John's loomed over them. Cyril, Beth, and Henry were waiting for them. Since she had had dinner with Henry, Glenda felt a lot more comfortable with him. She decided that Henry, like Cyril, was a real friend. Nothing more than that, but it was good to have friends. Now he smiled at her and put out his hand. 'Come along,' he said. 'We've kept seats for you. The whole chapel is crowded.'

They moved swiftly along the corridors and through the two quads. People were pushing and shoving to get into the chapel. Glenda felt her heart beat faster. She remembered the other time she had stood alone in this place. As she reached the door her eyes automatically rose to search out the shape of the man who so intrigued her. He was there. Her heart stopped and her breathing grew shallow. Why was she so deeply affected? He was only a young man playing the organ for a choir who were about to sing Christmas carols. She didn't even know him.

She walked quietly behind Cyril, hoping that somehow his great mass would protect her from . . . From *what*? she told herself crossly. You don't even know him and maybe you never will. She sat in her pew next to Molly and she stared at the back of the young man's neck. He was far away, but even at a distance she could see that his turtleneck was loose around his throat. He doesn't eat enough, she thought. His wrists stuck out like fish bones. He's too thin. He has nobody to cook for him. Immediately a wave of solicitude ran over her. She would know how to take care of him. Still warmed by the thought, she saw his head turn and his huge blue eyes blazed at her.

'*O holy night,*' the choir sang, '*the stars are brightly shining.*'

For Glenda the stars were shining brightly indeed. 'Who's that fellow?' Glenda prodded Cyril.

'Who?' Cyril asked, immersed in the music.

'Playing the organ, silly.' Glenda's voice hissed with anxiety. How could she meet him?

'Oh, 'im. That's Clive Alexander. 'E's the only millionaire in our party, though personally I question his devotion to politics. Seems he'd rather play music than decide on the important issues. Odd bloke, Clive. Why? You're not interested in 'im, are you?' Glenda said nothing, and Cyril understood her silence. 'Don't be nuts, Glenda. The man's an absolute lunatic, I hear. Potty. You have all the men in Cambridge you could possibly want, and you have to go and pick a loony. Stands to reason, don't it?' Cyril's voice was mournful. 'I suppose you want to reform him or something.'

Glenda laughed. 'I just want to feed him, and that's a very different thing.'

'Well you can't feed him 'ere, so there's an end to it. Now shut up and listen to the concert and you won't have any trouble. And no, I will not introduce you to him. So there.'

'I'll meet him myself, thank you very much.' Glenda fell silent and she sat on the edge of her pew. And watching him play, and hearing the incredible sensitivity with which he paused and held notes, making the middle voices below the melodies sing out, Glenda felt the stirrings of profound emotion. For the first time, she began to understand the feelings that had prompted other women before her to write books, compose poetry, give birth, and sacrifice themselves. Anyone who can play music with such emotion, she sensed, must be attuned to all the subtle sensations which life has to offer. And being that sensitive, he must also be vulnerable to being hurt. Glenda found herself wanting nothing more than to hold the young musician and to keep him safe.

She told herself she was being silly. Certainly premature about everything. And after all she had come to Cambridge to study . . . But her feelings could not be easily reasoned away.

Chapter 52

'Know the feeling well. It's what put the *dick* in *addiction*.'

Glenda glared at Molly who lay sprawled on her bed. Georgina made a face. 'Always the soul of tact. Molly, isn't that just a touch crude?'

'Crude but true.' Molly dropped her head back and blew a very large smoke ring. 'That's the way it goes. I should know. I've made a fool of myself enough times over men. Just cos some guy turned me on, I went ahead like an idiot and talked myself into thinking I loved him. You ever heard of anything so stupid? But women do it all the time.'

Glenda paused. 'But how can you be sure you're *not* feeling something real?'

'First of all, sweetie, you don't know the guy, so you're just projecting all your fantasies on him. And then if it hits you kinda like *whammo!*, that's definitely not love. It's addiction.'

Glenda sat on the floor. She said thoughtfully, 'It's not really a whammo feeling. I feel more . . . well, sort of exultant. It's as if the whole world has suddenly been re-coloured, you know? The air ripples and I breathe champagne.' She laughed. 'I can hear for myself how stupid that sounds, but I mean . . . I feel as if I've always walked around with some sort of barrier around me, like a thick coat, and now since I've seen him I've taken it off, or it's come off by itself for some reason, and all of a sudden all of my feelings seem more . . . Oh, I don't know. Alert. Awake. Alive. And of course nothing's happened yet, but still there's this strong feeling that you just *know* that you two will be getting to know each other. And everything feels exciting . . . Fatima, you must know what I'm talking about. Didn't you feel that way the first time you met Majid?'

Fatima shrugged. 'We grew up together. I always knew we would be married, so love between us is rather calm and peaceful. It was my destiny to marry Majid. You see we believe in kismet. I am sure I was married to Majid in another lifetime. But then I don't think he was a revolutionary.'

Glenda looked at Fatima. She knew that she had not heard from Majid, and that she was worried. Nevertheless, part of Glenda wanted to give Fatima a bit of a shake. Sometimes she could be so distant.

She turned to Georgina. Georgina gave Glenda the benefit of her absolutely gorgeous smile. 'I know what you mean,' she said. 'First time I saw Jonathan, I felt myself become a different person than I had been before. More passionate. More – womanly.' She raised her eyebrows. Her face glowed.

Molly nodded. 'More womanly, huh? Well, Georgina, maybe there's some life in you yet. Am I crazy, or do I detect a bit of dangerous human emotion creeping into the great British reserve?'

Georgina just laughed. 'But listen, Glenda. Seriously. You should watch out with this chap. His family are a bad lot,' she said. 'My mother told me that ages ago when I first started going to parties. "Bad blood," she said about the Alexanders. And Clive Alexander has a terrible reputation.'

'Oh how could he have a bad reputation?' Glenda insisted. 'The poor man just plays some rather odd music sometimes, he cares about people or he wouldn't be trying to change the world with Cyril and Henry, and all he gets is an awful reputation.'

'No, not for that,' said Georgina. 'It's just that everyone knows he comes from a very odd family. His father is Lord Alexander, famous as a gambler and a boor, always hunting and shooting and fishing. His uncle Caspar is the QC who's known for never losing a case. And then there's Clive and Clive's younger brother Caspar. Named after his uncle, but with nothing like his brains. Awful man thinks he's a real Cambridge blood. Organizes the beagle hunting and goes around yok-yok-yoking. But the real problem is Clive's mother, Lady Jane. What a terror! Poor Clive. No wonder he's turned into pretty much a blasted-out beatnik. Too much LSD, or whatever they're all into these days. But maybe it's not drugs at all. They say he might be just a little –' she raised her finger to her head '– touched? Spends most of his time thinking he's Jack Kerouac.'

'Jack Kerouac?' asked Glenda.

Molly sat up. 'Don't you know anything? Jack Kerouac is the most brilliant writer of the Beat Generation. You British don't appreciate our American writers. Jack Kerouac wrote *On the Road*. Boy, what a book! I was high for a week after I read it. I was going out with a guy who had a big Harley Davidson, and we scorched our way over to San Francisco and we rode everywhere. Jack Kerouac rode with his far-out friends. What a dick that boyfriend had! What a dick!'

Glenda laughed. 'You seem to remember your boyfriends by their dicks, not their faces.'

'Sure,' Molly said. 'Just like men remember asses and tits. We *are* the same, remember?'

'You think so, do you?' said Georgina.

Glenda felt the tension of a challenge rise between Georgina and Molly.

'Well, you British broads may be different, but it's all the same to us in the States.'

Glenda wished she could leave and go to her room to contemplate the wonder of her new feelings. How could she meet Clive? Maybe if I hang about with Cyril enough, I'll bump into Clive . . .

The other three girls started talking in a largely abstract generalized way about the question of whether men and women in society should be equal and the same or equal but different. Glenda fell silent. She felt as if she were in a special place of her own. She could see and hear the others talking. She could watch the long spiral of smoke coming from Molly's cigarette, but around her was a crystal clear pane of glass. Inside her glass she sat content.

When she first saw Clive she remembered her music. *Chicaboom chicarack* . . . Now the music was playing softly in her mind as she held her eternal cup of Nescafé. I wonder if Clive drinks coffee, she thought. And I must get that book by Jack Kerouac.

Chapter 53

Molly arrived in Glenda's bedroom on a Saturday. 'Okay.' She threw herself on the floor. 'I've checked with Cyril, and he says there's a Commie meeting later on at the Black Lion pub. If you want to meet the guy, I guess that's your best bet.'

Glenda stopped writing. 'I'll get dressed.' This afternoon, Glenda had promised herself, she would finish her paper on early Victorian women writers. She decided the essay could wait. She found her dressing gown and left her room with Molly behind her. 'You wearing anything special, Molly?' she asked.

'A Mao jacket, I think, in with the company. Dirty yourself up a bit. Grime under the fingernails and slime on your hair. Sort of *de rigueur* with all this militant radical crap. And it helps to smell. Body odour is very authentic, you know.'

'Oh, Molly.' Glenda laughed. 'They all mean well, and they do want to help people.'

'Some of them do,' Molly answered and veered off towards her room. 'See you in an hour. I've got to dig out some clothes.'

Glenda made a face. *Dig up* was more like it. Still, although Molly was dreadfully messy, she was at least clean.

The car rushed toward town as if it shared Glenda's excitement. She sat beside Molly who was wearing her usual tight jeans with a peasant blouse. Glenda wore a wrap-around skirt and a blue and green tie-dyed T-shirt. Today she wore more make-up than usual. Her face was unused to foundation cream, and she feared that if she smiled she might crack at the edges. And the light pink lipstick she put so carefully on her mouth made her lips feel soggy. She should have left off the make-up, but when she looked into the mirror she had to admit that the pink lipstick accentuated her mouth and lit up her hazel-coloured eyes. Her chestnut hair was pulled back in a pony tail. She looked down at her hands. Her nails were long and clean. She smiled. I'd never be a very good radical, she thought. The idea of all those tatty clothes and the smell of incense everywhere disguising the unwashed made her feel ill. Too close to home, she thought. Too close to those days with the McCluskies. Now, only occasionally when she passed someone on the street who exuded that well-remembered sour smell, Glenda knew she flinched. She also avoided the parts of the town where the poor lived. Cambridge fortunately had very few parts of town that were not beautiful.

The car weaved its way through the streets and down to the river. The Black Lion pub was full, but Glenda could see Cyril's huge form at the back. As they moved towards the crowded table Glenda anxiously scanned the group that huddled around the tables. She saw Henry sitting next to Beth. And then she felt as if embers inside her chest had been fanned to flame. Sitting up against the wall by the fireplace with a guitar in his arms, one foot hooked up against the fireplace, his chair tilted as if it could fall at any moment, was Clive Alexander. He looked up as he felt the noise of their approach. The hand that had been caressing the guitar strings fell to his lap and he stared at Glenda. Glenda, feeling the colour rise in her cheeks, blessed the thick foundation. The sharp wind had coloured her cheeks anyway. She felt a huge spurt of energy force her to take the last few steps towards the table. 'Hello, everyone!' she said far too loudly.

Cyril looked up. Clive began to play the guitar again. Softly.

'Greetings,' Molly waved her hand amiably.

'Sit down, both of you,' Cyril ordered. 'We're in the middle of the meeting's agenda.'

Glenda glanced quickly at Clive and then she smiled. He grinned back. Glenda could tell at once that he was as bored by the idea of an agenda as she was. She sat down and hid her face in her hands. Cyril was reading down the list. 'Item four,' he droned. 'The money from the last dance to raise printing costs for the *Red Flag*.'

Henry looked down at his notes. 'I report,' he said, 'that we raised fifty pounds and seventeen pence – who's taking notes for this meeting?'

Cyril looked around. 'Beth.'

'Oh, so the woman's automatically the secretary!' Molly butted in, laughing. 'You men are all the same,' she said with theatrical exasperation. 'Why should Beth take the minutes? I thought you all were supposed to be liberated.'

Beth looked seriously at Molly. '*Liberated*, as you use the word, is a bourgeois concept. In Russia men and women are all equal. It doesn't matter who takes the notes.'

'Oh, excuse me! No, I guess it doesn't matter in Russia. Though, of course, women get to sit on tractors, but how many women do you see in the Politburo? But sister, if your goal in life is to fight for the privilege of driving a tractor, then be my guest.'

Glenda kicked Molly under the table. 'Shut up,' she whispered. 'It's their meeting.'

Molly leaned back in her chair, her hands in her pockets. Why can't Glenda cut to the chase and pick the guy up? she thought. Just go up to him and say, 'Wanna fuck?' The line had worked for her on a number of occasions. She gazed at Clive under her eyelashes. Maybe not, she thought. There was something about the man that made even Molly pause. In those long slim fingers she saw the possibility of pain. In the controlled sweep of his fingers on the guitar she heard sadness. Why does a man leaning against a wall playing a guitar suddenly make me feel as if I want to cry? No wonder Glenda's hooked on the guy. What is it about him?

Sitting beside Molly, Glenda strained her ears to hear the melody from the guitar. 'Item number five,' Cyril boomed. 'There's a meeting of the Maoists this evening.'

'Will the Trots intervene?' Henry asked.

'I don't know. It's not our business, anyway.'

Glenda could hear the guitar. The notes slid across the room into her lap. They felt as if they were personally pleading with her for help, for compassion, for the touch of an understanding human soul. *Help me.* Glenda felt her heart splitting in two. One part of her heart beat strong and secure. *Of course I will help you,* it said. But the other half wandered into a torrent of emotion, crying, *But how can I help you?* She looked up at Clive and their eyes locked.

Clive stood up and put the guitar down. He walked to the table and he held out his hand. Glenda looked at him, mesmerized. She put her hand in his and she felt the tug as he pulled her to her feet. Molly sat quietly in her chair. Wow, she thought, the guy has a definite charisma. I'll give him that.

Clive walked out of the pub, his hand still firmly holding Glenda's hand. Cyril looked up and groaned. 'There they go, the Beauty and the Beast,' he said loudly. Other faces in the room had been turned to the door to watch Clive leave.

'Goodness,' Henry said primly. 'Never seen our Clive so quick to go with a girl before.'

' 'E's not usually,' Cyril said. 'I hear that's his brother's department.' He glowered at Molly. 'You got Glenda into this, Molly, and if anything goes wrong, I'll hold you responsible.'

'Me?' Molly laughed. 'First of all, Cyril, I don't know how the hell you can say I'm responsible in the least bit. And second, she's a big girl. Glenda can look after herself. And third, I can't imagine you "holding" me at all. Ever.' But Molly wondered why she found her heart bumping.

Chapter 54

Glenda followed Clive as he ran lightly across pavements. While they flitted over the ground like a pair of starlings, Glenda felt her heart singing. Around them there were lights in the windows. Dusk had settled upon Cambridge. The quads were full of people swinging past them. Many looked like early evening bats with their gowns flying behind them. Girls walked by, their heads covered in warm scarves. It was cold. The wind pierced Glenda's skin with icy fangs.

Once out of the main gate and into the road, a shadow of fear stretched over Glenda. Where were they going and what was she doing with this strange man? He led her, his hand firm but distant in hers. They seemed to be able to run together without pausing for breath. Glenda felt a warm, flowing strength in her legs and her lungs filled with effortless air. She felt as if they were floating above the grass and then they reached the edge of the night-lipped river.

The banks were soggy with dew. The willows mourned the passing of the summer and beside them a punt filled with water lay sunk in the deep muddy embrace of the River Cam. Clive abruptly stopped running. 'I'll bet people have tried to warn you off me. Haven't they? You've probably even been told that I'm not quite right in the head.'

Glenda stood still. From afar Clive's whitewashed blue eyes had seemed menacing, but close up she could see that he had a lovely row of eyelashes. Now with the painful question in the air between them, she could see how vulnerable he was. He stood in the cold night air dressed only in a tattered black roll-neck jersey, a thin pair of black tight-legged jeans, and a pair of American sneakers with no socks. 'Aren't you cold?' Glenda asked.

'You haven't answered my question.' Clive was shaking, not with cold, Glenda realized, but with impatience for her answer.

'Yes. I've heard several things about you,' she answered. They still held hands and Glenda wished she could take off her sensible Marks and Spencer's coat and put it around his shoulders. The shoulders were thin and the hollows in his cheeks worried her. He so needs good feeding. Glenda sighed and watched the breath leave her warm mouth and dissipate in small droplets on the air. Beneath her feet she felt the pressed grass rise up against her heel. In her heart she wished to take this man into her arms and hold him, comfort him, make him smile. She wanted to see the red tide of love rise up his face. What had happened in his life to make him so sad and so desperate? 'I don't care what people say,' she said, looking directly at him. 'People talk all the time.'

Clive smiled. His smile was gentle. 'Glenda, you are a romantic. I've been watching you. Are you still a virgin?'

What a question to ask! Her mind whirred and gibbered. 'Is that your business?' she said, feeling sorrow that he should ask such a question and spoil the magic at the moment. He was just like Molly's version of all men. She could see Molly smiling in amusement. 'If you must know, yes, I am.' She dropped his hand and turned away.

Clive followed her and put his arm around her shoulders. She felt the animal warmth right through the thick wool of the coat. Clive put his hand under her chin and raised his eyebrows. 'Glenda, I'll let you in on a little secret. Just between the two of us.' She looked into his hypnotic eyes. 'I'm a virgin, too.' And he threw back his head and laughed. Glenda did not quite know what to make of this statement.

228

Was he teasing her? Even Cyril was no longer a virgin. How could a man this attractive never have slept with a girl? 'Do you know why you are still a virgin?' Clive asked.

Glenda found it difficult to get all her thoughts together. In her imagination the love of her life would come into her world and sweep her off on his horse. In her imagination the man would talk to her of sweet nothings and protest undying love. Here she stood with this man and they were having a clinical discussion on virginity on the banks of the dripping river. This was not romantic, or at least it was not what she had expected. 'I think I'd better get back,' Glenda said uneasily. 'Molly's waiting for me.'

'Let her wait. Answer my question.' Clive looked at her with such amusement on his face, Glenda felt patronized.

'If you must know, I have too much self-respect to throw myself away. I've never understood girls who feel virginity is something to get rid of, rather like a Kleenex tissue.'

'Well, it might further surprise you to know that I feel that way, too.' Clive stopped smiling. 'I've always found men faintly disgusting. In a beautiful pristine world, there should be no need for lust. Love, romantic love, is what we were born for, not brutal rutting.' Clive's face grew cold. Glenda watched him quietly. 'Anyway, my family is so fucked up, I don't think I'd ever want to have children.'

Glenda felt a stab of sympathy. 'What do you mean by that?'

They were walking now and Clive linked his arm into hers. He pulled her close to his thin body. She saw his profile in the evening light. His mouth was talking but his lips were shaking, trying to hide the tears she heard in his voice. 'My mother hates me. She wants me disinherited and the title and the estate to go to Caspar, my younger brother.' He sighed. Glenda felt the sound escape from his lungs and cause his thin ribcage to shudder. 'She's probably right. I'm no good at all the hunting and shooting and fishing that my father does. Nor am I any good at all the socializing she does.

I don't mind being disinherited, I suppose. I just don't like her telling everybody I'm mad. Bats, loony as a rabbit in a top hat.'

'But you don't seem mad at all, Clive. Just a little more honest than most people.' Glenda found herself speaking with sudden conviction. 'And if all your mother cares about is socializing and hunting, then maybe *she's* the one that's crazy. Why kill things that have a right to live?'

'Honest?'

'Yes.'

'No, I mean, how do you mean I'm honest?'

'Oh. Well, I mean, in things you say, getting right to the point and all . . .' She paused and looked into his eyes. 'I mean, we've only actually talked to each other for a couple of minutes, and straightaway you tell me about yourself and I understand, and I feel I want to tell you about myself.'

Clive smiled and squeezed her hand.

'And as for your mother's social life,' she continued, 'I can imagine what you mean. I mean, it's not like that with my mother, though. My mother's not that type. She's a housekeeper. She cooks for Renée and Abe. We live in the basement of their big house.' I don't care, she thought as the words came tumbling out of her mouth. He must know who I am. 'My mother has never been married. Actually I'm a bastard, I suppose.' The awful bitter word that had always branded her as different. A girl without a father. Not even a father that cared enough to see her born into this world. She was not even worth waiting for. 'And that, I guess, is the awful truth about me. I'm a housekeeper's daughter. A bastard.'

Clive pulled Glenda into his arms. He put his firm, warm lips on her mouth and he kissed her. The kiss was gentle and soft. Glenda relaxed. A long time ago a small boy with a blonde head kissed her exactly this way. A kiss full of innocence. She remembered the warm breeze, Sam's back, and her brown hand as she held him. She put her arms around Clive. 'I'm glad that I've found you,' he whispered. 'We are two orphans in a horrible cataclysm.'

'I'd better get back,' Glenda said a moment later, finding that time had mischievously run away and was hiding. 'Molly has the car and she'll be getting impatient by now.'

'Don't bother about Molly. I'll take you back myself. Together we will roar up to the Virgin's Retreat of Girton and together we will vanquish the menopausal maidens, your dons.'

'They're not all that bad, Clive,' Glenda laughed. 'Scraggs is excellent. She's a wonderful woman. Really.'

Clive frowned. 'I don't want to let you go. Let's go back and square up with Molly, and I'll buy you dinner.'

Glenda walked quietly beside Clive. Her heavy heart lightened. The months of waiting were over. Georgina and Fatima had found their loves, and now so had she. She looked up at him as they walked back through the main gate. His face was tortured, she thought. But maybe it was just a trick caused by the shadows. He's not crazy, she decided fiercely. He's just different. I can understand him. His mother must be a bitch.

The others were standing outside the pub. She could hear Cyril's voice. 'Good. We will meet again next week, and by then Beth will 'ave all the documents and the statistics.'

Who needs documents and statistics? Glenda thought. What on earth has politics got to do with real life? Real life is found in love, in the heightened awareness of sensation that you feel when you've discovered your love. Poor Cyril, always so serious.

Molly stood on the other side of Beth who seemed to be lecturing Molly. 'Glenda!' Molly shouted. 'Come and rescue me from this terrible female, if she is female. I don't want to be a communist. I don't have a communist bone in my body. Anyway, Beth, don't let me catch you doing anything capitalist, like drinking champagne. And no going to May balls either.' She looked at Glenda and winked. 'I don't suppose you approve of those things anyway.'

'Laugh while you can.' Beth spoke coldly to Molly. 'Your sort won't be here much longer.'

'You bet your sweet bippy we will, darlin'!' Molly screamed with laughter. 'I'm going to find myself an expensive piece of ass, get my degree, and then I'm off to Capitol Hill to seek men of influence. But don't worry, honey. When you're tilling the soil of Cambridge and planting your wheat in the paddy fields, I'll be under some senator or other, giving him the time of his life.'

Glenda hurried forward. She knew Molly in these ribald moods. 'Molly, Clive says he'll take me back to college. Is that all right?'

'Yes, dear. But don't keep me waiting up too long.' Molly nudged Glenda. 'What's he like?' she said in a hoarse whisper, loud enough for Clive to hear.

'Quite possibly mad, but still quite a decent sort,' Clive replied. 'Glenda likes me very much and after a good dinner with a wonderful bottle of Châteauneuf-du-Pape, she will like me even better. At about four o'clock next Tuesday, she will probably not only like me, but fall in love with me. Won't you, Glenda?' He turned and grinned at Glenda, his blue eyes dancing and flashing.

Glenda just laughed. She wished she could tell him the truth: Oh, if only you knew! I fell in love with you when you were just the Joker in a pack of cards. Glenda felt she was dying to get hold of Abe, to tell him that she had found her Joker and he was not wild. Well, at least not all that wild.

'Catchya later, kids,' Molly said. 'I'm outta here.'

Glenda stood holding Clive's hand until she saw the back of the little red car pull away up the road. 'Funny girl, your friend,' Clive said.

'Oh, that's just Molly. You'll like her when you get to know her. She's just very American.' Glenda knew Molly was hurt. Now there were three who had men in their lives:

232

Molly, for all her promiscuity, had no one. No one special, anyway. Damn, Glenda thought. Why do I know Molly is hurt? The thought caused a small purple pall to fall over her golden world. Still, Molly was her friend and she wished she had not caused her pain.

Chapter 55

Glenda very much wished she had brought a handbag with her. Her make-up felt hot and greasy. Walking slowly to St John's College, she wondered if she could find a lavatory to wipe the stuff off her face. The courtyards became unfamiliar and blurred. The rooms abutting on the quads, now full of light, seemed to swell and rock like galleons wafting along an invisible sea. The world expanded and contracted and Glenda walked carefully, fearful that she might trip and be seen as inelegant and insecure. Clive didn't need to talk; he strode purposefully beside her, his feet light on the grass.

Finally they came to a small door. 'In here,' he said. 'That's my set of rooms.' He pushed open the door and stood aside to let her in. How curious, Glenda thought. I feel like Alice, but although I'm not exactly *falling* down the hole, I'm going into it nonetheless. She ducked her head, even though the lintel of the door did not demand the gesture. The genuflection was more of an acknowledgement, privately made by Glenda, that she was entering a new world.

The sitting room was white and square. The rooms were at ground level, so the window had a deep seat. There were no curtains. The cushion in the seat was of a light brown, buttoned leather. The surface was shiny and scuffed. Glenda made her way to the seat and felt much safer once sitting down. There was a small gas fire. Burning low, it popped and hissed a welcome. Beside the fire was a plate with a loaf of bread, a knife, and a packet of butter in wrinkled paper. Someone had gouged out the heart of the butter. A long brass toasting fork lay up against the black marble surround. On top of the mantelpiece was a pier glass. Its golden frame enclosed an expanse of very old mirror. The image of Clive standing in the door became distorted and indistinct. Glenda looked at Clive, who was watching her through the glass. 'Alice in Wonderland,' he said.

Glenda's heart stopped. He can read my mind, she thought.

'No,' Clive continued pleasantly, 'I can't read your mind, but when I took these rooms, I thought of the same thing.' He shut the door behind him and then went to the fireplace and turned up the gas. There were two very big spoon-backed Victorian armchairs covered in green velvet sitting in a matronly fashion beside the fire. 'Perhaps, before you do sit, I'll show you the rest of the rooms.' He pushed open a door at the back of the sitting room. 'Here is my bedroom.' The bedroom had a neat, Spartan look. He walked across the room and opened another door. 'This used to be a private dining room, but I now keep my piano there.'

Glenda walked into the room. It was smaller than the sitting room and it had a stained glass window. Through the red curve of the head of Our Lady of Sorrows, the light from an outside street lamp filtered onto the piano. For a moment Glenda felt as if the room was covered in blood. She shook the image away and walked up to the piano. On the music rack she saw pieces by César Franck. She ran her hand over the satin-smooth finish of the Steinway piano. 'Renée has a Steinway too,' she said.

'Renée?'

'Renée Blanchard. The woman my mother works for. Well, really she's more than just that. She and Abe are like our family. Mum cooks and cleans, and Abe and Renée take care of us in return. I feel as if I have always lived with them. In a way I have.' And she laughed.

She walked ahead.

'Over there is the loo,' Clive said.

'I must go and wash my face.' Glenda went into the small

square bathroom and she listened while Clive's shoes walked him across the floor of the music room and back into the sitting room. There was something bleak about all three rooms, she decided. Even if Cyril and Henry were poor, their rooms had developed life. Slowly they had collected bits and pieces of furniture, most of it broken, rescued from one of the city dumps or roadsides, purloined after a boozy night out. But Clive's rooms felt empty. A pile of music on top of the piano. Some sheets of paper with hand-written notes. Several pencils. In the bathroom Glenda looked about. A small beer-bellied bath with two thick brass taps. An old-fashioned lavatory with a warm wooden seat.

A large gleaming handbasin with a mirror. Thick white towels on the towel rail. Behind the door a thick white bathrobe. Glenda leaned up against the bathrobe and smelled it. She breathed deeply. This must smell of him, she thought. She closed her eyes and concentrated. As she breathed in she caught the smell of blue cornflowers in thick hay. It was a smell captured from the height of summer. That's it, she realized. He smells like summer. And it was the fault of the rooms, not him, that they seemed rather lifeless.

Glenda was more of an autumn person, but now she knew Clive was happiest in the bright hot sun. She went over to the washbasin and splashed water over her face. The water was hot and torrential. She saw his well-used toothbrush in the tooth mug. The toothpaste was rolled neatly halfway up. The make-up washed off her face and disappeared down the drain hole. She looked up and laughed. Her face was pink and shiny from the hot water, but she felt much better. Glenda with make-up was quite different from Glenda without all that gunge. She wiped her face briefly on one of the immaculate white towels and studied the towel to see that she did not soil it. To her relief she had not. She gave a little self-conscious laugh and opened the door.

In the sitting room Clive had been toasting some pieces of crusty bread in front of the fire. The butter oozed on the bread and a small brown pot of tea stood by the fire gently steaming. 'Do you like Earl Grey?' He looked up at her and his eyes brightened. 'You look much nicer without that make-up, you know. Don't ever wear make-up again, will you?' His voice ended in a question mark and Glenda grinned.

She felt as if she had known this man all her life. 'All right,' she said companionably. 'I won't.'

'Here. Grab a slice of bread and I'll pour tea.'

'You really are organized.' Glenda was surprised. With Cyril and Henry, she always had to wash up dishes in their dirty sink.

His face was grim for a moment. 'Tell you what.' He brightened. 'Instead of going to a restaurant, this evening we can go over and visit Nanny. She'll cook dinner for us. My mother got rid of Nanny, or at least she thought she did, but I put Nanny in a house in Cambridge. She means everything to me.'

'Why did your mother do that?' Glenda was amazed. She had always read that the very rich kept their nannies rather like precious heirlooms.

'My mother casts off people like used handkerchiefs.' Clive spat out the words. 'Once I went away to Eton, she said there was no need for a nanny, so Nanny was sacked. My mother wouldn't give her a reference, so she had to get a job in a shop. I didn't have any money then, but last year I came into a bit of a trust fund and I found Nanny and gave her a house and enough money to keep her comfortably for the rest of her life. You see, Nanny really loved me and my mother didn't. I loved Nanny and my mother was jealous. My mother is a vicious bitch.'

Glenda was taken aback, not just by the force of his words, but by the tremendous anger that lay behind the words. She was not used to anyone describing a parent in such shocking terms. Molly was rude about her mother, but in a more playful way.

Clive suddenly realized that Glenda was shocked. 'Sorry,'

he said abruptly. 'There I go being honest again. We'll change the subject. Here.' He carefully poured the tea into a pretty cup and saucer. 'Do you have sugar?'

'No.' Glenda smiled. 'I don't like sugar in anything. I like bitter and sour things, like pickles.' She sipped the steaming tea. The smell of Earl Grey filled her nostrils. She looked at Clive through the steam. He was chewing his toast. His teeth dug into the butter that swelled at the imprint, and his tongue was pink and sure as it curled around his lips searching for crumbs.

Glenda sat and wondered. What would it be like to be touched by that tongue?

They both sat in silence and gazed into the mysterious blue flame of the gas fire. The gas threw up jets of flame and a darkness settled behind them in the room. Neither of them moved.

Chapter 56

Glenda realized with a slight sense of shock that Clive intended to put her on the back of his magnificent Harley Davidson motorbike. It had not occurred to her that he might own such a monster. She had imagined rather fondly that he might have a car like Abe's green Lagonda. But no. Here in front of her was the bike gleaming under the lamplight. She dearly wished she had worn a pair of trousers. 'What do you think of her?' Clive patted the great beast's side.

'Well,' Glenda paused. 'I've never ridden a motorbike before. I guess I'm a little nervous.'

'Nothing to it.' Clive sat astride the motorcycle. 'Just climb on behind me, and we're off. Lean when I do, and keep your head down.'

Glenda struggled inelegantly onto the back. She put her arms around Clive's waist and felt herself blush, glad that he could not see her red face. This was really too intimate for a first date. But then, she felt quite comfortable.

Clive revved the engine and the motorcycle growled, happy to be free and away. They tore down the road and soon Glenda caught the rhythm of the bike and the two bodies swooped and glided around the corners. Glenda opened her eyes and looked around. The trees and the shrubs were whizzing past. Clive crouched even lower on an open bit of road. 'Let's give her her head!' he yelled into the wind, opening up the throttle. The bike screamed and shot forward. Glenda felt an enormous feeling of exhilaration, understanding at once why Clive liked the bike so much. And she decided to buy herself a pair of jeans and a biking jacket. Molly would approve, she thought.

Finally, as the moon scudded across the sky, they dropped back to earth and the bike came to a quick halt in front of a small cottage on the outskirts of Cambridge. The area was new to Glenda. COE FEN – a small sign on the road beside the cottage proudly announced. The cottage had a light on in the front window. The roof was thatched. Before Glenda stood a picture of the perfect country cottage made real. The garden, entwined with rose bushes, now dormant, and laden with beds of hollyhock, reminded Glenda of her own secret garden, only this garden wasn't secret. It didn't need to be because there was nothing threatening the little oasis on a fen. Nearby she could hear the rushing sound of a river. From far away came the lonely hoot of a hunting owl. 'What do I call your nanny?' Glenda asked, suddenly nervous again. Here she was in the world of a man she had just met. He knew next to nothing of hers, but then there was nothing much to know: a girl living with her mother, a housekeeper. Clive had a much more exotic history.

'Call her Nanny Jenkins,' he said. He opened the little latch gate and walked up the pebbled path. The long prickled stems of the rose bushes guarded the cottage for the winter months ahead. In the beds piles of leaves and dead flowers submissively awaited the spring. Glenda's feet crunched on the pebbles. Glenda could hear the frost under her feet. Clive knocked on the oak-beamed door. There was a shuffle, and a tiny woman, who reminded Glenda of Mrs Tittlemouse, came to the door. 'Clive!' said the woman and she took him in her arms. 'Come in! Come in! And who's with you, dear? I haven't got my spectacles on.'

'This is a friend of mine called Glenda, Nanny. I brought her to show her off to you.'

'About time, too.' Nanny's voice was sharp. 'I wondered when I would see you with a girlfriend. Do come in, dear. Did he make you come here on that dreadful machine?'

Glenda nodded, but she smiled. 'I enjoyed it.'

Nanny Jenkins took Glenda's hand and looked very seriously at her. Glenda blinked. Nanny Jenkins had radar eyes, she realized. Glenda felt all her life lay in front of Nanny Jenkins. 'Hrump,' Nanny Jenkins snorted. 'I see you are a very nice young woman indeed. Well done, Clive. I'm glad she is not one of those dreadfully modern aggressive gels. They don't make them like they used to, you know.'

'Yes, Nanny,' Clive said, bowing to Nanny's will. 'I know they don't.'

'Still, you've made a good choice, dear. Come along and let's see what we have in the pot. Hungry, are you?'

'Starved,' said Glenda.

'Ah. Then you're not one for banting, I take it.'

A confused Glenda looked at Clive.

'Banting,' he explained. 'As in Mr Banting who came up with some diet or other. It's an old word for dieting.'

'Oh, I see. No.' Glenda turned to Nanny Jenkins. 'I never diet.'

'You've no need to, dear. I can see that.' Nanny Jenkins led the way into her little sitting room. Glenda felt even more as if she were entering the world of Beatrix Potter. In the sitting room was a round dining table covered in a white cloth. 'Clive dear, you come into the kitchen and give me a hand.'

Clive obediently left the room and Glenda was alone. Sitting in a nursing chair Glenda looked into the coal fire. Her memory slid back to the days when she and Minnie sat quietly together in front of their own coal fire. The difference was that this fire had adequate coal for fuel. The fire burnt strong and red. Minnie's coal, bought at the end of the road, had large amounts of poor quality anthracite in it and it burned badly and smoked. Minnie did her best, but the fire never really amounted to much; it was all they had. The fire and the radio kept them in contact with the outside world. Nanny had a television and a gramophone.

The room was decorated with country-style chintz. Bright swags of yellow flowers. On the mantelpiece sat two large Staffordshire dogs. Will I ever fit in with people like Nanny Jenkins? she wondered. Will Clive's mother take one look at me and decide I'm not one of them? 'Not quite one of us, dear,' Georgina would say when she was in a teasing mood. Only she never used the phrase against Glenda. Glenda knew, and had known for a long time, that she was NQOUD. Clive didn't mind, and Nanny Jenkins didn't seem to mind, but Clive's family would be another matter. She had seen Caspar, Clive's brother, around Cambridge. He seemed like one of the many Cambridge rugger boors. Huge and loud. Not at all like Clive.

Nanny came bustling in with a tray. 'Now sit you down, dear,' she said, 'and I'll serve.' On the tray was a large blue and white casserole filled with shepherd's pie. The pie oozed a rich brown gravy and the top was golden and crusty.

'You're the best cook in the world, Nanny,' Clive said as he spooned his shepherd's pie into his mouth. 'I wait all week for this meal,' he said happily.

Glenda was glad Minnie had taught her to cook. Food was obviously necessary to Clive. 'Seen the doctor lately?' Nanny asked.

Clive frowned and Glenda felt a sudden tension between the two of them. 'No.' Clive pushed his pie around on the plate. 'Let's not talk about that, Nanny,' he pleaded.

But Nanny would not be deterred. 'You know you must see him regularly. You promised.'

'What does he need the doctor for?' Glenda asked, puzzled. 'There's nothing wrong with him, is there?'

She looked at Clive. He shook his head.

'It's his nerves,' Nanny said firmly. 'It's his nerves. Runs in the family. And he always was delicate. I had to take ever such good care of him when he was a baby. Oh my, he could have some fits!'

Clive was frowning. 'Don't go on, Nanny,' he said with an edge in his voice.

'You've not been playing any of that awful music, have you, dear?' Nanny obviously was not dissuaded by Clive's anger.

'No,' he said. 'I haven't.'

'It's when he gets it into his head to play that awful music. Really, I put my hands over my ears and leave the room. What is it called? You told me once.' Clive was not eating. 'Go on, Clive, tell Glenda about it.'

'You mean the *diabolus in musica*,' he said, having no choice.

'Yes! That's it. Oh my, Glenda. Don't let him play it. It does dreadful things to him. It's music that's not meant to be played, you know.'

Glenda looked interested. That was what he was playing when I first saw him, she thought. 'Why can't you play it, Clive?'

'Really, this is rather a silly conversation.' Clive pushed back his lock of hair with a nervous hand. 'A lot of fuss made about nothing. It's just old-fashioned superstition. It's only a musical interval we're talking about. That's all. Halfway between a perfect fourth and a perfect fifth. But it wasn't allowed to be played in the Middle Ages because some old fuddy duddies decided that it was the music of the devil. A bit like the way some people think of rock and roll today. I

241

don't listen to any of their superstition. To me it's a lovely interval. If you listen hard, you can hear the harmony behind the apparent discord.' His eyes lit up. 'It really gives a very exciting twist to music, Glenda. I've some pieces that build largely on the "diabolic" interval. Franck used it. So did Chopin, on occasion. I'll play them for you one day.'

'Oh no, you won't!' Nanny was decisive. 'Give the poor girl an awful headache, it would. Now, I'll just clear up and we will have my apple pie and cheddar cheese. And enough talk about all this!'

Clive gave Glenda a quick conspiratorial glance with laughter in it, as if to say, People do get themselves worked up about the silliest things, don't they?

The apple pie was delicious, the apples properly buttery and the pastry light as a summer cloud. Glenda had never eaten a slice of prickly cheddar cheese with apple pie before and she approved of the taste. 'That's marvellous, Nanny Jenkins,' she said. She wiped her mouth. 'I'll wash up for you, if you like.'

'No. No one washes my pots but me,' Nanny said firmly, 'but we can leave Clive here by the fire and you help me dry.' Glenda followed Nanny's determined little figure into the kitchen. 'I love that boy,' Nanny said, without pausing for breath. She plunged her hands into a sink of soapy water. 'He wanted to buy me a large house with a maid, but I wouldn't let him. A small cottage is all I want. And my own independence. Horace from next door does the garden. I have all my own vegetables. Clive visits me often.'

'I can see he loves you very much, Nanny Jenkins.'

Nanny Jenkins smiled. 'Yes, dear,' she said. 'I'm like a mother he's never had, poor soul. *She* . . .' Nanny's nose quivered with disapproval. 'She never understood what a treasure she had in Clive.'

That's it, Glenda said to herself. He's a treasure.

'She preferred the other one,' Nanny continued. 'Not that Caspar's a bad lad, mind you, but he is a true Alexander.'

'Alexander,' Glenda mused. 'I know that name.' Her mind dredged back into the past. 'There's a barrister called Alexander, isn't there?' she asked.

'Ah, yes. Clive's uncle. That's Lord Alexander's brother, Caspar. And Clive's brother, Caspar, is called after him.'

'He defended a neighbour of mine, Mrs McCluskie, when she killed her husband.'

Nanny paused. 'I remember that case,' she said. 'It made all the newspapers, didn't it?'

'Yes, it did. Poor woman, I hope she's all right now.' Glenda dried the blue and white casserole.

Nanny carried on washing and rinsing. 'You realize,' she said in a cautious voice, 'that there is something not quite right in the Alexander family.'

Glenda looked at Nanny. 'You mean because Clive's mother is so awful to him?'

'Not just that. You should be careful.' There was a warning in her tone that Glenda chose not to heed.

'I can take care of myself,' Glenda said lightly. 'Anyway, there's nothing wrong with Clive. He's just a very sensitive man. If he had been born into an artistic family, he would have fitted right in.'

The warning was extinguished in Nanny's eyes. She knew enough about women to know that, at this point in her life, Glenda would not listen to anything she said. If she said too much, Glenda would consider her a traitor. This very determined girl was in love with her Clive, but – Nanny shook her head – she was stubborn for a girl her age, and she would learn the hard way.

Nanny hoped, as she saw the two of them out of the front door, that the path ahead would not be too hard and that Glenda would survive the danger. A great many of the old families in England carried a curse. The Alexander family was no exception. She watched Clive's gleaming head disappear in the moonlight and she sighed. She was getting old, she admitted to herself as she made herself a cup of hot milk and let in the fat ginger tom. She must take care of herself until she felt that Clive was safe. Would Glenda keep him safe and be able to deal with his mother? Nanny Jenkins didn't know. But she offered a hope to God in her nightly prayers. God bless Clive. And Glenda too, she said before she fell asleep.

The doors of Girton College were still open and the porter sat chatting to a friend. Clive hopped off the bike and drew Glenda to him in the shadow of the arch. A quick hurried kiss and he was gone. 'I'll telephone tomorrow,' he said and then he roared off.

Glenda went dreamily through the corridors to her room. She did not want to talk to anyone. She did not want to break the spell. Slowly she took off her clothes and decided not even to wash her face. It was free of make-up anyway, and this way she could retain the image of Clive's bathroom. She went to sleep dreaming of Clive in his bathrobe. Nanny Jenkins was beside the door with a rod in her hand. Why a rod? Glenda wondered even in sleep. How odd.

Chapter 57

The next morning Glenda felt three pairs of eyes scrutinizing her at breakfast. Molly had not been slow to spread the news. Other girls looked up from their toast and jam. They too had picked up on the rumour or heard the powerful motorbike roar off into the night. 'Well?' Molly demanded. 'What happened? Did you get a beautiful candlelit dinner?'

'No candles,' Glenda said, suddenly afraid of losing her happy memories. The hours with Clive had been so fine and so beautiful, she did not want Molly pawing over their happiness. 'We had a quiet meal and then I came home.'

'What do you think of him?' Georgina leaned forward, her cup of tea in her hand.

'He's very nice,' Glenda said lamely. 'I mean I don't know him very well, but he's gentle, and he loves music. I really must learn something about music. I like his motorbike.' She laughed feeling silly and inadequate. 'Anyway, it's much too early to say anything other than that he's nice.' She shrugged one shoulder higher than the other.

Molly stretched. 'I'm miles behind with my paper, and we have a tutorial this afternoon. Can I take a look at yours?'

'Sure.' Glenda was happy for the subject to change, and sat quietly drinking her tea.

Fatima was looking as frail as ever. Glenda now knew how much Fatima suffered being away from Majid. Before Clive, Glenda could not imagine being that attached to anyone except Minnie. But even then she was able to leave Minnie for Cambridge with just a few pangs of homesickness. Minnie was somebody on the end of a telephone. Minnie was her mother whom she would go back to for Christmas. But Clive . . . She felt an invisible gold thread held them together already. She felt as if suddenly her ear had become a telephonic instrument in its own right. Through it she could hear Clive's music and that unmistakeable, hesitating voice. Clive's voice, that could caress her like warm honey and make her want to bury herself in his arms and into his soft, slim body. Physical desire was not a fully understood quantity for Glenda. Before, she had known something of lust: she knew how to manage her own lust. But afterwards she lay startled that this body had such demands of its own. She was sure that that was what St Paul said was the thorn in his flesh. She almost admired Molly for her carefree acceptance of sex in her life. Now she must question Molly closely. Hopefully there were other methods of protection outside that ghastly rubber ring . . .

The day passed. Glenda sat in her room finishing her paper. How can I write this stuff? she thought. How can I write a paper on the feminist heroes? Women, like Florence Nightingale and Beatrice Webb, who changed the way the world thinks about women. And then I feel as if I couldn't care less how the world thinks about women. I just want to be with Clive, not sitting behind a book.

Scraggs never married. She had taught hundreds of Girton women, many of whom were now back to celebrate Girton's anniversary. Glenda felt guilty. She had been so busy settling in at Girton she did not get very involved with the anniversary plans, or even with the radical shifts that were occurring at the college itself. She did sign a petition asking for the girls to have greater autonomy over their lives, but other than that she preferred to keep to her own small group and to work hard. It was easier for Molly, she decided. Molly and Georgina had both been to boarding schools, so they were accustomed to joining organizations. Georgina sang in the choir and played hockey for Girton. Molly was involved in some Cambridge magazine and was also doing stage design for the Cambridge Footlights. Glenda and Fatima were both reluctant to get involved. This gave both of them time to spend together. She was curious about Fatima's religion. It was so foreign to her way of life. But she had to admit that Fatima was a delightful and amusing girl . . .

While Glenda studied, she realized that she must learn not to wait for a telephone call. If she put this much nervous energy into hoping for a call, she would be a wreck by the end of the week. Anyway, she had things to look forward to and take an interest in, such as her next tutorial with Scraggs. Glenda was afraid that Scraggs might notice that she looked different.

When she walked into Scraggs's room, she gazed at the floor and then she had to look up.

Scraggs did know. She had heard. Nothing is secret at Girton, Glenda reminded herself. It was like a massive family and all dramas were writ large. She saw a warm light in Miss Crompton's eyes and, she hoped, a twinkle. She took her seat and other girls filed in. Molly slumped down beside her clutching her crumpled paper. 'Finished,' she whispered. 'Hope Scraggs doesn't compare our two papers.'

'Today,' Scraggs began, 'I shall tell you about a group of young women who, between the 1880s and the onset of the First World War, decided to turn the tables on their men. A group of intellectuals, artists, and politicians grew up, calling themselves "The Souls". And central to this group were *women* of influence, led by Margot Asquith, who essentially became a group unto themselves.' There was a silence as the girls in the room found themselves paying attention. Even the sneering group of extremist feminists, who usually whispered at the back of the room, stayed silent. 'By the time these young intelligent women were in their early thirties, they had become bored with their fearfully restricted lives. It was not uncommon for young women in those days, you see, to feel stifled even to the point of suicide. You must imagine a society that treated women in the upper classes as utterly dependent on men. Divorce was practically unheard of. If there was a divorce, the woman almost always lost her children. Women were playthings, until Margot Asquith and her friends, Ettie Grenfell and Lady Elcho, got together.' Scraggs was beginning to smile. Her voice warmed.

'And the philosophy by which these women chose to live,' she said, 'was best described by a visitor amidst their circle, Wilfrid Scawen Blunt. "It was a maxim of their set," wrote Blunt, "that *Every woman shall have her man; but no man shall have his woman.*"' Now, I know that doesn't sound very radical to those of you who consider yourselves feminists today,' she paused, 'but let me tell you, it was dynamite in those days. Remember, those were the days when unmarried women were not allowed a savoury course after dinner in case the spices might inflame their senses. Overnight, men like Arthur Balfour and George Curzon, even Hugo, Lord Elcho himself, found the tables turned on them. Whereas men had previously been able to philander and their women were none the wiser, suddenly they found that women now quite cheerfully shared their men and then compared notes.' Scraggs laughed. 'In an odd way,' she said, 'that was a far more revolutionary concept of sisterhood than we have even now. Women have never shared their men in the way that men have often shared their women. Women have always been trained to compete for men.'

Glenda shifted in her seat. She could not imagine sharing Clive. 'Far out idea!' Molly muttered. 'About time women came out of the closet.' Georgina and Fatima were listening.

The debate continued in the classroom for most of the afternoon. Sonia, a militant lesbian, argued that *any* relationship with men diluted the cause of feminism. 'Men are the enemy,' she argued. 'Always have been.'

Molly loudly talked her down. 'Those of us who want men in our lives have the *right* to have men in our lives. I think it's oppressive for you to speak on our behalf.'

Scraggs just sat back and looked at Glenda. Glenda felt silly. Her feelings about Clive were too new for her to be sure of what she felt. For the moment she felt she treasured her feelings and didn't want them dissected by Scraggs, any more than she had wanted them picked apart by Molly.

Fatima surprised Glenda. She put up her hand and very quietly, with a good deal of dignity, explained that in her country women were not nearly so dependent on men. 'We have our mothers and all our female relatives. Men and women live very separately. Of course we marry, if it is arranged.'

There was a loud groan from Sonia and her friends. Fatima faced them rather fiercely. 'You presume too much knowledge about our ways,' she said sharply. 'We have far more say in our lives than you have in yours. Once we are in our women's compound, we women determine our lives. Our husbands know that if they make us unhappy, we can call on our family and go back. He loses the dowry and he loses face. But I ask you: what happens in your society if a man beats a woman and makes her unhappy?' There was a silence.

'She can always go back to her family,' Sonia said.

'She can't,' another girl spoke up. 'My mother was beaten by my father, and she couldn't go back to my grandmother's house because my father said he would come and smash her house up, so we had to stay.'

Glenda felt discordant music playing in her head, the dreadful notes banging and crashing. Why, she thought, did Sonia hold forth so much on social issues when in fact she was a rich upper middle class bitch? 'Here in our country, most women don't help each other,' Glenda found herself on her feet. 'There's nowhere to go because we don't have much family life left.' Poor Mrs McCluskie's face swam before her eyes. Her mother's grey tired face and Mrs Jones's hollow cough intruded into the peaceful book-lined room.

'Well,' Scraggs said, 'the Souls decided to do something about that. They became their own very early consciousness-raising group. Maybe the first.' She nodded at Fatima. 'You are right. Western women make very little effort to understand other countries. They merely spend their time gathering what they, in their Western minds, consider atrocities. It makes for good table talk in West Hampstead and perhaps it makes for some good journalism. But most of it is false. I do take your point about women in other civilizations taking care of each other. I am afraid,' she said, 'we as women in this country have rather lost that ability.' The bell sounded and the girls stood up.

The afternoon faded outside the window. Glenda took her paper up to Miss Crompton and put it on her desk. 'I don't know about sharing men,' Glenda said, 'but I do see that women need to support each other.'

'Glenda,' Scraggs smiled, 'you already have three good friends and I hear you have taken to a motorcycle.'

Glenda looked at Miss Crompton. She did know.

'But which is most interesting? The motorcycle or the man atop the motorcycle?' Scraggs teased.

'Both,' Glenda laughed.

'Then I am happy for you. As long as it doesn't impede your work. So often I lose a really promising student to a boyfriend.'

'Oh, it won't affect my work at all,' Glenda said. 'I spent my life getting here. I promise it won't.'

Scraggs sighed as she saw Glenda leave the room with that troublemaker Molly. Between Molly and Clive Alexander, she knew, Glenda would have to put up a fight to find time to get her work done. Still, the girl might look frail, but she is tough underneath. Scraggs knew this because she read Glenda's well-reasoned papers with pleasure. There goes a fine mind, she thought, and pray God nobody destroys it.

Evening fell and Julie, an old friend of Scraggs's, came in for a glass of sherry. Both women sat in the shadows in a pool of silence. Ivy broke the silence first. 'I was telling the students about the Souls,' she said.

Julie laughed. 'How did they take it?'

'They listened. Some of the more politically minded missed the point, but I think the brighter ones have gone off to think about it.'

'We are old souls compared to them.' Julie sipped her sherry. 'Thank goodness I never allowed myself to let my life be defined by a man. I like men, but not as much as I like the company of women.'

Julie stretched. She was tall and slim. Ivy envied Julie her beauty, but then Julie confessed once long ago that she envied Ivy's academic mind. 'I don't have a first class mind like you have. I'm too frivolous.' Ivy shrugged it off in those far off days. Now she remembered and more recently she realized it was precisely her first class academic mind that barred her from ever getting married. Men found her formidable. So it was to be, she said to herself, and again the thought came into her mind as she watched her friend look out into the garden. At least if I am to be an old maid, Ivy thought, I have the students and I have Girton. A fierce love of this place sustained Ivy through sometimes lonely nights. 'We must go to Hall,' she said, and Julie nodded.

Ivy touched Julie's shoulder as she walked past her out into the corridor. Both women walked along in a companionable silence. College seemed such a safe place in such a sea of change.

Chapter 58

After dinner Georgina suggested that they go out for a drink. 'All this talk of Souls makes me restless,' she said.

'What makes you restless, Georgina,' Molly said, 'is the possibility that you might have to use your beautiful brains and think.'

'Think about what?' Georgina felt irritated. Molly could be so dreadfully American. Jonathan was American, but then he was a Boston Brahman and Boston Brahmans were often more English than the English. Jonathan did not even have what most people took for a Boston accent. He never said *kah* for *car* or *bah* for *bar*. If he did, Georgina would not have considered marrying him. Jonathan's *R*s were closer to *caw* and *baw*, in the mid-atlantic tradition. Molly, however, had a strong New Jersey accent. To Georgina, she sounded like a crow with a stick up its bottom. The thought made Georgina laugh.

'It will do us good to get out for an evening,' Fatima said in her precise English. 'I worry too much about Majid and I am worrying too much about the end of term papers.'

Glenda did not want to join them. She wanted to wait for Clive to call. Molly gave Glenda a slit-eyed look. 'Don't sit around the phone waiting for Clive to call,' she said. 'Make yourself unavailable. It'll do him good to know that you've gone out. Get someone to take a message. Get Sonia to tell him you're out with some friends.'

Glenda gave in. She felt tired of the wait. If she stayed in she would only strain to hear the telephone. If he telephones, he telephones, she thought. I can always ring him back.

Molly drove everyone to a pub a little way out of the city. She parked and they walked up the path to the front door. The pub, called the Black Raven, was small but warmly lit. 'What'll you have, ladies?' the barman called.

Molly tossed back her mane of hair and licked her lips. She never stops, Glenda thought, never. Not even with the barman and he looks about ninety years old.

Fatima ordered orange juice, Georgina a gin and tonic, and Glenda settled for half a pint of bitter. Molly, after much flirting and teasing and leaning on the bar, decided to drink a Bloody Mary. 'Not a virgin Bloody Mary,' she said loudly to the barman. 'Leave that to the others.' She nodded at the table.

Georgina rolled her eyes and Glenda felt her face freeze. Only Fatima looked serene. 'Molly would get on well with Fat Aunt,' Fatima observed. 'Both infidel women.'

Molly brought her drink back to the table. 'I heard that, Fatima,' she said. 'And I'll drink to infidelity.' She sipped her Bloody Mary. 'Now, let's all talk about the idea of sharing our men and swearing to become Souls forever.'

'I don't want to share Clive with any other woman. That seems a silly idea to me.'

'Very silly,' Georgina seconded.

Fatima surprised everybody. 'Eastern women are used to sharing their men,' she said. 'Not that I particularly want to share Majid, but if he decides to take a second wife, I won't stop him. I will always be his first wife. I don't want to have so many children, like other women in my country. Two, a boy and a girl, would be fine for me. But if Majid wants more, he can have another wife. And later on, when I no longer want to make love – if that happens – he can take a much younger wife. I don't mind.'

Molly shook her head. 'You Eastern women are really

something. You and your ideas of how to treat a man.'

Fatima sipped her orange juice and Glenda saw her glance at Molly. No wonder Eastern women are so attractive to men, Glenda thought. Fatima's eyes were brimming with liquid. They were soft and gentle, but, as Fatima continued to gaze at Molly, Glenda could see that Fatima concealed a very passionate nature behind the cool, well-dressed facade. 'We know many things, my dear Molly. We keep many secrets behind our masks. Out in the world we are covered from head to foot. Only the ankle can show for a minute, or the eyes. That is all we have to attract a man. So we learn at a very young age how to use both to our advantage. We learn how to cook or how to train our cooks. The man comes home after a hard day in the other world. Once inside his compound, he has his wife to make the nights pleasant. She pours scented water over his hands. She rubs his feet with sandalwood. She massages his back. And then she licks sherbet from his stomach and his private parts.'

Glenda paused mid-sip. 'Sherbet?' she said, scandalized.

Fatima smiled a quiet self-contained smile. 'You Western women know nothing about love. So many of you only know sex.' Her eyes touched briefly on Molly. There was laughter in Fatima's eyes. 'Sex is not love; sex is for animals. Love is pure and beautiful. Love is food and song and feeling and touching.'

'Then I suppose simple fucking is out of the question,' Molly shot in.

Fatima smiled again. 'We make love. We are taught to make love by the older women in the compound. But love is not like you understand it. Look at the words you have to describe the communion of souls. As you say, you *fuck*.' She wrinkled her nose. 'A cruel word, from the Middle Dutch *fokken*, meaning "to strike". Hitting. That's what your fucking is all about. Where is there love of woman, or the touch of a man's thigh?'

'Fine, Fatima,' said Molly. 'You win. I'll try some of this

Eastern stuff. Next time I screw a rugger bugger, I'll dump a load of sherbet on his dick and see what happens. I'll go into Mrs Henley's candy store, or sweet shop as you Brits call it, and I'll say, "Good morning, Mrs Henley. Can I please have half a pound of sherbet in a little paper bag for my next blow job?" I can hear Mrs Henley now: "Any particular flavour, dearie?"'

'Most amusing, Molly dear,' Fatima laughed. 'And, as you use the word bugger, you do know, of course, the derivation: it comes from the French *bougre*, which itself is from the Latin *Bulgarus*, meaning Bulgarian, because in the Ancient World, the Bulgarians were well-known infidels. Which brings us back to you, Molly.'

'No shit?' Molly said. 'Aren't *you* the walking dictionary tonight?'

'It is the mark of ignorance to shun somebody else's education,' Fatima said with a smile. 'Anyway,' she finished her orange juice, 'I feel very strongly that women should be close to each other. I find in the West that life is very cold without that warmth and strength. There are the four of us and we should agree to be friends for the rest of our lives. Even if some of us are more infidel than others,' she said with a glance to Molly, but the glance was affectionate.

'I agree with that,' Glenda said, looking around the table. 'I would always want to feel that the four of us are more than just friends, that we'll always be there for each other.'

'Absolutely,' Georgina said. 'Anyway, Jonathan is so straight, he'd never play around. And with all the free-love hippyism going on at Harvard Square, Jonathan has remained steadfastly Jonathan. Maybe that's why I love him – he's so predictable.'

Glenda thought about Clive. Had he telephoned while they were sitting there? Would he be dreadfully disappointed that she wasn't in?

She was relieved when the bell sounded for the last round.

254

Molly bought the last drinks. 'Shall we drink to the four of ourselves as Souls?'

'Oh no,' Georgina groaned.

Fatima looked dubious. 'This doesn't mean we have to take a blood oath that "Every woman shall have her man; but no man shall have his woman", does it?'

'If you're really opposed to the idea, I guess not,' Molly conceded. 'We can be Souls in any way we want to be Souls. It can mean whatever we want, just for us. Like "the Cambridge ladies who live in furnished souls are unbeautiful and have comfortable minds."'

Glenda laughed. 'That's a good one. Sounds like a quotation from something.'

'e.e. cummings, actually,' Georgina joined in. 'Very good, Molly. I didn't know you could quote.'

Molly bowed her head graciously, as if accepting a stage ovation. 'I didn't get to Cambridge on beauty alone, you know.'

Fatima could not help letting out a chuckle.

'Well, here's one for you,' Georgina shot back. 'From Donne, this is.

And now good morrow to our waking souls,
Which watch not one another out of fear;
For love, all love of other sights controls,
And makes one little room, an everywhere.
Let sea-discoverers to new worlds have gone,
Let maps to others, worlds on worlds have shown,
Let us possess one world, each hath one, and is one.'

'Why, Georgina,' said Molly with a wide smile. 'You make me quiver all over. That's positively romantic!'

'Hm,' Georgina agreed. 'Not a bad product of the great British reserve, wouldn't you say?' All four friends laughed.

'Okay then,' said Molly, raising her glass. 'Do we agree? We'll be Souls, and stay friends for ever.'

'Then count me in,' Georgina said, raising her glass.

'Let's promise,' said Glenda, 'when we leave Girton, that we'll try to meet at least once a year.'

'One day,' Fatima added, 'we might all meet in Turaq.'

'I'll drink to that,' Molly said. They sipped from their glasses. When she had swallowed, Molly said, 'And you'll give us a live demonstration with the sherbet, huh?'

Fatima pointed a finger at Molly. 'I'll do more than that. I'll get Fat Aunt to show you the oldest position in *The Book of the Minarets*.'

'Yeah? Tell me about it now.'

Fatima laughed harder. 'A secret is a secret, Molly. You have a lot to learn. There are a thousand positions and the greatest of all is one called "The Ten Thousand Winds of Heaven."'

Molly, her mind quickly trying to imagine, was speechless.

'Come on.' Glenda hurried them up to the car.

All the way back she sat in silence while the others discussed the Christmas holidays. Once they were back in college, she ran to find Sonia. 'Yes, he did telephone,' Sonia said. 'He left this number and said to telephone him no matter what time you return. Honestly, Glenda, how can you be so blighted by a mere male?'

'You wouldn't know,' Glenda found herself saying. She got to the telephone and dialled.

'Where have you been?' Clive's voice was breathless and shaky.

'Oh, Clive, I went out for a drink with Molly and the girls. I'm awfully sorry.' Why am I sorry? she thought. I haven't done anything wrong.

'I thought something awful might have happened to you, Glenda. I've been so worried.'

'But I'm fine, Clive. Really. How was your day?'

'Not very good.' He sounded miserable.

Glenda wished she could fly into town and comfort him. 'What happened?'

'Nothing much, just a touch of the black dog.'

'The black dog?'

'Oh, it's nothing really. Just a bit of the doldrums. It walks in and sits beside me. I can't shake it off.'

'Do you want to collect me tomorrow? I'm free after four o'clock.'

'Yes. That would be good.' Clive's voice sounded a little less desperate. 'Don't be out, Glenda. Will you?'

She could hear the small abandoned boy pleading in this man's voice. 'Of course not, Clive.'

'Good night then, Glenda.'

'Good night, Clive.' She very much wanted to call him darling, but she was too shy. She put the phone down first and then wished she hadn't. I must learn to be more careful, she thought. He really is very sensitive.

Chapter 59

Clive seemed preoccupied when he picked Glenda up outside the gates of Girton. 'Everything all right?' she nervously asked.

He looked tired and strained. There were fine lines about his pale blue eyes. 'I'm okay,' he said shortly, and then, as Glenda climbed onto the bike, he threw over his shoulder an invitation to visit his mother next weekend. 'I've never taken a girl home,' he said. They zoomed off towards the city.

The wind screamed in Glenda's ears. She hugged the thought of the visit. She wanted so much to find out more about this mysterious man. Now the days and the nights for Glenda were filled with the magic of being alive. She found herself reciting bits of poetry, riding her bike by herself over to Grantchester, taking a picnic and sitting with her back up against one of the graves, wandering around the church fascinated by its history and by the fact that Rupert Brooke was commemorated there. How marvellous, she thought, that this beautiful young poet could write such compelling poetry! How like Clive he looked, she thought.

Nobody else at Cambridge that she knew refused to discuss their futures. Clive alone insisted that he had no future. 'I will have to run the family estate until mother tips me out,' was as far as he would go. Glenda tried to find other sides of him by asking him what he read. 'Jack Kerouac is the only person worth reading,' he would reply.

Now they were going off to meet some of Clive's friends.

They pulled up outside a fly-blown cafe, the sort of cafe that was abundant in Hounslow. But it had none of the friendly charm of Joe's Cafe where she and Minnie used to sit with Phil Clough. This cafe had a naked bulb dangling from the ceiling above a long grey counter that was covered by grey smeared glass. Under the glass were some ancient-looking doughnuts. There were five tables, each with four rickety chairs. The tablecloths were green checked oilskin. The decor had not changed in the last twenty years. Plastic daffodils stood in green plastic pots on the tables. They were covered with dust and smudges of tomato ketchup, no doubt hurled by offended customers. On each table there were empty cruets and bulbous plastic tomatoes brown-edged with ketchup. At one table four people sat and looked up expectantly when Clive came in.

Glenda thought she had arrived at a freak show. Maybe, she thought, this is one of Molly's silly pranks dreamed up with her arty-farty theatre group. The tall, lank man in a jumper which looked even more threadbare than Clive's pullover stood up. He was dirty and smelled like a goat. Oh no, Glenda inwardly groaned. One of those dreadful existentialists who wear berets on their thin greasy hair and keep soggy fags hanging out of their mouths.

'Glenda, this is Bix,' Clive introduced. And Clive, she noticed, had the same expression on his face as when she had met him in the pub during Cyril's communist meeting, an expression that showed intelligence, vulnerability, humour, and a mind full of secrets. There was something in the expression that Glenda found irresistible.

'Glenda?' Bix put out a long unwashed hand. Bix's expression was anything but attractive. No, she realized. He might not be an existentialist after all; he might just be genuinely grotty.

Glenda did not want to touch the hand or inspect the dirty-rimmed finger nails. 'Glenda,' she confirmed and, being polite, she took his hand.

'Sheila,' he introduced with a jerk of his head.

Sheila sat next to him at the table. Sheila was a conspicuous leftover from the Fifties. She had a high beehive and a figure-hugging, V-necked jersey outlining her big breasts that were straining like two poodles on a tight leash.

'Hello,' Glenda said, thinking, I escaped Hounslow only to find Hounslow has now moved to Cambridge.

'And there are Stella and Ken,' Clive carried on with the introductions. Stella looked at Glenda through rat-thin eyes. Ken just nodded. He had a bad case of National Health teeth. Maybe, Glenda thought charitably, I can grow to like these people. Maybe.

Clive pushed a chair out for her and she sat down. 'Coffee?' Clive asked.

'Thanks,' Glenda said. She sat looking at these people and promised herself she would find something good about each one of them. Stella, whom mentally she dubbed Rat Face, was going to be the most difficult. Glenda wished she was back at Girton. Some of the girls there were ugly, but at least most of them were clever and interesting. ''Ow you been, Clive?' Sheila asked.

Glenda winced. I hope I never sounded like that, she thought, even when I lived in Hounslow. Clive turned his head from the counter. He had called for an order for coffee through a not very reassuring hole in the wall. 'Not too bad,' Clive said. 'How about yourself?' Clive sounded as if he was talking to the workers on his estate. Maybe that's why he likes these people, Glenda reasoned. The estate boys were his only friends during his early years, he had told her. His brother Caspar was too busy out mutilating things to spend much time with Clive.

Bix grinned. His multicoloured teeth were enormous. ''Ow's the bike?'

'She's great.' Clive returned to the table with two cups of coffee. The coffee was greasy and almost cold, but she forced it down. Glenda gazed into the cups and listened to the talk rattle on about motorbikes. Soon it was time to take to the road.

'Where are we going?' Glenda asked apprehensively.

'Say, everyone. Shall we take a run out to Ely and drop in on Gerontius?' Clive asked. 'Anyone else in the mood for chilli and corned beef hash?'

'How do you know he'll have chilli and hash?' Glenda said.

Ken laughed. 'Gerontius *always* has a pot of chilli and hash on the simmer. You're in fer a treat. 'E cooks really good, dun'e, Clive?'

'Yes,' Clive answered. 'For an old beatnik relic from the Fifties.'

Then Glenda understood why she had been brought to this awful cafe. It was the appeal of the Fifties, of everything that was dreadful and tacky about that era. Cheap and shoddy, Glenda thought as they left the place. The three bikes stretched across the road, only unwillingly giving way to oncoming cars. Glenda felt suddenly silly and awkward as she clung nervously to Clive. Why couldn't he have a comfortable car like everybody else? Why, when he's supposed to be so rich, does Clive have such a dreary set of rooms? Except for his piano and books, no money was spent on anything. The bikes hurled themselves out of the city, across the fens, heading for Ely.

Glenda hoped very much that she might get a chance to see inside Ely Cathedral, but she rather doubted it. And anyway, she was not sure she would want to be seen in

260

the company of such derelicts. At least Clive is clean, she comforted herself.

Once in the small streets of Ely they parked outside a small row of cottages. Gerontius evidently had heard the roar of the three motorcycle engines, and stood at the doorway to greet them. Gerontius Glenda knew only from Clive's description. He was an American. No connection to *The Hound of Heaven* by Francis Thompson, Clive had explained, but a much loved friend who knew it all. Glenda hoped she would like him.

Looking at him, Glenda could see why Clive had described him as the original Kerouac fan. He must have been at least fifty and he was dressed in a huge leather biking jacket and greasy blue jeans. On his feet he wore tattered sneakers. 'Used to be a stable for horses,' Gerontius said, indicating the house as he let them in. The American's voice was nasal and had such a twang Glenda was reminded of a guitar string plucked the wrong way. They followed his forbidding bulk into a small, square sitting room.

Glenda looked around. It could have been a very pretty little cottage, she thought. Next to the sitting room was a small kitchen leading out onto a tiny lawn. But it was obvious that Gerontius had no housekeeping attributes at all. The place was filthy. Gerontius obviously never went upstairs to sleep, because grey sheets lay on top of the sofa. Next to it was the burnt-out shell of a chair. Dishes and plates with rinds of food lay about the floor. 'I'll put a light under the pot,' Gerontius said and squeezed his huge self into the kitchen. 'Chilli and hash okay for everyone?'

Everyone let out a happy groan of yes, as if they had awaited and finally heard a favourite refrain.

The guests sank onto the floor and waited. Gerontius came back with two bottles of red wine. 'Californian,' he said. 'Get it from the PX.' He handed Clive some dirty glasses.

Clive smiled. The bottles were already open and the wine

smelled sour. 'Go on, Glenda,' Rat-faced Stella said. ''ave a glass. It won't hurt you none.'

'I don't drink during the day,' Glenda said, trying to recall a time when she had felt less at ease. She wanted to add 'I never drink with people like you' but she bit her lip. She very much wished Molly was here. Molly would fit in perfectly and would somehow make the occasion fun.

They all sat rather self-consciously around the floor finding nothing to say. Glenda realized miserably that it was perhaps her fault. They knew she did not like them. They certainly did not like her. Only Gerontius was oblivious. He was kindly and fat. His chilli was hot and to her surprise Glenda found she liked it and finally she rather liked him.

He began a long conversation with Clive about California. 'Dig it,' he said. 'When you hit the road all along Big Sur, you are flying, man. Totally flying. Like some crazy seagull or something. You got the cliffs on one side of you, and the wide open sea on the other. Just like a seagull, man. Or even like an albatross.'

Clive's eyes glittered with excitement. 'I've got to see that,' he said.

As Gerontius talked, Glenda found herself, like Clive, caught up in his descriptions. She imagined the huge Californian sun setting outside the window in Ely. She heard the long blue rolling waves break outside in the street. 'Even the Pigs are good-natured there,' Gerontius said. 'Pretty much. They leave bikers alone. They know we have our own code, just like they have their own Fuzz code. But it's cool. We don't shit on them and they don't shit on us. And we're good to our chicks.'

When it was time to go Clive went out to rev up the bike. Glenda helped Gerontius carry the plates back into the kitchen. 'You serious about that guy?' Gerontius's eyes peered at her.

'Yes,' Glenda said.

Gerontius shook his big head. 'Well, sister, it must be in your karma.'

'What does that mean?' Glenda asked rather sharply.

'Hey, I don't know if I would tell you, even if I could. I mean, I can't interfere with your karma. It would affect mine.'

'Oh.' Glenda felt put out. 'I see.'

He put a big hand on her shoulder. 'The road will be hard, darlin',' he said. 'You sure you're ready?'

Glenda smiled and pulled away. 'Must run. I hear Clive calling.'

'Okay, man. See you again.'

'Later, alligator,' Glenda shouted as she ran through the door.

On the way back to college Glenda decided she hoped she would see Gerontius again. The others she could do quite happily without.

Chapter 60

On the way back Glenda asked herself why, in particular, she disliked Clive's friends so much. Perhaps it was because, if she had not struggled for so many years, she could have been sitting on the other side of the table, like Stella and Sheila. The thought was agonizing. How narrowly she had escaped the awful trap that divided England so neatly and surgically down the middle! The Haves versus the Have-nots. It was particularly painful when a Have-not battled her way up and vaulted over the line dividing the two. For a Have-not to decamp meant an ever-present sense of the pit below. Georgina, Fatima, and Molly never even thought about the division. For them the world was a certain place. Their lifestyles were fixed and immutable. For Glenda, however, the fine line trembled and swayed in a wind of uncertainty. And sitting facing her were her accusers: Stella and Ken, Bix and Sheila. They knew she was really one of them, and no amount of clean underwear or expensive clothes donated by Renée and Abe could hide her sisterhood.

Glenda clung to Clive's back and waited until the bike shuddered to a halt outside the Girton porter's house. 'I'll let you off here,' Clive said. 'It's late and I don't want to wake anybody up.' He hopped off the bike and helped her off.

Glenda looked at his pale face. How kind he is, she thought. 'Clive,' she asked nervously, 'why do you like those people so much? I mean, I can see why you like Gerontius. But Ken, and Bix, and . . . ?'

Clive laughed. 'I like them because they are other.'

'Other?'

'Other. Other than my brother Caspar and his aristocratic, barbarian friends. Other than little debs who go around calling themselves Caroline Snoddington-Snodbury and only worry about what to wear at Ascot.'

'And am I other?' she asked.

'Yes. In a way, I suppose you are. But . . .'

'And is that why you like me?'

'No, Glenda.' He smiled warmly. 'I like Glenda because she's Glenda.' He squeezed her body in a comfortable embrace. He paused, then said, 'I like them because they accept me. Gerontius knew Jack Kerouac, you know. *Actually* knew him! Marvellous man and writer. As for Bix and the others, they simply accept me.'

'Cyril and Henry accept you, don't they? Molly accepts you . . .'

Clive said 'Yes' in a small voice and then he breathed as if a butterfly was fighting in his chest. 'But Ken and Stella and the others don't think I'm mad.' The last sentence burst forth as though the thought had been held far too long.

Glenda touched his cheek. 'Don't be silly, Clive. You're not mad at all. Why do you say that?'

'Because my mother thinks I'm mad. Everybody in my

family thinks I'm mad, bad, and evil.' He laughed. 'Not much of a write-up, is it?'

Glenda felt furiously angry. She, to her immense surprise, found herself pulling Clive into her arms and holding him fiercely. 'You're not mad or bad. You're nothing of the sort. I won't even let you say those things about yourself. Whatever happens, I'm your friend, and I'll see that nobody ever harms you. There is nothing wrong with you, Clive.' She stopped and let her arms fall to her side. There was a moment of silence and she saw tears come up in Clive's eyes.

'You don't know me very well yet, Glenda. You think you do but you don't. Nanny's right: I have these funny "turns", as she calls them. It isn't a doctor I go to see, you know, it's a psychiatrist. He says I'm a borderline personality. And I have these injections. If I don't have them, I go off the wall.' The tears were now suddenly running down his face.

'Clive,' she said, startled. 'Clive. Really, it's all right. You've just been a bit lonely, that's all.' Glenda put her arm loosely around his shoulders. 'Don't cry, Clive. You have me now and I'll look after you.'

Clive looked at her through the blur of his tears. 'No girl's ever said that to me before. You're right. I have been lonely.' His voice dropped to a whisper. 'You can't imagine what it's like to feel as if your head is about to explode. To feel that you're possessed by a raging demon that makes you do all sorts of things you don't want to do. When walls talk to you and trees scream. You feel that there are eyes everywhere watching you and whispering about you.' Clive trembled.

'It's all over, Clive. I'm here now. You have me.' Glenda pulled him gently close and they stood quietly. 'I know what this is about. It's about your mother, isn't it? You're nervous about us seeing her this weekend.'

He nodded his head.

'Well, don't worry. We'll handle your mother together.'

Clive stiffened. 'She's a very tough woman, my mother. No one gets the better of her.'

'No one needs to get the better of her,' Glenda said sooth-ingly. 'I just intend to see that you don't suffer. You should meet my mum, if you think your mother's tough. Minnie – that's my mother's name – she's the toughest woman I've ever known. But in a good way.'

'I'd love to meet her some day.'

'You shall.' She hugged his body and kissed him on the lips. 'You'll be all right?'

Clive kissed her back and in his kiss she felt a real yearning.

A yearning for what? she thought as she walked up the drive. Not even for sex. More a yearning to belong. A sense of longing. A need to find a safe harbour. Well I can be that, she thought resolutely. I certainly can be that for him. He so much needs protecting.

Chapter 61

The Alexander family house was beautifully situated between two cedars of Lebanon and vast rolling lawns. The drive up to the huge oak door was immaculate. Two men were raking the gravel as Clive's motorbike swept past. One of them shouted, 'Welcome home, sir!'

Clive waved. 'Thanks, George!' he yelled and they con-tinued up the drive, finally coming to rest in front of the massive porticoes of what once had been a fortress. 'Yes,' Clive said as he saw the surprise in Glenda's eyes. 'The old homestead was a fourteenth century fortified castle. Bits of it still remain, such as the turrets. He waved his hand and Glenda looked upwards.

Together the turrets and the jagged battlements atop the stone building created an atmosphere of austere strength, permanence and impenetrability. Glenda felt as if the staunch facade before her was the Alexander family itself: unwelcom-ing, prepared to do battle, and certainly not impressed by a creature of her smallness.

She shivered but said nothing. After all her bragging to Clive that she could take care of him, she could not afford to let herself get rattled at this stage.

George hurried up behind them and took the two shoulder bags off the back of the bike. 'Park it in the garage in its usual place, George, will you?'

'Yes, sir.' George tugged at his cap and Glenda smiled. Having people to run after you like that would take some getting used to, she thought.

An elderly, shrivelled man came down the wide stone stairs outside the house. 'Glad to see you again, sir.' The man had an air of polished ivory, yellow and faded, as if he seldom saw the sun. His eyes squinted in the daylight. The lids were pink and they fluttered nervously. 'Let me take the bags, sir,' he said and they followed him into the huge cavernous doorway which led in to the big square hall.

Glenda stood transfixed. From all the walls, animal heads gazed down at her with button-black eyes. All of them entombed in their final death throes. She was appalled. There were giant deer heads, fox heads, badgers' paws and tails divorced from bodies, and a tremendous eagle posed in mid-flight.

Clive said, 'That's Caspar and my father for you. I told you: they murder anything that moves. Looks like a wildlife graveyard, don't you think? Come on. Let's find your room. Thomas,' he said to the old man, 'where has Gwen put my guest?'

Thomas shuffled his feet. 'In the green room.'

'Ha!' Clive cried with bitter amusement. 'That would be mother's doing. She's given you a whole suite to yourself.'

Glenda laughed. 'I don't mind,' she said, wondering what a whole suite was. 'It'll be nice to have some space after the tiny rooms in college.'

'There you are, Miss,' Thomas said cheerfully.

'Oh, I see.' Stretching before Glenda was virtually the

whole wing of the castle. 'How magnificent!' she breathed. The green room was a series of rooms running across the fort. She walked to the window and looked out on the scarred remains of centuries of war. Beyond the ramparts she could see a perfectly kept Italian belvedere. She knew about landscaping from the coffee-table books Renée had in her drawing room. 'Isn't that beautiful? How absolutely wonderful!' She stood at the window, watching the evening light draw its fingers wearily over the park below. At the end of the belvedere was the glint of water and in the air the sounds of a few cold lonely crows making noises before retiring to their nests. There were no lights outside. No other houses. Just the vague shapes of a herd of cows and the rumble of the bull calling his females to his side.

'I'll send Milly up to unpack and draw your bath,' Thomas said.

He left the suite. Clive and Glenda were alone together.

'You're going to inherit all this?' Glenda asked.

'Not if my mother can help it. She wants it all to go to my brother Caspar.'

'And what does your father want?'

'I don't know,' Clive said. 'He thinks I'm a wimp and a waster. And he does whatever my mother tells him to do. We *all* do what she wants us to do. Anyway, I'd better go and change for dinner.' He smiled at her for a moment, then left the room.

Glenda was glad she had borrowed several dinner dresses off Georgina. Thank goodness for Georgina!

It was Georgina who coached her through the tortuous ways of the country weekend. 'Don't tip until you leave,' she reminded Glenda before she set out. 'And when the hostess gets up after pudding, you leave with her. Don't talk about sex, religion, or politics.'

'You don't have to worry about sex,' Molly helpfully chipped in. 'Your British upper crusts don't know anything about sex.'

Glenda wished Molly was with her now. Dear, brash Molly, with her directness, but warm heart.

There was a small knock on the door. 'It's Milly, Miss Stanhope.' The young woman entered. 'I've come to run your bath and turn down the bed. First I'll put your things away.'

'Don't bother to do that, Milly,' Glenda smiled. 'Anyway, do call me Glenda.'

Milly's face stiffened. 'I can't do that, Miss.'

'Why not?' Glenda said cheerfully. 'We're both about the same age.'

'Yes, Miss, but Madam would never allow. I'd be in awful trouble.' Her voice dropped.

'Oh, I understand. Then I'm stuck with Miss, I suppose.'

'Thank you, Miss.' Milly went over to the massive oak bed. Glenda wished she had borrowed one of Georgina's leather suitcases. Her Co-op shoulderbag looked shabby and tacky sitting on the wine-red counterpane.

Milly expertly unpacked and then asked, 'Which dress shall you be wearing for dinner, Miss?'

'The black one, I think.' Glenda looked on, feeling helpless.

Milly picked up a pair of panties and, smoothing them professionally, laid them beside the dress on the bed. Glenda was unused to anyone except her mother touching her personal underwear, and here was an absolute stranger calmly handling what had hitherto been entirely private in Glenda's life. 'Shall I draw your bath while you undress?'

Glenda's case was now sitting on a luggage rack at the far end of the bedroom. The bag seemed to leer at Glenda. 'Er, no. But thank you,' Glenda said swiftly. 'I can manage to run my own bath. You needn't do that. I can do it for myself.' She found herself tripping over words in an effort not to sound rude. No one except Minnie had ever seen Glenda without her clothes on and that had been many years ago. How on earth did these people live? she marvelled. Did they think that the people working for them had no feelings?

'Really,' she said quickly. 'I'll be fine.'

'All right, Miss,' Milly said uncertainly. 'I'll leave you now. The gong will sound twice. One is the ten-minute warning, and the second is to tell everybody to get to the refectory before Madam arrives. She does not tolerate lateness.'

'What will she do to me? Lock me up in a tower?' Glenda laughed. She stopped laughing as she saw the look of fear in Milly's eyes. 'Sorry,' she apologized. 'I didn't mean to be rude.'

Milly shook her head and glided to the door. She gazed sombrely at Glenda. 'Nobody,' she said softly, 'ever laughs at Madam. It's not safe, Miss. Not safe at all.'

She shut the door quietly, leaving Glenda standing in the middle of the room feeling foolish. I'd better watch what I say, she thought. And she busied herself getting ready for dinner.

Chapter 62

The gong sounded and Glenda felt very flustered. She wore Georgina's black taffeta evening gown. The dress fitted her waist, for Georgina was as slender as Glenda, but it was a little long since Georgina was a few inches taller. Still, Glenda thought, no one will know. She wore her Marks and Spencer's knickers under her Marks and Spencer's black lacy petticoat. Thank goodness for Marks and Spencer's!

She was thinking about Molly when she heard the first gong and then a knock on the door. 'Ready?' Clive pushed his head around the door.

Glenda looked at him in awe. 'You look smashing,' she said, forgetting her attempts at posh English. 'Simply smashing, Clive.'

Clive grinned. He was wearing a black dinner jacket, a plain white shirt with a stiff front, and a crimson cummerbund. His black bow-tie sat under his chin, a model of perfect decorum. He did look wonderful. She felt a powerful surge of attraction for him. 'I feel like an idiot,' he said, 'but the old bag insists on it. We all have to change for dinner every evening.'

'What's wrong with that?' Glenda asked as they hurried down the corridor.

'It's a bloody bore, that's what's wrong. But you look beautiful, I must say.' And he gave her a quick kiss behind her ear. She giggled.

Glenda didn't have much time to look at the magnificent paintings that hung on the walls or the elaborately coloured carpets that lay on the floors. All she knew was that she was now walking with jewels in her eyes from the colours in the paintings and her feet trod on magic as they moved swiftly down apparently endless halls. Finally Clive led her into a sitting room, like one of the many they had passed, but this one was set out for a pre-dinner drink. Two footmen in blue and white livery stood silently by the door.

Inside, the small bamboo tables beside the Chinese lacquered chairs held silver dishes with delicate canapés. Glenda looked at them with wonder. How many hours must it have taken to make those puffballs of delight? Even Minnie could not make anything so wonderful. Glenda could see little piles of caviar. Hard little black balls which must be the Russian, and on another tray sat little boat-shaped pastries filled with grey caviar. That must be from the Caspian Sea, she thought feeling proud of her lessons from Renée and Abe. At least all those years of being taught table manners meant that she could hold her own in this huge house. The size intimidated her and so did the two people bearing down upon them at this moment.

With a gasp she realized that Lord Philip Alexander looked exactly like his brother Caspar Alexander, QC, whom she remembered from her childhood. The same rolling gait, vast belly, and thick blubbery lips. He smiled at Glenda. 'Hullo,' he said quite nicely. 'So, Clive old son,' without taking his porcine eyes off Glenda, 'finally declaring your stake in manhood, are you?'

'*Really*, father,' said Clive.

'And you've chosen y'self a fine looking girl to do it with,' Lord Philip continued, unperturbed. 'Tell me, my dear. What do you and my son have to talk about? D'ya hunt?'

For a moment Glenda felt nonplussed. 'No, I don't actually.'

'Well then, that's one thing the two of you have in common. D'ya shoot?'

'No.'

'Of course not, my dear. Of course you don't. Not a feminine creature such as you. Painting's more for you, is it?' His Lordship inquired hopefully. 'Lovely little water-colours of the countryside, that sort of thing?'

Glenda shook her head.

'Then I'm at a loss. What *do* you do?'

'Well,' Glenda hesitated. 'I've always liked to read.'

Lord Philip nodded with difficulty, as if he did not catch her meaning. 'Books?' He looked uncertain. 'Yes, Clive was always one for the books. And that piano of his, too. But surely you don't sit reading all day. What else can you do?'

There was a silence and Glenda looked at the floor. She was aware of Clive by her side. He, too, was silent. They looked at each other. Then Glenda took in a deep breath and gazed at Lord Philip Alexander. 'I *think*,' she said. 'That is what I do.'

'Really?' Philip's voice throbbed with astonishment. 'You *think*. How extraordinary! Thinking! Do you hear that, my dear?' he called across the room. 'Clive's young lady friend says she *thinks*.'

His Lordship stuffed his mouth with a canapé and the flakes of pastry fell down his dinner jacket. He had a monocle dangling on his fat stomach.

'No doubt she does.' The quiet voice was Lady Jane Alexander's. She was bony and thin. She wore, to Glenda's surprise, a pair of spandex tights under her black dinner jacket. The neck of the shirt was open. At her neck hung a huge square-cut emerald. Between the fingers of her right hand was a very long black cigarette holder encircled with diamonds. I am *sure* they're diamonds, Glenda thought. 'Do be seated, my dear,' said Lady Jane.

Glenda sat down on an overstuffed brocade chair. She felt the slither of the material against her thighs. 'And,' Clive's mother continued as she beckoned forward one of the footmen, 'what would you like to drink?'

'A gin and tonic, please,' Glenda said. Actually she would much rather have had a soft drink, but a gin and tonic seemed the only answer in a room like this. Georgina, she knew, would have asked for a gin and tonic. This evening Glenda kept an invisible Georgina beside her to serve as her model for how to behave.

'With lemon or lime?' Lady Jane's eyes narrowed. This little tart will be easy, she thought. No family behind this one.

'Lime.'

Lord Alexander wandered out of the circle to the window. 'Don't know what's become of the young these days,' Glenda could hear him muttering. 'Too much thinking. Taxes the mind, it does. Now in my day, one had hunt balls to worry about.'

Glenda wanted to laugh and did not dare look at Clive. He sat back in his chair rather as if he was in the nursery with Nanny Jenkins. Then Glenda realized that Clive had been doing this evening ritual for years, coming down first with Nanny Jenkins by the hand and later on his own. What an ordeal, what a ghastly ordeal for him! She looked at Lady Jane. The woman gazed back. There was nothing in those eyes, Glenda concluded, but malice. It was evil that kept this woman alive. Vicious, plotting evil.

'And are you related to the divine Stanhopes that live in Buckinghamshire?' Jane's eyebrows had risen. Take that, you common little girl, the left eyebrow was now saying.

Glenda sat still. She knows I'm not, her heart argued. *Let 'er 'ave it!* she heard Minnie's voice in her ear. *Let the mean-arsed bitch have it!* 'No,' Glenda said calmly. 'I'm not related to anyone. I have no dad and me mum is an 'ousekeeper.'

'I see.' The right eyebrow now joined the left and they quivered so much that Glenda wondered if they could fly from Lady Jane's forehead and go off into the night air as bats.

'Come on, mother.' Clive's voice was impatient. 'Must we have the third degree? Glenda is my friend, and we don't all have to be spawned in the top drawer, you know. Who decides who's in the top drawer anyway?'

Jane was about to answer when there was a loud thudding of feet. The huge figure rushing into the dining room was Caspar, Clive's brother. Caspar looked exactly like old Lord Alexander, only younger.

'Sorry I'm late, mother.' Caspar bent over Jane's chair. He gave his mother an audibly juicy kiss that exploded in the quiet room. Glenda was relieved that her drink was arriving. The second footman handed her a black caviar canapé on a dish and she took it.

'Mother would make life hell if *I* was ever late,' Clive whispered.

'Don't worry about it,' Glenda said comfortingly. 'Anyway, what can she do? She can't shoot you, can she?'

Clive smiled. He had been watching Glenda when she spoke to his mother and he was amazed to find she was not afraid of her. In fact he felt Glenda rather enjoyed the odd barney. He did not. Quarrels and tensions made him dreadfully ill.

'Let's go in to dinner,' Lord Alexander walked across to Glenda and took her by the arm. 'Come along, little thinker.' He tucked Glenda's arm under his. Glenda felt as if she was a small London tugboat trying to negotiate with a large foreign oil-tanker.

'This way,' Philip said, firmly pulling Glenda along. 'I do hope we have pheasant for dinner. Shot them myself several weeks ago. Can't eat 'em, you know, 'til you can run a spoon up the backside and see the first maggot.'

Glenda was sickened.

'Didn't know that, did you?' Lord Philip looked down at her face, which Glenda knew was either white or green. She didn't really care which colour she was; she just didn't want to throw up on the nice carpets.

The old man looked down again. Not bad features, he thought. And the hair's good. Not my type, though. But this one had fire in her. Philip had never seen Jane discomfited by a young chip like this one. Might do the old mare some good, he thought.

They stopped in front of an open door. Philip cooed, 'Ah, how wonderful! Food!'

Milly was waiting by the door and Glenda smiled at her. Milly nodded briefly, but her eyes fled to her mistress's face. Lady Jane was angry with Glenda, but she hid her anger by paying attention to Caspar. Clive trailed behind.

'Now, darling,' Jane said to Glenda when they reached the long table, 'you sit next to Philip as our guest of honour. Then the family can fall in.'

She deftly pushed Caspar into the chair next to Glenda and then sat down with Clive isolated on her other side. Once everyone was seated, Milly obediently went off to the kitchen.

And then a parade of dishes appeared as if by magic. Asparagus. Glenda watched nervously and realized that this family ate asparagus with their hands. Renée and Abe used knives and forks, but she was glad she remembered Renée's dictum: watch, and if you don't see how it's done, ask your neighbour. Glenda was determined that she would not have to ask Lord Philip or Lady Jane for anything.

There was not much conversation. In between courses,

Caspar and his father conversed loudly about the various animals which the gamekeeper kept stocked. Soon would come the shoots for Christmas. The pheasant did arrive and Glenda gingerly pushed hers around the plate, attempting to hide it under a wedge of potatoes. 'Delicious, don't you think?' Jane said, grinning.

'Absolutely wonderful,' Glenda replied and took a bite of the thick gamey flesh. Well, she thought as she chewed determinedly, I've made it this far without throwing up.

After the pheasant came roast beef, followed by a sorbet and then fruit and cheese.

No wonder the old man is so fat, Glenda thought. Even Clive must put on weight when he is here. Glenda felt bloated, desperate for fresh air.

'Let the two of us go off and have some girl talk,' Lady Jane declared as the servants cleared the table. 'We'll leave the men to talk shop.'

Glenda looked at Clive who said nothing and had eaten very little. Don't worry, her eyes signalled his. I'm all right.

She stood up and followed Jane back to the Chinese sitting room. 'Another drink?' Jane enquired. The same two footmen stood rock-still in the doorway.

'No, thank you,' Glenda said politely. 'The wine was excellent.' Indeed, Glenda was feeling quite light-headed.

'Tell me, dear. How long have you known Clive?' Jane asked, sitting down and affixing a black Sobranie cigarette to her holder.

'For the last few months.'

'Coffee?' Jane asked. One of the footmen pushed a trolley towards Jane. 'Hurry up!' Jane looked at the man. 'He's far too slow, you know.' Glenda was embarrassed. 'Milk?' Jane asked sweetly. Glenda nodded.

The cups were tiny and the coffee very strong. Glenda wanted to ask for sugar, but decided not to. She was impatient with this woman and bored. She wanted to be with Clive. This was a beautiful house and there was so much to explore.

'Do tell, darling, all about your life at Girton. I never went up, you know. No, too much to do in London. Such fun, before the war ruined everything. They bombed Wheelers. Can you imagine that, bombing Wheelers? I had to move to the White Elephant for lunch after that. Germans are so beastly, don't you think?'

Glenda carefully lowered her coffee cup onto its saucer without making a clinking sound. 'I don't know any Germans, but they can't *all* be beastly.' She watched the corner of Jane's mouth twitch. Ah, she thought, she can't bear to be contradicted.

They chatted until they were joined by the men. 'Come along, Glenda,' Clive said. 'Let's go for a walk. I need some fresh air.' He glared at his mother.

'So do I,' Glenda whispered as they left the room.

'Dear Clive,' she heard Jane saying in her fluting high voice. 'So egalitarian, don't you think?'

Chapter 63

Clive bundled Glenda up in a bulky hunting jacket. The sleeves hung down to her knees, but it was mercifully warm. They slipped out of the front door and Glenda looked nervously up at the turret. The windows were blank.

'Thank God to be out of there,' Clive said. 'Place bothers me, but my psychiatrist says I'm deluded. I often hear voices arguing at night. And horrible sounds, Glenda! I hate staying here. I'm always afraid I'll have one of my turns.'

'You won't while I'm with you, Clive. You won't need to. And it seems perfectly normal to be upset around your family. If your psychiatrist thinks they're so wonderful, maybe he's the one who's deluded.'

Clive let out a great laugh, picked Glenda up in his arms, and whirled around. 'Oh, you're fantastic, Glenda! Really you are.' He put her down and looked into her eyes. 'I've been so very frightened of them, you know. And it gives mother such horrid satisfaction every time I have a turn. That's the worst part of it all. "There! You see, Philip?" she shouts. "The boy can't control himself. You simply must disinherit him. He should never have been born."' Clive dropped his head. 'If your own mother thinks you should have never been born, what right do you have to live?' His voice was torn with sorrow.

Glenda felt his pain go through her. 'Did you ever read Kahlil Gibran?'

Clive shook his head. ''fraid not.'

'Well, I got a copy of one of his books from Fatima. Gibran wrote what he called *The Prophet*. He was Lebanese, and a very religious man. He wrote a poem which I liked so much, I memorized the beginning.

Your children are not your children.
They are the sons and daughters of Life's longing for
    itself.
They come through you but not from you,
And though they are with you yet they belong
    not to you.

Only you can own yourself. You see?'

They were walking down the dark road among the strong old oak trees. The bare branches fanned out over their heads and the moon gleamed a self-satisfied cold gleam, bathing the park in iridescence. 'That's it!' He cried out with such evident glee that Glenda felt herself very much in love, so innocent and boyish and pure Clive seemed. 'You've hit it on the head. "Your children are not your children." Imagine the liberation of that line! If only I could really believe that.'

'But it's true,' she said.

'Glenda, my family is so big and so powerful, and they all stick together like glue. If one of them murdered someone, nothing would happen. We have such a parcel of barristers and judges in the family, he'd be sure to get off.' Clive laughed a high-pitched sound. 'The great British aristocrats are actually a great bunch of psychopaths. Don't you see that? Ever heard of the saying "Judge's Rules"?'

Glenda shook her head.

'Well, in law there are supposed to be rules laid down to protect people. But actually the joke is that there are no rules. The judges are a law unto themselves.' Clive giggled a tenor giggle that frightened Glenda.

'Clive . . .' she began, pressing his hand.

'Don't you see, Glenda?' Clive's eyes were wide in the moonlight. 'That's why I get into such trouble, because I tell the truth. You were right – I'm honest. At least I try to be. I try to say the truth, and what's more, I try to *think* the truth. I try to see what's really happening. But sometimes the truth can be absolutely terrifying, at least in a family like mine. Enough to depress the hell out of me.' He laughed. 'If you tell the truth in a family like mine, then you're the one they say is mad. Tell me I'm not mad, Glenda. Please tell me I'm not.' Clive's mood suddenly became that of a little boy in need of comfort.

'Come on, Clive.' Glenda put her arm around his thin shoulders. His coat was threadbare and he shivered. 'Let's turn round and go back. Of course, you're not mad. And I think you are the only sane one. The rest of them are nuts.' Particularly Jane, she thought, but she did not say this aloud.

'We'll go in through the kitchen,' Clive said, 'and see if Florence will let us have a cup of Ovaltine and some of her biscuits. I love her biscuits.'

Florence was a big smiling woman who was delighted to see Clive. 'Of course, sir,' she said. 'I'm so glad to see you back. It's been a while, hasn't it?' Her round face was innocent of any rebuke.

Glenda realized how much the staff loved Clive. He knew them all and their many relations. Florence made the two cups of Ovaltine in the big kitchen and Glenda wished they could live down there instead of in the glamorous rooms upstairs. The kitchen was still very Victorian. It had two orange double agas for cooking. 'Here.' Florence put the mugs on a tray with a plate of oatmeal biscuits. 'I'm cooking treacle tart for your lunch tomorrow, sir. I know how much you like it.'

Clive's cheeks shone a happy red. 'Florrie, you're a saint.'

She followed Clive up the stairs and along the dark corridors. They reached the green suite and she opened the door. The lamp was lit and the bed was turned down, her nightdress lying on it like a poor relation. Glenda blushed. Damn, she thought, I never thought of that. Was Clive going to ask to make love to her? A moment of panic shook her to her knees. She had no precautions. And anyway she wouldn't know what to do. She did not want a recurrence of the event she had shared with Cyril. Glenda felt fear grip her soul.

'I'll put the tray on the coffee table over here,' Clive said cheerfully. How his moods change! Glenda thought. In the last hour he had gone from near hysteria to being a small boy, and now he was about to drink his Ovaltine quite happily. 'Come and sit down, Glenda. Try one of Florrie's biscuits. She's been with us for ages and she's one of the best cooks in England. Mother wouldn't have it any other way. She always has to have the best. Tomorrow is Saturday and we'll have to put up with her charity friends. Awful bunch, they are.'

'I know what you mean,' she said. 'My mother got involved with raising money for a court case once. So Renée invited all the London rich to help out. Funny lot, most of them were. Some were okay, though.'

'The London rich are occasionally interesting, but the Home Counties crowd should be interred in their tweeds. Positively revolting. All the women look like horses and the men look like beagles with their noses up the ladies' bottoms. I hate them all.'

'Well, we'll make it through tomorrow. It can't be that bad, and we can always have a good giggle afterwards.'

Clive was draining his Ovaltine when he said suddenly, 'Glenda, can I sleep in your bed tonight?'

Glenda was startled. She said, 'How do you mean? *Sleep* as in *sleep*, or . . .'

There was a silence and then Clive grinned. He took Glenda's hand and said with infinite affection in his voice, 'Glenda, I am going to marry you. Ever since the first moment I saw you, I knew you were the only woman I could ever love. I don't want to make it sordid and sleep with you now. Or, for that matter, before we are married. Tomorrow I'll announce it to mother and father, and then we can be formally engaged. Next year I'll be twenty-one. And provided my mother hasn't managed to get me incarcerated or institution-alized, we'll have money and we can get married when we've finished Cambridge.'

Glenda felt tears rising in her eyes. 'You really do want to marry me?' She was awe-struck.

'Yes, I do.' He smiled and pulled her close. 'Sometimes life can be very simple.' He kissed her. Glenda felt as if a shaft of sunlight had entered the room and encircled them both. She felt as if she experienced God's hand on her shoulder. She felt omnipotent. 'Let's go to bed,' she said.

'You will marry me, won't you?'

'Of course I will,' she said. 'But first I'm going to go to the bathroom and put on my nightdress.'

'Do you think your mother will mind?'

'Mind? She'll be delighted,' Glenda said, 'as long as I finish my degree. That's extremely important.'

'Yes, I know it is,' he said. 'We can still be married though, can't we?'

Glenda kissed him and picked up her nightdress. She went into the bathroom and with her toothbrush in her hand she gazed at her pink face in the mirror. Good heavens, she thought, it's as easy as that. I fall in love with the first man in my life and he wants to marry me. Glenda very much wanted to be married to Clive. Let Jane try to threaten Clive, she thought, and it will be over my dead body.

Clive was sleeping quietly beside her. Their embraces had been tender but innocent. Glenda, sleeping lightly herself, thought she heard the door open. She tried blearily to listen into the dark room, but there was no sound. She put her arm around Clive protectively and went back to sleep.

She did not see a tall thin woman holding a candle stand for a moment behind the crack of the open door. 'So that's how she's doing it,' the woman whispered into the dark of the night. 'Pussy power.' The figure glided back into the shadows and the light bobbed along the hall. 'Doesn't matter if that little nobody snares him; she's no match for me,' the walking shadow muttered and she blew the candle out.

Chapter 64

Glenda awoke with a start. Then she remembered that Clive had asked to sleep in her bed the night before. And she remembered with perfect clarity that he had asked her to marry him and that she had agreed. Glenda propped herself up on her left arm and beheld Clive. He was sleeping soundly, his blonde eyelashes resting lightly on the curve of his cheekbone. Glenda leaned over and kissed him gently. Clive stretched and blinked. 'Where am I?' he said, startled.

'You're in my bed, silly.'

Clive pulled himself up on the bed and whistled. 'I slept so well. You make me feel safe, you know. And do you remember everything from last night?'

'Sure,' Glenda said, sounding like Molly. 'Of course I do.'

Clive looked at the ceiling. 'And you still want to marry me?'

'Sure,' Glenda said, with a hard American R. She dropped the American accent and after a moment said, 'I do, really, Clive.'

Clive put his arm around her. 'That's done then. I'll break the news at breakfast. My father will be out hunting with Caspar, but then it doesn't matter what he thinks. He always does exactly what he's told by mother. I'd better go back to my room and get changed.' Clive got out of bed.

Glenda had no knowledge of a naked man other than what she had seen in films or art books. Clive was slender but well made. He did look a little like Glenda's favourite statue of David. His penis did not look threatening, nor did it resemble any of the monstrous objects described by Molly. Clive was totally uninhibited by the nakedness. He stretched and Glenda watched the arch in his back. How she would love to run her hands down the arch over his buttocks and down to the soles of his neat shapely feet! Glenda felt herself blushing. Really, she told herself, don't be so silly. But the thoughts kept nagging at her belly and she felt herself warming between her legs, that old flame throbbing. It was like a remembered friend. Now, however, the act was not one of lonely satisfaction but one of a communion with another much loved body, unveiled here for the first time.

Clive stepped into her bathroom and walked back into the bedroom wrapped in a big fluffy terry-towelling robe. He gathered up his dinner jacket and other clothes and leaned over Glenda. Glenda found herself responding ardently to the touch of his lips. She felt Clive tighten and she pulled away. 'I'm sorry,' she said, laughing reassuringly. She detected a look of fear in Clive's eyes.

'Don't apologize,' Clive said softly, but Glenda still saw not just fear but also confusion. It was as if he had made a calculation and that calculation had let him down. 'See you at breakfast,' he said.

Had she frightened him away? Glenda agonized. Had she been too brazen? 'We'll beard the lioness in her den,' Clive smiled. 'See you soon.' And he left the room.

Glenda collapsed back against the pillows. 'Thank you, God,' she prayed. She lay there looking out of the window at a grey, wet day. Saturday, she thought, usually the nicest day of the week. Still, she pushed herself back up on the bed and hugged her knees, today I am going to be engaged. What to wear? she pondered.

The gong sounded only once for breakfast, Clive had explained, so when she heard the great boom explode in the middle of the castle she finished brushing her hair and went down the long corridor towards the noise of people.

She neared a small room off the main hall. Milly was lurking at the doorway and smiled miserably at Glenda. 'Is this where I go for breakfast?' Glenda asked.

Milly nodded. Her eyes revealed that she had been crying.

'What's the matter, Milly?'

There was nobody in the breakfast room yet so Milly followed Glenda in. 'It's my boyfriend,' she said, sniffing. 'Madam doesn't let me have visitors, so 'e don't come here no more.'

'Can't you get another job? Surely anything is better than slaving in this house.'

Milly shook her head. 'If I work hard, I can make my way up to being a housekeeper, like Gwen. And then,' she sniffed again, 'I get other people waiting on me. I never 'ad much education, you see. I'm a little slow, and me social worker found me this job and I'm good at it. I really wanted to be a nurse, but I can't read.'

Glenda heard the sound of high heels tapping their way to the door. 'I think I hear Lady Jane coming.'

'Yes, Miss,' Milly said. Her subservience troubled Glenda, but a stab of pity shot through her. That could have been me, she thought looking at Milly's broken-back slouch. Glenda had seen those resigned shoulders on so many children at the primary school. Maybe, she thought, when Clive and I get a home of our own we can take Milly with us. Anything to get her away from Jane.

Jane made an entry. Somehow, Glenda thought as Jane

came forward to air-kiss her face, Jane gets most things wrong. Today she was dressed in black. Long tight toreador pants with a black silk shirt tucked into the top of the trousers and a studded belt with an aggressive Mexican silver clasp. 'Like it?' Jane asked as she drew her body away. Jane pointed to the belt. 'I got it in Acapulco. You should have seen the cliff-divers there! Such beautiful brown bodies . . .'

Glenda recoiled from the heavy smell of perfume that Jane left clinging to Glenda's white poplin shirt. 'Very nice,' she said.

'Where's Clive?' Jane took her seat at the breakfast table. The chairs were comfortable wicker basket. The table, made of plain wood, had a red check cloth over it and the breakfast service was simple country French plate. The teapot and cups were Victorian. Altogether this room had been put together with a much kinder hand than the other rather boastful rooms. Glenda looked around. It was a warm blue and white swagged chintzy room.

'What a lovely room,' Glenda said.

'You like it? Philip's mother did this room. It used to be her sewing room. It is rather pretty, but a little chichi. Where's Clive?'

'Good morning, mother.' Clive's voice interrupted the conversation.

'Well, you do look chipper today, darling. Sleep well?'

'Never better.' Clive's voice didn't miss a beat.

'Why, look at you!' said Jane. Glenda sat frozen. Clive was wearing a light polo-necked shirt over a pair of dun-coloured trousers. Glenda had never seen Clive looking so confident. Even his mother's teasing voice, which usually reduced him to silence, couldn't shake his self-assurance. Glenda smiled. 'Do you want tea, Clive?' she said. She reached out to pour him his tea.

A long white hand shot across the table and held Glenda's wrist in a claw-like grip. 'Milly pours the tea in this house,' explained Lady Jane.

Glenda sat back, startled by Lady Jane's animal speed and by the strength of her grip. 'Of course,' she said.

Milly, who had been standing behind Jane, leaned forward. Her eyes asked for forgiveness. Glenda looked at the girl. Hazel eyes forgave blue eyes and ignored the black eyes.

'Mother,' Clive said once the tea was poured, 'I am very happy to tell you that Glenda and I have decided to become formally engaged.'

The silence was enormous. It expanded and filled the room while little flames of anger flickered at the table. Glenda could feel Jane's attempts to control herself. Fury hung over Jane's shoulders and a long green rope of hatred wound itself around Glenda's neck. Glenda coughed, hoping to break the silence. 'This is what you have decided?' Her words were cut from ice.

'Yes,' Clive said, unrepentant. 'I have decided. After all, next year I shall be twenty-one. I shall have the farm in Norfolk.'

Imagine, Glenda thought, our own home already! She listened to Clive and his mother, feeling very removed now from the conversation. She felt as if she was listening to the wireless. A play, perhaps, in which the protagonists talked at many deep levels, and it was up to the listener not just to hear the words but also to understand the undercurrents. The undercurrents in this conversation seemed dark and treacherous indeed. 'Did you not think, darling,' Jane now had control of herself and her voice had become the familiar rasping vehicle for confounding the world and all of Jane's enemies, 'that you should perhaps have consulted your father and myself first?'

'No,' Clive answered, his head thrown back.

Clive, Glenda realized, was beginning to enjoy this moment. 'No, I did not. It's my life and I've made my choice whom I am to marry. I chose Glenda.'

'I see.' Jane paused and picked up her cigarette holder. 'Does Glenda know about your medical history?'

Glenda was aware that Jane was scrutinizing her face. 'Yes, she does know all about my medical history,' Clive said. His voice was defensive.

'And that you can never have children because of your medical history?'

'Of course, I know all about that,' Glenda butted in vehemently. 'I don't care if we have children or not. And anyway, I don't think there is anything wrong with Clive. I see no reason not to have children, if we want them.'

'I see. You are a medical expert, are you, Glenda?'

Glenda flushed. 'No, of course I'm not. But I am a good judge of character.'

'Of course, dear.' Jane's voice flattened its head, like a cobra about to strike. 'A housekeeper's daughter would have access to so many interesting characters.'

Glenda decided to ignore the shot. She finished her tea, making slurping noises like Phil Clough. She laughed secretly when she saw Jane wince. If Jane wanted to fight with her new daughter-in-law, then Glenda would show her how to fight street-style. Gloves off. Jane may have the establishment behind her, but Glenda had a formidable pair of fists.

'It's only,' said Jane, trying another tack, 'that the stress of taking on too much responsibility may be too much for dear Clive. Not everyone does well under pressure. And being responsible for property entails a good deal of stress.'

Glenda smiled sweetly. 'I'd say Clive's held up pretty well already, given the pressure he's had to cope with.' She turned to him. 'Come on, Clive. Let's go for a ride. We can wrap up and I think the rain has stopped.'

'What a perfect idea!' Clive blinked and shook his head, and they left the room.

Milly watched Jane reach for the telephone. 'Get me Caspar,' she said to the switchboard. 'No, not my son — his uncle.'

The invisible pair of hands that ran the telephones in the castle sighed. Madam was in one of her foul moods.

'Hello, Caspar? Jane. Clive has just dragged in a horrible piece of common skirt and now has the cheek to tell me he wants to marry her.'

'He can marry if he wants to. There is nothing to stop him.'

'But what if the bitch gives birth to a boy? That will ruin everything.'

There was a moment when the hands could hear Caspar Alexander QC, sucking on his cigar. 'You've told him he can't have children, haven't you?'

'Yes, I have, but what if they decide to get an independent doctor's advice? These days being mad is considered quite fashionable.'

'Don't do anything until I come down next week.' Caspar's soothing tones crept down the telephone. 'Just a little hiccough, that's all it is. By the way, how are the charities doing? I need to find a home for a sum of money.'

'Oh good!' Jane's voice quivered. Money always made her feel so sexual. 'I could do with a little injection into my agoraphobia fund – it's all the rage now. Thank you so much, dearest Caspar.'

'Think nothing of it, darling.'

Jane put the phone down and sighed. Milly had left the room. Her luncheon guests were due to arrive in the next few hours. Pity about old Caspar, she thought. Why were the Alexander men so boorish? And then she had to produce a child like Clive. What a beautiful baby he was . . . Her eyes glazed. But then he never did like her, from the moment he was born. He refused her breast milk, and she had been prepared to risk marking her beautiful breasts with stretchmarks just for him. Ungrateful from the day he was born. Not like Caspar who suckled as eagerly as her husband. Sex, she thought. It's all the Alexander men thought about. That and killing things.

She could hear the two men coming down the corridor. I

do hope they've changed their clothes, she thought. 'What's for breakfast?' Philip yelled.

Jane sighed again. Swine, she thought. The lot of them. Now she would have to break the news of Clive's engagement to them. Not that they would care. Her son Caspar quite wanted the inheritance, but not enough to fight for it. But Jane would fight for him. She had to have him inherit the huge fortune. Caspar she could control, and the ability to control meant more to Jane than any other emotion in the world. Control of money meant power, and power was the only aphrodisiac Jane understood. Between her legs lay a much explored but completely blighted frozen lake. Not a tremor of joy or ecstasy ever shook her body. Only at the moment when money touched her hand did her mouth begin to tremble.

Chapter 65

'Whew!' Clive breathed in relief. 'Thank goodness that's over! The old bitch nearly blew a gasket.'

'Yes, she did.' Glenda didn't know whether to be frightened or amused.

'There's an old family diamond I can get off her for your engagement ring.'

'No, Clive,' she said firmly. 'I don't want anything from your mother. You can get me a ring of your choice.'

'All right then.' Clive jumped in the air, pulling down a branch from a tree. 'You know, Glenda, for the first time in my life I feel really happy. I never thought I'd know what the word joy meant. But I do feel it.' He stopped and looked at Glenda. The day was harsh and raw. 'Yes, it feels like Beethoven. The world is singing his Ninth.' He laughed out loud and held his arms out to the winter countryside. 'Hear it?'

Glenda felt herself sharing Clive's spontaneous exhilaration. She felt powerful and strong. She felt she could handle Clive's mother. A sudden playfulness rising within her, she lowered her head and looked at Clive across the curtain of chestnut hair that fell over her forehead. She grumbled like a charging bull and hurled herself at Clive's midriff. He caught her in his arms and let himself be knocked to the soggy, leaf-mould earth. He embraced her and together they rolled on the ground in a friendly wrestle.

'I must telephone mum,' she smiled up at him. 'Let's ring her from a phone box. I know this sounds silly, but I feel as if your mother has all the telephone lines in the house tapped.'

'You're not silly,' Clive said, catching his breath. 'She does. She has the master telephone in her bedroom. If a call comes in, a red light flashes and then she can listen in. She knows all about father's little affairs, you know. His mistresses, the ones he likes to spank.' Clive rolled his eyes comically. 'My father has very poor taste when it comes to sex.' He helped Glenda to her feet and they began to walk.

'Does it upset you?'

Clive put his arms around Glenda and leaned his forehead against hers. 'Nothing upsets me any more,' he said. 'And I gave up on those two a long time ago. Caspar is all right, but he is just like father. Anyway, it's a beautiful day to me and I'm in love with the most wonderful girl in the world, and I want to take you to Fen Farm. The family owns it, and it's about the only property that means anything to me. I love Fen Farm. When we're married, that's where we shall live. I'll introduce you to Mark and Paul. We grew up together, when I was allowed to spend time on the farm as a boy. Those two are probably the best friends I've got in the world. Now they run the farm with their wives. Mrs Robinson is the housekeeper and –'

'Do we really have to have all these people to look after us?' They were approaching the stables where the motorbike was parked.

Clive stopped and looked astonished. 'What do you mean, Glenda? These are people I grew up with. They all expect to work for me. They care about me and I care about them. I don't think employment has to imply subjugation. What do you want me to do? Throw them out so they can go and work in the local factory?'

'I didn't mean it that way. I mean, you can't forget, I'm a servant's daughter myself, I guess. And it's just such a strange idea that there will be people working for me.' Glenda walked quietly beside him. 'Well, then, do you think we could have Milly at Fen Farm? She's not really very happy with your mother.'

'I don't blame her. Mother is awful to servants. Of course. I'll get her for your personal maid. Then mother can't object.'

The bike spat gravel and they were off. 'We can't be too long,' Clive said over his shoulder. 'Mother's appalling friends will be hunkering down for lunch. Still, you'll see why I love the farm so much.'

Fen Farm rose out of the flat, grey, winter ponds of Norfolk. The land was damp. The motorbike whined down the empty road and Glenda felt she was riding in one of those grainy black and white films made by angry young men. She heard the cranking of the old film reels and envisioned white, dusty light shining from the square hole in the wall. Slowly she could see the shape of Fen Farm emerge out of the loam. The farm was shrouded with wisps of grey mist, but unlike the Alexander's castle it gave off no sulphurous whiff of evil. Rather the mist was warm and friendly, like a mother's shawl casually thrown over the back of a chair.

The bike pulled up beside a small door leading into a flagstoned passage. Against the wall were piled baskets of fresh vegetables. A small dumpy woman stood waiting to greet them. 'Master Clive! You should've told me yourself that you were coming.'

'You sound like you knew anyway. This is Mrs Robinson,'

Clive said, giving the small woman a hug.

'Your mother called and said to remind you to get back in time for luncheon.'

Clive grimaced. 'Blast mother! She's a witch with a very long reach.'

'Now, now, master Clive. Don't say nasty things about your mother. She is a wonderful woman.' Glenda was not fooled: Mrs Robinson's eyes did not believe what her mouth was saying. The eyes agreed with Clive. But then Mrs Robinson was a servant, Glenda thought, and it was not a servant's place to criticize employers. 'Pity you can't stay,' Mrs Robinson said. 'I've a lovely brace of grouse shot by Paul. Still, you can take them home for His Lordship. He likes grouse. How is he, and master Caspar?'

'Fine, fine.' Clive trailed behind Mrs Robinson. They walked up a passageway and came to a heavy door. Clive pushed it open and stood at the door for a moment. I can see why he loves this place, Glenda thought. The old vaulted ceiling spoke of hundreds of years of human habitation. This building, with its quiet, mullioned windows had always taken care of people. Men, women, and children of long ago had crowded into this room. Outside in the flagged courtyard the winter wind moaned, not of evil or death, but it told stories of the farm that offered shelter. Mrs Robinson said, 'I'll get on now, dear. You take Miss Glenda around the other rooms.'

Clive held Glenda's hand. 'Here,' he pushed open a door, 'is the nursery.'

Glenda smiled. 'One day our son will lie in that crib.' Clive winced and Glenda felt it. Damn! she thought. How tactless of me! 'Clive,' Glenda pulled his arm, 'we can have children if we want. You mustn't let your mother get to you. There is nothing wrong with you.'

'Well, there's not many who'd agree with you.' Clive gave her a sad smile.

Glenda went over to the window. 'What a beautiful courtyard!' she said.

Clive joined her. 'Yes, it is. I love this house and the people who live here. They are my family, far more than mother and father. I didn't see much of my parents when I was little. Caspar and I would be put on the train in London, with Nanny Jenkins, and shunted down here for Mrs Robinson and the servants to look after us. We lived here full-time when we were little and then when we went to school. We were in London until I went away to Eton. Don't really know much about my parents, except what I read in mother's diary.'

'You don't read her diary, do you?' Glenda was shocked.

Clive laughed. 'That's how I know about her telephone. When she's out, I get into her room. You've got to keep tabs on the wicked queen, you know. Her diary is remarkably interesting. She uses men just like Kleenex.'

'I thought only Molly did that,' Glenda said, trying to lighten up the situation.

Clive grinned a queer, twisted grin. 'Molly has a sense of humour. There's salvation in that. Mother has none. She's merely evil. Anyway, we'd better hurry. We have to get back to drink hemlock with her.'

Glenda followed Clive down the many stairs to the front hall. 'Let's go,' he said, his mood strained and his eyes troubled.

'After lunch with your mother, why don't we go back to Cambridge?' Glenda suggested. 'You're so much happier away from her.'

'I don't want the bitch to see that she can run me off the territory. I have to cope with her, Glenda. If ever I felt she could get the better of me, I'd be lost.' With that haunting phrase ringing in Glenda's ears, they rode their way back to the castle.

Chapter 66

Most of the wealthy women of Cambridgeshire seemed to be crowded into the main dining room. At least fifty or sixty, Glenda guessed. She and Clive were slightly late, so Glenda found herself gazing into fifty or sixty pairs of disapproving eyes, with one black glittering pair out-glowering the rest. 'Ah!' Lady Jane Alexander rose to her feet. 'The moment we've all been waiting for, darlings. The arrival of my soon-to-be daughter-in-law. Do meet Glenda Stanhope. She is from London, or rather shall we say Ealing, formerly a resident of that worthy borough Hounslow?' Glenda felt herself sinking. 'And her mother is a housekeeper for the well-known actress, Renée Blanchard.' There were murmurs at the notion that anyone would want to know a mere actress.

'Will your mother be announcing the engagement in *The Times*, dear?' A large woman with the face of a petrified frog leaned forward.

'Of course,' Glenda said stoutly. Glenda took particular care, when speaking, to see that her voice gave no hint that she ever, even in earliest childhood, had dropped an H. She felt like Eliza Dolittle. Fortunately her H's did not let her down and she relaxed.

It looked as if half the sheep from the Cambridge fields had come to lunch and died in their seats. If these are aristocratic genes, she thought, it's a good job Clive is going to get a load of my working-class ones. Glenda found herself sitting next to a pretty young girl. 'I'm Sally Humblebottom. Awful name, I know, but there it is.'

Glenda smiled. At least there was one person she could more or less talk to. 'Who are we raising money for?' Glenda asked.

'Oh, I don't really know.' Sally helped herself to the tray. 'Goodie!' she said. 'I do love salmon.'

Glenda served herself and wondered why the aristocracy had to eat so much. Not much else to do, she reasoned. She put her hand over her wine glass. 'Not for me,' she said firmly.

The two footmen quietly passed around the room. Mouths were chewing. Good heavens, Glenda thought. This lot eat like Cyril. She bowed her head after looking across the table at Clive. He appeared rather pale. Still, she comforted herself, at least he was eating.

The meal seemed to go on for ages. And then Jane tapped her glass with a fork. *Pinggg*. Voices stopped mid-sentence and mouths hung open, some filled with food, some empty. 'Ladies,' she said, 'today we are gathered to raise money for abandoned children.' There was a discreet murmur of approval. 'Also, of course, my pet charity is in need of money, that is, the charity that takes care of homeless animals.' Now there was an outright roar of approval. 'Last year we raised fifteen thousand pounds for the abandoned children's society and twenty-two thousand for the abandoned animals. I think we should give ourselves a little clap for that fine effort.'

Glenda wished she were back at Girton. The women there would have none of this. Scraggs would sit with that funny light in her eyes when she did not approve of something, which was usually Molly. Sally Humblebottom, sitting next to Glenda, harped on about a hunt ball she had attended a few days before. 'And you should have heard the music. They'd imported the band from London. It was beautiful, absolutely beautiful. Nanny took care of Anastasia and we danced all night long. Such fun, don't you think?'

'We had to take up charitable work,' a woman said, 'because England is getting so left-wing, you know.'

Glenda blinked. 'Really? I thought it was only a few people at Cambridge.'

'Oh, no!' Sally swung her long blonde hair. 'It's those dirty hippies and reds, if you know what I mean.'

Glenda very much wanted to be away from here. 'Coffee is served in the morning room, madam,' the man on the left of the door intoned. At least I'll be able to sit next to Clive, she thought, and she followed the herd into the morning room.

'Well, dear, what do you think of my fund-raising efforts?'

Clive was at her elbow and Lady Jane was staring into her face. 'Um,' Glenda said, having not thought anything about Jane's efforts, 'I can't help but think that if you simply paid out what it cost to feed all these people, you could probably support your abandoned animals for a year. And there would probably be some left over for the abandoned children as well.'

There was a gasp of horror. All eyes homed in on Glenda, who stood her ground. 'You don't understand, Glenda,' Lady Jane rasped. 'That is not how charitable work is done.'

'She understands only too well, mother,' Clive put in, unable to resist. 'You do all your socializing this way and you hope when the revolution comes they don't shoot you. But they will, you know, dear.'

'That's enough, Clive. You're drunk. Go to your room.'

'Yes, mother,' Clive said with mock timidity. He pulled Glenda along behind him. 'I'm off to the dog-house, ladies,' he said and he began to run. He and Glenda flew down the corridors, both giggling.

'I had to say that,' Glenda said. 'I'm so sorry.'

'Don't be!' Clive said, shaking with laughter. 'You are quite right. I feel I've been rude enough to her to last the whole weekend. Let's pack and get the hell out of here.'

'Thank goodness.' Glenda was panting. Before she left the dining room Glenda noticed that the two men at the door had tried to stifle their laughter. That'll give Florence in the kitchen something to laugh over, and she hoped Milly would hear too.

'Last one out of here is a monkey,' Clive yelled.

Chapter 67

'Where are we going?' Glenda screamed the words into the wind. The bike roared and strained, impatient to be out of the gates and away. Glenda felt her spirits rising as they escaped from the miasma that surrounded Clive's mother.

'We'll spend the night in Ely with Gerontius. I need to talk to him.'

Glenda felt Clive's back go rigid. His shoulders felt like iron. He's feeling awful, she could tell, despite his good humour. Maybe having a mother like that, she figured, is what made him so strange at times. There was a far away quality in Clive that Glenda was beginning to find unsettling. It was as if, when life became painful, he retreated to a private dimension. He could still be seen and Glenda knew he could still see all that went on around him, yet he was somehow removed and insulated. Never mind, Glenda told herself. Gerontius will know what to do.

They came into Ely and the shops were full of people doing their Christmas shopping. 'Let me just stop at the chemist's, Glenda,' Clive said. 'I've an awful headache and I need some aspirin.'

The bike stood still. Glenda watched Clive push diffidently through the crowded shop. She looked into the shop and saw a woman with an enormous belly. Two small children clung to her skirt and she had a big black eye. She was poor and tattered. Glenda winced. She remembered Mrs McCluskie looking like that. A fierce rage burned in Glenda's throat. I'll never go back to those days, she thought. I would never marry a man who could be violent . . .

Clive came back and he was smiling. 'I've taken four aspirins. Hopefully that should do the trick.' They took off to Gerontius' house round the corner and up the road.

'Hey, man! Good to see you!' Gerontius seemed quite

unsurprised that they should turn up at his door. The cottage was as pretty and as unkempt as usual.

'Can we stay for the night, Gerontius?' Clive asked. 'We've been over at my mother's and she's been true to her usual beastly form. By the way, we are engaged to be married, Glenda and I.'

'I must telephone mum,' Glenda broke into the conversation. 'I really must.'

'Help yourself. There's the phone.' Gerontius waved a none too clean hand at Glenda. 'Come on, Clive. I'll go and look round the kitchen and see what we have to eat.'

'Mum,' Glenda said. 'I'm engaged to Clive.' There was a silence.

'That's a bit quick, isn't it, Glenda?'

'I know, but he's really nice, mum. You'll like him.'

'I've no doubt I will.' Minnie's voice was warm and encouraging.

'And a friend of Clive's mother asked whether you planned to announce the engagement in *The Times*.'

'Of course I will, love. Don't you worry about that. I'll do it all proper so you won't be ashamed of your old mum.'

'I would never be ashamed of you. You know that.' Glenda felt dreadful. One fear in all her happiness was that one day Minnie would have to meet the Alexanders, and she could just imagine their basilisk-like stares.

'You told me so much about him in your last few letters,' Minnie said with a mild, affectionate, nagging facetiousness.

'I'm sorry, mum. I do mean to write more often, but it's end of term papers and things like that . . . I'm so very busy.' She could hear her new posh voice talking by itself.

'Never mind, duck.' Minnie was reassuring. 'We 'ave the holidays coming up, and you're bringing that nice American girl with you?'

'Yeah, Molly is nice, but she's also . . . Well, she's very American, you know. Her language . . .'

298

'Don't mind me,' Minnie chuckled. 'I can give as good as I get.'

'Yes. I know.' And mentally Glenda added *But not to Lady Jane.* 'I'll see you in a few weeks.'

'When do I get to meet your intended?'

'My fiancé, mother,' Glenda said in some exasperation. 'He's my fiancé.'

'Oh! Hoity-toity, are we?'

'No, mum, I didn't mean to sound like that,' Glenda said. 'I don't know. I'll ask him. Tell Renée and Abe, won't you?'

'I will, darling. Goodbye.'

'Goodbye.'

The goodbyes hung in the air as she walked into the small kitchen. Clive looked up. 'Mum's really pleased,' Glenda said. Clive leaned over and hugged her. 'Look, I'll cook the meal and you two can talk,' she offered.

'Sounds cool,' Gerontius nodded his head. His huge wattles shook as he walked from the kitchen with Clive.

'Don't take your old lady too seriously,' Glenda heard Gerontius say. 'I mean, your folks can't do anything to you but take away your money, right? And money's not everything.'

'She hates me, Gerontius.' Clive's voice was tense and thin. 'What did I ever do to get hated like that?'

'Nothing, man.' Gerontius sat down on the old armchair that protested his weight loudly. 'You don't have to do anything to set off an uptight bitch. Like, they're just born evil. Bad karma. But you gotta hang loose, Clive. Don't let her get you down. She's a dinosaur. Let her deal with her own karma. Don't let her screw around with yours. Every time you let her get on to your path, you mess yourself up. Stay clear. Ride your bike. The road's your own. Say, "No fucking way, mom. I'm not living like you."'

Clive grinned. He could not imagine saying *No fucking way* to his mother, but he wished he could.

Glenda listened as she began the horrendous task of

attempting to clean the kitchen. There were dried splashes of chilli sauce everywhere. She found some hamburgers encrusted with ice in the freezer. In the fridge she discovered a small lettuce, some good olive oil, and a tin of Crosse and Blackwell tomato soup. That will have to do, she thought. On the table was an open bottle of chianti. What a pity, she thought, that such a lovely cottage has to be owned by such a messy person.

Still, she could hear Gerontius comforting Clive. 'You create your own happiness. You can't, like, shake your fists at the heavens and say it's God's fault or the government's fault, because it isn't. We're born alone and we all die alone.' He paused and Glenda felt her back stiffening.

'I hadn't thought about that,' Clive said slowly. 'You're right, you know. But it's not the title or the money I mind about, Gerontius. It's the fact that I do want to keep Fen Farm. And not just for Glenda and me. There's Mrs Robinson and there's Mark and Paul and their families.'

Glenda went to the arch that led into the sitting room. Gerontius was pulling at his wispy beard, and his left hand was stroking his nearly bald head. 'Well,' he said, blowing out a huge amount of cigarette smoke. 'If Fen Farm is meant to be yours, it will be yours. It's as simple as that. God called your name before you were born, man. Do you want to make God laugh?' Gerontius asked, smiling. Clive nodded and grinned. 'Then tell him your plans!' Gerontius wheezed. 'Yeah, that's it! Tell him your plans! And He'll crack up laughing, because He's got plans of His own, man. He's already got the plan. Anyway, let's celebrate your engagement tonight. Enough of your lousy parents with their lousy karma. I smell hamburgers!' he roared. 'What have you got there, Glenda?'

'Hamburgers.'

'Far out! Let's have an incredible meal and we'll all get drunk. You can sleep upstairs in the master bedroom. And I've got a fucking shower you can use. You dig it? An

American with a shower! Must be the only one in this crazy country!'

Glenda smiled. My goodness, she thought, the sheets. 'Do you have any clean sheets?' she asked nervously.

Gerontius looked at her and he laughed. 'Yeah, man. But if you're going to marry Clive, you'll have to get over clean sheets. 'Cos some day we're gonna hit the road, all of us. And when we travel in the wide open Wild West, there aren't gonna be any clean sheets, you know?'

'I know,' Glenda said and then she set her mouth. 'We might be beatniks, Clive and I, but there is no need to be dirty.'

Gerontius roared. 'That's telling 'em!' he said. 'Maybe Clive's old lady will get pushed out by his new old lady.'

'Maybe she will,' Glenda said, one eyebrow raised. 'Now where are my clean sheets?'

Chapter 68

There weren't any clean sheets, but Glenda found a bedspread in the back of a cupboard. She sniffed the blankets. Not too bad, she said to herself. Clive was standing by the door of the bedroom. The room had slanting dormer windows and looked out over the back garden into a lot of other back gardens. The night was frosty and falling fast. 'Clive,' Glenda beheld him with great affection, 'you look tired.'

'It's my head.' He looked very white. 'It hurts. I have some special pills to take, but I left them in college.'

'Never mind. Take some more aspirin.' No such thing as a glass in the bathroom, she grumbled to herself as she walked downstairs.

Gerontius was lying in a huge mound on top of the old sofa. He looked up. 'Clive about to get one of his headaches?' he asked.

Glenda nodded.

'I thought so.' Gerontius shook his head. 'Always happens when he's been jousting with that dragon-mother of his.'

'What sort of headaches are they?' Glenda was concerned. 'He looks so pale.'

'I dunno, but they're bad, bad suckers when he gets them.'

Glenda climbed back up the narrow stairs and saw Clive sitting on the bed, his head in his hands. He was rocking backwards and forwards. She sat down beside him. 'Here, Clive. Take the pills.'

'They won't help,' Clive gasped. 'Aspirin won't touch it. Nothing helps.' He was groaning through clenched teeth.

'Is this a migraine headache?'

'Sort of.' Clive rolled over. 'Can you turn the light off, Glenda? It's killing me.'

'Look. I'll go back to Cambridge and get your pills.'

Clive shook his head. 'They don't really help either,' he said. 'Not once the headache has taken hold. Nothing helps. Just lie down beside me and try to go to sleep.'

Glenda lay beside him. She did not dare touch him. She could feel his spasms of pain and she knew that even the touch of her hand was too much for him to bear. She had to wait and leave him alone in the deep well of his suffering. Lord, she prayed, heal him from this terrible pain. But she knew the prayer was hollow. All those years of poverty made Glenda realize that one could not simply importune God. If, as Gerontius said, Clive's headaches were a result of visiting his mother, then the visits would have to be reconsidered.

Glenda lay in the dark and tried to untangle Clive's relationship with this woman. Had she always hated him? Had there once been a loving connection that had gone foul? Glenda eventually slipped into an exhausted sleep, only to be awakened with a start.

Clive was banging his head against the wall. 'I can't bear it!' he was screaming. 'I can't bear the pain!' She heard

Gerontius running up the stairs. His huge form squeezed into the doorway.

'I can't put on the light, Gerontius. It hurts his eyes too much.'

'Don't put on the light!' Clive screamed. 'Don't put on the lights!'

Gerontius looked down at the two of them. He felt a great sadness wash over him. Both of them looked so young and frightened. Clive curled up in a ball writhing in pain, and Glenda white and uncertain. 'Here,' Gerontius said softly. 'Get this down him.' He handed Glenda a glass of water and a pill.

'What is it?' she said.

'Don't worry about that,' Gerontius smiled. 'It's a major league little tablet. It'll knock him out. And by the time he comes to, hopefully the headache will be gone.'

She lifted Clive's head and he rolled his eyes up. He looked as if he were dead. 'Just sip this, Clive,' she said, awkwardly trying to hold him steady.

'I can't,' he gasped.

'Yes, you can. Here you go.' She got the pill down his throat and he lay back on the bed, breathing quickly. 'Is this as bad as it gets?' Glenda asked. 'I mean, I heard Cyril and others saying that he . . . well, he gets upset. The very first time I saw him he was playing this terrifying music. And Nanny Jenkins says that I have to be careful if he starts to play like that . . .' She was quiet for a moment. 'I felt so sorry for him . . .' She looked at Gerontius. 'Does it get any worse?'

'It depends what you mean, honey,' he said softly. 'Like, Clive shows people his pain. Most people keeps theirs all inside. That's what makes him such a wild, really different, and, like, brilliant guy, you know? It's what gives his music so much passion and depth, and everything. He's really in touch and tuned in. But that's gotta hurt him, too, you know? It's like, uh, we all have an inside world that's secret, you know? Really secret. We talk to our inner selves. Only sometimes Clive's inside world sometimes leaks out. Can you deal with that?'

'Yes. I think so.'

'Yeah, I think you can. They call him crazy, but he's not crazy. Not in a bad way anyway.' He screwed up his face in a strange smile.

Clive stopped moving. He moaned and then fell silent.

Glenda put her hand on his forehead. He opened his lips and let out a sigh. 'He's out of it,' Gerontius said. 'He'll sleep now for a good few hours. Get some sleep yourself, little momma. You could use it.'

Glenda let herself fall back on the bed beside Clive. 'Good night, Gerontius. And thanks.'

'Good night, sugar pie.' And Gerontius was gone, back down the narrow wooden steps.

She heard him rearrange the bed and she heard the groan of the bed springs. She closed her eyes and she thought, Well, whatever happens I will not be frightened. He is not mad; he just needs to be understood. And Gerontius is right: the same things that make Clive brilliant and talented and perceptive also make life painful for him. She put her arm gently around Clive's sleeping body and she smelled the sweet honey smell of the man she loved.

Chapter 69

Clive travelled slowly back to Cambridge. He was white, with circles under his eyes. But the headache was gone. Glenda, her arms around him, wondered how he could bear such pain. 'I've had headaches like that for years,' he said. 'The doctors say it's migraine. But I don't have them regularly. I do get a warning. Little silver specks before my eyes and things like that, but there isn't much I can do. Still,' he grinned wanly as they climbed onto the bike, 'it's over now and I can relax.'

As he drove Glenda back to Girton, he wondered how he was going to tell her about the fits. Not only the fits, he thought, but that I'm impotent. It must be the medication doing it to me, he thought. There is so much I can't tell her. His thoughts made him miserable. He so much wanted to stay with Glenda. She was the first person that made him feel real. When he was with her, he felt anchored to the ground. Other girls who had interested him for a while were so mysterious that he felt they spoke another language. Other girls tossed their hair, raised their eyebrows, rolled their eyes, licked their lips, crossed their legs, swung their feet, in a language that drove Clive to despair. Caspar laughed at him when he tried to describe his feelings. 'All they want is a good shag, Clive, not a Freudian analysis. You read too many books. Go down and try a few barmaids. Get some practice. Go with the old man and spank a few bottoms . . .' Clive recoiled from conversations like that.

In Glenda he found a girl who had no sign language. She said what she said and she meant it. There were no deep undercurrents waiting to sweep Clive away. No treacherous rocks to watch out for. So far they lived side by side happily. He did not need to wait terrified that he could not meet her every need. Years ago, when the boys found that petting girls and going all the way was now permissible, he had tried. But the open-mouthed, splay-legged girls in bushes outside the great houses at balls and dances disconcerted him. This was not the romantic idea of lovemaking that he had in mind.

Anyway, he thought glumly as they entered into the busy streets of Cambridge, I can't get it up, so all the thinking is really rather academic. Maybe, he thought hopefully, something will happen. He felt reassured. He could feel Glenda's warm arms around him and he turned up the street to Girton. 'I'll telephone you tonight,' he said.

Glenda was pleased. 'I feel as if I've been away for ages,' she said gazing up at the steady red brick walls of Girton.

'So do I,' Clive said. 'Sorry about the headache.'

'Don't worry,' Glenda said and she kissed him. 'I just hate to see you in that much pain.'

Clive put his arms around her and gave her a hug. 'Well, you've seen the worst of it,' he said. 'I mean my family. And you survived them all.'

Glenda laughed. 'My future in-laws, you mean? I can handle them.' She waved a hand and ran up the path.

Clive stood and watched her go. He shook his head at the wonder of it all. He was in love. He sang all the way back to college.

Chapter 70

Christmas was coming very soon. Most Sundays Clive drove Glenda over to Coe Fen where they had tea with Nanny Jenkins. Their announcement in *The Times* looked splendid, and Minnie telephoned to say she was ever so pleased. Clive bought Glenda an engagement ring of her own, one that had never touched Lady Jane's finger.

On the first Sunday after they had chosen the ring together, she proudly showed it to Nanny Jenkins. 'Lovely, dear,' Nanny said. 'I prefer diamonds, but those are very nice emeralds.' Nanny put on her glasses and took Glenda's hand. She peered at the emeralds and moved Glenda's hand to refract the light. 'Very nice setting. Elizabethan, am I right?'

'Of course you are,' Clive said. 'When are you ever wrong?'

Nanny turned Glenda's hand over and studied the palm. 'Long life,' she said. 'Good health.' She spread Glenda's hand out. 'Hmm,' she said. 'I see a good marriage to one man and children. At least three.' She caught herself, and Glenda felt her stiffen. 'I didn't mean that, dear. I just get carried away. Always do the palmistry for the local fête, you know. Nothing in it, of course. All a lot of nonsense, but people like to hear nonsense. Come along. We must sit down. The pot is brewing nicely.' Nanny bustled off.

Glenda looked at Clive. 'Poor old Nanny,' she said directly. 'Everyone seems so afraid even to mention the possibility of children.'

Clive scratched his head. 'Dr Umberto says very clearly what a mistake it would be for me to have children. Unfair to hand on problems like mine to future generations, that sort of thing.'

'But that's ridiculous. And it gets more ridiculous every time I hear it.' Glenda was outraged. 'Dr Umberto can go to hell. Clive, you can have as many children as you want. Don't listen to any of that stuff.' But Clive's face held an unconvinced expression.

Glenda exhaled and she patted Clive's cheek. 'Come on,' she said. 'We can talk another time. Nanny's waiting for us.'

Clive followed her into the sitting room, his shoulders bowed with the weight of hidden knowledge. He remembered Nanny holding him down and strapping him to the bed until he got too big for her and she had to ask for help. He remembered the dreadful day when two big men preceded Dr Umberto into the room where he writhed and convulsed on the floor. He saw Nanny Jenkins cowering over in the corner, crying, 'Don't hurt him! Please don't hurt him.' He remembered Dr Umberto's voice booming through the mistless time of eternal pain. 'Why didn't you tell anybody that this was going on?' 'He'll be all right?' he heard Nanny plead, and then came the long injection and blissful extinction. He saw Nanny no more until he found her years later. Before he came through the little dark hall, he remembered his mother's sneering white face. 'Nanny's gone,' his mother said, 'and now things are going to be quite different. You will see Dr Umberto once a week and you will have medication for life . . .'

'Sit down, dear,' Nanny said and pulled out a chair. Clive sat down, aware of a sickly taste in the back of his throat.

Glenda noticed how natural it felt to be in Nanny's cottage. Being with Nanny Jenkins felt very much like being home with Minnie. Nanny was a woman who made a home for everybody she loved. Here Glenda felt safe with Clive. Nothing could reach them or hurt them. They were two castaways, but this was their port. Now they had Gerontius and, of course, Minnie. Soon Clive would visit London and meet Glenda's family.

She sat back in the chair and gazed at the fire. Two weeks and they would be gone. Clive had to spend Christmas with his family. Cyril and Henry would make their way to Hounslow with Beth, and Glenda would take Molly to Ealing. A network of people, she thought. That's what Cambridge is all about. People strung together like beads. Later the clasp would be broken, but for all those beads, wherever they might roll across the world, Cambridge would always be long winter nights, mighty architecture, cosmic music, and talk. Such talk.

She felt reflective as she sat that night in front of the little fire. This is a happy moment of my life, she thought and she looked at Clive.

'A penny for them?' he said.

She shook her head. 'It would take much more than a penny, love,' she said.

The little word *love* flew to Clive's heart and folded its wings and rested. 'I'll miss you, Glenda,' he said.

'Only a few weeks and then you'll be down.'

'Getting all lovey-dovey,' Nanny said, 'just as my back is turned? I don't know . . .' She grumbled her way out to the kitchen. 'The young these days.' Nanny came back into the sitting room and made herself comfortable in an armchair. 'Play something for us, Clive. Won't you?'

Clive raised his eyebrows. Glenda looked up from the fire and said, 'Yes, please, Clive.'

'Very well then.' He walked to the small spinet in the corner of the room. He lifted the fall-board and sat down on the bench. 'What shall we have?' His fingers stroked the keys while he collected his thoughts. 'Ah. Something in keeping with this lovely little piano's size and scope.' He began to play the opening presto from Haydn's E minor Sonata.

Glenda and Nanny listened. Clive's touch was sure. His fingers, with magnificent swiftness, easily managed beautiful crescendi and mysterious diminuendos, shading nuances with amazing delicacy, shifting mood even between the two halves of a beat. Glenda heard, as if for the first time, just how lucid and brilliant a talent he really did possess. And, she decided, it's precisely his ability to switch emotions so quickly that gives his music such sensitivity. Indeed, she knew, his soul was instinctively artistic. And if his vulnerability also left him susceptible to headaches or depressions, then it was a small price to pay for the privilege of being close to a spirit so profound. She loved him very much.

When he was finished, Nanny rose from her seat and kissed his cheek. He held his hand to Glenda to pull her to her feet, and gave her hand a squeeze. She honestly felt delighted to touch the fingers that held such expressive capabilities. He turned and started to collect teacups and saucers.

'Don't clear up, dears,' Nanny said. 'Just come and say goodbye now. The ice looks bad tonight and I don't want an accident.'

'Good night, Nanny Jenkins,' Glenda said, kissing her soft cheek.

'You may call me just "Nanny", dear,' she said generously. 'You're practically one of the family now.'

Glenda beamed. She followed Clive out to the little picket gate. 'She is such a nice woman, isn't she?'

'I love her,' he said. 'And I love you.'

'I love you, Clive.' Glenda hugged him. She felt he needed a lot of hugging. He had a body that had been devoid of love. She could feel the loss in him and the instinctive shyness of his frame when she touched him. Almost fear, as if she might

309

award him a hug, and then somehow the hug would turn into a blow.

It would take time for him to trust her, she realized, and also, she thought as the bike found its way back to her college, time for there to be no secrets between them. A long time. But she would wait for however long it would take for trust to come. As they rode back, she heard the precise melodic notes of Haydn play above the motorbike's engine.

Chapter 71

Only one more week, Glenda thought. She was sitting with Clive in their usual pub, waiting for Cyril and Beth. 'I'll telephone you on Christmas Day,' she said, squeezing his hand.

'I'll be incarcerated in my cell at mother's,' Clive said gloomily.

'Oh, Clive. Why don't you tell her you're ill and can't make it?'

'You must be joking! If I told her I was ill, it would only go on record to show how sickly I am. Anyway I'm never ill.'

How awful, Glenda thought. 'I rather like being ill sometimes. Mum always tucks me up with a good book and rushes around making things I like to eat. When we are married –' Glenda felt herself thrilling to her own words, '– I'll take care of you and fuss over you.'

Clive smiled a luminous smile that lit up his pale blue eyes. 'I can't imagine a more paradisiacal promise.'

They were interrupted by Molly. She came into the pub with what seemed to Glenda to be a brawl of women. Brawl was the only word that Glenda could think of to describe Molly's friends.

'Hi.' Molly came over to the table. 'You two lovebirds waiting for Cyril?'

Glenda nodded and dropped Clive's hand. She knew that Molly, for the moment, saw handholding as evidence of men's oppression of women. 'All I want,' Molly would say, 'is to be pressed against a mattress when I need to be oppressed. Not seduced into a life of servitude by some fucking male chauvinist pig.' Molly was going through a militant stage. She spent a lot of time with Sonia and her cronies.

'Would you like a drink, Molly?' Clive offered.

Glenda winced. She expected Molly to throw back her hair and announce loudly that she could buy her own fucking drinks; instead Molly folded herself into a chair and took Glenda's hands in her own. 'Actually, honey,' she said with a quick look at Sonia who was occupied talking to her sisters, 'I really just want to say I hope that you will both be very happy.'

Glenda was amazed but she said nothing. 'Thanks,' Clive said. 'Now what can I get for you?'

'Nothing now,' said Molly. 'You'll ruin my reputation. If you have to marry a man, Glenda, I'm glad it's Clive.' Clive gave a small chivalrous bow of the head and left to get another drink. 'Look,' Molly continued, 'I know we haven't seen much of each other, but we will have time when we get to London. I've missed you, chuchy face.'

'I've missed you, too, Molly, but we'll have time.'

'See you!' Molly shouted over her shoulder.

Glenda waved. She had indeed rather lost touch with the other girls for the last several weeks, so much of her time was spent with Clive.

But now she heard Cyril's voice outside the pub. 'There's more of us than I'd anticipated,' she heard him say. He was rubbing his hands from the cold. He wore a very old duffel coat he must have bagged from a passing tramp. Really, Beth should look after him better. Glenda felt cross. Beth followed Cyril and glared at Glenda. 'Traitor,' she spat.

Cyril turned. 'Don't be silly, Beth,' he said. 'Glenda isn't a traitor. She's engaged to Clive. They're friends of ours.'

Beth sniffed a long soulful sniff. ''E's no friend of mine, not since he's been absent from the last four club meetings,' she said. 'Always knew he's nothing but a toffee-nosed capitalist swine underneath it all.'

'Maybe Clive simply decided,' Glenda said in his defence, for he was at the bar getting drinks, 'he'd rather spend some of his time loving one woman close-up than saving mankind from a distance. And that woman happens to be me.'

Sonia, who was listening to the exchange, laughed loudly. 'Serves you right, Beth!' she yelled. 'You're one to talk! For all your words of equality, the men talk all evening and you get the drinks. Where are the other women in your group?' Beth went an angry shade of red and her lips tightened. 'Back at home with the kids, aren't they?' Sonia carried on. 'While the men sort out the rest of the world. Your women are ironing shirts and cooking tomorrow's dinner. That's why women belong with us, not with you.'

'Shut up, Sonia. Go piss up a rope,' Cyril retorted, 'if you can manage that.'

Glenda sighed. She had hoped for a meeting of great minds in the socialist party, evenings spent in intricate Fabianist discussions. Instead the evenings usually ended in arguments before they even began. Why, oh why, Glenda thought, can't people just get together and get things changed? Why must there be millions of little splinter groups all at each other's throats? What did a Marxist or a Militant left-wing whatch-amacallit ever do to see that mum and I didn't freeze? Nothing, that's what.

Clive returned carrying a shandy, and a beer for himself. It was Mrs Jones, old and infirm in her shop, that helped Glenda and her mother. And the social worker. Glenda had forgotten her name, but she remembered her kindly, concerned face. But these people sitting here were not going to do anything for anyone, with the possible exception of Cyril and maybe Henry. That's why Glenda put up with the noise and the smoke. 'Do you understand all this carry on?'

312

she asked Clive as he slid into his seat.

'Much of it's a waste of time,' he shrugged. 'But I follow most of it. There's so much turmoil now. The war in Vietnam, rioting in Paris and in the States. I follow it because I must, I suppose. I feel guilty that people are homeless and don't have enough to eat. To tell you the truth, Glenda, underneath it all I really live for my music. That's what keeps me alive. Do you understand that?'

'I do. It's like my books. I get into my world and sometimes I feel I might never come back, particularly if it's a good book. *The Alexandria Quartet* was such an adventure, it took me weeks to come back to earth.'

'Tell you what.' Clive drained his drink. 'Let's skip out of here and go off to the chapel. I need to practise some more carols and a bit of Bach. I am also working an organ transcription of the most amazing work, originally for a cappella choir actually. William Byrd's *Sacred Service*. Most beautiful and complex religious music I've ever heard. As much as ten-part harmony in such passages.'

'I'd love to hear it.' Glenda stood up and nodded to Cyril who flashed his knowing eyes across the room. Glenda lifted a shoulder in recognition and then felt guilty when she saw Cyril's answering nod sprinkle the table with regret. Cyril was like a pepperpot – shake him and his feelings all fall out. She was fond of Cyril, but could never return his love. Still, he had Beth. Poor man, Glenda thought judiciously as they sneaked out, like naughty but happy, truant kids.

Chapter 72

The last few days before the end of term were a time of many arrangements. There were telephone calls between Minnie and Glenda. Chinchilla apparently had turned up – manless and alone – from America. She was staying with Renée for Christmas. Down the phone she asked what Glenda wanted for Christmas. A decent suitcase, please, was Glenda's answer, but nothing that costs too much. 'Don't worry about the expense, doll.' From the sound of it, Chinchilla's voice had acquired a breath of California laid-backness. 'I'm off-loaded but unloaded, if you know what I mean.'

Glenda grinned into the telephone receiver. 'You don't sound too miserable.' She heard Chinchilla sigh.

'You can't win 'em all. And if you don't, you can always collect in the courts. Gee, America is great for women.'

'I'm bringing Molly down for Christmas. You'll love her. And, oh, did you hear? I'm engaged.'

'I'm so happy for you, baby! Minnie is all excited about it. Oh, Glenda, it will be a lovely Christmas for all of us.'

Yes, Glenda thought. A wonderful Christmas for everyone except Clive. And her throat contracted with pity.

It was also a time of excitement for both Georgina and Fatima, for their fiancés had come to spend several days before Christmas. Jonathan's term at business school in America had ended a week earlier than Cambridge, so he was able to join Georgina. He shared a room at a local hotel with Majid, who flew in from Paris. Majid arrived with the rather difficult news that, due to a worsening of the political situation in Turaq, all of Fatima's family would have to leave quickly. Yes, he assured Fatima, they would be fine, but it would be some time before they were settled at an address in some other country. Fatima was worried indeed, but Majid assured her that Allah would ensure their safety.

In the pre-Christmas rush, all the friends made quick plans to spend time together before leaving for their holidays. Glenda telephoned Clive. 'Molly and I are on our way,' she told him. 'We'll meet you at the pub. We're supposed to join up with Fatima and Majid. Georgina and Jonathan have gone to Trinity to dine at the high table, but we plebs will eat at the pub.'

'I'm looking forward to seeing you.' His voice sounded wretched and flat.

'Clive?' Glenda was alarmed. 'What's the matter?'

'Oh nothing. Much. I had one of my little turns last night. That's all. I just feel a little groggy. I'll be all right. See you in the pub.'

'Wait, Clive. Are you sure you're all right? Tell me. What happened?'

'Really, it was nothing. I was just playing piano in my rooms and the room started to spin a bit and my head felt like a sheet of cotton wool being torn apart, and I guess I blacked out, because when I came to I was lying on the floor by the piano. But really, I'm fine now. It was nothing. Suppose I'm a little nervous about Christmas at home. That's all. Nothing. Really.'

'You should have phoned me.'

'Glenda, don't worry. Promise. I'm fine. See you at the pub.' And he hung up.

Glenda put the telephone down, very much wishing she wasn't leaving Clive over Christmas. If he could get away from that awful family of his, she was sure he would be healthy and at peace for good.

She ran downstairs to the car. Molly was waiting under the arch. 'Majid and Fatima are in town,' Molly said. 'I said we'd meet in the bar.' The car purred down the road. 'Now that all three of you have men in your lives, you won't have that much time for me.'

'Don't be silly, Molly.' Glenda looked at her profile. 'My girlfriends are just as important to me as Clive. I knew you before him, and I'm certainly not one of these women who bags a man and then is never seen again. I had a friend once called Ruth. She was my only friend, but the day she got engaged was the day she never really wanted to see me again. Anyway, remember our vow? We are Souls, aren't we?'

'Sure,' Molly said, comforted. 'Sure we are. Actually I'm

really excited about Christmas. I never had Christmas before. Of course we got invited to gentile houses over the season, but I've never seen the whole thing through. I'll make you some potato *latkes* with apple sauce. That's what we do for Chanukah which falls around the same time.'

'Do you think you'll be homesick?'

'Nah.' Molly revved the engine. 'I'll miss my dad. He's really neat, but my mom will be looking up her pussy with a mirror with all her girlfriends. It's big this year.'

'I beg your pardon? I think I missed a step.'

'It's the new American feminist thing. You know, self-examination. Getting to know your own body. The idea, and whether it's true or not I have no way of knowing, is that for centuries women have been alienated from their own bodies. So now everyone is supposed to sit with a hand mirror and "find themselves" all over again. In my mom's case, before I left, she and her girlfriends were having a women's meeting in order to "Get Acquainted with their Genitals".'

'You're joking,' Glenda said, her face red.

'I promise you I'm not.'

'Did your mother actually let you be there?'

Molly laughed. 'She isn't *that* liberated yet, though I dread the day she is. Anyway, what America did ten years ago is happening in England now. So you're safe here for a while. It seems you're always ten years behind us. But you watch. Hand mirrors will be here before long.'

Glenda pushed her hair back off her forehead. 'Sounds like Sonia will be the first to try. I don't see why you spend so much time with Sonia and her crowd. Molly, you don't really hate men like the rest of them, do you?'

'Hate men? Get real. How could I hate men?' Molly put her hand on her horn and blasted the man she overtook. 'No, I'm just a good old-fashioned narcissistic exhibitionist, and I like being at the centre of things. My shrink says I'm a hopeless case, but I don't care, Glenda. I want to *live*.'

'You sound like Gerontius. That's what he says. There's a

line in Kerouac's *On the Road* which he keeps quoting, ". . . the ones who are mad to live, mad to talk, mad to be saved, desirous of everything at the same time, the ones who never yawn or say a commonplace thing, but burn, burn, burn like fabulous yellow roman candles exploding like spiders across the stars . . ." Isn't that fabulous? That's why I love Clive. He's never boring. He's always busy.'

They were approaching the lights of the town. 'Make sure he doesn't burn himself out too early, Glenda.' Molly's face was in shadows. 'Be careful that you don't get hurt. From what you tell me, his family sounds very rich and powerful, like mine. They play hard ball when they play.'

'You mean "supping with panthers", as they say?'

'Yeah, you've got to know what you're taking on.'

'But I don't particularly want to take them on. It sounds like a fight. We're not in it for a fight. Clive isn't even sure he *wants* to inherit the family title. Part of him is quite happy to let his brother Caspar have the whole damn thing. He just wants Fen Farm and enough money to keep it going. After all, he grew up with all the people who now live there, and he knows that if he lets his mother take Fen Farm, she'll sack everybody. They all live in tied cottages which Clive intends to give them, so they'll always have a roof over their heads. But first he must inherit the title. His mother wants to destroy him, as far as I can see. She insists that he gives up *everything*.'

'She's probably in love with him, but can't have him, so that's her problem. You know, a sort of Jocasta complex. The Ancient Greeks got it right. Mothers wanting to fuck their sons.'

'Molly, you have a definite flair for the crude. You make everything sound so gross.'

'It *is* gross, Glenda. Take my word for it, it *is* gross. You should see my mother with my older brother Chucky. He's as bent as a pretzel. He'll be taking her to the movies for the rest of his life, if he doesn't commit suicide first.'

'Let's change the subject.' Glenda was growing uncomfortable. She needed time to think, to store these sentences away and take them out and consider them at her leisure. 'Do look at the lights. Isn't Cambridge fabulous at Christmas-time?'

'Cambridge is fabulous at any time. You know, I really like this place. And I can't wait to have a real American shower at your house. "My cup runneth over", as our own King David said.'

'Manischewitz, yourself.' Glenda grinned.

They pulled up outside the pub and entered the warm room.

'Over here!' She heard Fatima's high voice calling.

Molly and Glenda pushed their way through rough coats and dripping backs. The weather was cold and people were talking under their pink chafed noses and rubbing together their chilled hands. Fatima was sitting at their usual table with a tall dark-haired man who, Glenda knew, must be Majid. 'Hello,' she said. 'I'm Glenda.'

Majid took her hand and smiled. 'You are just as I imagined,' he said. His voice was soft, like a cat purring, Glenda thought. His hair was thick and wavy and he had long, slanted eyes.

Molly gaped. 'He's beautiful, Fatima. How did you land him? Got any spare brothers?' she enquired.

Majid smiled, his lips parting to show bright white teeth. 'Not for forward American girls, Molly,' he said with a hint of disapproval. Molly sat down. 'I'll get some drinks. What would you like, Glenda?'

'I'd love a gin and tonic please.'

'And you, Molly?'

Molly looked up. 'Forward American girls drink screwdrivers,' she said. 'Heavy on the screw.' Glenda kicked Molly under the table, but Fatima just smiled, her eyes alight. 'Wonderful buns,' Molly whispered loudly as Majid left the table.

'Please, Molly,' Glenda said. 'Don't be awful.'

'Not to worry,' Fatima said. 'Majid can handle Molly. He has seven spoilt sisters of his own and fourteen half-sisters.'

Molly leaned back in her chair. 'Christmas must be fun at his house,' she said, 'or Chanukah, or whatever it is you do to celebrate when you celebrate.'

'How typical,' said Fatima with teasing disapproval. 'Flaunting your ignorance again. Why, you Americans are even worse than the British. We honour our Prophet, but we serve Allah our God. He is also the God of Ibrahim, and Ishaq, and Ya'qoob, the same God the Judeo-Christians worship. We have Ramadan, when we fast and then we celebrate at the end of Ramadan. Do try and learn about how the rest of the world lives. And then maybe America won't make such a mess of its foreign policy.'

'I can't worry about foreign policy,' Molly stated, 'when I don't even understand my personal politics. I'm supposed to worry about women sewing up their vaginas to please men in Africa, and Chinese women binding up their feet. Then I'm supposed to understand the difference between a radical feminist and a radical lesbian militant. I tell you, it takes all my time just working out who believes in what. No wonder I don't have time to do my papers for old Scraggs. I'm going to have a lousy report, and mom is going to yell and dad will say I'm only young once. Life is so predictable.'

'For you it is,' Fatima said, and Glenda watched the light in her eyes dim.

'Any news on your family?' Glenda said quietly.

Fatima glanced quickly around the room and then she leaned forward and said, 'The family will leave on the Eve of Christmas. There will be much festivity, for there are many in Turaq who celebrate Christmas. The border guards will have been drinking. As Muslims they are not supposed to drink, though many of them do. Mummy and the family will slip through, dressed as peasants going to another town to visit family, and then away to the airport where some of Majid's friends will be waiting with an aeroplane.'

'Where will they go? Do you know?'

'No.' Fatima shook her head. 'Maybe London, but mummy doesn't want to live in England. She hates the British for their colonial history. She would like to go to Singapore. Majid says the less I know the safer I will be, so I must wait.'

The door of the pub opened. Glenda saw Georgina's blonde hair and behind her the tall figure of Jonathan. They swept through the pub. Automatically, people stepped aside as the couple made their way to the table. How different the rich are, Glenda thought. It was not that Georgina pushed her way through the crowd, but that the crowd fell back, a gesture of instinctive deference to the genuinely well-bred.

'Darling.' Georgina hugged Glenda. 'Meet Jonathan. You should have seen the high table, such marvellous Queen Anne silver. Fabulous dinner. I loved every moment of it. Snuff boxes. Of course, the ladies left the table before the port.'

Molly frowned. 'British men hate women,' she said. 'After dinner the women get thrown out.'

'You don't understand, Molly. Jonathan, this is Molly, our very liberated American friend. You really don't understand. We women don't *want* to stay with the men, boring old things that they are. They either talk shop or tell rather dull dirty jokes. Now, we women go to a drawing room where we *really* talk. Who's in Bed with Whom. Much better title for *Who's Who*, don't you think?'

Glenda laughed. She loved Georgina when she was in one of her funny moods. 'And who *is* in bed with whom?' Majid asked, smiling at Georgina.

'That's for the Souls to know and for you to find out,' Georgina said.

'What is this Souls thing?' Majid asked. He lifted his glass and looked quizzically at Fatima. 'I hope you are being a good little fiancée and not joining anything I would not approve of.'

'Oh, you wouldn't approve of this club, Majid,' Molly said.

'Our motto is: Every woman shall have her man but no man shall have his woman. *And*,' she leaned forward, 'we all get to share each other's men.'

Glenda said, 'Hey, Molly, hang on! We didn't agree on that bit.'

'Nor did we categorically rule out the possibility,' Molly said, staring at Majid.

'Well, then, Molly,' Majid's eyes narrowed, 'if you plan to live according to some of men's rules, you must live according to all men's rules. When women no longer want or need the protection of men, then you have only the law of the jungle left.' He threw back his head and laughed. It was a huge laugh. It tore the air and startled the people in the pub.

Fatima was smiling. She was used to her husband-to-be. She loved his sense of humour and the way he could enjoy life to the full.

Georgina looked amused and Jonathan grinned. 'You'd better listen to Majid, Molly,' he said. 'It's rough out there.'

'You mean in your world at Harvard?'

'Not just there. I mean when you set out to take on the male world.'

'How much do you know about feminism?' Molly demanded.

'Molly,' Jonathan said quietly so that Molly had to strain to hear him. 'No man in his right mind gives a monkey's about the women's movement. A small handful will exploit the idea to gain women's votes, and maybe for a few years a token number of women will be let into the boardrooms. But the pendulum will swing back and women will go home to their families and their children once again. Read your history, baby. Read your history.'

Molly's chin jutted out. 'I will not read *your* history,' she said. 'I read women's history, and I'm telling you we will not back down. I really can't stay here and listen to any more of this male chauvinist piggery. You are a bastard, Jonathan, an utter bastard.'

'Quite right,' Jonathan said, taking Molly's chair. 'Absolutely right. And I'm going to marry Georgina,' he said loudly as Molly turned to leave, 'and she is going to be barefoot and in the kitchen and permanently pregnant and happy in bed. Aren't you, darling?'

Molly was gone.

Georgina frowned. 'Jonathan, must you be such a frightful tease? You know you don't mean that.'

Jonathan spread out his long legs under the table. 'But I can't help being the devil's advocate from time to time. A pity though. Molly is too pretty to be a feminist, don't you think?'

'I think we'd better get out of here before Molly comes back with Sonia and her friends and surgically does you some under-the-table damage,' Glenda said, 'Come on. I can see Clive coming. Let's all relax and talk about something peaceful for a change, shall we?'

Chapter 73

Saying goodbye to Clive was one of the most miserable moments of Glenda's life. 'I don't want to leave you,' she whispered as she clung to him the night before she was due to drive down to London with Molly.

'I'll be all right,' Clive said, holding her close. In the last weeks they often melted into each other's arms when they were alone together. Or they held hands joyously as they sauntered around Cambridge. Glenda wished she and Clive could live there in an enchanted eternity. 'Really, I'll be fine. I've always got Gerontius and Bix and the others within arm's reach.'

Glenda held his sweet face between her hands. 'I'll think of you all the time until I see you again.'

'I'll telephone you every day,' Clive said. 'And then I'll be at the Savoy and we can have dinner on New Year's Eve. Why don't you bring your mother and Renée and Abe? I'd love to meet them. And what better an evening to celebrate our engagement?' He grinned. 'The smoked salmon at the Savoy is the best in the world, you know.'

'So I hear, but I've never been there. That would be lovely.'

Glenda unwillingly pulled away. They had not talked about Clive's family. There was no need to. There was nothing to say.

Clive walked Glenda to the front door of college. 'I'll telephone you tomorrow night,' he said.

Glenda waved and watched him walk down the path. Why does the back of his neck look so heart-breakingly vulnerable? she wondered.

Glenda sat quietly through the whole drive to London, trying not to weep. Don't be so silly, she thought, it's only ten days. But her heart felt like a rusty sieve shot full of holes. If this is what love is like, she thought, then some of it is very painful.

Molly drove. After a long silence she said, 'Jonathan and Majid are sharp people, you know. I'm not sure I like men like them. They have no respect for women.'

Glenda's mind shifted gear. 'Face it, Molly, you do come on a bit too strong sometimes.'

Molly pouted. 'That's what comes from having four brothers. My mom adores them all and I had to fight to get any attention. Funny, in a way. I mean, I know how to joke with guys and to play around, but I don't know how to really talk to a guy. Either I fuck them or they fuck me over.'

'Maybe if you didn't leap into bed so fast, you might find that men are human, just like the rest of us.'

'Maybe so,' Molly said with a sigh. 'You sleeping with Clive?'

Glenda stared straight ahead through the windscreen. 'I'm

not ready for that yet. We've talked about it, but I don't want to be like the other girls, always counting the days of the month and panicking in case I'm pregnant. You have to remember, I grew up with my mother only. I watched her suffer and struggle. We were poor, Molly, so poor you can't imagine what it was like. Anyway, I want to get my degree and then get married. After that,' she stretched, 'we can make love whenever we want. I know that's not a fashionable attitude, and Georgina and Fatima and I get teased for thinking that way, but that's how it's going to be. Besides, it's nobody's business but our own.'

Molly watched the road intently. 'I guess my problem is that I don't want to end up like my mom.'

Glenda smiled. 'You've said that so many times before. You can't end up like your mother. You're Molly. Different. An individual in her own right.'

'I know all that, but I mean she got married so young to dad. And then BANG. She had five children. No, she's just an airhead. She spends her mornings at exercise classes. She throws awful pots and paints muddy pictures that hang all over the house. She pretends to have opinions, but mostly she just reads the book reviews column in the *New York Times*. Really, there's no one home, if you know what I mean. My dad loves her in an abstract sort of way. He treats her like a china doll and pats her on the head if she gets upset. Whenever he gets a piece of her ass, he goes out and buys her something real useful like a new household appliance. We can always tell when he's had some – he runs around the house all bright-eyed and bushy-tailed. Not that he gets it too often. She has the Great American Bad Back. It used to be headaches, but now it's the back. Her chiropractor must be making a fortune from my mom and her friends. Just think of the money!' She turned her eyes momentarily towards Glenda. 'I want more in my life. Not just pussy power, which is what men let us have.'

'If that's what you want,' Glenda said, 'then I'm sure you'll get it. But so far you've had more sex than anybody else I know.'

'That's just because sex hasn't caught on outside the States yet, but it will.' Molly grinned and pushed her foot down hard on the pedal. 'What do you think the Peace Corps is all about? Americans taking sex to Africa and India and all over the world. Make love, not war. Chew gum while having orgasms. "Look, Ma! No rules!"'

'But there are rules. And you know it. And you can break them, if you must. But don't whine if you end up on your own. I know that Sonia sounds pretty convincing with her friends, but she's a rich girl with more money than sense. And for now it all sounds too good to be true. Give her another thirty years, then where will she be?'

'Oh, in some commune humping her anarchist friends, I suppose. I'll be on Capitol Hill in Congress, making money, lots and lots of money. That's where I'll be. Or maybe on Wall Street.'

'I'll be married to Clive,' Glenda said dreamily. 'We'll live on Fen Farm and have lots and lots of children, whatever his beastly mother says.'

'I hope so,' Molly said.

'Turn right here, and then go left.'

The car wound its way through the familiar London streets. As they reached Chiswick High Road, Glenda began to feel excited. Home, she thought. Mum and Renée and Abe waiting for me.

Molly stopped the car outside the house in Ealing. For a moment Glenda sat still. This was the house she felt she left as a child. Only a few months later, but aeons in time, she was now coming back as a woman. It was as if she could see herself walking down the stairs, her old self, young and vulnerable, easily hurt and shy. Now she was about to walk up those welcoming stairs no longer so vulnerable, but in love and engaged to be married.

She smiled at Molly. 'Come on,' she said. 'I'll introduce you.'

The door opened and Abe ran down the stairs and grabbed Glenda. 'Hiya, honey!' He gave her a hug. 'We missed you. This must be Molly.' Molly put out her hand and Abe shook it heartily. 'It'll be nice having a compatriot around the house,' he said.

Renée came down the steps and appeared behind Abe. She swooped and pulled Glenda into her arms. Glenda relaxed, feeling Renée's warm breasts and caressing hands. How I've missed them, she thought. So open and so caring. Scraggs could never hug any of the girls like that. But she knew she would miss Scraggs, alone in her beautiful library. I hope she has a good Christmas, she thought as she waited for Abe to take the two suitcases from the car.

'Yoohoo, Glenda! I'm down 'ere.' Minnie was waving frantically from the basement flat.

'Mum!' Glenda went flying down the steps. 'Oh mum!' She hugged Minnie.

'Well,' she said, 'you've not grown any taller.' Minnie pushed Glenda away so she could appraise her completely. 'You look lovely,' she said.

Molly walked down the steps behind Glenda. ''Ello, Molly. Glad you could come. Renée's given you a bed so you don't have to share with Glenda.'

'Great,' Molly said. 'That's wonderful.'

'Glenda, let's get you unpacked. Abe, take Molly up with you, and Glenda and I'll be up in a jiffy for lunch.'

When they were alone with the door securely shut, Minnie looked at her daughter and then she took Glenda's hand and examined the ring. 'Are you sure you know what you're doing, love?'

'You'll like him, mum. I promise. He's gentle and kind and I love him very much.'

'That's all right then,' Minnie said. 'It's just that talking over the phone isn't much good. I just had to see your face.

326

And you do look happy. Very 'appy.'

'Are you happy about it, mum?'

'Yes.' Minnie smiled.

'And Clive has asked us all to dinner at the Savoy to celebrate the New Year and our engagement.'

'The Savoy! That's nice.' Minnie paused. 'Glenda, you're not –' Minnie suddenly looked concerned. 'You're not . . . You know.'

'No, mum, not until we're married. We've both decided that.' Visions from early childhood, visions of Hounslow, of Jack's grey underpants, swam into Glenda's head. The endless 'uncles'. Oh no, she thought, I'm not doing any of that.

Minnie was clearly relieved. 'It's not that I'm an angel or anything,' Minnie said. 'It's funny. It's all right when it's you, but it's not all right when it's your daughter. Know what I mean?' Minnie washed her hands in the kitchen sink. 'Come along, love,' she said. 'Wash and get ready, and we'll go upstairs.'

Chapter 74

The tall Christmas tree shone and sparkled in the drawing room. Under the tree were piles of red-wrapped parcels. Glenda smiled. How many years had gone by with this familiar scene, central to her life? The smell of pine. The discipline of Christmas.

Minnie started her Christmas in October. Having learnt Renée's cookery book recipes by heart, she bottled her peaches in brandy and she baked her Christmas cake that usually required ornate amounts of marzipan. 'First grind the almonds, then add an equal amount of confectioner's sugar . . .' This year she had not been there to take part in the weeks of preparation, but she was glad to be home, even glad enough to put aside, for a moment, the ache of Clive.

Molly came down the stairs. She, too, was grinning. 'Nice

pad you've got here,' she said to Abe. 'Terrific shower. After lunch I'm going to lock myself in there for the whole afternoon.'

There was a knock on the front door and Chinchilla swept in. 'How marvellous to see you, darling!' Chinchilla's hair brushed Glenda's face. 'And this must be Molly.'

Molly looked impressed. She knew that Renée was a well-known English actress, but Chinchilla had made it to Hollywood. Chinchilla threw her arms around Abe and then similarly embraced Renée. 'I'll just go and see Minnie in the kitchen, and then I'll be back,' she said.

'Wow!' Molly's eyes were huge. 'Did you get a load of those diamonds?'

'Diamonds are Chinchilla's speciality,' Renée said wryly. 'She earns them.'

Molly stared back. There was no malice in Renée's voice; it was just a fact.

Chinchilla came into the room carrying a soup tureen, Minnie behind her with hot, fresh, crusty garlic bread. The smell of the garlic and the sight of the long, homemade white loaves filled Glenda with happiness. The food at Girton was good, but not this good. Glenda loved gazpacho soup. She gazed down at the black pepper flecks in among the bright red of the crushed Roma tomatoes and she thought of the paintings of the Impressionists. Cooking is just like painting, she thought, only in pots instead of on canvas. She very much wished she could frame this soup and hang it on the wall with her mother's signature at the bottom.

'Abe and I have something to tell you all,' Renée began. She nervously pushed her long hair back behind her ears. The years had been kinder to Renée than they had to Chinchilla. Chinchilla now had wrinkles under her chin that no amount of face-tucks could obliterate and Glenda noticed a little sagging under her arms. Today Chinchilla wore a familiar lavender-coloured cocktail dress. Rather elaborate for a family get-together, but she was still beautiful. Her blonde hair was also shaded lavender to match her shoes and her cocktail bag. She must be the only woman in London to still wear small cloche hats and gloves, Glenda thought.

Renée, however, seemed to have avoided signs of growing old. There were no tired lines on her face and she was as slim and youthful as the first day when Glenda saw her, except for a more pronounced streak of grey that ran from her widow's peak down the two wings of her hair. The wings were still a glossy black. Abe too was grizzled, but still the same Abe. Maybe happiness keeps you young, thought Glenda. Renée said, 'Abe and I are getting married.'

'Oh how wonderful!' Glenda cried out.

'Not right away,' said Renée. 'But soon. In a year or two. The main thing is that we decided we will.'

'Gee, congratulations.' Molly wasn't smiling. 'But why get married?' she said.

Glenda frowned at Molly. 'Don't give us one of your feminist lectures. Really, mum, Molly is awful. She has these hairy feminist friends who think you don't have to get married. I don't know why they have to be so anti-romance. Even after Clive and I decided to get married, he wanted to do things right, so he proposed to me again on his knees and he brought me red roses and chocolates later on. Why not?'

'Because he might be on his knees when he proposes to you, but just you wait until he gets up,' Molly said. 'Sometimes it feels like all men are male chauvinist pigs.' Molly suddenly realized that Abe was in the room. 'Of course not you, Abe. I'm sorry. You're black, so you're oppressed too.'

'Thanks, Molly. It's nice to know my suffering doesn't go unnoticed,' he said wryly. 'But listen, Renée and I are getting married because we want to get married. How's that for freedom? I love Renée enough to make my commitment public and before God. Those are important vows. If you take a vow before God that you will do all the things you say, then it can't be broken.' He glanced at Renée and there was such a warm surge of love and happiness between them that

Glenda felt them both glow. That's what I feel for Clive, she thought. Chinchilla sat rather silently.

'Now you're at university, Glenda,' Renée continued, 'we are thinking of moving to New York. Don't worry. We're not rushing into anything. It will take a couple of years to sell up here, and I have theatre commitments for the next few seasons. But in, what, two years or so, we should have moved to New York. And that's probably when we'll get married. And it's important to us to know that you will all be all right here. You'll probably be done with university by that time anyway. I've discussed this with your mother. We plan to invest in a small restaurant for Minnie. And Chinchilla wants to come in on it, too. Chiswick could use a good restaurant and Minnie needs a wider audience for her cooking, she's learned to cook so well.'

Minnie was beaming. 'I'll 'ave me own place, Glen. And after all, New York is only across the pond these days. People come and go whenever they want. Don't they, Chinchilla?'

'I'm not going or coming for a while,' Chinchilla said. 'I'm tired of the States, and LA, and all those boring suntans and the same white teeth. Martini bellies on all the men and sneakers on their feet. My! You can't imagine what it's like to live in the land of grown men wearing sneakers and baseball caps! They can be such children, American men. Spoiled, self-indulgent children. No thank you. I'm on the lookout for an English rotter instead. At least he'll speak English and wear decent shoes.'

Glenda watched Chinchilla. The trouble with Chinchilla, she thought, finishing her soup, is that *she* is a spoiled and selfish woman. But I love her anyway.

Molly said, 'May I say, ma'am, that you ought to read *The Feminine Mystique*? I think you'd find it very interesting.'

Chinchilla smiled at Molly. 'I have no intention of turning into a women's libber. It's thanks to them there are no men left to marry. The good men have taken to the hills. And the men who are left know they don't *have* to get married any more, so they won't.

'Women civilize men. Without us they would be a grunting pack of monsters. Don't underestimate the treachery of men or their brutality. Women asked to be treated as equals, and they are. So now we're unprotected. It's open warfare between men and women, and the bloodshed comes from women. They're getting it all now. Jobs, babies, homes, and no men.' Chinchilla's voice was bitter. 'But never mind. I'm going to bury myself in the restaurant and make a lot of money. Sod men!'

'*Brava!*' Molly cheered. 'Sod men!'

Renée laughed. 'Dear, dear,' she said. 'What a heart-warming conversation. Aren't you going to ask what the restaurant will be called?'

'What?' Glenda asked.

'We're thinking of La Pousada,' Minnie broke in. 'I think Portuguese food and wine is going to come into its own. Glenda, give me a hand with the next course, will you?'

Chapter 75

Christmas passed by in a gorgeous panorama of sights and sounds. Molly drove to Harrods to collect Christmas crackers for Renée. Glenda sat beside her, loving the lights and the decorations in the West End. 'Everything looks so small and cosy compared to America,' Molly said. 'Everything here's all so compact. You don't have any shopping malls.'

'No,' said Glenda, 'but we do have Carnaby Street and Biba's. Want to take a look? That's the shop the feminists are threatening to bomb,' Glenda continued. 'I love the place.' They parked outside the glittering front doors. Inside Glenda felt she was in a fairy story. Rows and rows of marvellous coloured scarves. 'This shop's designed by Mary Quant. Now *there's* a liberated woman for you.' Glenda smiled at Molly as they walked around. 'What do you think?'

'Fer to die!' Molly said and rolled her eyes. 'I've never seen anything like this!'

Glenda laughed. 'Face it. All the best ideas come from England.'

'I simply must have this purple eyeshadow. And look how well it goes with this purple nail polish! And look, Glenda! I'll just die if I don't have that cigarette holder.' Molly was off on one of her shopping rampages.

The two girls returned home with bags of loot. Glenda followed Molly up the stairs to her room. She had bought herself only a jumper, but she did not envy Molly. I have Clive, she realized. When I have my degree I'll get married. That's what I want out of life. Not a load of make-up or frilly underwear.

She sat on the bed and pretended to listen while Molly chattered away, but her mind was full of other thoughts. Clive would be ringing as he did every night. After the last *Goodbye, darling, I love you*, she went to bed content. Minnie was going to have her own place. Chinchilla would keep her company in the restaurant. Glenda was glad that soon Minnie would no longer have to do housework. And running a restaurant she could meet a lot of people. Maybe Minnie would get married one day, but even if she did not, there was always room for her at Fen Farm. Now it was just a matter of waiting for New Year's Eve and the moment when she would be in Clive's arms again at the Savoy. Everybody was curious to meet Clive and she knew they would not be disappointed.

When Glenda went downstairs, Minnie was poring over the *Chiswick and Brentford Times*. 'Look, dear,' she said. 'A sweet little cottage right by the river. What do you think?'

'I think that would be marvellous, mum. Does it have a garden?'

'Just a little one, but enough so I can grow my own vegetables and a rose bush or two.'

Glenda smiled at her mother. 'And geraniums?' she said, remembering the straggly, soot-encrusted geraniums in the kitchen window in Hounslow.

'Yes.' Minnie remembered also. 'Geraniums.' Mother and daughter looked at each other in perfect accord. There was no need to bring up the grim, grey past. *Let us leave all that behind us* hung on the air. Minnie leaned forward and gave Glenda a peck on the cheek. 'I'm proud of you, Glenda,' she said. 'Really I am.'

'I know, mum, and I'm glad.'

Chapter 76

Abe handed the keys of his Lagonda to the doorman at the Savoy. As the group stepped from the car, Clive came out onto the apron of the hotel. 'Here, Fred,' he said, 'let me give you a hand.'

'Thank you, sir,' he said.

Clive helped Renée out of the car and smiled at Glenda. 'Fred and I go back a long way. He's known me since Nanny carried me here in her arms.'

Glenda looked up at the brightly lit entrance. 'Isn't it magnificent?' she said.

Renée gave a happy sigh of agreement. 'It truly is. Only hotel in London worth staying in,' she said. 'Come, Glenda. I don't want to keep Reno waiting.'

'Reno?'

'Reno is the best restaurant manager in town,' Renée said.

Glenda trailed behind Renée, feeling a little dowdy. Minnie trotted after her. Glenda wished her mother was not wearing her usual tight mini-skirt. Mum's too old for a mini, she thought. Molly was wearing dark glasses under which she had her new purple eye make-up, and her mouth was a blotch of crushed blackberries. She wore a bright red dress and Glenda knew she had black frilly knickers underneath, if she was wearing any knickers at all. Renée sailed along the smooth floors waving a languid hand at people who looked up and smiled at her in recognition.

Reno came forward with a smile on his handsome face. He kissed Renée's hand. 'Lovely to see you again, madame,' he said with a bow.

They followed him into the River Restaurant. 'Ahh!' Renée breathed, and she looked at Clive who was hovering beside Glenda. 'What a treat! And Reno and I have so much to catch up on don't we, Reno?'

'We have not seen much of you this last year,' Reno said.

'No, darling. I've been working awfully hard at the theatre. We are thinking of going to New York. What do you think?'

Reno shrugged an expressive shoulder. 'It will be a loss for the Savoy. But New York is exciting. I will give you the names of some good restaurants, if you would like, but of course, you would have to have your smoked salmon flown in. The Americans, they . . . Smoked salmon is still rather new to them.'

At the table he pulled a chair out for Molly who looked bewildered at the numbers of spoons and forks. 'Are all your guests here, sir?' he asked Clive.

Clive raised a questioning eyebrow to Renée. 'Chinchilla will be along in a moment,' Renée said. Reno nodded and left the table. 'Now, Clive,' Renée began, 'now that we are all seated, shall we say hello?'

'I feel as if I've known you all for ages,' Clive said. 'Glenda talks so much about you, I hardly feel we need to introduce ourselves. You must be Minnie,' he said, taking Minnie's hand.

'Yes, thank you,' said Minnie nervously and Glenda winced. She knew Clive would not mind, but she also knew that Clive's mother would tease him unmercifully, had she witnessed this scene.

Clive shook hands with Abe and Renée as well and said

his hellos to Molly. 'Let's have champagne,' he said. 'Shall we?'

Soon they were joined by Chinchilla. The menus were placed before the diners and there was a moment's silence. The menu was enormous and Glenda decided the best thing to do was to follow Clive. 'I'll have what you're having,' she said. Moments later she sat with a glass of champagne in her hand and looked at the bubbles. I hope our life will be like that, she thought.

By the time midnight struck, they were sitting in Clive's suite, still with a glass of champagne. Everyone was laughing and talking. Molly looked animated, even if she had not found herself a man. 'I like this joint,' she said, having prowled around the bedrooms and two bathrooms. 'Can I move in? You could fit a football team in the bath. *And* it has a shower.'

Clive smiled and took Glenda's hand. 'When Glenda and I are married, you'll be welcome, but I'd want Glenda around to see that you don't have a football team in my bathroom.'

'One day I'll have a suite of my own,' Molly said, slightly drunk.

Minnie sat by the fire, and Abe and Renée were out on the balcony, their arms around each other. Renée opened the french windows and everyone heard the thrilling sound of Big Ben chiming in the New Year. Renée walked back as the great peals of the bells rang out over London. 'This has been a perfect Christmas,' she said, 'and the Queen's speech was wonderful.' She raised her glass. 'Here's to the two happy couples. Here's to Minnie and Chinchilla's restaurant, and here's to Molly who one day will be running the Capitol, and here's to the royal family. God bless us all.'

Clive pulled Glenda by the hand when everyone had seconded the toast and sipped from their glasses. 'Let's slip outside,' he said. 'We haven't had a moment to ourselves.' Outside the air was stingingly cold. Clive looked absolutely magnificent in his tuxedo. He put his arm around Glenda against the cold night air. 'How was your Christmas?' he said.

'Beautiful, but I missed you. How was yours?'

'Bloody awful, as usual. Father ran around with his disgusting old cronies killing everything in sight, and mother moaned and bitched. She's rather furious about us getting married, you know.'

'Tough,' Glenda said simply.

Clive chuckled. 'She wants us to have a godawful big public wedding at St Peter's in Eaton Square.'

'We won't,' Glenda said, suddenly making up her mind. 'Don't say anything to anyone except mum. When the time comes, we'll go off quietly and get married in a registry office. We simply can't have your mother telling us when and where to get married. It's none of her bloody business.' And, she thought privately, I won't have Lady Jane and her awful friends jeering at Mum. 'Anyway, it's two years away.'

'I know,' he said, 'but I can wait, darling. I'll always love you.'

'I believe you,' Glenda said, 'and you don't know how happy that makes me.'

'For better or worse?' Clive said.

Glenda nodded. 'Yes, but it will always be better,' she said and she hugged Clive.

'I hope so,' Clive said, but the word 'hope' flew off the balcony and plunged into the Thames. There was a last silver flash and then it was swept away, screaming. Glenda turned and went into the suite. She did not hear the warning.

BOOK THREE

Chapter 77

Standing in her cap and gown, clutching her degree in her hand, Glenda was unaware of anything but the proud smile on her mother's face. Far away she could see Scraggs sitting on the platform, her face drowned in a sea of bobbing caps. Beside Glenda, Molly sat quietly for once, as even she was overawed by the event. Georgina and Fatima sat the other side. Georgina had obtained a first, as everyone had expected. But Glenda was happy with her upper two. She did not expect a first; she was just glad that she had done well and now she had the rest of her life to look forward to.

After the ceremony was over there were numerous goodbyes. Goodbye to Fatima, who was going over to Paris to see Majid and then to join her family, now in Singapore. Goodbye to Molly on her way back to New Jersey and then to Washington, DC, where a job as a messenger on the floor of the Congress awaited her. It was not the congressional position she would ultimately desire, but it was a start. 'I'll lay 'em all, Glenda,' Molly promised.

Glenda hugged Molly tight. 'No, you won't, silly. I'll be over to see you once we're married.'

Clive wasn't at the ceremony. Glenda knew he had not been well. He was with Nanny Jenkins. Over the telephone his voice had been high and uncertain, pouring down the phone, overflowing the mouth piece. 'I can't come. Terribly sorry. I'm having a little trouble. Nothing to worry about. It won't go away, or maybe it will. I can't tell yet, but I'll tell you when I see you. When will I see you?'

'Before I leave Cambridge with mum. Calm down. What's the matter?'

'Nothing is the matter, but the gate won't shut.' A long silence.

'Clive, are you still there?'

Nanny's firm voice. 'He's all right, Glenda. He's just a little overtired and needs some rest.'

Glenda felt guilty now as she watched Molly disappear in her little red car. Molly was taking the car with her back to New Jersey, so she was driving to Southampton to take a boat home. Fatima was gone and Georgina was due to come and say goodbye. Minnie, Abe and Renée were waiting for Glenda downstairs in the Great Hall. Still, Glenda thought as she stood at her window for the last time, I'll still have Georgina to visit in this country.

A lovely, hazy Cambridge late spring day. The willows beside the pond bent their heads and wept. They were losing yet another batch of Girton girls. No, you aren't, Glenda whispered back. You'll never lose us. You will always be with us wherever we go. Cambridge is not just an experience, it's a way of life. Years later, when I pick up a jar of Nescafé, the sudden smell of the coffee when I rip off the seal will bring this moment back. The willow pond, the ducks waggling their behinds in the sunshine. My room where I lived almost exclusively in the last year studying for my degree. The Brahms piano concerto on the record player, the sound of madrigals swinging on the warm wind. The dons, the tutors, and above all the books. Hundreds and hundreds of books, all preserved by doughty women who cared that women should be educated as well as men. No other college anywhere in the world was so exciting. Nowhere else could contain the determination and the excellence found at Girton. Tears fell down Glenda's cheeks and she realized how much she would indeed miss 'That Infidel Place'.

For months now, even when she went with Clive to the farm, she had dreamed of the day she would leave. The freedom to be away from books and lectures, papers, noise, other women . . . All jumbled up in the last months of study. She ached for the calm of her own room in Ealing, for free days when she could just lie about and dream. Time had no time in this last year. She neglected everyone. Her mother understood and Clive said he understood, but did he? Had this illness been brought on by her neglect? Was he really as ill as his mother said? Thoughts, like dusty bats, crowded into her head . . .

There was a knock at the door and Georgina came in. 'My goodness, Glenda. You do look down.'

'It's Clive. He's not well again. I'm worried about him.'

Georgina smiled. 'We blue-bloods are a tougher lot than you think. He'll be all right. Listen, I've got to go now. Mother is waiting outside with a pack of foaming dogs in the Land Rover. I'll ring you in London and arrange for the two of you to come down and spend some time with us. Jonathan is coming over.' She hugged Glenda. 'At least we still have each other. I'm going to miss Fatima. And come to think of it, I'll even miss Molly.' They stood together for a moment and Georgina looked into the descending twilight. 'This really is the end of an era for me. Soon I'll be married and then I'll be Mrs Jonathan Montague.' She laughed. 'Will you be my maid of honour, Glenda?'

'I'd love to. I'd ask you to be mine, but we're thinking of a way to get married quietly, to blight Clive's mother's fond hopes. But, yes, I'd love to be yours.'

'Wonderful. Come on then. Collect your bags, and let's go down the stairs for the last time. Gosh, I can't remember how many times I've walked down these corridors.'

The corridors were empty. Abe had taken most of Glenda's boxes to the car before the ceremony. They were returning to the house in Ealing which had now been sold. Glenda offered to help Minnie move into her pretty little house by the river in Chiswick. Chinchilla had missed the ceremony because she was in Portugal buying dishes for the new restaurant. What a time of sea change! Glenda thought as they walked down the corridors where voices no longer echoed. The sounds of many feet, flying along or walking slowly, had cleared.

She remembered the day she arrived. How young she was! Shy and quiet she sat that first night after meeting Georgina. This was the same Georgina who, like Glenda, had grown in assurance as well as in knowledge. Both of them walked down to the Great Hall for the last time as students. Tomorrow they would be regular members of the rest of the world, but for this moment they were still students. Glenda felt an uneasy lump in her throat. I'll be all right, she thought, when I get home.

The drive back was long and boring. Glenda spent much of it asleep. She dreamed uneasily about Clive. Too busy much of the time to analyse his behaviour, she did think there was beginning to be a pattern to it. He would be fine for a while and then he would get very quiet and withdrawn. Then he seemed to spiral into a more and more frantic way of behaving. His words would come out backwards and sometimes, when he was agitated, they made no sense at all. She had learned that it was lithium which Dr Umberto injected into Clive when he seemed too upset. The lithium injections did calm him down. She knew from reading about lithium that he must at all times drink plenty of water, or any liquid, for lithium is very dehydrating . . . In her dream she tossed and turned as she saw his face. It looked piteous, as was his voice the last time she talked to him.

She flitted in and out of wakefulness until she felt the car pull up at the house. 'Come on, sweetheart.' Abe pulled her gently back into life. 'We've got to celebrate.'

Glenda clung onto his arm for a moment. He and Renée were leaving for New York in a few days. Renée and Abe, her rocks, her salvation. 'Why are we all breaking up?' Glenda said. 'Why can't we go back to being how we were? We were so happy.' The word *happy* touched all of them standing on the pavement in the lamplight.

'We'll all be happy again, honey,' Abe said. 'We're not leaving you for good. We're always on the end of a phone. Times change and people move on. Soon you'll be married to Clive and have a home and a life of your own.'

Minnie took Glenda's arm. 'Don't worry, love,' she said. 'You're just a bit upset. Let's go downstairs and tidy up and then we'll have dinner. Just the four of us. Won't that be nice?'

'Yes,' Glenda said, feeling dejected. 'It will be nice, but it won't ever be the same again.'

Once downstairs she sat on her bed and stared at the floor. 'I don't know if I do want to grow up, mum. I want to stay as we were when I was up at Cambridge and happy with Clive and taking my degree. Now it's all over. I have my degree. Now I have to think about a real future. Damn growing up! It's a foolish thing to do. I don't want to be an adult. What fun do adults have?'

'I have fun,' Minnie said, standing at the door. 'I'm ever so excited about the restaurant. Tomorrow I'll take you over and you can see for yourself. Chinchilla gets into London tomorrow. She's pissed off that she couldn't come to Cambridge, but she has a lovely dinner set for you as a present.' Minnie chattered on. Slowly Glenda found herself caught up in her mother's enthusiasm.

'He's much better,' Nanny said when Glenda telephoned after dinner. 'Dr Umberto has given him his injection and he's sleeping.'

'Tell him I called, Nanny. Won't you?'

'I will,' came the comforting reply.

Glenda climbed into bed and fell asleep. The same moon shines over my room in Cambridge that shines over my room in Ealing. For some reason that thought reassured her.

Chapter 78

Six months later, Glenda, living with Minnie, had worked various odd-jobs around London – part-time clerical work at the British Museum, a bit of research work for a literary radio programme at the BBC – but she had yet to find her place.

Minnie's little cottage in Chiswick was subdued after the days that celebrated Christmas had gone by. The Christmas tree stood in the corner of the sitting room, dropping needles and smelling of pine. Glenda watched the pine needles as they lay browning on the floor. 'You know, mum, I feel like a pine needle. Look at them.' She stretched out on the floor on her stomach, very aware of the warm coal fire. 'I mean, I've done a lot of sitting about, and haven't really started doing anything much. My life seems to have got a bit stuck.'

Minnie yawned. 'Everyone feels like that some time. I'm tired, love. We're nearly finished setting up La Pousada. Chinchilla's done a lovely job.' Minnie got up and then crouched down beside Glenda.

Her mother's warm body smells instantly reminded Glenda of childhood. She rolled onto her back and squinted up at her mother. 'I'm not too young to get married to Clive, am I?'

'Well,' Minnie said, 'couldn't you wait a little while longer? Maybe just till next summer. Just so you know you're sure. July is a nice time for a wedding.'

Glenda propped herself up on one arm. 'July is a good time,' she said softly, thinking of Girton and the huge trees alive with thick, green leaves. She must stop pining, she realized. 'I do miss Cambridge, you know. I mean, I can always go back to visit, but from now on I don't belong there any more. I never thought I'd miss it so much. It hurts. You wait for your childhood to be over, and you push yourself through years of school. They come and go. And then three whole years at Cambridge . . . Clive doesn't see why I don't move in at the farm and live with him.' She saw Minnie's face tighten. 'Don't worry, mum. I won't get pregnant. I know how hard it was for us. I can wait. And so can Clive.'

'Then he must be a very remarkable young man.' A slightly sharp note crept into her voice, as Minnie realized how extraordinary it was that Clive and Glenda had *not* yet slept together. Certainly she was glad her daughter's virtue remained intact, but then again no one could be expected to wait forever. Yet that was exactly what Clive seemed to be doing. The thought struck Minnie: Was Clive quite normal? 'You mean to say you'll live together, but not 'ave sex?'

'That's right. That's how it's been for the past three years. We both know we're not ready. Or he's not, anyway. I could work on the farm with Clive, but after working so hard for my degree, I would like to get a real job and earn some money that's really mine. There's a job open at a private museum just outside Cambridge. It's just what I want to do. I asked Scraggs to give me a reference and she said she would. It's an exhibition of manuscripts, original manuscripts, some of Virginia Woolf's writing, and her contemporaries, like Dora Carrington. Carrington was such a wonderful painter. Much better than the male Bloomsburys, but she was a woman so nobody paid any attention. There are some of her letters to Lytton Strachey, and a few of her paintings. I'll have to arrange all the loans from the various executive trusts. It will be fun. And quite fascinating. I wish Molly were here to do it with me. Which reminds me – she's due to ring tonight. If you hear the phone in the middle of the night, don't worry. It's just Molly forgetting the time difference. She usually gets drunk and then rings when the mood takes her.' Glenda sat up and put her face up for a kiss.

Minnie noticed how quickly she seemed to have changed the subject. She did not quite know what to say about Clive, so she said nothing. She would keep her doubts to herself. She smiled. 'I'm glad you're so happy,' she said. 'I can't get away for Renée's wedding, but you might go.'

'Sure, I'd love to. And I'd love to see New York.'

Minnie left the room.

Glenda turned onto her stomach and gazed at the brown needles. Those two, she thought, are Renée and Abe in New York. And that one by itself off to the side is Fatima surrounded by her family in Singapore. Fatima seemed very happy to be back with her family. She sent Glenda a black silk robe and a golden sari. She intended to wear it at the farm next time she visited Clive. That would be the coming weekend so that they could be together for New Year's Eve. She watched the plume of smoke extending itself from the ashtray. The familiar smell of her mother's cigarette filled her nostrils. Minnie was much happier now she had a home and soon-to-be business of her own. Glenda had not realized that, for all the years they lived with Renée and Abe, Minnie had so much missed having her own home. There was a lightness in Minnie's walk and a smile on her face that Glenda had not seen before. Glenda knew that as much as Minnie loved her cottage and pottered in the garden now bare and brown, she was beginning to love the farm. Clive had moved Nanny Jenkins from her cottage near Cambridge to Fen Farm in Norfolk so that she would be close at hand. Glenda was pleased, having grown to love Nanny. And she felt she had known the servants on the farm all her life. Paul and Mark and their wives were now old friends.

She loved visiting the farm. The room she stayed in there was at the head of the stairs. It was a pretty room, all white with a matching white bathroom. The floor was covered with thick white carpet and the armchairs matched the pink and green curtains. Every evening now Milly, who had been given permission to leave Lady Jane's fortress, made a fire for Glenda and turned down her bed. She would have drawn the bath and laid out Glenda's clothes if Glenda had not said no to that.

But — and there was a *but* when she visited him on the

farm – sometimes Clive was so withdrawn he didn't seem to notice that she existed. Sometimes for hours he would be playing his piano. He played beautifully. Magnificently, in fact. But it almost seemed to keep him from human contact . . .

As she lay on her stomach, she looked at a nest of needles and she thought about the Chinese game of sticks. There is the pile of sticks, she thought, which is really the Alexander family and here am I with the master stick and I have to untangle this awful mess. Somewhere at the bottom of the pile is Clive and I have to rescue him. She imagined the two of them leaping out of the nest of evil pine needles, she and Clive on the back of the Harley Davidson, exultant in their escape. She brushed the pile of needles into a heap. We'll get away, she thought. Of course we will.

Then she shivered. She had a memory of walking around the huge lawn outside the farmhouse last week. It was dusk and an owl hooted. Owls hooted all the time at the farm. It was as if there was a perpetual Greek chorus of owls warning, warning . . . Don't be silly, you're just being morbid, she scolded herself, lying on the floor in London. It's just that it is a dull, flat, dripping time of year on the fens.

The telephone shattered her concentration. 'Hi!' Molly yelled. 'What are you doing?'

'I'm lying on the floor thinking morbid thoughts,' Glenda replied, the phone extension snaking across the room.

'You done it with Clive yet?'

'Molly!' Glenda giggled. 'Is that all you think about?''

'You know it is. Listen, I gave up being a congressional gofer. Instead I got a job in a Washington law firm, starting next month. I can get my credits working there and then move on to higher or lower things, depending on how you look at it. There's the cutest guy in the firm who's just my type. What are you going to do?'

'Any luck, I'm hoping to set up an exhibition at a museum

just outside Cambridge, and I'll be moving in with Clive at the farm after the New Year.'

'Moving in, with *no nooky*?' Molly's voice sounded incredulous.

Glenda said, 'Not all of us live for nooky, you know. I can't believe you're spending all this money on a long distance phone call just to talk about nooky. Don't you have any other news?'

'Oh yes. I had a perfectly dreadful Chanukah with all my brothers' drooling kids and their equally repulsive wives. Eight days of plates of food, Manischewitz wine, and relations dripping their kreplach onto their plates and sneezing chopped liver all over each other. Can you imagine anything less appetizing? I'll never eat chopped liver again. What a bunch of *mishuginahs*. My grandma was good, though. She just goes on about what a good girl I always was and how brilliant I still am. Makes my mother puke. How was your Christmas?'

'Very quiet, now that Renée and Abe are gone. Chinchilla came over for the meal, and then I went up to Cambridge to see Clive. Odd, really. He seemed very remote, and often he seemed to be listening to something else. But I read a lot and sat by the huge log fire and thought about us all. We both went down to visit Georgina.'

'I phoned Fatima a couple of days ago,' Molly interrupted. 'Majid is back in Paris. But Fatima loves being with her mother and sisters out in Singapore. Apparently Fat Aunt is quite a character. They don't have to wear the veil in Singapore, but Fatima wears it anyway. She says she likes to be anonymous. Did she send you the sort of stuff she's wearing?'

'Yes,' Glenda said. 'In fact I'm going to stoke up the fires at the farm and wear it for Clive.'

'Maybe he'll give in as you sway in, covered in sexy silk and fall into his arms, saying, "Take me, Clive. I'm yours." '

'You've been reading too many romance novels, dear,' Glenda said.

'Sure I have. What's a horny girl to do? I miss you, sugar,' Molly said.

'I miss you, too, Molly, and the other two Souls. I miss you all very much. And I miss Cambridge . . . ' Glenda felt her eyes filling with tears.

'Not a bad old dump, Girton.' Molly sighed. 'Boy, I never thought I'd miss the place.'

'It's not just the place. I think it's a way of life that's gone. Now we have our degrees, we have to get on with what is loosely called an adult life, and I'm not sure I'm ready to be an adult. Earning money has its advantages, but the world out there is a cold place.'

'Sure as hell is. Still, Washington is full of wicked debauched people, so I'm in good company. Okay, love. I must get to bed.'

'Bye, Molly. Sleep tight. Mind the bugs don't bite.'

'I'm at a party, dope,' Molly said. 'I'm on someone else's phone. I'm off back to the apartment to see who I can pick up.'

'Good luck and a happy new year. And speak to you soon.'

Glenda put the telephone down and struggled to her feet. 'Christmas pud,' she said out loud and put the phone back on the hook. 'Too much Christmas pud.' She went up the stairs to her bed. I'm glad I'm not Molly, she thought. I'm glad that I have Clive and we are secure. Poor Molly, so restless.

On the river outside her window a tugboat hooted.

Chapter 79

In the middle of dinner, after several glasses of wine, Glenda felt Clive's mood change. He seemed angry, not with her, but with some nameless thing. The room felt jagged and full of menace. After dinner Mrs Robinson cleared the table and Clive, who had been silent for the rest of the meal, pushed his chair aside and said, 'I'm tired, Glenda. I'll go up to bed.'

Glenda spent the next two hours curled up in a heap of misery. Now she was living with Clive and the New Year had come and gone. She lay on the sofa looking into the hot fire that roared and crackled. The last year had brought her so much happiness. Her mother and Chinchilla were completely absorbed in the launch of their new restaurant. Glenda warmed as she remembered her first visit with her mother. Such lovely, gleaming, big thick plates, blues and greens. Portuguese *fado* flowing in the heavily spiced air, the voice sobbing and complaining . . .

Glenda's chest heaved. I'm finally living with the man I love, but why, she thought wearily, am I so unhappy? Molly is rushing about Washington. Fatima is happy in Singapore. Her last letter was full of information about the open-air markets and the smells of cumin and coriander. Georgina was waiting to see them in a week's time, and then Glenda had a job to come back to, for indeed she had just heard that she got the position as exhibition co-ordinator at the museum outside Cambridge. She loved Clive. He brought out all the tenderness and passion Glenda knew she had within her to give to the man she loved. His original mind kept her intellectually stretched. His sensitivity and generosity were touching. His physical beauty stirred her, and in truth she did feel a thrill just looking at him, a thrill that was both aesthetic and sensual . . . But, she thought, he doesn't want that from me. She hugged herself. Maybe I'm too pushy for him. Maybe men who grow up in public schools can't take too much affection. Still, I'll try, she thought. I must try.

She went upstairs to her own room and put on her night-dress. Not particularly glamorous by comparison, she thought, looking at the golden sari hanging in the cupboard, but at least he knows that I'm not trying to seduce him. She walked up the corridor to the big bedroom where Clive now lay looking like an effigy of a dead knight in a chapel.

'You seem cross or something.' Glenda was sitting on the

end of Clive's bed. He lay with his arms crossed above the sheets. 'Clive?' Glenda cleared her throat. 'Are you angry about something, Clive?'

Clive stared at the ceiling. He did not answer.

'Please tell me, Clive. Don't shut me away. I can't help you if you shut me away.'

Clive began to breathe heavily. 'I can't explain,' he said in a lost voice.

'Just try. Don't worry about the words. Just say it. Anything.'

'I can't. I'm afraid of what I say. I can't control my words and I can't control my thoughts. There. I've said it.' Clive's breathing became easier. 'Dr Umberto changed my medicine. I now take pills, but they don't help much. I don't have to drink liquids all the time, but I just feel knocked out. I can't feel feelings.' His hands wrenched at his chest. 'Glenda,' he said, sweat showing on his brow, 'I feel as if I'm drowning.'

Glenda lay down beside him and put her mouth to his ear. 'You're not drowning, darling. We have each other, and I won't let you drown.'

Clive clutched at her. He put his arms around her and squeezed her so hard she felt she might break in two. But at least Clive was responding. This was so much better than the silence and the sideways smiles as if acknowledging people who weren't there. She lay for a moment feeling happy. 'Can you tell me what you're feeling now?' she asked.

Clive was quiet in her arms. 'Well, I'm feeling as if my inside world has become my outside world. What I thought was fantasy is now reality. Broken bones, jagged moons, black ravens, dark tombstones . . . All in my head.' He shifted uncomfortably. 'Sometimes in my bed. Glenda, don't leave me. Stay with me tonight. I can't bear the nightmares. You know about my nightmares?'

'We all have nightmares from time to time.' She stroked his golden head.

'They hardly trouble me when you're here,' he said.

He lay quiet for several moments. 'Clive,' Glenda said in a soft voice, 'Clive, maybe if you tried to say what was bothering you. I mean, underneath everything else . . . What's on your mind? What makes you so frightened? If you could just put what you're afraid of into words – really afraid of, I mean – then maybe you . . . The nightmares wouldn't be quite so horrific.'

Clive was silent. Then he said, 'It's all too much. Everything. It's more than I can handle. There are things I *have* to do, things I should do . . . But it's all so very difficult . . .'

'Like what, Clive?' Glenda urged gently. 'What things do you have to do?'

'Well, last week when I was up in London, I had a meeting with our accountants. Since I'm the eldest son and past twenty-one, they have to keep me informed about family business. If I ask. And for ages I haven't bothered with the family money matters, because I thought I'd just let them take the lot and leave me alone. But now I want to look after you. And there's so many people I want to keep all right. There's Mark and Paul and Mrs Robinson . . .'

'And Nanny,' said Glenda. 'Yes, I see that you feel responsible for everyone.'

'Yes, and Nanny. But to keep them all right, I can't let my mother take away Fen Farm, and if she had her way she'd take *everything* from me. So that's why I went to see the accountant. I should have told you before . . .'

'I would have come with you, if you'd wanted.'

'Yes. I know you would. But this was something I wanted to take care of myself. At least I thought I could. But it was all rather frightening, sitting there with the accountant and him giving me descriptions of the family's assets and debts and all. I followed what he was saying – he probably thought I couldn't – and I suddenly realized how much it takes to keep everything going. I'm not even talking about the castle, and all that. But the farm, and all the people on it. Everyone on the farm means the world to me, I've known them so long. And it will take so much management to keep everyone safe. So much planning, if my mother ever decides she'd rather get rid of the place. Not that it's an immediate problem. The family's still solid in terms of land and buildings, and of course the factories in Hong Kong. But I'm afraid of mother deciding on everything, which is really what she does, because if she ever feels like it, there might not *be* any Fen Farm. It all might be sold off . . . ' He rubbed his eyes with his hands. 'Paul and Mark and their families will be ousted from their tenanted cottages. I simply can't watch that happen.' He lowered his hands and stared at the ceiling. 'And that's when I started to think that to keep even what we need, just the little group of us, I might have to fight for everything. The castle, the title, the business, all of it. Just to keep ourselves safe. And that would take a fight like the end of the world.' He stopped talking.

She put her head on his chest. She could hear his heart beating and she felt his thin ribs against her hair. 'You know, there *is* no end of the world. Your mother can never destroy you, even if she took away every penny, because you'd still have me. And I love you whether you have the farm or not. Really, it doesn't matter.' Beneath her head, she felt Clive's body begin to relax. 'But you must realize, you're not alone any more. You don't have to take on your mother or anybody else all by yourself. I'm with you. And we have friends. We have Georgina, and Jonathan . . . We can handle your mother together. I have no doubt.'

Glenda slipped under the blankets and snuggled up to Clive's sweet-smelling body. Clive turned his face to her, smiling. 'You know, you're very beautiful.' He looked at her in the moonlight.

There was a moment of promise in the room, as if two souls reached out for union and communion was nearly found. But the moment passed. Clive shook his head. He kissed her lightly on the lips. 'We'd better go to sleep,' he said, rolling away suddenly, his back to her. 'But lie beside me for the night, would you?' he said into his pillow.

Glenda kissed the back of his head and put her arm around his waist. She nuzzled her face into his neck and deeply inhaled his smell.

Clive was already asleep.

Glenda sighed. Her body could not release the tension of unfulfilment. Her mind was confounded.

She dreamed she was making love with Clive, their bodies twisted together like ropes hanging off a boat. And the spray and the spume glistened over them until they both lay exhausted on the deck of a schooner, the planks of the deck hot under her back and the sea water dripping on her face. Clive's big blue eyes enveloped her and then he floated away, his mouth forming a scream that she could not comprehend. And then she saw his mother's face grinning.

Chapter 80

Georgina and Jonathan were waiting outside the manor house to greet them. Glenda climbed off the bike and stretched. 'I'm stiff,' she said, kissing Georgina.

Clive laughed and shook hands with Jonathan. 'Good to see you again.' He looks happy, Glenda thought. His face was flushed from the wind. They had driven hard and fast from Norfolk to Dorset, Glenda nervously looking over her shoulders for police cars. This was the first long run they had taken since Gerontius left for California.

Kerouac was dead, Gerontius had telephoned Clive. 'Died of a heart attack. I'm going home to travel his road. I can't take this fucking reserved country any longer, man. I need California.' Clive seemed to put his bike away in the shed as a form of mourning for his hero, and, as was his way, he said little or nothing about the death except that he had promised Gerontius that they would visit him on the West Coast at some point. Now after the long journey, seeing Clive's obvious happiness to be back on his bike, Glenda knew that this promise must be kept. And the trip would also get him away from his awful family.

But for now, standing beside Georgina, Glenda realized the difference between this lovely, spacious, square-fronted Georgian house bathed in a weak winter sunshine and the farm they had left behind. Fen Farm was a farm with an uncertain future. A threat hung over the roofs of the house and the barns. And for all its beauty, it was a place for owls and bats and the sudden high pitched squeal of a dying rabbit, the sound hideous with surprise, and the red, bleeding tooth and talons of its assassins.

Georgina's family manor sat, as it had for centuries, like a placid grandmother who had given birth to all the small cottages on the estate, the high-roofed Dutch barns and the various outhouses. Her chimney smoked with contentment and breathed a welcome of logs of pine and spruce. The door opened and Georgina called, 'Brooks, they're here.'

Brooks came out smiling in the sunlight and squinting. 'Welcome,' he said as he took the two bags off the back of the bike. 'I'll carry these to your rooms, sir,' he said to Clive.

Georgina grinned. 'Separate bedrooms?' she said, looking at Glenda.

'Separate bedrooms would be fine,' Glenda smiled back. 'And you?'

Jonathan shifted his feet uncomfortably. 'If you two women are going to gossip, Clive and I will go inside and get a drink. Really,' he said to Clive in his Boston drawl. 'Women! Whatever next?'

Clive smiled and looked over his shoulder at Glenda. He waved as he walked away. 'Glenda says it's something about their secret club. Something about Souls, she says.'

'Ah yes, I've heard this from Georgina. "Every woman shall have her man and no man shall have his woman". That's what that girl Molly wanted it to mean, anyway. That

355

sort of thing. Although Georgina says it has something to do with comfortable furnished souls and the fine minds of Cambridge women. It mystifies me, really.' There was a momentary silence as their feet crunched over the gravel.

'Rum saying, about women having their men and the men not having them, and all,' Clive said. 'Wonder what it means.'

'Don't bother wondering,' Jonathan said. 'Don't even try to think about it. Women don't know what they want anyway. If you try to understand them, they'll just scramble up your brains.' Jonathan looked back. 'What on earth do they find to talk about? Look at them both, jabbering away.'

'Maybe there's a lot to be envied in the feminine soul. At least, some feminine souls,' Clive said meaningfully.

Jonathan ignored the comment. 'I see the stock market is up. It's looking good. How's business your end?'

'Terrible,' Clive said. 'Maybe. I don't know.'

'Oh good.' Jonathan pulled him into the library and poured a scotch. He raised his glass. 'Want one?'

Clive shook his head.

'I don't mean to sound rude,' Jonathan apologized, 'but I do like a really good challenge to put the brain to.'

Clive sat down in an armchair. 'Then I'm your man.' Funny, Clive thought, sitting comfortably and glad to be able to talk to someone outside the family about his financial fears. When I'm with Glenda talking about *real* things is so easy, but with another man we talk always on the surface. For a moment he felt the familiar envious feeling he always had when the four Souls were together. Four heads bent in unison like fat sunflowers loaded with seeds of words. Criss-crosses of bursting black words. Meanings, eyebrows, hand signals. Lips, teeth and laughing tongues. Eyes flashing. All a secret mysterious world shared by women. Men were forever outside those boundaries. Men were slow and ponderous. Their minds running along straight highways. Women were like rivers with tributaries rushing off to find other pieces of land.

Once the land was theirs, they fructified it and . . .

'You see, Clive?' Jonathan leaned forward.

Clive jumped. He had let his mind wander, but at least it had wandered safely and he felt under control.

'Really you need a good audit and some legal guidance. That's what my office can offer you.'

Clive looked at Jonathan. He saw a tall man with a solid chin. Jonathan's eyes were widely set apart and he wore designer spectacles. It was a kind face, Clive decided, but a bit ruthless. American moguls played rough. His own father did not like Yanks, as he called them. All the more reason to use Jonathan and his very powerful corporate law firm.

'Lord Silver is our head man in London. He would take a personal and legal interest in helping you.'

Why? Clive wondered, but didn't ask.

Lord Silver had lost all his family in Germany, thanks to the pro-Nazi antics and propaganda put out by men like Lord Alexander and his rotten brother Caspar. Jonathan felt that those details need not be added for Clive's benefit. If he knew what his father got up to in the war, it would be shame enough. Psychopathic bastards, the great English aristocrats. Jonathan had no time for them. They were arrogant and careless in business and Jonathan only enjoyed fleecing them. 'What does Glenda think about all this?' Jonathan enquired. Women were always a nuisance in business, always interfering, and so bloody subjective.

Clive smiled. 'Glenda is very practical. She gets it from her mother who is a little tiger. Glenda also knows what it's like to be poor.' He paused. 'She feels I should fight for what's mine, if that's what I want.'

'And is it what you want?'

'What do I want? I want to be safe. I want Glenda to be safe. That's what I want for Fen Farm and for everyone who lives there. But with my mother sitting on the throne and ruling over there, I've begun to wonder if we'll ever be safe unless I manage to take control over *everything*. More than

357

I want. That's what bothers me. I don't want ever to see the farm in particular taken away. These are the people I love. But my mother – ' Clive grimaced. 'She'd sell everything down the river for a new mink coat.' He stood up.

Jonathan watched Clive walk over to the window. He felt a momentary stab of sorrow for the slight figure. 'It will be a hard fight, Clive, if you ever do take your mother on. Nobody parts with money or titles easily. Do you think you'd be up to it?'

Clive nodded. 'I have Glenda beside me, and she's such a support. You have no idea how much I love that girl. She's like a pine tree.' He turned. 'We are both lucky men, you and I.'

Jonathan smiled. He had two little brackets that fitted around his mouth neatly. It was a neat smile, a careful smile, but there was not much warmth. Maybe, Clive thought, you can't be too warm when your life is engaged in calculated battles. He hoped there would be some warmth for Georgina's sake.

'Where have the womenfolk gone to?' Jonathan stood up. 'I'm starving, Clive. We'll probably find them in the drawing room still gossiping.'

Clive followed Jonathan down the hall. The house was as square inside as it was outside.

'Balderdash, nonsense, nonsense, gammon and spinach!' A loud voice could be heard in the porch. 'Get my bloody boots off, James, and don't you ever drive like that again. My word! We nearly ran over the vicar. Not a bad idea, mind you. The wretched man can't speak the Queen's English, but still, it won't do for the local magistrate to get caught running over the vicar.'

'Who could that be?' Clive said, standing still.

'Don't worry, dear boy. That's the mater, Georgina's mother. Bit of a war-horse, but quite sweet when you get to know her.'

'By George, Jonathan. Is that you lurking in the hall? Who's that with you?'

'Clive Alexander, Julia. You remember Georgina's friend, Glenda, from Girton.'

'No, not offhand. Can't say that I do. Georgina had that very nice gel from where was it? Africa?'

Jonathan intervened. 'Not Africa, dear. Turaq. Her name was Fatima Nicnojad.'

'Ah yes, that's it. Fatima. She believed in arranged marriages. Come here, Clive, and let me inspect you.' Julia Lampsetter bore down on Clive who felt as if he was rather an unpleasant piece of dog mess lying on some green grass. Julia peered at him through a huge lorgnette. 'Umm,' she said slowly, her small moustache bristling. 'You must be one of Philip Alexander's boys. Knew your father when I came out. Devil of a man, perfectly dreadful. Married one of the Twistleton sisters. Very spoiled gels. Very spoiled indeed. Has your father improved?'

Clive looked at Julia and he realized he very much liked her. 'Afraid not,' he said. 'Still murdering everything in sight and chasing barmaids.' Clive laughed.

'Men!' Julia said in disgust. 'They don't change, do they, Jonathan?'

Jonathan put up his hand. 'I'm American, Julia, and we don't behave as badly as you Brits.'

'You don't, eh?' Julia looked him up and down. 'Well, just look at you, Jonathan. A grown man in jeans and sneakers, as you call them. Will you ever grow up? Poor Dody would turn in his grave if he saw a pair of plimsolls – as we so *rightly* call them – anywhere but on a tennis court. You're lucky he is not still around. Where are the gels? Pull the bell and tell them we must change for dinner. Not black tie tonight. We have no visitors. All Georgina's friends go into the guest book as family. Just formal suits. I'll see you in the library for a drink in an hour.' She went upstairs.

'Whew!' Clive said, feeling the energy depart with its owner. 'What an energetic woman.'

'The backbone of England, women like her,' Jonathan agreed. 'Boy, is she fierce on her magistrate's bench! And she knows everybody. James is her chauffeur, but he's also her eyes and ears. Anyway, let's get going. She hates anyone to be late, and Georgina takes forever in the bathroom. Why can't these English houses have more bathrooms?'

'We think bathing is weakening, and a good steeped smell keeps you warm.' Clive went off happily to find Glenda. He could see he would enjoy his weekend.

Chapter 81

Glenda felt a heavy weight lift from her. Sometimes at Fen Farm she felt as if the grey mists might enshroud her. When Gerontius, or Bix and Sheila, or Ken and Stella visited, she could relax. She had learned to like them, she admitted to herself. Something about their cheerful imperviousness to misfortune buoyed her. Jobs could be lost, futures fade, but still the dazzling tones of Thelonius Monk played on the record player in the drawing room, while the poems of Gary Snyder, Leroy Jones, and Lawrence Ferlinghetti were read aloud. Gerontius, before he left for the States, had sat tracing postcards from his friends in Prague, Beirut, or Barcelona. Then the farm would become alight.

But not for long. The motorbikes would roar away and Mrs Robinson carried supper into the dining room. Clive, sitting, sometimes looked so unreachable that Glenda could only watch him helplessly. At least now he was not alone. The rich, she realized, were never alone; they were always surrounded by people who were paid to look after them. Even Nanny Jenkins at the end of the day might sympathize greatly with Clive, but she was paid and trained not to criticize anyone else in the family. Minnie would never have survived in the homes of the English rich. But then Minnie and Glenda had never been subjected to the slave-like mentality that fitted so neatly around those that worked in the great houses.

What made Georgina's home bearable and even light-hearted was that Georgina's mother, unlike Lady Jane, was a very benevolent dictator. True the servants moved through the house silently, but often Mrs Lampsetter stopped to enquire into their family life.

Clive felt at ease here and spent a lot of time talking to Jonathan. They appeared to be developing a good friendship. Jonathan had all the worldly know-how and confidence, a good pillar for Clive to lean against, and Clive's artistic nature seemed to open new possibilities of feeling for Jonathan. For an hour or two at a time, Clive would play Chopin, Scarlatti and Beethoven on the grand piano in the Lampsetters' house, and Jonathan would sit and listen. 'Like a front row seat in Symphony Hall,' Jonathan marvelled aloud.

Overall, Glenda did enjoy the stay. The rooms were high and wide and the countryside warmer and less barren than in Cambridgeshire. Occasionally Glenda missed the wide Cambridge skies. Here in the Dorset countryside the earth was soft and loamy, but the skies were hidden behind the hills that fringed the valleys, punctuated by sheep, white against the dark fields.

Major Lampsetter was a tall, quiet, balding man. His nose was permanently pinched where his glasses gripped the beak and his eyes were blue, like Georgina's. Since leaving the army, he had been a solicitor in Dorchester. Most of his clients these days, he remarked during dinner one evening, seemed to be the new rich – 'The fellows who have moved and intend to build concrete houses all over the place.'

Mrs Lampsetter smiled at him and Glenda watched closely. Recently, Glenda realized, she watched everything very closely. She did not feel that here she was 'supping with panthers', more that she was dining with two amiable tabby cats. Hopefully they were as contented as they seemed, but by now Glenda was losing her previously insouciant innocence. Like Alice in Wonderland, she knew that things were not what they seemed, as they once were in Ealing. When she was with her mother at Minnie's house by the river in Chiswick, Glenda felt a normal size. But in these big houses with tall ceilings and other humans moving to and fro, silently doing the bidding of their masters, Glenda felt as if she had yet again taken a swig from the bottle and was shrunk to a tiny size . . . Which was silly, as she was sitting at a long oval table next to Georgina and spooning her mulligatawny soup and trying to remember to push the spoon the right way, not to slurp, and then watch the soup recede like a low tide across the bottom of her soup plate, and pray that she did not let it leak in a humiliating puddle over the other side.

'Glenda?' Mrs Lampsetter broke her concentration. 'Georgina tells me you've been offered a post compiling a collection of some sort.'

Glenda nodded, her mouth full of toast. How on earth, she wondered, does one drink soup, eat a piece of toast, and talk, all at the same time? She coughed and little spurts of toast fell down the front of her dress. She blushed and finally, at the risk of asphyxiation, she spluttered, 'Yes. In Cambridge – well, actually just outside Cambridge – to help out on an exhibition of women's writing, poetry, and art. The parameters are not too strictly defined, which pleases me.'

'Go on, dear, this sounds very interesting. Whom are you including?'

'Um, the usual Bloomsburys, Virginia Woolf, of course. But I really want to show some of Dora Carrington's work. She was such a good painter. Only Lyttton Strachey genuinely encouraged her. Clive Bell was jealous and so were many of the others. Anyway, in those days, women had little chance. I'd like to include some of the American poets. H. D., the imagist, and even earlier – Edna St Vincent Millay.'

Glenda heard herself repeat what she had previously told Minnie of the exhibition, but at the Lampsetters', she noticed, everyone knew what she was talking about.

Major Lampsetter leaned back and smiled. 'I've got the very thing for you in the library. A notebook of Dora Carrington's.'

'An original? Why, that's wonderful!' Glenda carefully put her spoon down. There was a peaceful moment of silence which Glenda treasured. The soup was rich and thick, full of spices from another country. India, Glenda imagined. She was the only one in the room who did not know for certain. She must ask Clive when they were alone together. The maid came in carrying her tray and took the plates from the table. Chests were eased up, legs uncrossed and recrossed, napkins fluttered while the maid returned and swept the table clear of toast crumbs. She paused by Glenda who had left a rewarding heap to be corralled and then bullied into the dark maw of the tortoise-backed dustpan.

Clive was sitting next to Georgina. Glenda looked at his face. He was smiling, but not the worrying smile that made her think he was hearing things that no one else could hear. He was following the conversation with his eyes. He was fully in the room and in the small circle. Glenda realized that for months now she had been policing Clive, watching him as if with the aid of an invisible microscope. Somehow if she watched and observed enough, she might find out what was troubling him. Perhaps Clive was a beautiful species of butterfly in a rare tropical forest and there was only one of him in the world, like the Little Prince and his rose. If he was unique, he could not be compared, and then no one had the right to deem him mad . . .

She breathed in deeply. Jonathan's spectacles glittered in the overhead candelabra and refracted the light. He had an even voice with soft vowels.

The room receded. The plates fell in front of her and she ate. Suddenly Glenda wished she was sitting in the little

Chiswick sitting room with Chinchilla and her mother, eating a take-away Chinese. She wondered if Mrs Lampsetter had ever eaten a take-away Chinese in her life . . .

Mrs Lampsetter rose from the table. 'Come along, girls. Let's leave the boys alone with Pa. How about a cup of coffee in the library?'

'I've love one,' Georgina said.

Glenda followed them out of the room. Oh dear, why do they have so many rules? Why can't we just drink a cup of coffee all together? Where was the cosy little family group down Hounslow way? Mum and Dad and the kids all sitting together having tea. Tom, mum, Sam, and me sitting in Cambersand with the big bowl of fresh crab, Tom sucking his fingers and me with my white bread, bent over, bursting like a goose-feathered mattress, wiping up the last of the HP sauce . . .

Glenda walked behind the two tall, blonde women up the corridor. This was the class that made people great, but it didn't necessarily make them interesting. The thought was very disloyal, Glenda scolded herself. They are kind people, Glenda told herself. And she resigned herself to listening to talk about horses and flower shows.

Chapter 82

On Saturday, Glenda slept until late because at the Lampsetters' there was no farm rooster to demand that everyone wake with him at daylight. 'Nine o'clock?' she gasped. Breakfast had been announced for eight: she was late.

When she reached the dining room, having hurriedly dressed, she found the place empty except for Mrs Lampsetter who sat alone in front of a cup of tea. 'Don't worry, dear,' Mrs Lampsetter smiled. 'I thought you might like to sleep in. The others have gone for a ride. They'll be back by luncheon. Do sit down and I'll ring for some toast. Unless you'd prefer porridge?'

'Toast would be lovely.'

'Tea or coffee?'

All these choices, Glenda thought. Why not bacon and eggs and a mug of tea? The table did look pretty in the pale sunlight and when the toast came in its silver toast rack, it sat pretty, neatly divided into triangles. Her own personal butter rolled on several slivers of ice and a small jar of marmalade was served with a spoon. Glenda tried not to sigh. Breakfasts at Clive's mother's house were even more formal, but mostly buffet-style because the Alexanders had so many guests.

Today the room felt more relaxed than it had last night, but still Glenda began to suffer a particularly strange ache. The others had gone riding. Just as well, she thought, because she couldn't ride. Thanks to Georgina's efforts at Girton to teach her, she could play tennis, but not cricket or hockey. Games had been taught at her grammar school, but she was a blue-stocking – one of the girls designed to be academically inclined but not terribly popular among the other students. And blue-stockings were never encouraged to play games. That sort of physical effort was left to girls with sturdy legs and mottled blue elbows. If anybody had warned me, Glenda thought, that playing games was an absolutely necessary part of joining the British establishment, I would have learned to ride on the donkeys at Cambersand. Then again, even when I play tennis I will never look like Georgina who moves as if she had been born with a tennis racquet in her hands. Molly, trained by an American coach, had a ferocious game, but it was very American – all slams and smashes. At college Georgina used to beat Molly by moving like a willow tree, her long arms stroking the ball, her feet rising and her arms falling, while the ball spun and returned, until Molly, exhausted from her slamming and spinning, miscalculated, and gracefully Georgina ran up to the net, her hand extended.

That was — is — Georgina, Glenda thought, sipping her tea. The tea scalded her mouth, but she could not protect herself because an exploratory sip sounded like a fog horn in the quiet of this room and Mrs Lampsetter was reading *The Times*.

'I see the Henley girl is getting married to one of the Ferguson twins.' Mrs Lampsetter's blue eyes were warm and friendly. 'Well, our own arrangements are going forward. I do like Jonathan. Such a dear boy, and so good to Georgina. Did she tell you that they've been over to Boston for a quick visit, and Georgina is very happy with Jonathan's relatives?'

Glenda nodded, trying not to cry. Her mouth hurt. 'We were so busy talking about Girton last night, we've saved the getting married conversation for tonight.'

Georgina had looked unusually excited. 'I have something to tell you,' she had said before she bent to kiss Glenda good night. Glenda was intrigued. Georgina was rarely this excited about anything. Now she was out, so Glenda had to wait with patience. Her mouth felt too burnt to eat toast, so she added more milk to her tea and drank it slowly.

'Not hungry, dear?' Mrs Lampsetter gazed at Glenda's toast rack.

'Not really,' Glenda stared back.

'Well,' Mrs Lampsetter said, returning her eyes to *The Times*. 'The Queen is off to Sandringham with all her corgis, bless her royal heart . . . Why don't you run along and go for a walk? Nothing like fresh Dorset air to bring back an appetite. Oh dear! Poor old Henry dead, and only in his seventies! Far too young to die . . . But if one must live in London, what does one expect?' She smiled brightly at Glenda. 'Come along, dear. The devil finds work for idle hands, you know.'

Glenda felt dismissed, not unkindly dismissed, but dismissed nonetheless. I have nothing to say to her, Glenda thought miserably. I really don't have anything to say to anyone. She wished more than ever she was back with Minnie in Chiswick. Or helping the dish washer in the hot, crowded, little restaurant. I miss the noise of people, she thought. I miss crowded streets. I miss life . . . What a silly thing to think! There's plenty of life here. Yes, but it is all ordered. All events in this house and all these houses, except the farm, seem to be poured through a large colander so that they fall to the ground neatly, with no character. Nothing ever happens in this house.

She put on her coat in the cloakroom that was full of gumboots and fishing tackle. Mrs Lampsetter (Glenda's thoughts continued) sends someone to jail on a Friday. The man is taken off and his wife and children are told they can visit him once a fortnight. She comes back to her house and she is sad she had to do it, but the house takes away feelings that exist outside. Once inside here, the tranquility permeates everywhere.

Glenda found herself almost running down the drive. She wanted to get away from the house and the grounds. If she stayed any longer she might become part of the warp and the weft of the history surrounding the house. She might become like Milly who, even if she did work for Clive at the farm, had nothing for herself. Try as Glenda might, Milly was wedded to the idea of her own servility. Tugging of the forelock she would do if she had a forelock to tug, Glenda thought. Not everybody was that way, certainly not Nanny Jenkins. It seemed that only the nannies and the cooks retained their individuality. Maybe it was because they had powers of their own: power over the children, power over the stomachs. That must be it, Glenda thought. There has to be a subterranean power structure. The rich controlled those who toiled for them but did not see that some of those who worked so invisibly paid them back. She thought of the two silent blue-liveried footmen who waited on Lady Jane and her friends. She remembered the look in their eyes. Did the chattering women honestly believe themselves superior to the two men who stood watching them with speechless contempt? Undoubtedly Sally Humblebottom would not even consider the question. Humblebottom . . . Sally . . . Glenda sped down the drive.

The pain in Glenda's belly got worse. She began to trot, her hands curled into fists and her breath came white in the cold of the day. Finally she reached the tall gates, open, leading to a dirt track. Far down the road she could see the main road. The track was muddy, but Glenda rather enjoyed the mud sticking to her sensible country shoes. She slowed down and saw a whitewashed typical Dorset cottage. It was snugly reeded and the door was closed. A child of about twelve was standing by the gate holding a bright red bicycle. 'Hello,' Glenda said, glad to see a child, a genuine human being with a runny nose and blue knees under her rather flimsy coat. Glenda remembered the sting of cold knees and the warmth of mucus. She waited to see if the child would run the back of her hand across her nose, a well-remembered gesture and one that used to drive Minnie wild. The child looked at Glenda. For a moment their eyes met and Glenda saw in the child's eyes that she herself was regarded as one of those people who came from the grand manor house up the road. Little girls are warned, Glenda thought sorrowfully, not to talk to those funny strangers from up the road. The girl turned her face, dropped the bike and fled.

Glenda stood by the bicycle. It lay hurt and surprised, its front wheel spinning. Glenda picked the bike up and leaned it against the fence. She turned and walked back. She put her hands in her coat pockets and began to trudge. She was tired and out of breath. I am lonely, she thought. I don't belong here, do I? she asked the trees as she walked past. The trees did not answer. In the cold they were fermenting deep inside their trunks. No time to bother with humans and questions. The sorrow that Glenda felt curled into a small ball. I must ignore it, she thought. Besides, Clive and I can make a world of our own. We don't have to live in a stultified world like the Lampsetters', even if it is comfortable.

Chapter 83

'We did it, Glenda.' Georgina was sitting on her own bed, wrapped in a big fluffy dressing gown. She was naked underneath, and pink from a hot bath.

'Did what, Georgina?' Glenda was not in a good mood.

'Jonathan and I made love.'

Glenda sat down on the floor. 'Where? Here, in your parents' house?'

'No, silly. Remember I told you we were going over to Boston to meet some of his family a few weeks ago?'

'Yes. Your mother said you had a good time.'

'We did,' Georgina giggled. Her cheeks were bright.

'But I thought you said you'd wait, like Fatima and me.'

'I know we should have, but our new house was ready and the bed was huge. So we went to a party for us given by Jonathan's uncle in the country. And on the way home Jonathan had the key in his pocket. We didn't mean to do it, but we were full of champagne. So we did.'

'What was it like?'

'Lovely,' Georgina said. 'A bit messy, but lovely. I'm not a virgin any longer! I can't wait to tell Molly.'

'Do you feel different?'

Georgina paused. 'I don't know. I've waited so long, it's all a bit of a let down. Making love is fun, Jonathan's people are all right, I have heaps of things to organize for the wedding . . . I don't know what I feel. It made Jonathan very happy. But then he hasn't been a virgin for ages.'

'Does that make any difference?'

'A man should know what he's doing,' Georgina said. 'It's a bit like a bull with a cow.'

'Oh really? That doesn't sound very romantic.'

'Life isn't very romantic.'

'What about the Souls?' Glenda protested. 'That's a romantic idea. Women who are friends forever.'

'I'm still a Soul, silly, and we are still four of the best friends on earth. Getting married is something I've always wanted to do, and then I'll have four children and live just like mother. She's happy.'

'Yes, she seems very happy,' Glenda said slowly. 'Don't you think happiness can be boring sometimes, Georgina?'

'No. Not for the moment.' She looked down at her engagement ring and the diamond sparkled. 'You'd better go to bed, darling. Jonathan is due here in a minute.'

Glenda rose to her feet. 'Good night, Georgina.'

'Good night.' Georgina hugged Glenda to her.

Glenda could feel the heat from her, a smell she had not smelled before. Usually Georgina smelled of a gentle floral perfume. Tonight she smelled briny, but also floral, a thick heavy scent. Wax magnolias, Glenda reflected as she walked out of the room.

She wandered down the corridor to find Clive in his room. She pushed open the door. 'Clive,' she said. He was reading. He lay in bed with the bedside light shining on his fair hair. In his hands he held a thick book.

'Shhh, darling,' he said. 'I've borrowed this book from Major Lampsetter. Must read it from beginning to end.' He put the book down and brushed a lock of fair hair from his forehead. 'If I can finish this book before I leave, I can put together my argument for increased breeding on the estate. I really think I'm on to something. I know it's boring for you, but you do have Georgina. Come here and kiss me good night, and then I'll burn the midnight oil. Nice to see breeding rather than shooting on a country estate for a change.' He kissed Glenda perfunctorily on the brow. He said distractedly, 'I'll see you tomorrow.'

Glenda walked down the corridor with tears in her eyes. She had been dismissed by everybody. If only, she thought, as she climbed into her solitary bed, if only I could go downstairs behind the green doors and have a good giggle with the maids.

Chapter 84

'Everything's going very well, mum.' Glenda was sitting by the empty grate in her mother's sitting room. 'I love the job. So much to do, getting the exhibits together. So much to research. I love being with Clive at the farm . . . But somehow the world seems to have come to a standstill. Clive and I talk about getting married, but we don't do much except talk and then drop the subject.' She wriggled to get more comfortable in her armchair.

Minnie inhaled from her cigarette. She looked at her daughter through the curling smoke. 'You still don't sleep together, do you?' she asked with some difficulty.

'No. We don't. And that's not my idea any more; it's his. I feel bad about pushing him though. He's got so much on his plate. He really is working hard with Jonathan and this man called Lord Silver to get audited accounts for his family business so he can get a grip on things. And everyone knows his mother is just waiting for the day she can push for Clive to stand down and hand his title over to his brother Caspar. So, with all that going on, I'm not surprised he has no energy. He does love me, mum. I know that. We're great together. There's never been anyone I've had better conversations with. It's just that . . . ' Glenda looked down at her hands miserably. 'I would like to make love. Does that sound silly?'

Minnie snorted. 'Course not. Sounds normal to me. Any girl your age wants to make love. I certainly did.' There was a moment of awkward silence until Minnie, with a slight tremor in her voice said, 'I've always meant to apologize to you one day. I was very selfish when you were young, what with all me boyfriends and everything.'

'You mean the "uncles"?'

Minnie made a face. 'I shouldn't have done it really. It wasn't good for you. I knew that at the time, but . . . ' she paused to let out a stream of smoke.

'Don't apologize, mum,' Glenda said hurriedly. 'There's no need.' She seemed eager to change the subject. 'You know, I've been doing a lot of thinking since I stayed with Georgina and her family. I could write off Clive's lot as just mean and evil and rich. I almost agree with Cyril, they ought to be blasted off the face of the earth. I'd throw the first bomb. But Georgina's family are not like that. In fact Mrs Lampsetter and her husband work hard. Not just for themselves, but for the community they live in.' Glenda drew her knees up under her chin and wrapped her hands around her legs. 'You see, mum, it's not the lack of sex that worries me. That can wait. We have the rest of our lives. The problem's more complicated than that. When I'm with Georgina and Jonathan and their friends – and they've visited us a lot the last few months – I find I get bored. Not so much with Jonathan, because he has a very funny sense of humour and he makes me laugh, but with Georgina and her women friends . . . I simply can't get excited by glass pasta containers or whether I should have a marble slab for rolling my pastry. I haven't been to Greece, and I don't want to spend my mornings shopping with Georgina at Harrods. Georgina has a list at Harrods and at Peter Jones, and she visits both shops to see who has already bought what for her wedding. Well! I tell you, with all the carry-on over Georgina's wedding, I plan to elope.'

Minnie's eyebrows went up. 'What on earth will Clive's parents say?'

'They won't be able to say anything. I feel that Clive and I will never get married if we have to go through all that nonsense. I'm only a bridesmaid for Georgina, and already I've been prodded and poked and measured and . . . Oh mum, the trouble with all this is that I get bored. Awfully, desperately, hopelessly bored. Molly understands. She's flying in for the wedding and Georgina has sent her a heap of instructions about having her dress made in New Jersey. Molly says she plans to throw the instructions away and come in a mink-lined bikini. At least we'll be standing together as bridesmaids, but we'll probably giggle right the way through. If I can keep Molly's hands off the ushers, it would be a miracle. She reckons she could ball the lot.'

Minnie smiled. 'At least Molly doesn't have any problems with sex.' Minnie stood up. 'Ready for tea, love? I'm on a diet now, so I've just made some cold ham and salad. You sit.' Minnie stubbed out her cigarette. 'Just sit, love, and I'll get it for you.'

'Please let me help.' The sentence came out of Glenda's mouth like a loud wail and suddenly she was crying. Huge sobs rushed from her chest. 'Please, mum, let me help' turned into 'Please, mum, help me.'

Minnie rushed to Glenda and pulled her into her arms. She rocked her child back and forth. 'What is it, Glenda? What could be the matter?' Minnie was white.

'I don't know, mum. I just don't know. I'm so lost. Just when I think I have everything I've always wanted, I find I have nothing. I *am* nothing. I don't fit in with anyone. Georgina has Jonathan and a house in Boston. Clive has a farm and his fight with his family. Molly is working in a law firm in Washington, and I have nothing. I don't even have Clive. Nobody has Clive. He just has his music. And if I try to cook for him Mrs Robinson is nice to me, but I feel I have to leave the kitchen. So he thanks Mrs Robinson for all his food. If I go outside and try to pick flowers for Clive, Mark or Paul comes up and says, "I shouldn't pick that one, miss, it's not ready yet." I don't know anything about gardening. I can't cook well. I can't ride or play bridge. I'm a hopeless failure.'

Minnie sat back on her heels. 'How could they do this to my baby?' she said softly. She held Glenda's face in her hands. Her eyes were swollen and mucus was running down her chin.

Glenda smiled. 'I feel just like a kid I saw the other day. The kid's face was swollen and cold and snot ran down from her nose. Even *she* wouldn't talk to me. She ran away because she thought I was a posh visitor from the manor house. Actually I was so lonely I went for a walk all by myself.' Glenda sniffed.

'Come on, love,' Minnie said, pulling Glenda to her feet. 'You come into the kitchen with me and we'll eat in there. You know, I felt just the same as you when you were ever so young and we moved in with Abe and Renée. They were good to me – couldn't have been better. But I had so much to learn.'

Glenda stood by the kitchen table and she grinned. She saw a rainbow of colour through the last of the huge tears that dripped from her eyes. 'I haven't seen one of those salads since I left home.'

Minnie laughed. 'I don't care what anybody says; I like a good English salad with sliced boiled eggs, sliced beetroot, ham and potato. You can't beat it. Come on, sit down, and I'll . . . No, love, *you* can get the salad cream. Look, it's over there.'

Glenda picked up the bottle and took off the top. She stuck her finger into the bottle and gave a huge sigh. 'You see?' she said as she slid into her chair. 'I'll always be Glenda from Hounslow, even if I do marry Clive. I'll still be Glenda Stanhope, pretending to be Glenda Alexander. Ages ago, centuries ago, a Chinese philosopher wondered . . . Hang on, I'll try and remember it exactly. "Once I dreamt I was a butterfly. Suddenly I awoke. Now I do not know whether I was then a man dreaming that I was a butterfly, or am now a butterfly dreaming that I am a man." '

Minnie sat quietly for a moment. 'I need another cigarette,' she said. 'Trouble is, Glenda, most of England is wondering if they are butterflies. In the old days, you knew who you were. You knew Mrs Latham would come and lay you out when you died, just as she did your mother and your grandmother. There's no Mrs Latham now. Everybody gets thrown into the mortuary and you take your luck with strangers.' She sighed. 'But we're lucky, Glenda, you and I.'

'No, don't ever say *we* are lucky, mum. I'm lucky. You never were. And the only reason I'm lucky is that you worked hard for me. That's why I am where I am.' She sighed. 'It's not your fault, all this depression. It's mine. I don't see myself as a butterfly, more like a cabbage moth, a bit ugly and clumsy compared to Georgina and her friends. When they come into a room they smell different. They look different. There's a sort of light around them.'

'Yes, that's what they call privilege. We're not privileged people, you and me, but it doesn't matter, doesn't mean we're not as good as them,' she said fiercely.

'I know it doesn't. But being privileged helps. Anyway,' Glenda said, serving herself four neatly halved eggs on a bed of green lettuce, 'what the hell do the privileged know about a proper egg salad? And I'll be off to see Molly in June.'

'That'll give you a break.'

'Don't mind me, mum. A lot of it is just that the fens are very grim this time of the year. In a couple of weeks, spring will have arrived and I'll be fine.'

Minnie very much hoped so. She watched her daughter eat her salad. Minnie had a beau, as Chinchilla called him, and Minnie wanted Glenda to be as happy as she was. So far she had said nothing to Glenda, but soon she would.

Chapter 85

Glenda realized when she returned to Norfolk that there was something which was paralyzing the farm. She got out of the taxi, paid the driver, and watched him drive off into the distance. For a moment she very much wished to be back in the warmth and safety of the car with the cheerful taxi driver. The doors and the windows of the farm stared blankly at her. There were no sounds of the animals in the barns or in the fields. It was as if they knew they must be quiet. She heard her own footsteps crunch up the drive and she felt an unwillingness invade her body. Three years, she thought, going on four, I have fought with Clive's condition. But she still could not say for certain exactly what his condition was. For ages she had refused to let herself think of anything else but Clive. How was Clive? What mood was he in? Sometimes he would greet her, his eyes alight with what appeared to be love and excitement. Then there were the other times when he seemed driven by an inner agitation that sent him spinning onto the edge of a spiral that finally left him red-eyed, exhausted and sad. For too many hours to count she had watched him as he strode up and down, declaiming poetry. Beat poetry, he said, but it was nothing Glenda could find in her books. His poetry was wild words that had no meaning. Gerontius could calm him down, even long distance. When Clive seemed upset, Glenda reached for the telephone and dialled California.

Today, filled with the thought of a trip to New York and several weeks with Renée and Abe, she felt herself looking forward to getting away. The thought made her wonder.

She pushed open the door and saw Mrs Robinson in the kitchen. They stood for a moment and looked at each other. This is ridiculous, Glenda thought. 'How is he?' Glenda asked, realizing that her eyebrows naturally raised themselves for this question and that her mouth was pursed with the strain of the inquiry.

'He's asleep now.' Mrs Robinson said the *now* very slowly. 'Dr Umberto has been. He doesn't do well without you, you know.'

Glenda walked into the kitchen. 'I do know that, Mrs Robinson, but sometimes I must be able to get away.'

Mrs Robinson said, 'Yes.'

'I simply can't live my whole life for Clive and his moods, or whatever it is.'

'I had a talk to Dr Umberto today.' Mrs Robinson folded her hands together as if in prayer. She sat heavily on a kitchen chair. 'I asked him straight if there was any hope of change. He said that Mr Clive is a manic depressive, or possibly a borderline schizophrenic. I don't know.' She sighed and then she shook her head. 'He's such a nice young man. He seems so kind and good. I can't bear to see him like this. Last night he was like a lost soul. Howling and crying he was. I wouldn't wish this on a dog.'

Glenda shut her eyes. 'Oh God.' She put her hand over Mrs Robinson's clasped hands. 'Believe me, I want to comfort but sometimes I just can't. There are some things I simply must do. I must go to New York. I promised Renée and Abe I'd be there for their wedding. Anyway, to tell you the truth, I need some time alone. Some time to think for myself.' She smiled. 'I'll go and see Clive. Somehow or other we will all get through this, Mrs Robinson. Clive is loved by so many people, and I really do believe that love is an entity. If you love someone simply and wholly, they will get well.'

'If they want to,' Mrs Robinson added. 'Sometimes, with that mother of his, I wonder if he can ever get well. She's been round here, you know.'

Glenda stiffened. 'When?'

'Yesterday afternoon. There was an awful argument, until Lady Jane slammed out the door and took off. No wonder he was so upset.'

'I'll go and see him.'

Clive lay on his bed fully dressed. His head was turned to the door and the fading sun through the window lit up his pale face. Seeing him, Glenda felt a three year old sob fill her throat. Why did he look so vulnerable?

He was wearing his usual torn, black turtleneck sweater and his tight black jeans. He hadn't even removed his cowboy

377

boots, she noticed. There were dark circles under his eyes. Beside his bed were yet more pills and a glass of water. Dr Umberto and his pills, Glenda thought bitterly. Dr Umberto with his unctuous hands and his pince-nez glasses. Don't deal with any problems, Clive, just swallow more pills. Glenda thought of Dr Umberto as an evil spider. Dr Umberto in league with the she-devil. No wonder Clive was out of it: a visit from the devil followed by Dr Umberto was enough to send anyone over the edge. She wished she had been there to protect him and she felt guilty that she had been happily tucked away with Minnie eating her boiled eggs with salad cream from a jar. She should have been here holding up a cross and a bunch of garlic to keep away the real demons. Surely, she thought, if the devil was a real person it would be personified in Lady Jane Alexander.

She looked down at the stone floor of the bedroom and at the red Aubusson carpet by the bed. 'Clive?' she said softly. She put out her hand and stroked his face. 'Clive?' She could see that he heard her, though he was miles away.

A broken smile slipped across his drugged face. 'Is that you?' he whispered, trying to open his eyes.

'Yes, darling.' Glenda knelt down. 'I've only been away a few days, love. Not very long.'

Clive sighed. 'When you're away, it feels like forever. Mother said you might not come back.' He opened his eyes. 'She said you would never marry me.' His voice shook. 'She was here today. Or yesterday. She said I'm not to ask all those questions about the estate and that it's none of my business. She doesn't want me talking to the accountant.' Clive sat up. His eyes were wide and frightened.

'Clive,' she held his hand, 'it *is* your business. It's all your business.'

'She says I have to stand down because I'm sick, too sick to claim the title.'

'She's said that a thousand times before, Clive.' Glenda sat patiently. 'But she's just trying to bully you. There's nothing she can do. Jonathan talked to Lord Silver and the good lord says it takes an Act of Parliament to remove a hereditary title. Besides, she would have to prove you were unfit.'

'What does that mean?' Clive looked desperately at Glenda. 'Does that mean she would have to prove I was mad? That shouldn't be difficult.' He threw himself back on the bed. 'That shouldn't be difficult at all.'

'Clive, come on downstairs and let's talk. Why don't you have a bath and change your clothes, and I'll ask Mrs Robinson if I can cook tonight. We'll have dinner, just the two of us. Okay?'

'I'm glad you're back,' Clive smiled.

'So am I.'

Glenda went down the wide stairs and through the hall to the kitchen. 'May I cook tonight, Mrs Robinson?' She saw Mrs Robinson's face tighten and then soften.

'Of course, dear. I was going to serve cold chicken and rice, but it can wait until tomorrow.'

Glenda suppressed a grin. Mrs Robinson's cold chicken and rice was a shared joke with Clive. Clive couldn't believe anybody could cook something that tasted like boiled facecloths.

She went into the pantry to look for food. A lasagna, she decided. I'll make him a wicked Italian lasagna dripping with mozzarella and fresh tomatoes from the greenhouse. She went off to find Mark, hoping he might have some fresh basil. The smell of fresh basil sweating in a pool of yellow farm butter and red wine intoxicated her. Tonight she must tell Clive that she would be away for three weeks in America.

On her last night before she left for the wedding, Glenda tried to talk to Clive. 'Darling,' she said as she lay beside him in her nightgown. 'It won't be long. And when I get back let's talk seriously about getting married.'

Clive stared at the ceiling. 'I don't want you to go,' he said. 'I'm afraid without you.'

'You can't be. Don't be.' Glenda leaned over him, her hair brushing his chest. 'I talked to Jonathan, and he'll be in London at Lord Silver's office, so if anything comes up or your mother tries to threaten you, you telephone him. I have his home number in Chelsea, if you need him at night. Darling— ' Glenda felt an ache of longing, not necessarily for sex, but an emptiness that needed filling and could only be filled by the union of two bodies. It was not lust so late at night, rather a cosmic loneliness. She touched his face with her lips and then recoiled as she felt the unresponsive skin. 'Clive, what is it? Don't you want me? I mean, I've never really talked about this to you before, but I think we should.'

Clive rolled away and put his face in his hands.

'Look, Clive, we've been together for more than three years and I'm a normal woman. I know I'm a virgin, and so are you, but we should want each other. There's nothing wrong in that, is there?'

'No. Nothing wrong. Perfectly normal,' Clive said into his hands.

Glenda touched his shoulder. 'I would love to be loved by you,' she said softly. 'We are going to get married anyway, so I can't see the harm, can you?'

Clive shook his head. 'No,' he said in a voice muffled by his hands.

'Then why can't we? Georgina and Jonathan make love. You can tell it when you're with them, by the way they are with each other.' Glenda leaned her head back against her own pillow. 'There's a sort of golden cord between them. A happiness that is theirs alone. They really belong to each other, like the vows say. "With my body I thee worship . . . " ' She sighed. 'Probably the most beautiful words in the world . . . I don't mean that we have to make love tonight, or any other night in particular. We *can* wait until we're married, if that's what you want. But that's not the point. The point is, even if we do get married, will you *want* to make love to me?'

Clive kept his back to her.

'Clive, you must answer.' Glenda was getting cross. She leaned over him again and took one hand away from his face. She saw that he was crying. 'Oh Clive, I don't mean to hurt you.'

He pulled his hand free. 'You're not,' he said. 'You see, I don't know if I can make love to you. It's not–' and he gasped as the sobs rushed through his body '– it's not that I don't want to. I just can't. Oh Glenda!' he said, burying himself in her arms. 'I'm impotent. But I didn't want to tell you in case you went off me. You won't will you? I thought maybe if we were married and secure, things might change.' He hugged her tightly.

'Oh. I see.' Glenda felt her heart beating. She hardly knew what to say. 'And that's why – that's why, for all these years, you've pulled away from me?'

Clive nodded. 'I couldn't tell you. I just couldn't.'

Glenda held him. At last, she thought, the secret is out. 'Darling,' she said, 'you should have told me from the start. Of course, it wouldn't put me off you. I would have understood. That's all. But please, don't be afraid to talk about it. Or anything. Talk to me. What is it that makes you . . . ?' In all honesty, she herself found it difficult to discuss. But she was so relieved that Clive had opened up to her, she wanted to keep talking. 'I mean, do you understand it yourself?'

'No. Not really.'

'Well, what does it feel like?'

'It feels . . . I feel – I feel afraid. Simple as that. I feel something terrible will happen if I let myself go.'

'But, Clive, you can trust me. I'd never hurt you.'

'I know that, Glenda. At least my mind knows that.' He laughed softly. 'But try telling that to my body.'

She kissed his neck. 'Body, you can trust me.'

He kissed her mouth. 'Well, body says he does know that, but he wants a little more time to believe it.'

She hugged him. 'You can have as much time as you want, as long as I know you love me.'

He returned her embrace.

'Whatever happens,' she said, 'we'll get married and we will work this out.'

Clive was asleep almost instantly with a smile on his tear-stained face. He's still full of drugs, she thought. That's half his problem. Anyway, I can always ask Molly. I don't know a thing about impotence, but she will.

She fell asleep with Clive in her arms, feeling closer to him than she had for months.

Chapter 86

Glenda had never before flown in an airplane, neither had she ever expected to travel first class. Chinchilla coached her all the way to the airport. Glenda sat beside her mother in the back of the car. Chinchilla drove up the M4 furiously. They passed the little house where poor Mrs McCluskie had killed her husband and they went by the Town Hall where Mr Oppenheim, with his triple wart, wished to be king. Time had not treated the new Town Hall well. It already looked rather forlorn and shabby. Glenda grinned at her mother. 'We won in the end, didn't we, mum? We've left Hounslow forever.'

'Don't drink alcohol on the plane,' Chinchilla said, her pale purple hair flying in the wind.

Minnie sat next to Glenda and squeezed her hand. 'Glenda, I was going to tell you before, but I've been so busy and you've been . . . well, you've been so preoccupied.'

Glenda was only half-listening, her mind still reeling with Clive's confession. A ride to the airport with Minnie gave her no time to discuss this revelation. Besides, would Minnie know anything about impotence? Chinchilla certainly would, but this was neither the time nor the place. 'What, mum?'

'I've found a wonderful man.'

'Really?' Glenda was instantly interested. 'What's his name?'

'George,' Minnie beamed. ''Is name is George and he works as the barman in the Coach and Horses. 'E really is lovely and good to me. I know you'll like 'im, love. He's short and walks with a limp which 'e got from the war. 'E reminds me a lot of Phil Clough, you know.'

'Well then, he must be all right.'

'Do go to the bathroom before you get on the airplane,' Chinchilla continued. 'But as you're travelling first class, it won't be too bad. It's the poor cattle section one has to feel sorry for.'

Glenda winced as Chinchilla hurtled past a lorry. The lorry hooted and shook with fury. Chinchilla stuck out a finger and raced on. 'I do hope we get there,' Glenda muttered.

'Oh, we will, love. Don't worry. Chinchilla's an excellent driver.'

Inside the Heathrow departure terminal Glenda walked over to the bookshop. She left Chinchilla and Minnie having a cup of coffee in the upstairs coffee lounge. She browsed through the books and magazines. There were several magazines that looked pornographic and several others that purported to deal with human emotions, but perhaps some of the women's magazines might have an agony aunt holding forth on the subject of impotence. She surreptitiously tried to flip back the pages of *Other Women* to see if there were any other frustrated females who were partnered by men that couldn't. She realized that she felt totally ashamed to be doing this. Certainly she knew in her mind that it was not her fault that Clive could not make love to her, but, all the same, in her heart she felt that, were she beautiful enough or perhaps sexy enough, she could overcome his impotence and they would live happily ever after. Somehow it *was* her fault. The woman beside her was gazing down at the letters page. 'Silly buggers, some of these women,' she hissed at

Glenda. 'Bored 'ousewives, that's their problem. Too much time to moon about. Imagine making your problems public! Stupid, that's what I call it. Plain daft.'

Glenda blushed and hurriedly shut the magazine. She pulled out as many different magazines as she could and tucked them under her arm. 'My!' the girl on the desk said. 'We *are* going for a long journey, aren't we?'

'Yes,' Glenda mumbled, still blushing. And then she rushed back to the safety of Minnie and Chinchilla.

The magazines lay in a huge pile beside her as she sipped her coffee. 'Now, you've packed enough pairs of knickers, love, 'aven't you?'

'Mum, I am twenty-two years old, not two.' Glenda wriggled.

'Of course you are, but a mum has to know these things.' Chinchilla smiled. 'Excited, dear?'

'Very,' Glenda smiled. 'I need this break, some time for myself.' If only she could take Chinchilla aside and talk to her alone . . . Maybe when I come back, Glenda thought. Unbidden, into her heart a small voice whispered, *If* you come back. Glenda looked at her mother and her friend and then she looked around the airport. Yes, she thought, *if* I come back.

Chapter 87

Glenda always imagined New York to be rather sober. She had seen copies of *The New Yorker* when she stayed with Georgina. The men and women portrayed in the magazine seemed faintly supercilious. They shared jokes that were incomprehensible to Glenda. Jonathan wasn't much help. 'Brits never understand American humour,' he said. 'There are two sorts. There's WASP humour, which is very dry, and then there's Jewish humour.'

'I understand Jewish humour,' Glenda retorted. 'Ruth's

family were always making jokes and using Yiddish expressions. But WASP humour I think you have to be born into.'

She was pleasantly surprised when she left the plane and walked through La Guardia Airport. The place much more resembled a huge circus than an airport. There were hippies, smelling of incense and pot, with children on their backs and guitars in their hands. Along the walkways small groups of shaven smiling boys and girls wrapped in orange robes chanted like they did in Oxford Street. Her hands full of luggage, she saw groups of young soldiers, on their way to, or coming from, war in Vietnam. Those in their fresh uniforms on their way out looked bright and confident, but those on their way back, she realized, looked hunted and defeated.

The whole world in all its various colours and ethnic robes seemed present just as Glenda arrived: stately black men in dashikis, white turbanned Sikhs, and women – lots and lots of women. Not working-class women clutching their children in the London airport on their way to an annual holiday for two weeks in Spain. Those women she left behind her, waiting for Dad to come out of the pub at the airport and breathe beer on the rest of the family while Mum sits trying to control the children. No, these were American businesswomen. Glenda watched, fascinated. Immaculate in pant-suits or long skirts and matching coats, these women walked purposefully along the floor trailing their matching luggage on trolleys. Glenda felt like a country bumpkin. She had two mismatched suitcases. One, given by Chinchilla, looked all right, but the other was a cheap brown affair and Glenda wished she could set fire to it now.

At last she saw the ticket counter and, waiting beside it, the tall figure of Abe. In England, Abe always appeared the exception; here he was the norm. America was a huge mixture of everyone, all pouring in and out of the airport like sand in an egg-timer. Abe was waving and pushing his way through the sea of humanity to find her. She closed her

eyes and felt herself melt when he picked her up in his arms
and virtually carried her the last few feet to where Renée
stood. There were tears in Renée's wide brown eyes as she
looked down at Glenda. She pulled Glenda into her arms and
hugged her. 'I've missed you, darling,' she said in her slow
gravelly voice. 'We both have, so very much.'

Glenda found herself crying. Pent up tears rolled down her
face. 'And I've missed you,' she sobbed. Together they left
the airport terminal. Abe summoned a cab and they climbed
in.

The car barrelled around the streets of the city, sliding and
hooting. Glenda grinned. She was too excited to be sad for
long. 'I've seen taxi drivers like this in the cinema,' she
laughed, holding on to Renée's arm. 'Are you sure we'll get
there alive?'

'Look over there,' Renée pointed out. 'Central Park.'

Glenda was shocked at the dirt and the garbage.

Renée watched her, amused. 'I'm afraid it's not like Hyde
Park, darling.'

Glenda was amazed at the change in Renée's face. 'You
look marvellous,' she said. 'What's happened?'

Renée smiled. 'Everything's happened. I just wonder why
I took so long to get to New York.'

'You didn't think anything would beat London, that's
why.' Abe put his arm around Glenda who was squashed
quite happily between their two warm bodies. Abe's arm felt
good and solid. Not tentative, as Clive's sometimes felt. Just
big and comfortable and male.

After half an hour of driving down city streets filled with
homeless people scurrying like beaten animals, some carrying
packs on their backs or pushing prams in front of them full
of rubbish, the car stopped in a long quiet road. Large brown
houses stood to attention, their windows blank and unseeing.
Frosty tall trees guarded them.

Renée got out first. Abe fished into his capacious pockets
to pay the driver. Renée walked up the flat stairs and turned

the key in the lock. 'Mrs Fogarty's taken off,' she remarked.

'Taken off?' said Glenda.

'Oh nothing. She's our housekeeper, and she has a witless, toothless husband who goes on drinking binges. She can't live with him and she can't live without him. So we have a house rule. When he's sober he stays downstairs and does the heavy cleaning and the gardening. But when he has a binge, she throws him out until he's sobered up. Today of all days she has to go and fish him out of Bellevue. He often beats someone up and then has himself admitted until he dries out. A pity really. He's quite a nice man, and Bridget is such a good cook I'll put up with anything. Abe will take your suitcases up to your room and I'll see what Bridget's left us for dinner. Come along, Glenda.'

Renée was surprised to see Glenda looking rather pale. She left Glenda only a short time ago and, although they wrote to each other frequently, Glenda had obviously shared nothing of what was causing her unrest. Renée knew she must make time to spend with Glenda. After the wedding, she promised herself.

'Look.' Renée opened the door of the biggest fridge Glenda had ever seen in her life. Inside the vast space sat four plates of lobster tails, the pink roe lying across a neat bank of fresh caviar. A salad, some smoked salmon, and yellow honeydew melon halves draped with the palest pink prosciutto. 'Abe's chosen the champagne. We've been drinking a very nice Taittinger recently. So dry and light.' Renée babbled on, watching Glenda's face relax. 'Why don't you go upstairs and have a real American shower, and then we can go out to lunch. Dinner is already organized, thanks to Bridget.'

'Thanks.' Glenda was grateful she had cleaned her teeth in the airplane bathroom, but she still felt as if her teeth were wearing socks, and she was sweaty and musty.

Her bedroom was on the third floor. Abe and Renée had the top floor to themselves, including a big bedroom, a his-and-hers bathroom, and a study set so high that the tops of the trees peered in curiously. Renée led Glenda down the stairs and pushed open the door to her bedroom.

'I'll leave you now. Pop downstairs when you're ready. I'll be in the drawing room.'

Glenda walked across the room and leaned her head against the windowpane. She wondered where Clive was. The pain of separating from him clutched at her. The fingers were strong and they pried into her heart. She imagined the fingers had nails that were hard and yellow. They pinched and made her catch her breath. This is silly, she said to herself firmly. I'm only here for three weeks and I can telephone him any time I want to.

She shook herself and turned to inspect the room. It was large and square like the rest of the house. A creamy brown carpet with a deep pile lay across the floor and continued into the bathroom. The bed was expansive with thick white bed covers. The furniture throughout the room was white and a heavy gold-framed mirror on the wall made the room seem even larger.

The bathroom was nearly as big. Glenda loved the round, bright red sunken tub. The lavatory, hand basin, and bidet all had the same gold handles. She turned the bath taps on. A hot whoosh and a cloud of steam enveloped her face. She threw off her clothes and stood naked, inspecting herself in the bathroom mirror. 'Twenty-two and still a virgin,' she said out loud. 'I'll have to *give* it away at this rate.' Still, she thought as she turned to step down into the tub, I don't look too bad for an unused virgin. I must telephone Molly. She'll have some ideas.

Glenda slid into the water and watched it climb slowly up her body until it reached her pink nipples. They responded with joy to the embrace of the water. She reached for a big jar of salts that sat on the end of the bath. Ahhh! she breathed. This is the life of decadence. I could get used to this life. Yes, very used to it indeed.

Chapter 88

'Well, I'm here, Molly.' Glenda found her voice quivering with excitement.

Lunch had been fun. Glenda was used to the quiet respectful hue of an English restaurant, the subdued hum of the *maître d'* floating silently round her table, waiters interpreting his nods and eyebrow signals. Lunch in New York was rather like feeding time at the zoo, and Americans had rather different table manners. 'Who are these people?' Glenda asked Renée.

Renée waved across the room at a man who sat behind his paunch. A cheroot in his mouth dribbled ash onto his plate. His lips were big and swollen. He was almost bald except for a few wisps of grey hair and a surprisingly bristly moustache. 'That's Larry over there,' she said. 'He's a television producer. An absolute bastard, but I love him anyway. I don't know why there are so many rats in the television business. You'd have thought the theatre was bad enough, but television's even worse. All these people are leftovers from the McCarthy era, but they have interesting stories to tell. I can listen for hours.'

Glenda was left with a mental image of the New York intellectual elite loudly slurping Hungarian cooking.

'I've just had my first glimpse of the New York intelligentsia,' Glenda recounted to Molly down the telephone. She found herself laughing. 'I had some wine and I feel a tiny bit drunk, sort of high.'

'That's New York, baby,' Molly said. 'It's intoxicating. Washington's dull by comparison. But you ain't seen nothing till you've seen the New Jersey Turnpike. The quintessential American experience. I got some time off here at the firm. Can't wait to drive up and join you. When can I come and take you off to stay at my parents' house? It'd be a good break for both of us.'

'How about after the wedding on Saturday? You're coming for that?'

'Sure. Wouldn't miss it for the world. Another good man bites the dust. Maybe one day I'll be the lucky bride with red knickers.'

'Any offers yet?'

'Nah, only banana boys. I'm off to the Caribbean at the end of July. They say diving is the *in* thing at the moment, and at least you get assigned a buddy on a dive-boat, instead of having to find one for oneself. Anyway, the Caribbean men are desperate to get off their islands. They'll do anything for a trip to America. Want to come?'

'Can't. Clive and I are thinking of going to LA to join Gerontius for a while. They want to do something vague like ride the same roads as Jack Kerouac. He died you know, suddenly, of a heart attack. I could tell Clive was really upset.' Glenda paused and her momentary excitement deflated like a balloon. 'But don't let's talk about it. I need a break from England.' She realized that she had been about to say *from Clive*.

Molly heard the hesitation. 'You mean Clive, don't you? Everyone needs a break from England. England is a sort of international disease. I rolled on the floor and kissed the carpet when I got home, and I spent my first week under the shower. I rushed into the supermarket and stuffed the fridge with food and then – oh joy, oh bliss! – I ran to my local deli and bought tons and tons of pastrami. Was I happy! I'm never going back to that bleak little island full of moaning. That's what the English do, they bitch and moan. Complaining is the national pastime. "How are you?" "Mustn't complain." Oh Glenda, I intend to kidnap you and never let you go back.'

Glenda glanced around her room. She was wrapped in a huge woolly towel. 'I might not go back,' she said lightly. 'So far everything is so huge and so comfortable.' She sat down on the bed and she found herself shaking with laughter. 'I might even be tempted to come down to the Caribbean and chase banana boys with you.'

'You do that. Anyway, pack your prettiest underwear for Saturday and I'll take you home and we'll go out and boogie.'

'It's a deal,' Glenda said. She put down the telephone and sat for a moment. Why did she always have to be so responsible? If the wicked were to flourish like the green bay tree, why couldn't she be a happy leaf? What was wrong with her? Here she was, miserable and lonely for Clive, and there was Molly doing more than just flourishing – positively thriving. It was indecent.

She dressed and went downstairs. 'Tea time,' Renée said. Glenda heard a shuffling and a thumping in the kitchen. 'Bridget Fogarty is back,' Renée explained.

'A cup of tea would be wonderful.'

Renée sat down in her familiar spoon-back armchair and Glenda sat beside her on the nursing chair that she had sat on as a child. 'Nothing much changes, Renée,' Glenda said, looking at all the old familiar furniture moved to a new place. 'Even that shawl you brought back from Spain is still on the piano. I feel so content here.'

'You've been sad, haven't you?'

Glenda lowered her eyes. 'In some ways, yes, I guess I have. In other ways, Clive and I are terribly happy together. There's a peace between us. An understanding.'

'Mmm.' Renée looked up and smiled at Mrs Fogarty as she carried in the tea tray. 'Thank you so much. Bridget, this is Glenda.'

Bridget Fogarty said hello with a tilt of her head and put the tea tray down. 'I cooked you a chocolate cake, miss. I hear there's a sugar shortage in England.'

'That was during the war, Bridget. But thanks. I love chocolate cake.' The thing looked like a monster. It sat on the plate and glared at Glenda. Bridget Fogarty wandered off towards the kitchen.

Renée giggled. 'Cakes are not her thing. We can always dump it down the lavatory.' Renée took a large knife and tried to impale the cake. The cake paid her out by slipping off the plate and onto the floor where it oozed weakly at them. Renée and Glenda were on their knees trying to scrape up the mess when Abe arrived.

'Oh. I see.' He surveyed the scene. 'An orgiastic chocolate experience. I've got the plane tickets, darling.'

Glenda's eyebrows went up. 'Where are you going?'

'Just a week in Italy after the wedding,' said Renée. 'You don't mind, do you?'

'Don't worry about that.' Glenda licked her finger. The chocolate cake was laced with a bitter almond flavour. 'Gosh, is she trying to kill you? This tastes terrible. Molly says I can go and stay with her for a while. She owes her parents a visit anyway.'

'Good.' Renée sat back in the chair looking at the mess on the floor. 'I'll have to take the damn cake out into the garden and bury it along with all the others. Then I'll tell Bridget I dropped my plate and she can clean up the rest of the mess. Funny, I'm looking forward to getting away from New York. You wouldn't believe it, but even here things get too small and incestuous at times. Every so often I have to get back to Europe just to keep in touch with civilization. I make an awful lot of money in the theatre here, but I miss the feeling of history in Europe. I miss the museums and I miss the architecture . . . Listen, when Abe and I are back, let's you and I take a couple of days off and go down to Boston. I want to show you the Gardner Museum built by Isabella Stewart Gardner. Now there was a good Soul, or whatever you call yourselves.'

'Yes, Souls,' Glenda said. 'The four of us are soul-mates.'

'Well, Isabella Stewart Gardner lived an absolutely scandalous life. Had all the men she wanted whether they were married or not, made a fortune, plundered Europe, brought back all its best artwork, stuck it haphazardly into a transplanted Italian villa right in the middle of Boston, had herself painted, and then died almost penniless. But she lived, oh boy, did she live! I've got to go to the theatre tonight. I'm in a play called *Requiem*. Don't come to watch, as it's the last night dress rehearsals. I'm not doing this play for money. I'm doing it because I believe in what it has to say. You might come tomorrow with Abe. I banned him so far from seeing it. I warn you, it's not just Off Broadway, it's Way the Hell Off Broadway. Like far out, out of sight.'

'You mean it's controversial and men won't like it, and it's men who back the theatre.'

Renée nodded. 'Exactly,' she said. 'While I'm not a feminist, every so often I will tip my hat to an individual woman who actually wrote a book or a play or made a film that was not mere rhetoric. In this case the play says things that need saying. Come on, Glenda. Let's sneak this cake out and, Abe, you go to the kitchen and keep Bridget Fog busy while we do the dirty deed. Ha! The neighbours will think I have a private graveyard out there. One day the police will be banging on the door demanding entry. "Guilty, my lord, of burying Bridget Fogarty's cakes."

' "That will be three years in the slammer!" '

Glenda giggled. It was good to be home.

Chapter 89

The next night Glenda was in the audience for the opening night of *Requiem*. Alone on the stage Renée sat propped up in a hospital bed. The spotlight was on her. Behind her in darkness was another bed. Glenda shivered. The audience, nervous, shuffled its feet. This had to be Off Broadway. Nobody wanted to watch a play about other people's madness.

Renée looked dishevelled. She was not the warm, vibrant Renée that Glenda knew. This was a distraught woman, a tired woman, a woman who had given too much for too long and now was locked away in a mental hospital. 'Lucy lies quiet in her white-walled cell. Asleep, she dreams of childhood: harebells, dead dogs, cats and a sled. Raging father, sobbing mother stand at the head of her bed.' As the words floated over the auditorium, a shadowy figure rose from the bed behind Renée and this fair-headed wraith began to dance. The awful thing for Glenda was that the wraith had the same terrible vulnerability as Clive. Whoever had been chosen to play this part knew suffering.

The long arms groped their way into the light. The face looked as if it was carved out of cream cheese. The eyes did not look directly at anyone but played a game with themselves in the top of the head, and the mouth smiled a yellow pumpkin smile. 'Rows of bodies lie beneath this cell,' Renée continued in a conversational tone, 'all motionless, all dead, oblivious in valium.' A moment's pause while the people in the audience caught their breath in a guilty complicity.

Glenda wondered how many of them had the little round comforting bottles in their pockets. Clive had bottles of pills, so many bottles . . . Glenda listened intently.

'An orchestrated silence. No trouble now to anyone. Sad silent sleep, madness under strict control.'

The bird-like figure elongated its body and began to dance, to dance not the accepted dance of a body entwined in music but rather the movements of a human being in inner turmoil forced to move to fight off the paralysis of pain. Glenda watched. Then we are not alone, she thought. If this woman can express this sort of feelings, then Clive and I are not alone and we must be able to find help.

The character of the psychiatrist walked up beside Renée's bed, his long lean shadow blotted her out as he reminded Renée that she was an unreasonable woman, an hysteric, a danger to herself and to others. Her poor grieving husband stood in the wings with his cheque book and a crate of claret for Christmas, a present to keep the psychiatrist on his side. The play continued.

The audience was at some times wrapped in a silence and then embarrassed into more coughing and shuffling. Here were two rebellious women locked up together, watched over and wardened like dangerous animals.

Finally, as the play came to its painful ending, there was a marvellous moment of hope. The final act was a triumph when the psychiatrist, followed by his nursing staff and students, invaded the ward. Both women patients sat meekly in their beds, but they had a plan. As the psychiatrist silently mouthed his objections to the two women and prophesied more retribution, the lights went down. Renée, carrying a candle in her hand, approached the audience. She gazed at them and Glenda felt that she was staring at her. There must be hope, Glenda thought. She strained to hear the words. The audience watched Renée. 'Until we all refuse to be separated by labels called madness or mental illness, until we stop the tyranny of those who label themselves sane and others dissident and therefore mad, we will continue to be locked up as we are. Both of us chose not to stay, but then we are free to go because this is a play.' She took the dancer's hand and the spotlight bobbed back into the centre of the stage and then around the side and out of sight.

The lights came up slowly and the audience could see all the professional supporters of the psychiatrist chattering away hysterically at each other. The two beds were empty and the curtain came down. Renée and her dancing friend had got away.

Glenda turned to Abe who sat with tears in his eyes. Abe knew some of the struggle Renée had at various times in her life when things were difficult. He always took her in his arms and waited for troubles to pass. He hoped marriage would make her even more secure, but tonight he knew she had been nervous and he loved her for it.

Glenda was surprised by the pain she felt. 'It's that moment of hope, you know,' she gasped. 'I was all right when I thought there was nothing that they could do. But when they both escaped, I felt as if something was ripped out in my heart.' She began to cry.

Abe grabbed her arm and hustled her backstage. 'Hang on, honey,' he said. 'We'll go and find Renée.'

It was a very small theatre and the dressing rooms were dark and grim. Renée sat at her mirror, just staring. Abe put his head around the door. 'Can we come in, honey?'

'Sure.' Renée looked as old and tired as she had on the stage. She shook her head. 'I'm too long in the tooth for this role,' she said.

Glenda hugged Renée. 'You're not,' she said fiercely. She was crying. Wild sobs tore at her chest.

Renée held her hard. 'Go ahead and cry, Glenda. You have a lot to cry about.'

'I'm scared, Renée. I can't save him all by myself.'

'Shh. Shhh.' Renée rocked her as she did when she was a child. 'Of course you can't, darling.'

'Then will you help me?' Glenda looked imploringly into Renée's eyes.

'Yes, I will,' she said simply. 'I've done a lot of research for this play and I know a lot of good people who don't look at labels but at the people underneath the labels. I'll always be there if you need me. Now dry your eyes and have a glass of champagne and we'll go out and celebrate. How was I, Abe darling?' Renée stood up.

She'll always look like a little girl in search of approval, Abe thought as he beheld her with affection. 'You were wonderful,' he said. 'Just wonderful.'

Renée put her arm around Glenda's shoulders. 'Feeling better?'

Glenda smiled. 'I'll telephone Clive from the restaurant. I need to hear his voice. Isn't love a funny thing? Clive is like my brother and my best friend all rolled into one. Maybe it's because I never had a brother.'

'Maybe,' said Renée.

*   *   *

The restaurant was noisy. People came over to talk to Renée while Abe watched protectively. Glenda, standing at the telephone booth, gazed at her empty chair from across the room. She felt naked and exposed. Hard lecherous men's eyes watched her – pretty girl on her own in a telephone booth. New York was a city of rapacious men. Lizards, their designer clothes and gold wristwatches were salamander crests. Gold-tipped western boots. Silk suits, slithery ties. Glenda made a face.

Then she heard the soothing sound of an English telephone. She imagined it ringing in the drawing room, the old-fashioned handset burring gently. 'Hello?' she jumped at Clive's soft voice. 'I'm ringing from a restaurant. We've just been to watch Renée's play.'

'How was it?' Clive's voice sounded healthy and happy.

Glenda relaxed. 'Very good,' she said.

'What was it about, darling?'

Glenda hesitated. Clive sounded balanced and cheerful. 'Oh, nothing. Just a play about two women. I enjoyed it. What are you doing, Clive?'

'Well, it's the middle of the night . . . '

'Oh, I'm sorry. I didn't mean to wake you. I forgot all about the time difference. I just wanted to say hello to you and hear you.'

'Don't worry,' Clive said. 'I was up anyway. I've been reading poems and lolling about in front of the fire. I do miss you, Glenda.'

'I know.' Glenda pulled a face. 'But I'll be back soon, darling. Anything exciting happened on the farm?'

'Not much. The sow had fifteen piglets. She's full of milk, and they're so funny. Tiny, bald, little things with snouts.' Clive was laughing.

'I must go, Clive. I can see my food arriving at the table. I'm glad to hear your voice.'

Clive blew her a kiss. 'Speak to you tomorrow.'

'Love you, Clive,' Glenda said. She put down the telephone and stood still for a moment. Why did she always feel so hungry after she cried? she wondered. And why do I get into such a state over Clive when he is just fine?

She noticed a plump man on her left looking at her through cold, predatory, blue eyes. She shivered and walked back to her chair. His eyes, she thought, looked exactly like Dr Umberto's eyes. She sat down at the table and she raised her glass. 'To your marriage and eventually to mine,' she smiled at Abe and Renée.

Abe and Renée raised their glasses. 'To us,' they said in unison.

There were shadows in Renée's eyes unseen by Glenda. Renée knew the world that Clive inhabited and it was not an easy one to escape. She looked fondly at Glenda. Glenda would be hurt many times in the coming years, but Renée would be there to help her. And above all, she had faith in Glenda, the little trembling child that had come into Renée's life. The same little girl that suffered night terrors for years after the dreadful McCluskie murder. Glenda knew what fear was, and pain. She would survive.

Chapter 90

Glenda tried to suppress tears, tears not of sorrow but of happiness. How stupid! she scolded herself. She stood next to Renée, who looked amazing in a long, sweeping, velvet dress. Abe stood beside her, handsome in a dark grey suit. Next to him was his tiny, grizzly-haired mother. Glenda smiled through her tears. Abe's mother might be tiny, but she was ferocious. He picked up his mother and kissed her soundly. I want that, Glenda thought. I want to be picked up and kissed soundly. I want to be married.

She watched as the Justice of the Peace read out the vows. 'I do,' Renée said in her resonant, strong voice. Abe, too, repeated the vows. Both, unified in their love, now publicly proclaimed it in front of people who loved them. For once Molly was listening and quiet. I wonder, Glenda thought, if Molly is as moved as I am?

The short ceremony over, Renée turned and threw the orchid at Glenda. She reached out and scooped the flower, hugging it to her breast. The huge orchid flopped over her nose and then she pulled it down and looked into the giant mouth. What a wonderful colour, she noticed. A Rousseau-like jungle lay before her eyes. She saw a panther with Clive's eyes staring implacably at her. Suddenly she felt guilty: All day long she had not thought about Clive. I will telephone him, she promised herself. I must see if he is all right.

Then her other side came through. Of course, he's all right. And why do you make yourself feel guilty? Why can't you just have a really good time and be happy? All your life you looked after and felt responsible for your mother. When you were free of that you got into a relationship with a sick man . . .

He is *not* sick, Glenda reminded her tormentor.

Yeah, the tormentor sneered back. You and who else think he's not sick?

Go away, Glenda said fiercely.

She went up to Renée and gave her a big hug. 'It's all legal now,' Glenda said, reaching for Abe. For a moment the three of them were united. Abe's mother Bella pushed her way into the hug.

Abe's face was wreathed in warm happy smiles. 'She's made an honest man out of me, mom.'

'About time, too.' Bella smiled at her tall son. 'You make sure he behaves,' she said with a finger pointed at Renée.

'Come on, everyone.' Renée shooed the guests out of the room.

Outside, in the City Hall corridor, a long queue of people waited to get married. Glenda looked at the impatient couples. Some had been planning this day for many months. They wore special outfits and carried bottles of champagne. They were surrounded by families and friends. Others had decided in a rush and stood awkwardly beside each other. Glenda felt she could see them internally screaming that the idea had been a mistake all along but they were too far gone to stop what was going to be a bad relationship. A man stood and loomed over his young wife-to-be and Glenda was reminded of PC McCluskie. The man had a tight face underneath which, Glenda felt, he boiled with rage. I wonder, she thought, if I picked Clive because he has no violent feelings. Except when he had a turn, Clive was the calmest, most peaceful man she had ever met. Maybe, she thought.

She hurried out to follow Renée and Abe to the cab stand.

Bridget Fog was proud of the effort she had put into the little marriage feast. Before she added the final touches to the table she folded her hands in prayers to Our Lady. Not for Renée and Abe – she knew they would be happy, and anyway they had a permanent place in her goodnight prayers – but for Glenda who had arrived looking unhappy and drawn. Still the prayers were working and the girl genuinely looked a lot better.

The big room at the brownstone was filled with friends and well-wishers. Studio directors, actors, and actresses filed through the house. Everywhere Glenda looked she saw animated discussions. She did not feel herself to be any part of these people. They were beautifully dressed and very clever. They had clever laughs and eyes that roved like retrievers retrieving ducks that had been shot down on a lake. A man stopped Glenda and asked her what she did. 'I've been running a long-term exhibition on women writers and painters at a small, private museum.'

'How *interesting*!' the man said, making the word *interesting* explode with energy.

'Actually, it is.' Glenda watched his eyes slide round her, tracing the lines of other people's bodies, watching for the crook of an interested finger or the tip of a sexually inclined head. 'The exhibition runs for another few weeks and then, after that, I don't know.'

'Do you know the newlyweds?' the young man asked.

'Yes, very well.'

'Um. Odd, you know. A white woman marrying a black man. Don't see that often.'

'How dare you?' Glenda felt the colour rise in her cheeks and her voice wobbled. Damn, she thought. Why can't I just get angry.

'See you around,' the man said and he slid away.

Glenda walked out of the drawing room and passed Molly who was sitting on the stairs with an elegant young actor whom Glenda recognized from the play the other night. 'Hi.' Molly grinned up at Glenda. 'You look pissed off.'

'I am pissed off. People can be so terrible.'

'Meet Valentine,' Molly said. 'Sit down. Have a drink. And loosen up, will you?'

Glenda looked at Molly. Her eyes were bright and her speech was beginning to slur. That's all I need, Glenda thought. Molly drunk and out for the evening with this man. Glenda said hello to the dark-haired man sitting beside Molly. She said, 'I'm afraid I'm not in a good mood. Please forgive me.'

Valentine laughed. Glenda noticed how beautiful his white teeth were and how well he laughed. She looked at Molly. She was not going to spend tonight on her own, not when she knew Abe and Renée would be celebrating their honeymoon together. She would be far too lonely in such a big house. 'Souls, Molly,' she said, gazing down at her friend. 'Remember? We are Souls. We stick together.'

Molly laughed. 'I haven't forgotten. Don't worry.'

Valentine looked puzzled. 'Souls?'

Molly dimpled at him. 'That's for me to know and for you to find out. Have another drink.'

Glenda left them and walked up the stairs. She telephoned

Clive. He sounded busy and quite happy. She put the telephone down and sat on her bed. She wished she could get into bed and sleep, the way Clive slept when he was depressed. She shook her shoulders. Go away, you dreadful old crow, she said. Depression lifted its head for a few moments. It was crouched in the corner of her room. She could see the skeleton with its huge, hooded cloak. Be gone, she said.

Glenda left the phantasmic thing in the room and went downstairs. I shall find someone I like to talk to, she promised herself.

Valentine detached himself from Molly's side. 'I was waiting to see you again,' he said, taking Glenda's hand and noticing her ring. 'Engaged to be married, I see.' He turned her hand over. 'Never mind, princess. Maybe I can make you a better offer.'

Glenda tried not to giggle. Valentine looked very serious. And she saw his dark blue eyes twinkle. 'Souls,' Molly reminded her as she stormed past.

Glenda shrugged her shoulders. Why not? she thought. That's what the original Souls were all about, sharing men.

Valentine put his arm around Glenda's shoulders. 'How about dinner tonight?'

'Oh, I can't. I've promised Molly.'

He looked intrigued. 'You seriously mean to say you're turning down a date with me to spend the night with your girlfriend? Is this a feminist statement, or are you two an item?'

Glenda looked at him out of the corner of her eye. 'That,' she said, 'is for us to know and for you to find out.' She laughed and walked away. She knew Valentine was looking at her. She also knew he was interested. Really she would rather spend the evening with Molly which she knew, of course, was exactly what she would do.

But just being desired, Glenda felt wicked and she much enjoyed the feeling.

Chapter 91

After the guests were gone, and Renée and Abe had run laughing down the front steps, Bella came up to Glenda and said, 'I'm going now. Goodbye.'

Glenda looked at the strong little woman. 'Wouldn't you like to stay the night with us?'

'No,' she said firmly. 'I don't like New York. I'm a Southerner, and we Southerners don't ever like this place. I want to get back to my home and to the good weather.' She smiled. 'You take care of yourself, child. One day you can come and visit me in my own county, and I'll show you round.'

Glenda hugged Bella. 'You can be the grandmother I never had,' she said, feeling the thin bird-like bones through the thick overcoat.

Bella stood back a moment and studied Glenda. 'You needs all the grandmothers you can get. Just take the Greyhound bus and come down. Greyhound bus is the only way to travel. The people are so friendly and so nice to you.' Her face hardened. 'Not like the trains where the ticket collectors push and shove you around. Still,' she beamed, 'my boy is married and that's all of them off my hands.' She shook her head and picked up her suitcase. 'Bye now.' And she left.

'I can see where Abe gets his independence,' Glenda remarked as she settled down on the sofa next to Molly.

'I had a nanny like her once.' Molly lay back, her face still flushed with champagne.

In the kitchen Glenda could hear Bridget grumbling to her husband. They can clean up, she thought. Thank God for servants. She suppressed a guilty urge. 'You know, Molly, I'm really trying to discipline myself to stop feeling guilty. I *always* seem to feel guilty. I mean, don't you feel you should be helping Bridget Fog?'

'Nope. I don't feel guilty at all. She's paid to clean up. I'm not. The trouble with you, Glenda, is that you don't have anything real in your life to be guilty about. Guilt can be a rather delicious emotion, if you've done something truly wrong. With guilt, not only did you enjoy the moment itself, but then you also get to savour it for ever after by feeling guilty about it.'

'Like what?' Glenda asked.

'Well, like fucking your mom's lover.'

'Molly, you didn't. You're making that up?'

'You think I'm making it up, do you?' Molly sat up, her eyes brimming with laughter. 'Ha! It was only a few weeks ago. Mom went off to a conference. The whole time I was away at Cambridge she spent retraining to be a special Ed teacher. She brought back this gorgeous hunk called Tucker. Real WASP material. I knew she'd balled him because she told me, but she'd never tell dad.'

'She *told* you?'

'We're old enough to be friends now. Dad doesn't suspect. He's sort of The Man In The Grey Woolly Suit, you know? The guy that pays the bills every month and in return his wife thinks he's boring. That's how mom sees him anyway.'

'Don't you mind?'

'Well, I don't think he's boring. If my mother does, that's her problem. Anyway, it's their business, I suppose. Besides, one day when mom was in town I balled Tucker. Amazing. WASPs don't even buzz when they come. All very quiet and dignified. "Was it as good for you as it was for me?" All very formal and controlled.' Molly grinned. 'All this in the middle of the day out by the pool. I thought one of the gardeners might catch us, which made it all the more exciting. Then mom came back and Tucker disappeared. He made his excuses later that night and he left again. This time for good. WASPs and their little Anglo-Saxon consciences . . . Still, he wasn't circumcised, you know.'

'Did it make any difference?'

'Not really. It just reminded me of an umbrella.'

'Oh.' Glenda tried to look knowing. 'How interesting.'

'Oh, go on, Glenda. You don't know what I'm talking about, do you? You need to go out and get laid, that's what you need to do. And then you can feel guilty for the rest of your life because you didn't wait for Clive.'

Glenda felt herself blushing. 'You mean Valentine, don't you?'

'Race you for him.' Molly lay back on the sofa. 'It would be worth the experience to ball the same man as you, and then we can compare notes.'

Glenda almost began to think about the idea, just as a little exercise in imagination, but she was tired.

'Valentine says we can go to a party in his loft tomorrow night,' said Molly, half-closing her eyes, letting the champagne lull her again. 'We could put off going to New Jersey for another twenty-four hours, couldn't we?'

'I don't see why not.' Glenda yawned. 'I'm tired, Molly. I ate too much.'

Molly stretched. 'I'm worn out, too. You know, Glenda, it's good to see you. I've missed you. And Fatima, and even Georgina. I never thought I'd miss Georgina.'

'I bet you never thought Georgina would break her vow of chastity. She's been making love with Jonathan. She looks quite different, more energetic, less — I don't know — aloof.'

'No wonder.' Molly held her arms out to hug Glenda. 'Nooky is the best thing for your complexion. The very best.'

'Well that explains it,' Glenda laughed. '*My* face is beginning to break out. Look.' She pointed to a lump on her cheek.

'We'll have to do something about that.' Molly kissed Glenda. 'Good night, hon,' she said. 'Let's go to bed.'

Glenda laughed. 'You sound so lecherous, I'd better barricade my door.'

'You do that.' Molly stood up. 'I'll let you know if I feel a bit of sisterly passion come over me. My dyke friends say it's the best. I'll think about it when I've exhausted all the men in the world. But I think that might take me a lifetime.'

'It well might.' Glenda trailed up the stairs. 'Good night.' She could hear Bridget Fog stumping about the dining room. She fell into bed and she realized that she did not feel at all guilty letting someone else do the clearing up. I'm learning, she told herself.

Chapter 92

Dressing to go to Valentine's party, Glenda realized she was nervous. It was one thing to joke with Molly about seducing Valentine, and quite another to allow herself even to play with the notion of going to bed with him. Molly had planted a seed, and Glenda, try as she might, could not uproot the little plant that was beginning to grow. 'What do I do about contraceptives?' she heard herself ask Molly at breakfast. 'God, what a stupid thing to say!' she quickly pounced on herself, mortified.

'Condom,' Molly said simply, answering the question and ignoring the self-recrimination. 'You can pick one up at any drug store.'

'You mean I'm supposed to have to buy one and give it to him?'

'Why not? You're responsible for yourself these days, Glenda. Women have a right to take care of their own bodies.'

'You sound just like one of those books, banging on about the virtue of hairy legs and the joys of bad breath. I can't hand Valentine a French letter and say, "Here, put this on, I just happen to have it sitting in my handbag." Come to think of it, by that time I won't be carrying a handbag.'

Molly grinned. 'Don't fuss, Glenda. I've got a ton of condoms floating around. If you're afraid to go out and buy one, I'll give you one. Or two or three. It's not difficult. You just roll it onto his erection and try and keep a straight face. I usually get the giggles.'

'Why don't you use the pill or the cap?'

Molly made a face. 'Because I like myself too much to risk the pill, and I certainly am not about to squat on the floor fiddling around with a disgusting bit of rubber inside *myself*. No, if a man doesn't want to wear a condom I don't want to make love to him. I decided all that years ago when girl-friends of mine were running about on the pill and then found out they were suffering from the most awful infections. No thank you! Not for me.'

Glenda swallowed her coffee nervously. 'I don't *have* to seduce him tonight, so maybe I'll just carry around a condom for a while and give it time to get used to my handbag.'

Molly got up. 'Suit yourself. But maybe I'll get there first.'

'Be my guest.' Glenda realized that she would much rather Molly had him first and they could giggle about the night's events – much better that than having to risk herself. 'I can't believe that I'm sitting here talking about giving up my virginity to a man I've only met for a few minutes.'

'Has to be someone,' said Molly.

They spent the rest of the day leisurely wandering about a big expensive shopping mall. 'What sort of underwear have you got on?' Molly suddenly asked Glenda as they passed a lingerie shop.

'Marks and Spencer's. Why?'

'You can't seduce anybody in Marks and Spencer's under-wear. It's not the underwear; it's the family image. He doesn't know it's Marks and Spencer's, but you do. You slip off your pants and remember that your mother bought them for you. And your bra . . . No, no, no. It doesn't work. Look, let's go in here and I'll buy you a teddy.'

'A teddy?' Glenda laughed. 'What on earth is a teddy? We don't have those in England.'

'Oh yes, you do. You've just never looked for one before.'

They entered the shop and Glenda was amused. Not only did they sell sexy underwear and nightgowns but also there were several shelves full of men's expensive leather briefcases. 'Clever, isn't it?' Molly said. 'A man forgets his mistress's birthday, so he pops into this shop. And he has to take his purchase home, so he buys a briefcase which he can lock and keep in his study until he gets time to sneak out and visit his Other Woman. Huh! Now, if she were a Soul like us, she would telephone his wife and they could make plans to discomfort him. Like his wife could come down and buy exactly the same piece of lingerie and leave him wondering if it was a coincidence, if she had a lover, or if she suspected him . . . *This*,' Molly said, drawing a piece of red silk that looked rather like a bathing suit, 'is a teddy.'

'Oh.' Glenda stared at it. 'How do you pee?'

'For heaven's sake, Glenda, how romantic can you get? I show you the sexiest piece of underwear, and all you can say is *"How do you pee?"* Is that what you think of when you see something sexy?' She let her hands flop, and they made a slapping sound against her sides. 'I think I'm wasting my time.'

'No, you're not, Molly. I can't help being practical. After all, not all of us live in the lap of centrally heated luxury. I live in a draughty, freezing cold farm where the loo is about a million miles away from my bedroom and the water gets so cold you could break it with a pickaxe.'

'Trust the English.' Molly handed her the teddy. 'No wonder you're all so chaste. Here, go over there and try it on.'

In a small booth with a curtain, Glenda took off her clothes and slipped on the teddy. What a dreadfully vulgar word, she thought. A teddy. Teddies were warm, furry, little bears. Oh, I suppose that's what it must mean. She looked down at her pubic hair. Trust the Americans to think of everything in terms of cutesy little bears. Make everything safe and sanitized. Lavatory paper, towel rolls, and now sex. What an extraordinary country. She looked at herself in the long mirror. I do look nice, she decided. The silk swished around her body. It does feel sexy. She turned her back to the mirror and looked over her shoulder. Umm, not bad, Valentine. Her heart beat fast and she slipped off the teddy and pulled on her own clothes. She did up the snaps in the crotch of the garment. She imagined long, manly fingers undoing the snaps and she blushed. Not tonight, Glenda, she said to herself. Let Molly try first.

She walked back to the counter wearing a smile near to laughter. 'Thanks a lot, Molly. It's a really nice present.'

Molly took out her wallet. 'Don't thank me,' she said. 'Thank American Express.'

Chapter 93

The party was well under way when Molly arrived, clutching a rather reluctant Glenda. 'I feel silly,' Glenda said quietly to Molly. 'I mean, I can't believe I've got this funny-looking teddy on and I'm carrying a condom in my bag. What happens if I open my bag and the condom falls out? What am I supposed to say? "Oh sorry. Brought this along in case I felt like some sex." '

'What's wrong with that?' Molly was exasperated. It had taken her nearly an hour to persuade Glenda that she did not want to go to bed early but to come to this party. 'Look, you don't have to sleep with Valentine. You can just go and have a good time. Honestly, Glenda, you're getting very boring. Three-quarters of the world are bonking away, and you won't do it. Even Georgina's doing it. I mean, if she can do it, so can you.'

'Yes, but she's doing it with the man she'll marry.'

'*Glenda*,' Molly pushed her up the long flight of stairs to the loft, 'shut up. And let's just enjoy ourselves. Okay?'

Quite how they were supposed to enjoy themselves, Glenda thought she would never find out. They pushed open the heavy metal door to the loft. For a moment they both stood still. The walls were huge, with a skylight running around the top. The outdoor darkness could be seen through the skylight. They were high above New York and Glenda could see stars. The loft was full of people milling about. She saw pictures. Immense blown-up photographs of a black model, her tongue sticking out of her mouth, licking a variety of objects. The photographs were black and white, but the artist had retouched the tongue with a brassy red paint and the background was flat and blue. The model appeared sad, Glenda deemed.

She looked around. The crowd could have been picked randomly off the streets of New York. There were people dressed like hippies. Molly wore an Alice's Restaurant type of outfit. Glenda wore a small black dress that hugged her figure tightly, but had the skirt cut on the cross so it swung out from her knees. She liked her black high-heeled shoes. She gazed at rows of women who wore jeans, faded and torn, and working men's shirts, and no make-up. Molly took her arm. 'Our sisters,' she said. 'God help us. Come on. They have absolutely no sense of humour. Let's go and find men. Real men.'

Several couples danced on the floor. Glenda couldn't decide if they were men or women or a bit of both. She did see Timmy, Renée's hairdresser. 'Let's talk to Timmy,' she said. 'One friendly face.'

Valentine came up behind them as they made their way to the back of the loft. 'Ah, there you are! I've been looking for the two of you. Come along and let me introduce you to *tout* New York.' He put a suggestive hand under Glenda's arm. Glenda was instantly nervous. What if his hand could feel the edge of her breast in the ridiculous teddy under-garment? She very much wished she was not wearing any-thing so silly. She should have stuck to her Marks and Spencer's pretty knickers and her bras. Damn Molly and her sexual revolution ideas! What was wrong with letting men do all the chasing? Why should women gallop about knocking themselves out after men? I won't even get a box of chocolates or some flowers out of this, she thought. All I'm supposed to do is wriggle about on a bed with some strange man and then get up and go home. Oh dear, she remembered, the French letter. She held tightly onto her handbag. She imagined Lady Bracknell's voice. 'A *handbag*? You were found in a *handbag*?' She imagined for a split second the whole loft freezing, a single spotlight falling on her and her handbag, revealing to the world the awful moment with this little round silver package at her feet.

Glenda unfroze. Don't be so silly, she reminded herself.

Valentine was pushing them forward at a great rate. What a bunch of twisted people, Glenda thought. At least Renée's friends were published poets and painters. These people looked like escapees from the New York subway. At last they reached Timmy. 'Glenda!' he said and wrapped his long spider-like arms around her. 'Renée and Abe get off safely?'

'Yes, they did.' Glenda was glad to be with Timmy.

'Come on, Valentine. I want to dance.' Molly dragged Valentine onto the floor and ground her pelvis against his. She winked at Glenda as she led him off. Glenda tried to wink back. Always was a rotten winker, she comforted herself.

Timmy stood with his arm loosely around her shoulders. Timmy, she knew, was only interested in men. Feeling safe, she gazed about. Over in the corner a huge bear of a man crouched on one knee, playing the guitar. 'Who's that?' she pointed at him.

'That's Amerjit.'

Glenda listened to his music. 'What is he playing?'

Timmy took her hand. He said, 'You'll like him. He's straighter than all the others.'

Glenda followed Timmy and they both sat down quietly by Amerjit who played on as if he had not noticed their shadows cross the floor and settle in two quiet puddles. The music was neither European nor American. Glenda felt drawn to this large silent man. His thick fingers delicately

picked at the cat gut that strung his guitar. Glenda felt a
sense of peace flow over her. Here, in the middle of this
electric writhing atmosphere, was an oasis of calm created by
a silent figure who moved only his fingers. The rest of the
body, slumped behind the guitar, was wrapped up in the
music. His heavy head with long, black hair fell over his
shoulders.

Then he looked up. And Glenda saw his eyes like new
moons gleam for a second. 'Who are you?' he asked quietly.

'I'm . . . I'm Glenda.'

'Ah.' He continued to play.

She stretched her legs and the song came to an end.

He sat for a moment depleted, then said, 'My name is
Amerjit.'

'I know. Timmy told me.'

Amerjit got to his feet. 'Come,' he said. 'We'll get some
orange juice. I'm parched.' He put his enormous hand on
Glenda's shoulder and she felt as if an electric current came
from his hand down into her body. She walked beside him,
past Molly who was snogging with Valentine.

They found a table full of bottles. No orange juice. 'Well,'
Amerjit said amicably. 'We'll have to go out and get some
juice.' He pulled Glenda towards the big doors. 'Come along,'
he said. 'I don't drink alcohol and the food is just junk. I
know a Cypriot deli where we can get some decent food. Do
you like tahina?'

'I don't know what that is.' Glenda felt a little foolish.

Amerjit was loping down the stairs two at a time. She had
to run very fast to keep up with him. 'Why are you wearing
those awful shoes?' he asked.

'I don't usually wear high heels,' she said, panting. 'But I
tried to please Molly. She's my friend. I should have told
her that I was going out shopping with you.'

'Don't worry. We won't be long.' They burst into a bright,
hard, clear New York night. The effect was rather like being
spat out of a black hole into an electric hallucination. Neon

flashed and twirled. Cars bleated and beeped. People rushed past in that peculiar New York way, as if they were rushing to attend a funeral. Frightened faces. Sly eyes. Everybody notices everything, she thought as they walked along the pavement.

Amerjit had his arm around her and she walked safely, feeling he could control any situation. They came to the all-night deli. Amerjit grinned under his thick moustache. She could see his fine, square, white teeth. I wonder if he is a Moslem like Fatima, Glenda thought. He doesn't drink alcohol . . .

'I'm a Buddhist,' Amerjit said and Glenda jumped. 'I could feel you wondering,' he explained. He pushed open the door. 'Ahh!' he breathed. 'Real food.'

'That,' he said at a counter, pointing to a ceramic bowl overflowing with white paste, 'is tahina. Let me have a tub please,' Amerjit asked the blonde, dumpy lady. 'And we need some pitta bread and some taramasalata. Come, let's sit at the table and eat quietly. Do you wish for a glass of wine?'

Glenda shook her head. 'No thanks. I have a slight head-ache from all the noise at the party. I find the smell of incense and pot makes me feel quite sick.'

'Quite sick,' Amerjit echoed. 'How English you are! I agree. It is sick-making because it is foul air.'

'Where are you from?' Glenda asked.

'From nowhere in particular. I began this conscious life in Beirut. I was conceived there by a woman I call my mother and a man I call my father. He was a businessman. A material man. He made much money and it was my choice to resist the temptation of all his money and all his possessions.' Glenda looked startled. 'Yes,' he said, seeing her face, 'I chose to be reincarnated to these two people. They have spent many lives unable to divest themselves of material possessions Therefore they cannot attain nirvana. My father passed on, but my mother . . . ' He shook his head. 'She is a dear, dear woman, but a very young soul. She is blighted by her need for sweetmeats and jewels. I am very fond of her nevertheless.'

'What are you doing in New York?'

Amerjit looked amused. 'What are *you* doing in New York?'

'Running away.' Glenda gasped. Why on earth had she said that? 'I didn't mean that the way it sounded. It just slipped out.'

Amerjit inclined his head. 'You should not run away. Whatever you run from will always pursue. Look,' he said. 'I will teach you a teaching, but not today. We need a calm mountain.'

'There aren't any calm mountains in New York City.' Glenda was beginning to enjoy herself.

'If we need one, one will come.'

Glenda tried again. 'What are you doing in New York?'

'Living,' Amerjit answered. 'Just living. I take each day as it comes. Like today. At last, after aeons apart, we meet again.'

'You mean you knew me before? Like in another life?'

'Yes,' he said. 'I remember you well. You don't remember me, but you will. You will.' Amerjit licked his fingers clean.

She watched this very simple, secure man. He was wearing a big, brown overcoat and underneath it a flowing robe. Anywhere else he would have looked odd, but not in New York. She was the one who looked odd. She had left her coat in the loft and it was chilly outside.

When they left the deli, Amerjit tucked her under his coat next to his warm body. 'We'll go back,' he said, 'and find your friend.'

Molly was nowhere to be found. Timmy said he last saw her with Valentine. He lifted his chin. 'They're probably balling in one of the bedrooms. I shouldn't go looking, though.'

Glenda looked at Timmy and wrinkled her nose at the thought. Amerjit picked up his guitar, saying, 'Don't worry.

414

She'll surface. We can sit on the mattress over there and I'll play you some Tibetan music.'

Glenda lay beside Amerjit, comfortably curled up. She felt like a small well-loved cat. Finally she fell asleep, her head full of tiny flute-like notes. Great, was her last thought. Molly is doing it and I'm lying next to a man who knew me many lives ago. I wonder how well he knew me . . . At least my French letter is safe. She slid off into a deep and dreamless sleep.

Chapter 94

Glenda awoke. She opened one eye and surveyed her knees. Her feet were curled up under her. She was lying next to a very large man almost buried in his overcoat. He smelled of lavender, English country lavender, she decided. But how could this man find such a smell in New York? Yes, she was in New York and the memory slithered back. She had come to this loft with Molly who had run off with Valentine. She put out her hands and searched for her handbag. Had she done anything she should not have? She found the bag: it was shut, so nothing had been done with haste. She pulled it to her and then decided to take a look.

She struggled into an upright position and opened the clasp. She looked up and saw a warm pair of brown eyes gazing down at her. 'Did you sleep well?' a big deep voice asked her. She looked at the man curiously. She could not quite remember his name. She was embarrassed. Imagine, she thought, spending the night on a mattress with some strange man and not even remembering his name! 'Amerjit,' the man said softly. 'How were your dreams?'

Glenda paused, the handbag in her hands. 'Actually, I don't think I did dream.'

'Dreaming is very, very important, you know.'

'Really?' Glenda sat up and looked at her discarded shoes.

415

They lay abandoned on the floor of the loft, one upright and empty, the other on its side. Well, she thought, the shoes looked as if they had a good time. Glenda was glad to be sitting against this nice warm man. She remembered the Cypriot deli, the delicious tahina, late night stars, and the walk back under his coat.

People were appearing, looking as if they had slept in haystacks, their hair all messy and their eyes bleary. 'I wonder where Molly is?'

Amerjit smiled. 'She will be with Valentine a little while more, and then she will come and find us. She will not feel well because she had too much to drink and too much to smoke. She will be sad.'

'Sad? Molly's never sad. You don't know her.'

'I know women like her,' he said. 'You don't have to know Molly to know just how sad she is. You only see with one pair of eyes, Glenda.'

'I *have* only one pair of eyes.'

Amerjit gave a soft chuckle. 'You have a third eye. Look.' He put his long forefinger on Glenda's brow. 'Feel.' He stroked an area above her nose. 'Can you feel your third eye?'

'Well, I can feel a sort of hole, I suppose. But what do you do with that?'

'You see without seeing.'

Glenda laughed. 'All this philosophy before breakfast.'

Amerjit paused. Then he laughed. 'You are right. Your Christian Christ always fed his people before he taught them.'

'Are you going to teach me then?' Glenda sat silent as she waited for an answer. She knew, and she knew not why, that she was going to be with this man for a while. But not for long. He in his movements and in his hands communicated with her without speaking. This was not a relationship for life, but he was here to teach. She very much wanted to learn.

He stood up. Glenda sat on the floor, staring up at him. 'Don't worry,' he said. 'I'm not leaving you. I'm just going to run out and bring you some breakfast. I won't be long.'

When he left the mattress Glenda felt bereft. Not the same sense of loss as when she left Clive . . . She realized with a pang of guilt that she had not telephoned him. I'll telephone him tonight, she promised herself. Oh dear. Tonight they should be in New Jersey with Molly's family.

She saw Molly coming towards her with Valentine at her side. Molly's mascara had run down one cheek. Her eyes were red from smoking pot and her lips were swollen. She was grinning a lopsided grin. 'Amerjit deserted you?' Valentine inquired. His eyes were like ice-picks.

'No. He's just gone to get me some breakfast.'

'Breakfast. Good idea. Think I'll do the same,' Valentine said. 'Which direction was the Wonder Guru of New York heading?'

Glenda shrugged. 'I don't know. Why do you call him the Wonder Guru of New York?'

Valentine turned. 'Because he saves his come for himself,' he said viciously. 'Women like that. It's some sort of heathen practice.' He saw that Glenda was upset. 'If you can't stand the heat, get out of the kitchen,' Valentine hissed.

Glenda shook off Valentine's anger. 'There's no heat in my kitchen,' she said coolly. 'Besides, that's a dreadful cliché, as is most of your life, Valentine. I'm choosy about whom I share my kitchen with.'

Molly snorted. 'Give it to him, honey!' She sat down beside Glenda.

'Well, I'm out of here. I gotta take a shower. See you around, Molly.' Valentine waved his hand and disappeared into the straggling crowd that were making their way out of the loft and fanning out into the subways.

'Oh houf.' Molly groaned. 'Boy, he's like a battering ram.'

'Did you actually enjoy making love with him?'

'Get real,' Molly said. She lay back on the mattress. 'No,

417

I didn't. I found out too late he's a man who hates women but he's heavily disguised as a womanizer. Anyway, last night I decided that sex was not a spectator sport, and I decided from now on to keep it personal. All those asses and tits everywhere. Yeuck. Maybe orgies aren't my scene. Not a pretty picture. So how about you? Did you score?'

'No, Molly, I didn't *score*. But I had a really nice time with Amerjit. He's fascinating, and I know he has a lot to teach me.'

'I'll bet.' Molly lowered an arm over her eyes. 'Why don't you bring him along with us to good old New Joisey?'

'Won't your parents mind?'

'Mind? They're used to all my boyfriends turning up. Anyway, only dad's home. You'll see mom at the end of the week.'

'I'll ask him.' Glenda felt very pleased. 'You'll like him, Molly.'

'I'd like anybody who's going to bring me breakfast,' Molly said. 'I've got an awful hangover.' She groaned.

When Molly saw breakfast laid out before her, she groaned again. 'What?' she said, outraged. 'No coffee? And what the hell is this, Amerjit?'

'Garlic and whole grains,' he said. 'A sort of Indian pudding. Eat. It will make you feel better.'

'If I don't throw up first.' Molly grimaced. She took a spoonful. 'Not too bad though,' she acknowledged.

Amerjit handed Glenda a glass of pineapple juice. 'Drink,' he said quietly. Glenda watched him watching Molly. 'You feel better now?' he said sympathetically.

Molly nodded. She ate the warm porridge.

'It fills the stomach with good things,' Amerjit explained, 'and the garlic heals the excess of the night before.'

Molly squinted at him. 'What do you mean *the excess of the night before*? I was screwing.'

'I know.' Amerjit was calm. 'I could see you.'

'See me?' Molly exploded. 'Don't be ridiculous! I was at the other end of the loft.'

'I can still see you,' Amerjit said reasonably.

'How?'

'With my third eye.'

'Feel,' Glenda interrupted. 'Run your finger over and above your nose.' Molly followed Glenda's directions. 'All you have to know is how to open that third eye. That's what Amerjit is going to teach me.'

'Amerjit,' Molly said, 'you'll just have to come with us and stay. I need a third eye. Definitely I need a third eye. If I don't land a man, I can always be a fortune-teller.'

Amerjit smiled. 'I'll come.'

'Don't you need to go home and pack?' asked Molly.

'I go where I go and I acquire what I acquire. If I need it, I think it into being. Thought,' he said, 'creates matter. You understand?'

'Whoa.' Molly got to her feet. 'You give me brain ache.'

'But yes,' he said. 'There are a few things I might collect.'

'Fine,' Molly said. 'Glenda and I'll get cleaned up. We'll swing by your place, then make for the New Joisey Turnpike. I'll always remember the New Jersey Turnpike. I lost my virginity there at a rest stop.'

Amerjit was behind her. 'Actually,' he said in his rather precise voice, 'you lost your virginity thousands of years ago and you will not stop losing it, even now, many lives later.'

'Tell me about it.' Molly shot down the stairs with Glenda after her. 'Hey, Glenda, do I want this guy knowing all about me?'

'*I* do,' she said very firmly. 'I know I do.'

Chapter 95

Suddenly life felt very odd to Glenda. She was sitting in a car being driven erratically by Molly. The long roads, filled with honking New York drivers, rushed past them. Amerjit sat in the back. He had a carpet-bag with him that seemed to be stuffed with books. While Glenda winced and tried not to brake on an imaginary foot-pedal as cars swept by, Amerjit seemed oblivious to the world of the highway. Molly had little to say, so Glenda sat back and thought about the busy week behind her.

Renée and Abe must be in Italy by now, she thought. Lucky things. But then she felt lucky herself. Normally she hated parties, but Amerjit had made last night a very special time. He was like a solid island between her reality back in England and the unreality which was New York. Time with Amerjit was time out, Glenda decided. Maybe she should not be her usual worry-wart self, but just 'go with the flow', as Molly kept describing her life in America.

Everywhere Glenda looked, people of her age had tuned in and dropped out. America seemed to be awash with young people. Where were the old or the suburban middle-aged Americans? Glenda did not know. Maybe they had taken fright and were living in the deserts in foxholes. Certainly, if one followed the news on television and read the *New York Times*, middle-aged, suburban Americans seemed to have lived a life of many crimes. They were racist, bourgeois, capitalist paper tigers. They were responsible for crimes, wars, and drug addiction. Glenda was fascinated by the amount of ridicule targeted against these middle-aged, suburban evil-doers. Making money was now a dreadful crime, the underground newspapers thundered. For Glenda the sight of the Revolutionary Brigade of Weather People looked more like terrorists than reformers, with their raised fists and guns.

420

But no, they were to be regarded as the saviours of the American way of life, and apple-pie Mom and car-washing Dad must be wasted by bazookas and a hail of rhetoric. Still, maybe things would be quieter in New Jersey.

Things were quieter in New Jersey. The urban revolution had not yet reached Charleston Street in Upper Montclair. Molly pulled up in front of a large square mansion and hooted the horn. A very tall man came out of the house and bowed low. 'Miss Molly,' he said. 'How delightful to see you.'

'Hi, Jasper.' Molly hopped out of the car.

Jasper peered into the car and smiled at Glenda and then he saw Amerjit. Glenda watched his face change. No, she thought. Things aren't that different in New Jersey. Amerjit smiled at Jasper. 'Good day, my good fellow,' he said and he climbed out of the car. Amerjit towered over Jasper. He beamed down at the man and handed him his carpet-bag. 'Kindly take this to my room.' Amerjit opened the door for Glenda. Molly was already in the house.

They followed Jasper. Molly came into the hall. 'Dad's waiting for us in the family room,' she said.

Night was drawing in and the family room was warm and friendly. Jeff Rosenthal, Molly's father, was short and compact. He was almost bald and Glenda noticed that he wore very expensive shoes. The light-coloured leather was soft and beautifully polished. 'What can I getcha to drink?' he offered, being a good host.

Amerjit smiled. 'I would like to wash,' he said, 'and then I will drink orange juice, thank you.'

Glenda said, 'I'd like to wash also.'

'Okay, you two,' Molly said. 'You're in the second bedroom on the right.'

Glenda blushed. Damn Molly, she thought. I don't even get a choice. But she felt too insecure to argue. She followed Amerjit out of the room. 'We don't have to share the same room,' she began.

Amerjit put his hand over hers. 'Don't worry,' he said.

421

'We can share a room together. I was not raised with this passion for privacy. I'm used to living in one big room with all my family. We sleep together, children, women . . . Privacy is a luxury not known to the rest of the world.'

Glenda walked up the spiral stairs. 'What a beautiful house,' she commented.

'Beautiful, yes. Functional also.' He made a face. 'But soon it will kill my spirit. Too much carpet, too much everything.'

They turned the corner and walked into the bedroom. Glenda was relieved to find two queen-sized beds. Amerjit's carpet-bag lay on one bed and her suitcase on the other.

'Let's get washed.' She imitated Jeff's New Jersey accent. 'And then let's go downstairs.'

'I do hope we don't have hamburgers for dinner.' Amerjit looked mournful. 'I will have to find a Middle Eastern deli somewhere. I can't live without my grain food. Americans eat cow, so much cow.'

Amerjit is out of luck, Glenda thought as Jasper served dinner. It wasn't hamburgers; even worse, it was pot roast – a lump of meat welded together by fat. Glenda looked across the table at Amerjit. He ate his meat obediently. With his right hand he mopped up the gravy with bread and pushed it into his mouth. 'Tell me, Amerjit,' Jeff said, 'what d'ya do?'

Amerjit looked across the table at Molly who grinned. 'In your sense of the word, I don't do anything.'

Jeff looked concerned. 'You must do *something*. I mean, are you on welfare?'

'No. Welfare is not a concept for me. Where I come from we are considered religious men. In India we are called *saddhus*, or the unenlightened call us gurus. I do not like the idea of guru.'

Jeff's bewilderment was visible. 'Guru? You mean you smoke funny stuff and walk around chanting?'

Amerjit took another mouthful of pot roast. He chewed slowly.

'*Dad.*' Molly leaned forward. 'Amerjit is a sort of teacher.'

'Where do you teach?'

'Wherever I happen to be.'

Jeff rolled his eyes. 'I dunno,' he said. 'I don't understand you young people at all. Molly, mom says she'll be back Friday, so until then can you organize the house? I'm really tired of running the business and then coming home and having to make decisions about dinner and the shopping. Just tell Jasper what you want, and he'll get it delivered.'

Amerjit's face lit up. 'I need couscous, Molly.'

'Sure thing.' Molly sipped her glass of wine. 'We'll lighten up dad's taste buds and lower his cholesterol.'

'You're not going to order foreign food, are you, Molly? I got sicker than a dog in Puerto Vallarta last year. I told mom we shouldn't eat the local food, but would she listen? Not mom. "Come on, Jeffrey," she said. "If the natives can eat it, so can we." ' Jeff shuddered. 'Tamales at nine dollars a plate. Anyway,' Jeff looked at Amerjit, 'where did you say you came from?'

'Many places.' Amerjit wiped his beard. 'I mostly live in Singapore.'

'Singapore? That's where Fatima's family live now.' Glenda was excited. 'Hopefully I'll get there one of these days. It all sounds so romantic.'

Amerjit's face softened. 'Singapore is a very beautiful place. Very tranquil people live in peace there.' He sighed and Glenda felt a grieving in him. For what? she wondered. Maybe for the market described by Fatima or the beautiful flowers and the smells and the sounds of the jungle that so entranced Fatima that she found it hard to leave for Paris. She realized how much she missed Fatima. Then she realized she really missed Georgina. The four Souls were so comfortable with each other.

Molly and her father were deep in conversation. Glenda

watched the two of them together and she could see why Molly had such difficulty in forming relationships with men. Molly and Jeff looked more married than most married couples. They sat side by side and seemed to fit together like a highly-polished, wooden jigsaw puzzle. And more strongly perhaps than at any other moment of her life, Glenda wished that she had a father of her own.

They ended the meal with coffee. Amerjit refused the coffee. 'You don't drink wine or any alcohol, and you don't drink coffee. What do you do, for heaven's sake?' Jeff asked with some exasperation.

Amerjit just smiled. 'Depressants like alcohol and stimulants like coffee take away the energy from my aura. See?' he stretched out a large brown hand. 'Put your hand under mine, palm facing up.'

Jeff put out his hand, a smile of disbelief etched around his mouth. He sat and Amerjit gazed at his own hand intently.

'What do you feel?' Amerjit said.

Jeff stifled an impulse to pull his hand away. 'My hand is getting hot,' he admitted reluctantly.

'It is not generally known, but all human beings can raise their body temperature by ten to fourteen degrees. One simply centres the mind and then moves the blood to the desired part of the body to create heat. You can even heal an injury this way.'

'Holy smoke!' Jeff said. 'As easy as that!'

'Everything in the universe is easy,' he said. 'Everything is harmonious. Only man destroys.'

'Wow,' Molly said. 'Let's spend the rest of the evening practising. Just think what I could do with a knack like that?'

Glenda looked across the table. Why, she thought, must everything be sex with Molly? And then she reddened. She had been thinking the same thing, and she had been thinking it about Amerjit. Oh dear, she said to herself. This is likely to be difficult.

Chapter 96

Glenda stood in the big bedroom wondering what she should do. Amerjit was loping around, shedding clothes onto the floor. 'I cannot possibly sleep on a bed,' he said. 'Much too soft. Bad for the back. People here have bad backs because they lie on soft beds. And,' he said, 'do you notice how Western people defecate?'

Glenda sat down on the bed. 'No,' she said faintly. 'I hadn't really given it much thought.'

'They sit on the toilet!' Amerjit snorted. 'Just imagine! No proper evacuation. Then they get cancer of the bowel and wonder why. Serves them right.'

'How should they go to the lavatory then?'

'They should squat.' By now Amerjit was entirely naked.

Glenda looked at his huge, brown, golden body and she was confused by a feeling of warm honey that slid up her thighs. She very much wanted to be pressed in his long, strong arms and to feel her naked stomach against his.

Amerjit stood in front of her and then pulled her along to the bathroom. 'See?' he said as he hopped on to the lavatory and squatted on the rim. 'Like this.' Amerjit defecated neatly into the bowl. 'Very good,' he said cheerfully, examining his product. 'Very good indeed. You see? This is result of eating grains. Our first breakfast together.'

Glenda was stricken with embarrassment. She had never seen a man so enjoy being naked before, and certainly she had never seen a man defecate.

'Now,' Amerjit said wandering back into the bedroom, 'I give you a piece of twig to clean your teeth.'

'Thanks. That's very kind of you.'

Amerjit pulled out two aged and crabbed roots from his carpet-bag. He lay down on the mattress on the floor and began meticulously cleaning his teeth. 'Take your clothes off,' he instructed. 'It is getting late and I must sleep.'

Glenda rifled around in her suitcase and came up holding her very virginal nightdress. 'I'll be back in a minute,' she said, slinking into the bathroom. I must have a bath, she thought. Maybe if I lie in hot water I can calm down.

She sat rigidly upright in the hot water and considered her options. She thought for a while and then realized she hadn't got any. She might try to preserve herself, but she had no idea of Amerjit's agenda. Part of her wanted very badly to roll about his mattress in an orgy of lust, and the other part of her wished to hold fast to her childhood innocence like a monkey clinging to its mother. And, of course, she thought of Clive and started to feel guilty. But not quite guilty. He seemed so far away and . . . No, more than that, this was an episode in her life and she felt herself giving herself permission to do something that she was probably going to do anyway and it wasn't really intended to have anything to do with Clive. Certainly she would never hurt him in any way but maybe this was something she needed to go through and to learn what she could . . .

She sighed. I can't sit here for ever. She observed her water-ribbed fingers. I've got to get out. She heaved herself out of the bath and picked up the piece of twig she had left on the wash basin. She picked gingerly at her teeth. Smells good, she thought, huffing a little air up to her nostrils. Well, at least my breath doesn't smell bad. She pulled on her long warm flannel nightdress and she opened the door.

Amerjit reclined on his mattress, his arms under his head. 'Come here.'

Fearfully she approached him. She was unable to stop looking at his genitals. How like the big orchid that Renée threw at the wedding! Molly would really admire his balls. They were huge.

She tried not to think any more. She dropped to her knees and fell into Amerjit's open arms. At first she felt as if she was swallowed up in his warm, hairy embrace. It was dark in his chest and she pushed her head up to get some air. His mouth hovered over hers. Then he turned her over onto her back and gently began to stroke her thighs. Lazily, and for what seemed like many erotic hours, he tickled her and stroked her. He inserted the tip of his tongue into her ear and into her belly button. Slowly he moved down her body while she moaned and writhed and begged him never to stop. Finally he put the tip of his tongue into her vagina and she clung to him in ecstasy.

She fell back and gasped. 'Is that what it's all about?' she said, opening her eyes and feeling the loss of the throbbing agony. She was breathing hard.

Amerjit lay with her head in the crook of his arm. 'Yes. That is what it is all about.'

'Am I still a virgin?' Glenda asked.

'In a physical way, yes. But not emotionally.'

'Oh.' Glenda paused. 'I thought sex meant you had to do it. You know. Put yourself inside me.' She pointed between Amerjit's legs where his penis lay, flaccid.

He gave a great bellow of laughter. 'Oh you sweet idiot!' he said. 'Have you read no Eastern philosophy? Do you not know anything of the tantric pleasures of the flesh? Tonight I must sleep. But tomorrow I will teach you from the *Kama Sutra of Vatsyayana*. You have much to learn.' He shut his eyes and began to snore.

Glenda lay beside him, feeling a little bereft. She certainly had been missing something in her life. This method of making love seemed far removed from Molly's descriptions. I wish I could talk to Fatima, she thought as she slid off into a deep, delicious sleep. And her only thought of Clive before sleeping was that some day she would have many beautiful things to share with him.

Chapter 97

Glenda wondered how the mouth that kissed her and the fingers that caressed her could eat toast with such unconcern. She watched Amerjit while she sipped her coffee. She felt as if a million fire ants were trampling over her body. She thought that Jeff Rosenthal must know that she had made love with Amerjit in his house. If he did, he gave no sign of recognition. Jeff sat quiet and grey in his chair, eating his scrambled eggs. The butler, Jasper, moved silently around the table, stopping imperceptibly when he passed Amerjit. Glenda sat struggling with her feelings.

For so long she had felt unconnected to the world. There was the world, spinning around on its axis, and there was Glenda, standing beside the huge globe, her finger in her mouth, wondering how or why the world existed at all. She felt herself a closed system, a satellite planet spinning around the world, watching carefully but without much understanding. Into that sealed unit her mother, Renée, and Abe had forged a path. Then Fatima, Georgina, and Molly. But apart from them, other people had been merely insubstantial shadows. In a strange way, she realized, Clive was still a shadow to her – a permanent shadow. With Amerjit, however, Glenda felt for the first time to be entirely part of the world.

She knew with sorrow that these weeks with Amerjit would not last. Amerjit would become a shadow, a happy, dancing shadow who would fade from her life, leaving memories for the rest of her life. 'Teachers always come when you need them,' he had said last night. A lot of what he told her had faded in the bright light of this morning, but she would have time at the end to remember. For now all she wanted to do was to run away with Amerjit. Run away from this comfortable, luxurious New Jersey house. She felt stifled as she watched Mr Rosenthal eat slowly and methodically. Molly was smoking and watching Amerjit under her eyelashes. Amerjit was downing large glasses of orange juice. He seemed perfectly at ease, even in this house, but then he was at ease anywhere he went. 'Will you be in for lunch?' Jasper enquired.

'I have eaten enough until dinner,' Amerjit said firmly.

Mr Rosenthal pushed back his chair. 'Gotta run,' he said, kissing Molly full on the lips. Glenda was startled.

Molly seemed unconcerned. 'Bye, dad,' she said. 'Are you home tonight?'

'I'll be late, honey. It's stock-taking. But I'll be back in time to tuck you in.'

'Good,' said Molly. Jeff left, Molly's eyes following him. She turned to Glenda. 'Want to come with me to the mall?'

Glenda shook her head. 'I hate malls. You know I do. I think I'll just hang around the house, if that's all right.'

'Well, I have mall fever coming over me.' Molly laughed. 'You go off with Amerjit and I'll be shopping. You know what they say – when the going gets tough, the tough go shopping.'

And then it hit Glenda: Molly was jealous. Glenda felt like laughing. After all Molly's talk about Souls and sharing men, here she was behaving like a dog without a bone. Too bad, Glenda thought. She pushed away her usual guilty feeling. I have a right to have some fun. I've been the good little virgin for far too long. 'Okay, Molly. We'll see you.'

Amerjit watched the interaction between the two women. Glenda would suffer. She would cause herself suffering with her impetuousness. But Molly . . . He mentally shook his head. Molly was blind to everything. She was caught in the sticky web of her father's emotions. Amerjit had not met the mother, but he could guess down to the last dyed blonde hair what she would be like. The Americans, he thought, have a mould for that sort of woman which they fill with latex and stamp them out. Molly was in danger of becoming the product of such a mould. *My heart belongs to Daddy*, he thought, remembering the old song. He heaved himself out of his chair and took Glenda's hand. 'Let's run away,' he whispered to her.

'How did you guess?' she whispered back, surprised.

Amerjit stood up. 'I shall go to our room and maybe read for a while. Glenda, do you wish to study?'

Glenda smiled, rose, and took his hand.

'Jasper, I won't be in for lunch,' Molly said as Glenda and Amerjit left the dining room.

'Who is that fellow?' Jasper frowned as he heard the front door bang.

'Oh, Amerjit's a friend of Glenda's. He's okay, Jasper.'

'Then there is no need to count the silver?'

'No,' Molly said. 'He's perfectly safe. A little strange maybe, but safe.'

Jasper sniffed. 'No good will come of it. Mark my words.'

'I will, Jasper. I always do.' Molly climbed up the stairs hearing Jasper's disapproving footsteps thud down the hall. Damn, she thought. I never thought I'd be jealous of Glenda, goody-goody Glenda. She walked into her bedroom and looked at herself in the mirror. 'Nice ass,' she said, turning round. 'I'll call up Mike. He's home and usually hot for a good lay.'

'Mike,' she said on the telephone, 'are you busy?' She smiled as she heard his enthusiastic reply. 'Okay, I'll go shopping and then I'll be around for a bite to eat.' She drawled the last words and giggled. Mike felt he owed his life to her, ever since she taught him how to pinch his prick before he came so he could wait for her to orgasm. Funny how men revere their pricks, she thought. If I were a true feminist, I'd say they suffered from clit envy. Still, she squirted a good measure of perfume over her shoulders, I like men too much. She imagined the exhausted look of pleasure on Mike's face and then the gratitude . . .

It's easy to keep them happy. Eventually they get like Dad,

430

grey and tired with wives who don't love them. I won't do
that, she promised herself as she picked up her pocketbook,
searched for a packet of cigarettes, and popped her lighter
into the purse. I'll never tie myself down to a businessman
in a blue woolly suit. Never. She left the house and walked
into the triple garage. Her new white Corvette sat waiting
for her. Dad's a doll though, she thought fondly. How can
any other man be as good as dad? She revved the engine and
then was embarrassed by a fleeting glimpse of herself in bed
with her father. That was a long time ago, she told herself.
And I was a little girl. There was nothing sexual in the
memory, just an unspoken closeness between the two of
them that existed even now. The man I'm with will have to
be a hell of a man, she thought as she backed out of the
garage with a squeal of tyres.

Chapter 98

They made love on the mattress on the floor. Glenda was
initially embarrassed when she saw the mattress neatly made
up by the housekeeper, but soon she forgot herself in the
delightful sensual experience of making love with Amerjit.
He was tender, slow, and gentle with her. She discovered
that, even if her head knew little about the act of making
love, her heart had known all along.
    In the few moments when her soul returned to her body
and she lay exhausted and sweating on the mattress, she felt
the animal exuberance of the stretched muscles in her back
and in her thighs and the automatic responses of her body to
the thrusting that far exceeded any imaginings or lonely
longings of her own. After the third climax, she was deeply
shaken to the centre of her yet undiscovered self. She found
herself shaking and then weeping, not with sorrow, as she
first expected, but with a cosmic gratitude that this pleasure
had been given to her and that the possibility of this great

unwinding and expanding in a golden universe now existed. She lay utterly content.

She opened her eyes and smiled at Amerjit. He was leaning over her, his eyes laughing. 'You didn't . . . ' she hesitated to say the word.

'I never do.' He took her hand in his and lay flat on his back.

'Why not? Don't you want to?'

'No. I am on my last incarnation, and my seed shall not be spilled this time around. There are to be no more Amerjits.'

'Don't you mind?'

Amerjit shook his head. 'I am to be spared the worst of what is to come. But then, great evil can only exist in the presence of even greater good. Both these energies go hand in hand. I get as much pleasure in making love as you do. Besides,' he laughed, 'you don't get pregnant this way.'

Glenda stretched. 'How did you learn not to come?'

Amerjit propped himself up on his arm and bent down and gently licked the sweat from her forehead. 'It is an ancient technique. When you are rested, I will teach you to meditate. This is necessary for your equilibrium.'

'It is also necessary for my equilibrium to telephone Clive.'

'Leave him alone,' he said. 'Let him get on with his life. You are too attached. So is he. You tell me about his mother. You both allow her to be the enemy. All negative feelings come from attachment. Learn to detach yourself, unhook yourself. Telephone Clive later, after you have meditated.'

Glenda sat up and regarded him. He glowed in the half-light of the drawn-back curtains. She felt a heat in him. She wished she could stay forever in the warmth of his shadow. The world outside the door had become unimportant. This man had made sense of the inner world she inhabited, and she was no longer alone. Her feelings for Clive had not disappeared. She was not in love with the man at her side, rather he was time out in the universe, a badly needed time

432

out. Sometimes, she thought, words don't explain feelings. Words can't express thoughts that haven't been thought yet. Scraggs would not have accepted that sloppy definition from her. Glenda smiled. 'How did you say it, the other day – "Thought creates matter?" '

'Yes, that's right. In your own Bible, Jesus says, "Ask and you shall receive." What a rebel, that man! What a revolutionary!' He stood. 'I must relieve myself.' He vanished into the bathroom, leaving the door open.

Glenda heard the front door slam and she heard Molly run up the stairs. She just managed to pull a sheet across her naked body when Molly threw open the door. She watched Molly's eyes rake the floor and come to rest on the mattress. 'My, my, Glenda. You look a little flustered.'

Glenda lay back on the pillow and hoped Amerjit would stay in the bathroom. 'We'll be down in a minute.' She held the sheet protectively over her breasts.

Molly backed out of the doorway and shut the door. There were tears in her eyes. Why did she feel used and bruised, and why did Glenda look so radiant? Both of them had screwed. The same act, only with two different men. Maybe Amerjit knew a lot more than Mike. She would have to find out.

Dinner was a quiet event. Amerjit eyed the hamburgers with loathing. 'Everything fried,' he muttered. 'No wonder they all get sick.'

Glenda kicked his ankle.

Jeff Rosenthal was tired. He sat opposite his wife's empty chair and wished she would come home. 'Have you heard from mom?' Molly asked.

'No, sweetheart. Once she gets into a conference with all those girlfriends of hers, they conference all day and visit with each other all night. It seems to me that they forget they were ever married.'

Glenda was aware of his loneliness and wondered how

Molly's mother could desert such a nice man.

'Still, she'll be home in a couple of days,' he said, his doggy eyes beginning to shine. 'You'd love mom,' he said to Glenda. 'She's the life and soul of any party. Everybody loves her. She's very artistic, too.' He pointed to some perfectly dreadful paintings that hung on the walls.

Glenda saw Molly's face harden. Poor Molly, she thought, another awful, strident woman for a mother. Thank God Molly has a good heart. Glenda munched her way through the hamburger, miserably aware that she would rather be eating a delicious meal at an exotic restaurant somewhere with Amerjit. But they had tonight to come, many more nights before she had to go back to England and to Clive.

'Clive,' she said later on the telephone, 'I've met the most fabulous man. His name's Amerjit. He's a sort of teacher.'

'What sort of teacher?' Clive's voice was faint and anxious. 'I can't hear you very well. The line's all fuzzy.'

'Are you all right, darling?' Glenda was instantly concerned.

'Oh, I'm all right. I just had a tiring session with Dr Umberto. I don't know what sort of psychiatrist he thinks he is. He depresses the hell out of me.'

'You're not having any of those things Nanny Jenkins calls "funny turns", are you?'

'No.' Clive sounded far away. 'I'm fine. Just a bit tired. I've been playing the piano half the night. I'll go to bed now.'

'It's two o'clock in the morning your time, isn't it?' Glenda imagined him sitting at his Steinway grand.

'Yes, but you know I'm up late.'

Glenda cleared her throat. 'If you want me to come home, you only have to say so. You know that, Clive. I really do love you, and I do want to marry you,' as if only now had she learned how true were the declarations of love that she had been making all along. I do love him, she said to herself when she put down the telephone.

She found herself dancing into the family room where Amerjit sat gazing solemnly at the television. 'American baseball,' he said to Jeff Rosenthal. 'A very interesting pastime. Grown men hitting and chasing a white ball. Very interesting.'

Jeff Rosenthal agreed distractedly. He sure as hell hoped that this huge intrusion into his everyday life would not spend the game talking, and he sure as hell didn't want him sitting next to him on his couch when he wanted his wife next to him. His wife, who always smelled of face powder and painted her mouth red. He hoped this heathen was not getting any nooky with the girl in his room when he, Jeff Rosenthal, lay alone in his double bed contemplating his wife's backboard. Headache jokes should be banned, he thought, looking at the rows and rows of men cheering on the Boston Red Sox. What he would give to be at Fenway Park with one of the boys, but the boys were all gone and he was alone with his beloved Molly and her friends. Well, at least this man didn't stink out the place, like some of Molly's other boyfriends.

Chapter 99

Glenda felt as if she and Amerjit were turning endless cartwheels of happiness. Amerjit seemed always to be in a good mood. Nothing clouded his eyes or his face, not even the arrival of Mrs Rosenthal.

Helen Rosenthal was considerably taller than her daughter. Her bleached hair hung to her shoulders and the effect of the blonde hair was an immediate conflict with the dark eyebrows and tear-washed brown eyes. 'How *wonderful*!' she said when she grasped Amerjit's hand. 'Jeffrey tells me you're an Indian. I don't mean an American Indian but a *real* Indian all the way from India?'

'No, madam,' Amerjit said, bowing low, making Glenda

want to giggle. 'I am from many places. I was conceived and born in Beirut but my parents were from elsewhere.'

'Oh, I see.' Helen gave her husband a startled look. 'I thought you said he was Indian, honey.'

Jeff munched solidly on his sandwich of pale pink luncheon meat. 'I thought,' he said, still chewing, 'he said he was Indian. Well, at least I guessed he was Indian, or something like that.'

Helen drew her attention away from Amerjit and graced Glenda with her bright, all-consuming smile. 'Glenda!' She put her hand out into the air as if answering prayer. 'You are Molly's best friend. I've heard so much about you! How *marvellous*! How *wonderful*!' The force of the *wonderful* almost knocked Glenda off her chair.

What on earth can I say? Glenda's brain ached with the effort. Helen, a few moments earlier, had rushed into the dining room, dropping her suitcase on the floor for Jasper to pick up after her. She had enveloped Molly in her long spider-monkey arms. Flinging Molly back onto her seat, she had grabbed Jeff with a hug. 'How I missed you all!' she had beamed at the assembled table.

Now Glenda struggled for air. 'Did you enjoy your conference?' she asked.

Helen sat down in her chair and hacked at the square piece of luncheon meat on the plate. 'Sure. We got a lot sorted out. You know – abortion on demand, day care centres . . . the whole shebang.'

'Mom's fighting for the right of women to pee in men's bathrooms,' Molly grinned at Amerjit. 'Aren't you, mom?'

'My generation fights for *all* the things you take for granted, sweetheart, like going to Cambridge.'

'Yeah,' Molly snorted. 'A few women did the fighting, and the rest of you went to conferences, drank white wine, and pretended you never left college. The "happiest days of your lives." '

'No.' Helen shook her head. 'Those were happy days, but

436

our best days n ' and she smiled at Jeff who smiled moistly back– ' – the very *best* days of all,' Helen Rosenthal continued, 'were those wonderful days when you and the boys were babies and dad and I had a smaller house and only one maid. How we struggled!'

Glenda watched Mrs Rosenthal and could quite see why Molly disliked her. She was not a bad woman, just stupid. She was like a pot of Ponds Cold Cream. Smear it on and it disappears. Mrs Rosenthal was a performance. Molly was at least real.

When the New Jersey visit was over, Molly took the long way round, returning to Washington, DC by way of New York, in order to spend the drive with Glenda, she said. Molly pulled her car up in front of Renée's house, and then drove off to take Amerjit to his home.

Glenda was happy to be back in Renée's world. The house breathed softly and calmly. Molly's house had seemed perpetually busy, not the humans who appeared to move about lethargically, but the rooms themselves. Everywhere in Molly's house objects intruded. Vases were full of flowers, not real flowers but silk flowers or sprays of fake flowers that required a touch to verify the lie. Maybe that had been it, Glenda thought as she sat peacefully in Renée's drawing room. Maybe everything in the Rosenthals' house except Amerjit and Molly was fake. Fake people.

She eyed the shelves of books that lined the walls of Renée's drawing room. Here the floor was bare boards, lying long and polished. Every piece in the room had been chosen for personal reasons. She could see Abe's hand in the placing of the rugs on the floor and Renée's love of Victorian paintings was evident on the walls. The Rosenthal home carried Helen's banal paintings and some other artists' monstrous attempts at American modern abstract art. The floors were drowned in huge shaggy-pile fitted carpets. The books lying about were coffee-table volumes intended to be seen

437

but never read. And everywhere was the frightening feeling of exuberant amounts of money spent on anything at all. Even the mall where they shopped horrified Glenda. Piles and piles of food lay loose on the counters. Outside the poor and the hungry went by, the vast mass of American shoppers oblivious to this horrid army of the dispossessed.

Glenda supposed that the gaps between people of different financial situations depended on the individuals involved. If Mrs Fogarty needs anything extra, she knows that she is family, and Renée and Abe will take care of her and Mr Fogarty. The gap between Helen Rosenthal and her Jamaican housekeeper would never be bridged. Both women stood either side of a line that would never disappear with a friendly remark or even the recognition that both of them were women, sharing the same ills and strains of being a woman in the twentieth century. Glenda was glad to be out of that house.

She missed Amerjit . . . But tomorrow it would be Boston with Renée. And Renée always had so much to say.

Chapter 100

Glenda fell in love with Boston. New York was all excitement. It sparkled and sent rockets up her spine, but Boston had an altogether different feel. The city was vibrant but respectful of its people and its buildings.

All day long Glenda and Renée talked. Glenda felt as if a torrent of feeling flowed between the both of them as they sauntered along the Fenway on their way to the Gardner museum. Once there, they had lunch in the small cafeteria. Surrounded by students dressed in clothes that called for peace and love, Glenda felt uneasy. So many of those people of her age were neither peaceful nor loving. To Glenda's mind, they were promiscuous and furious. But part of Glenda could sympathize. If she had had to endure Molly's sterile family life, and if that was at all typical of the American middle-class lifestyle, she too would probably break away and rebel. Molly, unfortunately, only rebelled in the bedroom. 'I do worry about Molly,' Glenda said.

'Yes,' said Renée. 'I can see that. The poor woman is confused by all the rhetoric being spewed out these days. Abe is considered to be to the right of Attila the Hun by his friends. He won't get involved in all the Black Panther business. He says he's a black man living in a white society and he gets his respect by the way he lives, not by shooting guns or threatening violence. To tell you the truth, Glenda, in my long life I've observed most men to be quite simple people. Feed them and love them and they will love you back.'

'You've always said that, haven't you, Renée?'

Renée was eating a chicken sandwich on rye bread. Mustard dripped between her fingers. 'Um,' she remarked. 'Delicious.'

'I'll miss moments like this when I'm back in England.' Glenda looked around her. She took a forkful from her waldorf salad. 'Still I'll be glad to see Clive. After talking it all out, I think I can begin to see a way of coping with his family. The problem's not the father, as you pointed out, or his brother Caspar. It's his bitch of a mother.'

Renée's eyebrows raised. 'Yes, but don't underestimate the uncle Caspar. Do you remember the barrister that we used when we defended Mrs McCluskie?'

'How could I not? He gave a good performance and he got her off, but he seemed so remote, like a god descending into the underworld by way of Mount Parnassus.'

'Well, just remember he stands to gain a lot more control if they get rid of Clive. Caspar junior is a thick lad, like his father, and they can control him quite easily. When we've finished lunch,' Renée said, 'we'll see the Gothic Room upstairs, and then I'll take you into town and have a look at the wharves.'

Glenda licked the last of the mayonnaise from her fork. 'That was lovely,' she said, feeling full from her salad but not bloated. 'Amerjit would approve of my lunch. He doesn't like people eating meat. Says red meat is for savages. It inflames the passions.' Glenda grinned. 'He does very well without meat, I must admit.'

'Ah ha! Then you did.'

'Did I ever!' she said. 'I was beginning to feel like the last virgin in the world, but I'm glad I waited. You know, it would have been such a shame if it had happened in a bad way, with some man who didn't care for me or about me. I know I ought to feel that I've betrayed Clive, but in a funny way I don't. I feel Amerjit has given me something I can give to Clive. I know what making love is all about, and I'm not afraid of it any more. It's the world's most natural act. It's not like Molly's dreadful descriptions. But then, she's usually so doped or drunk at the time she can't remember much of what happens, except that "screwing", as she calls it, is always accompanied by a haze of alcohol and cigarette smoke. Yuk. Very unattractive.' She decided to wait to tell Renée about Clive's impotence. That would be something to discuss when the lights were out and she could sit on Renée's bed in the safety of a hotel suite and explain.

After a long and gorgeous dinner at Joe Tecce's restaurant in the Italian North End of Boston, the two women returned to the elegant hotel in the Back Bay. The lobby was like so many hotels at night – still busy but relaxed. People who had flooded out to catch airplanes or boats or trains were long since gone. The staff stood or sat in clumps, discussing the day's dramas. The few guests that straggled in did so almost apologetically.

'A lovely dinner,' Glenda said dreamily in the lift, replete with fresh pasta, parma ham and chianti. 'Really lovely. And a wonderful day. Thank you, Renée.' She leaned forward and kissed Renée on the cheek.

Renée hugged her. 'I've enjoyed every moment of it. And we still have most of tomorrow.'

The hotel suite was filled with flowers. Glenda stood at the big picture windows looking out at the Boston skyline. The skyscrapers seemed to grow out of the earth as if they had been planted by a mighty hand centuries ago. The lights shivered across the city.

Renée, her bath finished, sat in the drawing room of the suite and watched the fire in the grate. They did not need a fire, but Renée felt Glenda needed to talk. A fire always helps people to tell their secrets. Renée loved live fires. The embers slipping slowly into the pile of wood ash helped heal the hurt and she sensed that Glenda had wounds to tend to.

Glenda joined her before the fire. 'How about some champagne? The wonderful thing about being mildly famous is that people always give you champagne.' Renée walked over to the bar fridge. She took out a long, slim, green bottle. 'Quite a nice Moët. A good year, too.' Expertly, she turned the cork with her strong hands and the bottle gave a satisfying pop.

'I'll never understand how you do that,' Glenda laughed. 'You taught me ages ago, but I still mess it up. Clive's good at it though.' She sighed. 'He's good at so many things.' She took the glass of champagne from Renée. She liked the sides where the cold champagne had brought up strands of little bubbles. She sniffed the rim of the glass. 'Ummmm. How delicious! What a perfect way to end the day – sitting in this beautiful room, drinking champagne. Clive and I often do this. He has an excellent cellar put down by his grandfather. The farm has a wine cellar, and I love going down there. Clive says he'll put down some port when his son is born, and I agreed, but only if he buys champagne for my daughter. If we have children.' She grinned and held up the glass. 'Now that you're already married, we must drink to Clive and me.'

Renée held up her glass. 'And I hope you will be as happy as Abe and I.' They sipped. Renée's eyes remained fixed on

Glenda. 'Glenda,' she said. 'I can see there's something you need to say.'

It took two glasses of champagne before Glenda was able to tell Renée that Clive was impotent. Renée listened. The fire gleamed on the threads of grey in her hair. She leaned forward as if to make sure she lost none of the words that came out of Glenda's mouth. She was silent until Glenda stopped talking. 'So you see, I don't know quite what to do.'

Renée sat back for a moment. 'I'm not surprised he's impotent. First of all, he has that dreadful mother hovering over him all the time. He needs to get away from her, far away. And, what's more, they've kept him drugged up with endless pills. Exactly how long have they been drugging him?'

'Since he was about eight.'

'*Eight?*' Renée was shocked. 'No wonder, poor man!' She looked grim. 'Oh, it's horrid, what parents do! Frightened children are put on phenobarbitol. Or the doctors put kids on downers if the mother claims the child is hyperactive. And then the parents wonder why their children become drug addicts! They've always been addicts, thanks to the people who are supposed to love them . . . Oh, Glenda, I honestly don't think Clive *is* impotent. I just think he needs to get away from his mother and to get off *all* the medication. That's my opinion.'

'I'm so relieved to hear you say that. I can go to bed without worrying tonight.' She stood up and stretched.

Renée looked at her small form. Making love really rounds women out, Renée thought. It fills up their skin and makes their eyes sparkle. 'Don't worry, Glenda.' Renée stood up and put her arms around Glenda's shoulder. 'You teach Clive all that Amerjit taught you, and he'll be a happy man. There's one young man who will survive the great English public school tradition that sex is for dogs and horses, and women are only for bearing children.' She laughed and left for her room.

442

Chapter 101

Glenda and Renée were back in New York. 'Amerjit,' Glenda said, answering the phone, 'I leave the day after tomorrow. I must get back to England. I'm starting to worry about Clive. I telephoned just now, and Nanny Jenkins says he's away for a few days. She sounded a little strained. So I'd better get back. I'll shop tomorrow and then I want to see you and say goodbye.'

'Very well.' Amerjit also sounded a little strained.

'Are you all right?' Glenda was sitting in Renée's drawing room with a cup of coffee by her side. 'Where are you calling from?' No reply. 'I'll shop all day – shop till I drop, as Molly says – and then I'll come by at about six. Is that all right?'

'Very all right.' Amerjit's voice brightened. 'Have you spoken to your friend Molly?'

'No, I've been away. I was just about to ring her. Why?'

'She is a very pushy girl.' Amerjit sounded quite outraged.

'Oh no, Amerjit. What's she done now?'

'She tried to jump on me when she brought me home after we dropped you off at Renée's house.'

Glenda found herself laughing. Renée and Abe stopped talking and looked across the room at Glenda. 'Surely you can cope with a grope, Amerjit.'

'I am not used to that kind of behaviour,' he said stiffly.

'So what did you do? Oh, never mind. You can tell me all about it when I come over. But where are you calling from?'

Amerjit was quiet for a moment. 'Good question,' he said. 'Where am I? Let me see. Abdulla, where am I?' he shouted to someone in the room. 'Ah. I see. I am in the Village on LaGuardia Place.' He gave her the street number. 'You have that?'

'Yes. Got that written down. Sleep well, Amerjit, and I'm glad you know where you are.'

'So am I,' he said. 'You tell that girlfriend of yours that she is no good.'

'I tell her that all the time. It gets me nowhere. Molly is Molly.' Glenda put down the phone. 'Molly tried to rape Amerjit,' she explained.

Renée made a face. 'You'd think a man like that could take care of himself.'

Abe looked up. 'Deep down, Renée, men are cowards when it comes to women. That's why they don't want them in the armed force. Women drill-sergeants . . . Can you imagine? They'd have to issue the men with lead-lined jock straps.'

'And Molly would buy herself a blow-torch for Christmas.' Glenda stretched. 'I'll just telephone her and then I'm off to bed. I'll contact the airlines tomorrow and reschedule my ticket. I feel so anxious, Renée. It's as if something is bothering me and I can't quite shake it off.'

'Don't worry,' Renée said. 'Have a good night's sleep, and you'll feel better in the morning.'

In her room after her bath Glenda picked up the telephone. 'Well, Sister Soul,' she said when she heard Molly's voice, 'you tried to pull a fast one.'

'I didn't.' Molly was defensive. 'And I always said I thought part of our deal as Souls ought to include sharing men. Particularly when the man in question looks like Amerjit. Besides, he's fair game. You don't want him, or do you?'

'It's not a question of wanting him or not wanting him. Amerjit isn't like that. I just resent the fact that you embarrassed him.'

'Embarrassed him?' Molly's voice rose. 'I didn't merely embarrass him; he ran into his bathroom and locked the door. Serves him right. He shouldn't have asked me in for a drink. These days that's a loaded invitation.'

Glenda discovered that she felt quite hurt by Molly. 'Listen, I've got to go back to England the day after tomorrow. So I'll say goodbye now. Keep in touch.'

'I will,' Molly said in a casual tone.

Glenda felt the coolness and she put down the phone. 'Oh why do men have to spoil everything?' she muttered.

In the deep-pile shag carpet, with a pillow under her head, Molly lay smoking in the bedroom of her Washington apartment. The telephone sat beside her. She felt a lump growing in her throat. Why did Amerjit prefer Glenda? I'm a much better lay. She got up and walked to her wardrobe in her bathroom. 'Sure I am,' she said out loud. She extinguished her cigarette and then she sighed. I guess it's just me and my right hand again. She lay, later that night, convulsed with lonely desire.

She looked toward the hallway and wished her father was there to stick his head around the door and say, 'Good night, honeybunch.' But the doorway was empty.

Molly gasped. And she rolled over into her pillow and cried. She recognized that she was crying for a great many years ago. She was crying for the father that brought her home parcels and put her on his knee and sang, 'Hickory Dickory Dock, the mouse ran up the clock.' Only now the clock was not ticking for the mouse but ticking away time for Molly. Tick tick tock, and she heard a loud BOOM.

Chapter 102

Glenda felt warm and contented once she arrived at Amerjit's flat. Apartment, she corrected herself. He stood at the door and hugged her. Her concern about Clive and her anger towards Molly were put aside. Inside the beautiful, elegant apartment she looked around. 'Gosh, Amerjit. Who owns this place?'

'It is owned by Amado, and another friend of mine called Tony from Somalia. We are all exiles from our countries.' He took Glenda's hand. 'Come. I have made supper for the two of us.' He led Glenda to a beautifully fitted kitchen.

Glenda watched Amerjit as he moved around the gas grill, stirring an amazing number of pots. She used to watch Abe cook, only Abe was a very American cook. He threw things on the barbecue, but at least he used plenty of garlic and his hominy grits were excellent. The smell rising from Amerjit's pots made her happy. 'Can I help?'

'No.' Amerjit seemed preoccupied.

Glenda wondered if they were going to make love. In anticipation she had bathed very carefully and she was wearing her one-piece, obscenely-named teddy. Still, it felt sexy under her clothes. Her hair shone with a vinegar rinse and her eyes she had painted carefully. She looked down at her fingernails – a very fine pink polish that matched her toenails. She knew that Amerjit disliked any sort of make-up, as did Clive, but Glenda enjoyed making herself up on occasion, and now, as a woman of the world, she did not intend letting either Amerjit or Clive dictate what she should wear. She leaned against the steel countertop. 'I'm sorry Molly did that to you. I telephoned her and told her off. Do you still feel upset with her?'

Amerjit stirred his pots. 'It is you who should be upset with her. Her intention had nothing to do with me. Her intention – which is what matters – was to take something away from you.'

Glenda stood, looking at Amerjit. Why must he always be so right? she thought. 'Well, when we were at university a few years ago, we all agreed that we would be Souls.'

Amerjit raised his head and he frowned. 'And were you not souls already?'

'No, a special kind of Souls. You see, we were studying Victorian literature and our professor pointed out that in those days men systematically betrayed women. Men could have all the affairs they wanted, and women had no choice but to tolerate the situation. There was no such thing as divorce except in the most scandalous situations, and even then the woman lost everything – her home, the children, and probably any money she owned in her own right. So we decided to take a vow to call ourselves Souls, which really just meant being special friends for life. But Molly wanted us to adopt the motto of the group of women who created their society called The Souls. The motto was "Every woman shall have her man; but no man shall have his woman." We – that's the four of us, Molly, Georgina, Fatima, and I – we all thought of it as a bit of a lark except for Molly, of course. But the other three of us were still virgins. Honestly, I don't see how anyone can share men. Fatima says if she marries Majid in a traditional Turaqi marriage, she would accept other wives. I can't believe I could do that, but then I'm not Fatima.'

'Quite.'

'Oh, but that doesn't mean Fatima *will* have to put up with other wives. Majid says he'd never dream of taking on a second wife. He only wants Fatima.'

'He has adopted the Western attitude then?'

'Maybe,' said Glenda. 'But one thing we did decide when we were at university was that it isn't right for men to be the only ones with choices in their lives. If the men in Fatima's country could have many wives and everyone thought it was all right, then maybe it was time for women to take equal privileges for themselves. Why should a woman *have* to have only one man? That's what the Souls were about. Getting rid of some of the *have-to*s. That's the way I thought of it, anyway.'

Amerjit laughed. 'I see. A university experiment in idealism.'

Glenda was not sure whether or not to be offended. 'At the time, we believed that a new form of equality was needed, and I still think . . . ' she started to say.

'But you cannot be serious!' he interrupted. 'Surely you see the difference, don't you? There is a very big difference between an ancient tradition of polygamy throughout much of the world, whether the modern West likes it or not, and four university girls agreeing to invent a new tradition of sexual liberation.' Amerjit stopped stirring his sauce and smiled at Glenda. 'Eastern concepts cannot be flown across to the West and opened like a can of Coca Cola. You see this jug? What is the importance of the jug? Is it the jug itself or is it the empty space between the walls of the jug?'

Glenda looked at the art deco jug in his hand. Its lines were angular and the mouth deeply lipped. 'The jug,' she said.

'Why?' Amerjit demanded. 'Why do you say that?'

'Well, because the jug holds the liquid, doesn't it?'

'There you are,' Amerjit said. 'To the Eastern mind it is the space, the emptiness, of the jug that matters. Without it the whole thing would be a useless lump. And the same for the spaces between the spokes of a wheel. It is they that define the wheel. First there is nothingness. Your people call it the void. And from that all else arises. I am ready now,' he said. He put several sauces into small dishes on a tray and he walked from the kitchen into a huge dining room.

The picture windows showed the skyline of Manhattan. 'The view is unbelievable,' Glenda said, following him slowly. All around the room were African statues. The walls were hung with vivid African paintings.

Amerjit put the tray down and placed two bowls on the table in front of Glenda. She looked at the small bowls of food. 'Is that the same dip that we had at the Cypriot delicatessen?'

'Yes, tahina. Sesame paste with garlic and pitta bread. Very good for you. Very ancient food. Here we have a little dhal, lentils with onions and garlic. And this is a secret recipe, known only to me, to make a curry most exotic.' He grinned. 'This recipe was created by a maharani to seduce her maharajah. Very perfumed.' He kissed his finger and thumb. 'Try it. First we eat the fresh yoghurt and cucumber.' He placed some flat round bread on her plate. 'No knives and forks,' he said. 'We eat with our right hands.'

Glenda tasted the yoghurt. 'It prickles,' she said, surprised.

448

The cucumber was cold and the fresh mint in the yoghurt caught her breath. 'How refreshing!'

'Yes, this is the proper way to eat. You live much longer. The West eats too much animal fat.' He frowned.

'You're in a very grumpy mood, Amerjit.' Glenda wiped up the last of the yoghurt. 'What's the matter?'

He sighed. 'I have to leave tomorrow on business.' He shook his head. 'Ayee. Life is hard. I don't want to get involved with the rest of the human race, but I must. There are things that must happen for my brothers, and so I must go.' He put his bread down and looked intently at Glenda. 'I will not see you again.'

Glenda's eyes asked him a question.

'No,' he answered. 'Not one last night of love. Not for us. It would leave us too open. You must go home after we finish eating. I have things to do, so there is not time for love. Take with you what we have given each other. Remember how to meditate and avoid fear. Fear is a great distraction from the task at hand. You have a perilous task at hand. Your path does lie with this Clive of yours, but you must be prepared to encounter difficulty. It is not for me to interfere in your karma. If I do, we will form a bad attachment and you will have to repeat this cycle.

'I give you this thought. Hold it to you like a mantra: action by non-action. That is the Buddha's way. But,' he said, spooning a little curry onto her pile of rice, 'if you do decide to act, make the action swift and terrible. So much is lost by people who cannot take action efficiently. Be in a constant state of readiness, like the warrior. For all that the universe seeks peace, life is also a war.'

Glenda mopped up her curry. The smell in her nostrils intoxicated her. 'Oh, Amerjit. You do make everything sound so gloomy.'

'Things are gloomy, as you say.' Amerjit smiled. 'But they are also ungloomy, if you live for the moment and not for tomorrow. We have a few hours left with each other. What do you think of the curry?'

'I like it. Actually, I more than like it. I love it.' Glenda was surprised at how full she felt. The little dishes were empty, but she felt light and satiated.

'Food is more important than sex.' Amerjit parodied an American accent, 'You are what you eat, honey.'

Glenda giggled. 'You sound just like Helen Rosenthal.'

Amerjit laughed. 'And the food at her house must have been the worst I have ever had in my life.'

'Well, it was wonderful for me. In England we simply don't have the loads of food they have in the States. We don't have all that fast food. I'll miss my McDonald's hamburgers.'

'God help you the day you do.' Amerjit cleared up the plates. His big hands were deft at stacking the little plates and bowls on the tray. 'Let's clean up, and then we will meditate before you leave.'

Sitting beside him with her back straight, Glenda felt her crossed legs going into spasms. Amerjit put out his hand and rubbed her feet. He stroked both her legs until the cramps ended and Glenda felt a peace spreading over her in the dark of the sitting room. Again they looked out over the Manhattan skyline. Glenda in her trance began to feel afraid. She opened her eyes slightly, hoping to ward off the revelation from her third eye. It was too late.

Over the skyscrapers, outlined by a string of lights, Lady Jane Alexander's face appeared, huge and full of evil. Her two long teeth pointed down over her bottom lip. She was a caricature of herself. She smiled. Glenda remembered Amerjit's warning: Feel no fear. 'Of whom shall I be afraid?' she reminded herself. It was a phrase from the Bible. She held onto that thought and she beamed her will at Jane's face. At first the vision flared back red and angry. Then slowly the face began to crumble as Glenda geared up her one-pointed attack. The flames, red and blue, began to burn on Jane's face and with a dreadful cry she disappeared.

Glenda found herself slowly coming back to consciousness. 'Whew!' she said out loud. 'That was a battle.'

Amerjit moved his head. 'Why do you think meditating is all peace and light and Coca Cola? If you take on a battle, you fight the battle on all levels – the physical, the emotional, the psychic, the spiritual, the astral. And you must be very careful or else the battle might overpower you on every level. Perhaps this is what makes your beloved Clive suffer so. The battle wearies him. But you can help him. Fight one battle at a time. Some day you should read the Hindu text, the *Mahabharata*. It tells of Arjuna's battle with the Kauravas. Very instructive. Now you must go, Glenda. It is getting late and I have so much to do.'

Glenda put her hand on Amerjit's knee. 'Will I never see you again?' She felt a great sadness.

'You will always be with me, just as I will always be with you. If you need me, call for me, and I will be beside you in thought. As we create matter from our thoughts, so we have created each other. Wherever we go, the silver cord binds us.' He kissed Glenda carefully and gently.

She got to her feet and left Amerjit still sitting on the floor. She saw by the tilt of his head he was going back into a deep meditation. She picked up her coat and bag and quietly closed the door behind her. She walked down the long hall to the lift. At the building's front door she summoned a taxi. A chapter finished, a door closed, but not fully closed. A door in her heart would always be open for Amerjit. She was comforted.

Chapter 103

Glenda caught the night flight to London. 'Don't come and say goodbye,' she begged Abe and Renée. 'I think I'd be a puddle of tears.' She felt the ache of the goodbye with Amerjit. To compound that pang by travelling to the airport with Abe and Renée would be more than she could bear. 'I want so much to get back to Clive,' she said as she kissed Renée goodbye before climbing into a taxi. 'But part of me's a bit afraid of what I will find.'

'Everything will be all right,' Renée reassured. 'Don't worry so much. We're only a phone call away. There's only a small pond between us.'

She hugged Abe and then she fell into the waiting American yellow cab.

Leaning back in the car, listening to the flow of the cab driver's reminiscences of his war years in Portsmouth, Glenda let her thoughts stray. By tomorrow I will be at the farm with Clive . . .

Glenda was surprised to see Nanny Jenkins and an embarrassed, red-faced Mark at Heathrow Airport. Mark took her suitcase from her after saying a rather gruff hello. Nanny looked pink and flustered. 'Glenda,' she began after Glenda kissed her on her downy red cheek, 'we have something to tell you. You see, Clive had a rather bad turn a few days ago. Actually it was the day you called and I told you he had gone away.' She paused. 'Mark dear, please let's stop for a minute.' They were walking up the long hall towards the exit to the car park. Mark stood still, his head hanging down and his mouth unsmiling.

Glenda said, 'Nanny, what's wrong?' She felt a cold terror seize her heart. 'Is Clive all right?'

'He is all right, but he's in hospital. Dr Umberto insisted, Glenda. There was nothing we could do. I don't know what went wrong that day. He was playing his piano very happily . . .'

'Did anyone come and see him?'

'No. No one came to see him.'

Glenda looked closely at Nanny Jenkins. 'You're *sure*, Nanny?' Now, after Amerjit, she saw and heard things far more clearly. 'There is something you're not telling me.'

Nanny's lips were pinched and white. 'I was told not to tell you,' she whispered.

'Lady Jane?' Glenda felt anger boiling up inside her. 'What's that bitch done to him, Nanny?' She saw Nanny's face redden. Damn, she thought, I must take care. Nanny was Nanny and would be loyal all her life to Jane. 'You tell me, Mark, if Nanny can't.'

Mark said, 'I heard that Lady Alexander had telephoned and told 'im he would 'ave to sell the farm. That's what I 'eard. I may be wrong, but I 'eard the music later in the afternoon. I was swilling out the pigs, cleaning the muck and the mud, and then I 'eard it. I put me hands over me ears and I went in to find Nanny Jenkins. I said, "Can't you do nothing about that noise?" I asks Nanny. "It's a frightful sound when Master Clive plays like that." He was shouting and shouting, and still playing. Miss Glenda, it was like the devil himself was after him. That music, it's bad music. I don't like it.' He picked up the suitcase.

'Anyway,' Nanny decided to take back the conversation, 'we came to collect you and to take you to see him.'

'Where is he? Is he in Cambridge?'

'No. There was not a suitable –' she hesitated, picking her words carefully, '– er, *hospital* in Cambridge. So he's been put in a private hospital run by Dr Umberto in West London.'

'What sort of hospital? You don't mean a mental hospital?'

They crossed the road in front of the car park and Mark went ahead to bring the Land Rover. Nanny squinted miserably. 'I'm afraid so.' Two tears formed in her eyes. 'That's the second time I saw him carried off by strangers. The first time was long ago when he was a little boy of eight. I never thought I'd see it again. I got permission for you to visit, though. Even if he's not awake, I'm sure when he hears your voice, he'll wake up. And even if he doesn't wake up, he'll hear you and know you're there anyway. I'm sure of it. He's been asleep for days.'

Glenda was stunned. 'But why would I need permission to see my own fiancé?'

'You're not his next of kin. Lady Jane had to sign him in, you see.'

Glenda did not see, but for the moment she knew the details were unimportant. They needed to get to the hospital. She must see Clive. Oh God, she prayed, please take care of him. Let nothing awful happen to him. She prayed all the way to the hospital.

The hospital was a large, uncompromising building. The doors slid open like the jaws of a huge clam and then snapped shut. 'Visitors over there,' a large burly woman, her upper lip shadowed with hair, pushed Glenda aside. 'Get out of the way,' she said. 'You're blocking the corridor.'

Mark intervened. 'We're here to see Clive Alexander.'

'Do you have permission to see him?'

Mark gestured at Glenda. 'Miss Glenda is his fiancée. She's got permission from his parents.'

Glenda realized that in the small world of a hospital Clive was a bit of an event. Not as good as a film star or a pop star, but still a member of the British aristocracy. The woman's eyes widened. In them Glenda could see intense envy. How else, but through her job, would a little nobody like the woman that stood before her ever get to meet real aristocrats and have power over their lives? Glenda felt deep resentment for the woman, but she tried to keep herself in check. Remain unattached, she said to her inner self. Unattached to this woman's hatred and envy.

'This way,' the woman said abruptly.

They were frog-marched along a corridor and up several lifts until they came to a large waiting room. 'You stay here,' the woman said, pointing at Nanny Jenkins and Mark. 'You,' she pulled Glenda's sleeve, 'come with me.'

They arrived at a big steel door. The woman inserted a key and pulled Glenda through. Inside the door was another world. A long corridor ran down between glass-walled rooms. From the ceiling to waist-height the glass exposed the occupants to anybody passing by. They lay between glass and concrete as if they were framed and already dead. Indeed, to Glenda's horror, many did appear as if they were dead. There were people who were so thin they looked like Auschwitz inmates. 'What are these people here for?' Glenda whispered.

'Oh, they're the anorexics. Manipulative buggers, the lot of them.'

'Where is Clive?' Glenda was shaking but she tried to keep herself steady.

'He's in the locked ward. Didn't do himself any good at all. Came in here shrieking and raving. Upset all the patients and he hit the doctor.'

'He hit Dr Umberto?'

'Mmm,' the nurse grumbled with great satisfaction. 'A very silly thing to do. Dr Umberto saw to him properly, he did. Funny if he wakes up in a month of Sundays.'

Glenda walked quietly beside the nurse. They stood at the last door of the ward. 'Here.' The nurse pushed open the door.

Glenda saw Clive's blonde head on the pillow. She ran the rest of the way. 'Clive!' she said as she bent low to kiss his cheek. 'Clive,' she cried quietly. 'I'm here.' She paused and pulled away part of the sheet. She tried not to shriek. She dropped to her knees and put her arms protectively around his head. 'You've shaved his hair!' She looked down at the two bald patches on Clive's forehead. 'What have you done to him?' she blazed and she found herself shaking.

'I didn't do nothing,' the nurse whined, suddenly frightened by Glenda's intensity. 'I didn't do nothing at all. He did it to himself. You can't go round hitting doctors, you know.'

'Where is Dr Umberto?'

'In his office.'

'Clive,' Glenda touched the oblivious head. 'You *will* get

455

better. I'll stay with mum and I'll be here every day.' She kissed him. Then she straightened herself. She said firmly, 'Take me to Dr Umberto, please.'

As she was joined in her march along the corridors by Nanny and Mark, Glenda had a mental dialogue with Amerjit. 'No, Glenda,' he said. 'You must not attach your anger to these events. If you do, you will cause anger in others and then you will have a negative outcome. You must consult with this man and you must make him feel important. Puff him up like a toad.' Glenda knew he was right and she felt comforted. Amerjit had taught her well.

'Ah, Dr Umberto!' she said in his office. 'How kind of you to let me visit! I am so very relieved to find Clive in your expert hands.'

'Do sit down, Miss Stanhope. Yes, I'm afraid Clive went into a very nasty manic episode. He needed a little treatment. Soon he will be well again. Such a miracle, the medical techniques. He came in raving and shouting and quite dangerous – to himself as well as to others. A little treatment and he is as quiet as a mouse. There is no pain, and he will wake up with no memory of the episode at all. Isn't that nice?'

'A miracle, as you say. Tell me, what sort of treatment did he have?' she asked, sounding innocent.

'Oh it's called ECT, electroconvulsive therapy. We've been using it for years. Perfectly safe.'

'ECT. You mean shock therapy?'

'I won't make this difficult for you, dear.' He included Nanny Jenkins and Mark who were still standing in the doorway. 'Yes, some people call it shock treatment. Simply the passing of an electrical current through the brain to make the patient better. Just a little voltage, and then all is well again. How about we have a cup of tea, Miss Stanhope, and then you can get back to Norfolk?'

'Well, I've decided to stay with my mother until Clive gets out. You see, I have to meet Clive's adviser, Jonathan

Montague. Works with Lord Silver. Do you know Lord Silver, by any chance?'

'Of course, of course. Everybody knows Lord Silver. Splendid fellow. Jew, isn't he?'

Glenda nodded, delighted. You anti-Semitic bastard. She felt as if her words were in a bubble above them. She would only have to pull the string and the bubble would break and the words spill like mucus all over his thin, balding head. 'Yes, I believe so. Thank you, but I can't stay for tea. I must get along. Jonathan and I will be seeing Lord Silver tomorrow. He will be so distressed to hear that Clive is not well. Clive and I were planning a long holiday in a few weeks' time.'

'Uh.' Umberto rubbed his hands. 'Well, you tell Lord Silver that I will be more than happy to receive a telephone call from him. We have one of his family in the hospital now. Nice girl, but so difficult. Not, of course, Lord Silver's immediate family. A distant cousin. The Silvers have such excellent sherry. They never forget my crate at Christmas.'

'How kind of them.' Glenda stood up and shook Dr Umberto's yellowing hand. 'I'll say goodbye and I will see you tomorrow. I can visit whenever I like, I imagine. I shall bring some books and read to Clive.'

'He won't hear you,' Dr Umberto said.

'I don't mind,' she said. 'I love to read. In fact I can sit and read all day. I never get bored.'

Glenda felt Dr Umberto's eyes through her back. She's a difficult one, he thought. I'd better talk to Jane.

Later, when Dr Umberto was quite sure that she had left the building, he made a phone call. 'You didn't tell me that Miss Stanhope knows Lord Silver.'

Jane Alexander was quiet for a second. 'Well, I know that Jonathan Montague is working for Lord Silver in the London office, but I didn't know that Glenda personally had any dealings with the man.'

'That does change things, Lady Jane. We shall have to let him go this time.'

'Damn.' Jane sucked in her cigarette smoke.

'This is the first record of his being committed since he was a child. You'll need more proof before you can put him away for life, Jane.'

'Don't worry,' Lady Jane said. 'I'm prepared to be patient.' She laughed and even Dr Umberto's heart froze.

Chapter 104

Mark and Nanny dropped her off outside her mother's house in Chiswick. 'I'll let you know as soon as I get Clive out,' Glenda reassured. Nanny sat in the back of the car, her small figure frozen with doubt and with guilt. She knew that, even if not this time, there would come a time when Jane would want Clive locked away for the rest of his life. As much as this thought shocked Nanny, she knew these things happened among the very rich. The poor didn't have spare rooms in large houses to hide their embarrassing relatives. The poor had no capital or land or inheritances to squabble over. This would not be the first time a strong family incarcerated its weaker member. Her heart went out to Glenda, fumbling with her key on the lonely doorstep. Nanny sighed and Mark looked at her through the driving mirror.

'Awful, isn't it?' he said.

'Yes,' Nanny said shortly. 'Terrible. There is nothing we can do.' For a moment their eyes colluded.

Then Mark broke the tension. 'Lady Jane didn't reckon on Miss Glenda.' And he grinned. 'If I were a betting man, I'd put my money on Glenda. How about you?'

Nanny's fingers trembled as she folded them carefully. 'I don't know,' she said. 'There's so many of them and only one of her.'

'Jonathan Montague speaking.' Jonathan's soothing, sane voice answered the telephone.

Glenda was furious with herself; she could not control her hysteria. Out of the window went Amerjit's lessons. She felt the horror of the beds and the seismic shock of seeing Clive's shaven head, his utter vulnerability, his torpor – Clive, who was usually so vital and alive and would have been so pleased to see her, lying in that alien place, a place that Glenda never dreamed existed. 'It's Clive,' she garbled her words, 'he's in hospital.'

'Has he been hurt?'

'No, no. It's not that. Oh Jonathan! It's awful!' She felt fresh sobs tear at her throat. Her tongue was too big for her mouth and her nose started to run. She had no handkerchief so she was forced to sniff.

'Do you have anybody else there with you, Glenda?'

The question threw her for a moment and she was forced to concentrate. 'No,' she said. 'Mum's at the restaurant.'

'Who can you call to keep you company?'

'No one.' And then she remembered. 'I have Cyril's telephone number.'

'Call him when we're finished talking. Now start again.' The diversionary device worked. Glenda was now calmer. 'I wasn't told that Clive had had a turn.'

'Not just a depression or a headache – something worse. He's locked up in a hospital in Hammersmith.'

'What do you mean by locked up?'

Glenda had to give a wry grin. How Jonathan, she thought. So precise. 'I gather he is under some sort of order so he can't get out until it's lifted.'

'By whom?'

'Well, I suppose his mother and Dr Umberto.'

'Ah. I see. Sounds like it was against his will.' Jonathan was thinking out loud. 'How is Clive?'

'I don't know. He's so drugged he was asleep. Unconscious. But, Jonathan, the awful part is –' she faltered '– they shaved his head. Dr Umberto said they gave him ECT.' She heard a silence. 'Jonathan, are you still there?'

459

'I am.' Jonathan's voice was steely. 'I'll have a word with Lord Silver about this. I don't like it at all. You stay where you are and give Cyril a ring.'

'I'd like to telephone Georgina and ask if we can stay for a while when he's out. I really don't like the idea of going back to Norfolk. Not right away. Too close to his mother in Cambridgeshire. I don't want him anywhere near the bitch until he's much stronger.'

'You do that. I'll get on with getting him out, and I'll see you down in Dorset.'

'Do you think you *can* get him out?'

'I know I can.' Jonathan sounded so positive, Glenda felt herself relax.

'I can never thank you enough,' she said simply.

'You don't need to,' he said and put down the telephone.

Georgina agreed eagerly. 'Of course,' she said. 'I'd love to see both of you.'

'Oh, I need some time to talk to you face to face. I mean, it's all so upsetting, so . . . I can bear all of it except his shaved head, Georgina. I don't know why it hit me so hard.'

'Telephone Cyril, darling, and try not to worry. I promise, Jonathan will sort it all out. He's brilliant. He always wins.'

'So does Jane. She's the most ruthless woman I've ever known. When the policeman used to beat his wife and kids when I was little, at least you knew something had happened. But this . . . This is much worse. It's so silent, what goes on in Clive's family. Everything done in secret. No bruises to see. Telephones ring, people talk behind our backs . . . I don't know. I've been away for three weeks, three whole normal weeks, and now I'm back to it. To be honest, I had the worst feeling of dread on the airplane the whole way home.' She gave a short, cheerless laugh. 'Now I know why. If Jane hit Clive, or even me, we'd know something was happening, but it's not like that. She's all smiles and "darlings" when we see her. And then there's a telephone call.

It wouldn't even have been nasty, just a hint that the farm has to be sold for financial reasons, and the ground shifts under Clive's feet. He hates her so much and that makes him feel guilty. That's what this fit is about, if you ask me, but he can't control himself and he can't allow himself to hate her. I do understand it all much better now. But I still don't know what to do.'

Georgina was listening. 'Why don't you just get on with it and marry him, Glenda? Marry him and get out of the country for a while. Clive has never been away from his family, and maybe going abroad might do him good. Go to Rome or Paris. They're both lovely places.'

'Well, we've talked about going to LA. Gerontius left a while ago and we promised we would go out and ride with him.'

'That's what you should do then,' Georgina said. 'It would be good for both of you. Listen, I'm sorry to have to run, but mummy will be home soon and I'm cooking lunch. Did you see Molly while you were in New York?'

'Did I see Molly?' Glenda was disgruntled. 'Molly tried to exercise her right as a Soul to pinch a man who was interested in me.'

'Really? How exciting! Tell me all about it when you come down. Don't worry, Glenda. He'll be all right. Lord Silver, or "Our Lord" as we call him, can fix anything.'

Cyril was right, Glenda thought as she fished about in her handbag. It's not what you know in this country; it's who you know. She was very, very thankful that she knew Jonathan Montague.

'Cyril?' she said. 'I'm ringing you for help.'

'All right.' Cyril's loud reassuring voice sounded as if he was standing next to her. 'What's the problem?'

'Clive's been highjacked into a mental hospital by his mother and the family psychiatrist, Dr Umberto. I've just arrived back in the country and I'm still reeling from the

461

shock. Jonathan Montague is going to get hold of Lord Silver, so I'm not worried, but I'm badly shaken. I didn't know you could cart people off like that.'

Cyril snorted. 'Well, it's about time you woke up, Glenda. They do it all the time.'

'They?' Glenda asked. 'I didn't realize there was a *they*.'

'Tell you what, Glenda. Why don't you meet me for lunch? I can get away in about an hour. Meet you at Busie's Bar in the Strand.'

'Okay then. We can talk.' Glenda put the phone down and then she lifted it again. 'Mum,' she said, 'it's Glenda.'

'Nice to hear your voice, love.' Minnie sounded pleased.

'I'm at your house, mum. I flew through the night and I've just come off the airplane and Nanny and Mark took me to see Clive. He's been locked up in a mental hospital.'

'Do you want me to come home, love? I'll just be a minute.'

'No, it's all right. I'm having lunch with Cyril. He knows a lot about these things. Jonathan's looking into it all for me. Can I stay with you until we get Clive out?'

'Of course you can, Glenda. You don't even have to ask. You know that.'

'Thanks, mum. You're ever such a good mother.'

'And don't you forget it,' Minnie said. 'But that's what mums are for. I'll be back early and I'll bring something back for you from the restaurant. Chinchilla says she wants to come too. Is that okay?'

'Tell her I'd love to see her.' Glenda put down the telephone and went upstairs to wash her face and shake out her clothes. She now felt tired. The rush of adrenaline that carried her through the events of the morning had subsided. She felt battered. She sat on the side of her bed and then she remembered that Jonathan said to wait for his call. She went downstairs and telephoned him. 'Jonathan,' she said, 'I've got to go out and can't just sit here and wait.'

'You go out,' Jonathan replied.

'I'm meeting Cyril. We'll be at Busie's Bar on the Strand, if you need me.'

'Don't worry about a thing, Glenda.' Jonathan's voice was light. 'Lord Silver said he'll fix everything.'

'I'll go back this evening and sit with Clive.'

'Hopefully you can do more than just sit with him in a couple of days.'

'You mean take him home?'

'Why not? Keep your fingers crossed.'

Glenda smiled for the first time that day. 'Thank you, Jonathan.'

'You're most welcome. Have a nice day,' he teased.

For once, Glenda did not get cross at the expression. 'I will,' she said.

I'll take a bus to the Strand, she thought as she walked from Minnie's house. I need to sit among ordinary people like myself.

Chapter 105

Cyril was waiting for her when she arrived at the restaurant. 'Order the steak,' he said. 'The rest of the menu is lousy.'

Still the same Cyril. Just as bossy.

Cyril grinned. Cambridge had done him a lot of good. He had not necessarily become more socially acceptable; he was simply more confident in who he was. 'How is 'e then?' Cyril looked around impatiently for a waiter.

His accent is still the same, Glenda observed. Even Cambridge couldn't change that. 'He wasn't awake when I was there this morning, but I'll go back at five o'clock. Hopefully I'll have had a call from Jonathan and we can get him out soon.'

'Jonathan?' Cyril snorted. 'E's working with that Lord Silver. 'Well then. You shan't 'ave any problems. Old Lord Silver is a member of the establishment. Probably one of the most powerful. You'll get 'im out. He'll put the fear of God into Umberto, the old fraud.'

'You really think Dr Umberto's a fraud?'

'I know he is.'

'How do you know?'

'It's part of my job to know these things.'

'I see.' Glenda leaned back in her chair and her heart began beating. She knew that Cyril was now something dreadfully hush-hush in the Foreign Office and that he wouldn't talk about it to anyone. She also knew that Cyril would love her all her life and that her well-being was more important to him than any oath he took. 'Can you tell me anything about him?'

Cyril shook his head. 'No, I mustn't. But you can always let him know that you are on to him. He'll think you know more than you do, and that'll make 'im back off.'

'Does Jane Alexander know anything about this?'

'She has him by the short and curlies on another matter.'

'Thank you,' said a voice. A hand reached for the menus.

Cyril looked up at the waiter. 'A bottle of the house red, ta.'

The steaks looked thin and pitiful measured against the huge T-bone steaks that Glenda had enjoyed in America. Recent events had blocked America from her mind, she realized. 'Can you at least tell me what hold Jane has over him?'

'Oh yes. That's not a matter of secrecy. The Alexanders got him out of Romania during the War. So 'e owes them one, and she never lets him forget. Our other information is rather more personal.' Cyril cut into his steak. 'Not uncommon for 'eadshrinkers to want to hide things. Most psychiatrists are nuts. That's why they're psychiatrists.'

Cyril's table manners hadn't changed, Glenda thought, any more than his accent. But this comforted her. Cyril was just the same. The Foreign Office evidently had taken him on board for his unusual intelligence, not for his etiquette.

464

He was like the dome of St Paul's – always there for her.

She ate her steak. 'Does Dr Umberto have anything over Jane?'

'For years now he's supplied her with pills. You know, slimming pills, sleeping pills. Dr Happy, they call him. Now she's completely hooked. Uppers, downers, the lot. Whatever she wants, he's her supplier.'

'So if I report them both to the police, they can do something about them.'

Cyril choked. 'Oh dear, dear!' he said, his eyes brimming with laughter. 'You really are a nana, aren't you, Glenda? Haven't you learned anything in all your time among the great upper middle classes? There's one law for the rich and another for the poor. It's whether you're a person like us – from Hounslow like us, Glenda – in which case you get screwed all the time, or one of them, in which case you do the screwing. They're the establishment and they live like ticks off our backs. You could go to the police and nothing would happen except that one of them would pick up the telephone and tell the policeman in question that you were an unfortunate neurotic woman. Deluded, of course. You know, poor thing. And the whole thing would be dropped. Mind you, if Lady Jane thought you'd take any action against her to separate her from her precious money, all I can say is that I'd sleep with both my eyes open if I were you. She gives new meaning to the word ruthless.'

'You mean she would kill me.'

'*She* wouldn't kill you, love, but someone else would. Just a little accident, you know. Found dead in a ditch.'

'Do you really mean all this or are you just frightening me?'

Cyril stopped chewing. He pointed at her with his steak-knife. 'I'm warning you, Glenda. You joked about supping with panthers when you first met Clive. Well, now you're in the company of the panthers all right, and look at what the likes of them did to Oscar Wilde, our greatest poet and

465

playwright. Look at what lengths they went to in order to destroy him. He bucked the establishment and they in turn killed 'im. And D. H. Lawrence, he told the naked awful truth. Exposed the mean, greedy little nobodies that these people were. Take care, Glenda. Take very good care of yourself. The panthers mean business.'

Glenda felt her appetite recede. She pushed her plate away. 'Point taken. Thanks for the advice. Thank goodness we have Lord Silver on our side.'

Cyril looked up at her, his eyes concerned. 'I'll keep you informed, if I hear anything on the grapevine. But if I were you I'd get Clive out of the country for a while and don't tell anyone – and I mean anyone – except Jonathan where you're going. The less anybody knows the better. Leave all the business side of the estate to Lord Silver and let him fight it out. He's one of the panthers himself, but 'e's on your side in this one. And 'e enjoys the tooth and the claw of it all. But you and Clive are non-starters in this game.'

They were drinking their coffee when a telephone call was announced for Glenda. She followed the waiter to a telephone on a glass desk. 'Hello?' she said nervously.

'Good news,' Jonathan said. 'You can't take him out tonight – still too groggy. But he'll be released tomorrow morning.'

'Then I'll sit with him all night tonight,' Glenda said firmly.

'Is that really necessary?' Jonathan asked.

Cyril, Glenda realized, was considerably more sussed – to use a word of Cyril's – than was Jonathan. 'Absolutely necessary,' she said.

'Okay. I'll see you in Dorset.'

'Jonathan, thank you.'

Jonathan laughed and put down the telephone.

'They'll let Clive out tomorrow morning.' Glenda finished her coffee in one gulp. 'Will they let me stay with Clive?' she asked anxiously.

'Lesson numero uno,' Cyril replied, paying the bill. They

stepped outside through the restaurant's door. 'Come along. I'll walk you back to Carlton Terrace. Lesson numero uno is that you do what you want to do and if they don't like it, you make a huge fuss.' Cyril stopped and then started to swing his arms around and around at an alarming rate. He made some terrible faces and then he began to hop about the pavement in a bad imitation of a gorilla. Two policemen were approaching and Glenda instinctively whispered, 'Cyril, police!'

Cyril went on hopping about while astonished passers-by flattened themselves to the wall. Some scurried away frightened, some laughed. The two policemen hurried towards Cyril. Cyril jumped up and down and ran around both the men in ever-diminishing circles until it looked as if he was going to knock them down. The policemen surveyed this huge man dressed in a dark pin-striped suit with a bowler hat and umbrella. 'Are you all right, sir?' they said.

Cyril came to a stop, panting. 'Perfectly,' he said in impeccable English. 'Thank you, my kind fellows. Just a little constitutional until I go back to the FO, you know.'

'Very good, sir. Wouldn't want to think there was anything wrong.' They walked on, their hands firmly behind their backs. 'A bit eccentric,' Glenda heard the older policeman say to the younger. 'They get like that, those toffs. It's the in-breeding.'

'See?' Cyril was perspiring. 'If I was dressed shabbily, I'd be in the nick by now. Wear a suit and hat and they're only too quick to help. The secret is to look like one of them. Get yourself a big diamond ring and a string of large pearls. Out-class everybody.' By this time they were approaching Carlton Terrace. Cyril gave Glenda a loud sploshy kiss on the left ear. 'Look after y'self, and keep in touch.'

'I will,' Glenda said and she ran down the stairs to walk through St James's Park. 'Honk,' went the pelicans as she walked by. 'Honk yourself, pelicans,' she called, feeling herself up to the fight. I'm off to do battle with Nurse Watts, and that's only for starters. Cyril was well worth listening to, she decided.

Chapter 106

The trees were young and green. Late spring cast shadows across Buckingham Palace on Glenda's taxi drive to Chiswick to pick up her bag. She looked at the flag pole atop the Palace. The Queen was in residence – all is well with the world.

Minnie was home by the time Glenda floated in on a tide of euphoria. 'Mum,' she said, seeing Minnie in the kitchen, 'he's coming out tomorrow. Jonathan's arranging for a private ambulance to take us down to Dorset. Georgina says we should just get married down there. Her mother can organize it. Then we should go abroad for a while. I think it's a good idea.'

'You really do want to marry Clive? You're sure?' Minnie came into the hall and hugged her daughter.

'Absolutely sure,' she said. 'I watched him yesterday lying on his pillow . . . Oh, mum, he looked so lost.'

'It's not pity, is it, Glenda?'

'No, of course not. Nobody knows Clive as I do because he's so shy. But when we're together, it's magic between us. Both of us like a lot of quiet. We have a lovely life together on the farm. Really. I read and he plays his piano. Or he takes out his horses or potters around in the vegetable garden. Even I'm getting good at growing things. You'll be amazed when you see my tomatoes, mum. They'll be ripe before too long.'

'Then I don't see why you don't get on and just get married.'

'I'll talk to Clive tonight at the hospital.'

'Do you want me to come with you? To help you look after him, I mean.'

'Thanks, but we should be fine. I'll just go upstairs and

pack a few things and then I'll come down and we can have a cup of tea before I go and deal with Nurse Watts.'

'I'd better make the tea strong,' Minnie said.

Nurse Watts was put out. 'The very idea!' she huffed. 'You'll leave when the normal visiting hours are over, I tell you. Spending the night indeed! Who do you think you are?'

'But Nurse Watts,' Glenda said, her cheeks pink with anger, 'who the hell are *you* to give me orders? You are a nobody. I am engaged to this man and I intend to stay with him until he is out of this awful hellhole.' She was shouting by now. She saw Dr Umberto's secretary stick her head into the visitors' room where Glenda was creating an uproar.

'Get on your bike, Nurse Watts!' a large visitor was cheering. Definitely not a relative of one of the *private* patients, Glenda thought cheerfully.

The other visitors were sitting on their hands, their mouths down-turned with disapproval, letting their loved ones get zapped with electricity, Glenda thought. 'Dr Umberto will see you now.' The secretary shot her neck out behind the door, looking like an elderly tortoise reaching for cover.

'Thank you,' Glenda said and she swept out of the room. As she passed Nurse Watts she said, 'Be sure to see that I have a cup of tea waiting for me in the ward.'

Nurse Watts had steam coming out of her ears.

That was easy, Glenda muttered as she strode down the hall. All I have to do is shout Balderdash, balderdash! like Georgina's mother and Dr Umberto will run.

As it turned out, a very meek Dr Umberto rose from his desk and put out a defeated hand. 'Well, Miss Stanhope, you do indeed have friends in high places. I had a word with Lord Silver and we agreed that Clive can be driven to Dorset tomorrow with you. I trust you are willing?'

Glenda nodded. Old shark, she thought. You've been caught though. Usually Dr Umberto stood up and tucked his hands under his frock coat.

'Normally I'd like to keep him here for at least three weeks, but I gather the Dorset house has servants who can take care of him satisfactorily. So why take up a perfectly good bed when he can be moved quite comfortably? Now run along.' Dr Umberto waved his hand dismissively.

'I shall stay with him all night,' Glenda said, clutching her suitcase.

'Of course, dear. Of course. If you must.' Dr Umberto showed Glenda out of the room with a flourish. 'Do . . . do anything Miss Stanhope asks,' Dr Umberto murmured to an astonished Nurse Watts.

Glenda grinned at the nurse. They walked in a studied silence to the locked ward. Glenda ran up to Clive's bed. 'Thank goodness, Clive,' she said, folding him in her arms. 'Are you all right?'

'I'm fine. My mouth is parched and I have a funny taste on my tongue.' He ran his hand over his hair. 'Seem to have lost some hair. What on earth is going on, Glenda? Why am I here?'

'You don't remember?'

'Not a thing. The nurses won't say anything. When can I get out?'

'Tomorrow. But, Clive, don't let's talk now, all right?' Glenda remembered Cyril's face. 'Don't say anything. I'm staying here with you until the ambulance comes tomorrow morning at ten and takes us both down to Georgina's house. Then we can talk.'

'Damn!' Dr Umberto put down the headphones in his drawer. Every bed was bugged in the locked ward. That way Dr Umberto learned a lot about his patients. Blackmail might come in handy in certain cases. Damn the girl! She suspects me. I wonder how much she knows.

'She knows nothing.' Lady Jane's voice was bored. 'She's just a little nobody. Clive will soon tire of her. Let them go for a while. He'll be back in a few weeks. He can't stay away from his beloved farm for too long. There'll be plenty of opportunities. Don't worry about it. And Umberto, darling, I need a little extra help. My head, you know. Have you anything for me?'

'I know,' Umberto said, not much relishing the fact that for him the practice of medicine had come to *this*. 'I'll be down in a few days.'

'See that you are,' she said, hanging up. She studied a long, shining, red fingernail.

'Scrub my back, Caspar. There's a darling.'

Casper dutifully scrubbed his naked mother's back.

'Ahhh, that's lovely!' Jane said and she slid into the deep, pink, frothy bath water. 'You were always such a wonderful son to me. Give your mother a kiss.'

Obediently Caspar leaned over the bath and kissed his mother on the lips. He was impatient to get off for the shoot. Old dingbat, he thought as he left the bathroom. Leathery tits. No wonder Clive is nuts.

He ran off to find his father. Now there's a sane man. 'Hullo! Wait for me!' he shouted as the beaters walked down the bridle path. Ah, a good clear sky and the air still. A good day for putting up pheasant.

Chapter 107

The chair by Clive's bed was uncomfortable. Glenda sat and read aloud from her book of American poetry, a favourite of Clive's. Clive enjoyed listening to the Black Mountain poems and the Ferlinghetti descriptions in 'A Coney Island of the Mind.'

Dinner was served on plastic trays with rounded spoons for the sloppy stew and the rice pudding. Clive lifted his eyebrows. 'Not even decent skin.'

'Clive, did you try to . . . ' Then Glenda remembered and pulled herself together. This was not a safe place, even if it purported to be a place to heal the emotionally sick.

471

Finally he fell asleep.

Late into the hours of the night Glenda sat in her chair, keeping watch over Clive. She was in the unsettling state of being too agitated to sleep, yet too tired to steer her own thoughts. Instead her thoughts had power of their own to hold her mind and subject her to varied and sometimes unpleasant sensations.

She began to feel guilty. Perhaps, she observed, this was a guilt that she should have felt earlier. All at once it seemed to her that her relationship with Amerjit had somehow brought about Clive's bad turn. Had she betrayed Clive? She had not meant to. No part of her had sought to hurt Clive by getting to know Amerjit, yet juxtaposed against her return was her discovery that Clive was hospitalized, and the two events felt mysteriously intertwined. Then again, she told herself, her time with Amerjit had nothing to do with Clive. She had been seeking something for herself. She had learned something and had enriched herself. Was that really harmful to Clive? No, she certainly had not intended . . .

Had Glenda been older, she might have felt more guilty about Amerjit. But Glenda was still at an age when all sorts of things can be reconciled with conscience in the name of finding new experience. She found herself incapable of regretting Amerjit altogether.

She had learned, she said to herself. Through her life she had seen all sorts of relationships in all stations of society. She had seen marriage in poverty – the bestial, violent, marriage of the McCluskies. And she had seen the brutality of the aristocratic world as well, maybe less straightforward than in working class life, but no less real. Between Lord Philip and Lady Jane Alexander, there was little love lost, if one could use the word *love* at all to name the visible hostility that existed between them.

In the middle there was the stultified suburban coupling and coping that Molly's parents had in New Jersey, the boredom and the monotony that could be found on the faces

472

of the middle-class. The face of the woman sitting beside her on the plane over to New York, an unctuous woman with a self-satisfied, made-up, puffed-out face . . . Why had that woman bothered Glenda so much? A total stranger . . . Glenda drifted and in a brief near-dream found herself back on the airplane again looking at the woman. She shook herself and returned to Clive's hospital bedside. The woman was a vision of the last thing in the world Glenda ever wanted to become.

And that was just it – with Clive, Glenda would never become like that woman. Neither would she be poor again and destined to return to a Hounslow slum, nor fall into any of the traps that most people fell into. She and Clive were different. Clive was special. He was artistic and intelligent and sensitive. He had a perceptiveness that let him see the world from a different angle, a view that was fascinating. How many men found genuine pleasure in sitting and having Ferlinghetti read to them? Certainly not Jeff Rosenthal, and probably not the husband of the woman on the plane . . .

Clive and Glenda together would have a life free from all the mistakes that everyone else made. Theirs would be an unconventional but happy relationship, like Renée's and Abe's, each of them freed from the constraints of their individual class backgrounds, each finding new worlds together.

What had Minnie asked? Are you sure it isn't just pity, Glenda? No, of course not. How could Minnie ask such a question? That wasn't it at all. Their love for each other was about other things, about daring to be unconventional together and set apart from most people's mediocre existence . . .

Glenda shook her head to rouse herself, for she was beginning to slip away.

True, their life together at Fen Farm had yet to take on any real shape, but when they were married it would. Clive spent most of his days working side by side with Paul and

Mark, doing all the things it took to keep a farm going. And Glenda in her days made the drive to Cambridgeshire to the private museum to run the exhibition. But the exhibition was ending now and she was not sure how she would fill her days, though her nights were full of Clive's beautiful piano-playing and poetry read aloud and sitting by the fire, sometimes with friends, and listening to jazz, and . . . Yes, marriage would solidify their life into a lifestyle. More time together, that's what was needed. She had run away to New York to Renée's wedding too early, before they each had time to set themselves up in real life. Bad timing, that's what it was. Just unfortunate. And maybe the disturbance of her going had unsettled Clive. That, and Lady Jane making a point of threatening him at all times.

But she and Clive would be together now, settling back into days on the farm. And they would have their nights together and the nights would be . . . She wanted nights of love. Nights filled with the warm tingly sensations she had learned from Amerjit. Yes, she would have that with Clive. She'd help him overcome his little problem. She would show Clive, unlock him. Once she got him to trust her. Trust and peace and happiness would come through marriage. And perhaps in time she would help him sort out whatever it was that caused such horrors in the Alexander family, horrors that manifested in Clive's emotional flights into darkness. What had Lady Jane done to him to make him this way? Glenda would help him . . .

Glenda's eyes started to close.

In marriage all would be good. She wanted the experience of knowing that goodness with Clive, as she had wanted the experiences which Amerjit had to offer. That was her mission, her purpose – to create the experience of marriage with Clive. Thought creates matter . . .

Glenda's chin began to drop toward her breastbone.

And she was good at doing something she set out to do. She got herself into Cambridge by putting her mind to it.

And now she would put her mind to seeing that she and Clive were married.

Glenda's neck relaxed.

Chapter 108

She awoke early in the morning. Glenda watched the nurses filing into the room at five o'clock. They all looked fresh and tidy. The room was frowsty and her mouth felt as if full of dried corn meal. She swallowed and waited for a cup of refreshing tea. She could hear the trolley clanging in the next room. A nurse came up shaking a thermometer. 'Time to take the patient's temperature.'

'You're not waking him up.' Glenda took the nurse by the wrist. 'He doesn't have a fever, and we're leaving this morning. Let him alone.'

The nurse looked uncertain. 'But it's rules, Miss. All patients must have their temperatures taken in the morning.'

'Well, break the rule and tell them I said so.' Glenda pushed the nurse aside. She stood up and she stretched. 'For goodness sake, woman! Don't you ever break the rules?'

The young nurse looked at her and then she smiled. 'Yes,' she said. 'It's a damn silly rule.' She walked off.

Glenda grunted. At least someone in here has a heart.

Clive turned over. The tea trolley came towards the bed. Oh good. A nice, steaming hot cup of tea. 'Thank you,' she said to the orderly. Not long now. Not long. She took the thick, white plastic mug in her hands and she watched the trolley bully its way around the beds.

The journey down to Dorset felt odd. The ambulance was an old, luxurious Citroën Safari. Painted white outside, inside it was cream. There was a bed with a bench beside it.

Clive was wheeled to the ambulance by Nurse Watts. Glenda followed, carrying their suitcases. Nurse Watts slammed the door on them and then said venomously, 'I hope I do not see you again. Either of you.'

'Fuck off,' Glenda said cheerfully and then laughed at Nurse Watts' horrified face.

Clive sat on the bed and shook his head. 'That startled the old bag! What a frightful place.'

'I didn't know pits like that still existed.'

Clive lay back on the bed and the car pulled away from the kerb and began to nose its way out of London. He turned and looked out the window. 'I don't know, Glenda. Maybe we've kept our heads in the sand for far too long. Maybe Cyril and Beth were right. This country *is* in an awful mess and something must be done about it all. I was in a semi-private hospital. What must it be like in a state hospital?'

'Like Dante's *Inferno*, I should imagine.' Glenda lay down on the bench. 'Anyway, I'm not going to think about anything now. I'm exhausted.'

'Sleep, darling,' he said and he bent over and kissed her. 'I'll look after you. Just sleep.'

Glenda slipped away and did not wake up until Clive pushed her shoulder gently. 'We're here.'

'Where?' Glenda awoke with a start. She sat up and looked at the inside of an ambulance. 'Oh. We're on our way to Georgina's house, aren't we? I had such awful dreams, Clive.' The ambulance turned into the drive.

'I didn't wake you up when we stopped for petrol or for lunch. You looked so zonked. The driver and the attendant were really very nice. Look, Glenda! How marvellous to be in Dorset! Look at the trees! I feel as if I missed the whole month of May.'

'You haven't. Just a week.'

'A week is a long time to miss. So much can happen in a week.'

Glenda watched the ambulance slide to a stop in front of the manor house. 'Yes, a week is a long time, but it takes

just a second to change a life. Clive, will you marry me?'
The words were hurried.

Clive looked surprised. 'Of course, Glenda. But we've
known that all along, haven't we?'

'I don't mean far off in the future. I mean let's get married
now. As soon as possible. Georgina's mother is a Justice of
the Peace and a magistrate. She'll know the local Registrar
who could do the ceremony. Then we can run away to LA
and find Gerontius and start making a life for ourselves.' She
heard feet shushing up to the double doors and the sound of
the handle being turned. 'Say yes, Clive. Let's do it.'

Clive grinned and took Glenda's hand. 'Yes.' He squeezed
her hand. 'I've always dreamed of running away. I could be
like the Little Prince, travelling to a distant world.'

Glenda looked at him as the door opened and others
intruded into their lives. How like the Little Prince he looks,
she thought, watching Clive climb out of the ambulance. His
neck was thin and his hair wispy and blonde. His brilliant
blue eyes shone with happiness. She followed him, bending
double before she jumped out of the back of the vehicle.
'Georgina!' she said, hugging the tall, elegant figure.

Georgina hugged her back. 'How is he?' she asked
anxiously. Clive had wandered off to pick a daisy on the
lawn.

'He's fine now, Georgina. But it was a dreadful ordeal. We
can't let that happen again.'

'Exactly what did happen?' Georgina looked puzzled.

'Wait until Jonathan arrives later tonight. Then we can all
talk about it. Do you think your mother would know someone
who could marry us?' Glenda felt self-conscious.

'The Registrar's an old friend of hers. I'm sure she'd be
glad to arrange it. Anyway, she's in the house fussing about
her flowers. We can ask her.'

Clive came sauntering back carrying a small posy of daisies.
'For you, my wife,' he said and stretched out his hand.

'Thank you,' Glenda smiled at him, taking the little bunch

477

of flowers, feeling for him incredible love. The gong sounded across the May-filled lawn for sherry. 'Oh goodness. We haven't changed.' Glenda put her hand to her mouth.

'Not to bother. Ma knew you'd be late, so we're having a sort of nanny high tea. Pa loves high tea. Reminds him of his nursery days.' She led the way into the house. The two suitcases had already been carried in. 'You both pop upstairs and have a quick wash and I'll tell mummy that you're here.'

Glenda looked at the now familiar guest bedroom. She knew Clive would be brushing his hair nearby. Funny how much you know about a man whom you live with. Clive always brushed his hair before he washed his face and cleaned his teeth. Glenda always washed her face before brushing her hair. As soon as possible they would be married and preserve these routines for the rest of their lives. She reminded herself to tell the people at the museum that she wouldn't be doing any future exhibitions with them. Paramount in her mind was the need for her and Clive to escape . . .

In daylight reflection, she wondered again. Escape from what? Was she just being paranoid? No, she didn't think so. She promised herself she would wait to talk to Jonathan. He was so good about this sort of thing.

'Do you think I'm making a fuss?'

Jonathan sat in a large brown leather armchair in the library. Georgina was sitting at his feet, her arm resting on his knee. Clive and Glenda sat opposite them. Coffee cups were on the low table with small liqueur glasses. Clive drank only mineral water from a larger glass. 'No, I don't think you're being neurotic. Funny,' Jonathan paused. 'Here we are in the biggest upheaval since before the war. Left-wing lunatics trying to instigate and infiltrate all over the place. Right-wing hardliners not knowing whether to jump ship with their riches or stay and fight it out with private armies. The government under suspicion. Allegations of Reds under the Prime Minister's bed. All this going on, and Clive's being attacked by his own mother.'

'I know.' Glenda reached out and took Clive's hand. She knew Clive hated to talk about his mother to anyone but herself. 'Darling, we do have to tell Jonathan. He can look after things for us while we're away.'

'Yes,' Clive said forlornly. 'I suppose you're right. Thanks, Jonathan. I do feel I would be better off if I do get away for a while. I don't feel very steady after that last . . . er, episode.'

Jonathan leaned forward. 'Can you try to explain what happened and how you managed to find yourself in the hospital.'

'Well. Let's see. All I can remember is feeling rather odd on that day. A bit depressed. The sun doesn't shine on those days. It feels as if I'm living in a negative. You know, like a roll of black and white film. What's inside looks as if it's outside, and what's outside goes inside. It makes even the people you know look funny and woozy.' Jonathan, Clive could see, was frowning. 'I know it's difficult to understand if it's never happened to you.' Clive felt defensive.

Glenda squeezed his hand. 'Go on,' she said. 'I understand.'

'Then I was playing quite happily on the piano and the telephone rang. I answered it and it was my mother. I heard her say something about the farm having to turn a profit or else it might be time to think about selling it. And suddenly I felt as if I was falling backwards and this awful music kept rising and falling in my mind. I think I went back to the piano and began to play. It was a piece built upon the interval of the augmented fourth, the *diabolus in musica*. The devil's music. Always a good way of letting out the upset, you know. Playing piano. Great release. But this time it didn't do much for me.'

'What happened next?' Jonathan asked.

'I'm not sure, exactly. I remember playing, and the pain in my head got worse and worse and then . . . I guess I passed out for a very long time.'

Glenda sat quietly, listening.

Jonathan was silent for a moment, thinking everything through. 'Clive,' he said at last, 'you leave me with power of attorney, and I'll see that your bank accounts are kept straight and the servants paid. Take as much as you need for the trip. If you need more, just let me know. Don't tell anybody where you're going.'

'You can contact us by telephoning Renée.' Glenda smiled. 'You can trust her absolutely. I'll phone in from time to time to see if there are any messages.'

Mrs Lampsetter appeared at the door. 'Georgina tells me you dears wish to be married.' She glanced fondly at the young couple. 'It's a bit unorthodox to do it away from family, but then the Alexanders never do anything the right way. And Jane will be furious.' Julia Lampsetter looked delighted at the idea of infuriating Lady Jane. 'It will take her ages to find out you're married. What a hoot! When she asks, I shall say – ,' Mrs Lampsetter collected her considerable bulk and stuck her nose in the air ' – I shall say, "It was just tickety-boo, my dear. Just tickety-boo! What a shame you weren't there!" What about Saturday afternoon? I can arrange for the Registrar to marry you on Saturday, and I do so think weddings should happen on a Saturday, whenever possible. Then we can all go to church on Sunday and have a little party. Just a little one, because Georgina tells me you want to keep it all a secret.'

'That would be wonderful,' Glenda said.

Mrs Lampsetter wandered off, clutching her large grey dressing gown round her and hanging on to a very decrepit hot water bottle. 'Good night, mother,' Georgina called.

'Don't stay up too late, darlings.'

That little lot in the library are a decent bunch of young people, she murmured to herself. Need more like them around nowadays. She settled herself in the big four-poster bed beside her husband. We just have to hope the future of the country is in their hands and not in the clutches of the awful rabbit-toothed, knotted-hankie brigade. She rather doubted the former and did not want to think about the latter.

Chapter 109

'Two days to go to my wedding,' Glenda telephoned her mother.

'I'll come down by train,' Minnie said. 'Chinchilla and I can stay at a local hotel.'

'You can stay with us. There's plenty of room.'

'No thanks, love.' Minnie's voice was firm. 'I'd be out of place, if you know what I mean. I could do with an 'oliday. Chinchilla and I can 'ave a shufty round town.'

'Oh, mum, I can't believe I'm really getting married.'

'I'm pleased, Glenda. Really I am. 'E's a nice young man. Me boyfriend and I are happy for you.'

Glenda put the telephone down and went to find Georgina.

'Ma notified the registry office yesterday, so they can post the banns. She told a little fib about your being resident here with us, but then ma always says rules were made to be broken.'

Glenda found herself laughing. 'Your mother is quite the revolutionary in her own way.'

'Yes. Always has been. She and her mafia friends in the Women's Institute run things around here. They know everything about everyone and they bully the hell out of all their husbands. You would think the bank manager runs the bank? Think again. His wife makes the decisions and he says "Yes, dear." Anyway let's go into Dorchester and get you something to wear. You said you needed a new outfit.'

'I do. And something old, and something borrowed, all that stuff that goes with getting married.'

'You know,' Glenda sat beside Georgina in the Land Rover, 'I much prefer getting married this way. I rather dreaded the

481

idea of a big wedding with just mum and Chinchilla on my side of the church and the entire Alexander clan on the other. I suppose I could have asked Cyril and even Beth. I last saw her plodding around the road carrying a banner. Poor old Beth, she did hope to marry Cyril, you know.'

'I don't think many of our generation will get married. Most of them are so confused they don't know what they want. Come to think of it, Glenda, our generation of Girton girls were the generation that openly declared that they would rather live with men than get married. So that's what they get: they live with their men and then the men run off and marry someone else. *Plus ça change*.'

Glenda thought she heard a hint of envy in Georgina's voice. 'You do want to marry Jonathan, don't you, Georgina?'

Georgina straightened her back. Her hands gripped the steering wheel. 'I suppose, when you shoot into my life with all your problems . . . ' She looked across at Glenda. 'I don't mean that unkindly. What I'm trying to say is that it's as if I live in this world on a large motorway. Everything appears to roll along so smoothly that sometimes I don't feel I'm even alive. I will be married in the autumn. The same hats will be there that were at a wedding I attended at the beginning of the year. We'll drink the same champagne, eat the same small smoked salmon sandwiches on brown bread. What would happen if the bread was white? Oh horror! Talk of the town! The Lampsetters served their smoked salmon on white bread! Next thing you know they'll be tampering with the cucumber and egg sandwiches too. Stop press – "Twenty nuns raped and disembowelled in Dorchester." Headlines in the papers – "Lampsetters served cucumber and egg sandwiches on wrong bread *again*. Must they be run out of the polo club?" It is all very trivial. At least when I do marry Jonathan, I'll be living some of the time in Boston. House is set up already. And Boston simply can't be as boring as here. Lucky you, Glenda. You get to rush off on your honeymoon and buzz about with Clive, while I get to groom the horses and decide what colour the youngest bridesmaids' dresses ought to be. Most people now seem to have a disgusting habit of dressing the little monsters in lime green.'

'Georgina! I don't think I've ever heard you talk this way before.'

'Could be I haven't felt this way before. Or maybe I have and I just never knew it.'

'Well, what do you feel? It sounds as if you're not sure you want to go ahead with . . . '

'No,' Georgina cut in. 'I just . . . ' She stopped. Her eyes concentrated on driving. When she talked again, her voice had refound its usual calm tenor. 'I took a glimpse, you see. I mean, for all the trouble you and Clive are having, with his parents and everything, the two of you are still free. You can go anywhere and live as you please.' Glenda started to speak but Georgina held up a hand. 'Yes, I know it's not quite that easy, but that's how it feels, from the outside at least. My life is so planned that . . . I don't know. I glimpsed your freedom and for a moment I imagined myself breaking loose.'

'You can if you want to,' Glenda said after a silence. 'Break loose.'

'No.' Georgina smiled. 'This is what I want. I think. I want to marry Jonathan and have the house here and the house in Boston. The whole thing. It's what I want.' She laughed. 'But I can still have fun imagining, you know? My mind runs away sometimes and I think silly things, like what would it be like to have a wedding completely dressed in black with bridesmaids dressed in purple? Anyway,' she grinned, 'I ought to at least wear red knickers.'

'So should I. I haven't really had time to tell you about Amerjit.'

'Oh? This sounds exciting. Do tell!' Georgina changed gears at the lights. They were on the outskirts of Dorchester. A leafy road, hidden houses behind protective walls, led into the centre of town, but both women were oblivious to all but their discussion.

Glenda walked beside Georgina, looking in the shop windows. How small and quaint the streets of Dorchester were after the huge stores in Manhattan! The two friends found a table in a pub and Glenda looked around her. Different faces, she thought. Not so hunted or driven as the faces had been in New York. Hopefully LA will be as laid back as Clive says it is. Anyway, nothing to worry about. Jonathan is taking care of everything. Odd, Georgina doesn't seem to be so sure of getting married.

They went to a restaurant for some lunch.

'We'll be back for your wedding,' Glenda said. Two bulging pasties sat on their table along with two glasses of white wine.

'Well. Here's to Saturday and *your* wedding.' Georgina raised her glass.

'And here's to yours in September.' They each sipped. 'In between I'll have a couple of months in America.'

'And I'll spend those same months rotting in the country. Still, I'll get up to town from time to time. And Fatima says she might be coming over from Paris. You know, she's quite fed up waiting for Majid to marry her. She says she's the oldest virgin in Paris. I told her to give in gracefully. She says it isn't a question of giving in. Majid is hardly ever there.'

Lunch over, they wandered into the streets. 'It is an odd feeling, the four of us so split up,' Glenda said. 'Still, we'll all be together again at your wedding and maybe we shall have to call a special Souls meeting before you go off to Boston.' They found the car and drove back in a companionable silence.

Chapter 110

'Don't worry about a thing.' Jonathan drove Clive and Glenda to the airport. Their marriage ceremony was over. Clive had been very tense in fear that the local paper had picked up the news that the heir to the Alexander fortune and title had sneaked off to a small registry office and married a commoner. 'Don't worry,' Major Lampsetter said just before the ceremony. 'I had a word with the chap who runs the paper.' Clive relaxed.

Glenda remembered as she sat in the back of the car, holding his hand in hers, the thrilling moment when she said 'I do.' Somehow those words cemented for her all the months of waiting, the years that had gone into the sharing of their lives together. When Clive slipped her gold wedding ring onto her finger, a knot was formed in her heart – Clive and Glenda forever entwined. Nothing could loosen the bond or the commitment made in this room. She turned and she saw her mother's face. There were tears in Minnie's eyes. Tears of loss, but also of comfort. Glenda was now married.

The car sped up the road to London. It was a long drive. Jonathan drove steadily. Clive was tired and he dozed against the cushions. Glenda looked at the strong uncompromising back of Jonathan's head. Jonathan would take care of everything: tell the staff at the farm that they would be back, run the accounts and keep an eye on the panthers. Jonathan was still a young panther himself, but his claws were sharp and he was learning.

Glenda did not relish sitting in the tourist section of the plane. 'I forgot to tell you,' Clive explained, his face alight with happiness. 'I decided that we should be like other people. Most people don't travel first class, so neither should we. I've always hated being stuck up in front with all that lobster and

485

champagne stuff. You don't mind, do you, darling?'

'No,' Glenda said, suppressing an evil desire to shout that she had been most people all her life, and being most people was nothing to be coveted.

They settled down in their squashed seats next to an enormous woman with a loudly crying baby. Glenda sat back and waited for take-off. In her purse she had a thousand pounds in traveller's cheques – a present from Minnie and Chinchilla. Business at the restaurant was successful indeed. 'We didn't buy you anything because we knew you were going away.'

'Don't worry, mum,' Glenda said, seeing concern in her mother's eyes. 'I can get all the things a bride is supposed to have when I get back.'

Now she realized there was nothing to get. Fen Farm, now her home, was almost too full of things.

The baby had decided that Clive was definitely its best friend and was smiling and slobbering enthusiastically all over him. Clive was a little nonplussed. Good, Glenda grinned. Let him have a slice of real life. Jonathan wouldn't have been caught dead in the cattle section of the airplane. Then again, Jonathan would never try to play with a baby. However inept Clive's attempts were, he was trying. 'Round and round the garden,' Clive held the baby's fat hand in his, 'like a teddy bear . . . ' The baby gurgled and then threw up on Clive's hand.

The mother pulled out a grim, soiled nappy and carefully wiped the baby's face. 'My nanny taught me that rhyme,' Clive said. He rummaged about in the pocket of the seat, looking hopefully for something to wipe his hand with.

'Your *nanny*?' the mother squealed. 'Blimey! I thought nannies had gorn out with *Winnie the Pooh*.'

'Now *there's* a wonderful book.' Clive's voice was wistful. Here at last was a safe subject. '*Winnie the Pooh*.'

'Don't know. Never read it. I mean, waste your time reading a book about a fucking bear? Whatever for?'

'What do you read then?'

'Oh, you know. Everything. *News of the World*, and *The Sun* of course.' The baby, tired of playing with his new friend, went to sleep and the woman buried her face in the baby's neck and shut her eyes.

Clive turned his eyes to Glenda. She laughed. He looked so helpless, his hand cupped around the little pile of vomit. 'Here,' she said and pulled out a handkerchief. 'Don't get too friendly with the natives, Clive.'

Clive frowned and the plane shook before take-off. Glenda held his clean hand. 'You'll have to wait until the seat belt sign is off and then you can go and wash your hand.'

'I do hope the little brat doesn't shriek the place down all night.'

'It would serve you right, Clive,' she whispered, in case the fat woman was listening. 'When will you learn that there's nothing automatically noble about being a member of the working class? They can be as mean and stubborn as anyone.'

'I don't want to believe that.'

'Well, don't. But just remember, I was one of them, only I escaped.'

The baby alternately screamed and gurgled all through the flight. Glenda rolled herself into a ball and curled up, her back to the baby and its monstrous mother. Clive twitched and occasionally Glenda opened her eyes to see him attempting to occupy the baby. She knew Clive was trying to ensure that she got a good night's sleep and she loved him for it. Nevertheless, she wished he were not so romantic about the daily lives of ordinary people. A month in the torpid streets of Hounslow should sort him out. Or perhaps not. She wasn't sure. There was something about Clive that was naturally egalitarian. He could be anywhere and he would talk to people in his shy way with genuine concern and interest. People responded to him. Even the fat woman unbended. 'I'm a farmer,' Glenda heard him say in one of her waking moments.

She watched him leave his seat to get some juice to refill the baby's bottle. He will make a great father, she thought and then she remembered. His 'turns' would be inherited, Dr Umberto claimed. Then again, Glenda thought before returning to sleep, if the Alexanders were bent on keeping Clive from inheriting the full estate, what could serve their interests better than dissuading him from having an heir of his own? Well, Glenda might have some plans of *her* own.

She fell asleep, full of excited anticipation for their honeymoon.

Chapter 111

Los Angeles airport was loud and bustling, but very different from New York. The weather was hot and damp. Some people wore shorts and T-shirts, and it seemed that many women were against the idea of shaving under their arms. The porters ran around shouting and threatening the travellers. LaGuardia airport in New York had been exciting; LA airport was angry. 'Want a porter?' A man pushed his face into Clive's.

'No, thank you,' he said reasonably. 'I can carry the bags myself.' Clive's tone was firm. He arched his eyebrows and gazed at the man who, seeing steel in Clive's eyes, pulled away muttering.

They pushed their way through the crowd and walked outside. 'The Hollywood Holiday Inn, please,' Clive said to a taxi driver.

Clive and Glenda sat back in the air-conditioned cab. 'It's hotter than I expected,' Glenda said, glad for the air-conditioning.

'Hm. As soon as we've checked into the hotel and unpacked we can go out and find a clothes shop if you like.'

'Store, you mean. American is a different language.'

'I hope you like the Holiday Inn.'

'Sure I'll like the Holiday Inn. I already like the taxi. I thought for one horrid moment you were going to make us catch a bus.'

'I'm not *that* nuts.' He took her hand. 'You know, Glenda, you must remember, apart from spending time with the people at the farm, I tend to lead a very isolated life. I didn't mean to upset the woman on the plane. I just take for granted that everyone has nannies and servants and things like that. But I want to merge here in LA. I want to live like Gerontius. Oh. Did I tell you? He's coming for dinner.'

'Gerontius in a posh restaurant?'

'He won't mind.'

'It's not him I'm worried about. He isn't planning to wear his especially disgusting shirt, is he? The one with all the beans stuck to it?'

Glenda was out of luck. Gerontius rolled into the hotel and the nervous receptionist stood horror-struck. Gerontius leaned forward, his breath stinking with garlic, and roared, 'Take me to my friends. Here, little lady. I'm Gerontius. And this is my friend Tex.' Tex was as thin as Gerontius was fat. Tex wore his clothes and his ten-gallon hat like props from a cowboy film.

'Who have you come to see?' the girl enquired, trying to free herself from Gerontius's sweaty grasp.

'I have come to see my friend The Honourable Clive Alexander and his new wife.'

'Take a seat over there, please.' The girl waved a hand and hoped the dreadful apparitions would disappear for ever.

Both the men settled themselves, their backs against the wall of the lobby. Gerontius began his usual recitation at the top of his voice. Hotel personnel were running in and out of the lobby. The manager had been told that Gerontius was visiting The Honourable Clive Alexander. He checked the register – yes, they did have a Clive Alexander. Suppose he really was a lord or something, they couldn't very well throw Gerontius out. No, they would have to play this one

489

carefully. Meanwhile, hotel guests were scuttling about.

'Please, Mister . . . Um . . . The Honourable, er, whoever you are, could you come down quick? There is a man down here who says he is your friend.'

'Down in a minute.'

'Any chance you could make it sooner?'

Clive laughed. The final word held a special pleading. Gerontius must be up to his usual tricks. 'I'll be down right away. Don't worry about Gerontius. He's quite harmless.'

The manager put the phone down. He certainly hoped so.

Gerontius drew breath and then bellowed 'It took Allen Ginsberg, the great genius of our nation, to strip off stark naked and howl this poem. It took that for the frigging generation of empty-minded adults of America to realize that America had its own poetry, its own literature, its own experience. Read the Beat poets! Listen to the music! Be proud to be American! Europe is finished, a whore who fucked herself insensible. She stole from the rest of the world and now screams for help from the very countries she robbed.'

Clive arrived by the lift, Glenda at his shoulder. 'Gerontius!' Clive walked up to his old friend and hugged him.

'Glenda!' Gerontius pulled her into his warm embrace and Glenda found herself forgiving him his smells and even the shirt. 'Meet Tex. He'll be riding with us. I have your Hog outside. Your Hog,' he explained to Glenda, 'is your Harley. Your ride, your bike. It's big and it's beautiful.' They trooped out of the hotel and stood admiring the great machine. 'Dual Glide, 1200 cc's. Cruises smooth at eighty-five on the open road without a shiver or a quiver.'

The open road. The words stuck in Glenda's brain. This was going to be home for the next few months, this huge monstrous motorcycle. Already Clive had changed. Gone was the slightly hunted look in his eye. He even seemed bigger and more confident.

'Well done, Gerontius,' said Clive. 'She's a beauty. Thanks a lot.'

'Yeah, well you should thank your buddy Jonathan. He called me from England and took care of all the business side of things. Got the bread here and shit like that so I could buy the bike for you.'

'Yes. Well done Jonathan,' said Clive.

'Funny. He's not a bad guy to talk to on the phone but you can tell from his voice he sure as hell isn't a biker.'

'No,' Clive smiled. 'Somehow I can't imagine Jonathan on a bike. Oh, Gerontius! I wish we were setting off right now! Today!'

Glenda sensed Clive's impatience to be off. 'First,' she said, 'I intend to have a hot bath and a good meal and a decent night's sleep. Where are we staying tomorrow night?'

'With friends,' Gerontius said. 'With friends.'

'Oh.' Glenda did not like to ask if they had showers or four-star gourmet kitchens.

Dinner was a tortuous affair for Glenda. She had never seen Gerontius in a plush setting, nor did she wish to ever again. Tex had little to say. He pushed amazing amounts of food into his mouth, washing down what was left after some hard masticating with loud gulps of beer. Gerontius, too, enjoyed his food very audibly. A volley of grunts and burps announced his pleasure in ordering and his anticipation of eating. A series of cushion-ripping farts heralded the fact that he had not only eaten his food but was now well into the process of digesting it. 'It's polite to burp in China,' he explained, catching Glenda's eye.

'Is it?' she said, trying to relax. The tables around them were noticeably empty. The waiters hovered cautiously. They had been told that Clive was a noble lord from England and they must put up with his eccentricities and those of his friends. After all, the British Royal Family were dearly loved in America. All the manager could do was to retire to his back room and pray that they were not staying long.

Later that night, after packing Gerontius off with Tex supporting his now very drunk friend, Glenda was in the bedroom,
sitting on her bed, cutting off the labels of her new clothes.
Married to Clive, she felt less guilty spending the money that
was now rightfully shared. Before she had tried to contribute
what little she could from her salary, but now, her job gone,
she had a new job, and that was making Clive happy. After
a long refreshing bath, she lay beside him in the comfortable
king-size bed. That was what she loved about America: the
sheer comfort which the American people demanded and
got — a big bathtub and piles of clean, feathery towels,
complimentary bottles of shampoo and conditioner, and little
kits of this and that to make travellers welcome. Clive, nearly
asleep, pulled her close to his warm body. 'I'm tired, darling,'
he said, 'from last night on the plane. Mind if I go to sleep?'

'No, not at all.' Glenda lay quietly in his dreaming arms.
I don't mind, she told herself. But she knew she did mind.
She very much minded. This was her honeymoon, and yet
again she lay beside the man she loved, sterile with desire.

Finally she slept.

Chapter 112

Breakfast was hurried. Gerontius would be coming by the
hotel at eight o'clock to lead them off. Glenda sat up and
surveyed the hotel bedroom. 'Clive,' she said, 'is this my
last bath for a very long time?'

Clive grunted. He was in the bathroom brushing his teeth.
'Come on, Glenda.' He walked out of the room, a towel
around his waist. 'Don't fuss. It's an adventure, and you can
spoil an adventure if you keep picking away at it like a wart.
Of course there'll be bathrooms. Anyway, Gerontius says
most bus stations have perfectly good washrooms.'

'Oh goody,' Glenda said wryly. She ran the bath deep and
full. Here I am, she thought, with my beloved but impotent

husband embarking on a nightmare journey across America. She stared at her toes. Maybe once we get away and Clive feels happy, something might happen and we'll be able to make love.

She almost regretted her lovemaking with Amerjit. Before Amerjit, she knew feelings of lust and desire, but they were diffuse. Now, since her body had shared space and time with another willing body, she felt the sadness and loss of that communion.

She pulled on her new jeans. In her pack she carried an anorak, sweatshirts, two long T-shirts for sleeping in, and some socks. On her feet she had a flashy pair of American sneakers. *Sneakers*. She smiled. New words, she thought. All the time, new words. She looked at her London clothes lying forlornly on the bed. 'What shall we do with our going-home clothes?'

'Throw them away,' Clive said. 'We might never go home.' He seemed in such a happy mood, Glenda decided to put aside her troubles and her tremulous moans and just relax. 'The bike is burning a hole downstairs waiting to go. Do you really have to have breakfast? We can stop later on the highway.'

'Clive, Gerontius isn't due for another half hour. I'll order some coffee and bacon and eggs. You need to eat, you know. This is a long trip.'

Glenda dawdled over her coffee appreciating the smell and the density of the liquid. Her orange juice was freshly squeezed and the crisp bacon lay beautifully against the golden stomach of the egg. I shall miss this comfort, she thought.

Clive, toying impatiently with his egg, looked across the table. 'Don't worry, darling,' he said. 'After the first few days, you'll get the hang of it. You'll love it. Promise.'

'I hope so.' Glenda finished her coffee.

'Let's go downstairs and grab Gerontius before he scandalizes the hotel again.'

'Ready when you are.'

Clive slipped his backpack onto his shoulders and handed Glenda hers.

Gerontius was waiting quietly in a chair in the foyer. His eyes were enthusiastic. 'Nothing like it, man,' he said punching Clive on the arm. 'We're out of here.'

Clive paid the bill at the front desk, straightened his shoulders, and took Glenda's hand. 'Here we go.'

They walked through the front door into the early morning, hazy, wavering Los Angeles sunshine. The bike parked in the car-park did not seem so large this morning. Clive turned the key, and pressed the starter button. The motorcycle roared. 'Man, this Hog was born to be a tiger.'

Tex pulled his black motorcycle up next to the red bike. 'We're gotta get my old lady, and then we'll cruise up Highway Number One to Frisco. We should be there in time to spend the night in my home.'

Glenda felt immediate relief. At least they would have a roof over their heads. She crouched against Clive and they took off.

Gerontius led the way, weaving through traffic. Clive followed. Glenda could feel he was nervous. His back was stiff and his body did not curve as it usually did. The bike was new and he had to concentrate on the American road signs. 'See that I stay on the right side of the road,' he shouted at Glenda. She held her hand up in a thumbs-up signal and squeezed his waist.

They rode for half an hour until they came to the northern outskirts of the city. In a relatively poor area, they drew to a halt outside a small, blue, frame house. 'You coming, Mama?' Tex called out to the open door.

His old lady has a very large bike, Glenda observed.

She loomed out of the door, carrying a big bundle wrapped in a red checked tablecloth. 'Well, you're not riding with that thing flapping around behind you, are you?' Tex complained.

494

'I sure am.' Tex's old lady grinned at Glenda. 'We two going to ride together.' She squeezed Glenda's hand. Glenda looked into her black face. The eyes were big and round and her hair was driftwood white.

'Glad to meet you,' Glenda said with a genuine smile.

'Don't worry. I've ridden with these guys for many years. They'll do as they're told.'

Tex waited for Mama to straddle her bike and the engine to roll. Gerontius gunned his bike and the convoy took off.

'Where are we heading for first?' Glenda screamed in Clive's ear.

'Big Sur.'

Glenda sat back.

In open stretches they streamed four bikes abreast down the freeway. The early morning traffic trundling in and out of LA was enormous, a vast constipation of cars and trucks. The four bikes looped and wheeled and squealed around the slower cars. Tex whooped and yelled with glee. Gerontius howled his poetry into the wind, and Big Mama urged everyone on.

Glenda found herself letting out a few quiet whoops of her own. 'Gets to you, doesn't it?' Clive said as they finished the freeway and began to cut up into the road that would bring them to the bright Pacific Ocean. Gulls flew overhead. The wind was warm and the air smelled of salt and palm trees. Hibiscus bloomed beside bougainvillea in riotous colour. Glenda could see why Jack Kerouac would have loved these roads. She watched men walking on the beaches. Tall, golden men with surfboards under their arms and crowds of young girls perched on the edge of the ocean waiting for their boyfriends to come hurling in on the waves. Tucked inside the waves boys balanced on their boards with grace. It took her breath away.

The road ran parallel to the beach and the motor cycles began to climb. The beach fell below as the road raised itself over the shoulders of rocks and passes. They climbed twisting roads and they dipped along the cliffs over the sea until the sun stood high over their heads.

They came to San Francisco. 'The Golden Gate Bridge!' she screamed in Clive's ear. He laughed aloud as they kicked their machines across the beautiful bridge toward the city that shone in the pink light of the setting sun.

They followed Tex who ran them through the centre of San Francisco's downtown traffic. Glenda laughed up and down the rollercoaster roads. They crossed the tracks of the clanging trollies. San Francisco sang with life, not the lightning crackling of electric New York, but the healthy joyousness of a Pacific song. Zoom!

Glenda realized she was tired. Her back ached and her neck was stiff. She was glad when they came to a side road covered with shady trees. They pulled into a yard, square and tidy, next to a frame house with shutters. 'Here we are,' Tex said. '*Mia casa*. Welcome.' He parked his bike and stretched.

Everyone bent to touch their toes and stretched to snap out their backs. 'My poor little buns,' Gerontius groaned, clutching his bottom. 'Both asleep.' He slapped himself loudly with both hands. 'Wake up, back there! What I need is a long cold drink of beer.'

'Knew you were coming, man. Fridge is all stocked. Mama gets my room. Clive, you and Glenda take the guest room. Gerontius and me can stay in the living room.'

Glenda was relieved to see that the guest bedroom lived up to its name. It was clean and neat and thank goodness had its own little bathroom tucked up under the porch. Mama was fussing about in the kitchen when Glenda came out. Night was fast falling over the city. Glenda called, 'I'll give you a hand in a minute, Mama. I just want to go outside and take a look.'

Clive was standing outside the front door. She walked up beside him and he put his arm around her. He pulled her to him and kissed her gently. They stood looking at the stars that were beginning to emerge in the blanket of the night. 'I feel free, Glenda.' Clive talked softly. 'For the first time in my life I feel as I am, really me.' He tightened his arm around her waist. 'There's just the two of us and our friends and nobody else knows where we are. Isn't it wonderful?'

Glenda kissed his lips.

He said, 'You've been very patient with me. It won't be long. I promise you.'

They stood silently for a moment until Glenda disengaged her arm and said, 'I'd better go in and help Mama.' She sniffed her way into the kitchen.

When they were all sitting down to the evening meal Glenda felt a sense of peace settle over her body. Clive was right. No one knew where they were, not even Minnie. It was a strange but light-hearted feeling.

In bed, one with an old wooden headboard, she reached out for Clive. He, eyes still alight with the day's journey, reached for her also. They laughed as they bumped heads. Clive pulled Glenda to him and he began to kiss her with an urgency she had never known in him before. She melted into his body and he ran his lips over her breasts and under her arms. Go on, she prayed but not out loud.

She felt him attempting to enter her and she widened her hips to accommodate him. He slipped inside her and began to rock. She could tell he was nervous, for his movements were tense and ungraceful. He kissed her, but their teeth clicked together. She reached up and held his face between her hands. 'Sshh,' she said. 'It's all right.'

'Sorry.' Clive gave a self-conscious little laugh. 'I'm afraid of hurting you.' He stopped moving his hips.

'You won't,' she said, her voice reassuring and encouraging.

'Yes, but I've heard a woman's first time is painful.'

She hated having to lie to him, but she had no choice.

'Look. You're inside me already, and there's no pain. It feels wonderful.'

'Really? I'm not tearing you, or making you bleed, or anything nasty?' He reached down between their legs. When he pulled his hand back up, there was no blood on his fingers.

I can't tell him, Glenda thought. I'll never tell him. 'I guess,' she said, 'not all women bleed their first time. Some just don't.'

Clive smiled at her, his face above hers. 'Really no pain?'

Glenda smiled back. 'Pleasure,' she said.

'In that case . . . ' Clive began to rock again.

But Glenda sensed that his tension had not left him. His mouth was still tight, his back rigid. Then she felt his penis inside her begin to slacken. Of course he's anxious, she told herself. She didn't want to say anything to make him retreat back to the fear that had kept him from her so long, but she did want to help him. 'Clive,' she said gently.

'Hm?' He stopped, but remained inside her.

'Clive, don't worry so much. Don't even think about what you're doing or what movements you're making. Just relax. Let it flow. Here,' she said. She held his head with her hands. 'Start by kissing me. Let the rest of you be still. Just kiss me. Softly.'

His mouth touched hers and she kissed him with little kisses until she felt his lips relax. He began to respond. She heard his breathing quicken. He kissed her lips harder. Suddenly his hips tightened again. 'No rush,' she said. 'No need. Gently. Like playing the piano. A lovely piece of music.' She kissed him. 'No hurry.' Her tongue moistened his lips. 'Let the notes follow each other naturally.' His mouth returned her kiss. '*Adagio*,' she said between kisses.

'*Piano e dolce*,' he replied, catching on, the corners of his kissing mouth rising in a happy smile. 'Soft and sweet.'

'Yes,' she laughed lightly, feeling her own body genuinely respond. 'It's the slow movement we're playing. All the time in the universe.' Her own hips started to rock beneath him.

Clive let out a gasp as her movements stroked him and filled him with electric sensation. '*Crescendo*,' he whispered in her ear, his hands moving lightly over her skin.

'Beautiful,' she said honestly. He was sensitive now, growing confident. He expressed the same grace that she had heard in his music for years. Their bodies moved together in concert.

'That was the most remarkable experience I've ever had,' Clive said, lying back against his pillow with his arm around her. Entirely satisfied herself, Glenda rested her cheek against his chest. 'I found myself thinking the most amazing things.'

'Like what?'

'Like . . . Oh, let's see. Sounds silly, but I thought of Mozart's *Sinfonia Concertante*. Second movement. The slow movement, as you say. I mean I actually *heard* the music in my head. Pure heavenly beauty. I heard the violin and the viola playing together, and it was like listening to the two of us. Two sympathetic instruments rolling and turning in closely held harmony, soaring together through a cosmos of sound and colour and pleasure and beauty and . . . I saw lights, Glenda. I actually saw beautiful white lights.' He laughed and she could hear his usual tone of shy self-mockery slip into his laughter. 'But you'll think I'm talking nonsense. I'm talking much too much, at any rate. It's just that it's an incredible experience and really I never even imagined that anything could . . . '

'Clive,' said Glenda, turning her face up towards his and kissing him on the mouth. 'I love you very much.'

He hugged her with all the love that was in him. 'You're amazing, Glenda,' he said. 'Utterly miraculous. And the way your body moves . . . A true miracle. If I didn't know better, I'd swear you'd done this before.' He spoke with unblemished innocence, without trace of edge or suspicion.

Glenda said nothing, but kissed his neck, and rested her cheek against his chest. She would keep her secret forever.

When she heard his breathing expand into soft snores, she

499

propped herself on her arm and watched him. He was so gentle and trusting in his sleep and a smile still rested on his lips. She did love her husband very much. This time spent away from the rest of the world would be their eternal honeymoon.

Chapter 113

As the days passed, Glenda realized that the farther they drew away from civilization, the more Clive left behind his old self, the tortured and twisted self. He began to shine anew. His shoulders were broader. With all the food cooked on the camp sites, he ate hungrily each night. Both of them now were brown and tanned. Glenda no longer fussed about being clean. Many nights there was not enough water to bathe, but she learned to like the slightly sharp smell of her own sweat. She always cleaned her teeth and she learned to wear her clothes dirty and dusty from the day before. Her fingernails were chipped from collecting wood and washing clothes, when they had enough water to fill their washing bucket. 'I never imagined that some day the most important thing in life would be a washing bucket,' she laughed one day in the early morning sunlight outside their camp of tents. Clive laughed with her. Indeed, she seemed happiest when life was this simple.

Clive kissed her. In her warm and secret place she could feel last night, another night of lovemaking. She remembered the welcome sigh they both gave as they slipped into the exterior moment of black ecstasy shot through with silver light. Explosions, Clive had called them. 'They've been a long time coming,' he had said into her ear, 'but well worth the wait.'

Salt Lake City far behind them, they were in the Rocky Mountains, the guardian mountains that lay like a continent-sized dragon protecting California from its Eastern neighbours. The mornings were now cool and the mist on Glenda's face washed it better than any face cream could.

Near Denver they rolled into the house of a friend of Gerontius who said sure, they could stay for the night, they could stay for as long as they wanted, man. It was a beautiful mountain house with redwood decks and big glass picture windows all around looking out onto the surrealistic beauty of stony mountain peaks stretching up impossibly high into the sky. Tex and Gerontius grabbed some beers from the fridge and lay out on a sundeck watching the clouds float past. Mama made herself right at home in the kitchen, and what pleased Glenda most of all was the hot tub. Carrying a bottle of champagne and two glasses, Clive joined Glenda in the tub. They kissed and then caressed.

Clive plunged into her and he fell as Icarus fell from the sun. As he fell he called Glenda's name and when he opened his eyes he lay close in her arms, his head on her wet, warm shoulder.

'Hmmm,' Glenda said. 'That was huge.'

'Ungh,' Clive grunted, too tired and too content to move yet. 'We must buy a hot tub when we get home,' he said in a quiet voice when he had caught his breath. 'We really must.'

Glenda reached over and poured the champagne. 'Here,' she said, 'let's drink to American bathrooms and hot tubs and showers and making love in all of them.'

Clive lifted his glass.

They drank more champagne until, groggy, they made their way back to the big king-sized bed. They lay side by side, holding hands. He stared at the ceiling. 'Glenda,' he said. 'Do you . . . ? Well, do you use anything, you know, I mean, so that you don't get pregnant?'

She shook her head. 'I meant to tell you, but everything happened so fast. I mean, we rushed off and got married within a few days, and I didn't really have any time to get anything organized.' She ran a finger around the features of his face. 'Anyway, I don't really mind if I get pregnant. Do you?'

'Um. Only because I've been told that I mustn't have a child in case –'

'In case *what*, Clive? You've been perfectly all right while we've been away from England.'

'Yes, I know.' There was a long familiar Clive-silence. Glenda had learned over the years not to push him. It was hard sometimes when she was used to Minnie's quick talk and the intimacy of their in-depth conversations. And for all that Clive could be sensitive and insightful, there were other moments when he grew quickly taciturn and uncommunicative. She felt she needed to wait for him to put out his tentative head like a tortoise.

'I know we . . . Well, it's not *we*.' Clive began after a pause. 'It's *me* really. I don't talk much about my feelings, but since we've been on the road I feel so different. I can talk and I can make jokes. They don't think I'm a failure or sick or anything. To them I'm just Clive. I don't even take pills any more. I threw them away.' He gave Glenda a guilty smile. 'Is that bad of me?'

'No, it isn't bad of you – it's your life and you decide what you want to do. Anyway, I never did think you needed pills. You seem so much better without them. You need to learn how to talk. That's all.'

'Yes. I did try when I was smaller. Believe it or not, father used to try. He tried taking me for walks, but we had nothing to say to each other. I tried talking about the breeding seasons, but my father isn't interested. So we would walk up and down the grounds, with him hurrumphing and me trailing miserably by his side. Caspar was so much more the son he wanted. But then, of course, there was my mother.' He shivered and Glenda pulled the blankets up around his naked body. '*She* talked. How that woman could talk! She wanted me to be a girl. The sister and the best friend she never had. She nearly talked me to death. I had to go everywhere with her, with Nanny trotting behind, so if I did anything unpleasant she would hand me over like a parcel.

'I remember one day I told her to get out of my bathroom, that I was far too old for her to try and get into my bath. And she backed out. I frightened her, because I was screaming at her. From then it was open warfare between us. I had defied her, I had told her a truth that she did not want to hear. I was my own person and not part of her court.' Clive was breathing heavily.

Glenda watched him. No wonder he had fits, she thought. All that pain and anger filed away in neat boxes, now slowly erupting. Well, let it erupt, she said to herself. If he can get it out, his brain won't have to short-circuit itself trying to hold the awful memories down. She imagined Lady Jane in the early days when Clive was a vulnerable boy just reaching adolescence. She remembered Jane's countenance when she turned her greedy, lustful eyes onto her sons. There was no forbidden territory in Jane's life – not even her sons. No act of terrorism, whether it was emotional or sexual, that she did not allow herself. After all, she was Lady Jane Alexander, and the Alexanders and their ilk had always been above the law.

Clive pulled Glenda to him and held her tight. 'I feel so clean and so light,' he said. 'I feel wonderful.'

'Let's do it agin,' Glenda whispered, feeling him rise.

'For you,' Clive said, 'any time.' And his voice faded away.

Chapter 114

They zoomed south, racing through Los Alamos, New Mexico as fast as they could, lest they pick up nuclear contamination which Gerontius assured them leaked from every doorway and window in any building even remotely connected with the government. From the Jemez Mountains they headed to the Sangre de Cristo range, the high blue guardians of Santa

Fe which sat right at the meeting place of red-soiled, pine tree covered mountains and high, dry, sagebrush dusty desert.

It was a clear, spectacular magenta sunset evening when they reached the camp site. The red earth glowed rose. They got off their bikes and bow-leggedly made their way to the little store where they registered themselves for the night. The camp site owner, an ex-biker himself, pulled out free beers for everyone. Glenda sat with her feet on the barstool, eating a bag of sour cream and onion flavoured potato chips. She was tanned and healthy. 'We have a bathroom block and with good hot showers,' the man grinned at them all. 'Get you feeling clean and new in no time. And we have fresh pizza delivered every day. You finish your beers and I'll be along with some pizza.'

Mama shared a happy exchange of glances with Glenda: they would not have to cook that night. Her old face was still lined, but the ride had eased the lines out. 'My,' she said, 'I'm having fun. Come along, girl. Let's get some clean clothes and wash our bodies. I stink worse than a skunk.'

Glenda ambled out behind her. She took her wash bag out of their travelling backpacks. The hot water gushed down Glenda's body. She ran her flannel up and down her body and under her breasts. She washed her buttocks, still sore and aching from the motorcycle seat. She washed between her legs, enjoying the erotic friction of the rough flannel and the heat of the soapy water. 'Your Clive is really coming along,' she heard Mama's voice come from over the partition between the shower stalls.

'Yes. He's wanted to do this ride for so long, and we were both a bit nervous at first.' The words escaped from the water and the steam and hung loudly in the air. They were alone in the showers.

'He sure is putting on weight, Glenda.'

'That's your good cooking. And the riding gives him an appetite. Normally he doesn't eat much. When I get home I'll make sure we eat plenty of beans and chilli. That will keep his weight up.' Glenda turned the water off and put a towel around her body. 'Anyway, food's not really his problem, Mama.'

She wondered why hot water brought out this need to confess. So far she had kept her secret from Mama, much as she liked this big, warm woman. Her problems with Clive had been hers alone. Now maybe this far away from England it is safe to ask or to tell a woman so much older and so much wiser than herself.

'He has fits, Mama. I don't mean epileptic fits. They tested him for that and for a hundred other things. They can't find anything wrong with him neurologically, but they say he isn't normal mentally, and they keep him on pills, though he hasn't been taking them during this trip, and he seems fine to me. Better, in fact. Just before we left . . . Well, we sort of ran away. Got married and then ran away. He had a kind of fit while I was in New York. I found him in a mental hospital when I got back. His doctor had given him ECT.' The memory of the ordeal made her eyes fill with tears.

Mama turned off her shower and put a hand over the stall and clutched Glenda's shoulder. 'The bastards,' she said. 'The stinking bastards. I'd have cut the doctor's throat.' Mama struggled with an old multi-coloured kimono tied ineffectively around her bulky body. She shambled out of her stall and stood in front of Glenda, shaking her fist. 'Don't you *ever* let them do that to him again.'

'I won't,' Glenda promised.

'What's Clive's problem anyway?' Mama asked when they had finished showering and were walking outside.

'His mother,' Glenda answered. 'That's all. His mother. You wouldn't think it was a problem, but it is.' She sighed and said, 'We do have to go back. We can't always live like this.' She gestured at the trees and the little clean camp sites, at the motorcycles sitting obediently in front of the shop.

Through the window she saw the men talking furiously about their bikes, about the roads they had ridden. Hands slapping, heads nodding, wiping puffs of beer foam off their whiskers.

'Then, honey, you got to do something to that lady.'

'I know, but what? Lady Jane Alexander is very powerful and . . . ' Glenda watched a bat swoop low to catch a gnat. 'See that bat? She's evil, just like that. Do you know what I mean, that some people can be truly evil, so evil that you believe there's nothing that was ever good in them?'

'Sure,' Mama said. 'I've known plenty of evil men in my time. But evil women . . . That's a whole new subject. Women who can't love are like black widow spiders. They sting you to death.'

'That's Jane, all right.'

Mama said, 'You protect your man. You're much stronger than you think you are. You can do it.'

'I hope so,' said Glenda. 'I do love him.' The hope rose on the night air and fulfilled itself with a soft kiss on Clive's entranced cheek.

Chapter 115

Santa Fe was a wild place. Low adobe buildings squatted around a grass square in the centre of town. In the clear, pure air the deep indigo mountains could be seen rising up behind the pink-brown earth buildings. Next to the Palace of the Governors, Indians sat, their backs against the pale adobe wall, selling turquoise and silver belt buckles and bracelets. The air smelled of spicy Hispanic cooking. Clive and Glenda hardly felt that they were in America at all, but in some distant country in a high, mountainous continent of its own.

They had lunch in an outdoor cafe across the street from the colonial-style public library. They sat and watched the people walk by, people of all sorts, for Santa Fe was a centre, a meeting place, a town that had a varied home-grown life and attracted far-outs from every place else. Cowboys sauntered along with hats and boots and big wide belts. Hippy couples strolled past with hands intimately tucked into each other's back pockets. The friends sat at their table and felt a buzz, felt connected to it all, because this was in, this was the scene, and they were part of the heart of it.

Gerontius got friendly with the cafe waitress, and, during her coffee break, he went off with her into the library across the street to peruse with her among the back stacks. Glenda watched it all. She thought the waitress looked like a nice young kid, and she knew that Gerontius would view the episode as an experience, a happening, an afternoon's encounter with no strings attached. When Gerontius returned to the table a half hour later and sat his bulky self down with a satisfied grin and slapped the waitress's bottom while she went off to refill their coffee cups, Glenda found herself fighting an involuntary sense of disappointment. They were all supposed to be free, but somehow this didn't look cool at all.

They hung out around the plaza for the rest of the afternoon and ended up having dinner in a health food restaurant off Galisteo Street. While they munched their way through bean sprouts, alfalfa sprouts, white rice, tofu, and soy sauce, Gerontius made eye contact with a female diner across the restaurant. He excused himself from the table, 'for some fresh air,' he said. And he walked to the side door which led to an alley. The young woman across the room walked out after him.

Glenda was surprised. Tex and Clive were lost in conversation, planning a day's ride up to the nearby town of Taos. Glenda whispered to Mama. 'I didn't know Gerontius was like that.'

'Listen, sweetie. Tex and Gerontius may be friends of mine, but they sure as hell don't know how to treat women. I've known them both for a long time.' She paused. 'Men have it made in the shade these days,' she said, leaning forward. 'They just take what they want and then they split.

But your guy's different. You've got a good man in Clive.'
She smiled at Glenda. 'He's straight and true. Don't you let
him go.'

Glenda sat back in her chair and waited for Gerontius to
re-emerge through the side door.

'Nice chick,' Gerontius said, swinging his huge thigh over
his bike as they made ready to head back to the camp site for
the night. 'Hope to pass by another time!' he called out. The
girl waved but Glenda saw a look of disillusionment in her
eyes.

'Santa Fe, land of Fanta Se,' Gerontius sang as they
swooped out of town and into the cool, black night.

Suddenly Glenda felt safe and happy to be sitting on Clive's
bike. She hugged his torso and leaned her head against his
back. Their life together was simple. If only she and he could
ride forever towards the huge Sangre de Cristo mountains.
The bike flew and they flew with it. She never wanted this
moment to stop.

Chapter 116

'I am *not* staying another night in Madrid. This is an awful
place. I'm tired of Gerontius's women. I don't intend to live
in an abandoned miner's shack, nor will I eat any more hippy
food. I didn't leave Hounslow to end up with a bunch of us
living like derelicts, playing destitute, chanting silly words,
and pretending to love the world. I hate this place. I hate
these people. And I've come to believe that Jack Kerouac was
a psychopath with a loony mother.'

Clive stood in the dusty murk of a falling-down house.
They had spent weeks living in the New Mexico town of
Madrid to the southeast of Santa Fe. Once a coal-mining
centre along the Turquoise Trail, Madrid had stood for years
as a ghost town, until some members of the new American
counterculture had decided that living in the old, condemned,

ramshackle buildings was about the funkiest thing they could imagine. Gerontius had taken up with a girl who lived in Madrid and, feeling right at home there, he had persuaded his fellow motorcycle travellers to move in with him.

Receiving the weight of Glenda's wrath, Clive looked at his wife, who was shaking with anger. For a moment he felt afraid of her and then he smiled. 'You know,' he said, 'maybe you're right. I'm rather tired of all this camping and hanging about myself. What do you want to do?'

'Run away,' Glenda said firmly. 'Book a luxurious suite at the La Fonda Hotel in Santa Fe, and spend our last weekend in America in comfort.'

Clive grinned as if wickedly. 'What a fabulous idea. Let's say goodbye and we'll split.'

Mama was reassuring. 'Goodbye, honey,' she said, squeezing Glenda until she thought her bones would burst. 'You take care of yourself and the guy.'

'I will. And I'll miss you, Mama.'

'Life moves on,' Mama replied.

Glenda realized that for Mama life did move on. There were no deep relationships that could tie her down to any particular place. Mama lived very much for the moment, and a few weeks from now even this journey, which meant so much to Glenda, would be just a happy memory for Mama. A pleasant trip among many.

Tex shook Glenda's hand. He too was ready to race down the road back to LA. Only Gerontius seemed genuinely grieved to see them go. 'I already miss you, man,' he said, bear-hugging Clive. 'Take care of her,' he said, waving an embarrassed paw at Glenda.

'Goes without saying,' said Clive, escorting Glenda out of the beaten-up house.

They climbed onto their bike and took off, past the seedy houses and dirty roads, and away into the immense, clean countryside. New Mexico *is* beautiful, Glenda thought. But it would be better off if they left New Mexico to the New Mexicans and got rid of all the boring hippies.

The bike hummed on its last ride. 'What will you do with the Hog?' Glenda screamed into Clive's ear.

'I'm going to find an old cowboy on the Plaza and hand it over to him.'

Glenda grinned, not really believing him.

They parked outside the La Fonda hotel, right on the Plaza in the centre of town. After Clive negotiated a comfortable suite and booked dinner in the dining room, they went out. Clive approached a man sitting on a bench with a bottle of Jack Daniels. 'Can you ride a Harley?' Clive asked.

'Sure as shit,' the man said. 'I can ride anything. Been a lot of things in my time.' The man was garrulous. Years of whiskey strained his voice.

'Well then.' Clive put the key to the motorcycle in his hand. 'See that red bike over there?' The man followed Clive's finger and his eyes widened. 'It's yours. We've got to go back to England and the bike needs an owner. The papers are under the seat. I hope it gives you a lot of happiness.'

'I'll be darned,' he said. 'You sure, mister?'

'Very sure.'

Clive took Glenda's hand and they walked back to the hotel. Glenda saw the man standing over the bike, his fingers tentatively touching the big black leather seat. 'Goodbye, Hog,' she said.

'Sweet old Hog,' Clive echoed.

Later that night, as they lay in the comfortable king-sized bed, Glenda laughed. 'Making love,' she said, 'is much better after a hot bath and an excellent meal, don't you think?'

'Hmm.' Clive pulled her close. 'Listen, I've been thinking about what you said. Yes, I know Jack Kerouac was a psychopath in many ways. Didn't show much conscience in his relationships either. But he was still a bloody good writer.'

Glenda hugged Clive. 'He was,' she said, 'and I enjoy

reading his books. But I've grown out of trying to live like one of his characters. I like our real life together. I loved the trip, but next time, can we do it in a comfortable car?'

'Hmm,' Clive mumbled, drowsily. 'Next time.'

BOOK FOUR

Chapter 117

The years rolled by. At the time of their marriage, Glenda had hoped for a more solidified lifestyle to emerge. Their life together did indeed take shape, but it was not necessarily the shape that Glenda would have wished for. Clive got on with working around Fen Farm, helping out Mark and Paul in whatever needed to be done. The bigger concerns, the matters of money and bookkeeping, he left to Glenda. In no time, Glenda found that she had a full-time job just administrating the farm and the lives of its staff and their families. About all that Glenda found herself looking forward to were the business meetings with Jonathan Montague in London when he acted as her business adviser in matters concerning the affairs of the farm.

And as for Lady Jane, she remained at once peripheral to their world yet omnipresent. She let Glenda and Clive get on with their lives to a certain extent, and even allowed them to miss a family Christmas or two. When Glenda and Clive were summoned to the Alexander house for special occasions, Lady Jane treated Glenda with a coldness, and was like a mighty Queen receiving into her court a not very impressive dignitary from a not terribly important country.

But every few months, whenever Clive started to feel secure in his life on Fen Farm, Lady Jane's car would suddenly appear in the drive and she would step out and knock on the door. Glenda always wished she could hide on such occasions. Jane would sit in the sitting room and be given a cup of tea and would look with patronizing disapproval on the world that Glenda and Clive were trying to create together. 'How's the sheep-rearing, Clive?' she would say. 'If that's what you're doing. Sheep, is it?' And she'd give her little cold laugh and sip her tea.

'He's doing an excellent job,' Glenda would put in on his behalf.

'Yes, no doubt he is,' Lady Jane would smile. 'This does seem to be about the right size for him to manage, doesn't it? Nothing too much. Clive, you really ought to come home more often and see how very well your brother Caspar's getting on. He's been overseeing training for the hounds, you know. Lovely pack, really. No one can wait for the next hunt. But, of course, that never was your interest, was it? Still, I suppose there's no harm in letting you stay on here with your sheep, or whatever.

'Still keeping your old Nanny with you, I see. Clive, you always were such a sentimental sort. But never mind. This place suits you all so well. Always was rather a sweet little farm. Shame if we'd ever have to sell it. But small farm freeholdings are no longer the thing they once were, are they?' And, rising from her seat to go, she'd smile with icy warmth and say, 'Do look after him, dear Glenda, and see that he takes his pills on schedule, won't you?' Returning from America, Clive had gone back on lithium, advised by Dr Umberto that it was the most sensible thing to do.

In any one of a thousand ways, Lady Jane saw to it that they never felt the farm to be their own. She kept them thinking that they were the voiceless tenants and she the mistress of their fate who, on a whim, could take everything from them. Their life together developed into a stasis. They were neither particularly trapped nor particularly free. The only thing that seemed inarguably permanent was a vague sense of insecurity. Glenda was not sure where her life had taken her.

After a visit from Lady Jane, Clive's face would be white and drained for days. Where was the man who raced about the Wild West on his red motorcycle? Where was the man who made love to Glenda with such gentle abandon? Not here, not here, not in the marshy dampness that hovered around Fen Farm.

In the years that had passed since the honeymoon in America, Clive had remained completely sane. Quiet and withdrawn, but sane. And for that Glenda was grateful. Nanny Jenkins was so old she spent most of her days sitting in an armchair in the library, wrapped in a soft blue cashmere blanket. Most evenings Clive sat beside her and they reminisced. Nanny lived mostly in the nursery which she had shared with Clive when he was a baby. Clive seemed to take comfort from his talks with Nanny. Her pale, translucent hand stroked his cheeks until he left her, still smiling, and Mark or Paul would come to carry her to her bedroom.

Every now and then, Clive and Glenda did make love, but not often. Glenda began to grow restless.

Glenda and Georgina were in the drawing room of the farm, drinking tea. Outside Jonathan and Clive stood on the October lawn talking. Sitting with Georgina in the splendid blaze of autumn, Glenda talked about their shared memories. 'So, Fatima says marriage to Majid makes no difference. He is still away a hell of a lot of the time, but she goes back and forth to Singapore. She's in Paris at the moment, isn't she?'

Georgina took out a letter from her handbag and smoothed it on her knee. 'Yes. And she suggests that we all ought to try to plan a get-together in Singapore this year.'

'Oh, I'd love that,' Glenda said, shaking her head as if discussing an idea too treasured to ever really happen. 'I could use the break. I wonder if Molly would come.'

'I'm sure she would. She's the most mobile of the lot of us. Two divorces behind her. I told her last time I saw her that one could be considered unfortunate, and two careless, but the third time round she'd better get it right.'

Glenda sipped her tea. 'I don't think Molly'll ever find a man who will spoil her like her father did. Most men don't want Jewish American Princesses for wives. I keep getting letters from her from all over the Caribbean. She certainly has cultivated cheque-book sex to an art form. She says she takes out her cheque book, picks up a pen and waits. Eventually a dive master at whatever resort she's at comes along, names a price, and then she takes him off and screws his brains out. I don't know, Georgina. Whatever happened to the good old days when it was men who treated women as sex objects?'

'Long gone, dear Soul. Long gone. Here we sit, two matronly women in our thirties, nattering about Molly's sex life.'

There was a silence. Neither woman wanted to mention the lacunae in the middle of their own beds. Georgina had left her four boys in the charge of their nanny in Dorset. She was trying to recapture some of the fun that she seemed to have left behind her so shortly after her wedding to Jonathan. She sighed. 'Life is surprisingly hard, Glenda. I know I have no right to moan. I have servants and a nanny. But still my days revolve around driving the kids to school and music lessons and rugger matches. We'll be going back to Boston full-time in a few years so that the boys can go to prep school and then on to the Ivy League. I don't know why it has to be an American Ivy League. They're not a patch on Cambridge. But Jonathan insists. I feel so restless. Jonathan is away such a lot.'

Glenda knew all about Jonathan's absences, but she said nothing. Recently Glenda had been meeting Jonathan in London for lunches more and more often and, occasionally, for dinner. The meetings went on with Clive's full knowledge: he was relieved that Glenda could manage things so well. The summer months demanded too much of his time to have to leave the farm for business appointments. Glenda showed a definite knack for the figures and the balance sheets, the projections and negotiations.

It was in fact under Jonathan's guidance that Glenda expanded her attention beyond the simple running of the farm.

Clive did have, after all, a seat on the board of the Alexander family's estate, including the varied holding companies and corporations and businesses. Though he never showed a personal interest in exercising his voting power as a member, he was quite pleased for Glenda to be his proxy. And as a present Clive used some of his assets to buy Glenda some stock of her own. In time, Glenda found her focus shifting from merely running the farm to playing a part in the bigger issues. Naturally Lady Jane did not welcome any of Glenda's involvement.

The major decision facing the Board of Directors of the Alexanders' holding company was whether or not to pull out of Hong Kong. Lady Jane Alexander, the principal shareholder, was against leaving Hong Kong. Lord Philip backed his wife, but weakly. Caspar tended to vote in a block with his parents. Jonathan, as friend and adviser to Clive and Glenda, was adamant that Clive's assets must be protected by the company's divesting itself of Hong Kong assets. 'If you stay you might lose everything,' Jonathan warned Glenda and Clive. 'You must get out and put your money instead either in Gibraltar or in an off-shore bank, perhaps in the Cayman Islands.'

Glenda felt she benefited greatly from the time she spent with Jonathan. He seemed so confident and sure. He inspired in her feelings of . . . She did not understand quite what she felt. Why must her heart beat faster whenever she saw Jonathan? It was not that she did not love Clive – she did and she always would. But why the desire to be with Jonathan? It was worse than desire. It was an awful ache. Why did she find reasons to telephone him at his office? Why did she make not strictly necessary trips to London and haunt friends' parties in case he was there? Just to watch his broad shoulders, or to see him bend over some other woman's face. Then, an emotion not unlike jealousy would jab home a red hot rod into her heart and she would move forward. 'Fancy meeting you here!' but his eyes would also acknowledge that together they were dancing a dangerous pavane.

In times of need, she tried summoning her memories of Amerjit's instruction. Be detached, she told herself. Meditate on keeping your course . . . Amerjit had said that his image would be by her side when she needed him, but he hid from her. She knew, without knowing, that Amerjit would let her go through this alone . . .

'I'll just check the stove, Georgina.'

Georgina walked into the big, pleasant, square kitchen behind Glenda. She watched Glenda, slim as ever, walk over to the aga and stir some pots. Glenda looked tired, Georgina thought. No, not tired, just faded. Her once bright chestnut hair was pulled back in a pony tail and her jersey hung large across her thin shoulders. 'How's your mother, Glenda?'

'Mum? Oh, she's fine.' A warm note came into her voice. 'The restaurant's thriving. She and Chinchilla have a ball. She got rid of her boyfriend, George Whatwashisname. Said she was too old to put up with a man in her life. She won't come out here until next summer. Says she'll be damned if she'll be found deep-frozen in a bed in this house. I'm used to the cold now. I really don't feel it. I just wrap myself up like an old bundle and wait for the spring. Here you are. Want to help carry some things to the table?'

'Mmmm. The lasagna looks great,' Jonathan beamed at her from across the table.

Glenda blushed. 'Thank you.'

'By the way,' Jonathan continued. 'I was just talking to Clive and he thinks you and I need to meet at least once a week up in London to keep our fingers on all the manoeuvring of the Board of Management. I've spoken to Lord Silver and he feels that if we don't keep moving Jane might manage to secure sufficient votes from the other members of the family to overrule yours and Clive's votes entirely. You too are a member of the board and hold stock in your own right. The man we have to watch is Clive's Uncle Caspar. He knows we should get out of Hong Kong now before anything disastrous happens in China, but he is easily swayed by Jane.'

A fine buzzing began in Clive's head. He sat looking strained. But he pulled himself back from the threatened abyss. 'I think lunch in London will do you the world of good, Glenda. You can see your mother and spare me those odious trips. I hate being off the farm.'

Glenda turned to Georgina. 'And you,' she said, 'can come and shop.'

'I'll pass, thanks.' Georgina laughed. 'I hardly ever shop any more. Don't really have the time. I stay home with the dogs and the horses and the boys. They are my life. I feel absolutely out of place in London. I feel like an old country bumpkin among all the women shooting about in their pin-striped suits. Gosh, I remember the times when only men carried briefcases. Now women do as well. It's all very confusing for a middle-aged lady like me.'

'Middle-aged indeed!' Glenda protested. 'You're only thirty-five.'

'Sometimes I feel a lot older,' Georgina said. 'Maybe I need reminding that I'm not dead yet. But I do like the idea of all four of us meeting up in Singapore. How about it, Jonathan? Just an innocent girls' junket to the exotic East?'

'It won't be that innocent with Molly around,' Jonathan grunted. 'She tried to get off with me at my own wedding.'

Georgina chuckled. 'I know. I bet her you wouldn't, but she said for the sake of the Souls' Club she had to try.'

Glenda's mental eyebrows went up. So, Molly tried . . . Glenda got rid of the idea very quickly. Maybe if the meetings in London go on too late, I'll have to stay up there for a night or two. Who knows? Maybe.

She led everyone from the table to the library for coffee and liqueurs. Glenda swirled the thick green crème de menthe in front of her. She could see Jonathan's immaculately shod feet stretched out before her. He was wearing blue argyle socks and the hems of his trousers bit his ankle. Glenda felt life flow in her veins.

That night she made love effortlessly to Clive. 'Did you enjoy that?' she said breathlessly.

Clive nodded. He looked at Glenda's shining face. 'I think time out from here would do you some good.'

Glenda lay on her back. She felt restive and alive and electric and . . . Oh, why must it all be so complicated? Tomorrow she would telephone Fatima and Molly and suggest a meeting in Singapore. Running away again, she told herself. But what's wrong with that? I haven't been away by myself – really away – since New York before we got married. And Clive's a lot steadier now. And it will keep me away from London and . . . Just some time with my friends in Singapore. That's what I need.

Yes, that seemed a good, virtuous plan.

Chapter 118

The four Souls made plans to be together in Singapore in February. In the weeks before the trip, Glenda got on with her daily farm life with Clive. Weekly, she had the adventure of travelling to London to meet with Jonathan.

Today, upstairs, she polished her nails, painted her toenails, and depilated her legs and underarms. Silly thing to do, she said to herself. Normally I'd let it grow all through the winter . . . Who the hell sees my legs except Clive anyway? And as for my underarms . . . A slight red spot burned in her cheeks.

She pulled on a soft tweed skirt and a suede blouse. Under the blouse and skirt she wore a black clean pair of silk camiknickers and a matching black lacy petticoat. She put her perfume in her handbag and leaned towards her mirror. 'I like the smell of "Femme".' She mouthed the words in the mirror and smiled at her delicately painted lips. Her eyes she outlined with eyeliner and finished off with a very pale purple shadow. Lunch in the Savoy's River Restaurant would be perfect.

Her hands were clenched on the wheel of her car and her throat tightened in anticipation. As she drove up the long motorway in the early morning of the new day, she remembered the red bike now somewhere in New Mexico. Occasionally she and Clive received a cryptic message from Gerontius, a card from Las Vegas or a note from Idaho. The man travelled. Clive's face did not light up with envy. Clive still played the piano but no longer the awful notes of the *diabolus in musica*. He seemed to live like a candle fluttering in the wind. And I . . . Glenda shifted gears. I live like a woman on the banks of some great river with only my hand immersed so I can feel the temperature but do nothing about sliding in and letting my body roll in the current.

She could think of moments of great joy with Clive when they were one . . . And even now there were still the quiet pleasures of their life together – books still to be read in the library, the fire in the grate, and Clive sitting in his chair, reading a score or playing the piano. The roses in summer around the big oak tree and the courtyard filled with herbs that let their perfume lie around her feet as she walked out into the grounds. She loved her daily walk around the kitchen garden with her basket and the deep sense of communion with this earth that now was as much hers as it was Clive's.

Nevertheless, life was a little listless for Glenda.

Glenda slowed down at a red light. Chiswick roundabout. Chiswick, where her mother lived. She herself was a different Glenda from the young woman who had sat in her mother's small cottage by the river and dreamed of her marriage to Clive. Now a svelte, immaculately dressed Glenda drove the rest of the way to the Savoy slowly and carefully.

She handed her keys to Fred the doorman and she smiled. 'Is Mr Montague here yet?' she asked.

Fred grinned broadly. 'He arrived ten minutes ago, and said to meet him in the American Bar for a drink before lunch.'

Glenda swept through the hotel's revolving doors, turned left, and made her way across the carpeted lobby to the stairs. She heard a wall of words, American voices interrupted by English tones.

She walked into the bar. The room hushed and a great many male eyes looked at this beautiful woman. She looked around for Jonathan. She spotted him and walked forward.

Jonathan stood up and smiled. 'Drink?'

'A large gin and tonic.' Glenda felt at home. Behind her a man left the bar and headed for a telephone booth. 'Lady Jane?' His hand gripped the telephone with excitement. 'She's lunching with Jonathan Montague at the Savoy.'

'Thank you, Nigel,' Jane's voice was cool. 'Do keep an eye on the darling girl. We wouldn't want her to get into any trouble, would we? Do remember that Glenda and Jonathan's wife are the best of friends.'

There was an innuendo in Jane's voice that made the back of Nigel's neck quiver. How many men had been in Jane's bed? he wondered. Nigel was old now and his hair silver, but he had been in the castle in past years. He had taken part in the games with the leather mask and the hoods. Whips on naked flesh. The thought of the welts made his tongue tingle. 'Can I see you again, Jane?' he whispered.

'It depends on your news, Nigel. If you have something really good to tell me, I might consider it. Just for old times' sake. You haven't forgotten my room in the tower, have you?'

'I'll never forget that room. Never, Jane.'

'And for the news you've given me already, the cheque is in the mail, as they say in America.'

'Thank you, Jane.' Nigel put down the telephone. I'll watch, he thought. You bet.

*

Lunch in the River Restaurant thrilled Glenda. She turned her head to see the other guests and counted herself to be fortunate sitting here looking out of the huge glass windows over the Thames. The handsome manager of the dining room held her chair for her and, when she was seated, arranged her napkin. From the cordial handshake the manager gave to Jonathan, Glenda realized that the man was fond of Jonathan and therefore of her as well. Jonathan bent his fair head over the menu and began to order. This was so unlike Clive, who was always hesitant and unable to make up his mind. Glenda relaxed. It was a change to be with a man who knew what he wanted. 'Smoked salmon?' he asked Glenda.

'Sounds perfect.'

'They do a very good lobster here. Very simple, but specially flown in.'

Glenda smiled.

Jonathan cleared his throat. Incredible smile she has, he thought. He ordered the food. And he ordered the wine without consulting the wine list. 'A bottle of Pouilly Fuissé, please,' he said. 'I'm afraid I always order the Fuissé. It's my favourite.'

'Don't apologize.' Glenda looked down at her hands and made a note to wear rubber gloves more. Her hands were rough from gardening.

'As you know, Glenda,' he began when the manager and waiters had moved away from the table, 'things in general have been going very well indeed. Clive has been solid and steady. The farm itself is now in the black, largely thanks to Clive's hard work and your administration. I think even Lord Philip Alexander is reconciled to the fact that his son can do the job properly. It's really Jane we have to watch. And the old man is so weak about Jane. She can bully him into almost anything.'

'Yes. She tries it on me, but she doesn't get anywhere. We stay away from her as much as we can but we do have to attend those damned awful shareholders' meetings where moribund members of the family show up and agree with her. They're terrified of change. Good heavens! These are people who helped found empires. But now that the empires are crumbling, they can't pull out. It's not British to leave a sinking ship, I suppose. Holding your nose and jumping into a sea full of sharks. That's what's going to happen over there in Hong Kong. At least that's what I think. The idea of capitalism can't be created overnight, throughout mainland China, I mean. At first, if change does come to China, it will be a free-for-all, everyone getting what they want for themselves. Then maybe things will settle down and we can go back in.'

'I say, Glenda!' Jonathan looked at her, astonished. 'You have been doing your homework.'

'You forget, Jonathan,' Glenda felt annoyed, 'I've got a perfectly good degree from Girton and so has your wife.'

'Yes, but you'd never guess Georgina went to university,' Jonathan said. 'No,' he continued, 'she's so wrapped up in the village and the boys, I hardly ever spend time with her. And then if I do, it's usually a long discussion about whether one of the boys should have polio shots, or whether we ought to donate even more money to propping up our near-derelict church.' He sighed. 'Seems ages since we were young.'

Glenda picked up her fork. 'A trip to Singapore will do Georgina the world of good. The trip Clive and I took to America changed my life, Jonathan. I didn't know there was anywhere in the world with skies as huge and as blue as New Mexico. What a fabulous place! We lived for those months from day to day. I couldn't do it now. I wouldn't want to. But it loosened my hold on life. Before I left for America, I felt so confused. The months after university were empty and dry. I felt Cambridge had been such a central part of my life, I would never get used to being without it. But I have.' She tasted the pink salmon and patted her lips with her napkin.

Jonathan looked across at Glenda. He so much wanted to take her by the hand, walk with her upstairs, and make love to her. It would not be the first time he had taken a woman upstairs. Women very rarely said no to Jonathan Montague. He loved them all. But he loved his wife . . . This was the first time he felt a twinge of anxiety. What was it about Glenda that made his hands tremble? It wasn't that she was more beautiful than Georgina, though Georgina had put on quite a lot of weight. Maybe it was that Jonathan recognized that he could talk to her as he would talk to a man. Most women had little to say. They read reviews of books and went to the theatre. The left-wingers pounded on about the government and the suffering of the poor and the homeless with little regard for the fact that they had just dined in one of the most exclusive hotels in England and that their lust was now being slaked on a bed in a suite, the price of which would keep a homeless family for several months. No, the left-wing women were boring. And the right-wingers moaned prettily in bed, but you couldn't tell how real any of it was. Jonathan usually gave his Tory mistresses an extra bottle of champagne before making love to them. With the others he just pleased himelf.

Glenda was different. 'I think,' he said, trying to keep his mind on matters in hand, 'we need to have a meeting with Lord Silver next week. We need to look at the shares you and Clive hold in Hong Kong. Could be time to think about divesting and, as I mentioned, maybe setting up something in the Cayman Islands with the capital.'

'Molly's been there. She says it's beautiful.'

Jonathan laughed. 'Yes, but we're not talking about sun-bathing or scuba-diving.' At some point Molly was on his list for a re-think. He grinned. 'Molly still up to her usual tricks?'

Glenda's hazel eyes beamed. 'Sometimes I think she's utterly incorrigible. She spends her holidays down in the Caribbean picking up "Banana Boys", as she calls them. I do hope she behaves herself in Singapore. But I'm afraid the sight of the beautiful Malay men might be much too much for her.'

'Or for you?' Jonathan's voice was probing.

'Oh, Jonathan. You know I'm the faithful type. So is Clive. We've never looked at anyone else, either of us. Anyway, who would want me with my hands all rough from gardening?'

I would. The words were there in the open, but unsaid.

Glenda quickly squeezed lemon over the remaining smoked salmon and put it in her mouth so as not to speak. Jonathan went on talking, but the words lay between the salt and the black pepper, pulsating.

They finished their meal and left the table. Jonathan's protective hand was on her arm as he led her out to the Strand entrance of the Savoy. Fred was there with her car door open. Jonathan regretted the final steps to the revolving door. He so much wanted to take a turn to the left and into the small lift, a quick journey up, and then post-prandial ecstasy . . . But it was not to be. Not today.

Glenda climbed into the car and drove out into the traffic of the Strand. She felt thrilled with herself. Already she had a mission to perform. I will review all the facts and the figures and study up on the Cayman Islands all week. Why should she not know as much about the business as Jonathan did? If Girton had taught her anything, it had given her the confidence to know that she could do whatever she liked.

She drove down the motorway with a sense of loss. She pushed her foot hard on the accelerator.

Chapter 119

'You know . . .' Glenda was sitting next to Chinchilla. Minnie was standing by the table clearing up the dishes. The three of them were the only ones in the restaurant. Glenda had finished her weekly meeting with Jonathan. In a fit of guilt a few weeks back, she had decided to make the weekly meetings safe by having dinner with her mother and Chinchilla afterwards. 'I was talking to Molly the other day and we ended up discussing the idea that in men's eyes women have a Fuckability Factor.'

Chinchilla's eyebrows went up. 'The things you young women talk about.' She grinned.

'Oh come on, Chinchilla,' Minnie said with a nudge. 'Remember us before we hit menopause?'

'I don't know about you, Minnie, but menopause hasn't held me back any. Go on about your theory, Glenda.'

'Well, if I walked into the Savoy, say, at the age of sixty with grey hair, even if I was immaculately dressed, the staff would acknowledge me of course, but I would be absolutely invisible to the men in the American Bar.'

'Right you are,' Minnie nodded. 'I know exactly what you mean. Not that I've reached that age yet, meself. But it's starting to 'appen. I can walk down Chiswick High Road and it's as if I don't exist. I go into Boots and, apart from Mona who knows me, the men buying things in the shop will actually push past me. It's frightening, I tell you. I feel as small as a speck of dust.'

'Well, I found myself feeling that way, so I went out and bought myself new shoes and some smart clothes and I found a hairdresser called Gary in Bolton Gardens. And now when I walk into the Savoy, men's eyes automatically turn.' Glenda paused and sipped her coffee. 'I've entered the Fuckability Zone.' She laughed. 'Molly never left it. Georgina's turned into a mother of four and a bit fat about the waist, might be heading for the periphery of the zone. I'm still in there, though, with a lot of artificial help.'

'I always dreaded the Big M,' Chinchilla said. 'All the horrific tales of hot flushes and night sweats.'

Minnie lit a cigarette and sat down. 'Nah,' she said. 'Wasn't like that. Not for me, anyways. Oh, I suppose some women have a dreadful time, but most of us don't. You only hear about the ones who do. After all, it's the women who have the menopause while the doctors, who are mostly men, make all the money. Nothing changes.'

Glenda sat at the table devoutly wishing she could be back with Jonathan. Clive was waiting for her at the farm, but she was safely in her mother's company.

They closed the restaurant and climbed into Glenda's Volvo. Chiswick High Road was a road she knew well. Not all that much had changed since Glenda was a child, except for a big refuge for battered wives up towards the Gunnersbury roundabout. The desperate women had painted *Battered Wives Need A Refuge* in big white letters on the wall in front of the house. So they do, Glenda thought as the car passed the front door, the light shining out into the dark night. A figure in shadow, with small children clinging to her knees, was just entering. Poor Mrs McCluskie, thought Glenda. Still so many women like her. 'Whatever happened to Mrs McCluskie, mum?'

'Now isn't it funny you should mention 'er!' Minnie said loudly. 'I heard about her only the other day. She's married to ever such a nice man, but two of her boys have gone to the bad. I take stuff into that refuge there from time to time. It's packed to the ceiling with mums and kids, but it's a very happy place. Shame, really.'

The car drove into the small garage beside Minnie's house near the river. They got out. Chinchilla was spending the night. Glenda stretched out on the sofa bed in the small sitting room. A last cup of coffee by her side, she put her head on her arm and looked at the ceiling. I haven't done anything, she thought. But why am I feeling so guilty?

Next week was Christmas. She had planned to have Christmas Day with Clive down here in London. Whenever possible, Glenda now made sure they were busy over family holidays. So sorry, Jane, she rehearsed in her mind. We can't possibly come over on Christmas Day. I promised my mother I'd be there. And then we simply must dash down to

Georgina's for the rest of Christmas. New Year's Eve? Perhaps, but I can't promise. As you know, I'm off to Singapore in February and there are so many plans to make. She imagined Jane's face, her cruel eyes glistening.

With Glenda firmly in control of Clive's life, Jane was finding it increasingly hard to rattle him. Even her threatening telephone calls seemed to leave him less moved. It's as though the bitch has mesmerized him, thought Jane. Glenda slept in Chiswick while in Cambridgeshire Jane drummed her fingernails. There would be little chance of her handing full control of all the family wealth to Caspar if Clive carried on like such a sane person. She would have to do something about that, have to tilt him over the edge, but Glenda was not making things easy for her. 'Nigel,' she said, waking the man up in his bed.

Nigel groped for the phone. 'Ummmm?' he said, not wishing his bed partner to hear Jane's name.

'Has that cow climbed into bed with Jonathan Montague?'

'No, not yet,' Nigel whispered down the telephone. 'At least, not as far as I know.'

'Well keep tailing her.'

'Right.'

'Who've you got there, Nigel?'

'Me? Oh, nobody you'd know.'

'Not your archbishop, I suppose.'

Nigel dropped the phone back on the hook. Bloody woman is clairvoyant, he thought as he watched the old man snoring by his side. Pillow talk, that's what he was doing. Pillow talking with a man old enough to be his father. Sometimes this job disgusted him, but not often. He must take Jane up on her offer. But first things first.

Chapter 120

Glenda studied hard and found that she was enjoying herself. Now along with *The Times* she read *The Financial Times* and *The Economist*. As she drew closer and closer to the world of high finance, she found herself getting bored with the few local contacts with her neighbours. Even discussions about the running of the farm seemed tedious. She did not want to know when to harvest or how many tons of hay they would put into the strong old barns. She was enchanted instead by the more abstract yet more substantial world of shares and assets. Numbers and percentages began to flash in her head and she very much enjoyed the light of admiration in Jonathan's eyes when she understood a particular point. 'My goodness!' he said more than once. 'You really are good.' The approval made Glenda glow.

Clive noticed the difference and teased her about her fascination with the books and newspapers. He also noticed her new, immaculate clothes, the brightness in her eyes, and the swing of her hips. 'Are you sure,' he one day asked anxiously, 'that you're happy down here?'

'Of course I'm sure,' Glenda smiled. Her double life suited her. All the fantasy and excitement of London and Jonathan she kept separate from the quiet, steady, loving farm.

I've done nothing wrong, she told herself as she left yet again to see Jonathan. Not to see *Jonathan*, she argued all the way up in the car. To do business and to save Clive time and worry.

A few days before Christmas, Glenda was making a list of things to pack for their trip down to Georgina's. By her side sat the Christmas presents. Two for Minnie and Chinchilla. She sat on her heels on the floor and was dreamily wondering if Jonathan would like her cashmere – not *her*, silly. The gift was from both Clive and herself. She had chosen it though, walking miles and miles around South Molton Street and down through Covent Garden, and finally finding the ultimate in a cashmere jersey. Pale cream with a V-neck. Jonathan wore his shirt collars inside his jerseys. She liked that about him. It made him look rich and dependable.

There was an awful wail from the library. It rose to a desperate scream. Glenda froze. She jumped to her feet and started running. The screams were agonizing and as she ran she prayed. *Dear God*, she pleaded, *not again*. She had not heard such sounds for a long, long time. She had forgotten that Clive could howl like that. Why had she forgotten? The memory was unbearable.

She turned the corner of the library before Mrs Robinson caught up with her. Clive was on his knees, his head in Nanny Jenkins's lap. Nanny was dead. Glenda was very sure of that. Nanny sat, her thin hands folded and her head bowed. She sat so still and so quietly that nothing moved in the library, not even the air. It was the absence of Nanny's frail breathing that was most frightening. Glenda knelt down beside Clive and touched him gently. 'Clive, it's all right.'

'She's dead.' Clive was quieter now. 'She's dead.' He lifted his head and looked into Glenda's face. 'I loved her, Glenda. And she loved me. And now she's gone.' Tears poured down his face and his eyes were hopeless.

Glenda took him by the shoulders. 'Come on,' she said. 'I'll take you upstairs.'

Clive flinched. 'I don't want to leave her yet. I need to talk to her.' He looked around the room. Mark and Paul and Milly were in the doorway and Mrs Robinson was standing in the room. 'Please leave me alone with her,' Clive begged. 'I just want to talk to her for a while.'

The staff left.

'Do you want me to stay?' said Glenda.

Clive shook his head. 'I must be by myself.'

Glenda left the room, her eyes full of tears. Nanny had been a benign influence in the house, a small rosy apple, who puttered and pottered and adored Clive. Still, Glenda reminded herself, he has me now and we will fight for what is ours together. She felt a pang of guilt for her double life, but then she picked up the list and uneasily continued with her notes.

Night-time fell and she went to the door of the library. Clive was still there. He sat in front of his Nanny, his hands clasped around his knees and he talked to her. Glenda could see he was recounting his childhood. And she stood helplessly as he cried, clutching the small motionless form in his arms. He stroked the dead woman's cheeks and he kissed her hands.

Finally Glenda went to bed.

Later she felt Clive crash into the bed beside her and he fell asleep.

The funeral was a quiet affair. Only the staff of the farm were invited. For once Clive was firm with his mother. 'No, thank you,' he said. 'There's really no need for you to come.'

Jane slammed the telephone down. Philip Alexander looked alarmed. 'What's the matter?' he said.

'Nanny's dead and Clive won't let me come to the funeral.'

'Why d'you want to go? She's only a servant.'

Jane looked at Philip through narrowed eyes. What a dolt the man was. What a boring, indecent dolt. She would welcome any event, any pretext, to invade Glenda and Clive. After all, Glenda was the only woman ever to argue with Jane and she wanted to know what gave the woman such backbone. It can't have been that common little tart of a mother of hers. Still, she had weekly telephone calls from Nigel and he had confirmed that Jonathan had a suite upstairs at the Savoy that he occasionally used for his trysts. It shouldn't be long before Glenda became a notch on his belt and Jane would have the information that would send Clive off the deep end forever.

She grinned and looked at her handsome, strapping,

younger son Caspar and imagined herself watching him take his seat in the House of Lords. As she walked past him, she ran her hand over his chest and bent down and kissed him.

Philip escorted her to the door. 'You're supposed to kiss *me* like that, not your son,' he protested.

'Wouldn't you just love it,' Jane grinned. She stepped elegantly out of the castle door into the waiting Rolls Royce.

For days after the funeral Clive was quiet. Glenda suspended her visits to London. She felt a thorn of disappointment, but Clive worried her. He appeared white and worn. She took him for walks during the day and at night they sat by the brightly flaming fire. She tried to interest him in a new litter of pigs. Usually Clive loved little piglets. 'What *is* it, Clive?' she finally said, a little tired of the mourning. 'Everybody has to die eventually. Nanny was ready to go, darling. Nobody can live for ever.'

'I don't know.' Clive watched the fire leap in the hearth. 'Nanny was the one person who never betrayed me. She was the only sure thing in my life. If Nanny hadn't been there all those years, I would be dead by now. I could trust her absolutely.'

'You can trust me absolutely.' Glenda felt wretched. 'You know that.'

'Yes. I do, Glenda.' He exhaled slowly. 'You are my last hope. Before I had you and Nanny – now there is just you.'

Glenda changed the subject. 'In a few days we'll be out of this place and down at Georgina's. You can do lots of riding with Jonathan, and Georgina and I can sit about and gossip.'

Clive smiled a wan, strained smile. 'I will try to cheer up, Glenda. Really I will.'

'The New Year will bring a good year for us, Clive. And we will resolve this thing with the Board of Management. We will get the Hong Kong interests safely sold and the money tucked away and working for us. It will give us something of our own, entirely clear of your family. And then you and I can relax.' Glenda stood up and walked towards the kitchen. 'I'm going to make you a super big pizza,' she said. 'That'll get your appetite back.'

Clive watched her go out of the room.

He has the eyes of a beaten puppy, she thought. She rolled out the dough and suddenly wondered how she would survive the coming solid weeks unbroken by a trip to London.

The night before they left for Dorset, Glenda sat cross-legged on the bed. She had her wedding ring suspended on a piece of thread. 'Yes goes round and round,' she muttered, 'and no is back and forwards.' She used to play this divining game with Molly at Girton. In fact it was a Soul game, a game to discover if your lover loved you or indeed if you loved him. It made them giggle and fall about and slosh more wine down their throats. Tonight Glenda felt that this was no game at all. Her feelings for Jonathan had taken on an almost rabid quality. She had not seen him for three weeks now and she had no excuse to call. Georgina she called almost daily with a forced cheerfulness, just to hear the name *Jonathan* on Georgina's lips or to be able to say the name herself. How could a thing like a name hold such force in her life? She wandered about the farm in pain. She wished she could disintegrate in the mud. Anything would be better than this awful, wrenching pain. There was no cure, she knew, and no antidote. She re-read *Wuthering Heights*. She shuddered as she heard Heathcliff's wild cries across the moors. 'Cathy! Cathy!' she heard in the howling fen winds. *Jonathan, Jonathan*, she found herself sobbing. Tonight she sat and promised herself one question. 'Does he love me?' she asked the ring. Slowly she felt the ring gather force. Her heart beat wildly. She held her breath and began to feel faint. The ring swung back and forth, back and forth. *No*, it said decisively.

Glenda felt a sickening moment of disappointment. Then she broke the thread and put the ring back on her finger. 'An old piece of rubbish. Superstition,' she grumbled, and ran downstairs to find Clive.

He was mourning so deeply that he had little noticed her obsessive behaviour. She took his hand and she kissed his cheek. Let us two shipwrecks sit this out together, she thought. I really have no control over myself any more. This feeling can't be love. It's more like a dreadful nightmare.

Chapter 121

Minnie noticed Clive's strained face. He had lost weight in the days after the funeral and now he looked skeletal. 'Is he all right, love?' she asked Glenda with genuine concern.

'He'll get over it in time, mum. Don't worry.' Glenda so much wished she could throw her arms around her mother and tell her about Jonathan, but she knew she could not. Minnie would never let a man obsess her like that. Even Chinchilla, now with her restaurant a great success, seemed less and less interested in men. Maybe I'm just different, Glenda thought as she and Clive left Chiswick for the long drive to Dorset. Maybe no one else in the world feels the way I do. I feel as if a curse has been laid upon me and I can't break free.

She sat beside Clive. He was driving his dark green Jaguar. The car was quiet and rolled down the road as if it were alone. Clive's face was taut. There were lines under his eyes. 'What I can't bear,' he said, breaking the silence, 'I just can't bear the thought of the earth around Nanny. The thought that she will be cold and lonely and . . . Oh God!' he groaned. 'I shall never see her again. Touch her soft cheek. I'm sorry, Glenda. I must be boring you.'

'No, you're not.' Glenda put her hand on his arm. 'I know how you feel. I miss her too.' But she was thinking about how much she would miss Jonathan when she was in Singapore. It will be the only thing that I can do. Get away and give myself a break. Maybe something good will come of it.

They got down late. Georgina gave the staff the night off, and served a light supper in front of the drawing room fire. She carried in a butler's tray of plates heaped with smoked salmon and brown bread. 'Nothing like a light supper on Christmas Eve,' she announced and Glenda jumped. She had completely forgotten that it was Christmas Eve. 'I'm sorry.' Georgina looked compassionately at Clive. 'I am so sorry about Nanny, darling. I know how you must feel. I lost my Nanny before I lost my mother, and I don't know which was worse.'

The boys were all asleep, so Glenda and Clive sat alone with Georgina and Jonathan in the comfortable drawing room.

At Georgina's feet sprawled a red setter. 'Get up, you lazy thing, and go and take care of your puppies.' The setter yawned, her pink tongue hanging out of her mouth, and she grinned a wide jowly smile.

Glenda felt a fraud. Here she sat, trying not to stare at Jonathan. Jonathan sat opposite her. The country Jonathan was far more informal than the London Jonathan. He sat with his yellow sweater tied around his shoulders. Plain penny loafers on his feet and a dark tweed hacking jacket lying beside him.

'You know,' Jonathan said in his rather clipped English, 'we are becoming talked about.' Glenda raised her eyebrows. 'Yes,' Jonathan continued. 'I get teased. "Who is that beautiful young woman you've been lunching with?" That kind of office chatter. I told them that you are my wife's best friend. Purely business, I said. But they wouldn't believe me.'

Georgina laughed. 'Men,' she said. 'They have such dirty minds.'

'So do women,' said Clive.

Glenda felt a flash of electricity between her thighs. She said as casually as possible, 'After the trip to Singapore we'll

538

go back to talking business, but this Christmas I just want to laze about.'

'I get *The Wall Street Journal*,' Jonathan said, 'even out in this neck of the woods, if you want to have a read.'

'Thanks,' said Glenda. 'I'll read it after you.'

'Seriously,' said Jonathan when he and Glenda were alone for a moment in the hallway, 'people *are* beginning to notice us together. And we don't need any gossip around. So I think it would be best if from now on we had lunch upstairs in my suite at the Savoy instead of at the restaurant. Far more private that way, don't you think?'

'Lunch in the suite?' Glenda said, trying not to let her voice tremble. 'Well, if you think it's best.'

Christmas passed both slowly and in a flash. Slowly, as the hours slid by while she and Georgina splashed about in the house's heated indoor swimming pool with the four boys. Two of them kept pushing each other into the pool. The smaller two never left Georgina alone. 'Hey!' Glenda yelled. 'Leave your mother alone and go and play.' She shooed the two whining children out of the study and sat Georgina down. 'I didn't realize children took up so much time.'

'Twenty-four hours a day,' Georgina said, letting herself sit down heavily. 'I can't tell you how much I'm looking forward to this trip to Singapore. I do need a break. I sometimes think I'll go mad if I have to put on another shoe or find another sock. How can one's life become a matter of shoes and socks? You remember at Girton when I said I wanted a little girl? Golly, look what I got! Four boys. Oh, Girton seems a million light years away.' She sat, over-plump and pink in an armchair.

Glenda felt a momentary rush of pity for Georgina. Where was the immaculate, slim girl who had run up to Abe's Lagonda, the first friendly face that Glenda saw at Cambridge? Where was the brightest brain at Girton? Lost, lost among

539

too many years of looking after Jonathan's houses and his children. Lost in the years of housekeeping. All the doing, all the giving. 'Do you feel it's been worthwhile?' Glenda asked.

Georgina did not immediately answer. 'I don't know,' she said at last, her head on one side. 'I need to get away, and then I'll need to come back. Ask me again when we get back.'

Chapter 122

Glenda and Georgina flew together to Paris, the first step on their journey. There they met up with Fatima, who lived in Paris with Majid. Molly had flown to Paris a day or two early, to sample, she explained, the French waiters.

Fatima looked no different than she had when they last said goodbye to her. Molly did look older and was prematurely a little grey at the temples. Majid was still the same tall, hawk-like character. He enfolded Georgina and Glenda in his warm arms and for a moment Glenda was comforted. 'Gee, Glenda, you've smartened up.'

Glenda rolled her eyes. 'Shut up, Molly. Didn't anyone ever tell you it isn't polite to make personal comments?'

Molly looked surprised and somewhat hurt. Glenda did not seem like the same Glenda. 'I didn't mean to be rude.'

'Then don't be.' Glenda was herself surprised at the venom in her own voice. There really was no need to be angry. Maybe, Glenda reasoned with herself, she would have to put this awful pain on hold. She would ruin the trip if she could not get the obsession out of her mind. She realized what she actually wanted to do was to say, 'Sorry, girls, but I'm catching the next plane back to London,' but she knew she could not do that. Too much planning and anticipation had gone into this trip. 'Sorry, Molly.' Glenda squeezed Molly's plump shoulder. 'I didn't mean to snap. I'm tired and the flight was bumpy.'

'Dah, don't worry. I thought you'd probably got the mean reds.'

'You would,' Glenda laughed.

They made their way up through Fatima's and Majid's restaurant into the flat above. The flat was very elegant. A big brass tray sat on four legs. Fatima sank gracefully to the floor and rang a bell. A Moroccan woman, lean and lithe, floated into the room. 'Tea, please,' Fatima requested. The woman bowed and left.

Georgina looked around the room. 'This is lovely, Fatima. What beautiful Bukhara rugs.'

'They come from Majid's family. You will not see many more of these now that the borders to Afghanistan are closing. They are beautiful. I love the colours. They shine so in the sunlight. They remind me of Turaq.' Fatima sighed and Majid looked tenderly at her.

'Not long now,' he said softly. 'Dictators only last a time before they are thrown off and the people will be free to choose again.'

A great steaming urn of tea arrived. Fatima handed out the cups and they all sipped the hot, sweet tea appreciatively.

Glenda sat cross-legged and uncomfortable. English legs were never designed for sitting on the floor, she thought. Georgina's knees stuck up at a ridiculous angle and Molly, with utter lack of modesty, sat with her legs wide apart, slurping her tea loudly.

That night, after a delicious meal of couscous and tiny sweet cakes, Glenda was only half-awakened from her sleep by Molly who was sharing the guest room. Molly slipped out of bed and stumbled, cursing loudly. She left the room and walked down the narrow hall.

Molly was bored. She was not used to going to bed before one or two in the morning. Noticing the lights on downstairs in the restaurant, she walked down the stairway and pushed open the door.

Majid was sitting at one of the tables, his head bent over the receipt book. She looked at him and smiled. How handsome he is, she thought. What a lay.

She sat beside him.

'What's the matter, Molly? Can't sleep?'

'Insomniac old me.' Molly pulled a pack of cigarettes out of the sleeve of her Japanese kimono. She lit the cigarette and inhaled deeply and waited for Majid to say something.

He was silent. He looked down at his receipt book and continued to check the day's taking.

Molly was a little unsettled. Usually a man, seeing the sexual beckoning in her eyes, responded. Not always was the invitation to bed accepted, but at least there was a recognition that she was extremely attractive. Molly waited. Majid continued to write.

'What's wrong?' Molly said. 'You scared or something?'

'No.' Majid stopped writing. 'I am not scared. I am in love with my wife and I don't find you attractive.'

Molly sat in a stunned silence. Nobody had ever said that to her before. 'What do you mean I'm not attractive?'

'Exactly that.'

'What about Fatima telling us about men like you having four wives?'

'I'm a modern man. I do not want or need four wives. I've got all I can handle with Fatima. Your problem, if you don't mind me saying, is that you are your daddy's spoiled little girl and you need to grow up.'

Molly smashed her cigarette into a thick white ashtray. 'Sod you!' Molly stood. 'You're just trying to be hurtful.'

'I'm not. Look, Molly. I've known you for many years and everything Fatima tells me about you fills me with regret. You are used meat now. That is what you have let yourself become. You think you are funny letting many men have you for free, but it is not funny. It is just horrifying and sad. If you don't sort out your relationship with your father, you shall be a lonely old woman. You gave your heart

542

to your father many years ago. You need to get it back
again. He puts up with your rotten behaviour. A decent man
will not.' And Majid lowered his head and continued to write.

Molly was stupefied. She walked away. The trek back to
the guest bedroom seemed to go on for ever.

In bed she lay on her back, listening to Glenda breathe.
She knew Majid was telling the truth. But for so long she
had relied on pussy power to get what she wanted. How
would she make a new beginning? Could she? What would
it be like to live in a world where there were no sexual
messages, a world where her breasts and her buttocks had no
exchange rate? She was still young enough to be powerful.
Her mother had now joined the women who, past a certain
age, did not seem to exist. Her mother's group of friends
were by now largely divorced. Their husbands, after years
of bitching, had run off with young women or cut loose,
paid alimony, and abandoned ship. Her mother still had a
grip on her father, but the protests and accusations were
muted now. Her mother knew she was exchangeable. Her
father, in all probability, never would swap her mother for a
newer model, but the threat was there. Now her mother,
having giving up on her own affairs, clung possessively to
her father's arm when they walked down the road. Any
young friend of Molly's was kindly greeted, but treated with
suspicion. How much longer could Molly buy the warm,
young, brown bodies in the Caribbean? Another ten years,
tops . . .

Molly fell into a restless, jagged sleep.

Chapter 123

'I'm sick and tired of men. From now on, *I'll* use *them*.'
Molly sat in a defiant heap on the airplane. Her legs were
crossed like razors and her mouth bitter.

'So what's new?' said Glenda. 'You've always used men.'

543

'Men have used *her*,' Fatima corrected with a smile. Molly squinted at Fatima. Had Majid told Fatima of his midnight encounter? Fatima gazed serenely back at Molly. 'By the way,' she said, 'I've news for you all. I am pregnant.'

Glenda wiggled her toes in her first-class socks. 'Fatima! How wonderful!'

She felt an awful pang of jealousy. Pregnancy was something she had never managed to achieve. Anyway, she reasoned, pregnancy now with Jonathan so much on her mind might not be a good idea.

Georgina rang the buzzer for the stewardess. 'Champagne,' she said, grinning at Fatima. 'Do tell Majid to have a crate ready for the birth. Champagne keeps away the baby-blahs. I should know. I had the blahs with all four boys. Whether it's the shock of having a baby, or just the sheer exhaustion, I couldn't say. Even with a nanny around the whole thing is an ordeal and it gets worse as they get older. I do miss the little buggers, though. I sent them all some extra tuck. I feel so guilty. I don't know why. It's time I had some time to myself.'

Glenda looked out of the window. 'Hmm,' she said. 'It is good to be away. Of course, I do worry about Clive. He's had headaches lately. Since Nanny died.'

Georgina said, 'Clive will be all right, Glenda. All men have their Achilles' heel. You should see Jonathan when the weather gets cold. He spends most of the winter with his head under a towel inhaling from a bowl of steam. I can't bear the smell of Vick any longer. He honks like an old man in the morning, and he blows his nose right in the sink too. It's disgusting.'

'Good heavens, Georgina!' Glenda was genuinely astonished. She felt defensive on Jonathan's behalf. 'I never thought of Jonathan like that. He always looks so immaculate and healthy.'

'Yes, he looks so, but underneath he's just as neurotic as

544

any other man. He gets ill and demands his mother, or else he lies in bed moaning.'

Glenda sipped her glass of champagne. 'But I always thought of him as so strong. So good at taking care of you. I've often envied you the way Jonathan took over your life and paid all the bills and looked after all the boring details of dealing with the rest of the world.'

'Oh, he does all that. But he's never around when the lavatory is blocked. I have to get the plunger myself. And if one of the boys is ill, Jonathan always seem to have an appointment in New York or Jakarta. Life is very convenient for Jonathan. And when anything becomes inconvenient, he simply becomes absent.'

Glenda wondered if Georgina suspected her feelings for Jonathan . . .

'Well anyway –' Molly was on her second glass of champagne. She watched the diminutive Malay and Chinese stewardesses handing out hot towels to the passengers. ' – I intend to get me a hairless little Chinese lover and I'm going to try out the newest thrill.'

'Do tell.' Glenda was always amused by Molly and her endless perversity.

'This is the very latest trick,' Molly said, warming to her subject. 'You cut a tiny hole in his scrotum, and you insert a cocktail straw and blow.' She grinned. 'He gets the greatest come in his life, or he dies of an embolism. It's terribly dangerous, but great fun.'

'Why do you like such dangerous games?' Fatima sat next to Molly. She put her hand on Molly's knee. 'If you kill a man, you will go to jail. Particularly in Singapore. Our Prime Minister is a very just man. Why take the risk?'

'Because I'm bored. I'm very, very bored.'

'And you're lonely, Molly.'

'Shit, Fatima! You're not my psychiatrist.'

'Well, in all these years your psychiatrist hasn't done you

very much good. The trouble with you, Molly, is that you don't like men.'

'I don't like men, Fatima? You're telling me *I* don't like men? You must be out of your mind. My problem is that I like men too much.'

Fatima shook her head. 'You wait until you meet Fat Aunt. You'll see what I mean.'

'You mean I'm some sort of dyke, don't you?'

'Ha! Not at all. You just don't like men. Real men are very uncomplicated. They like to eat and make love and get on with their lives, which have very little to do with the women they love.'

'That's true,' Georgina smiled. 'I hardly ever see Jonathan.'

Glenda thought about this. Then she said, 'And Clive is usually out on the farm. I see him at night if I'm lucky, if some cow isn't calving. Molly, I think you really want to get married again and you won't admit it.'

'Sure,' Molly said, 'and wear a jail sentence around my neck for the next forty years? No, you're all wrong. All of you are way the hell off base. I like my life. I'm a partner in my law firm. I can do whatever I like. I have my own apartment and I can pick and choose any man I want. I've tried marriage. Twice. And it doesn't suit me.'

'Ah,' Glenda said, 'but you haven't hit the unfuckable zone yet. I was telling mum and Chinchilla about what you had said. Even Chinchilla – and she's only in her early fifties – notices it. Suddenly you pass from fuckability to invisibility. Men don't know that you exist. Not all men, but most. That's the awful thing about being a woman and growing old. Women don't feel that way about men because usually, as men get older, they become more powerful and wealthy, and power and wealth are the greatest aphrodisiacs to women. But for women it's a one-way slide into decay.'

'I don't mind growing older,' Georgina said defensively, 'because I always have a happy picture of myself ending up sitting in a wheelchair with no teeth and a bottle of gin.'

Fatima smiled. 'In Islam we are taught by the Koran to respect our elders. The older a woman gets, the wiser she is deemed. We all honour my mother and defer to her. She is the head of the household. You will see when we get there.'

'Well, there ain't much to honour about my mother,' said Molly, having another glass of champagne. 'She drips about in a see-through nightie in the morning. She smells bad. She uses so much air-freshener around the house, the whole place stinks like wet underpants.'

I think my mother is just fine as she is, Glenda decided as she watched the trays coming down the aisle.

In a minute, conversation was stopped by the arrival of a gorgeous dinner, plates resplendent with lotus buds, delicately fried rice, slices of pale pink papaya, and deep orange mangos.

After dinner the women slept. Glenda was pleased to feel that although the pain was still there, she had enjoyed her flight so far. Tomorrow they would be in Singapore and hopefully she could forget Jonathan for a while.

Chapter 124

When Glenda walked into the airport, she felt like a frightened child. She noticed a strange smell and asked Fatima about it. The smell more than anything else made clear to Glenda that she had entered a very different world. Part of the smell was beautiful and part of it putrid.

'Oh that. It's called durian. See the man with the fruit over there?' A man was holding what appeared to be a large prickly football in his hand.

'How can he bear to carry it? It stinks.' Molly held her nose.

'Yes,' said Fatima. 'But the taste is magnificent. Many people, once they've tasted it, find themselves always seeking

547

more. And for centuries it's been seen as a powerful aphrodisiac.'

This statement gave Molly pause. She raised her eyebrows and leaned her head to the side in a gesture which said: Hmm, might be worth trying.

Georgina sailed serenely ahead of the others looking as if she owned the airport and the other passengers were merely friends and acquaintances.

They stepped out of the air-conditioned airport and into the sudden wave of heat. Glenda thought she would not be able to breathe ever again. The solid wall of heat hit the back of her throat. In front of the airport a long white limousine stood waiting. A fat plain woman with a friendly face, wrapped in layers of cloth and a veil, put out her hand to greet Fatima. Fatima put two hands together and bowed. 'This is my aunt,' she said. The three women stood silently by, except for Georgina who bowed back and smiled.

'I've heard so much about you,' she said.

Fat Aunt laughed.

Fatima climbed eagerly into the car. 'I can't wait to get home and get out of these beastly Western clothes. They are so hot and useless in this climate. I have ordered robes for all three of you, if you want to wear them.'

Molly grinned as she lay back in the car. 'Yeah, right,' she said. 'How am I going to find a man with my body swaddled in these clothes in this heat?'

Fatima smiled. 'You will stay with my family, and none of the men would dare touch you as you are my honoured guest.'

Fat Aunt was shaking with laughter. Tears poured out of her tightly squeezed eyes. 'You want a man!' she said and the words pop-pop-popped out of her mouth. 'I'll take you where you will find men.'

'No you won't,' Fatima gave a serious frown. 'She'll take you to the local brothel and that is where the rough men go.'

Molly's face fell. 'No fucking,' she said, 'for three whole weeks? You sincerely mean that?'

'You shall enjoy yourself nonetheless.'

The car pulled up in front of a huge house with many balconies. Hibiscus bloomed in the garden. Tall spears of plumed bamboo guarded the door. The chauffeur opened the door of the car and several men came running to carry the luggage. Glenda looked about the garden. She loved the smell of the flowers and the dark green of the lawn. Fatima led the way into the house, Glenda and Georgina following. Molly trailed along behind Fat Aunt as if going to an execution.

Later that night they left the house all dressed in silk. The four of them were escorted by Fat Aunt's son, Nayim. Nayim was tall with a happy, sunny disposition. The women put on their black silken robes and Glenda found herself entranced by the idea of being genuinely anonymous. Now she pulled the silk across her face and looked at the twinkling Singapore night as they sped by in the polished limousine. The car stopped in a street filled with tables. 'We will eat here,' Nayim said.

The chauffeur opened the door and Nayim waved him away. 'About two hours,' Nayim said.

Still covered the women sat down. Other eyes stared in astonishment. 'Look,' Glenda heard a Chinese man sitting near them. 'Round eyes behind the veils.'

She stared at him in amusement. 'We must look odd,' she said to Georgina.

'I rather like my robe,' Georgina laughed.

A waiter appeared and Nayim ordered dim sum. 'Chinese dumplings filled with little tastes. Special tastes. You will like them.'

Molly looked hopefully at Nayim, but he smiled back benignly.

Nayim said to Fatima, 'Your mother will come to the house tomorrow. She is in J. B.'

'Johore Bahru,' Fatima translated helpfully.

'Why do you sound so English?' Molly wanted to know.

'Because I went to school in England,' Nayim said. 'Most of my family opt for education in the States, but I preferred an English education. Classical, don't you know. Greek and Latin and all that.'

The waiter arrived, carrying a pile of steaming bamboo baskets in his hand. Tier upon tier, they looked ready to topple.

Glenda sat in the hot moonlight, savouring her small dumplings. Behind her parrots chattered, chained to perches. People walked in and out of the street. 'Who are those beautiful women?' Glenda asked Nayim.

Nayim laughed. 'Beautiful, yes. But they aren't women at all. They are very famous, the Bugis Street male prostitutes. It is said they can do things women cannot do.'

'Umph.' Molly snorted. 'Give me a pack of cocktail straws and let me at them.'

Fatima frowned. 'Please, Molly. We don't talk like that in front of men.'

'Then what *do* you talk about?'

Fatima looked down at her plate. 'Tell me, Nayim,' she said. 'How is mother?'

Molly flounced in her chair, alone and ignored.

The male prostitutes wandered up and down between the tables. Occasionally one would take a man or a woman by the hand and they would rush down the streets with quickened steps. It all seemed so very innocent and peaceful to Glenda. She sat beside Georgina who ate her way through course after course of Chinese food. 'It's absolutely delicious,' Georgina said. 'Absolutely the most delicious meal I've ever had.'

Nayim grinned. 'There's more to come. Singapore has the best food in the world.'

For a moment Glenda did indeed forget Jonathan.

Chapter 125

Glenda went to bed with her head full of the sights and the sounds of Singapore. From the moment the Singapore Airways plane had taken off from Paris, she had felt transported into another world. Perfumed, mysterious, and many-layered. The people of Singapore, the night in Bugis Street translated into so many shapes and colours. Faces with high cheek bones, flat noses. The streets multi-coloured and full of smells. She had enjoyed the night wrapped only in her silk gown. The silk was sinuous, and she felt desirable. No longer dressed in tight, revealing clothes, she could choose to look or not to look at a man. It was her decision to raise or lower her eyes.

Before she slept she thought about Jonathan and then realized she was annoyed with Georgina. How dare she say that Jonathan put his head under a towel all winter, or that he honked mucus in the mornings! That made him less of a man in Glenda's eyes. That's silly, she told herself. Of course he does things all men do. But then she felt as if Georgina had violated some private part of her fantasy of Jonathan as the consummate, all-caring, all-perfect man. I do hope he doesn't pick his nose, she thought, or clean his ears with his little finger. Shut up, she told herself fiercely, and leave a fantasy untarnished. She turned over and fell asleep.

The days flew. Molly grumbled a little, but soon found herself enraptured by the bustle and the business of Singapore. 'The whole city is like one gigantic marketplace,' Molly said, flourishing her chequebook wherever she went. The other three usually staggered back to the house carrying Molly's many purchases.

'You don't need *all* these things,' Georgina remonstrated.

'Yes, well shopping's a good subsitute for sex,' Molly said

stoutly. 'Fatima has put me on a strictly no-sex diet, so I have no choice but to shop until I drop.'

'More likely till *we* drop.' Glenda collapsed onto the red velvet sofa in the house. The women lived in the inner courtyard among a bewildering array of aunts and female *amahs*. As they were without their husbands, Fatima, Georgina and Glenda lived with the single women.

Only Molly objected. 'I could be quite happy out there with Nayim and the other men,' she pointed out.

'But they wouldn't want you out there,' Fatima was adamant, 'any more than we would want the men in here.' They had removed their black robes and were sitting at ease with their shoes off. Fat Aunt called for tea. Fatima slipped onto the floor. 'There has to be mystery between men and women, or else . . .' She was interrupted by a commotion at the door.

Fatima's mother came in. Fatima got to her feet and crossed the room. Georgina and Glenda stood up. The elderly lady came across the floor with her hand outstretched. 'Ah!' she said. 'Did you shop well?'

'Yes, thank you,' they said.

Glenda watched Fatima lead her mother to a place of honour on the sofa. Mrs Nicnojad smiled at Glenda and Glenda smiled back. The small woman had her hair in a tight bun and her black eyes were watchful. In them lay a great depth of understanding. 'My husband tells me he had breakfast with all of you and he much enjoyed the experience.' She tilted her head to Fatima. 'And my daughter tells me she is pregnant, may Allah be praised!' She put her hands together.

Outside the house Glenda could hear the *muezzin* calling the people to prayer. How can a country not be good, she thought, when people pray five times a day?

Mrs Nicnojad settled herself into the sofa and they began to chat. Conversation, Glenda realized, was circumlocutory. 'How is Majid, darling?' Mrs Nicnojad took Fatima's hand.

'He is well, mother. I spoke to him last night. He is anxious that I do not do too much rushing about because of the baby.' She grinned and looked at Molly. 'Of course, if I told him I was living the life of a camel, carrying Molly's many parcels, he would be furious.'

What a strange and formal distance there was between Fatima and her mother! thought Glenda. But still the bonds were felt, deep and strong. 'Nayim says he is taking you out to see the Chinese theatre tonight. My, he is having a fine time!' Mrs Nicnojad laughed. 'Escorting four pretty women around Singapore! He shall ask his friend Prapanas to join you this evening.'

Molly looked instantly hopeful. 'Prapanas?'

'A very good man. A very good man indeed. He is a barrister and a cousin to the Sultan of Johore. Actually he is of royal blood, a sultan in his own right.'

'No kidding?' Molly beamed and was met by a look of disapproval from Fatima's eyes.

'*No*, Molly,' she jumped in.

Mrs Nicnojad looked at Molly. 'Maybe you might try to influence events in our way,' she said.

'How do you mean?' Molly asked slightly defensively.

'Open eagerness, as you are quick to show, does not always attract,' said Mrs Nicnojad with a wry smile. 'We have other ways, such as subtlety and patience.'

Molly stared back and then lowered her eyelids. 'Maybe,' she said ruefully. 'It sure doesn't seem to work my way.'

Mrs Nicnojad laughed and stood up.

Fat Aunt came bustling in with the tea. 'Won't you stay?' she asked.

Mrs Nicnojad shook her head. 'I must join my husband. We will walk together, now that the air is cooler. He loves his walks in the garden and so do I.'

Watching her go, Glenda felt envious. There were no contradictions for Mrs Nicnojad. She was the mistress of this huge house and all who lived within it. There must be at least twenty servants . . . Glenda sipped the hot, sweet tea.

Maybe twelve women in the compound, and eighteen men, including Mr Nicnojad. It was a community within itself.

The *amah* that came in to collect the tea service had long, black, wet hair. Fatima smiled at the girl. 'I see,' she said and she put her hand to her face and giggled.

'Did I miss something?' Molly asked as the girl left the room. 'What's so funny?'

'She is Malay,' Fatima explained. 'She has been making love to her husband. That is why her hair is wet.'

'You're joking,' said Molly. 'All this you can tell from wet hair?'

'That's why she bathed at this time of day.'

'Not fair!' Molly said. 'Everybody's getting some except for me.'

'Come on. Let's go upstairs and get ready.'

It was warm that night, but the heat was soothing against the skin. The car stopped at Raffles Hotel where they were to meet Nayim and Prapanas. The four women went to the Long Bar and sat down. Around them bamboo tables and chairs were filled with people eating and drinking. 'This is the hotel where Somerset Maugham used to drink and Noel Coward played his famous songs,' Fatima pointed out.

The four friends were talking when Nayim and Prapanas arrived. Molly for once was subdued. Though her usual habit was to sit carelessly with her legs wide apart, tonight she sat quietly and simply gazed at Prapanas, raising her lowered eyes. Prapanas returned the look. He was tall and striking. He had fair hair and blue eyes, but his skin was honey-gold. 'Good evening, ladies,' he said, his eyes lingering on Molly.

Nayim sat down and waved his hand for a waiter. 'By golly,' he said. 'We'd better hurry or we'll be late. After the performance we can all go and eat at a steamboat restaurant. You'll like the steamboat. They serve all sorts of things on little plates, and you can cook anything you like from the plates in the boiling water, and then we put the vegetables in and you drink the soup.'

They did enjoy the *wayang*. The actors moved about the stage in bright costumes as ancient stories of gentle maidens and fierce warlords were reenacted. The music was discordant but slowly Glenda could hear a pattern in the sounds and the rhythms of clashing gongs. In the trees parrots cried encouragement and the stars were huge in the thick black sky.

The steamboat restaurant was crowded with many people. A great shining urn of boiling liquid was placed on the table. On plates big piles of pink butterfly shrimp and pieces of lobster were garnished with curls of onions and garlic. Sliced *bok choy* and fresh green spinach added colour to the meal as did the pale pieces of pork and thin wedges of beef. Prapanas showed Molly how to pick up the shrimp with her chopsticks, the two of them laughing. Molly's eyes shone.

On the way home they dropped Nayim and Prapanas at the Raffles Hotel. 'May I call you tomorrow?' Prapanas asked Molly, leaving the car.

'Please do,' Molly said in her best English manner.

'Huh.' Glenda leaned forward as the car took off. 'I hope you are not planning to use a straw on him.'

'Oh Glenda. How crude.' Molly lay languorously back in the seat. 'Actually, I think I'll take Mrs Nicnojad's advice. I'll try it her way. The soft sell.'

Fatima said, 'Mother gives good advice.'

Glenda thought only briefly of Jonathan as she prepared herself for bed. She remembered that she ought to telephone Clive. The day had been too busy and too full. Living in the women's compound seemed to make the idea of an all-important relationship with a man – or even an obsession about a man – rather remote. Men were satellite planets, not the central sun, in this world of women.

Chapter 126

For the rest of the holiday, Prapanas seemed to live in the outer courtyard. He brought Molly back in the evening and her eyes glowed. There was a carefree bounce in her step that made her seem younger. 'I see, child. You are smitten with your sultan,' Mrs Nicnojad teased gently.

Molly beamed. 'I'm doing it your way,' she said. 'I get quite a kick out of saying no.'

Mrs Nicnojad raised her small shapely hand. 'Men have to chase. It is in their biology. If they catch the hare, they have no more interest. Instead the hare must wait but must know when to run.'

'What is the secret then?' Molly asked.

Glenda and Georgina stopped talking and listened. 'The secret is that the hare never stops running.' Mrs Nicnojad chuckled. 'To this day, my dear husband does not know what I will do. I keep him guessing. I say to him, "Today I am going to Johore Bahru and I *might* be back tomorrow." '

Molly laughed. 'And I always thought *women* were oppressed.'

Mrs Nicnojad smiled. 'The poor are always oppressed anywhere. They have no choices. But, Molly, you will never be oppressed.'

Molly grinned at Glenda. 'I never thought life could be such fun. We get to go out and do all sorts of things instead of just screwing.'

'And your cocktail straw technique?' said Glenda.

Molly laughed self-consciously. 'Somehow I don't think Prapanas would be into that. Anyway, I've decided to give my perverse side a break. In fact, I'm even thinking of giving up my shrink. Her life is more of a mess than mine is. And it would save Daddy-O an awful lot of money if I gave the therapy a rest.'

The days passed. Glenda and Georgina practised the bits of Chinese they had picked up. 'Good morning, Georgina.'

'Hi Zao,' Georgina shot back.

'Okay. How about, Hello.'

'Ni hao.'

Glenda was feeling more comfortable around Georgina. The days were so busy she did not have much time to brood about Jonathan. Down the telephone Clive seemed happy and said he had seen Jonathan in London for lunch once or twice, and Jonathan rang him every couple of days. That's good of Jonathan, Glenda thought. He really does care for Clive.

Georgina blossomed in Singapore. Everything interested her. Georgina bought herself a large square crocodile handbag and a matching pair of shoes. She also bought a Rolex watch for her husband at a price far less than what it would have been in England or America. Glenda very much wished that she too could buy something for Jonathan, but she felt intimidated by her guilty secret. Of course she could buy him something. After all, they were old friends. But the obsession held her back.

For Clive she had six shirts made from slub silk, neck size fifteen. Privately she wished she could order another six shirts for Jonathan, neck size at least sixteen.

The few days before they left Singapore, Glenda spent time in the deepest part of the city dragging Georgina with her. 'We are the only white women down here,' Georgina said uneasily, but she soon learned that no one would hurt her. They wandered along Thieves' Alley. Glenda bought herself a ring. A large oval piece of turquoise opened into a little cavity with the Buddha sitting cross-legged in this tiny shrine. Glenda smiled at the wild mountain man who held the ring. He put it on her finger.

She also bought three jade bracelets. 'Good for health,' the man said.

Glenda and Georgina wandered further. Stopping for coffee, they sat on two chairs, a rickety table between them. 'Funny,' Georgina said, looking at the crowds that surged up and down the road, buying, spitting, laughing, 'I shall be rather sorry when we go home. I hate to admit it, but much of my life is somewhat boring, you know? Of course, I miss Jonathan. At least I think I do. He's away so much, I almost feel myself only part-time married. I haven't really missed him that much.'

I have. Glenda sat silently. 'It will be nice to get back to the farm. Spring will be coming, and I love to watch the garden come to life.' *Lying bitch,* she scolded herself. *You just want to get to the suite in the Savoy.* Only two days away, and the old obsession came back full force. Glenda could hardly wait to get on the airplane.

Molly, parted from her sultan, moped all the way back. 'I'm in love,' she said, dramatically throwing herself down on her seat. 'And he says he loves me. Just imagine. Little Molly Rosenthal, a sultan's wife. Wait till I tell Dad.'

They landed in Paris. Only Glenda and Georgina would continue on to London, for Fatima was returning to her life in the restaurant with Majid, and Molly was staying in Paris for a few days to get in just a bit more shopping.

Fatima, after much hugging and kissing, walked away through Customs and towards her husband. Molly said, 'Bye, guys. See you soon.'

At London's Heathrow, Clive was there to meet both women with apologies from Jonathan. 'He says he's sorry, Georgina, but he had to go to Rome. The chauffeur is here to take you back to Dorset.'

It was Glenda who tried not to burst into tears of disappointment. She had so longed for this moment. Even if she could not touch Jonathan other than in a quick hug, she had wanted at least to see him.

Clive kissed Glenda and took her suitcase. 'I've got you a nice present,' Glenda said, hoping the disappointment would not show in her voice.

'Seeing you again is present enough,' Clive smiled. 'Let's get going. I have a special meal for you and a wonderful bottle of champagne.'

Glenda followed Clive through the crowded airport. She sat beside him in the car. She looked out of the window and realized that she had indeed been to another part of the world. England appeared small and dirty. The people looked miserable. The car made its way through Islington. 'Grizzly Isly,' she said.

'A mess, isn't? Anyway, we'll be out of the traffic and the city soon and back in the country. We have several new lambs on the farm. A bit early really, but they're beautiful and safe. I'm feeding one on a bottle. The mother had two and not enough milk. You'll love him, the lamb, I mean.'

'What have you called him?'

'Baa Lamb, I'm afraid.'

Glenda laughed.

Chapter 127

It was two weeks before Glenda was able to see Jonathan. During that time she wandered about the farm. Baa Lamb followed her around like a puppy. On the trees the leaves were just shooting out pale green tips. The farm seemed to be ready to awaken after the long winter.

'Only three weeks away from here,' Glenda said, standing by the window, 'and I feel as if I've been gone forever.'

Clive sat in the study, reading a book on the Romantic poets. 'I know,' he said, looking up. 'I missed you as if you *had* been away forever. How's it feel now that you're back? All settled in again?'

Glenda walked behind his chair and kissed the top of his

golden head. Clive let the book fall on his lap. He reached his hands up behind him and held on to Glenda's neck. She let herself be pulled downward until her cheek rested against the top of his head. 'I'm driving up tomorrow to have lunch with Jonathan and then I'll give myself a treat and go shopping,' she said casually. 'Is there anything you want?'

Clive stretched. 'Would you see if Fortnum's have some Patum Peperium? We're all out down here.'

Glenda's heart was racing. 'Yes,' she said. 'Of course.'

As she packed early the next morning, her hands were shaking. She was going to spend the night with her mother. She packed a long, clinging, black satin negligée. 'For my mother,' she said out loud. 'Ha! I should coco.'

The drive up to town was long and boring. Over and over again she played a tape which she had borrowed from Clive: Beethoven's 'Archduke Trio.' The music soothed her and helped her to pay attention to the road. She longed to put down her foot and zoom, but she held back.

Finally she arrived at the Savoy and rushed through the entrance, leaving a surprised Fred the doorman holding the key to her car. 'Sorry, Fred. Can't talk,' she said. 'I'm in a hurry.' She turned the corner and ran up the stairs to the American Bar. Jonathan was there. Oh, so very much there.

He sat with his back to her and she came up behind him and put her hand on his shoulder. Her hand felt as if on fire and for a moment she entertained the wild fear that she might burn him right through his suit.

Jonathan stood up. She wanted to kiss his cheek, but he held out his hand for her to shake. 'Do sit down. Gin and tonic, as usual?'

'Everything as usual,' she said quickly. She felt herself tingle.

They discussed this and that, mostly that. The figures were good from Hong Kong. The battle at the moment lay fallow. Jane seemed to have other fish to fry. 'By the way,' Jonathan said, 'after we finish this session, I'll take you up to see the suite. In the future, you should get here a quarter of an hour early and let yourself in. Here's the key.' He took a key out of his pocket and handed it to her. 'I'll come along fifteen minutes later. That way we'll cut down on the gossip. I know it's ridiculous, but the City is always a-tattle with one rumour or another.'

Glenda slipped the key into her handbag and realized that tonight she would indeed be sleeping at her mother's. This took away most of her tension and she was able to relax.

Jonathan was a fund of gossip. 'While you've been away, everyone I know seems to have changed partners.'

'Oh, Molly found herself a beau. A man named Prapanas. He's a cousin to the Sultan of Johore. A sultan himself, in fact.'

'Well. You all seem to have had a magnificent time,' he said.

Glenda sat with her handbag next to her, the key safely inside.

She finished her drink with difficulty. Finally they stood up and made their way across the lobby and went into the lift.

Nigel was standing by the front desk. He saw them go. He waited until they came back down again. Not even enough time for a quickie, he thought. Jonathan must be taking this one step at a time.

Nigel was soon on the telephone. 'All set to go.'

'Really?' Jane's voice was interested.

'Yes, really.'

'All right. Will you make the necessary telephone call?'

Nigel smiled. 'With pleasure.'

'Next week? Same day?'

'I think so. Should be all set next Wednesday. I can't be sure, but I'll be there watching.'

'Good.' Jane put down the telephone. She called Dr Umberto at his home. 'Darling,' she said. 'I'm afraid I have the

561

most frightful premonition that Clive will not be too well next Wednesday. How about you come down here and stay Tuesday night with me and then we can go over and visit Clive, just to see that the dear boy's all right?'

'Certainly, Lady Jane. Anything you say.' Dr Umberto put down the telephone, wondering what she'd cooked up now. Whatever it was, he wouldn't want to be in Clive's shoes. Jane frightened him.

Chapter 128

The week went fast. Glenda felt frantic. She felt as if she was a hastily torn piece of paper. Ripped from her normal life, she felt jagged and sharp. She operated most of the time in a daze. Sometimes she would spring to life and rush around, madly cleaning, or walking in the garden. He was withdrawn again and thin in the cheeks. She knew he dared not hint at the question, except to say, 'Darling, are you sure you're not working too hard?'

Impatiently flicking the pages of *The Financial Times*, she replied, 'No, I'm not working hard enough.' This was true, at least when she compared her own efforts to Jonathan's workaholic habits.

He found a pretext to ring every day. Clive watched her face light up when she heard the telephone ring. He also watched her face when the call was not from Jonathan.

She talked to Molly in Washington, DC. 'What about the New Jersey Turnpike?'

'What *about* the New Jersey Turnpike?' Back came the same gravelly voice that Glenda loved.

'You still taking your lovers there, to truckstops along the road?'

Molly laughed. 'Listen, Sweetie, I've reformed. I put my shrink on tranquillizers. I told her she was an asshole. She told me I wasn't dealing with my latent hostile feelings

562

towards my mother. I told her she was full of crap. I ain't got no *latent* hostile feelings towards my mother. My hostility is right out there in the open. That's when I went on to explain that she, my therapist, was, is and always will be an asshole and I don't have to spend hours lying on a couch to know that.

'Anyway, Prapanas will be coming over in a week to talk to Dad. Guess what? He wants to make an honest woman out of me.'

Glenda was genuinely pleased.

Molly's voice was warm and comfortable. 'I guess I'm just a late bloomer.'

When the conversation ended and Glenda put the telephone down, tears rose in her eyes. Oh dear, she thought. This is to be one of those awful days when I feel so guilty I would like to go down to the lake, pick a bunch of weeds, and drown myself. Ophelia got it right. She sighed. I couldn't do that to Clive. But then I'm planning to . . . And she let the thought slide.

So far she had never actually articulated, even within herself, the idea that she might sleep with Jonathan. She had held her imagination back, allowing it only a peep into the suite, a glance at the bedroom door from the middle of the drawing room. No further. Always in her mind there was a gulf between the actual act and the foreplay. Luncheon served, she imagined, on a trolley. Both of them sitting politely at their table. A servant there to keep the occasion formal and after that . . . Nothing for the moment, except a delicious, forbidden shiver.

Monday ran by with the sun on its heels and the wind blowing the trees about. Tuesday threatened to sulk and to shower. And then came Wednesday morning.

She packed her suitcase without the silk negligée. Don't be silly, she reasoned. She could not admit that she might want to use it in the middle of the day. If we . . . If we *what*?

she thought as she impatiently collected her toothbrush and toothpaste. Well, if we do, and I don't have the negligée in my suitcase, I can't be guilty of premeditation. *You see, my lord*, a sonorous voice in her head proclaimed, *the accused had no previous intention of committing adultery.* Adultery. What a horrible word. So cold. I will be an adulteress. What does it feel like to stare in the mirror and clean your teeth after you have been adulterated? Spoiled, gone bad, corrupt?

She looked at herself in the bathroom mirror. 'Get on with it,' she said.

She picked up the suitcase and ran down the stairs. 'Goodbye, darling,' she kissed Clive lightly on the forehead.

'Do you have the last list of shares to be sold?'

'Yes,' Glenda called over her shoulder. 'I do.' She walked out to the car, trying not to run. How awful I am! How very dreadful! Madame Bovary had nothing on me. I am a loose woman. She berated herself and debated with herself all the way to London.

She could no longer wonder about the day . . . She fought to stay on the road. She cut her way through aggressive drivers until she arrived at the sanctuary of the Savoy's courtyard on the Strand. From here on, her life assumed another quality. She was not simply the Hon Mrs Glenda Alexander; she was Glenda Alexander, a director of a firm on a business trip to discuss facts and statistics.

Fred was not on duty today. His absence disconcerted her. She strode into the lobby feeling the key to the suite burning a hole in her purse. Go straight up, Jonathan had said. They know you at the front desk. She walked behind the porter who carried her small suitcase. She looked about her. A vaguely familiar face loomed behind her. A regular at the American Bar, she thought.

The lift slid up the floors and disgorged her and the quiet respectful porter into the silent hall. Their footsteps were hushed in the carpet. The young man took her proferred key

564

and opened the door of the suite. Glenda smiled. The suite was full of huge bunches of flowers. A room service trolley stood isolated in the spacious room. She could see a bottle of champagne and covered plates. She laughed a little excited laugh. It was all so very much like the old romantic films she had watched as a child with Minnie. She tipped the porter who put her suitcase down by the door. She walked over to the big windows and gazed out at the tiny specks below. People going about their boring lives, people working in the great and beautiful city of London to make money to go home to their wives and children . . . She jumped as the telephone rang.

Maybe Jonathan would be late. She walked over the carpet and put out a hesitant hand. The telephone purred again. She lifted the receiver. 'Hello?' she said. There was a silence. She said, 'Jonathan?' She thought she heard a small gasp. She put down the telephone.

At the farm Clive stood by his telephone. A few minutes earlier, a strange man's voice had spoken gruffly down the line. 'I think you should check on your wife.' Clive did not want to hear the words, but he knew they gave confirmation of thoughts he had refused to consider. 'Ring the Savoy. Ask for Suite 240, that's Jonathan Montague's suite.' He heard a click as the telephone on the other end of the line was hung up.

Clive remained with the telephone in his hand. He wouldn't do it . . . He would do it. The thoughts were chaotic in his head. How could he not trust her? How could he trust her? Everyone was gone from his universe. He felt the familiar pain in his head. He knew he must telephone before the thing gripped him. He dialled the Savoy and asked for Suite 240. He heard Glenda's hello and then he heard the name Jonathan. Her voice sounded almost afraid.

Clive dropped the telephone and held his hands over his ears. The pain was excruciating. He lay on the floor, screaming and rolling.

Mark and Paul ran into the room, Mrs Robinson behind them. 'Oh no!' Mrs Robinson clasped her hands in a frantic prayer. 'Not again.'

They paused as Mark held Clive's writhing body. 'It's Lady Jane at the end of the drive,' Paul said, leaning out of the window. 'Must be psychic, the old bat.'

Mrs Robinson dropped to her knees and tried to help Mark hold Clive still.

Jane Alexander swept into the room with Dr Umberto beside her. 'What's happened?' Jane said angrily.

'I don't know, Lady Jane,' Mrs Robinson began. 'He seemed fine a minute ago, then all of a sudden . . .'

'I thought I'd come by for a visit and bring along Clive's old friend Dr Umberto, and *this* is what we find?' Jane sounded furious. 'This is inexcusable.'

Paul and Mark stood helplessly as Dr Umberto swiftly took out a syringe from his bag and inserted the needle into Clive's arm. They relaxed as they saw his thrashing body crumple and his eyes close. He was no longer with them. He was gone, somewhere else. But at least the dreadful screams and the pain were also gone.

'He'd better come with us,' said Dr Umberto.

Mark carried Clive to the car.

'Where's Glenda?' Jane asked. She could not help but allow the beginnings of a triumphant smile to emerge on her face, but it appeared as more of a crooked leer.

'She's away on business, madam.'

'Is she now? If she telephones, none of you are to tell her what happened. The poor woman will be so upset. You tell her to ring me. You will do that, won't you?' The threat in her voice lay like a coiled snake.

All three of them nodded.

'Fuck off, you old bitch,' Mark muttered as they watched the car pull away from the house.

'A cup of tea, I think.' Mrs Robinson bustled into the kitchen and dithered among the pots and the pans.

Chapter 129

Jonathan was five minutes late. Glenda heard his key in the door and she jumped awkwardly to her feet. 'Sorry, darling,' Jonathan said, giving her a gentle peck on the cheek. 'Held up in the traffic.'

'Did you telephone?'

'No,' Jonathan answered. 'Why?'

'Oh, I got a call, but no one was there.'

'Must have been a wrong number.'

'Hm.'

Jonathan strode over to the trolley. 'I think this deserves a glass of champagne before we get down to business.' He did not specify which business, but for the moment Glenda felt safe.

Anyway, they had to have lunch, she supposed. One didn't succumb to lust in the middle of lunch.

She had been so apprehensive that she realized to her surprise how hungry she was. 'What's on the menu today?'

Jonathan looked at her and smiled. There was something proprietorial about his smile. It made Glenda uncomfortable. 'I ordered lobster bisque, followed by duck in aspic with port, a small salad, and finally crème brûlée. How does that sound?' He lifted off the silver covers from the plates. The food sat on the trolley looking delightful and very innocent. He pulled the chair from the table and made a sweeping gesture. '*Asseyez-vous, mademoiselle.* Allow me to open your table napkin.' The pink table napkin fanned over her knees and she felt the palm of his hand on her thigh.

I could stop now, one part of her head prayed. *No*, the

other was resolute. I can't back out now. I'm too far in and I'd look like a silly little schoolgirl from Hounslow. That thought caused her to pause, her spoon in her hand.

'A penny for them.' Jonathan gazed at Glenda. 'What are you thinking about?'

'Oh. Nothing, Jonathan.' She realized, as the words came out of her mouth, that he would not understand. Clive would. He came from a different, dual world himself. He grew up and played with Mark and Paul, despite his own wealth, so he knew and understood poverty. Jonathan had never been exposed to that side of life. It passed him by.

She finished the soup and smiled. 'Lovely,' she said. 'Really lovely.'

Jonathan pushed his empty soup bowl away. 'Things are going quite well,' he said. 'Jane still seems in a mood to listen. I'm pleased.' A warm tone came into his voice. 'Come, let's have another glass of champagne. I've worked hard already this week and I could do with an afternoon off.'

Glenda's heart, always a coward, jumped with all the panic of a marlin suddenly caught on a hook. This, she understood in an instant, was real; this was not make believe. Glenda coughed.

She finished the glass of champagne and held out her glass for another. 'I've been thinking,' Jonathan said. 'I don't know what you got up to in Singapore, but Georgina has really quite changed.'

'How do you mean?'

They were both pecking away at their unwanted crème brûlée.

Jonathan leaned back in his chair, his eyes amused. 'Well, she says she had such a good time she wants to go skiing in Switzerland next year. Alone with some friends.' His eyebrows rose like swallows.

'Why not, Jonathan? The boys are at school full-time, and you travel all over the world. Why shouldn't she go to Switzerland?'

'Really, Glenda.' Jonathan's voice hardened. 'She is my wife, you know.'

Glenda froze. 'Yes, I know. But Georgina's got to have a life of her own. She can't just live for you and the boys. After all, she earned an excellent degree at Cambridge.'

Jonathan stood up and took Glenda by the hand. 'We can talk about all that later.' With practised grace he picked up the champagne bottle and the two glasses. He walked behind Glenda as she approached the bedroom door.

She felt as if she was about to attend a hanging. Her own hanging.

Once she was through the door, a lightning bolt of terror exploded inside her stomach. 'I feel sick,' she said helplessly. 'I drank too much champagne.'

'Don't worry, darling.' Jonathan's arms were around her. 'It's just nerves. You'll be all right in a minute.'

Glenda looked into Jonathan's face, now bearing down upon her own. 'You've done this before,' she said, pushing him away sharply.

Jonathan paused and loosened his grip. 'We're both grown-ups, you know.'

'I must go to the bathroom,' she whispered and she slipped from his grasp. She ran down the corridor into the bathroom and locked the door. She sat on the lavatory staring at the telephone. Who could have telephoned? she thought. Certainly not Clive. She slipped off her dress and stood in front of the mirror. There were goosebumps on her shoulders. She took a big fluffy dressing gown off the hook behind the door and wrapping herself in its comforting folds, she walked slowly down the corridor back into the bedroom. She waited and then said, 'Jonathan, I've decided not to do this.'

Jonathan was sitting on the bed. It was a large bed. His shoulders were hunched. He looked at Glenda. 'As you like.' Then he laughed. 'Imagine getting turned down by my best friend's wife!'

'If we did make love,' Glenda said slowly, 'I don't think

Clive would ever again be your best friend. And you and I would certainly not be friends any more. I think the guilt would drive me away. I couldn't live with such a secret. I suppose part of me realized that while I was in Singapore with Georgina. I couldn't feel close to her because I felt so guilty. Anyway, I don't think you love me, any more than you love other women you bring up here. And you *do* bring other women up here, don't you?'

Jonathan got up and walked across the room. He was wearing only a towel. He stood looking out of the bedroom window with his back to Glenda. 'Occasionally,' he said. 'But you're right about one thing. If I sleep with a woman, the affair runs its course and then we tend to fall apart. And that would have been unfortunate for you. I don't know what got into me.'

'I do. Mrs Nicnojad told us in Singapore.'

Jonathan turned. 'What was it then?'

'For you it was chasing the unobtainable. You knew you might not get me, so you had to try to prove something to yourself.'

'And for you?'

Glenda laughed and pushed her hands into the deep white soft pockets of the robe. 'For me, it's just like Molly says, "Who put the dick in addiction?" I got caught up in a fantasy. Somehow my own life didn't seem good enough, so I imagined a whole . . . I don't know. I pictured how *heightened* life could be. But really that's not what I want at all. Sounds funny, you know, but in a strange way I've never felt more married to Clive than I do right now.'

Jonathan's look revealed only partial comprehension.

Never mind, Glenda said to herself. It doesn't matter if he understands or not. 'Let's get dressed,' she said, 'and go back into the sitting room, ring for coffee, and stay friends, Jonathan. That's what I want.'

'Nobody needs to know anything about this, do they?' Jonathan looked anxious.

'I have to tell Georgina. Not about this, but about the fact that I was addicted to you.'

Jonathan made a face. 'Well,' he said, 'maybe I should confess and tell Georgina the whole thing and then ask her to forgive me. To tell you the truth, I've felt rather like a train hurtling off the rails these past few years. Life in the fast lane isn't all it's cracked up to be. Maybe I can convince Georgina she would like to go skiing with *me* – alone, I mean.'

'And you'd give up other women?'

Jonathan raised an eyebrow. 'How about you and your Souls?'

'We were children then. That was a long time ago. We didn't have any experience of life. And any talk we had about being unfaithful was just talk. Molly's mostly, and even she's outgrown that. Anyway, if you read about the real Souls now, they were an unhappy bunch of women. Infidelity simply doesn't work.'

She went back to the bathroom and pulled on her dress. She looked in the mirror and scowled at herself. 'Idiot,' she whispered. 'Insane idiot.' She walked down the hall into the drawing room and waited for Jonathan to join her.

He rang the bell. The waiter entered the suite, his eyes discreetly checking the room. Glenda looked at Jonathan. She tried not to giggle. When the waiter left she burst out laughing. 'Oh, Jonathan! And we're innocent!'

'I know,' Jonathan said ruefully. He put out his hand. 'Friends, Glenda?' he said.

'Yes, friends.'

Chapter 130

Glenda telephoned the farm later, near midnight. She was surprised to hear Mrs Robinson's uncertain voice. 'You're up late,' she said. 'Is Clive around?'

She heard whispering and the sound of the telephone receiver being passed from one person to another. Mark said, 'Clive was taken away by Dr Umberto and her Ladyship.'

There was a moment's bewildered pause. 'What's that?' Glenda said, certain she was dreaming.

'Clive got one of his headaches. He was screaming. I couldn't do anything with him. Lady Jane happened to be passing by with Dr Umberto and she came running in. I'm sorry, but there was nothing we could do.'

'You could have telephoned me.'

'We . . .' He hesitated. 'We was told not to tell you nothing, ma'am.' Mark's voice was formal and frightened. 'I oughtn't be talking to you now. Lady Jane said I was to tell you to telephone her if you rang up, and say nothing else. I'm not supposed to tell you none of this at all.'

'Where have they taken Clive, Mark? Please tell me.'

'To the doctor's clinic in London, I should think, ma'am.'

'All right. Thank you for telling me, Mark. You did the right thing.' Glenda's voice was trembling with controlled rage.

'Lady Jane just *happened* to be passing by,' she whispered to herself as she walked back to the kitchen.

'What's wrong, love?' Minnie was horrified at Glenda's ashen face.

'They've got Clive back in the clinic, mum. I'll have to go. I can't let them hurt him again.'

'I'll come with you.'

'No, you get some sleep. I'll go and deal with it.'

She went back to the telephone. 'Dr Umberto is at home and cannot be disturbed,' the prim night nurse on the line reprimanded Glenda. 'It is rather late, you know.'

'Well you can fucking well tell him to bloody get himself out of bed and be there when I arrive.'

'And who shall I say left the message?'

'Tell him it's Glenda Alexander. And he'd better get his arse round there.' And she hung up.

572

Her immediate instinct was to telephone Jonathan. Then she realized she could not. *Damn*, she thought. I've buggered up that relationship too.

She raced for the car and drove to Hammersmith. The car knew the way to the hospital. All the way there her mind waged war against itself. How on earth had this happened? Did Clive know about her meeting in the suite with Jonathan? Or was he suddenly struck down? It was such a long time since he had been ill. Glenda very much hoped that he would not go back to his former sickly pattern which, in its own way, had helped alienate her from him some time ago.

She realized as she drove to the hospital that in order to addict herself to Jonathan she had turned him into an idealized man – very far away from what Jonathan really was. Jonathan, over the years, had become selfish. Running around with his rich business friends, he had taken the world and other people's wives for granted. She had nearly succumbed herself. Had she slept with Jonathan, she would have been merely another notch on his belt. Another secret. Now she bitterly regretted her obsession with this man. Even more, she repented the gulf it had created between herself and Georgina. And between herself and Clive . . .

Above all, she prayed for Clive's sanity. 'Please, God,' she prayed, her hands white on the wheel of the car, 'please take care of him.'

She rushed through the glass doors of the hospital and saw Nurse Watts grimly waiting for her. 'How do you do, madam?' Nurse Watts began aggressively.

'Not very well, thank you. Where the fuck is Clive?' She marched up the highly polished hospital floors. The familiar stink of linoleum and too many human beings greeted her nostrils. All around her bright paintings leered down from the walls. Tall vases of bright flowers bloomed in the unnatural lighting.

'Dr Umberto is waiting for you in his office. He says he will take you along to see your husband.'

Glenda strode along the corridors and stood impassively in the lift. Upstairs they walked on in silence, Glenda raging inwardly.

Dr Umberto was standing by the window of his office, gazing out on the night traffic below. 'Ah,' he said pleasantly. 'Glenda.'

'Don't Glenda me. What have you done to Clive?'

Dr Umberto shook his head. 'Actually, I've done nothing to Clive, my dear. I merely walked in on him when he was struggling on the floor.'

'You mean you haven't –' Glenda's voice shook and she tried not to cry.

'No, I haven't done a thing. He's in a private room and should be waking up any time now. I gave him a little sedative. That's all. But before I take you to him, I have a confession to make.' Dr Umberto took a deep breath and returned to his desk. 'Many years ago, during the war, Jane Alexander helped me get out of Romania. She set me up in this clinic and all her rich friends came to me for treatment.' He made a face of helplessness. 'It goes without saying, I am eternally grateful to her. But sometimes the price she asks of me in return is too high. And this was one such occasion. Lady Jane would ruin me if she knew I was saying what I am about to say.' He sighed. 'I realize I am placing myself in your hands, but I feel I must try and save Clive's sanity. I would never want to hurt the boy. Man, now, of course. I've known him for so long.

'There is nothing organically or physically wrong with Clive. I should know. I've x-rayed and examined him often enough.'

Glenda felt herself relax. 'Do you really mean that? There's nothing wrong with him?' Hope crept into her voice.

'I've known Clive since he was little, and over the years I've grown very fond of him. Through all his troubles he has preserved his own integrity. And that is precisely his problem. In troubled families such as his, most of the family choose to retain the family secret and to play out their lives within its confines. But Clive sought health. That was his undoing. The source of conflict.'

'I'm afraid I don't quite understand.'

'Well.' The doctor took in a breath. 'Jane Alexander is a deeply disturbed woman, what we might call a narcissistic exhibitionist. A true narcissist, she lives a totally solipsistic life of her own. She loves only herself. What's worse, she has marked exhibitionistic tendencies as well. Exhibitionist personalities must at all times have an audience, and their rage against that portion of the world which refuses to admire them is immense. Jane demanded that her family be her audience. But she knew that Clive refused to join in the family game of letting her do whatever she wanted to do. So she grew to hate him.'

Dr Umberto moved in his chair. 'I don't know how she managed to get to Clive this time, but I do know that she's been wilfully trying to get him into hospital and then certified as incurably insane.'

I know how she got to him, Glenda thought. Then she remembered the vague face behind her in the lobby of the Savoy. Oh, yes. How stupid she had been! That face had been around far too often. 'Does Jane have spies?'

Dr Umberto nodded. 'Lady Jane spends her life plotting, I'm afraid. People with her condition do that.'

'But why?' Glenda asked. 'Why the whole thing? Why has she spent so much effort trying to have Clive proved insane?'

'It's odd, you know,' the doctor replied. 'If you asked her, probably the most honest answer she would give – honest in her terms – would be that she was trying to keep the family's money and estate from him. But that's far from the truth. I've come to believe that the situation has nothing to do with money. Nothing whatsoever, at the heart of the matter. The main reason she tries to destroy Clive is because she cannot tolerate his disapproval of her. If she could have him certified as insane, then that would be proof that he is wrong and she is right, that she *is* indeed worthy of the audience which she demands. But Clive always has been the dissenter.'

'So Jane is the one who needs treatment. Not Clive.'

'Yes,' Dr Umberto said, his voice oddly impersonal. 'She does need treatment. But even Freud writes that treatment for people like her is almost impossible. The ego is so defended that treatment is tantamount to trying to smash through an impenetrable brick wall. Anyway, if you could break down the wall in Lady Jane's case, I don't think you'd find a hurt child in there, the hurt child most people have hidden in their souls. Instead, I'm afraid, you would find nothing. Absolutely nothing. Hitler was a classic example of a narcissist, and look what he managed to do with the help of a willing audience.'

'She has been a Hitler in our lives. What can we do?'

'Nothing.' Dr Umberto rose. 'There is nothing you can do but put distance between yourselves and Lady Jane. She is obsessed with Clive, utterly obsessed. Now let's go and see the young man. He should be awake now.' He put his hand under Glenda's arm. 'What Clive needs is someone to spend time with him, helping him understand the tangled threads that tie him to his mother. He reacts to her without rage. He never allowed himself his rage. This expressed itself in the shutting down of outward emotions and finally to the headaches and the convulsions. I know someone who can help him. I can give you a referral. Also, I promise you that I will refuse to testify against Clive in any proceedings his mother might ever take against him. That's a decision I've reached.'

'Won't you attract some of Jane's rage yourself?'

Dr Umberto shrugged. 'Maybe,' he said. 'But believe it or not, I take my Hippocratic oath seriously. And I too must sleep at night.' They walked to the door of one of the private rooms along the hallway. 'Take him home when you like.' Dr Umberto bent his head and kissed Glenda's hand. She watched him walk away with amazement. Then she took a deep breath and pushed open the door.

Clive was lying on his back, looking at the ceiling. Glenda walked over to the bed and took his unresponsive hand. 'At least they haven't given me ECT,' he said in a monotone voice.

'I know. Dr Umberto told me. Clive,' she said. 'Tell me what happened.'

He looked at her severely for a moment, then returned his eyes to the ceiling. 'I got a telephone call from a chap who said you were in Jonathan's suite at the Savoy. And I felt I just had to ring. When I did I heard your voice, and you . . . Did you, Glenda . . . ?' His eyes were bright with tears.

'No, I didn't.' She couldn't bear the hopeful look that appeared immediately on his face. 'I realized at the last moment that it was you I loved.' She sat on the bed beside Clive and she looked down at her hands. 'Actually, I made a fool of myself. An awful fool. I didn't realize the difference between love and addiction. I made Jonathan into something he wasn't, and I hurt you.'

She shut her eyes to steady herself. 'You know, Clive, I don't know if this will make any sense to you.' She opened her eyes and looked into his sad face. 'Something inside of me has changed. It's as if . . . I don't know. As if . . . We've been married for years, yet today, really for the first time, I felt that I fully made the decision to be married to you. Today I took my vows. It's not that I haven't loved you before. I have. But my commitment to you was . . . I don't know. Maybe I never really understood what commitment meant. Not full, absolute till-death-us-do-part commitment anyway. I think there's been a hole in me. Something missing. Part of me – I hate to admit it – part of me has always looked after myself. I guess it's a habit I picked up as a young girl. I was determined to make a better life for myself, and people along the way . . . There's always been mum, of course. And Abe and Renée as friends. More than friends. But a man, one single man to love always, a man who I knew would love me always . . . Abe has always tried. And I do love him. But he's not a father. Maybe girls do need fathers after all.'

She shook her head. 'God, I hear myself talk and I know how inadequate it sounds. There's no excuse. I just . . . Clive, years ago, before we married, mum asked me if I was sure I loved you. And, it's funny, my mum asking me about loving a man. If you think about it, that's the one thing she's never done. Never with any commitment, anyway. You know how much I love my mother, but part of me is desperately afraid of ending up like her. Alone, and not really having someone to love . . . She asked if I was sure I loved you. I said I was, and I meant it. But now I think part of what I was feeling was simply that I had set my mind to something. And your life was in such a state. You needed someone so badly . . .'

Clive began to open his mouth.

'No, I don't mean that in an unkind way. But you did. And my life was no better, though I didn't even realize it. And I wanted to be that person for you, the one who would take care of you and make you happy. But it wasn't till today, Clive, *today*, that I really understood that our marriage isn't just about me making you happy. You make me happy too. You do. You understand me. You know me for who I am, Glenda from Hounslow, and you don't love me any the less for it. I can't imagine not having you in my life. And I realized –' her eyes filled with tears – 'that I do love you totally. That it's not just a question of looking after you. I just *love* you. You're part of me. There's no way in the world I would want to hurt you. It would be like cutting off my own hand. Maybe that's what the Bible means when it talks about two people becoming one flesh. It's as if our two souls are joined into one.'

She wiped her eyes. 'Strange. All this time, Georgina and Fatima and Molly and I went around calling ourselves the Souls. But you and I are the Souls, Clive. *We* are. To each other. That's what I want to build my life around.' She dropped her head and slow tears rolled down her cheeks.

'And the worst part of it,' she went on, 'is . . .' She shook her head and gave a sad laugh. 'Your mother's been trying to do you in for years. All her phone calls. All her threats that somehow we'd be pushed off the farm. Her efforts to drive you insane . . . In a strange way, there wasn't much she could really do. Not as long as we were strong together, because you were strong. But I was the one . . . I gave your mother the opportunity to get to you. In hurting you myself, I let her harm you. Isn't that a horrific thought?' Tears flowed freely from her eyes. 'Isn't it horrible?'

Clive lay silent. He lifted a finger and rubbed a tear into her skin. 'Funny,' he said, his voice steady, yet almost distracted. 'When you're lying in bed with a hospital ceiling to stare at and medicine whizzing around in your head, you get a chance to think.' He touched her nose with his forefinger, and then her chin, exploring. 'I've been thinking a lot. Lots of thoughts. Not all of them pleasant. Memories.' He touched her hair. 'Thoughts. Dreams. Remember I told you about the time I was in the bath? I asked my mother to get out. Told her to. Didn't want her to see me exposed. That was bad enough. She was so cross. But that wasn't all. I've been lying here thinking. I recall it quite clearly.' He let his hand fall to his side and he lifted his eyes to the ceiling.

'A couple of years later – must have been eight or nine – we were in bed with her. Her bed. Caspar and I. Caspar was laughing and giggling and I . . . I wasn't sure what to do. Maybe I laughed a little too. But I remember stopping. I sat up and watched the scene. Strange you know, but it was like being a million miles away. No, not that far. Just across the room, or looking down from the ceiling, but not actually *there* myself. She was naked, my mother, lying in her own bed with her breasts showing over the top of the sheets. And her shoulders, and the skin under her arms. And Caspar was in the bed with her, playing the tickling game. And my mother gave off the strangest smell . . . She looked so happy. Happiest I've ever seen her look. Happiest I can remember, anyway. So very happy to have both of us there all playing . . . And suddenly it seemed horrible to me. Absolutely horrible! Like a nightmare. I sat up. Sat back. And looked at them, Caspar and my mother, both all pink and excited together. And I pointed my finger at my mother – brave thing to do, now that I think about it. She looked like a harpie. Just like a bare-breasted harpie with haggard hair and vicious sharp teeth. I was very, very angry. I said, "Don't you ever touch me. Don't you ever come near me again." I ran away from her room. And that was that. From that moment, she decided I was mad. She hated me, wanted to kill me, just like some hideous dream. Get me out of the way. You see, she thought I had betrayed her. And for years I guess I believed she was right.'

He looked straight into Glenda's crying eyes. 'Do you know what I've been lying here thinking? I've been thinking, perhaps it would have been nice to have had a mother who loved me. Sounds strange, doesn't it? Someone who didn't want me dead.' He looked away. 'You and I found each other, Glenda. And I put my trust in you. When I heard your voice on the telephone, I . . . God. You were against me too.'

'Clive, I could never be against . . .'

'Sshhh,' he said, beginning to smile. 'I know. You weren't trying to. People make mistakes. My unhappiness is – was – from her, not from you. But whatever she did, I have to leave that behind. What you did, or didn't do, with Jonathan, I forgive you. I'm partly to blame myself, really. Couldn't have been easy for you, living with a loony for so long. But I'm beginning to get a handle on things now. Please forgive me.'

'Oh, Clive.'

'You say you still love me, and I believe you. And you should believe that I still love you.'

She put her arms around him. Tears were sliding down her cheeks.

'Don't cry, Glenda.' He hugged her close. 'Please don't cry. You haven't lost me. I'll always love you. Remember our vows? In sickness and in health, for better or for worse? They do mean we'll love each other always. Come on, darling, don't cry.'

They embraced – a long, quiet, innocent embrace.

Sitting up, Glenda said, 'We can go home to mum's place. I've been talking to Dr Umberto. He says there's nothing wrong with you.' She lay herself down on the bed beside him. 'You know, I think he likes you. I think he's liked you all along, but he's been too afraid of your mother to stand up to her. Now it seems he's prepared to be on your side. He says the only way we'll ever get rid of her is to move away.'

Clive sat up. She could feel his animation and his life. 'Screw it,' he said with liberated laughter.

'What?' She was unsure.

'Screw it all. I don't want the damned family title or their kind of life. Let Caspar take my seat in the House of Lords. I just want us to live our own quiet lives. I'm happiest mucking out the pigs and playing with Baa Lamb.'

Glenda looked at the lines under Clive's eyes. 'So am I,' she said.

'I'll talk to Caspar when we get home. He can have the lot. As long as we can sell our shares and Fen Farm and have enough to start up on our own. The castle and title and all the rest, that can be his. Good luck to him!'

'Then Jane will get just what she wants.'

'So what? I don't care if she's pleased or not,' said Clive. 'It's what *we* want that matters. What do *you* think? What do *you* want?'

Glenda inclined her head. 'I want us to get away from her. I want to pack up and take Mark, and Milly, and Paul, and Mrs Robinson away. All of us. Norfolk is too close to your mother in Cambridgeshire. None of us can ever live normal lives while she's around. Even they were too intimidated to telephone me when you were brought in. I wouldn't be here now if I hadn't rung up to say good night to you.' Glenda took Clive's hand. 'In a silly way, I almost had to lose you, Clive, to know what I was losing.'

Clive smiled. His face was still strained, but his eyes no longer rejected her. 'And what were you losing?'

'The most wonderful man in the world,' she said softly.

'Is there really nothing wrong with me?'

'Absolutely nothing. You just need someone to talk to. Dr Umberto says he knows someone who can help you. Someone to help you straighten your feelings out. Just for yourself. And we can get you off the pills for good. You'll be far better off without them.'

They left the hospital that night. Nurse Watts was nowhere to be seen.

Chapter 131

'So you see, mum, I turned Jonathan into something he was not.' Glenda sat with Minnie at a table in her mother's restaurant. 'Clive is having dinner with Caspar now and telling him about our plans. Tomorrow we go back to the farm and begin to clear up and get it sold. Jane will be furious, but it's such a relief to have made the decision. It's all over now. We'll both be free of her. I talked to Renée this afternoon before I came down here. It's like the end of a nightmare. I can't really believe we're through. Jane can't hurt us any more. And I'm free of my addiction to Jonathan.' She looked down at her plate. She had been pushing her food around. The restaurant was very crowded.

'Let's have coffee in the kitchen.' Minnie led the way. 'You know, I still feel guilty about them early years.' Minnie poured the coffee into Glenda's cup with great concentration. 'I feel I've changed so much. I don't think I can explain what it was like to be born so poor and to live for year after year without hope. Funny how your mind can change once you've something to hope for. Like you remember how I used to be about Jews? Well, I don't think like that now. I've travelled all over the place with Chinchilla and I realize that people are people everywhere. I mean, who'd have thought Dr Umberto could 'ave a change of heart?'

Glenda sipped the hot sweet coffee.

Minnie lit another cigarette. 'I ought to give these up,' she laughed and then she pushed her chair back. 'Actually, Glenda, part of having all those men around was boredom and loneliness. I didn't think there'd ever be anything else in my life. That was what women did in them days. You found a man and then you married him and that was that. You waited till he died, like old Mrs Jones, and then you lived on for a while by yourself until you finally died. I thought I'd be another gravestone in Hounslow's graveyard. Another polystyrene coffin in a welfare grave.' She shuddered. 'Thank God we both got away. So many didn't.'

'Ruth Schwartz didn't,' Glenda said. 'But then Cyril did. I talked to him a few weeks ago. The Foreign Office has posted him to Hong Kong. He's very excited. Still the same Cyril, though. Not an *h* to his name, but I do love him. I've promised that Clive and I will come out and visit. And I've been thinking it might be a *very* good idea. Once we sell the farm, we could go out to Hong Kong. And Clive could do with a total break, away from everything. It's time for Clive and me to do some travelling *together* again. Have some fun.' She finished her coffee. 'I'd better run. I don't want to keep Clive waiting for me.'

She realized how infinitely precious Clive had become to her. In a queer way it took all this for us to get closer together. Glenda drove down the Kings Road. Even at this late hour, people were roaming up and down. So many people, she thought, with nobody to go home to. She put her foot on the accelerator and roared into the night, eager to see her husband.

Chapter 132

Georgina was looking at Jonathan's bare bottom. She realized that she stared at his buttocks with a good deal of dislike. 'Talked to Glenda recently?' Jonathan said. He was putting on his socks the way he always put on his socks. First he wiped his feet clean of invisible sand. Next he leaned forward, grasped his toes in his right hand and inserted them into his sock as if they were dangerous animals. Then he repeated the motion with the other foot. Once he had his socks on, he padded naked to the bathroom, his penis – for once – hanging flaccidly between his thighs. Georgina realized also that she was very bored with Jonathan. The three weeks in Singapore convinced her that she must make a change in her life.

Now, when Jonathan came home from his business trips, she put her own life on hold. When he went away, she became again the real Georgina. She had fun with her father. They talked of the old days and about the garden. She often cooked gourmet meals and then her father would rummage around the wine cellar and find a good bottle of wine. She would go into town and visit her friends – a new baby born in the hospital, or a friend in bed. Life flowed by smoothly, punctuated by visits from the boys home from school. They grew longer and louder, but the house was hers . . .

She heard Jonathan urinating. Some men, she observed, pissed like horses and it goes on forever. She wished he would use another bathroom. He must have a huge bladder, she concluded. Georgina rolled over in bed.

'No, I haven't heard from Glenda,' she shouted, 'but I should be meeting her soon. Molly's coming into town and Fatima's flying in from France. We're having a get-together, and we've decided we won't wait so long between reunions any more.'

'But you were all in Singapore not long ago.'

'Yes. And now we want to see each other again.'

'Oh.'

She heard Jonathan put down the lavatory seat. She sat up, watching him as he walked back to the bed. Lovemaking with Jonathan had been a routine for Georgina for many years. That was another realization. Seeing Molly in love with Prapanas reminded Georgina of those years when she very much wanted Jonathan's body, but now she wrinkled her nose. He was no longer attractive to her, just an old habit. She observed the back of his head as he bent over his drawer to get a shirt, a shirt she had ironed without affection.

To Georgina's surprise, Jonathan did not leave the room. Fully dressed he sat on the bed beside her. 'I have something to tell you,' he began. 'I know this is going to hurt you, but I feel I must be honest with you.'

Georgina looked at her husband. 'What?' She did not intend for the word to come out like a bullet, but it did. The word crashed in Jonathan's face.

'I have been having affairs,' he said simply. Then he was silent.

'You have been having affairs?' Georgina's voice rose. 'With whom?'

'With several people. At a suite in the Savoy. And the last was nearly an affair with Glenda.'

'With *Glenda*?' Georgina was appalled. 'I don't believe you,' she said after a moment of thought. 'Glenda would never do a thing like that to me.'

Jonathan squeezed Georgina's hand. 'Yes, you're right. She wouldn't. That's why we didn't actually have an affair. Look, Georgina, I've been thinking. We need to do something about our marriage. I need to cut back on being abroad so much, and maybe we should go away together, just the two of us. We haven't had a break since our honeymoon, not a

585

real break. If we do go away, it's always with the boys. We need to find each other again.'

Georgina sat on the bed, rigid with pain. She had always half-wondered if Jonathan might be less than completely faithful, but she had never openly thought about it much. Why should he have affairs when she was automatically faithful? What had happened to Glenda? Certainly Georgina knew that Jonathan and Glenda were close friends, but it had been much closer than Georgina had suspected. The word *suspect* again came into her thoughts. How do you *suspect* a person if you do not entertain suspicion yourself? For the moment Georgina very much wanted to be on her own to make a decision. 'Why don't you pack a suitcase, Jonathan, book yourself into a hotel, and let me think about the rest of my life? You've betrayed me, not once but many times. I can't deal with how I feel so quickly. I want you to leave the house and I will think about it. Anyway, I want to talk to Glenda before I can know what to think. I'll see her in London next week. By the way, this suite you talk about. Have you the key?' Jonathan pulled his keyring out of his pocket and handed her the key. 'What's sauce for the goose, Jonathan, is gravy for the gander. Or something like that.' Jonathan left the room to find a suitcase.

Don't cry, Georgina told herself fiercely. Don't cry, whatever you do. At least wait until he's gone.

She waited. She heard her mother's voice in her head. *Noblesse oblige*, the voice whispered.

When she heard Jonathan's car drive down the road, she fell back on the bed sobbing. 'Oh why?' she cried. 'Why did he do this to me?'

Chapter 133

Clive opened the door to an absolutely distraught Jonathan. 'I had to come and see you, Clive. To apologize.'

Clive stood at the door, barring the way. His face was set and white.

'Please, Clive, let me in and I'll try to explain.'

Clive stood back and Jonathan walked into the farmhouse. 'Where's Glenda?' he said.

'She's in the sitting room. I don't know if she wants to see you.'

'I must see her. Please, Clive. Help me.'

'Why should I?' Clive's face was unmoved. 'You tried to seduce my wife.'

'I know, but thank God, Glenda didn't let me.'

'Yes, thank God, Jonathan, because if you had I would have shot you.'

Jonathan looked at Clive.

'Yes, I would have,' Clive said. 'You've been a spoiled brat for far too long, you know. Always thinking you can have whatever you want.' He paused. 'I'll go and find Glenda.'

Glenda was in fact in the library packing up a crate of books.

'Jonathan's here and he's in a state. He wants to see you.'

Glenda looked up, alarmed. 'A state? What about?'

'I don't know.'

'Oh, let him in. Let's hear what he has to say.'

Clive and Glenda stood arm in arm, studying Jonathan as he paced up and down the library floor. 'So you see, my life is in a mess. I told Georgina the truth and she's thrown me out. She says she'll be seeing you next week, Glenda. Please, please tell her I love her, and I've never really loved anyone else. Please ask her to let me back into her life. And I promise I'll never look at another woman.'

Glenda began to feel sorry for Jonathan. 'I'll try,' she said, 'but Georgina is the one you must convince.'

'Just ask her to give me a chance.'

When Jonathan had gone, Clive put his arm around Glenda's shoulder. 'You know,' he said, 'once the farm's sold up and we're all settled in the new place, how about we take a second honeymoon? We could visit Cyril in Hong Kong, as you suggested, and then we could go and spend some time in Japan. I've always wanted to go there. Always been a country of such wonderful artists and I hear the food's fantastic. What do you think?'

Glenda smiled and snuggled into his side. 'And, now that you know there's nothing wrong with you, maybe we could make babies all the way there and back.'

Clive giggled. 'I'm not certain I want to share you with babies, but it would be fun trying.'

They walked out of the farm and both laughed as Baa Lamb came bounding up to them. Clive tried to protect Glenda from Baa Lamb's impetuous leaps. Mark, standing next to Paul, watched them go in the sunlight. 'Do us all some good to be moving from here,' he said, 'and starting again.'

Chapter 134

Lady Jane's fingernails were drumming up a red-rimmed storm on her dressing table. 'Tell me again what Clive said.'

'Not *again*, mother.' Her son Caspar leaned wearily back on the chaise longue. They were in Jane's dressing room. Once upon a time Caspar had loved this room with its rows of dresses, shoes all neatly wrapped in grey shoe bags. The air was full of the smell of the powder his mother used and on the table sat the lipstick with which she so carefully outlined her thin mouth. Now she sat looking at him irritably through the mirror. He disliked that look. It was impersonal and conspiratorial. 'He just said that he really didn't want the title. Or the estate. And I was welcome to have it. He would just take the proceeds from Fen Farm so he could make a new home for himself and that whole bloody entourage he keeps with him, Paul and Mark and Mrs Robinson and such. Always was a sentimental sort, our Clive, believing himself responsible for everyone else. Really, mother. I've told you this so many times. Why can't you just accept it? You don't own him, you know.'

Jane shot Caspar a particularly furious look. 'He is my son.'

'He *was*, mother. He was. I don't think he's too fond of you now.'

Caspar felt guilty. Clive had spared his mother nothing. 'I don't ever want to see the old bitch again,' Clive had said. Caspar had been surprised at the intensity of Clive's hatred.

He watched Lady Jane pick up her silver brush and slide the bristles through her black hair. He noticed, with the practised eye of the philanderer, the little sagging slack under her arm. Well, he thought, even mother is showing her age.

'Time for a bit of a nip and tuck,' Caspar said getting to his feet. He walked over to his mother and pinched the offending loose pouch of flesh.

'Ouch.'

'I'm off, mother.'

'Shan't you stay and scrub my back, Caspar? I could do with a bath.'

Caspar looked down at her. 'No. I've got an appointment in London.' He left the room.

Tears rolled down Jane's face with theatrical ease. In the mirror she watched a drop slide slowly down her cheek. Oh shit, she thought. Her hand reached for the telephone. 'Umberto?' she said. 'Where is your report?'

'It's on its way, Lady Jane.' He disliked the way she used his surname. It made him feel like a slave. But then the whole world was Jane's slave, or so she thought.

'What is your recommendation?'

'I have no recommendation, Lady Jane.'

'What do you mean, you have no recommendation? Clive was in your hospital, wasn't he?'

'Certainly he was.'

'Well, what happened? What did he say?'

'That, my dear woman, is privileged and confidential.'

'Don't be so silly, Umberto. What on earth has got into everybody lately? Clive gives everything up and says he's running off forever with that common little tart of his, and everyone seems to think that's absolutely fine . . . What is *happening*?' Her voice rose.

'Just a moment of truth, perhaps.' Dr Umberto put down the telephone. He was shaking, but he felt a marked triumph.

Jane, sitting by herself in the empty castle, looked at her face in the mirror. She stood up and checked the evidence under her arm. Maybe a little plastic surgery was a good idea.

She turned her body to check that her dress lay fluid against her thighs. She picked up the telephone again. 'Darling?' she said to one of her many bored and beautiful friends, 'I've decided I need a bit of a nip and a tuck. Who do you recommend? Make sure it's someone divine and dreamy.' She listened and then she cackled, her mouth a thin, sharp razor just beginning to crumble at the edges.

EPILOGUE

London was shaken by a huge wind that blew newspapers about the streets and put its bossy hand behind people and shoved them around as in some great game of croquet. Glenda almost cannoned into Fred at the door when she arrived at the Savoy to have lunch with Georgina. 'Sorry, Fred, but it is windy.'

Fred grinned and took her car keys. 'I like the wind, myself,' he said. 'We've had a hot summer.'

Glenda walked into the Savoy and wandered around the display cabinets. Oh, she thought, that's a wonderful diamond. 'Thinking of buying it?' Georgina came up behind her.

'Sorry I'm a bit late, but that wind held everybody up.'

Georgina looked at Glenda. 'You've got an incredible tan. You really are brown. I'm afraid I haven't had much time to sunbathe, I've been so busy.'

They walked together down the stairs and sat in the foyer. A young man at the white piano gazed at them both. Glenda smiled back at him and then whispered to Georgina, 'I'm pleased to see we are still in the FF zone. No doubt we always will be. Molly tells me it's all in the mind. If she gives up on sex, then she is anonymous. Men never give up on sex, do they?' Glenda laughed. She could feel Georgina's unease. She realized she had been saying entirely the wrong things, but she was nervous. 'I can't believe Molly's actually getting married again. And to a sultan. Who would have guessed? Still, I think she's made the right choice. She deserves happiness.'

'Prapanas seems awfully nice,' said Georgina pleasantly.

'But you don't think Molly will expect us to genuflect every time we see her, just because she'll be a sultan's wife, do you?'

'Knowing Molly, I'd say she probably will.'

The two women laughed. And they fell silent once again.

'Darling,' Glenda began, picking at a plate of mixed nuts. 'Have *you* made a decision?'

Georgina nodded. 'You know, Glenda, in an odd way you did me a great favour.'

Glenda felt tears rise in her eyes. 'I felt as though I betrayed you, Georgina.'

'No. You didn't. You set me free. You see, I just followed on my mother's heels. I knew that however clever I was, I would only get a degree to please my father, and then I would get married to please my mother. And there's one thing I've learned from long, long talks with Jonathan. You know the most awful thing I discovered? It's that Jonathan and I have never really talked about anything. How can you be married to a man and just not talk to him? He wants us to go to Boston for good and send the boys to a good day school. He feels part of the problem for him is that he was away at prep school for most of his young life. You are trained there not to show any emotions. It's a world of men without women. But I think men need women to civilize them. Without women, men tend to behave like animals.'

Glenda listened. While they talked, a waiter took their orders for drinks. 'There's a lot of truth in what Chinchilla says,' Glenda put in. 'That men act alone and women act by connections.'

'Yes. Quite. So I've thought it all through.' Georgina relaxed with her gin and tonic. 'I'm still thinking it all through. And my decision is still a question mark, even to me. I mean, part of me says Jonathan and I should try and make our marriage work. I know my father would be quite happy to stay in the house with the cook and the maid in Dorset, and Jonathan and the boys and I would become

Boston-based. But there's another very big part of me that is not at all eager to go back to the same rut. In many ways I've compromised in our marriage. I never thought to question Jonathan, about whether or not he was faithful, about the way he treats me . . . Really! He'd like to forget, if he could, that I ever went to university myself, the way he behaves.

'And I suppose I've come out of it all feeling that one way or the other, if I stay with Jonathan or not, I'm no longer prepared to compromise myself. If Jonathan wants me, then he'll have to build his life around me for a change.' She was quiet for a moment, and then she laughed. Looking directly into Glenda's eyes, her own eyes alight with beauty, strength, and confidence, she said, 'And maybe I'm still a Soul. I still believe that men are mistaken if they think they own us. The fact is, I have Jonathan, but will he ever have me?'

Georgina put her hand on Glenda's arm. 'Now let's have some lunch. I'm starving. How was your trip with Clive? You must tell me all about it.'

'It was wonderful. Hong Kong was jammy and Japan was bonking, as Molly would say.' The two women moved gracefully toward their table. Heads turned. They sat smiling into each other's faces, all shadows gone, all golden bonds in place.

Hot Type
Kristy Daniels

When Tory Satterly starts at the second-rate afternoon paper, *The Sun*, she's just a lowly, overweight reporter, relegated to the women's pages and hopelessly in love with Russ Churchill, golden boy of the prestigious rival morning paper, *The Post*. But Tory is tenacious and she soon enters the hard news world of smouldering sex scandals and drug deals. As her career soars, Tory becomes a svelte and sexy woman equally at home at exclusive spas, Swiss resorts, and in the arms of multimillionaire Max Highsmith.

And when *The Post* and *The Sun* are merged, there's room for only one at the top. Russ Churchill becomes Tory's rival . . . as well as her lover. Which of them will get the plum job – the one they have both wanted all their lives?

FONTANA PAPERBACKS

Daughters
Consuelo Saah Baehr

Daughters is an unforgettable story of courage, love and hope; of two worlds – one ancient, one modern – and of the extraordinary women who bridge them.

Miriam Mishwe is born into a Palestinian Christian family in the last years of the nineteenth century. She marries a man chosen by her family, but centuries-old traditions are on the verge of upheaval.

Nadia is Miriam's daughter. Sent to a local British school, she adopts many modern ideas but is not yet ready to renounce her heritage.

Nijmeh, Nadia's daughter, is the one who will call herself by her English name, Star, and go to live in America. There she will face problems of a new and unknown kind . . .

'A long, richly textured novel filled with wonderful characters and an extraordinary sense of historical detail. Consuelo Saah Baehr has written a blockbuster with a heart.' Susan Isaacs, author of *Almost Paradise* and *Shining Through*

FONTANA PAPERBACKS

So Many Partings
Cathy Cash Spellman

Born in poverty in Ireland, the bastard son of an aristocrat and a pretty housemaid, Tom Dalton had lost everything he loved by the time he was eight.

Another immigrant in an indifferent city, he found a job in the punishing servitude of the dockyards. But soon he would tame the corruption of waterfront politics and carve a path to the opulent heights of New York society which would bring him wealth and power. It would also bring him the two women he loved – one whose ill-fated love would change his life, and one who would be his strength when his dreams turned into nightmares of betrayal and loss. Yet Tom Dalton was the only man who could shape a stronger dream from the bitter ashes of defeat – a dream that would endure as long as life itself.

Turbulent, triumphant – *So Many Partings* is an unforgettable novel in the great tradition of *Evergreen* and *A Woman of Substance*.

FONTANA PAPERBACKS

Shining Through
Susan Isaacs

'In 1940 when I was thirty-one and an old maid, while the whole world waited for war, I fell in love with John Berringer.'

Linda was a legal secretary; John Berringer was her indecently handsome, brilliant, unattainable boss, the man of her dreams. Four years later, Linda Voss Berringer emerged from the ruins of Berlin a self-determined woman of shining courage and a war hero.

Shining Through is the compulsive, engaging, heart-stopping saga of an American working girl and her transformation. Her story involves passion – a blazing affair with John Berringer; betrayal – when John's faithlessness rips their marriage apart; and intrigue – ultimately of a lethal kind when Linda joins the war as an OSS spy. Her story soars to its breathtaking conclusion in a blazing explosion of danger, death and unexpected love.

'Three cheers for Susan Isaacs, *Shining Through* keeps you turning the pages because you care what happens to the characters . . . her most ambitious novel to date.' *Daily Express*

'Give me the unashamed blockbuster any day, especially of the Susan Isaacs' tear-jerking, breath-catching variety . . . marvellously engaging.'
Financial Times

'Truly compulsive . . . has all the hallmarks of a runaway bestseller.' *Publishers Weekly*

FONTANA PAPERBACKS

Fontana Paperbacks: Fiction

Fontana is a leading paperback publisher of fiction.
Below are some recent titles.

- [ ] ULTIMATE PRIZES Susan Howarth £3.99
- [ ] THE CLONING OF JOANNA MAY Fay Weldon £3.50
- [ ] HOME RUN Gerald Seymour £3.99
- [ ] HOT TYPE Kristy Daniels £3.99
- [ ] BLACK RAIN Masuji Ibuse £3.99
- [ ] HOSTAGE TOWER John Denis £2.99
- [ ] PHOTO FINISH Ngaio Marsh £2.99

You can buy Fontana paperbacks at your local bookshop or
newsagent. Or you can order them from Fontana Paperbacks,
Cash Sales Department, Box 29, Douglas, Isle of Man. Please
send a cheque, postal or money order (not currency) worth the
purchase price plus 22p per book for postage (maximum postage
required is £3.00 for orders within the UK).

NAME (Block letters)_____

ADDRESS_____

_____

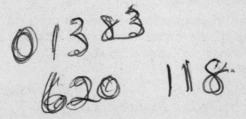